TO LOVE, HONOR AND OBEY

TO LOVE, HONOR AND OBEY

A Novel By Joan Cox

iUniverse, Inc.

New York Lincoln Shanghai

To Love, Honor and Obey

Copyright © 2004 by Tell Me A Story, Inc.

iUniverse books may be ordered through booksellers or by contacting:

iUniverse
2021 Pine Lake Road, Suite 100
Lincoln, NE 68512
www.iuniverse.com
1-800-Authors(1-800-288-4677)

ISBN: 0-595-33476-8

Printed in the United States of America

Here is to the one and only one,

And may that one be he!

Who is loved by one and only one,

And may that one be me!*

For JCC

*An old family toast (author unknown)

Acknowledgments

"To Love, Honor and Obey" marks a milestone for me…one that I was determined to reach because of my obsession with storytelling and my enduring admiration for my great-grandmother whom I was fortunate to have known. Being a closet pragmatist, I chose to take others along with me on this literary journey in order that they might read, edit, correct, critique, amplify, advise and hopefully, enjoy my work. If the novel shines, it is due to light reflected from the generous assistance of John Cox, Michael Cox, Michelle Cox, Heather Crabtree, Thomas Capshaw, Sandra Kramer and Michael Whicker. Thank you for propping me up along the way as I worked to make my dream a reality.

As a card-carrying member of a generation renowned for its ignorance of computers and anything electronic, I have been blessed with my very own computer guru…one who continues to be on duty twenty-four hours a day, seven days a week. Thank you, Michael Cox, for endowing me with your infinite patience and your electronic wizardry!

Heather Crabtree loaned her artistic talents to this project by designing a book cover that so perfectly evokes the era.

Thank you again…one and all!

CHAPTER 1

———————— ▼ ————————

Emma's eyes fluttered open at the sound. A faint breeze stirred the curtains around the edges of her bedroom window. Slowly shifting on the damp covers until she lay flat on her back, Emma peered into the black void before her and listened intently as she tried to identify the sound that had awakened her. Her distended belly shuddered as the unborn child awoke within her.

The sound came again. Emma could barely make out the faint outline of roses on her bedroom wallpaper. Gray flowers on white at this hour, but flowers which would burst into full crimson with the dawn. It was early…too early for Mr. Sweeney to be delivering milk so perhaps a stray cat seeking a final lick had sent an empty glass milk bottle tumbling down the stairs from the back porch.

Emma rolled onto her right side, straining to push herself upright on the mattress. Inching off the bed, she advanced cautiously through the darkness toward her bedroom widow over the porch to listen again. Finally alert, Emma heard the unmistakable sound of glass breaking. "What are those boys doing at this hour of the morning?" she wondered. She remembered distinctly that she had latched both the front door and the back door before climbing the stairs to her bedroom for the night.

Earlier that same summer, Emma had forgotten to latch the back door one night and the boys had escaped the confines of their small brick row house to terrorize the neighborhood horses up and down the back alley by banging loudly on all the shed doors with firewood intended for their mother's cookstove. Remembering that episode, Emma felt her way back to the edge of her nightstand that held a small pewter saucer and a lump of candle wax. Blindly she opened the drawer to grope for matches, struck one and lit the candle. Faint sounds were drifting up from below her room. "Those boys!" she thought. "They are going to get a good switching for this!"

Emma straightened the long white cotton nightgown that had wadded up around her thighs and heavy belly, where her third child squirmed within its confines. With the candle held aloft, she crept down the dark hallway, passing first the nursery she had been preparing for the new baby and then the boys' room. Emma shoved the flickering candle at arm's length into the darkness of George and Will's bedroom to verify that her suspicions were correct. Instead of two empty beds, she saw her seven year old twin boys sprawled dimly against the white sheets. A scraping sound floating up the stairwell to the second floor made her freeze. If not the boys, then who was downstairs in her house?

Turning her back to the twins' bedroom, Emma made her way cautiously to the top of the narrow staircase and, gripping the railing with one hand while holding the candle aloft in the other, she inched her way down into the gloom. Through the glow of candlelight, she could see that the front door remained undisturbed, still latched high up the frame. Holding the sputtering candle out in front of her, Emma peered into the small front parlor. Nothing seemed amiss. Next she tiptoed to the dining room and was startled to see that a chair was missing from the head of the table. Silently Emma crept toward the kitchen at the back of the house directly under her bedroom. As she fought to control the noise of her breathing, Emma could feel tiny hands and feet in her ribs. Her heart thudded wildly and sweat crawled irritatingly down her body. With the back of her hand, Emma pushed aside the dripping auburn hair from her forehead and eyes.

Able to discern a faint light coming from the kitchen, Emma blew out her flickering candle and continued to inch forward on bare feet until she had a complete view of the little kitchen. There, hunched over her kitchen table, sat the dark figure of a man busily devouring a leftover meat pie which she had fixed for her family's supper the previous day. In the pre-dawn light of a coal oil lantern, Emma recognized Cletus Donohue, the neighborhood handyman. She cleared her throat in order to try to speak and startled the intruder, who lurched sideways in the wooden chair nearly falling to the floor. Righting himself and pushing the remnants of pie toward a wooden bowl of apples on the other side of the enamel-topped table, Cletus rose and turned to face Emma.

As Cletus stood unsteadily over her, Emma caught her first whiff of alcohol and unwashed body parts. With the back of his sleeve, the thief brushed piecrust crumbs from his heavily bearded face. "Mornin' Miss Emma," he belched down at the diminutive woman as he swayed over her. "I was jest passin' by and figgered you'd have some vittles roundabouts for a hungry man like myself." Cletus belched loudly again before adding, "Knowin' you been without a man fer sech a long spell, I figgered you might could use a little company too. Whadya say?"

"I say you are very drunk, Cletus, and you had best be departing from my home immediately or I shall summon the constable," responded Emma defiantly, hands on her hips.

Cletus snickered, "Be my guess our fine constable's humpin' a fat whore right about now and don't give a pig's ass anyways as concerns the doin's in your house at this hour of the mornin'. We ain't disturbin' the peace, now is we?"

"Well, you are surely disturbing mine and I want you to leave my house immediately," ordered Emma as she turned and pointed toward the kitchen door with its broken windowpanes. Reaching out a hairy paw, Cletus grabbed the back of her nightgown and pulled Emma to him.

"Mind yourself, Cletus, for I am to term with this child of mine and I shall not be treated in such a rude and insolent manner!" Cletus laughed and then bent down to belch in her hair. Emma slapped the intruder across his face.

The smile faded abruptly from his lips and Cletus pinned Emma to the table, squeezing her breasts with both hands, feeling down her belly and then her thighs. "You been all alone too long, Miss Emma, but don't you fret none 'cause ol' Cletus here gonna take care of you this mornin'," he said spinning her around and slamming her belly against the table. Emma's heart pounded and the baby lurched inside her. With one hand, Cletus gripped her by the hair and pushed her face down on the table as he fumbled with the buttons of his trousers. Scarcely able to draw a breath, Emma's mind raced desperately for a way out of the attacker's grasp.

Just as Cletus raised her nightgown and shoved himself inside her, Emma caught sight of a paring knife in the bowl of apples. She used every thrust of his malodorous body to propel herself further across the table and closer to the bowl of apples with its knife. One more thrust...one more grunt from Cletus and Emma's outstretched hand reached into the bowl to grab the protruding wooden handle of the knife. With a swift, backward arcing motion of her right arm, Emma stabbed Cletus in the side.

Cursing in pain, Cletus withdrew from Emma and staggered back toward the cookstove. Emma turned and with the knife held low, stabbed him again, this time in the stomach. "Get out of here you...you...BASTARD!" she shouted. "If I ever see you around this neighborhood again, I shall finish you off...as God is my witness!" Still brandishing the bloody paring knife, Emma picked up her broom from the corner by the cookstove and began pummeling the bleeding man. As she drove him out the back door, Cletus fell down the stairs from the porch into the yard and dragged himself off into the graying dawn.

Emma shook violently as she shut the door. Only then did she realize that her feet were bleeding from the glass on the floor and that her nightgown was splattered with blood from Cletus. Gripping the edge of the soapstone sink, Emma tried to steady herself. She gasped for air, sucking in great breaths as if she would never be able to draw another and it was then she felt the telltale rush of warm water from between her legs. The baby was coming…forced from its safe haven by the hairy, foul intruder and there was no one to help Emma with the birth.

She had planned for her mother, Mary Miller, to deliver the baby. Mary was an experienced midwife and it was she who had delivered Emma's twin boys seven years earlier. Emma had assisted her mother on several occasions with the birthing of babies in their neighborhood and so she possessed a novice's knowledge of midwifery, but could she deliver this third child on her own in the faint light cast from a coal oil lantern in the middle of her kitchen floor?

Emma realized that she must immediately begin her preparations. Shaking the lantern which Cletus had left in his hasty and wounded departure, she found that the basin of oil was nearly full so she would have light by which to see in the darkened kitchen. Next she turned to her sink again and taking a dipper of water from the pail underneath the sink, Emma primed the water pump before urging the creaking apparatus to yield a half bucket of water. Righting the wooden dining room chair that had fallen over in her scuffle with Cletus and stripping off her nightgown, Emma sat heavily upon the chair. With a clean dish towel in one hand and a bar of lye soap in the other, she began to wash her body, saving her feet for last.

Cautiously Emma picked out the shards of glass from the soles of her feet and washed them too. After her sponge bath, Emma emptied the pail of water into the sink and gathered up the largest shards of glass which she placed in the dustbin. Taking up the broom once again, Emma swept up the remaining glass from around the back door and dumped it also into the dustbin.

She moved next to a wicker basket of freshly laundered sheets that she had washed, hung out to dry and folded earlier in the day. As she sat down gingerly upon the chair, Emma was slowly gripped by what she recognized as the first of many strong labor pains. It began at her back and slowly moved around her entire abdomen. Gripping the edges of the chair, she tried to focus on a point in the room. The old kitchen clock tick, tick, ticked a soothingly familiar chorus from its vantage point on the yellow wall directly in front of the small woman crouched upon the wooden chair. The time was 4:32 on the morning of July 13, 1889.

As the pain loosened its hold on Emma, she took in several deep breaths before reaching into the basket of sheets. With her teeth, she opened a small tear in the middle of one and then yanked the sheet in half. From the frayed edge, she tore several strips and placed them in a pile on top of the other half of the clean sheet on the floor next to the chair. With these strips of sheet, Emma planned to bind off the baby's umbilical cord and fashion a "necessary" for herself. Emma knew that she would bleed heavily after the baby's birth and she had to be prepared to stanch the flow of blood. As Emma continued with her crude preparations, she was gripped by another pain. Quickly she stuffed a piece of sheet into her mouth to stifle her outcry of pain. As the contraction subsided she removed the wadding from her mouth.

Emma picked up the bloody paring knife that she had tossed onto the floor and crept toward a cupboard by the wood-burning stove. Reaching high into the interior of the cupboard, she removed the last bottle of Edward's beloved whiskey. She inched her way back to the sink and pumped water into a bowl from the same cupboard. In the bowl, Emma washed the paring knife with lye soap and water, sterilized it with Edward's whiskey and then placed the knife alongside the pile of torn sheets.

Another pain held her in its agonizing vice as she chewed the wadding in her mouth. She must hurry now for the pains were coming closer together. Pushing the table to the far side of the kitchen, Emma grabbed up her nightgown and mopped up the amniotic fluid that had rushed from her body. She turned and stuffed the wet bundle into the cavernous black maw of the stove.

Reaching back into the basket of sheets, she removed the entire contents, making two pallets, one for herself and one for the baby. Tick, tick, tick. The old clock was watching her struggles and it was now time for Emma's final preparations. Panting, Emma crept around the kitchen, gathering up a second, larger mixing bowl to hold the afterbirth and a stack of fresh dish towels with which to clean and cover the infant after its birth. Another contraction racked her body and instinctively, Emma knew it was now time to crouch over the pallet of sheets. On her hands and knees and with the sheeting clenched in her teeth, Emma began to give birth.

Arching her back and raising her head high, Emma gave a great push and the pain sent her tumbling onto her side. Quickly she resumed her crouch and again she pushed, raising her head to fix her eyes on the face of the old clock. Over and over again she repeated the sequence until she knew it was time to lie prone on the sheets. Feeling between her legs, Emma's fingers traced the distinct bulge of the baby's head. On her back and with her knees bent wide apart, Emma gave several mighty heaves very quickly in succession until she felt the baby slip from her body. Grasping the baby with both hands she gently lifted it onto her belly and then reached for a dish towel. As she wiped mucous and blood from the tiny body she realized for the first time that she had a boy baby.

"Welcome to a new life, Edward John Richardson," she spoke softly to the slippery baby as she laid him gently between her legs to begin tying off his umbilical cord twice with two of the thin strips of sheeting. With the same paring knife that she had used to fend off her attacker earlier, Emma severed the cord between the two strips of sheet. For the first time in nine months, mother and child were separated.

Since the baby had not yet begun to breathe on his own, Emma grasped him by his tiny feet and hoisted him into the air while rendering a smack to the lifeless infant's back. Nothing. She wiped more mucous from inside the baby's mouth and nose, then hoisted him again by his dusky feet. Still nothing. Bringing him close to her face, she did what she had seen her mother do countless times. She placed her mouth over the small nose and sucked. Then covering the baby's nose and mouth with her mouth, she gently blew into the baby, hoisted him and thumped his back. Nothing. Again and again she repeated the maneuvers she had watched her mother perform so deftly until the air was suddenly filled with a loud wail. With great jubilation the old clock marked the hour of birth and the arrival of this tiny new life. It was fifteen minutes before six o'clock in the morning.

As Emma continued to clean herself and the baby, she realized that a beautiful new day had dawned outside the little kitchen along with this new life and for the first time she smiled. Emma covered herself with a clean sheet and propped herself up against the chair, offering her breast to the baby boy who lay swaddled in kitchen towels. Tiny Edward let out another wail before settling contentedly against his mother's breast. In the lull, Emma heard the unmistakable sound of feet running down the front stairs and scampering along the hall to the kitchen.

George and Will appeared simultaneously in the kitchen, clad only in their underwear, their dark hair sticking straight up from their heads. "Ma!" Will exclaimed. "What's that noise and watchya doin' down there on the floor?"

George sized up the situation first, "She has just gotten the baby, Dummy, and the only way she can get the baby is by lying down."

"How come?" asked Will, scratching his head.

"Because…" and George looked at his mother, "because the stork is afraid the mother will drop the new baby if she is standing up so he tells her to lie down."

The boys cautiously approached their mother where she lay on the floor with their new baby brother. Down on hands and knees, the twins stared in amazement at the bundle. "Gee, Ma, what is it?" Will asked.

"See for yourselves, boys," answered Emma as she gently removed the baby from her breast and peeled back the kitchen towel.

"Oh, lookit! It's another boy…just like us Georgie!" Will exclaimed.

"Do not call me 'Georgie', Dummy, and I can see that thing between his legs plain as I can see your ugly self," George replied haughtily to his twin.

"Boys, boys!" Emma scolded. "Not now! I need Nana's help and you are going to have to fetch her for me because she does not yet know that Edward John Richardson has been born. Can you do that for me?"

"Sure," the boys replied in unison.

"But first," Emma admonished them, "you must go pull on your pants and shirts and do not dillydally along the road and watch out for the milk wagon and do not run out in front of the horses and…"

"Ma, it will be okay! Will has me with him so I can make sure this will be done right. Straight to Nana's house and back. You will see. But, Ma?"

"Yes, George?"

"I was wondering if Pa is going to come home now that the new baby is here and named after him and all?"

"Oh, my darling George and Will! I do so wish that your Pa would return to see the new baby but I am quite afraid that business matters will keep him away a bit longer," Emma lied. She stroked the cheeks of her sons sadly for a moment before issuing the order, "Now scoot and bring Nana to me!"

As the boys raced each other down the hall and back upstairs, Emma heard Will ask George, "But I thought you said the stork brought new babies and I didn't see one nowheres, did you?"

"Willynilly, sometimes your head is like a block of wood. I can explain it all to you later. Now shut up!"

During the boys' absence, Emma removed the baby from her breast and rested him against her shoulder, as she gently stroked his back. Then she encouraged him to suckle again from the other breast but already the tiny boy was fast asleep when George and Will came cascading down the stairs, back down the hall and into the kitchen.

"Ma, the front door's locked," exclaimed Will breathlessly, "so what'll we do?"

George pointed to the back door, "This one is unlocked, stupid, so we can go out the back way."

"Hey, Ma, what happened to the glass?" Will asked.

"Oh…when the stork was delivering the baby earlier, the wind caught the door and banged it so hard against the wall, it just shattered," Emma grinned up at George's startled face. "Now you two run along and mind what I told you."

Both boys took off at a lope across the back yard, past the privy and the horse shed when Will exclaimed, "Wait! I've got to pee."

"You will just have to piss in your pants. You heard Ma, 'no dillydallying', so forget your privates and come on."

The twins raced down the dirt alley passing a large shed that housed the neighbors' horses, Flash and King.

"Sorry we can't stop, boys," Will hollered at the horses as they streaked on by, "but we're doing somethin' really 'portant today. We got ourselves a new baby!"

"Criminy, Will! Those are horses you are talking to and they do not speak English."

"Well, what do they speak?" demanded Will breathlessly.

"Horse," replied George tersely as they raced out into the dusty street, narrowly avoiding a collision with Mr. Sweeney's milk wagon.

"Mornin', Mr. Sweeney," bellowed Will to the startled milkman. "We got ourselves a new baby. Stork brung it," he called over his shoulder, adding, "and he's a dandy!"

As they raced down Longmeadow, George admonished Will, "Are you going to tell everybody in creation that we have a new baby? Remember what Ma said. Hurry up!"

"Georgie? 'Bout that stork deliverin' babies…what was it you was goin' to tell me?"

"Storks delivering babies is just a fairy tale. Where was that baby all this time, Will?"

"Whadya mean?" Will panted as the boys continued their race down Longmeadow toward the railroad tracks.

"I mean where was that baby inside Ma all this time?"

"Inside her stomach?"

"Exactly Will. And how do things get into Ma's stomach?" George asked his brother as the two boys raced along the dirt road, shoulder to shoulder.

"That's easy…through her mouth!" exclaimed Will triumphantly, still not getting the point.

"Therefore," concluded George for his brother's edification, "the baby had to be born out of her mouth. He had to come out the same way he got in there in the first place, kind of like…kind of like food coming out of your stomach when you get sick. You know, she just all of a sudden threw up that baby." As an afterthought, George added, "Of course it hurts a whole lot."

"Oh, yeah? Well, how do you know that?"

"Do you remember when Benjamin's mother had that baby about a year ago?"

"Yeah."

"Well, Benjamin told me that his mother yelled and screamed something fierce when the baby came out, just the way you do when you get to throwing up."

Will fell silent and the boys ran beside the railroad tracks kicking up the dust as they went. Will idolized his brother George, just fourteen minutes older than he, but possessed of a wisdom that routinely guided Will through some of life's dicier moments. After pondering the astonishing facts of birth as set forth by George for several long seconds, Will asked, "Then why did Ma tell us the fairy tale about the stork and all that?"

"Probably because that is what adults do when they think you are too stupid to understand the real truth," George huffed.

The two of them picked their feet up high as they ran across the railroad tracks and headed up the grassy knoll from High Point Avenue toward their grandmother's house. Arriving on Mary's front porch, the boys threw open the door and raced back toward the kitchen with Will shouting, "Nana! Nana! Where ya at?"

"It is Will and George and we have ourselves a brand new baby!"

Mary's diminutive figure appeared in the kitchen doorway, clad in her customary long black cotton skirt and blouse with a gold brooch at the center of her high collar. Her thick, black, glossy hair was parted in the middle and drawn severely back into a bun at the nape of her neck. Her only adornment other than the gold brooch was a pair of gold loop earrings. Her mother had pierced her ears when she was only a baby but Mary's late husband, James, had refused to allow his wife to pierce Emma's ears, stating flatly that it was a pagan ritual and had no place in a God-fearing home. Still, James never objected to his wife's fondness for her gold jewelry.

"What is all the fuss about, boys?" Mary asked wiping her hands on the white cotton apron that reached to the bottom of her dress hemline.

Elbowing each other out of the way in order to be the first to deliver the news to their adored grandmother, the boys fell against her skirts shouting in unison, "The baby's here, the baby is here!"

"Yep, and the stork just dropped him off too!" winked Will at George.

"You must come right away, Nana. Ma is lying on the kitchen floor and things are a terrible mess," George delivered the news breathlessly.

"Good heavens!" exclaimed Mary. "Why is your mother lying on the kitchen floor?" she asked looking from one boy's upturned face to the other.

Will looked at George and George looked at Will who replied, "Stork musta knocked her down when he busted in the back door," chuckled Will as he poked George in the ribs. The two boys shared a good laugh until they caught sight of Mary's ashen face.

"Come at once boys. Will! Go to the barn and saddle up Onion. George you run upstairs to my bedroom and fetch my black bag." Mary returned to the cook-stove, already too hot to touch, and removed first the dark blue enamel coffee pot with a corner of her apron and then the cast-iron skillet in which she had begun to fry fatback. Next she removed her apron, hanging it on a peg behind the back door. At the sink, she pumped water into a basin, undid the buttons on the cuffs of her blouse, rolled up her sleeves and began to scrub her hands and arms up to the elbows.

George came thudding into the kitchen with Mary's midwifery bag in hand about the same time that Will appeared at the backdoor scowling.

"Onion's givin' me trouble, Nana. That old horse just won't hold still…kicked the box out from under me and he's fartin' real bad. Guess you'll hafto help me."

Mary hustled the boys up the slope at the back of the house and into the barn. "Easy now, Onion! We are on a mission today and we do not have time for any of your foolishness," Mary chided the farting horse.

"Pee-yew!" exclaimed George holding his nose. "What makes him do that?"

"Do you not remember, George, why we call him Onion,?" Mary asked the child as she adjusted the bit and bridle and re-cinched the girth.

"Yeah, because he likes to eat those wild onions that grow in the field."

"Right. So I would bet you can guess what the old boy had for his supper yesterday." With that, Mary reached down, grabbed the front and back hems of her skirts, drew them up between her legs and tucked them into her waistband, making a garment akin to a pair of baggy britches. Pushing a wooden crate to the left side of the horse, Mary first stood upon the crate and then placed her left foot in the stirrup, hoisting herself onto Onion's broad back.

"Will go hold the door wide. Now mind me boys, you follow behind as lively as you can and do not go off somewhere. Come right to your mother's house or I shall have the constable after you." Reining the horse around, Mary walked him out into the sunlight and then urged Onion off at a trot. "Come along now boys," she called over her shoulder, "and make haste but not waste with my doctoring bag."

Onion expelled another malodorous blast of hot air prompting George to warn Will, "Do not follow the old fartbag too close, Will, because you know what is coming next." Will giggled and the two of them set off at a lope, following their grandmother's billowing black skirts astride the chestnut horse.

"Watch out you don't drop Nana's black bag," Will admonished his brother. "She'll switch the daylights out of our legs if we break any of her magic glass jars!"

Whenever the boys questioned Mary about the contents of her black bag, she always told them the worn leather satchel contained her 'healing magic' and that she would cast a spell on them if they dared to disturb its contents. The sound of clinking bottles was almost irresistible to the twins but they had been severely switched for far less than opening Mary's black bag so fear triumphed over curiosity and they arrived back at the row house on Locust Street with their grandmother's midwifery bag and its contents intact.

Mary guided the horse into Emma's empty shed next to a stool, dismounted and tied the horse's reins to an iron ring in the wall. She peered around the side of the shed and saw the boys hightailing it down the heavily rutted alley, black bag in hand. "Quickly, boys!" she urged them. Taking the bag from George's hand, she hurried across the sparse grass in Emma's back yard, onto the porch and then into the tiny yellow kitchen. "Oh, dear heaven!" Mary exclaimed at the sight that confronted her.

There was her only child, propped up against a dining room chair on the kitchen floor, draped in a white sheet, calmly nursing a newborn. Mary turned her gaze to the back door with its missing windowpane and then to the blood-stained linens. Immediately sizing up the situation, Mary directed the boys to take their wagon back to her house and fetch a load of firewood from her kitchen for Emma's stove. "Do not play around, George and Will, because I need lots of wood to boil water and cook some meals for our family today so you had best be off and mind you…do not dawdle!"

As the twins scampered out the back door to retrieve their wooden wagon from the shed, Mary knelt by Emma and eyed the empty bowl at her side, "Where is the afterbirth?"

"I have not yet passed it."

Mary rose to her feet, unbuttoned her sleeves, rolled them up again and began a second scrubbing at the sink. Kneeling beside her daughter, Mary took the baby from Emma and placed him on a clean dish towel near his mother. Then she began to knead Emma's belly like a mound of bread dough all the while feeling for the afterbirth to emerge. Once she was assured that she had retrieved all of the placenta and fetal membranes, Mary examined the mass, finally placing it in the bowl that Emma had ready at her side.

Next Mary took the kettle from the back of the stove and poured lukewarm water into another clean bowl. "I must wash you, dear, and change your necessary." Mary cleared her throat as she began to wash off all the traces of childbirth from her daughter's small body. "It would seem that you have done a splendid job of birthing here all by yourself. You must have had a good teacher," and Mary smiled into Emma's wan face. I am quite proud of your skills, Emma Miller Richardson. Well done! Now allow me to examine this tiny one here. Ah," exclaimed Mary as she removed the baby's swaddling towels, "so the boys were correct when they referred to this new arrival as 'him' but tell me, my darling, by what name are we calling this handsome boy child?"

"This would be Edward John Richardson, Mama, and is he not just ever so beautiful and look how tiny? Can you guess at his weight?"

"Oh, my sweet! Surely you do not intend to name him after the bugger that ran off and left you to do this by yourself, do you?"

"Mama, he is Edward's child and I want everyone, this baby included, to remember that simple fact. I want him to be able to hold his head high when people ask 'Who is your papa?'"

"Trust me, my dear girl, the question on everyone's lips these days is not who is his papa but rather, where is his papa!"

"Let us not argue now, Mama. I am so very much in need of rest. Can you please carry little Edward up the stairs and place him in the cradle next to my bed? I shall just wait here a bit and then perhaps you can help me to my feet. I do not feel that I can make it up the stairs by myself."

"Well, of course, we shall do just that although I should like to know how you came to be down here for the birthing instead of upstairs in the first place like we had planned and for which we had been prepared?"

"That is a long story, Mama, and not very important right now, but I shall tell you once I have regained my strength."

After the baby was tucked securely into his cradle by Emma's bed in the room above the kitchen, Mary helped her daughter to her feet, slipped a clean nightgown over her head and holding her firmly under the arms, guided her up the long flight of stairs to bed. As Emma looked at her sleeping infant with his dark hair and tiny hands, she imagined that any second Edward would come striding in the front door to take command of their lives and exercise dominion over her again. The culmination of events leading to Edward's sudden departure had been infinitely more painful to bear than the delivery of her child had been. Once the baby had exited her body, the pain was at an end, but the pain that Edward had so enjoyed inflicting upon Emma would endure long after his disappearance.

Edward, Emma's husband of nearly seven years, had stolen silently away from their home and their lives some three months earlier in the middle of a lovely, cool April night, abandoning his wife, his children and his responsibilities. His departure had been brutal and selfish, calculated to destroy those he left behind.

CHAPTER 2

▼

His head was bent low over the store ledger when she entered Hummel's store to make a purchase of flour, tea and sugar for Mary. Emma's long skirts swished across the dusty floor as she approached the wooden counter. Midway between a roll of white paper with its spindle of string and the imposing bulk of a brass cash register, he appeared to be totally engrossed in his pencil scratches on the ledger paper in front of him. Emma stood quietly at the counter's edge, directly in front of his bent head, waiting for some sign of recognition. As there was none, she took a moment to examine his black hair which she noted was a bit too long, in need of cutting, curling over his ears, waving back from his forehead, glossy and...without moving his head he startled her by saying, "Perhaps you think I am unaware of your presence, but the truth is I do not have to see you to know you are there for I have only to breathe the air that envelopes you to know of your proximity."

Edward abruptly raised his head to look into her brown eyes with his ice blue ones. Emma gasped, taking a half step back and self-consciously raising a hand to her lips. Edward laughed at her embarrassment, tucked the pencil behind his right ear then held out his right hand to shake hers. "Hello. Miss...what did you say your name is?"

"Actually...I did...did not say but it is...Emma," she stammered.

"Well, then, Miss Emma, the pleasure is most certainly mine," and he grabbed her hand, audaciously pressing it to his lips. "I am Edward, Mr. Hummel's new clerk, at your service and may I say that the fragrance which you are wearing is quite captivating," and Edward inhaled deeply. "Roses?" he guessed correctly.

Flushing uncontrollably, Emma withdrew her hand. "And you, sir, are more than a bit forward. Do you use this ploy to make the acquaintance of all the young ladies who frequent Hummel's?"

"Why, Miss Emma, you have wounded me," and Edward placed his right hand dramatically over his heart, all the while gazing into her eyes, "for you think me insincere!"

"Nonsense," Emma retorted, regaining her composure. "I am here for sugar, flour and that special blend of tea that my mother, Mary Miller, ordered. Has it come in yet?"

"Ah, we are to be all business then, are we? Pretending that it never happened!" Edward looked sorrowfully at Emma.

"I assure you that absolutely nothing has happened except that your impertinence is beginning to annoy me. Please be so kind as to fill my mother's order at once as I am not at leisure to waste another moment listening to your foolishness," fussed Emma tapping upon the counter.

"Very well, then, business it is," and Edward turned his back to her to search the shelves for Mary's supplies. He rang up Emma's purchases on the gleaming cash register and she handed him coins from her purse. Then Edward deftly arranged the items on a length of paper, wrapping the bundle and tying it tightly with string.

"Here you are, Miss Emma, or perhaps I should carry this home for you, as the parcel is rather heavy and awkward and I feel certain that Mr. Hummel could spare me for a few minutes."

"Absolutely not! You are a total stranger, and a rude one at that! Good day, Clerk Edward!"

"The pleasure was all mine, Miss Emma Miller," he said leaning over the counter until she could feel his breath upon her cheek. "When shall I see you again?"

"Never!" Emma snorted, snatching the package from him and sashaying out the double store front doors.

Without so much as a backward glance and with her head held high, Emma clasped the bundle to her side, sweeping up her skirts with a free hand before crossing the square to Longmeadow. Once the river snaked into view, she stopped to catch her breath and ponder the unsettling encounter with the handsome but aggressive clerk. Her heart raced and she felt quite giddy.

"What," she wondered, "had possessed this Edward...this clerk...Edward Noname to be so forward with her?" Never in all her life had she been so intimately approached by such a smooth-talking and wildly handsome dark-haired stranger. Much to her surprise, Emma realized that she had enjoyed every second of his flirtatious talk. Furthermore, she was certain that Clerk Edward Noname had enjoyed the dalliance himself for she had distinctly felt his pleasure coursing all the way through her body, even down to her toes.

Emma's feet scarcely touched the road as she made her way along Main Street, down Longmeadow, across the railroad tracks and up High Point Avenue where she lived with her parents, Mary and James Miller. Safely out of sight of Clerk Edward Noname, she once again lifted her skirts and raced up the broad expanse of lawn with its ancient garrison of majestic oaks, maples and tulip poplars and its unsullied view of the Southport River, to the large white frame house which sat atop the heavily shaded knoll. Her father was seated on the front porch in the swing with a glass of lemonade in one hand and the Grandview Courier in the other.

"What is your hurry there, my sweet?" James called from behind his newspaper to his only child.

"Oh, Papa! I have just seen...been...to Hummel's for flour and sugar for Mama's cakes and I had best be getting these ingredients right to the kitchen," she answered quite breathlessly.

James peered blankly over the edges of his paper at his daughter as she paused in front of him. "Are we having a party that I have forgotten?" asked James returning to the perusal of his paper.

"Papa, you are such a tease!" Emma scolded her father. "After building all those nice long wooden tables for the summer social at the church, I doubt very seriously that you would forget such a thing!" James just looked over the top of his paper and winked at his daughter.

Emma found her mother at the back of the house, dripping with perspiration, the sleeves of her white blouse rolled up above her elbows, busily creaming mounds of butter and sugar for her famous pound cakes in the enormous, old cracked bowl which Mary claimed was crucial to turning out a perfect cake.

"Thank you, my darling girl, for retrieving the extra flour and sugar for me...one cake would simply never do for the summer social." Mary paused to glance at her daughter, adding, "My, you look more flushed than if you had been standing over the stove all day. Are you feeling quite right, Emma?" asked Mary, casting an appraising eye over her daughter and touching the back of a flour-covered hand to her daughter's forehead.

"I am feeling fine, Mama. I was just in a hurry to get all the ingredients for your cakes because I know they will take a long time to bake and cool," Emma replied dipping her finger into the glossy mixture of sugar and butter in the mixing bowl. "May I have a glass of lemonade? I noticed Papa has one and it certainly did look inviting," Emma said changing the subject. "But you know it is a bit hotter than I thought so if you do not mind, I believe I shall just go to my room and remove my petticoat." Pouring herself a glass of lemonade from the icebox, Emma walked back down the long hall to the staircase and up to her room at the front of the house.

Emma stood for a moment with her back to the closed door as if trying to catch her breath when she caught sight of herself in the oval, cherry floor mirror which stood in a corner of her room. Advancing slowly toward her image, she placed the lemonade on her dresser and looked with fascination at her image reflected in the glass as if she were seeing herself for the first time. What was it that had so interested Clerk Edward Noname?

Slowly Emma unfastened the buttons at the side of her cotton skirt, letting it fall to the floor. Then her fingers moved to the white, whalebone buttons of her blouse, which she let fall to her feet. Her lace petticoat fluttered to the floor, leaving Emma standing before her image clad only in her white step-in. Reaching for the buttons across each shoulder, she let her undergarment slip down to the rest of her clothing. Moving the pile aside with a tiny foot, Emma stood gazing at herself, first the front and then with the help of her silver hand mirror, she scrutinized her backside. Turning to the long mirror again, her hands moved to unknot the white ribbon which caught up her auburn hair at the nape of her neck. She fluffed the long curls over her shoulders and peered at the woman looking back at her.

She smiled at her image. "Good teeth! That must be it!" she mused. Her father had always admonished her to check a horse's teeth before selecting an animal. The teeth told it all. Obviously, Edward Noname had seen her teeth but he certainly had not viewed anything below the jaw line. Still, in conversations with her female friends and snippets of overheard divulgences amongst ladies of the town, Emma had gleaned that men tended to be preoccupied with the female figure and specifically that portion which lay hidden underneath endless layers of clothing.

Just the previous week, Emma had heard Miss Rita, Grandview's school teacher, giggling to Mrs. Hummel that Mr. Sweeney always found an excuse to bring the milk directly inside her kitchen to the icebox for storage. Miss Rita had confided to Mrs. Hummel that Mr. Sweeney was inordinately fond of patting her buttocks, giving her a little squeeze as he did so. Recently, Mr. Sweeney had worked up the courage to give his favorite customer a little peck on the cheek before leaving to complete his deliveries. Miss Rita was seeking the wise counsel of Mrs. Hummel for she feared that she had allowed Mr. Sweeney to be rather forward with her. More laughter ensued as Emma had strained to catch every word of the ladies' gossip.

As she perused her body from head to toe, she wondered if Clerk Edward would like to give her buttocks a squeeze, and she turned to view herself from the back again. What exactly was it that men found so attractive about what lay concealed beneath the layers of women's clothing? Emma's ample breasts were such a nuisance to her, flouncing up and down awkwardly as she ran or when she worked Onion up into a rollicking canter across the meadow. Besides all that, every man on earth knew that the purpose of a woman's breasts was to suckle an infant. Her stomach was flat, punctuated with a tiny round navel and between her slightly muscled legs was a puff of auburn hair. Turning again to view her backside, Emma mused that perhaps it was her buttocks which so aroused the passions of Edward Noname, even as Miss Rita's so enflamed Mr. Sweeney. "Strange creatures, these men," reflected Emma silently, pulling up her step-in and re-buttoning her blouse and skirt. She kicked aside the detested petticoat, tied back her hair again and, without her shoes, went downstairs to sip lemonade with her father on the front porch.

James appeared just as she had left him, still reading the newspaper, legs idly moving the swing forward and backward. "Papa," she began.

"Uh-huh," responded James, never taking his eyes from the print.

"I was just wondering…how did you know that you loved Mama enough to want to marry her?"

James peered at his daughter over the top of the evening paper and then lowered his gaze to the printed text. Emma waited for a response as she sipped lemonade in the white wicker chair. James ignored his daughter's question.

"Papa? Did you hear me?" persisted Emma.

James looked a bit uncomfortable as he began, "Well, now…ahem…perhaps that is a question which you might want to pose to your mother."

"Do not be silly, Papa! I want to know how it was that you knew you loved Mama."

James cleared his throat, slid a finger around the inside of his shirt collar and replied, "Well, the truth of the matter is that I could not take my eyes off your mother from the very first instant I met her. She was absolutely the most beautiful woman I had ever seen. I have always told her that she cast a spell upon me and the spell has never been broken."

"Yes, yes…but did you check her teeth first or did you check her buttocks?" Emma asked, nonchalantly sipping her drink.

James choked on his lemonade, "What on the face of the earth has prompted you to ask such a question, my dear child?"

"It is just that you have always told me when considering the purchase of a horse, you must first check the teeth. Good teeth mean a good horse, right? But, I have heard lately that men check the buttocks of the women that they are considering for marriage and I wondered what might constitute good buttocks as opposed to bad buttocks?" Emma babbled at her astonished father.

At this, James could contain himself no longer. Throwing back his head, he began to laugh uncontrollably. When at last he caught his breath, he folded his newspaper and with it slapped Emma playfully on her knee. "Child, it is time for us to wash up for dinner. Perhaps you should seek the wise counsel of your mother for an answer to that very profound question. I feel certain that she would have a much more enlightened view of the subject than I," and still chuckling to himself, James went into the house banging the screen door with its fine white scrollwork behind him.

Emma lingered a while longer on the porch watching the boats ply the muddy waters of the Southport River. She could hear both her mother and her father laughing uproariously from the kitchen. Papa, it seemed, had told on her.

The next morning, Emma dressed in her customary summer attire of white cotton skirt and blouse but no petticoat this time. Spreading her legs beneath her skirt in front of the mirror, she checked her image to see if anyone could detect that she was not wearing the required garment. What a silly piece of clothing a petticoat was! Hot, bothersome and in her way when she rode Onion or ran across the field to her father's lumber mill down by the river. This morning, however, there would be no need to rush to her job at the mill for she had slept barely a wink, rising before the sun. Thoughts of Edward, Mr. Hummel's clerk, had crowded out sleep the previous night.

Emma felt amazingly refreshed and energized as she greeted her mother in the kitchen.

"Good morning, Mama!"

"Well now, this must be Miss Early Bird herself that I see before me! Is something going on at the mill today that I have forgotten?"

"Not that I recall," replied Emma taking one of her mother's freshly baked biscuits from the pan and slathering it with butter and cream gravy. Humming to herself, she poured a glass of cold milk and sat at the kitchen table to eat her breakfast. "Where is Papa?" Emma asked with her mouth full.

"For pity's sake, Emma! Swallow your food first. Papa left some time ago because he is anxious to load a big order of lumber onto the barge this morning. It has a long way to go and the builder in New Orleans wants his lumber right away."

"Oh, yes, I remember. Did you know that some of the hired men have been whispering that this man in New Orleans wants Papa's fine lumber to build himself a great house of ill-repute? Now, why would that man waste so much money to buy Papa's fine lumber in order to construct a house that he knows is going to have such an unfavorable reputation?" Emma asked naively.

Mary clattered the pots and pans at the sink, her back to Emma. Turning slowly toward her daughter and wiping her hands on her apron, she said, "I think perhaps it is time that you and I had a talk about men and women. After all, you began your monthlies when you were twelve and ever since you turned eighteen, you have been assisting me as a midwife." Mary paused to gauge the impact of her words upon her daughter who continued to devour her breakfast without looking up at her mother.

Clearing her throat, Mary tried again. "I know that you are well familiar with how and from where babies are born but it is my distinct impression that you know nothing of how they get into the womb of the mother in the first place. Am I correct?" she asked looking at the top of her daughter's head.

"Why would I need to know such a thing, Mama? I am not married and do not intend to have a baby. So do you not think such information is useless? Papa always says, 'Do not clutter up your mind with nonsense and things you do not need to know.'" Mary was about to protest when Emma rose from the kitchen table, gulped the rest of her milk and headed for the back door. "Did Papa take our lunch with him? Did he remember to take some pound cake for us too?"

"Yes, and no to the second question. Honestly, Emma, you are exasperating! The cakes are for the church picnic tomorrow, and mind, I do need your help frying all the chicken tomorrow morning so please do not make any plans to run off to the mill after your father, and," Mary wheeled around to face her daughter who was silhouetted against the light at the backdoor, "I see you are once again not wearing your petticoat, so upstairs with you this instant and put it on!"

"Oh, Mama! It is too hot and such a bother!"

"Right now! I cannot permit you go to the mill in that condition."

Ever since Emma had demonstrated an uncanny facility with addition, subtraction and multiplication at the age of fourteen, James had employed his daughter as the bookkeeper at his lumber mill for the sum of two cents a day. At first, Mary had protested vehemently. It was not ladylike for her daughter to be in the company of so many smelly, foul-tongued hired hands. James had pointed out to her that it was his mill and Emma would not be allowed near the barges or the wagons or the saws or the hired hands. Instead, he promised that his only child would sit in the office keeping track of their fortune as it pertained to the lumber business.

"She has a good head on her shoulders, Mary," he had offered, "just like her mother!" James prevailed in hiring his daughter.

Emma adored her father and followed him around the mill, the lumber yard and the loading dock with her paper and pencil in hand, making note of the heft of rough sawn white oak as opposed to yellow poplar, learning to price lumber by the board foot and overhearing her father negotiate the sale price of a wagonload of prime cherry. "Just smell that glorious fresh cut wood, Emma!" James would pause to admonish his apprentice. "After you have worked here a bit longer, you will come to know cherry from oak from poplar with your eyes closed, just by the smell." Emma dutifully inhaled deeply of the musty odors emanating from the neatly stacked piles of lumber, but to little avail. Wood was wood and it all smelled alike to her.

What truly interested Emma was the level of activity around the mill. No two days were ever the same and there was always some sort of weekly crisis like the time Herbert arrived too inebriated to operate the hoist for loading the barge, only to let go of the ropes, allowing them to snake out of the pulleys, spilling James Miller's precious lumber into the river. Then all the hired hands jumped into the water to swim after the cargo that was rapidly floating off downstream to join the Mississippi. Emma had enjoyed the fracas enormously, especially the antics of all the hired men as they splashed after the lumber. James had later shushed his daughter, warning her not to tell Mary that she had witnessed such an event for several of the men were naked to the waist.

She loved to sit on the top of a barrel seat that her father had fashioned for her. From her perch under the ancient oak that anchored the mill to the land, Emma listened to old Bill weave his stories of chicanery and deception that lead to his escape from behind Confederate lines. Emma always knew when old Bill was nearing the exciting denouement of one of his stories for he spat mightily into the dust beside his left shoe. James would then roll his eyes at Emma and jerk his thumb toward the mill door, indicating that she was to get back to work and so was old Bill.

Mary realized that her daughter was spending more and more time at the mill and subsequently less time at home. She felt frustrated by her failed efforts to interest Emma in the fine art of cooking on the wood-burning stove. Mary was exasperated by her daughter's inability to grasp the concept that flour, salt, leavening, lard and milk must be measured carefully, combined and kneaded with a light hand in order to ensure the desired result…a light, edible biscuit. Her father teased Emma that he could use her biscuits as ballast on the barges.

Emma consistently burned her mother's rabbit stew even after Mary had repeatedly instructed her to move the pot slowly to the cool side of the stove while stirring every fifteen minutes. Her excuse was always that she needed to read just one more page of the newspaper or her book so that she and Papa would be able to have a lively discussion of the issues over dinner.

Mary tried teaching her daughter to clean their spacious four bedroom home. Elizabeth was an elderly widow who came twice a week to the house to assist Mary with beating the carpets, washing the family's clothing and sluicing the pots. The latter was particularly abhorrent to Emma and consisted of lining up the chamber pots on the back lawn for their weekly soaping and bleaching in the sunlight.

It was because of his daughter's aversion to the chamber pot ritual that James was one of the first in Grandview to install indoor plumbing in the form of running water at their kitchen sink and a bathroom in a converted closet above the kitchen. Emma absolutely loved the running water and would linger in the bathtub until her mother would come to pound on the door, admonishing her, "Time is up or I shall appear to you and dry you off myself!"

Ironing was a task which Elizabeth seemed to enjoy immensely for it allowed her to remain in a fixed position, shifting the irons from the top of the stove to the board where she pressed the family's sheets and clothing. Knowing that Mary was worried about her daughter's lack of domestic skills, Elizabeth took on the task of teaching Emma to iron. At first, Emma seemed to be an apt pupil, carefully smoothing out the largest wrinkles from the sheets by hand as she placed the linens on the board. Lifting the hot iron from the stove with a folded towel around the handle, Emma then spit on the iron in order to make sure that it would sizzle as an indication that the correct temperature for ironing had been reached.

One afternoon as Emma guided the iron effortlessly over the sheets, she begged Elizabeth to tell her a story to make the time pass more quickly. Never one to pass up an opportunity to tell one of her stories, especially if she could squeeze in a moral or two for her young listener, Elizabeth launched into a favorite story about the day she assisted Mrs. Hummel at the birthing of Emma.

"And as I was saying," reminisced Elizabeth, "your poor mama was having a very difficult time of it as you were determined to stay put and Mary was determined to have you come out, so it was akin to a big tug of war such as we have at the socials, only without the mud in the middle." Elizabeth laughed, looking out the kitchen window, totally engrossed now in her story telling.

"Your dear sweet little mother was imploring Mrs. Hummel, me and most especially the good Lord with all of His angels to be merciful, saying, 'Please do something for I cannot go on like this much longer as the pain is too strong.' Then she turned to me and knowing that I am a God-fearing, church-going woman, Mary implored me to sing a hymn. So, I chose 'Rock of Ages' which I sang for her in a solemn manner as would befit a house of worship. But my dear Mary implored me, 'For the love of Jesus, sing it louder, Elizabeth! The pain is killing me,' and she rose up off the bed to glare at me in such a terrible fashion that she quite scared the daylights out of me so I commenced the hymn again…only much louder."

At this juncture of the story, Elizabeth began to sing raucously in her best contralto, "Rock of ages cleft for me. Let me hide myself in Thee," interrupting her singing only to narrate that every time she reached the end of a verse, Mary would exhort her to sing it again but louder. "And suddenly, Mrs. Hummel spied a tiny foot coming out and she commanded, 'By all that is holy, Mary, you must push like you're expelling the devil himself because the child is coming out feet first,' and your poor mother gave several more heaves and I sang louder than I have ever sung before and the next thing we knew you had arrived, feet first…dancing…or so your proud mama always claimed. Mary always said that you entered the world with a song in your heart and music in your toes."

The two women laughed at this juncture of the story like a couple of conspirators until Elizabeth wheeled around to face Emma who stood with hands on hips, laughing violently, iron resting on the clean white sheet. "Jesus the Almighty!" exclaimed Elizabeth. "The sheet is burning! Quick the pail!" Emma rushed over to the sink, filled the metal pail with water and handed it to the old housekeeper who immediately threw the pail and its contents at the ironing board whereupon there arose a great sizzling sound accompanied by a billowing cloud of steam and smoke.

Emma rushed to the ironing board, grabbed the still sputtering iron with a towel and set it back on the stove. Then she picked up the soggy, blackened sheet, put it up to her face, peered through the triangular hole and asked Elizabeth, "Does this mean that I am absolved from ironing?"

"Yes," replied Elizabeth, "and it also means that if I catch you in this kitchen ever again I shall beat your hide like I do one of your mother's rugs. Now go read a book while I clean up this mess before the missus returns."

Elizabeth never did tattle on her domestic protégé but then it was not necessary, for everyone in the family and her immediate circle of acquaintances knew
that Emma had two left feet in the kitchen and could barely boil water. Her coffee was such a joke that everyone teased her with such comments as, "Well,
Emma, could you make us a cup of coffee now and just remember I like mine
strong…so that the spoon stands up in the cup all by itself!" referring to the time
she had offered to make coffee for the hired hands at the mill and had ground up
a whole bag of beans for one pot of coffee.

Emma always flushed to the roots of her hair but the teasing failed to daunt
her for she secretly loathed cooking and household chores of any kind. "You had
best plan on marrying a wealthy man, dear Emma," her father had teased, "one
that can afford to hire a cook and a laundress for you!"

"Mama, why must we stand over this infernally hot stove on such a glorious
summer morning frying chicken of all things?" Emma scolded her mother, wiping the sweat which poured from her face and neck.

"We are responsible for frying four chickens to take to the picnic this afternoon and supplying three cakes. If everyone pitches in to help with the preparation of the food then many hands make the work less of a burden. Now mind
Emma that you do not burn that skillet of chicken there. Move the pan just a bit
off center. Pour some more buttermilk into the bowl over those chicken parts
which I just cut up and where did you put the lard pan?"

"Mama, you are a wonder!" responded Emma. "Your powers of concentration
far exceed those of anyone else! How can you possibly keep track of so many pots,
bowls and ingredients at one time?"

Turning to scrutinize her daughter's face, Mary wiped off her hands and
reached out to smooth back a drooping curl from Emma's forehead. "Domestic
chores are my forte. I can cook, keep house, needlepoint, quilt and garden. But,
as a hedge against difficult times, please remember that I can also deliver babies
from their mothers' wombs and people hereabouts are only too happy to pay me
for these services. I learned this skill early on because as a child, I watched in
despair as my own dear mother foundered after the untimely death of my father.
As a result, the three of us, my mother, my baby brother and I, all had to be taken
in by my mother's sister and her family. I vowed right then and there that one
day I would learn something useful and be able to take care of myself no matter
what befell me. Hard times taught me a very valuable lesson. Always remember
that before you take on the care of anyone else you must first learn to take care of
yourself."

Emma was thinking about her mother's words the next morning as she luxuri-
ated in a bubble bath above the kitchen. She had never before quite realized the
import of her mother's midwifery skills until the previous day. After all, there was
no need for Mary to assume any work that took her outside the comforts of her
home since James provided a very tidy living for the family with his lumber mill,
the only one in Grandview. Word had it that even across the Southport River in
the larger city of Clarksburg, James Miller's lumber was renowned. Orders had
also begun to stream in from such far away places as New Orleans.

As she soaped herself for the second time, Emma pondered her mother's
determination to maintain her status as the town's midwife. She wondered if her
mother felt the same sense of satisfaction after delivering a new baby that she felt
when she had balanced all of her father's accounts. Emma derived great satisfaction from being compensated for her bookkeeping skills. Her skills had worth
and so did she.

Emma continued to contemplate these weighty matters as she soaked in the
copper tub until her mother interrupted her reverie by knocking on the door.
"Child! You must complete your toilette! Papa is harnessing Onion and I have
the food packed. We must be off to church for the picnic!"

"At once, Mama!" Emma responded, rising immediately from the now cold
water and grabbing her towel. Hurriedly she dried, dressed and combed her hair
back, tying it with a pink satin ribbon. The buttons on her shoes would not
cooperate and she ran down the stairs barefooted, shoes and button hook in
hand. Dashing across the lawn, Emma could not help noticing how cool the grass
felt underfoot and how she wished she could go to the picnic barefooted, but
once in the carriage, she dutifully applied the hated strictures to her feet.

"What! No stockings?" Mary chided her daughter.

"No one will notice under my skirt, Mama."

"Just as long as you do not stand up on the swings in the oak tree. We would
not want any of those young fellows getting a glimpse of your bare legs!"

"I promise. No standing on the swings," and Emma avoided her mother's critical gaze.

After James guided their carriage up to the church hitching rail and tied
Onion's reins securely, he offered his hand to Mary as she descended. Emma did
not look up as she stuck out her right hand and moved her skirts aside with the
left. When her feet touched the ground, she looked at her mother and realized
that James was still holding onto Mary's hand. Quickly she looked to see who
held her hand and to her utter astonishment, there was Edward, grinning at her

with his perfect teeth, ice blue eyes crinkling at the corners and his magnificent, if unruly, black hair curling around his ears.

"I have been waiting for your arrival, Miss Emma Miller," Edward announced. Taken aback, Emma momentarily lost the ability to formulate words.

"Well, now Emma…how about introducing us to your gentleman friend, my dear," suggested James raising an eyebrow.

"Actually sir, I fear that Miss Emma does not know my surname as we were never formally introduced. Permit me to shake your hand, Mr. Miller, and introduce myself to you. I am Edward Richardson, Mr. Hummel's new clerk, recently arrived from Clarksburg," and he smiled broadly into the startled face of Emma's father.

"And this," said Edward turning to Mary, "must be Emma's lovely mother. I see the resemblance. Please permit me to offer you this small gift of rose hip tea as I know it to be a favorite of yours." While extending a small packet to her, Edward lightly grasped Mary's hand and Emma could have sworn that her mother actually blushed.

"Well then Edward, you are just the man we need. Come with me sir for we do have several baskets of the most delicious fried chicken and three absolutely splendid pound cakes to deliver to the picnic tables. One pound cake was not enough," James confided cordially to Edward. "No sir! My Mary had to bake three pound cakes," he bragged.

"I expect that Miss Emma is also to be credited with these tasty morsels that I see before me," smiled Edward.

Mary, James and Emma all exchanged glances.

"Well…um…er…yes. In a manner of speaking. To be sure, Emma was positively glued to her mother's side during all the cooking and baking…right Mary?"

"Oh, yes…quite right, James."

The trio moved on to the large oak trees shading the picnic tables that James had crafted at his mill.

"So, Emma my sweet, how is it that you failed to tell me about the dashingly handsome Edward Richardson and the circumstances of your meeting?" Mary said sotto voce to her daughter as she smiled and nodded to the passersby.

"Well I guess I did not think Mr. Hummel's store clerk was of much interest to you or Papa. I know he is of absolutely no interest to me," Emma sniffed as she walked away to join a group of girls who had gathered by the watering trough to admire a spirited dapple-gray mare belonging to the new preacher, Pastor Nesbitt.

Edward helped James place Mary's golden fried chicken and pound cakes on one of the long wooden tables in the shade to the side of the church before he spoke again.

"Looks like a grand feast, Mr. Miller, would you agree?"

"Indeed it does. Makes my mouth water just surveying the delectable assortment. Now do not breathe a word of this, for my Mary is a splendid cook, but Miss Rita makes the absolute best fried corn fritters over there," and James gestured to a brightly colored platter stacked high with the crispy bread and draped with a red and white napkin, "especially if you top them off with a hearty splash of sorghum."

"I shall certainly keep that in mind when heaping my plate this afternoon. Please excuse me now, sir, as I intend to teach that group of young men over yonder some of the finer points of the game of horseshoes. None among them seem capable of landing a ringer."

Out of her peripheral vision, Emma could plainly see Edward challenging the youths to a game of horseshoes but still she remained with her circle of friends chatting about the new preacher, his horse and the various dishes of food that they had all brought to the festivities for the afternoon picnic.

"Dear me, but it is ever so hot! You could positively fry potatoes on a stone today!" exclaimed Emma. "Does anyone else want to accompany me over to get a lemonade?" The rest of the girls declined so Emma feigned nonchalance as she strolled to the drink table which was closer yet to the horseshoe pits. As she chatted to a neighbor lady who was dipping up the lemonade, Emma kept one eye on Edward.

"My, what delightful lemonade this is! You absolutely must tell me how to make it!"

"Oh, it really isn't that difficult Emma but the secret is to remove each and every seed from the juice before adding the sugar only not too much sugar for that can make your skin crawl."

"Mmmm," responded Emma as she pretended to listen, all the while paying rapt attention to Edward.

Just as Emma turned to pluck a crisp cookie encrusted with sugar from the basket next to the lemonade pitcher, she felt a hand on her right shoulder. Startled, she turned abruptly, spilling some of the sticky drink onto her white blouse and coming within inches of Edward's handsome, sweaty face.

"Forgive me, Emma," apologized Edward as he retrieved a napkin from the table and offered it to her. "I did not mean to startle you. I just beat those lads at horseshoes and felt that I had worn out my welcome among them. Perhaps I could interest you in dining with me. Might we go help ourselves to some of that wonderful looking food? I personally have worked up a vast hunger and thirst."

"But…but…my mother and father," Emma stammered.

"Oh, of course. How rude of me. We shall ask them to join us."

Approaching a tight knot of church elders that included her father, Emma pulled at her father's sleeve. "Psst! Papa!"

James turned to his daughter, "Yes, dear, what is it?"

Speaking boldly, Emma announced, "Edward has invited me to eat with him so if you and Mama do not object, I should like to sit with him for a while."

Distracted at having to interrupt his conversation, James replied, "Yes, yes. By all means, but make sure that you two put a large dent in Mother's fried chicken," and he waved them off in the direction of the tables.

Suddenly free of parental obligation, Emma smiled as she and Edward filled their plates with picnic food and took seats at the farthest end of the last table, away from the gathering crowd. As the two of them engaged in polite chatter about the food, the crowd and the weather, Emma took stock of the young man seated before her. She had not dared to look below his face at the store, but now she let her eyes feast upon his upper body. His white shirt was worn rolled up at the sleeves, well above his elbows to reveal finely muscled arms with little hair. The shirt which was drenched with his sweat clung to broad shoulders. As he ate, Edward pushed his suspenders aside and Emma's attention was drawn to his thick neck and squarely cut jaw.

He caught her looking and said, "Have you filled up already, Emma? Just look at the desserts and think of your mother's cakes!" he reminded her.

Daintily wiping the corners of her mouth with the checkered napkin and clearing her throat, Emma said, "I eat three meals each and every day but it is not often that I am in the company of such a…an interesting man and I prefer the conversation to the food. Perhaps you would indulge me by telling me a bit about yourself Edward, as I know so little and it is my fond hope that you and I shall become friends," and then she lowered her eyes to her plate. Surely she had tipped her hand with that last remark as it was much too forward.

Edward seemed to take no notice of her breach of social etiquette and instead, unsettled her again by flashing that beautiful grin of perfect teeth at her. "Your wish is my command, fair lady. Let me think where to begin? Are you sure you want to hear the very boring story of my life?"

"Quite sure!" she responded, nibbling at Miss Rita's corn fritter.

"Well, then, I was born across the Southport River in Clarksburg some twenty seven years ago to John and Edwina Richardson, people of modest means. My father was a tenant farmer on the outskirts of town and I was my mother's only child, but as she was fond of saying, I more than made up for the other three that she lost.

I was the kind of child who always loved adventure, whether it was climbing to the top of the highest oak tree by our house or attempting to swim across the Southport at age eight to see what was on the other side. As a result, I suffered more than my share of broken bones, bloody noses, scraped knees and elbows than any other child in Clarksburg and Grandview combined, or so my mother used to claim. I even had the misfortune of an encounter with a bobcat one evening."

At this revelation, Emma's eyes widened and she exhorted Edward, "Do go on!"

"Yes, I was about six or seven and supposed to be asleep when I heard what I knew to be the wail of a bobcat coming from outside my bedroom window in the vicinity of the barn where my father put up his hay and kept a few chickens. When I crept by my parents' bedroom I could discern that they were otherwise engaged and had not heard the bobcat. So I made my way out the back of the house and by the light of the moon, to the barn door which I noted to be ajar. I threw the barn door wide open and could perceive that the bobcat was laying waste to my father's chickens and so I picked up the pitchfork and was advancing upon the creature when he turned and bit me severely in the leg several times while I continued to flog him with the pitchfork."

At this juncture of the narrative, Edward paused to gauge the reaction from Emma, who sat transfixed across the table from him. "Oh, you poor dear boy! It is a wonder that you did not bleed to death right there in the barn! What happened next?"

She was hooked! Edward knew it and now the fun of reeling her in had begun.

"Of course I was crying out in terrible pain and the bobcat also was howling madly with the pain that I had inflicted upon him with the pitchfork so my parents were alerted to my dilemma and came running from the house. Father discharged his old musket after the fleeing creature and then he and Mother rushed me into the house to tend to my wounds. Would you like to see them?" he asked Emma somberly.

"May I?" she flushed.

With out any further ado, Edward stuck out his right leg from under the ging-ham tablecloth and proceeded to raise his trouser leg above the knee. Emma moved to examine the now white scars as they appeared around his knee and on the inside of his calf. Gently, erotically she traced the pale welts with her finger-tips around his lower leg realizing as she did so that she was skating dangerously near the perimeters of decency. Looking up into his blue eyes which were fas-tened upon her face, Emma whispered, "Are there any others?"

Their eyes joined for several palpable moments before Edward answered, "Yes, many more on my upper thigh but I do believe your parents would set the con-stable upon me if I were to reveal them to you." They both laughed nervously and Emma took a large sip of lemonade to ease the burning feeling.

"You certainly were a most heroic lad, albeit an adventurous one, Edward. Now tell me, what of your schooling?"

"Hard work was more prized in my family than book learning. Oh, I learned to read and write but my father so desperately needed another pair of hands in the fields that I found it necessary to abandon my books at an early age in order to help him put food on our table."

"What of your parents? Where are they now? Still in Clarksburg?"

Edward looked over her shoulder and then down at the ground before responding. "They took ill with typhoid fever and died when I was ten," answered Edward his eyes briefly misting.

"Oh, do forgive me for intruding on such a painful memory. I had no idea that you had faced such brutal circumstances in life at such a tender age!" and Emma moved to his side to place her arm around his shoulders. Instinctively, Edward turned his head to rest it against her body and Emma sensed she had been struck by lightning. For a fleeting moment, she cradled his head to her bosom while murmuring, "I am so terribly sorry for your profound loss!"

In an instant, Emma regained her wits and swept from his side. "Do let us take stroll around the grounds a bit," and she slipped her arm through his as he continued to tell his story.

"Actually, Emma, I was most fortunate because my mother's sister, Aunt Lenore, saved me and helped me grow into the man that I am today. I truly owe it to her that I survived. You see, Aunt Lenore was a spinster lady and obviously without any hope of children of her own. Due to a disorder of birth, Aunt Lenore had been born with only one arm and therefore was not considered suitable mar-riage material by any of the men in Clarksburg. But do you know, there was absolutely nothing that woman could not do with one arm! She could sew, cook, keep house, wring a chicken's neck, pluck the feathers, eviscerate the fowl and cut it up for frying and…all with one hand!"

"And I perceive that you love her dearly. I wonder who is the luckier one, you or she? Might I have the pleasure of making the acquaintance of the second woman to cast such a spell upon you?"

"Sadly, Aunt Lenore was mortally injured in a buckboard accident some five years ago. Her horse shied, reared and pitched Aunt Lenore off the seat under the wheels of the buckboard. She never drew another conscious breath again. The day she died, I took that horse into the field beyond the house and shot him once through the head."

Emma shivered as she imagined the handsome Edward pointing a gun to the head of the hapless horse and pulling the trigger. Edward's tale of unrelenting sadness and woe staggered the senses and the imagination of Emma. There was so much to fathom about this handsome new friend of hers and her rush of feelings for him was overwhelming. Just at the very moment that Emma was feeling faint, James appeared calling, "Yoo-hoo! Emma! Time we had best be going home with your mother now for she is a bit tired. Come along dear and good evening to you, Edward. It was a pleasure to meet you," and James gave Edward's hand a good, strong shaking.

Emma looked stricken. Edward, noticing her expression, asked, "When may I see you again?" Then he laughed at Emma's puzzled expression by recalling, "The last time I asked you that question your answer was, 'Never.' May I be so bold as to hope for a more favorable answer this time?"

"Perhaps," was all that Emma replied as she turned to follow her father through the crowd.

CHAPTER 3

▼

The child, still nestled snugly in his tiny cradle, began to make sucking noises and abruptly ended Emma's post-birth nap. Sunlight flooded the room now and the roses bloomed brightly in a profusion of color from her bedroom walls. Edward had detested her choice of wallpaper but Emma took special delight every time she looked around the room in knowing she had prevailed in her selection, minor though it was, for it was usually Edward's decisions and taste that reigned supreme.

"Are you hungry, my little precious?" Emma cooed to her infant as she gently lifted him from his cradle. At his mother's touch, the baby began to wail hungrily until firmly attached to his mother's breast.

"Is that our darling little John that I hear?" called Mary from the foot of the steps.

"Yes, it is our darling little Edward, Mama!" countered Emma.

Mary entered her daughter's bedroom carrying a tray on which sat a small pitcher of ice water and several slices of buttered cinnamon bread.

"I noticed as I chipped the ice from the box for your pitcher of water that you are low and I took the liberty of sending the boys off to the icehouse to order up some more. With this heat what is left in the icebox will not last much longer," and Mary handed Emma a frosted glass of ice water which she drank straight down and handed back to her mother for a refill. "Strange," mused Mary, "but every time I see flecks of sawdust on a block of ice, it reminds me of your father."

"Well, there is nothing strange about it, Mama. After all, it is Papa's fine saw-dust that is used by the icehouse to store the blocks of ice." Changing the subject,

Emma added, "Just imagine how proud Papa would be of this little one here today!"

"Indeed he would be!" Mary paused, looking tenderly at the baby as he nursed. "It seems hard to believe that Papa has already been gone two whole years! He so adored Will and George and I know this baby would have brought a special joy to his heart also." Mary walked to the window and looked out at the roof over the back porch.

"I still think about old Bill finding him slumped against the oak tree at the mill and thinking that he was asleep, shook Papa's shoulder. James just keeled on over and in my mind's eye, I see the men from the mill carrying him back home to me...slowly...ever so slowly up the front slope. They laid him out on the porch and I threw myself upon him exhorting him, 'James! James! Do you hear me my darling?' And of course he never heard another word I said."

Mary looked around at her daughter and said, "Forgive me, Emma, but it is just that my emotions are running high...both from joy and sadness and today the two are very intimately connected so that I can barely discern one emotion from the other. That is what I am feeling today as I gaze upon the face of this bright and beautiful new life just beginning while remembering and longing for the one so recently ended." Emma reached out her hand to hold her mother's and the two women were joined in an intense moment of celebration and sorrow.

Just then, as if on cue, George and Will came thudding up the stairs to the back bedroom.

"Right, Nana! We ordered the ice and it'll be here in the morning," announced Will.

"And we even had a penny left over," chimed in George handing the coin to his grandmother.

"Well done, boys!" Mary praised her grandsons. "See what fine lads we have here, Emma! Who dares to suggest that we women have no men to care for us! You two might want to visit the kitchen and wash up those dirty hands before eating the nice cinnamon bread that I brought over for the two of you...and I put extra butter on the slices, just the way you like it! Now run along and eat but remember to drink your milk too!"

When the boys had run back down the stairs, Mary reached for the baby to burp him. Pulling the rocking chair closer to Emma's bed, she began to cuddle and rock the infant to sleep. Clearing her throat, she began talking quietly to her daughter.

"I have been doing some serious thinking the last three months and I want you to hear me out concerning several subjects. I have many concerns for the future of our family, which, as of this day, now numbers five. Of course, dear Papa will not be returning to help us although I feel certain that he would have implored God to allow him just a few more years with us. It would also seem that your Edward has vacated the premises forever. Therefore, that leaves you, a woman of twenty-nine and me, a woman of fifty, to raise three small children."

Mary paused to readjust the baby's swaddling while Emma ate her cinnamon bread in silence. "Between us we have two houses and a lumber mill. May I ask how much money you have left?"

"Twenty dollars in a tin under the floorboards in the closet," came Emma's reply.

"Twenty dollars will not last very long with another mouth to feed. Your work at the mill ended long ago with your confinement and now the loss of those wages has become permanent with the birth of the baby today. While I realize that the man Edward brought in to act as foreman...what is his name? Linley? Lyman?"

"Lowell, Mama."

"Yes...Lowell has been doing an adequate job, but the point is, that without a strong man such as your father or Edward around to boss the men, including Lyman..."

"Lowell, Mama."

"Including Lowell, the hired hands will soon slack off and run your father's mill right into the very ground, which is what he always told me they would do in his absence. Therefore, I am of the opinion that we must sell the mill at once to the highest bidder we can find."

Emma looked startled. "And," Mary continued, "I would propose that you and the three children move into my house which has the benefit of indoor plumbing and gaslight and that we rent out your home as a source of income. All of which would mean that we would have funds on which to live and raise these three boys for a while. In addition to which, I still command three dollars for every child I deliver."

Emma leaned back into the white pillows that Mary had stacked behind her head and gazed up at the ceiling with its horizontal crack. "I did not realize what a worry we are to you, Mama," Emma spoke at last. "What you say is true enough and in my present weakened condition I see the logic of your plan all too clearly."

"Splendid," replied Mary. "In anticipation of your acquiescence, I spoke with Linley..."

"Lowell, Mama."

"Yes, yes! Lowell…about renting your home for his family which he has put up in a couple of rented rooms in a house on the outskirts of town and with four children, he and his wife are feeling quite cramped. Of course, you will not be needing all this furniture so I promised to rent the house and most of the furnishings to Lowell and his family too. Is that agreeable to you, Emma?"

"It is agreeable. However, I would like to take the baby's crib and cradle and the rocking chair with me as those were mine as a baby, which you very well know. Papa made that crib and I could not bear to leave it behind."

"No one is asking you to, Emma. Only that we move just the most sentimental of objects because I already have a household full of furnishings."

"And I must take the beautiful oil lamp with its hand painted roses from my living room as it was a wedding gift from you and Papa." Already Emma was packing the wagon.

"Since we are in agreement about the decision to move, can we also pick a day?" Mary wanted to move her grandchildren and her daughter to her more spacious and luxuriously appointed home as soon as possible to make the task of caring for all of them during Emma's recovery from childbirth easier on her, both financially and physically.

"I will probably need a few days at least, Mama."

"You can make a list of what you want to take and I shall have old Bill round up the hired hands to assist us with the move. Now, we must tell the boys, would you agree? At least the ones old enough to understand," she concluded looking down at the dozing baby

"Yes, by all means, Mama."

Mary gazed at her little daughter, now rendered almost gaunt after the deliverance of her third child. "I hope that I have not overstepped my bounds here, my darling, but frankly in your weakened condition, I felt it imprudent to allow you to continue living in this fashion, in this…this…" and Mary waved a hand at her surroundings, searching for the right word, "hovel."

"Yes, Mama, I know the truth of your words. At the time of my marriage to Edward, it seemed like the perfect little love nest and of course it was all that Edward could afford for us. Recently I have come to despise this house and all that it represents. I cannot vacate the premises soon enough."

So it was that five days after giving birth to her third son, Emma, George and Will Richardson along with Mary Miller, loaded the new baby and their meager possessions onto a wagon. With the help of the mill hands, the women moved the little family into Mary Miller's home on High Point Avenue, atop a grassy knoll with its sweeping vistas of the Southport River.

The twin boys were ecstatic about the move as they adored their grandmother and the sanctuary of her large, comfortable home with its barn and horse, the porch out front with its swing and the endless supply of food that Mary prepared for them all. Later that night, after the boys were tucked into their beds down the hall and across from Emma's room, George and Will fell to whispering about the events of the day with its good and not so good points.

"Georgie?"

"Yes, Willynilly?"

"You know if Pa does come back, he won't be able to find us since we moved from our old house. He'll probably be searchin' for us the rest of his life and that makes me feel kinda sad. We'll be just like them marbles I lost two weeks ago. The ones that Nana said would never be found again." He made a faint sniffling sound into his pillow.

"Oh, come on now, Will!" admonished George. "Where is the first place Pa would look for us when he sees Lowell and his family in our old house?"

Will brightened, "The mill?"

"Does anybody live at that old mill? Come on, think!"

"Oh…you think he'd look here first!" exclaimed Will.

"Right, Will! Now, what really worries me is the bathtub and all that running water because you know what that means?"

"Yeah…a bath every night," Will responded dejectedly looking up at the ceiling. "You know, we might just get Nana to let us go swimming in the river instead, especially if we keep the firewood bin heaping full for her."

"Now, you know very well and good, Will, that Nana does not allow us to swim in that river because of the undertow. She says the only thing good about that river is the boats and the catfish. Otherwise, she tells us to stay away from the river."

"Yeah! It was that undertoad what took old Bill's boy clean under the water and never brung him back up," reminisced Will. "Funny thing is, I never have saw a toad in that river. Matter of fact, I've never in my whole life seen a toad big enough to carry a boy under the water."

"The word is undertow, Will. U-N-D-E-R-T-O-W," spelled George. "There is no such word as 'undertoad'. Sometimes I wonder if you are sleeping in that school room right under Miss Rita's nose!"

Life in the big house was different that summer, for Will and George not only had to share their mother and grandmother with the newest arrival, but they also had to take orders from two women. Life had become inexplicably complicated for the twins. Emma noticed that Will and George seemed rowdier than ever and more at loose ends. They talked more of their father and Emma did not know how much longer she would be able to spin the fairy tale that their father's absence was due to 'business'. On the rise too were her concerns about the family's finances. The sale of the mill was in progress and she was collecting rent from Lowell but it would not be enough to maintain the family for long and Emma feared for their future.

Seeking a diversion for the boys and herself as well, Emma decided to take George and Will on an excursion, across the Southport River by ferry and then into Clarksburg to see the sights of the big city. The twins had outgrown their shoes from the previous year and whereas the two had reveled in going barefooted all summer long, it was time once again to purchase new leather shoes for the boys, an expense she could ill afford. Still, with the trees showing their unmistakable signs of fall, Emma knew it was time to take her boys to the cobbler.

With Mary waving at the trio with one hand and cradling the baby with the other, they called their good-byes as Emma, Will and George skipped down the sloping lawn holding hands.

"This will be the most fun we've had in a long time!" exclaimed Will, already scanning the river for the arrival of the ferry from the far bank. "It's like we're going on an adventure! We're explorers!"

"Just make sure you two hold my hands or the railing on the ferry going across the river for I do not cherish the thought of jumping into that treacherous river to save you!" Emma admonished her sons.

"Otherwise the 'undertoad' might get us. Right Will?" George elbowed his brother who ignored the sarcasm.

Once safely across on the other side, the trio made their way up the long boardwalk to the main thoroughfare through the city. Both children were agog with the sights, sounds and smells of a bustling river city.

"Did you ever see such fine horses and carriages in your life, Ma?" George asked his mother. "Just look at that pair by the rail. They are the purest white I have ever seen! Probably somebody really important owns that rig."

"Yeah, most likely a king or somethin'," opined Will.

"We do not have kings in this country, Will. We elect a president," corrected Emma.

"And it is just us men that get to vote for him too," added George with an air of superiority.

"Maybe some day I'll get to vote for the president," remarked Will, excitedly swiveling his head in all directions to take in the sights.

"Yes, of course you will," replied Emma, "and who knows, perhaps some fine day even I shall have the right to vote for the president of these United States."

Arriving in front of a row of stores with large glass windows, the twins bolted for the closest one, pressing their noses to the panes and examining the displays of merchandise.

"This store sells candy and toys, Ma!" Will exclaimed over his shoulder to his mother.

"Indeed. And what does the next one sell, George?"

George raced to the next glass store front window. "It sells books. Hundreds of them! Just look for yourself, Ma!"

Delirious with their newly perceived freedom and the glut of merchandise to scrutinize, George and Will raced on far ahead of Emma, who called to them, "Come back here this instant!"

Heedless, the boys raced on up the boardwalk, weaving in and out of the pedestrian traffic as they ran. Losing sight of them, Emma began to feel a rising panic, so she lifted her skirts and moved swiftly past the stores, excusing herself as she bumped others in passing. Catching sight of George and Will who had paused in front of a bakery where they were exclaiming over the cakes, Emma moved to within reach of the twins. Sitting in the dusty street next to the board-walk and directly opposite the now immobile boys was a water barrel used to col-lect rain water from a downspout. Swiftly, Emma removed the top metal hoop from the barrel used to hold the staves in place and approached the unsuspecting boys. She slipped the hoop over their heads and down around their arms, thus fastening both boys together.

"Oh, Ma! Stop it!" they both began to wail in unison. "What did we do? We were just havin' some fun!"

"Yes and you were both disobeying me and ignoring my calls for you to return to my side." Emma marched her boys the length of Water Street through Clarks-burg with the aid of the barrel hoop to the cobbler's store. Once the twins had been properly fitted with new shoes for school, the trio exited the store onto the main thoroughfare again.

Carrying their new, high-topped leather shoes tied up in paper parcels, Will and George begged their mother to take them for a bite to eat as the display of iced cakes in the storefront window had made them both very hungry. "All right, but only if you will come with me to the horse fountain and wash off your feet again," Emma announced.

"If I have to keep washin' my feet, there ain't gonna be no more skin on my toes!" complained Will. "And they're just gonna get dirty again," he added.

"If you intend to accompany your mother into the Foggy Bend Hotel for lunch, you will both be required have to have socks and shoes on your feet," explained Emma as she produced a pair of socks for each boy from her purse. "Now come along as we have not got much longer before we need to be on the other side of the river so that I can feed your baby brother."

"Maybe Nana could just feed him some of them leftover fried 'tatoes that she made for our breakfast," offered Will.

"How is the baby going to eat those potatoes?" asked George, yanking wool socks over his damp feet.

"With a fork just like we do, Georgie."

"Did it ever occur to you, Dummy, that the baby has no teeth yet?"

"Well, neither does old Bill but he still eats 'tatoes 'cause I seen him."

"Because I saw him," corrected Emma.

"That makes two of us that seen him, Georgie," said Will pushing his face close to his brother's for emphasis, whereupon George pulled Will's nose and threatened to dunk him in the horse fountain.

"Boys! Boys! That is just about enough! If you continue on this way we shall return immediately to Grandview without anything to eat," scolded Emma.

With their new shoes on and hands held tightly by their mother, the boys and Emma stepped from the boardwalk to cross over the street to the Foggy Bend Hotel for an early lunch. Suddenly, horses, carriages and people began to part in the middle of the street to allow for the passage of the fire wagon. There were two firemen seated up in the front of the fire wagon. One fireman drove the team of black horses while the other clanged the big brass alarm bell to clear their way down the street.

"Would you look at that!" yelled George as the red fire wagon with its gleaming brass water tank and beautiful black horses sped past them in a cloud of dust.

"Yeah, and would you listen to that bell too!" replied Will just as loudly. "Now that's what I call a real BIG dinger!"

Once safely seated inside the hotel dining room, Emma ordered fried catfish, green beans and mashed potatoes for the three of them. The boys jabbered incessantly about the events of the day until the food arrived. The last items placed before the boys were finger bowls with pieces of lemon for washing the hands at the close of the meal. Having never seen a finger bowl before, Will automatically proceeded to squeeze the lemon into the water and drink it.

"Yecch!" belched Will. "This doesn't taste like very good lemonade to me! Somebody forgot to put the sugar in it."

Emma laughed and continued to be greatly amused by her two sons for the remainder of the meal. Their childish antics and conversation lifted her spirits greatly and eased her mind of the terrible worries that always crowded out the lighter moments in her life. For more than an hour, she allowed herself to relax and enjoy the time she was spending with her sons in the dining room at the hotel.

As Emma and the boys left the hotel, a printed flier tacked to a far column of the hotel's porch caught her attention. Before walking toward the river and the waiting ferry, Emma paused to read the flier: WANTED: NURSES TO ASSIST DOCTORS AT ANGEL OF MERCY HOSPITAL: TWO YEAR PRO-GRAMME INCLUDING FIRST YEAR OF SCHOOLING AND SECOND YEAR OF PRACTISE: DEGREE CONFERRED AFTER SUCCESSFUL COMPLETION OF TWO YEAR PROGRAMME WITH PASSING MARKS ON EXAMINATIONS, BOTH ORAL AND WRITTEN. APPLY TO: HEAD NURSE FANELLA WALKER, ANGEL OF MERCY HOSPITAL, 216 CHESTNUT STREET, CLARKSBURG.

Emma looked around and then tore the flier from its tack, hastily stuffing the paper into her purse.

"What did you take that for, Ma?" asked George.

"Oh, it contains some interesting and possibly useful information that I want to remember. Now let us hurry down to catch the ferry," and she whisked them away to the landing.

After all the boys had been fed, bathed and put to bed, Emma took out the crumpled flier and read its contents again. Then she approached her mother who was sitting in the swing on the front porch.

"Well, dear, tell me just how did your adventure go today? I, of course, have heard the boys' version but perhaps I best hear the truth of it now!" and Mary continued with her mending while motioning that Emma should sit beside her in the swing.

Emma smiled and shook her head, "Just as you might expect, Mama. Will and George were exuberant and kept me on my toes, either scolding or laughing at the two of them the entire morning."

"How was the food at the Foggy Bend Hotel? Do you remember that your father and I spent our honeymoon weekend there?"

"Yes, I do remember. The food was splendid and the catfish were some of the best I have ever eaten, but…" and here Emma smoothed out the flier in her lap, "what really caught my attention was this paper tacked to one of the hotel's col-umns," and Emma handed the paper to her mother.

Mary read its contents and asked, "Just what does this mean?"

"It means, Mama, that I have found a way to support this family. I shall apply to become a nurse." Noticing her mother's furrowed brow, she added, "You know how you are always telling me that I have a talent…a gift for assisting you with the birthing of babies and you are always telling me that I am an apt pupil, so might I not apply those same skills in training to become a nurse?"

Mary was silent for a while. "And what of your three children, Emma? Are they to accompany you across the river while you take your training for two years? Surely you have not forgotten the wee one who depends upon your milk for sustenance?"

"Mama, I know this is a huge favor that I am asking of you…but…would you…could you care for my three boys while I am away? I shall make every effort to schedule my absences to coincide with the baby's feeding schedule and George and Will adore you and mind you as if you were their mother already."

Mary's hands fell motionless with the needle in midair, thimble gleaming in the twilight of the lowering sun. "But I am fifty years old, Emma, and some days it feels more like I am double that. God made mothers young for a good reason…to run after young children and do not forget that!"

"But what you lack in physical vitality you more than make up for with your mental capabilities. You are the most organized, disciplined and patient woman on the face of the earth and these are qualities which we young women sadly lack due to our youth and inexperience."

"Nonsense, Emma! You do not have to woo me with compliments in order to get me to care for my grandchildren who have been the entire center of my universe following the death of your father. But why nursing and why now?"

"I lack skills that will fetch enough income to support this family. Two years ago following Papa's death, we realized that the mill would never again be an ideal place for me to work due to the difficulties encountered by Edward in trying to manage the hired hands. You are the midwife that everyone demands when it is time for the birthing of a baby, not me," Emma lightly patted her mother's arm. "I could earn a regular income and work regular hours and support this family as a nurse. Please, Mama, help me to help us! Edward is never going to return. I have realized that for a very long time now. He took the horse, left me a pittance and I have never to this day heard a single word from him and neither have the boys so I cannot escape the fact that it is now up to me to take on the burden of supporting the five of us. Unless, of course, you would rather that I choose a line of work such as women find at Miss Hattie's House of Splendor?" Emma giggled. Mary giggled.

"Oh, do not be ridiculous, Emma! But as long as we are having such a weighty discussion…one that will undoubtedly affect all of our futures for a very long time to come, I have a request to make of you in return."

"And that would be?"

"That you cease referring to the baby as 'Edward John'. I would prefer to have him known instead as 'John E. Richardson'," replied Mary.

"Done! From this moment on, we shall call the baby 'Johnny Richardson'," and the two women again laughed.

Sobering, Mary added, "Actually, I have a second request too. A simple but urgent one. You must tell your two oldest sons about their father. They must not be left in limbo concerning the whereabouts of their good-for-nothing father a moment longer. The sooner you tell them that Edward is not returning, the sooner they can bear the pain of parting."

"Yes, Mama, I shall honor that request as well, but I must apply to nursing school immediately. Therefore, tomorrow I plan to take the ferry to Clarksburg and apply to the head nurse at Angel of Mercy Hospital." The two women rose in unison from the swing and entered the darkened house. It had been decided. Emma would become a nurse.

CHAPTER 4

▼

Emma did not see Edward the week following the church picnic and she fretted daily that he had lost interest in her. Anyone as dashingly handsome as Edward and as articulate as he, was bound to make endless conquests over the course of a week. Emma returned home from the mill at the end of the workweek, ate her dinner and then excused herself to wash in the copper tub. She always felt grimy after a day spent at the mill for the sawdust permeated everything, especially her hair. She lathered herself twice with Mary's lavender-scented soap and then began to wash her hair, applying more of the soap at the base of her neck and around her forehead. Then with her fingers she began to work the soap through her long, auburn hair, pulling the soapy mass straight up from the top of her head into a cone shape. She stood to view herself in the mirror opposite the tub and laughed at her reflection. Easing back into the water, she closed her eyes.

The sound of footsteps coming up to the second floor reminded her that she had best be rinsing and getting to bed. Even with her head under the spigot of running water, Emma could hear her father calling to her through the bathroom door. James knocked several times to get her to turn off the water.

"Yes, Papa? What is it?"

"You have a gentleman caller, Emma."

"A what did you say?" asked Emma in disbelief.

"Edward Richardson is downstairs and has asked my permission to call on you this evening. He was all apologies for the lateness of the hour but Hummel wanted the store open late tonight and so your new friend Edward hoped you would still be able to receive him. What say? And by the way, he brought your mother a most lovely bunch of flowers and me a bit of tobacco for my pipe. Shall I tell him to go away and never return?" James stifled a laugh.

Horrified, Emma exclaimed from behind the bathroom door, "Do no such thing, Papa! Please go back downstairs and tell Edward that I shall be down to receive him directly."

"Your wish is my command, my darling daughter! But do hurry as your mother and I must now sit in the parlor and find some small amusements for ourselves until his departure and I am dead on my feet as it is."

"Yes, yes, Papa. I am nearly ready now," she replied toweling her hair dry and braiding it into a long queue that hung down her back. "Do go, for you are making me nervous standing just outside the door."

Hurriedly pulling on a fresh step-in, skirt and blouse but no petticoat, stockings or shoes and pinching her cheeks to add color, Emma took the stairs two at a time down to the front hall, where she could hear voices coming from the parlor. As Emma stood by the entrance to the parlor, Mary scanned her daughter's appearance disapprovingly, raising an eyebrow to let her know. Emma ignored Mary's look and turned to Edward, "What is it that brings the horseshoe champion of Grandview to our door at this hour of the evening?"

"If I were to tell you that I was just passing by, you would probably detect the ruse immediately. Therefore I must confess…it is an urgent hunger," and here Edward paused ever so slightly, "for a piece of your mother's fine cake," whereupon he turned to Mary. "May I possibly prevail upon you for the smallest slice of your famous pound cake? I have dreamed of little else ever since enjoying the delectable cakes which you brought to the church picnic. That is, assuming there was any cake left at the close of the picnic." Before the startled Mary could respond, he added, "I am quite sure you can imagine that a bachelor such as myself rarely has an opportunity to partake of such gastronomic delights."

"Why, Edward, dear boy, I am quite amused by your flattering words! My pound cakes, however, were entirely consumed at the church picnic but I made a fresh chocolate cake for our supper this evening. Perhaps a slice of that and a glass of lemonade would suffice," Mary responded flushing.

Emma stood looking at Edward in disbelief, thrown off guard by his little speech that he had quite obviously rehearsed many times before the mirror for the benefit of charming Mary while infuriating her.

"Since it is my mother's chocolate cake that you have come for, Edward," Emma finally managed to say, "I believe I shall just excuse myself for I suddenly feel quite tired," and she turned so abruptly, flinging her head around, that her pigtail caught in the wood scrollwork decorating the corners and sides of the entrance into the parlor. There she remained stuck, tugging at her hair which conspired to hold her fast.

"Allow me," chuckled Edward, moving to her side to free the captive. As he faced her with his hands working her hair, she could feel his breath upon her neck and the heat of his body.

"Of course you know," Edward smiled down into her dark eyes, "that I am a terrible tease and that the real reason for my visit was to see the Captive Maiden, who, unless my eyes deceive me, is standing right before me! Having set you free, fair maiden, you must now grant my wish," and so saying Edward made a deep bow in front of Emma.

Instinctively, Emma reached out and touched his black hair with the palm of her hand and getting into the spirit of his teasing replied, "Arise, Noble Edward, and escort the Captive Maiden to the porch to sit with her in the swing, lest the beasts of the night descend upon her."

At that, everyone enjoyed a huge laugh as Emma and Edward excused themselves to the front porch with generous slices of Mary's cake, lemonade and Edward holding an oil lamp.

The two were quiet for several long moments, enjoying the chocolate cake with its rich, buttery icing and the sunset over the Southport River. "Quite a lovely evening, would you agree, Emma?" Edward broke the silence first.

"Indeed," Emma responded.

"Emma, I am not one to mince words or to play foolish games," Edward began in earnest.

"Then just who was it on the church grounds playing horseshoes and trouncing those poor boys at the horseshoe pits?" Emma laughed. "Your twin brother, perhaps?"

Not amused, Edward responded, "I should have said 'I am not one to play foolish games of the heart,' but you interrupted my train of thought. Please let us be serious for a moment," and he took her plate of cake from her and set it on the wicker table next to the swing.

Emma wiped the corners of her mouth with her mother's good lace napkin, brown eyes riveted upon Edward's blue ones as he began again. "I have thought of little else but you since our meeting at Hummel's store and then again at the church picnic. Your image haunts my dreams at night. Daylight brings no relief and each time I hear Hummel's door creaking open, I turn...hoping that it is you I shall see. I am besotted and obsessed to the point that I went to work yesterday without my socks."

"Well, look here, Edward," she responded pulling up her skirt to reveal a leg bare to the knee, "I have forgotten mine as well."

At the sight of her bare leg, Edward responded by placing his hand gently under her knee and kissing the bare skin from her knee down to her ankle and as she did not resist, he kissed each toe individually, "You must never again wear stockings in my presence for if you do, I shall have to remove them."

Emma felt she would faint at the intimate touch of his lips upon her skin and the two of them sat for many long moments, Emma scarcely breathing and Edward cradling her bare leg, before they were brought around by the sound of Mary ascending the staircase and James opening the front door. Quickly the two of them regained their composure and Emma stood abruptly. "What a magnificent sunset it was this evening! Would you agree, Edward?"

"Oh, yes...absolutely breathtaking!"

"Edward, my boy," began James, "it is time for our family to retire. Do you need a lamp to see your way home?"

"No, sir, I shall be just fine. There is going to be a full moon tonight so I shall manage quite well without one, but thank you for your kind offer."

"Emma, do bid Edward good-night and follow your mother up the stairs. I am going into the kitchen for another swallow of lemonade and then I expect to see you upstairs too."

"Yes, Papa," was all that she said and James went back inside the big white house.

Seizing his opportunity, Edward moved toward Emma and drawing her to him with a hand in the small of her waist, he kissed her full on the lips and then on her neck. When he lifted his face, Emma kissed him back before pushing away. "I am quite undone," she whispered to him, "I must be off before Papa returns."

"But not before making a promise to me," said Edward lifting her hand for a final kiss.

"And what promise would you exact from me, Noble Edward?" she teased.

"I would ask," and here Edward dropped dramatically to one knee while still holding onto her hand, "that you promise your heart to me."

"I do so promise," was all that she whispered before vanishing abruptly into the house.

James was not surprised when the next day, old Bill approached him at the loading dock to say, "Someone's here to see you, Mr. James."

"Oh," was all that James replied.

"Yup. Good lookin' young fella what goes by the name of Edward Richman."

"Richardson," James corrected Bill.

"So then, you know the fella?"

"Yes, I believe I do. Give a hand here, Bill, as I may be up the way for a while and the boys are having trouble unloading these logs. Be sure to mind the pulleys, too, for I can ill afford to have these logs cavorting downstream to the Old Miss!"

James turned to walk up the dusty path toward the mill, mopping his sweaty brow with the back of his shirt-sleeve. The cicadas sang loudly from the banks of the Southport and heat shimmered off the tin roof of the mill as James approached the distant figure that he recognized as Edward Richardson, leaning against the giant oak.

"Hello, there, Mr. Miller," Edward called out to the approaching man as he walked forward with his hand extended. "I hope I have not come at a bad time but I have some urgent business which I should like to discuss with you. Hummel was very kind to give me a lunch break today. I promise not to take much of your time as I can see that you are just docking a large shipment of logs to process at the mill," said Edward as he wrung the outstretched hand.

"Come sit a spell under the oak tree, Edward, as it is much cooler there. I shall just go retrieve that pot of sassafras tea Mary made for me this morning."

When James returned, he produced two chipped enameled cups and a small canister of tea. Removing the lid, he poured them each a cup and settling back against the rough bark of the oak, James remarked, "The heat is almost intolerable today. Everything is so bone dry. We had best all pray for rain soon for I can tell you that these droughts affect the lumber crop hereabouts. Some say when you split a log open you can calculate how severe the dry spells have been by how deeply the knots penetrate the core of the tree. And I do not prize lumber with knots in it!"

A squirrel clung upside down on the trunk of the ancient oak, tail twitching furiously, loudly scolding both James and Edward. "Oh, pay her no attention! She is just a cantankerous old female guarding her nest up high in the tree. We call her 'Nettlesome' or 'Nettie' for short. Old girl thinks this is her very own tree and raises a terrible ruckus when we come to enjoy the shade. I always try to have a few peanuts in my pocket to mollify her wrath," whereupon James produced a dozen or so peanuts in the shell from his trouser pocket. "Here, go ahead," he motioned to Edward, "you appease the little tyrant. Just scatter them over yonder and see what happens."

Edward took the peanuts and did as he was instructed. Cautiously but with her tail still waving furiously over her head, Nettie descended the tree. Coming to within a few feet of Edward, she began to gather the nuts one at a time, sitting on her haunches each time as she opened a shell to extract and savor the nut, all the while keeping a sharp eye on the two men.

"There, there, Nettie old girl! Do be good and be quiet now as Mr. Richardson and I must have a conversation without all your noise. You were saying, Edward?"

"That is quite remarkable, sir! It is as if the squirrel understands you!"

"Quite possibly she does but right now, I would prefer to understand why you have made the long walk down here to the mill to speak with me in the heat of the day," ventured James.

"Well, sir, to proceed directly to the point of my visit, I have come to ask your permission to court your daughter."

James choked on his tea. "You have what?"

"I have come to beg you to allow me to court your daughter," Edward repeated more earnestly.

"I have got to hand it to you son, I do admire your," and here James was tempted to use the word "balls" but thought better of it, saying instead, "your pluck, for it seems to me that you have only just met my daughter."

"That is entirely correct sir but I recognized Emma as the woman of my dreams the moment I laid eyes on her. Have you ever had that feeling Mr. Miller?"

"Yes, as a matter of fact I have, but only once and once is enough to last a man a lifetime, provided, of course, that he has good eyesight!"

"I have keen vision, sir, and my vision is to court your daughter, with your permission, and then to ask for her hand in marriage, for I simply cannot bear the thought of living without her!" blurted out Edward without stopping for breath.

"Yes, yes…well then…" James stalled, hardly knowing where to go next with the conversation. Clearing his throat James ventured on, "Perhaps at this juncture I should inquire about your financial stability?"

"As you know sir, I am working for Mr. Hummel as his store clerk which involves keeping the books, stocking the merchandise, ringing up sales on the cash register, even cleaning out the storeroom when necessary and tending to Mr. Hummel's horse."

"And…er…what sum are you paid for all of your services, if I may ask?" questioned James.

"Mr. Hummel is quite generous with me and pays me a whole dollar a week plus my choice of either canned peaches or beans from the shelf each Friday."

"Ah! Well that is impressive, to be sure." James instantly regretted any hint of sarcasm. "Emma has told me of your background as a field hand for your father when you were a young lad but what of your employment during the time that you lived with your aunt?"

"Well, sir, I did just about everything and anything in order to help support my Aunt Lenore and me prior to her untimely death. I was apprenticed to the town smithy for several years and I became quite good at the trade until the pit fire raged out of control one hot fall day, consuming the blacksmith shop. The smithy accused me of setting the fire deliberately but in fact, I had fallen asleep just outside the door to escape the blistering heat. He dragged me to the constable's office and accused me of the fire. Fortunately, other townspeople had witnessed my slumber and stepped forward to exonerate me but the smithy ran me off so here I am." Edward looked almost apologetically at James.

"That is quite a tale, my boy. So much tragedy in such a young life! But I suppose each and every one of us has had our fair share of tragedy, young and old alike. So, what is it that you have learned from all your experiences, Edward?"

"What I have learned is that with the sweat of my own brow, the head on my shoulders and these two hands," here Edward held up his hands for James to inspect, "I can be successful at any trade, but the one element which I am so sadly lacking in my life at age twenty-seven…is the love of a decent and fine woman, such as your Emma. It is she who could provide me with children and thus make my life complete." Edward paused to calculate the effect his words were having on James.

James puffed on his pipe in profile, ostensibly scrutinizing his men on the dock. At last he spoke, "Very noble, my boy, very noble. Tell me, Edward, what is the one quality about my Emma that so attracts you?"

Without hesitation, Edward replied, "Her purity."

"Mmmm, I see," said James as he continued to puff deeply on his pipe.

"Purity is doubtless the greatest asset a woman can bring to a marriage. Would you not agree, sir?"

"Quite so, lad, quite so." Silence befell the two men as the cicadas enthusiastically droned their assent from unseen perches. "May we expect you for supper this evening, son?" James asked turning to the beaming Edward.

CHAPTER 5

▼

Emma arose early in the morning the day after her sojourn across the river to Clarksburg with the twins. Tiptoeing into the baby's room, she awakened the sleeping infant to breast-feed him and change his diaper. As she sat cradling the little child to her, Emma stroked his smooth dark hair, which was just beginning to fill in on the top of his tiny head. "How rare and precious such moments are!" she thought to herself, enjoying the stillness of the hour and the closeness with her baby. Just as she rested baby Johnny against her shoulder to burp him, Mary appeared in the doorway still clad in her nightdress.

"You are awake early today, dear. Did you have a fitful night?"

"Yes, Mama. Thoughts of applying to Nurse Fanella Walker kept me tossing and turning most of the night, so I believe the best thing for me to do is dress, eat a light breakfast and be off to submit my application. As you can see, Johnny has already been fed and changed. Would you please take him now so that I may dress?"

"Of course dear, but what of the big boys today, Emma? Do you have any special instructions for me in their regard?" Mary asked taking the infant in her arms.

"I know they will be a handful, as they usually are, but I was thinking that perhaps after breakfast they could each take a turn with the small scythe and cut the long grass around the barn for you. It surely needs to be done and the work will hopefully wear off some of their energy. With a bonnet securely fastened to your head and a chair to sit upon while holding Johnny, I imagined that you might be their straw boss."

"That sounds like a decent plan. When do you think you might return?"

"If I hurry, I can make the eight o'clock ferry and be back by noon in order to nurse the baby. Should I be late, try to pacify him with a sugar-tit and if all else fails pending my return, swing the baby, for he does love it so."

Emma dressed in her customary light skirt and blouse with all the proper undergarments and brushed her hair vigorously before pinning it up into a bun on the top of her head. Edward disliked the style and always wanted her hair to hang loose, flowing over her shoulders when they were together. But what did men know of hair styles anyhow? Quietly, she descended the staircase so as not to awaken George and Will. Once in the kitchen, Emma poured herself a glass of cold buttermilk and nibbled at a raisin scone.

"Well then, Mama, I am off!" she announced as Mary entered the kitchen now fully dressed and still holding Johnny.

"Do take care, my pet, and be watchful! Clarksburg can be dangerous for a woman alone."

"Have a good morning with the boys, Mama. Rest assured that I shall make all haste to return."

"Good luck!" Mary called after her daughter as she sallied forth to the landing and the ferry which would take her on a journey that was to last the rest of her life.

As she disembarked on the far bank of the Southport, Emma brushed off her skirt with her hands and straightened the pins in her hair. She wanted to make a good impression on the head nurse. Carefully picking her way through the rock hard ruts up the embankment to the boardwalk that she had so lightheartedly traversed the previous day with her boys, Emma was suddenly consumed with misgivings about the plan she had devised for the future of her family. It was too audacious and certainly would prove to be exceedingly taxing upon her physical self.

Emma paused in front of the bakery where she had finally corralled the twins less than twenty-four hours earlier. She could still see the imprint their faces had made on the glass as they exclaimed over the tempting pastries on display. "I owe it to each of my three sons to do this," she thought to herself, "and to Mama, but most especially I owe it to myself." With her head held high, she marched on up the hill, around the corner and through the front gates to Angel of Mercy Hospital.

Once inside the black wrought iron gates, Emma hesitated a moment to gain control of her knees which were threatening to give way. Breathing heavily and clinging unsteadily to a hitching post, she nonetheless managed to smile at a young man who doffed his hat in passing. Another deep breath and she made her

way along the wooden sidewalk, up the front steps and through the entrance to
the hospital itself.

The hospital was an imposing edifice of limestone with immaculate gray marble floors and on each wall there appeared a bewildering array of signs: CHILDREN'S WARD, arrow pointing up; WOMEN'S WARD, arrow also pointing up; CHIEF OF STAFF, arrow pointing left; PULMONARY WARD, arrow pointing right; SOLARIUM, arrow also pointing right; MEN'S WARD, arrow pointing straight; SURGERY, arrow pointing straight; MEDICAL LIBRARY, arrow pointing straight; NURSING, arrow pointing down; SUPPLIES AND LINENS, arrow pointing down and so forth until she at last saw the INFORMATION arrow, pointing straight. Making her way forward in the direction of "Information", Emma looked down and realized that she was standing on a beautiful rendering of a caduceus medical insignia made of highly polished black, pink and gray marble, which seemed to be the axis of the hospital and the bisecting point of all the corridors.

Approaching the information desk, Emma asked the young female receptionist if she might see Head Nurse Fanella Walker.

"Oh, that's quite impossible I'm afraid," was the disappointing answer, "for no one sees Nurse Walker without a scheduled appointment, unless of course you happen to have one. Do you?" and the skinny bespectacled receptionist with prominent teeth looked Emma over from head to toe.

"Actually, no, I am afraid I do not have an appointment. However, I have come in response to the flier that I obtained just yesterday which advertises that Nurse Walker is seeking applications from prospective nursing students, of whom I am one," and here Emma drew herself up to the full measure of her four foot and ten inch frame while returning the unsmiling look of the receptionist.

"No matter that you are Florence Nightingale herself, you will not gain admittance to see Nurse Walker without an appointment as I told you," sniffed the young woman.

Rapidly escalating discouragement at having traveled so far for such a worthy purpose only to be rebuffed by a hospital receptionist was fueling Emma's frustration.

"Just exactly what 'information' do you disseminate from your lofty perch?" Emma asked the startled receptionist tartly. "Never mind," added Emma turning upon her heel and retracing her steps back to the marble caduceus where she followed the arrow for NURSING that lead to a flight of stairs. Just as she was about to descend the staircase, Emma caught sight of a hospital laundress approaching to the left, precariously balancing a pile of soiled linens that towered well above her nose. The laundress and her pile of linens combined were taller than Emma. "Make way! Linens coming through!" The next thing Emma knew, she was pitching headlong down the flight of stairs.

When she awoke, Emma realized that she was stretched out on a table and covered with a white sheet. "Did I die?" she asked the face that hovered over her.

"Oh, my stars no, child, but you did have a nasty fall and that bump on your head is as big as a goose egg," smiled the kindly face.

Emma felt her forehead, which throbbed painfully. "Where am I and what happened?"

"Well, dear, you are in the lower quarters of Angel of Mercy Hospital in its nursing department following a spill down the stairs and I am Nurse Walker. Now who might you be?"

"Oh, my goodness!" exclaimed Emma trying to sit up.

"Easy there. You are going to feel a bit woozy for a while, I would expect. Allow me to look in your eyes once again. Close both eyes and when I count to three, please open them," Nurse Walker instructed Emma. Then she removed her pince-nez glasses and held one lens close to Emma's right eye. On the count of three she examined the pupil of the right eye first. "And again I shall count, one, two, three," whereupon the nurse examined the pupil of the left eye. "Good," she commented briskly. "Now follow my finger as I move it around and tell me if you are experiencing any nausea," she instructed Emma.

"No ma'am," responded Emma meekly.

"Do you see two of me?" she questioned her patient but when Emma looked confused she added, "Are you having double vision?"

"No ma'am," Emma again responded.

"Splendid! Then let us try to sit up," and here she took her patient under the armpits from behind and righted her on the table. "Slowly dear, so as not to pass out! And do let us have the legs dangle overboard a bit before we try to walk, right?"

"Yes, ma'am."

"All right, now try to walk to me child and should you lose your balance, fear not, for I promise to catch you."

Whereupon Emma made her way cautiously toward Nurse Walker.

"Fine dear! Absolutely fine! And now I propose to mix you a powder which I would like you to drink straight down for me. Can you do that?"

"Yes, ma'am," and obediently Emma drank down the milky liquid that Nurse Walker had mixed for her, handing the glass back and wiping her mouth with the back of her hand.

Finding her voice at last, Emma spoke, "I am so terribly sorry to have been such a bother to you as busy as you must be as head nurse of the hospital here."

"So you know me, child?" asked Nurse Walker.

"It was you I was coming to see when I fell. I had hoped to have an interview with you but the girl at the information desk said that I could not possibly see you without an appointment and it was then I determined that I would just follow the NURSING sign and beg you to see me anyway." Out of breath, Emma paused, rubbing her head, tears forming in the corners of her eyes.

"There, there, dear!" and Nurse Walker put her arm around the trembling Emma. "What was it that you were coming to see me about Miss…Miss?"

"Emma Richardson is my name, ma'am."

"Well, Miss Richardson, you certainly did get my attention in a most spectacular fashion, would you not you agree?" and she laughed

"Actually it is Mrs. Richardson, from Grandview, abandoned only this past Spring by my husband and having given birth recently to my third child and that is why I have come to see you to beg for admission into the school of nursing so that I may acquire a legitimate profession by which to support my three children and my mother and oh, my goodness! I am leaking milk!" Instinctively Emma placed her hands over the wet spots that were forming on her blouse over her breasts.

"I see. Perhaps we had better adjourn to my office where you can be more comfortable and you can tell me the whole story, slowly and in great detail, for I am most interested in your plight, Emma," soothed Nurse Walker, placing an arm around Emma's shoulders and leading her forward.

As she sat across the desk from Nurse Walker pouring out her heart to this total stranger, Emma had a chance finally to assess her listener. Much taller than Emma, Nurse Walker appeared to be a woman in her fifties with gray hair that she wore braided and pinned to the top of her head under her nurse's cap. Her face was deeply creased, without a trace of make-up and as white as her uniform. Her eyes were a lovely, bright green and almost disappeared when she smiled or laughed. Pince-nez glasses were anchored just under the collar of her uniform by a black ribbon and her front teeth had small spaces between each one. Her frame, while large, was covered by little flesh and she appeared almost gaunt.

"What a fascinating but tragic story, Emma," Nurse Walker was saying. She rested her chin on her intertwined fingers with her elbows propped up on the desk, contemplating Emma over the top of her pince-nez glasses that straddled her nose.

Worn out from her recitation, Emma sat quietly in the hard chair facing Nurse Walker who also sat without speaking for several long minutes. Emma began to fidget, feeling her leaking breasts again.

"I realize that you must be getting back to Grandview to nurse that infant of yours but I frankly feel that you are in no condition to make the journey unescorted. Did you come alone or did someone accompany you across?"

"I came alone," Emma responded.

"It is settled then, dear, I shall accompany you back home, provided that you could put me up for the remainder of the day and night. I can make adjustments to my schedule here and call on one of my subordinate nurses to fill in for me. How does that sound?"

"I believe the hospital has been aptly named," responded Emma, "for you are truly an angel of mercy!"

The two women disembarked from the ferry around noon and made their way slowly up from the dock, turning first onto Longmeadow and then onto High Point Avenue. In the distance, Emma could see the boys and her mother, holding the baby, on the front lawn of their home. George and Will seemed to be chasing a dog around in circles and laughing loudly as it rolled around on the ground with them.

As she drew closer, Emma could discern that the twin's new playmate was an ungainly, large puppy which so preoccupied all of them that they took no notice of the approaching women.

"Well, now is this any way to greet your mother?" Emma chided the boys teasingly. "Rolling around with a...a kangaroo!"

"Ma! Ma!" they both cried in unison running to her, arms outstretched. "Can't you see that's not a kangaroo?" Will asked in all seriousness.

"But of course, I can see quite clearly that it is a...hippopotamus!" Emma teased again.

Both boys looked at each other and then George announced, "See, Will, I told you Ma is getting old and really does need glasses. I had to find her hairpins the other day when she dropped them on the floor!"

Will took his mother's hand solicitously and lead her over to where the dog had collapsed in an exhausted heap. Hauling the dog upright so that his head reached to his mother's waist, Will took her hand and moved it down the dog's back. "Feel that, Ma? It's a DOG!"

"Well, I declare! I believe it is!" and Emma bent over to examine the black and brown dog. "It would appear that your new friend here has a bit more growing to do in order for his body to catch up with the size of these paws," laughed Emma.

"However, right now, I want all of you to come meet someone very special. This is Head Nurse Fanella Walker from Angel of Mercy Hospital in Clarksburg who has been so very kind to accompany your mother home after my nasty tumble down a flight of stairs."

Everyone began to shake the nurse's hand, talking at once and exclaiming over the prominent lump on Emma's forehead, while Johnny began to wail for his noontime feeding. With so much commotion, the dog decided to add his voice to the fray and began to bark and jump around all over again.

"Mama, I must excuse myself with the baby and feed him. Please make our guest comfortable as I promised her lodging in our home for the remainder of the day. I feel certain that she is hungry and thirsty after assisting me all this way," said Emma taking the wailing baby in her arms.

"Mrs. Miller, please permit me to escort Emma upstairs to her room and into her bed to feed the baby as I know that she is quite exhausted. Until I leave the comfort of your home, I shall consider her to be my patient."

The three women turned to walk up the steps to the front door with the boys bringing up the rear.

"Do not bring that dog into the house!" warned Mary. "Take him to the barn, give him a pan of water and remember to shut the door. The poor fellow is quite exhausted."

Nurse Walker reached for Johnny, "Emma do allow me to carry the baby up the stairs for you as I fear that you may still be a bit unsteady."

While Emma nursed the baby in her room and the boys ate their lunch at the kitchen table, Mary took a tray of food up to Emma's room and then carried a tray to the porch for herself and Nurse Walker.

"How very kind of you, Nurse Walker, to take such fine care of my daughter!"

"Please, Mary, call me Fannie, everyone does except for my students. Your daughter told me the story of her tragic circumstances and of her desire to support the family by becoming a nurse. What do you think of her plan? How realistic is it given her age and the number of children that she has?"

Mary wiped the crumbs from her skirt and placed the blue and white china plate back on the tray sitting on the wicker table. "You must understand, Fannie, that I have only one child and I therefore tend to think of her in superlatives. I am hardly capable of unbiased analysis. But, keeping my prejudices in mind, I would say to you that I have witnessed what was once a headstrong young girl mature into a determined, capable young woman, who puts her family first and foremost in all that she does. She is one who does not suffer fools lightly but when the need is real, would put her life on the line for anyone who needed her.

In spite of all this mother's falderal, I can personally attest to the fact that she has assisted me in the birthing of a dozen or so babies and she even birthed her own baby by herself in the wee hours of the morning."

"I have only known your daughter for a few hours, but I too judge her to be exactly as you have described," concluded Fannie. "In my twenty-eight years as a nurse, I have worked alongside and taught hundreds of young women so I rather fancy myself an expert on the subject of female capabilities, initiative, professionalism, call it what you will, I believe that Emma possesses it. It would seem that you concur with Emma's decision to enroll in nursing school for you must certainly be an integral part of the plan, having agreed, I assume, to bear the burden of the care of her children. Am I correct in this assumption, Mary?"

"Indeed, I have willingly agreed to assume the care of Emma's three children, who seem just as much a part of me as my daughter."

"It will not be an easy task for either of you," warned Fannie.

"My late husband, James, always used to tell Emma, 'You get out of life what you are willing to put into it. Plant and tend a bushel of seed and you shall reap a field of corn.'"

"Your husband was obviously a very wise man and judging from what I see in the two women whom he held so dear, I can tell that he was a very fine man as well. So, now that the particulars of character, suitability, inclination and dedication have been met to my satisfaction, what financial arrangements do we need to make to cover Emma's tuition?"

"May I ask the cost of the tuition?"

"It runs ten dollars per semester and over the two year period there are four semesters so the total would be forty dollars," replied Fannie.

"An astronomical sum for us at this juncture!" exhaled Mary looking off across the dark river.

"No need to despair, Mary. There are ways to make her studies affordable and I believe that I might have just the solution."

"Really?" Mary brightened.

"Yes, our 'greenies' and staff doctors always need assistance with the most menial of tasks. Some of them," laughed Fannie, "can hardly tie their own cravats without assistance so I always tell my students, if you are willing to perform slave labor for two years, then you can receive your tuition at half cost. What do you think of twenty dollars for the two years, Mary?"

"I believe we could scrape that together, especially if you would allow us to pay a bit each month as Emma progresses. Would that be acceptable?"

"Yes, of course, I could arrange that."

"But, Fannie, when you say 'slave' it causes me some concern. Could you elaborate about what Emma's duties to the staff doctors might be and what exactly is a 'greenie'?"

"Forgive me, Mary. I forget that not everyone understands our hospital jargon. A 'greenie' is a new doctor who is lacking in practical medical experience. Our 'greenies' routinely turn the hospital laboratory topsy-turvy with their experiments, cultures, autopsies, dissection of animals and the like. I select a few nursing students to restore the medical laboratory to working condition each day in exchange for credit toward their tuition.

I use the term 'slave' jokingly because some of the young men get to thinking that my students should do their laundry and cook their meals but I draw the line there. None of my girls will function as a domestic. They are there to work and perform chores only as they relate to the practice of medicine and only under my supervision. My girls do not draw a breath without me knowing how long it took them to exhale."

"Then there is the question of her schedule," continued Mary. "Emma, as you know, must suckle her infant every four hours. How can that be arranged?"

"That is a bit more difficult to solve. Ideally, my students have three hours of class in the morning, two hours of class in the afternoon and I assign each to a doctor, either individually or in groups, in order to follow him as he makes his rounds of the patients in the hospital. Emma would have to feed baby Johnny in there somewhere and the trip across the river and back would make the task impossible, unless she brought the baby with her, nursed him in between class and rounds, and then left him in the care of my nurses on the children's floor. Yes! Precisely!" exclaimed Fannie thumping the arm of the wicker chair for emphasis.

"You surely do clear the way to a solution quickly!" Mary congratulated Fannie.

"Which is just what we nurses are trained to do, Mary. We must think clearly and quickly because lives depend upon our speed and clarity of thought."

CHAPTER 6

▼

As he discerned that he had obtained the blessing of James Miller, Edward felt quite free to drop by the Miller home each evening after work, arriving conveniently just at the dinner hour. Mary persisted in her charade of asking Edward if he had eaten, to which the answer was invariably "no, ma'am," accompanied by a great sigh and hangdog expression, whereupon Mary would instruct Emma to set another place at the table, "For I shall never let it be said that we Millers turned away a starving man," smiling coyly at Edward all the while.

The Millers' habitual dinner guest reveled in Mary's cooking, shamelessly flattering her culinary talent while devouring copious amounts of food at each sitting, frequently scraping the platters and bowls of any food remnants to the keen annoyance of James, who delighted in taking Mary's leftovers to the mill the next day for his lunch. What really spiked the ire of James was that Edward always had the temerity at the end of dinner to turn to Mary and ask, "What was that I spied in the pantry for dessert? Was it one of your delectable cobblers? A peach pie perhaps?" Which inquiries would send Mary scurrying to the pantry to retrieve a large helping of pie for their uninvited guest.

"My word, lad! One would think that you had not eaten in a year judging from the manner in which you put away the food!" James was finally driven to comment one evening.

"Oh, forgive me sir! I do apologize but I have missed my dear Aunt Lenore's cooking so much these last few years and Mrs. Miller has been so gracious to invite me to dinner each evening…"

"Nonsense, Edward! You have just showed up on our doorstep each evening looking like something the cat dragged in from the field. You have quite obviously a shameless talent for playing upon the sympathies of my Mary."

"Papa!" interjected Emma.

"James!" scolded Mary.

James rose from his chair at the head of the table and looking squarely at Edward, announced, "Come with me to the porch, Edward. It is time you and I had a little talk."

Edward rose to accompany James to the front of the house while casting a glance at Emma who merely shrugged her shoulders. James sat in the swing and motioned for Edward to take a seat in the wicker chair to his left. Taking out his tobacco pouch and pipe, James worked several long minutes at filling, tamping and lighting the contents of its bowl. Sucking the smoke into his mouth and exhaling deeply through his nose, James at last spoke.

"At the risk of seeming rude, I feel the time has come to get some issues straight between us, man to man. You spoke to me some weeks ago of your love and devotion to my daughter, which is all noble and good. You asked permission to court Emma and I was pleased. However, I did not believe for a moment that I was acquiescing to a gargantuan food bill each week. Mary quite literally spends every spare moment of her day in the kitchen cooking for you."

"And I am quite flattered…" interrupted Edward.

"Shush, boy. I am not through."

Edward paled and then flushed red. Averting his gaze from James he suddenly feigned keen interest in the meanderings of a nuthatch up and down the tulip poplar tree by the porch.

"You need not fear the guillotine here, Edward, for I am not going to cut off your head. However, I am going to cut off your…" and James paused dramatically to puff on his pipe before finishing, "vittles if you do not agree with the logic of my proposal."

Relieved, Edward responded, "Please tell me of your proposal, sir."

"I would propose to hire you away from Hummel for the sum of seventy-five cents each week without the added benefit of beans or peaches, but with the understanding that you may eat at our table each evening. In addition, I would insist that you split and haul the scrap lumber from my mill to Mrs. Miller's kitchen for use in the cookstove. What do you say to that, Edward?"

"You drive a hard bargain, sir. What is it exactly that I would do at the mill? Keep the ledger books?"

"No indeed. I trust only Emma to do that. You would be a mill hand."

"A mill hand!" Edward exclaimed indignantly.

"Take it or leave it, boy. The alternative is to continue at Hummel's while subsisting on peaches and beans."

"I shall have to give it some thought," responded Edward.

"You do just that, but until you accept my proposal, do not seat yourself at my table again. Do you understand me, Edward?"

"Yes sir, I believe I do." Whereupon Edward rose, walked down the steps, across the lawn and out onto High Point Avenue. His next stop was Miss Hattie's House of Splendor.

James continued to smoke his pipe, blowing smoke rings out into the night air when Emma appeared at the screen door wiping her hands on a kitchen towel. Opening the door, she peered around the porch in the gathering darkness, "Where is Edward?" Emma asked.

"Gone," announced James. "Back to that rathole he crawled out of in the first place, I would wager."

"What did you say to him, Papa?" wailed Emma.

"I just told him that there is no longer any room at my table for a billy goat who passes each evening in my home under the pretext of courting my daughter but all the while eating everything that is not firmly nailed to my oak floors!"

"Please tell me you did not say such a thing to Edward!"

"And furthermore, I told him that he could earn his keep at my table by working for reduced wages at the mill and I told him that he could supply your poor dear mother with the firewood necessary to slavishly prepare all the food that he consumes," James paused to re-light his pipe.

"I feel positively faint!" exclaimed Emma slumping into the chair just recently vacated by Edward and fanning herself with the folded towel.

"I am sorry to distress you, my dear, but sometimes the truth is distressing. It has become quite apparent to me that this young man is using you as a method of filling his stomach each evening. He enters our home on the pretext of 'courting' you only to satisfy his gluttony at your mother's table!"

Here Emma began to cry into the kitchen towel. Mary, hearing Emma's sobs, appeared at the door. "What on earth has happened?" she demanded

"I have just decided to cut my food bill in half," proclaimed James rising and tapping out the contents of his pipe before entering the house.

Mary moved to Emma's side and taking her by the arm, guided the still sobbing girl over to the swing where Mary encircled her daughter with both arms. "There, there, deary! Life is a bit dreary! But soon enough it will be cheery!" Mary cooed, reminding Emma of the little doggerel verse that she used to recite for her when, as a child, the tears would flow.

The little ditty only made Emma cry harder. "Oh, Mama, Mama! Why did Papa have to go and spoil everything! I love Edward so and now Papa has driven him off because he does not want to feed him dinner any longer and I know I shall probably never see him again. After all…who would want a girl whose father is a mean-spirited pinchpenny?"

"Emma Miller! How dare you say such things about your father!"

"Well, it is the truth!"

"Your father is burdened with many responsibilities in life…responsibilities which he willingly shoulders for the benefit of you and me. He works long, hard hours at his mill to provide all of this for us," and Mary made a horizontal sweeping motion in front of her. "He has paid for all of this with his own blood, sweat and toil. It has taken him his whole life to do it. Nothing angers your father more than a man whom he perceives to be lazy or a man who takes from another man what he should be earning for himself. Your father has given countless young men opportunities to support themselves and their families over the years, but the moment he perceives that the man is lazy, your father refuses to pay him wages."

Emma had stopped crying now and was wiping her face off with the kitchen towel. Taking a handkerchief from her waistband, she blew her nose loudly several times. Mary gently pushed errant curls back from Emma's forehead with her index finger.

"Your papa is trying to safeguard you, Emma. He does not want some young huckster taking advantage of his daughter…making a slick pitch to achieve his own ends to the detriment of yours. Now, if Edward is half the man I think he is, I predict that he will come back and agree to Papa's terms."

"Really? You do think that, Mama?" Emma asked her mother mournfully, her eyes tearing again.

"If he does not return, then we shall both know that Papa was right in his assessment of Edward and you will have lost nothing except a future filled with trouble and pain."

Emma sat staring out into the gloom, contemplating her mother's words of wisdom.

A week passed and Edward did not return. Emma dutifully rose each dawn, dressed, breakfasted alone and trudged to the mill, kicking up little swirls of leaves as she made her way down to the river. The activities at the mill no longer held her interest. The antics, swearing and storytelling of the men bored her. She wore an habitual sullen expression and moped around the premises, prompting old Bill to whisper to Herbert, "Must be a bad time of the month. Just leave her alone." Returning home, Emma helped her mother with the evening meal, ate in silence, washed up the dishes, bathed and retired for the evening to her room, where she sat awake for hours, staring out her window into the darkness.

The change in Emma's behavior both at home and at the mill did not escape her parents' notice and they worried that she was sinking into a dark state of mind. Out of genuine concern for her daughter, Mary finally spoke to Emma about Edward and his absence, for it was she who had comforted the younger woman with her prediction that he would return. "Emma, I have a notion that you and I should go shopping at Hummel's today and restock the larder. What do you say?" Mary made her pitch to her daughter.

"Do you not feel that to be a bit forward, Mama?" was Emma's only reply.

"Forward? I see nothing forward about going to the store where I have traded all these years in order to restock my pantry shelves!" declared Mary. "And," she added, "because I shall be purchasing a large quantity of supplies, I do need an extra pair of hands. Now let us draw up the shopping list and be on our way."

There was a faint chill in the air as the two women began to make their way up Longmeadow to Court Street and Hummel's on the square. The maples were rapidly losing their leaves and rain had recently made the roads muddy, so the women crossed them gingerly, lifting their skirts ever so slightly as to avoid soiling their hems. Arriving at Hummel's, Emma held the door open for her mother who moved directly to the counter to greet Mr. Hummel. "Good morning!" she chirped brightly to the rotund proprietor, while scanning the store for Edward. Emma sulked into the store behind her mother, also scanning the interior for Edward.

"Top of the morning to you, Mrs. Miller!" cried Hummel upon seeing one of his favorite customers. "And what'll it be today? Well, I declare! Is that the beauteous Miss Emma that I see hiding behind her mama's skirts?"

"Indeed, Mr. Hummel and good morning to you," Emma managed.

Mary took out her list and feigned unusual interest in every scrap of merchandise in the store, trying to prolong her stay and give Edward a chance to appear. While her mother and Mr. Hummel made the rounds of the shelves and counters, Emma sat sullenly on one of the wooden chairs by the checkerboard atop an empty pickle barrel, aimlessly moving the pieces around with her finger. Suddenly, she heard her mother say, "I am surprised not to see that young and handsome clerk of yours. I had hoped to prevail upon him to assist us home with our order."

"Edward? Oh no, he doesn't work for me any longer," replied Hummel.

Emma froze in her chair. What was he saying? Edward was gone? Gone where? Emma felt a tide of rising panic washing over her. As nonchalantly as her knocking knees would allow, Emma made her way over to where Hummel and her mother were tallying up the goods and wrapping them into neat bundles. "Why...whatever is Grandview to do without its horseshoe champion?" Emma began lightly. Then more to the point, "Did he mention where he was going?"

"Yes, as matter of fact he did. Said he would be returning to Clarksburg. Had a better offer over there, more money and all. You know he's from Clarksburg. Probably has people over there. I was getting worried about him these last few months, though."

"Oh, really," Emma asked innocently, "and why was that?"

"The hours he was keeping."

"The hours?" Emma pressed.

"Well of course you know he slept in the storeroom at the back of my house and it was not unusual for me to hear that boy entering the premises at three in the morning and then he would turn around at six and come over here to the store to open up for me," replied Hummel handing the last of the parcels to Emma.

Unable to conceal the look of surprise on her face, Emma blurted out, "Where do you suppose he would go until that hour of the morning?"

"Probably where most of the young bucks in this town spend their time and money," Hummel answered. Seeing the uncomprehending look on Emma's face, he whispered, "Miss Hattie's."

Emma flashed her mother a stricken look and turned for the door. "Thank you, Mr. Hummel," Mary covered for her daughter's hasty departure. "Please do remember me to Mrs. Hummel and thank her for the delightful jar of jam that she sent over the other day with Will and George."

Mary scurried on out the door, trotting along to catch up with Emma who was moving rapidly out of sight. "Emma!" Mary called, "Do hold up a bit, for I cannot move as quickly as you do, especially with all these parcels!"

Emma paused and Mary caught up with her saying at once to Emma's contorted profile, "Now, do not take Hummel's words as gospel! You know he is little more than an old gossip. Why he spends the better part of each day trading stories with everyone who enters his store. That is one reason people go there...just to hear old Hummel spin a good one!" and Mary forced a laugh. Emma looked askance at her mother.

"What I do not understand," Emma said in a strangled voice as she began to walk down Longmeadow shoulder to shoulder with her mother, "is why Edward would leave Grandview without telling me...without so much as a good-bye. He spoke to me of marriage and to Papa as well!"

"Ah, so he wanted to marry your papa too?" Mary teased.

"Mama! Have pity on me and refrain from your teasing. This is serious!"

Later that night after Emma had retired to her room, James turned on the gaslights in the parlor and stoked up the fire in the fireplace to ward off the chill of fall. Mary took up her sewing and James turned to reading the Grandview Courier. The two sat in silence for a while, each self-absorbed. The gaslights hissed faintly at the fire which crackled loudly from its grate. Mary's needle flashed in the firelight as she deftly stitched colorful squares of fabric together, forming the top of a quilt that she was piecing together for their bed before winter came on hard that year. Pulling at his mustache as he read the newspaper articles, James was moved to comment quietly to his wife, "Emma seemed a bit worse for wear this evening."

"Indeed she was!" Mary answered tartly. "I should have liked to scalp Hummel this afternoon at the store!"

"For what transgression now?" James asked without looking up from his paper.

"He actually told Emma how he knew for a fact that Edward had left town to go back to Clarksburg. He also could not refrain from telling her that he had heard Edward entering the house at three o'clock in the morning on more than one occasion and when our Emma asked Hummel where he supposed Edward had been, the man had the nerve to surmise that Edward had been to Miss Hattie's House of Splendor!"

"He did what?" James looked up from his newspaper.

"You heard me. He mentioned Miss Hattie's to Emma!"

"The old tub of lard just gets a thrill out of saying such things to young women, is all. It titillates him, I do believe. Pay him no mind," admonished James.

"Well, I can assure you that Emma, upon hearing such gossip, has thought of little since and I must confess, I do not know quite how to console her."

"You simply tell her what I said, that Hummel is an old gossip and..."

"I already told her that to no effect," Mary sighed.

"Do you know for a fact that he has actually left Grandview for Clarksburg?" James asked Mary.

"According to Hummel he has left town and I would tend to believe him as Edward was boarding in his very own house."

"I could make some inquiries across the river," James continued.

"To what end? We know that he is gone so what would you do? Tack up fliers all over Clarksburg begging him to come back? Begging him to give up his river whores for the love of our daughter?"

"Tut, tut, Mary! You have already convicted the man and we know nothing for sure except that he has left. The only thing that I know for certain is that the man is an opportunistic parasite and I say good riddance! Other than that, I would not dare to speculate on the man's morals."

"Well, James Miller, I certainly could hazard a guess as to his morals. To lead our poor innocent daughter on like he did with talk of courting and betrothal, to sit each night with her in the swing for weeks and then just to vanish…and without a single word! I would say he is a man of low morals and totally devoid of scruples. I could see it the moment I looked into those immoral blue eyes of his!" Mary sputtered, thoroughly enjoying her trouncing of Edward.

"Now do not get yourself so lathered up as you know you will have difficulty sleeping this evening. Instead, come sit here beside me for a while," coaxed James patting the burgundy velvet upholstery on the settee next to his leg, "for I should very much enjoy the closeness of the lovely lady that I married. You know it just seems like yesterday that you and I were setting out together on this very same journey…" and Mary was persuaded to set aside her sewing along with her mounting worries about Emma.

CHAPTER 7

─────────── ▼ ───────────

Emma awakened late the morning after her return from Clarksburg with Nurse Walker the previous noon. Baby Johnny was wailing from his crib and she could hear the others downstairs in the kitchen preparing breakfast. Judging from the noise level drifting up to her room, Will and George were in high spirits, showing off for Nurse Walker, no doubt! As she swung her legs over the edge of the bed and prepared to stand up, Emma felt suddenly faint and slumped back onto the covers. Then she remembered the fall she had experienced the previous day and reached to test the lump on her head, which felt somewhat smaller but just as painful.

Looking across the room into her full-length mirror, she could see plainly the large purple mark on her forehead and she was instantly reminded of the purple marks that Edward used to leave on her body. Not on her face, to be sure, because then the hallmarks of his violence upon her would have been in plain view and Edward's beatings were calculated to leave no visible trace. He tormented and scarred the private parts of her body to which no one else had access.

Deliberately pushing such sinister thoughts from her mind, Emma rose again, more carefully and went to her wailing baby. Lifting him gently from his bed, she kissed the top of his dark head and his round little cheeks. Delighted to see his mother, baby Johnny stopped his crying and smiled a big toothless grin for her. "Oh, my precious! Did my little man have a nice visit to Sleepy Town? I do believe my nose tells me that your pants are quite full of something unmentionable! Let us see what we can do to correct that situation," and as soon as Emma removed the baby's diaper, Johnny proceeded to urinate all over the covers of her bed where she had taken him for a change and his feeding. "You would think an experienced mother would know better than that. What do you say Johnny? I guess it is this big ugly bump on my head that has caused me to forget the tricks that little boys play on their mamas!"

Emma continued talking sweetly to baby Johnny as she cleaned him up and fed him. It was the sort of one-sided conversation that all mothers have with their infants whereby the mother asks and answers her own questions put to her uncomprehending baby. "And is this sweet thing hungry? Yes, this big boy has worked up quite an appetite during the night. Do you see what a lovely fall day it is outside with the sun shinning so brightly? Yes, and you most certainly will want to take a ride in your baby buggy today to bask in the sunshine and see the colors for yourself."

After feeding baby Johnny, Emma descended the staircase cautiously, holding tightly to her infant with one hand and the balustrade with the other. Walking back to the kitchen, she could see the twins gathered around Nurse Walker who sat at her mother's worktable sipping coffee.

"Ma!" exclaimed Will, "Did you know that Nurse Fannie cuts people open and takes out their innards? She says there's a whole bunch of blood too! Just like when Pa used to cut open those squirrels and rabbits for stew. Only difference is, you can't keep their hides 'cause they need 'em back and naturally we can't eat people neither," proclaimed Will quite out of breath with his newly acquired knowledge of medicine.

"Really, Will? I can already tell that you are completely captivated by Nurse Walker. George, what have you learned from Nurse Walker this morning?" asked Emma getting into the spirit of the boys' fascination with their overnight visitor.

George seemed perplexed and then he added, "Well, I do not know if Nurse Fanny is an angel or the Holy Ghost that we talk about in church on Sunday," here George paused to scratch his head. "She dresses all in white just like a ghost and I heard her tell Nana that you think she is an 'angel of mercy' because she saved your life when you fell down the stairs. But the big problem is, no wings! Nurse Fannie does not have any wings," whereupon Will was moved to examine Nurse Walker's shoulder blades. "I already told you, Will, she does not have any wings! I already checked for them, Dummy!"

Stifling the urge to laugh, Emma regained her composure, "That is because earthly angels have no wings but when they are called home by God, they are given their wings in Heaven."

"So that's the reason!" chimed in Will, adding, "Can I ask for green wings when I get to Heaven? I don't want no white wings. Green is my favorite color," Will announced turning to Nurse Walker.

"You are definitely not going to Heaven, Will!" exclaimed George.

"Georgie! That's not nice! How'd you like it if I said you ain't goin' to Heaven?"

"Are not going to Heaven, Willynilly!"

"Are too!" shouted Will.

"Boys! Boys!" interjected Emma. "Let us be on our best behavior for our guest!"

Amused, Nurse Walker was moved to add, "Boys, I have it on good authority that as long as you both behave here on earth, mind your mother and your grandmother and grow up to be fine young men of good moral character, then St. Peter will allow you into Heaven."

"That settles that!" exclaimed George. "I am so hungry Nana! Can I have my pancakes now?"

The little group gathered around Mary's kitchen worktable for pancakes, crisply fried fatback, milk, coffee and more spirited conversation with the boys before Nurse Walker said farewell to her new friends. As they waved her off down the hill to the ferry, Emma exclaimed, "What an extraordinary woman she is! How very fortunate I am to have met her, given the extraordinary circumstances! Her presence in my life at this time is a good omen, would you agree, Mama?"

"Most definitely, Emma dear! I predict that your life is about to take a turn for the better."

After she dressed and put the baby down for his nap, Emma gathered the boys for a stroll outside for she had a promise still to keep.

"Perhaps we could take that new dog of yours for a walk down by the river, boys. What do you say to that?" Emma asked the twins. "By the way, just how did we acquire that dog?"

"I found the poor little dog all tangled up in honeysuckle vines around the edge of the woods by the pond," claimed George.

"Did not!" argued Will elbowing his brother out of the way. "That dog started cryin' something terrible, Ma, just when I came around the barn with the cutter..."

"Scythe," interjected Emma.

"Yep, that same thing and then I runned over and..."

"Ran, Will," corrected Emma.

"Ran over and there he was, just lookin' up at me!"

"Who was it that cut Brute free?" asked George glaring at Will while pulling out his folded silver pocketknife to show his mother and brother in the palm of his hand.

"Oh, so now we already have a name for the dog? Does this mean someone has decided to keep the animal without asking me?" Emma questioned her boys.

"Nana! She decided!" exclaimed both boys in unison, putting the blame on their absent grandmother.

"So, if I were to go straight to Nana this minute, she would tell me the same story?" Emma pressed her sons.

"Definitely," responded George.

"Just how did you two decide upon a name for the dog?" Emma continued.

Again came the answer, "Nana decided."

"Well, it would seem that this dog was all Nana's idea, from beginning to end."

"Yes," agreed the boys exchanging glances.

"But why did Nana choose the name 'Brute' for this fellow?" and here Emma stooped to scratch the friendly black dog with brown markings, fondling his ears.

"'Cause she said he had such big paws that she figured he's gonna grow up to be a brute."

"So, that is what we decided to name him," chimed in George.

With that, the dog began to lick Emma's face, making her laugh. "I shall let the two of you in on a little secret," giggled Emma rolling the squirming dog onto his back to scratch his belly.

"What, Ma?" asked Will delighted at the prospect of hearing a secret.

"Your own grandmother had a large black and brown dog as a girl. She adored that dog! He accompanied her everywhere, even to the schoolhouse. The school teacher back then used to swear that Prince, that is what Nana named him, could tell time, for each afternoon at three o'clock sharp, Prince would appear at the door of the schoolhouse to see your grandmother safely home. When Prince grew old and died, Nana cried for days," and Emma's eyes clouded briefly.

"Gosh, Ma! You never told us that before!" exclaimed George in amazement.

"There are many stories that I have never told you before but today I have something more important to tell the two of you. How about if the three of us sit over there for a bit," said Emma motioning to a large fallen tree some ten yards up from the water's edge.

Will and George scrambled up onto the tree trunk beside their mother, swinging their legs to and fro while Brute jumped wildly in the air as he attempted to grab their toes. Deep in thought, Emma gazed across the river into the brilliant sunshine glinting off the water.

"What was it you was gonna tell us?" asked Will, "Another secret?"

"A secret of sorts," replied Emma slowly, "and one that I have been keeping to myself for too long now." Emma's face began to contort as she struggled for control. "What I must tell the two of you today is very sad news…news about your father. You see…" Emma hesitated groping for the right words. "You remember last April when your father left and I told you that he was away on business for the mill?" she looked into the faces of her children.

"Is he dead?" interrupted George in a tone of panic.

"In a way," replied Emma.

"I knew it! Pa got smacked in the head with one of them big hoists of lumber that he was gonna barge down to New Orleans and it killed him just like it killed Pa's man, Ellis, last winter. Do you remember that?" wailed Will.

"No, no, Will! Nothing like that!" soothed Emma placing her arm around her trembling son. "Your father has simply vanished," Emma stated flatly.

"What is 'vanished', Ma?" demanded George, scowling.

"It means that he has disappeared without a trace," Emma answered.

"How could a man as big as Pa disappear?" pressed George.

"Yeah, how could he?" chimed in Will. "The magician at the church supper made the rabbit disappear but Pa's too big for that!"

"It is a different kind of 'disappear'," responded Emma, looking from one boy to the other. "You see, your Pa wanted to disappear…to no longer be part of our family…to never come back home to us again." Emma drew in her breath sharply and held it for several seconds, bracing for the storm that she knew was coming.

"Oh, no Ma! You are wrong! Pa loves us. He would never do such a thing. Why, we have a new baby that he has never seen and a new dog and…and…" George's tears rolled down his uncomprehending face.

"And besides, I just lost my tooth," cried Will pulling up his lip to remind his mother, "and Pa doesn't even know it yet and he always told me every time I lost a tooth it was a very special day for him because it meant I was growin' up!" wailed Will. "I just know Pa wants to be here to see me grow up!"

Both boys were weeping uncontrollably and sobs shook Emma's small frame as she gathered her sons to her in an attempt to console and to be consoled. The dog sat in a dejected heap at their feet looking up at the three of them and sensing their overwhelming grief, threw back his head and began to howl.

Taking her handkerchief from her waistband, Emma attempted to wipe George's face and nose with it.

"Get that thing off me!" shouted George, pushing his mother's arm away and jumping down from the log.

"Yeah, and don't touch me with it neither!" scolded Will with rising anger.

"This is all your fault, Ma!" yelled George into the startled face of his mother. "You drove Pa away!"

"George, whatever has possessed you to say such a thing to me?" Emma questioned her son, wiping her eyes with the handkerchief.

"You think I am just a little kid with no sense. Well, I know that you used to fight with Pa late at night when you thought we were sleeping. I could hear you slapping him and hollering at him too and that is why Pa left, because you were so mean to him!" yelled the indignant child.

"Yeah!" chimed in Will.

"There is no truth to what you have said, George. It was your father who beat me unmercifully, causing me to yell in pain," Emma tried to explain to the two raging boys that stood before her with tear-stained faces.

"I know how mad you get when you switch us, Ma," continued George in his tirade against his mother, "and it always scares us to death. Pa left because he was scared to death after you yelled at him and now he is too afraid to come home because of what you might do to him!"

"Yeah!" exclaimed Will again.

"Just like the time," George continued in a rage, "that I hit Benjamin with a stick across the face and you yelled at me. Told me you were going to tie me to a tree and leave me there all night long. Scared me and Will so bad that we both ran away and hid out for the rest of the day."

"Yeah!" said Will.

"And when we got hungry and came back that night, you got the biggest switch off the tulip poplar that you could find and beat the daylights out of my legs and Will's too."

"Yeah! And I didn't even do nothing neither!" managed Will, finally adding his voice to the fracas.

"Oh, heaven help me!" moaned Emma. "You boys have knotted up the facts, as you usually do, to fit inside your seven year old heads! Your father's departure was not my fault and I can assure…"

"Liar!" screamed George, his face purple with rage.

"Yeah…liar!" echoed Will.

"We are going straight to Nana this minute and tell her what you have done!" exclaimed George before adding, "Come on, Will! Run!"

The twins took off at a gallop along the river, retracing their steps through fallen leaves and over tree trunks to the yellowing meadow that signaled the edge of their grandmother's property. The big white house with its expansive porch came into view and the boys ran faster up the hill. Banging open the screen door, the twins raced through the house calling, "Nana! Nana? Where are you?" Not finding their grandmother downstairs, they climbed to the second floor, peering into each room and not finding her there either, the twins raced downstairs, banging loudly out the back door on their way to the barn.

Hearing their calls of distress, Mary emerged from the barn with Onion's currying brushes still clutched in her hands. "What is all this fuss I hear?" she asked smiling until she saw the looks on their faces.

Both boys dissolved into their grandmother's skirts, sobbing out the news that their father had disappeared from their lives forever, while naming their mother as the culprit responsible for causing all of their present misery. Mary listened in utter astonishment.

"She needs a switching for this, Nana!" concluded George.

"Yeah!" added Will. "And no dinner!"

"Boys, please come with me to the house. Will, take hold of Johnny's baby buggy and bring him along. We have much to talk about but first we must put some cool water on those faces of yours at the kitchen sink and have a drink for I fear that you are nearly overcome by the heat and so much emotion," and Mary wrapped her arms around her grandsons and led them firmly back into the house.

Emma sat on the ground next to the fallen log, a disheveled lump of a woman. Her skirts were soiled, one stocking was torn, her auburn hair was undone and cluttered with bits of leaves, her face was still streaked with wet tears and even the dog had abandoned her, preferring the company of Will and George to hers. Still looking off in the direction of the boys' escape, Emma let out an enormous sigh. Her head ached and she gingerly rubbed the site of the lump on her forehead. "How could so much go so wrong so quickly?" she wondered to herself, absently picking debris out of her hair. Had not Mary herself urged Emma to tell Will and George the unvarnished truth about their father? Now, she, their mother, their only provider, was the evil one and their father, the abusive devil, was considered a victim! How would she persuade the boys to understand the truth of her situation without revealing the terrifying details of abuse to a couple of seven year olds?

Pulling herself together, Emma rose slowly, straightened her clothing and made her way back to the house on High Point Avenue. She found the boys in the kitchen assisting Mary with the preparation of their evening meal. Baby Johnny lay sucking on a sugar-tit in his baby buggy that the boys had helped their grandmother carry up the back steps and into the house.

As Emma entered the kitchen quietly, she startled the boys by saying, "Your dog is hungry. You had best feed him and close him in the barn for the night," and turning to her mother added, "Thank you for taking care of Johnny. I shall take him upstairs to nurse now." Removing the cloth, which Mary had tied with a bit of sugar in it, from Johnny's mouth, Emma picked up the gurgling baby and made her way slowly up the long staircase.

She was surprised a few moments later to see her mother peer in through the door. "Emma, dear, I know that this afternoon was a bit of a disaster and I feel ever so much to blame as I am the one who insisted that you tell your sons the truth about their father. No matter what the consequences, it was the right course of action. You simply could not go on living a lie for those two. I have spoken at length with both Will and George and what I propose to cap off my little talk with them is an unveiling of the evidence. Therefore, in about the next half hour, I shall assemble the boys up here in your room, just prior to supper. Please go along with me and whatever request I make of you." Whereupon, Mary turned abruptly and went back downstairs.

True to her word, as Emma sat burping the baby over her shoulder, Mary, George and Will appeared at her door. "May we come in?" asked her mother politely.

"Of course," responded Emma closing her blouse and moving her fingers to re-button it.

"Do not bother with the buttons," she said quietly to Emma, "and please place Johnny on your bed." Emma did as she was told and then her mother added, "Now turn around with your back facing us and remove your clothing from the waist up."

"Mama!" Emma briefly protested.

"Do as I say, please, and boys, you look sharply at what you are about to see. Go ahead now Emma."

As she was instructed, Emma turned her back to Mary and the boys. She removed first her blouse and then lowered her step-in to her waist. There was an audible gasp from George and Will as they surveyed their mother's naked back. A thick purple scar snaked from her left shoulder horizontally across and down her back to the right side of her waist. "Now you can each see with your own eyes, Will and George, that both your mother and I spoke the truth about the beatings your father inflicted upon her. Those blows that you heard were directed at your mother and her yelling was due to the terrible pain that she experienced each time your father struck her."

Emma's sons wore expressions of complete shock. Finally tearing his eyes away from the hideous scar, George turned to his grandmother and asked, "May I touch it?"

"Ask your mother. The welt is on her back," replied Mary.

"May I, Ma?" George asked turning again to his mother's back.

"And me too?" chimed in the now subdued Will.

"Yes," was all that Emma replied quietly over her shoulder.

The boys stepped forward and each slowly traced the purple coil across her back with their small fingers. "Does it hurt, Ma?" George was finally able to manage.

"Not any longer," Emma murmured. What she could not tell her sons was that, whereas the beatings which Edward inflicted upon her body caused her physical pain, the mental pain of the beatings was far greater and would remain indelibly etched upon her spirit.

As Emma pulled her clothing back up to cover the ugly mark, Mary again addressed the hushed audience of two. "Your father beat your mother one night last April with his riding crop while she was heavy with baby Johnny and made that mark upon her back which you just saw with your own eyes. Your father had a fondness for alcohol, as I told you earlier, and the alcohol made him mean and violent. Some time during that same night, your father decided to run away. He took his clothing, all of the family's money that he could lay his hands on, the horse which Papa and I had given to your mother and left the house on Locust Street, never to return. He did not even bother to leave so much as a letter of explanation for your mother."

"Do we know where he is?" George asked sadly.

"We do not," his grandmother responded firmly.

"Is he ever coming back?" Will sniffled up at Mary.

"No," was the unflinching reply.

"So," responded George heaving a huge sigh, "Will, Johnny and I are orphans."

"Indeed you are not!" exclaimed Emma finally breaking her silence and gathering her twin sons to her where she sat in the pink upholstered chair. "Orphans have no parents or grandparents to take care of them and love them. The three of you have me and Nana to take care of you and we are going to continue to do just that. Never forget that the five of us are a family and we shall all stick together no matter what befalls us!"

"But I do have a request," interjected Mary, "and it would be that from this time forward, we shall all please refrain from speaking the name of Edward Richardson in this house again. He is gone from our midst of his own choosing, and I want him gone from our conversation as well. Is it understood?"

"Yes, Nana," the boys responded in unison.

"As you wish, Mama," answered Emma.

"Good! Then let us all go back downstairs and partake of the pheasant and sweet potato dinner that the boys and I have prepared for the four of us. We have, I believe, concluded matters up here."

CHAPTER 8

▼

Fall was rapidly closing in upon the little town of Grandview, turning its vantage point on the Southport River into a blaze of color. The trees were staging their famous annual gala in which all vied for first place in the Most Beautiful Foliage contest. Assisting the trees with their costuming was North Wind who ushered in Cooler Temperatures at night to transform the ordinary green attire of Summer into the spectacular ochre, bronze and persimmon of late September. It was suggested to the Sun that she begin to limit the time she spent on the streets and meadows of Grandview, where she now hung around as a distant and uninvited guest at the pageant. Rain crept silently in each evening to wash the trees and freshen them for their performance the next day, and West Wind gently blew upon the leaves to dry them for their grand finale.

With the boys at Hummel's one afternoon, Emma spied the notice she had been looking for tacked to the "Town Crier" board as Hummel called it. SCHOOL WILL BE IN SESSION THE FIRST MONDAY OF THE MONTH OF OCTOBER. CLASSES WILL COMMENCE AT 9:00 A.M. AND END AT 3:00 P.M. MONDAY THROUGH FRIDAY. CLASSES WILL ADJOURN FOR ALL THE USUAL AND CUSTOMARY HOLIDAYS. APPLY TO MISTRESS RITA WEAVER AT THE SCHOOLHOUSE ON THE CORNER OF VINE AND FIRST STREETS: DAILY 1:00 P.M. UNTIL 3:00 P.M.

"Well, boys, look here!" Emma exclaimed to the twins pointing to the notice. "Come read this for me, please," and haltingly George read the notice for his mother in his best singsong voice.

"It is about time we got to go back to school!" exclaimed George adding, "Summer is so long and I have read every book in Nana's house...some of them even two times."

"Not me! I don't want to go back to school, ever," fretted Will.

"And just why not?" asked Emma

"'Cause that Miss Rita always makes me stand up at the chalk board when we have our spelling lessons and she gives me the hardest words and makes me write them in front of the whole class and when I can't spell the words right, the class always calls me 'Dummy', just like Georgie does," Will related forlornly to his mother while picking out big, fat red apples from the wooden crates that stood adjacent to the gleaming brass cash register.

"Really?" responded his mother.

"Yeah. Georgie always thinks I'm sleepin' because I can't get it right but it's just because I'm not interested in spelling. It's a dumb thing and a stupid waste of time. Makes my head sweat to have to spell a word like tiger."

"And how would you spell tiger, Will, if you were at the chalkboard today?" Emma asked as she paid Hummel for their parcels and together with her sons carrying her purchases, headed out the door.

"Hmmm," Will thought for a minute. "Probably spell it 't-i-g-g-u-r', just like it sounds, right, Ma?"

"Not exactly, Will. I think it might be more like..."

"T-I-G-E-R," interrupted George in a very loud voice, unable to contain himself any longer.

"Why do I need to know how to spell tiger anyhow? I ain't never goin' to see one and even if I did I wouldn't walk up to him and say, 'Hello Mr. T-I-G-E-R, nice to see you today,'" reasoned Will.

"You need to learn to spell so you can read, Dummy!" exclaimed George.

"Well, who wants to read anyhow? I have to spend my time fishin' and swimmin' and ridin' Onion and takin' care of Johnny and helpin' Nana. There's just too many chores to do! I can't be wastin' time on readin'!"

"All right, all right, boys!" Emma scolded.

"Psst!" whispered George to Will behind Emma's back as she stopped to chat with a friend.

"Yeah, what?" Will whispered across to George, leaning back to scowl at his brother behind his mother's skirt.

"How about if I make you a deal?" asked George.

"What kind of a deal?" Will asked suspiciously of his brother.

"I promise to help you learn to read and spell in school this year if you help me do some of my chores. Fair?"

Will gazed up at the sky as if seeking Divine counsel before responding to his twin brother, "Okay, it's a fair deal!"

"What 'deal' are you two cooking up now?" Emma asked suddenly, having bid farewell to her friend.

"Oh, nothing, Ma," responded George disarmingly as he changed the subject to ask, "Do you think Nana will have those sugar cookies ready by the time we get back home? I have really worked up an appetite with all this shopping!"

So began a collaboration of energy and intellect between the brothers that would span the next five decades of their lives.

Emma missed opening day at the little corner schoolhouse as her classes had begun a week in advance of the children's. On her first morning of nursing school, she rose before dawn to bathe and dress, paying careful attention to all the details of her toilette according to Mary's strict training. Emma smiled at herself in the mirror as she recalled her mother's utter despair at her appearance when she had been a young girl.

"Will you never learn to put on those garments as I have taught you!" Mary had repeatedly chided Emma. Today, her mother would be proud of her as she carefully made her selections and laid them all out on the bed for final scrutiny: fresh step-in, dark stockings, two garters, petticoat, white blouse, navy blue skirt, all crispy pressed, without the usual burn marks and black high button shoes, gleaming with a fresh application of shoe blacking. Placing the buttonhook back on her dresser, she next tackled the unruly mass of auburn curls which hung to her shoulders.

Emma attacked her hair with the silver brush with its stiff boar bristles, brushing vigorously from the top of her scalp and down, swinging the hair first over her right shoulder and then her left to make sure that she had brushed down and out through all the curls. Next she removed a dark blue ribbon from her dresser drawer, pulled her hair back and away from her face, securing it there with a bow at the base of her neck. Finally, she surveyed her image in the full-length mirror, both front and back, by glancing over her shoulder.

"Mama would approve," she thought. Because of her diminutive size, Emma looked a decade younger, which caused her to fret that she might not gain the acceptance of her classmates when they learned that she was actually twenty-nine years old and the mother of three children. As if on cue with her musings, Johnny began to cry for his breakfast from the room next to hers and Emma rushed to feed the baby before he awakened the rest of the household. Preparing him carefully for the journey across the river, Emma swaddled baby Johnny in a soft, warm blanket and packed diapers, extra woolen soakers and a change of clothing for him in a leather valise.

Cradling the baby with her right arm and holding the valise with her left, Emma cautiously descended the long staircase and made her way back to the kitchen where she laid the baby in his buggy along with the valise. She poured herself a glass of milk and quickly ate an apple, tucking a second apple and a slice of bread into the leather bag for her lunch later that day.

As Emma opened the front door to leave the house, she was startled to see a piece of paper held down by rocks at all four corners, lying on the top step. On it was penciled in large capital letters: DEAR MA, WE HOPE YOU HAVE A GOOD DAY AT SCHOOL. BE CAREFUL CROSSING THE STREETS! LOVE GEORGE AND WILL. P.S. CAN YOU BRING US A CAKE FROM TOWN?

Tears rolled down Emma's face as she read the note from her boys. The misgivings that Emma had been experiencing ever since making the decision to enroll in nursing school suddenly loomed malevolently in her thoughts. How dare she even think of leaving her adored twin boys, and eventually her third child, with their grandmother for the next two years while she pursued a career in nursing?

The baby squirmed in her arms and Emma shifted her gaze from the paper to Johnny's toothless smiling face. "I must remind myself, dear little Johnny, that I am doing this for you and your brothers. It is not a capricious whim that drives me to seek a vocation. It is our survival!" Emma folded the paper, tucked it into the pocket of her skirt, gathered up the valise and without looking back, walked down to the ferry.

After the ferry docked on the opposite shore, Emma positioned the baby over her shoulder and picked up her valise to disembark at Water Street, the main thoroughfare up through the center of Clarksburg, past the bakery, past the Foggy Bend Hotel to Chestnut Street. With her head held high, her steps sure with purpose and her infant son sleeping on her shoulder, Emma again walked through the gates of Angel of Mercy Hospital, this time taking the flight of stairs up to the Children's Ward, as instructed by Nurse Walker.

At the nurses' station, Emma introduced herself to the woman behind the desk.

"Oh, yes, Emma Richardson, and this must be baby Johnny. Nurse Walker told us to expect you this morning." As the woman stepped forward to take

Johnny, Emma stepped back. "Please forgive me for not introducing myself, I am Nurse Eleanor Tyler and it is I who shall be caring for Johnny while you are in class or following one or more of our assorted doctors around the hospital," and she stuck out her hand, into which Emma placed her valise.

"May I please see the crib where Johnny will be sleeping? I shall be back at noon to feed him and in that valise you will find a change of clothing and diapers, he prefers his own blanket in which he is presently wrapped, if he should become fussy before his next feeding, I always walk him around a bit and…"

"Please do not fret so, Emma! I and the other women on the Children's Ward are highly skilled nurses who specialize in caring for seriously ill, and often, terminally ill children. We all have a light touch with our babies and very large, soft hearts. Rest assured, if anything were to arise concerning Johnny that I or the others did not feel capable of handling, we would fetch you at once. We are here to help you and Johnny. Let us do what we are trained to do so that you may study to be a fine nurse yourself."

Relief spread over Emma's face and she kissed her still dozing infant on a fat cheek before handing him over to Nurse Tyler. "Thank you so very much. I shall be back at noon," and Emma turned to walk down the stairs and back to the central hall where once again she found the staircase leading down to the nursing department. This time she was sure to look sharply left and right before beginning her descent.

At the bottom of the stairs was a hand-lettered sign that indicated nursing school applicants were to convene in room 02 with an arrow pointing straight ahead and in fact, Emma could see a small desk just ahead, around which milled a large group of young women. As she approached, she realized that all the new students were checking off their names on a sheet of paper, after which they received nametags to pin on their blouses. Emma's tag was hand-lettered: Student Nurse—Richardson. Pinning her tag to her upper left-hand shoulder, Emma peered into the classroom where about twenty or so students were already seated. The room was humming with conversation and laughter as Emma made her way to one of the long tables in the middle of the room.

"Is this seat taken?" she asked a young woman with hair the color of corn silk.

"No it is not. Please, join me," responded the woman pleasantly.

"Permit me to introduce myself. I am Emma Richardson from Grandview," whereupon Emma put out her hand to her fellow nursing student.

"Hello. I am Louise Bennington from Clarksburg, but you may call me Benni, everyone does."

"Benni?" Emma parroted.

Benni laughed. "When I was quite small and someone would ask me to say my name, I would always respond, 'Louise Benni' because I could not quite manage the last two syllables of my surname. My father, being the droll man that he is, nicknamed me Benni and it has stuck with me."

"I like that story," smiled Emma.

Benni cast an appraising eye over her new companion and making a wiping motion on her own left shoulder, pointed to Emma's left shoulder. "It looks to me like you must have either a baby brother or sister in your family."

Looking down at her shoulder, Emma realized that Johnny had left behind the unmistakable sign of a breast milk burp on her blouse. She took out her handkerchief to wipe the dribble away and replied, "Actually, I have a three month old son who delights in christening all my blouses in like fashion."

"You have a son?" stammered Benni. "But you are much too young!"

Smiling, Emma asked, "How old do you think I am?"

"I am nineteen," reasoned Benni, "so I guessed you to be a similar age."

"I am twenty-nine but because of my short stature, everyone thinks me quite young."

"How strange the two of us are!" exclaimed Benni. "I because of my name and you because of your age. It is a wonder that we were ever admitted to this fine school of nursing, being such odd fellows, so to speak."

The two were sharing a good laugh when Head Nurse Fanella Walker strode to the front of the classroom.

"Good morning, Students, and welcome to Angel of Mercy Hospital, soon to be known as 'Home Sweet Home' to all of you. Since I have personally met with each and every one of you during the past few weeks and months prior to the selection process, all of you undoubtedly recognize me to be Nurse Walker and you will kindly address me as such. I, in turn, shall call each of you by your surname, as for example, Conrad, Griffith, Richardson, Mayhugh, Bennington and so forth.

You thirty-five women seated before me this morning were hand-picked by me because I saw a spark in each and every one of you. Those sparks need some fanning, to be sure, but under my tutelage and that of other nurses and doctors on the staff here at Mercy, those sparks will combine and leap into a roaring fire that will warm, sustain and heal the legions of the sick, the diseased, the dying, the maimed, the suffering and the infirm that pass through these hallowed halls. We are the Sweet Savior's bulwark here on earth. We are His earthly angels of mercy and let us all remember that this is a most sacred mission for which we have been chosen. Do not disappoint the Divine Creator and heaven help you if you disappoint me!

At this point in my welcoming address, I always like to play a little game with my new nursing students to see if you know as much about your anatomy as my little patients do in the Children's Ward upstairs on the second floor. It goes like this. I shall call out a body part and you will respond by either pointing to or holding up the corresponding limb or area of your bodies."

All the girls giggled at the prospect of playing such a silly game. "Are we ready?"

"Yes!" the nursing students responded in unison.

"Yes, what?" persisted their instructor.

After a slight pause, the desired answer occurred to several in the class, "Yes Nurse Walker."

"Let us hear it from everyone!" exhorted their instructor, cupping her right hand behind her ear.

"Yes Nurse Walker!" came the response.

Cupping her ear again, their instructor once again exhorted the group, "Louder!"

"YES NURSE WALKER!" shouted the girls again in unison.

"Good! Let us begin then. Where are your elbows?" The girls looked around at each other in disbelief. "Do not worry, it will get harder as the months go by, and now once again, show me your elbows," whereupon seventy elbows were displayed for Nurse Walker.

"Excellent! And where are your ears, eyes, nose, mouth?" came in rapid succession with the appropriate pointing by the girls following just as rapidly.

"Splendid!" exclaimed Nurse Walker, pacing back and forth in front of the classroom. "Shoulder blades and breasts?" accompanied by much turning and patting. "Do not get the two confused, Bennington! Or is your head positioned on your body backward?" Much laughter ensued.

"Knees? Feet? Hands? Truly magnificent ladies, but enough of this silliness!" Nurse Walker moved to the side of the room and dragged two large easels to the front and center of the class.

Picking up a wooden pointer, she flipped up the cover sheets on artists' renderings of the male and female anatomies which were fastened to each of the easels. "Ladies, permit me to introduce you to Chart Female, as you will address her, and Chart Male, as you will address him," tapping each chart with her pointer as she spoke. "During the course of the next year, you will become intimately acquainted with their anatomies, inside and out, down to the most minute of details. Every hair follicle will receive your scrutiny until you know more about follicles, veins, hearts, bones, tissue, lungs, vertebrae than you know about anything else on earth. What say you to that?"

"YES NURSE WALKER!" came the desired response.

"And that is just the beginning of the fun that I have planned for you! For you will also learn to weigh, measure and mix medicines to be administered according to a patient's weight. You will learn to take body temperatures, both orally and rectally. You will locate and count the human pulse just here in the carotid artery," pointing to the side of her neck, "and here at the wrist and again here at the ankle," lifting her shoe and tapping at her ankle with the pointer.

One of the students in the back row leaned over to make a comment to another student which interruption was followed by an horrendous whack with Nurse Walker's pointer upon the front desk.

"Are you talking in my class without my permission?" Nurse Walker pointed to the offender with her stick.

The startled girl looked around for assistance from her classmates, but since none was forthcoming, she answered, "No Nurse Walker."

"What?" accompanied by the cupping motion.

"NO NURSE WALKER!"

"Good lungs on that one!" exclaimed Nurse Walker, smiling. "Now, when you wish to get my permission to speak you will do so by raising your hand thusly, to be recognized by me before one word escapes from your mouth. Do you understand, class?"

"YES NURSE WALKER!"

"Right. And as I was saying, you will learn to empty bedpans, administer bed baths, tend and dress wounds, set broken bones, deliver a baby, assist during surgeries and so forth and so on until your level of expertise far exceeds mine, or at least that is my fond hope for each and every one of you and do not disappoint me or..." and here she made a slashing motion across her throat with the pointer, "off with the head!"

"There is one element of your training which I have been saving for last, my personal favorite!" and she smiled hugely at the cowed women in front of her. We here at Angel of Mercy are blessed with a Chief of Staff without equal! His specialty is surgery and you will each have the good fortune at some point to make rounds with him and eventually to assist him in a surgical procedure. His name is Burris G. McKendrick. Now there are some who have whispered through these hallowed halls that the 'G' stands for God but I have it on good authority that the 'G' actually stands for 'Grant'. However, feel free to treat him with the same reverence and deference that you would the Higher Power because girls, around here, HE IS YOUR HIGHER POWER!"

"At this time," Nurse Walker beamed at her hushed audience, "we shall take a break to collect ourselves, after which I want you to line up single file just here," and she used the pointer to indicate the wall over to her right, "to sign for and receive your textbooks. You are now excused for fifteen minutes. Fail to return after that, and you will not be readmitted to class. BE PROMPT! I cannot abide tardiness!" and she waved them off with her pointer.

There were hushed murmurings as the thirty-five young women exited the room. Once back upstairs, the girls gathered on the caduceus to exclaim over their introduction into the realm of nursing as envisioned by Head Nurse Fanella Walker.

"It wasn't exactly what I had in mind," commented one distraught student.

"Are we to be treated like militia or morons?" asked another.

"It would seem that Nurse Walker is a bit, shall we say, 'sweet' on this Burris G. McKendrick," laughed another.

"The experience will be exactly what we make of it," came another voice from the crowd. All eyes swept the faces to find Emma's.

"And just what is that supposed to mean?" questioned a girl who stood next to Emma.

"It means," continued Emma, "that each and every one of us has it inside here," she tapped her head, "and inside here," she tapped over her heart, "to make this year of nursing school the pinnacle of our education to date. Let us all open ourselves up to this great and grand opportunity which stands before us."

"Hear ye! Hear ye!" chorused several of her compatriots. "Student Nurse Richardson for president!"

"Well, I do not know about the rest of you," laughed Emma, "but I cannot entertain the notion of running for president until after I have run to the water closet!"

With that, the students dispersed and when Emma returned to the caduceus, she found Benni scrutinizing all the signs posted along the walls.

"Now show me again, Student Nurse Bennington, just where those breasts of yours are located!" and both young women shared a laugh.

"That woman is positively exhausting, would you agree?" asked Benni.

"For a woman her age, she possess an abundance of energy which I very much admire and envy. I only hope that when I am her age, I may be blessed with half of what she has!" responded Emma. Changing the subject, Emma motioned to the front door and once outside for a stroll, she asked, "What of your family,

Benni? You mentioned your father. Is your mother still living? Do you have brothers and sisters?"

"Yes, my mother is quite well, although my poor father suffers from ill health. There are seven of us children and I am the fourth."

"So, you must have much younger siblings?" Emma linked her arm with Benni's as they walked slowly around the front lawn of the hospital.

"Yes, our baby brother is four, then two girls, me and finally my three older brothers," Benni smiled at Emma.

"Then," commented Emma, "as in so many other circumstances of our lives today, you girls are outnumbered by the boys in the family."

"What about you, Emma? Do you have brothers and sisters?"

"Sadly, I do not. I am an only daughter, living with my mother and my three sons."

"Please forgive me if I appear rude, but what has happened to your father and your husband?"

"My father died nearly two years ago and my husband ran away and left the four of us alone to fend for ourselves just this past April."

"Oh, I am so terribly sorry," sympathized Benni, her face clouding.

"Please do not be. Both my father's untimely death and Edward's hasty departure prompted my enrollment here in the school of nursing, where I have this day met you and all of the others. So you see, something good can always be fashioned from tragedy, if one is willing to adjust one's perspective."

With that, another nursing student came running toward them, exclaiming, "Time! Time! We're running out of time! We have to return downstairs before you-know-who slams the door in our faces!" All three girls sprinted for the front door.

Later that afternoon as Emma retraced her steps from Chestnut Street to the ferry, she stopped at the Water Street Bakery and picked out four little cakes covered with white icing and tiny sugar flowers. Cradling the dozing baby with one arm and setting the valise down on the floor, Emma fumbled with the coins in her purse, at last placing four pennies on the counter to pay for the sweets. "Oh, no, ma'am, after three o'clock in the afternoon all our cakes are two for one penny," said the clerk pushing two pennies back toward her hand. Then lowering her voice and checking in all directions, she added, "I have a wee one myself, ma'am, and I miss my baby terribly while I'm working here in the shop. Allow me to sweeten your package for you a bit," whereupon she slipped two additional cakes into the paper for Emma.

"You are most kind! I assure you that these lovely cakes will make my arrival at home this evening quite grand indeed. Thank you!"

Smiling broadly, the clerk placed Emma's package of cakes in her leather valise, handed it to her and then held the shop door open for Emma to leave. As Emma continued on down Water Street to the ferry, she thought to herself, "What an extraordinary day I have had! What a wonderful beginning to a new life!"

CHAPTER 9

▼

Later that same evening as she sat exhausted in the pink upholstered chair in her bedroom and nursed Johnny for the final time before putting the baby to bed, Emma rested her head against the back of the chair and looked across at the sepia-colored photographs on her dresser. Since she had dimmed the gaslights to encourage Johnny to fall asleep, Emma could barely make out the images in their gold frames, but light was not necessary for her to see the two men who had once possessed her heart. Emma closed her eyes and saw Papa with his high white starched collar, dark hair parted down the middle, the corners of his mustache reaching to the edge of his jaw, handsome and unsmiling. Next to him was Edward, teeth blazing, large, piercing light eyes, black hair tousled down to his stiff collar and tie. Both men were beyond her reach now, one by death and one by choice.

She had always given in to Edward's request for 'just one more chance'. She had tried to understand the cycle of drinking and beating and begging for redemption. He was so impossibly handsome and attentive when sober and so impossibly ugly and cruel when inebriated. It was as if Edward had become two people, the one she knew and loved and the stranger she hated. When had he begun to unravel?

Emma held the sleeping baby and tried to think back to the beginning of their troubles and then she laughed. Of course! It had been over food! Papa had scolded Edward about his rude consumption of food at her mother's table and his opportunistic attitude. Edward had responded by leaving town. Such a childish reaction but such a telling one. When Edward did not get his way, he always took his departure. Edward had perfected the art of departing. Sometimes he turned on his heel to depart the room where Emma was. Other times, he departed their household for the night. Most recently Edward had departed Grandview, leaving behind his wife and three children. Emma never knew where her husband went during his absences and she never asked, fearing his wrath. Then there were the rapturous re-appearances!

How long after the food episode was it before their joyous reunion? Three…four weeks? Emma remembered that it was fall. There had been a hint of frost in the late afternoon air when she took Onion for a gallop across the meadow down to the river. On a whim, she reined Onion around and headed toward the mill to encourage Papa to leave early and spend some time playing cards with her that evening after supper. As she slowed Onion to a walk and approached from the back of the mill, Emma could see a dark-haired man with his back to her talking to James. Her heart began to pound. At the sound of the horse's hooves upon the dirt road, the man turned toward Emma. Even in his gaunt, bruised and disheveled condition, she knew it to be Edward.

She reined in Onion and sat looking at Edward in disbelief and then at James who wore a similar look. James began walking toward the mill and as he passed Emma, still astride Onion, he winked.

"It would seem," offered James by way of explanation as he continued walking toward the mill, "that after a somewhat lengthy contemplation of my previous offer, Mr. Richardson has come to the wise conclusion to return to Grandview to accept employment here at the mill."

"Is it true?" Emma asked as she dismounted.

"Indeed it is!" exclaimed Edward unable to contain his delight at seeing Emma.

"But, where will you stay?" Emma pressed.

"Your father has most graciously offered me a cot in the office at the back of the mill and in exchange for my services at a reduced income, I am invited to eat at your mother's splendid table," whereupon he opened his arms to Emma.

"Oh, Edward!" and Emma fell into his embrace. "Why are you so thin? Why is your appearance so unkempt? How did you acquire so many bruises? What has happened to you these many weeks?"

Just as Edward was about to formulate an answer, James stuck his head out of the door to the mill, "Perhaps you two had best be getting to the house at once for Edward is still weak and in need of a good, hot meal, Emma. He also needs to bathe and requires a change of clothing. See what you can find for him in my closet."

After a soak in the copper tub, Edward appeared at the supper table in fresh clothing borrowed from James. "Mrs. Miller, I have sorely missed your marvelous hospitality," he began in earnest.

"La, la, la, Edward! You shameless flatterer!" and Mary's cheeks crimsoned as she heaped his plate with roasted chicken, mashed potatoes with gravy and stewed black eyed peas.

"Perhaps you should tell the ladies of your plight, Edward," suggested James as he buttered a thick slice of Mary's homemade bread. "Are we to have coffee this evening, my pet?" he added.

"Yes, James, right away," and Mary moved to the stove to pour a fresh cup for her husband.

"Well...er...as I was telling Mr. Miller just now, I left town so abruptly last summer after I discerned that I was quite umm...ill."

"Really, Edward? Ill with what?" asked Mary placing a cup of coffee at his place also.

"Ill with...with typhus, as I was telling it to Mr. Miller," responded Edward stuffing his mouth with food.

"Do slow down son. The food is not going to run off your plate!" admonished James.

"Papa, please!" exclaimed Emma, impatient to hear the details of Edward's absence.

"Yes, indeed, ill with typhus and so I knew immediately that I had to go across to Clarksburg to that fine hospital for treatment. I was close to dying, did you know that Emma?"

"Oh, you poor man!" soothed Emma touching Edward's arm.

"Yes, it was quite uncertain for a while if I would live or not," whereupon Edward dramatically dabbed at his forehead with his napkin. "Would you please pass the bread and butter? But, God was surely on my side, for with all the wonderful treatment that I received from the doctors and nurses, please pass the potatoes, I made a miraculous recovery, and a bit of that heavenly jam of yours, Mrs. Miller. Thank you."

"But what of your appearance?" intervened Emma, unable to take her eyes from Edward and unable to eat a bite of food.

"Well, I...my clothing was quite contaminated, you must realize and everything that I touched had to be burned, pass the peas, thank you. Might I have a dab of butter for those? Mrs. Miller, this is truly your finest meal!"

"Just how did you come to be so covered with bruises?" chimed in James, sitting back in his chair to sip the cup of hot coffee.

"Well, I am quite embarrassed to tell you," answered Edward reaching for a drumstick.

"Do try," admonished James again, "but mind that is the third helping of chicken and ought you not to ease up a bit there, seeing as how your constitution is on the delicate side now?"

"Oh, quite right," responded Edward devouring the chicken anyway. Wiping his mouth, he added, "When I left the hospital recently, I went…I had occasion to pass the fancy hotel over there in Clarksburg, you know the one…"

"The Foggy Bend," supplied Emma.

"Yes, the Foggy Bend. I was so taken with the menu which the hotel had posted out front at the dinner hour and so beside myself with hunger after having been hospitalized for so long and treated to a diet of thin broth, beaten biscuits with only chicory to drink, that I entered the hotel dining room and ordered dinner. I am ashamed of this fact for I had absolutely not one cent in my pockets, all of my money having gone for…to pay my hospital bill. I ate a delightful meal but when the waiter came to collect on the bill and I told him I was penniless, he summoned the hotel manager, who in turn had two thugs remove me from the premises, take me out the back door and beat me nearly senseless," recounted Edward to his attentive audience.

James surveyed Edward over the top of the blue and white coffee cup that he held in both hands, elbows resting on the table. "And here I thought you had come to your senses unaided, when in fact it was the beating that you sustained at the hands of a couple of thugs that changed your perspective!" James' laughter was met with scowls from the women.

Unfazed, Edward leaned over to Mary and in a conspiratorial tone asked, "Did you say that you had made a pecan pie?"

"Ye…" Mary began only to be interrupted by James.

"No. No pie tonight. It is much too late since I expect you to be up bright and early at the mill tomorrow morning, ready to learn the ropes from my men. That is the deal that we struck and by God, you will stick to your word and our handshake!" Rising from his chair at the head of the table, James continued, "I have a lantern which you may use to see your way to the mill for the night." Handing the lantern to Edward he added, "I exhort you to be careful to extinguish the flame before you sleep as I do not relish the thought of my lumber going up in smoke."

"I thought I might at least spend a few moments with Emma since I have been away from her for so long," whined Edward.

"A man in your condition needs rest more than female companionship. There will be plenty of time for that later. Now bid Emma good-night and follow me to the front door."

After James had ushered Edward out the front door and stood watching the lantern light fade in the direction of the mill, he returned to the kitchen and, rubbing his hands together, exclaimed to Mary, "Now how about a nice big piece of that pecan pie!"

The work at the mill was tedious for Edward as it required a physical stamina that he had not yet regained. Both old Bill and Herbert took pity on him, picking up the slack when they realized that James had singled Edward out for the more grueling chores. Emma continued with her clerical duties at the mill so that between her paperwork for her father and meals taken together at her mother's table, Emma saw Edward on a daily basis, but only under the watchful eye of her father.

As the Christmas season drew near and the mood in the Miller household became increasingly festive, Edward became emboldened to have a talk with Emma's father about his prospects as they pertained to his benefactor's daughter. One starry December evening just after supper, James excused himself to the front porch for a smoke, donning his heavy wool coat to ward off the cold wind that was blowing across the Southport.

"May I join you, sir?" asked Edward grabbing his coat.

"By all means," James responded cordially.

Teeth chattering into the wind, Edward began his carefully rehearsed speech while James fiddled with lighting his pipe, back turned to the numbing breeze.

Drawing his coat collar up tightly around his neck, Edward commenced, "Mr. Miller, it has been my very good fortune to be taken into the bosom of your family once again following my hospitalization for a lengthy and highly debilitating illness. You have been exceedingly forgiving and generous toward me and I am humbled by your spirit of caring, for you have fed and clothed me, given me work and put a roof over my head." James inhaled deeply and nodded his head in agreement while Edward continued.

"I feel that with the return of my health, thanks largely to the care of Mrs. Miller and her attention to my dietary needs, and the skills which I have acquired at the mill, that I am once again on solid ground. I have regained my footing, so to speak." Here Edward paused, hoping for some sign of approval from James, who merely puffed on his pipe and replied, "Mmmm…"

"It was my intention from last summer to ask for your daughter's hand in marriage, which intention was interrupted by my untimely absence due to…due to circumstances beyond my control." James stood in profile to Edward as if cast in stone, the only movement being the curling smoke from his pipe. "And, therefore," Edward continued boldly on, "it…is…my fondest hope that you will grant me your permission this evening to ask Miss Emma Miller to become my betrothed." Edward fairly choked on the last few words, his Adam's apple working furiously up and down his neck as he fought to control the urge to vomit on the porch.

"Are you going to be ill, boy?" James asked sharply turning to face Edward.

The suddenness of James' response startled Edward who lost his battle for control and rushed to the far side of the porch where he heaved up Mary's dinner.

"I tried to tell you, boy, that was one pork chop too many, but did you listen to me? No! And now you have gone and fouled my Mary's Christmas ornaments just there!" exclaimed James pointing with the end of his pipe to the little tree that dripped with brightly colored ornaments, regurgitated pork chops, bread dressing, stewed tomatoes, applesauce and coffee. "Moderation in all things, son! Moderation!"

Edward took out his handkerchief and began wiping his face, ashamed to have lost control in front of Emma's father. James tapped the tobacco embers from his pipe into the dirt of the flower bed and stepped down off the porch to grind them out with his shoe.

When Edward made a move to the front door, James admonished, "No sir! You are not going into the house like that," motioning to the front of Edward's coat. "We shall continue this conversation tomorrow, after you have cleaned up and hopefully it will be on an empty stomach. Good night, sir," and James entered the house, shutting the door firmly behind him.

Hearing the door close, Emma appeared in the front hall with a perplexed look on her face, "Where did Edward go now, Papa?"

"I believe he said he was ill again and bound for Timbuktu this time. Probably be gone for several years. Good-night, my darling girl," and he bent to kiss Emma on her curls. "Please tell your Mama that I have gone upstairs to soak away my worries in the tub."

A week later on Christmas Eve, the Millers welcomed a houseful of friends from Grandview into their home for supper as was their custom each year. Small evergreens at the front of the home held pinecones smeared with suet and then rolled in seeds for the birds. Strings of cranberries and popcorn and whole small ears of dried corn were all tied up with green and red ribbons. It was Mary's love of all creatures that prompted her to include the animals in their Christmas Eve feast.

"After all, James," Mary would remark each year, "the Babe was born in a barn with only beasts to bear witness. God did not bestow that honor lightly and we must therefore pay homage to the wild creatures who were present at the birth of the Holy Child."

"Of course dear, you are quite right," James would comment each year as he sat by the fireplace poking a needle and thread through endless cranberries, popcorn and with increasing frequency, his fingers.

Garlands of greenery were wound around the columns of the porch, and hanging from the front door and each window were large evergreen wreaths decorated with red bows. A light dusting of snow earlier in the day had transformed the Millers' home into the embodiment of Christmas.

Christmas from within the home was even more spectacular after Mary's annual pilgrimage to the attic. For weeks she would move through the house happily humming Christmas carols to herself as she placed her treasure trove of baubles, trinkets and ornaments on every table, mantel, tree and shelf in the home. The effect was always quite spectacular and everyone who was anyone in Grandview vied for an invitation to the Millers' Christmas Eve dinner.

The Millers' dining room table groaned under the weight of the sumptuous repast that Mary always prepared for their guests: roasted turkey, ham, mashed potatoes, sweet potatoes, bread dressing, her own canned lima beans and corn, giblet gravy, loaves of homemade bread to be eaten with Mary's own jams and jellies and the piece de resistance, Mary's Christmas cake. The latter was a three tier, dazzling white beauty that measured eighteen inches in diameter. Each year as she would begin to slice and serve the cake, Mary would laugh, "I see that some among us have been unable to resist sticking our fingers in the icing," and she would look over at the children who feigned ignorance.

The children all vied for the prize that Mary baked into one of the layers of the cake. Usually it was a large, brightly colored marble and who ever got the marble, had the honor of wearing a gold paper crown for the remainder of the evening to signify the birth of the King of Kings. The recipient of the marble and the gold crown was also rewarded with a seat next to James at the fireplace for the grand finale of the evening as he read the Christmas story from the family's large Bible. In spite of her repeated admonitions to the contrary, every third year or so, someone swallowed the marble and then much merriment ensued about the fate of the marble. In that case, the youngest child was selected to wear the crown by default.

As the evening wore on and guests began to leave, James and Mary would gather on their front porch bundled up against the cold and sing the traditional Christmas carols with their departing friends. The couple would stand braving the cold and wind until the last guests had departed, waving at the carriages as they jingled down the meadow in the moonlight toward High Point Avenue. Then, as was his custom, James would draw Mary to him with one arm while continuing to wave with the other, kiss her lightly on the forehead and remark, "Splendid Christmas Eve, my darling. You truly outdid yourself this year! I do not believe our friends left one scrap of food behind this year, did you notice?"

Edward, seizing upon the preoccupation of James and Mary with their departing dinner guests, chose that moment to pull Emma back into the house, down the hall and into the kitchen.

"Edward, whatever are you doing?" Emma laughed up into his handsome face as he indicated that she was to sit in a chair by Mary's worktable. There by the turkey carcass, Edward knelt in front of Emma and wordlessly offered up a small wrapped package. "For me? To open now?" she stammered. He nodded his head "yes."

She took the package from his outstretched palm and with trembling fingers began to fuss with the ribbon and paper. Peeling back the layers of tissue, she uncovered a delicate cameo brooch surrounded by a border of twisted gold. While Emma held the brooch in one hand, Edward took her other hand in both of his and gazing tenderly into her eyes said, "Emma, my heart's desire, I must ask you this question tonight or perish for I have agonized far too long over the details of asking. So here I am now, with only the silent and long cold remnants of Christmas Eve dinner as my witnesses, asking, will you marry me and be mine for all eternity?"

"Oh, Edward, my sweet! I am quite undone and confess to feeling a bit faint but it would be too rude to faint before giving you an answer." Here Emma began to sway slightly, "Yes, I shall marry you!" and with that, Emma slumped forward onto Edward's shoulder, sending the brooch skittering across the kitchen floor.

Just at that moment, Mary and James appeared at the kitchen door, smiling faces all crimson with winter's cold breath. Instantly scowling at his assessment of the scene before him, James shouted, "What in thunder have you done to her, son?"

"I...I..." stammered Edward, "I just asked her to marry me."

"Well, no wonder the poor dear fainted!" soothed Mary. "James, go fetch the smelling salts from the bathroom cabinet and be quick!" Turning back to

Edward, she added, "Here, let me help you set her upright. Mind you brace her carefully against your shoulder there while I apply the salts under her nose. James, hurry!" she called out into space.

"Almost there," he shouted in response, racing down the front hall.

Mary took the smelling salts and, bracing Emma's sagging head with one hand back against Edward's shoulder, she waved the salts under Emma's nose with the other. Emma responded by turning her head away from the salts and saying, "Phew!" Opening her eyes, she asked, "Why are we all sitting on the kitchen floor?" Then, her gaze came to rest on the lovely cameo across the floor and she remembered swooning.

"Oh, dear, I am so sorry to have caused everyone so much trouble," began Emma. "Such a magnificent evening, Mama and Papa! I was not my intention to spoil it!" and Emma wiped tears from the corners of her eyes.

"Nonsense, my darling," James reassured Emma while scowling darkly at Edward. "Let us get you to your feet again," and the three lifted Emma upright.

"Feeling steady?" asked Mary.

"Not at all," replied Emma.

"All right then, James and Edward, please take Emma to the front parlor while I prepare her a cup of hot tea." As Mary removed the zinc lid from the glass jar of loose tea, she spied the piece of jewelry on the floor. Reaching down, she picked up the cameo brooch to examine it. Placing it in her pocket, Mary took the steaming cup of tea into the parlor and handed it to her daughter. "Sip it slowly, dear, so as not to scald your mouth." Turning to Edward and removing the brooch from her dress pocket, Mary asked, "What of this lovely brooch? Is this a gift for Emma?"

"Indeed it is," responded Edward, now flushed himself. "Emma had just accepted my proposal of marriage and was holding the brooch when she fainted."

"Proposal of what?" bellowed James.

"Proposal of marriage," Edward replied meekly.

"Oh, so that is how you young men propose marriage these days! You advance upon your intended with a pin instead of a ring. Is that the newfangled way to do it? Did you stab her with the damned thing, Edward? Our Emma is not a fainter!" James admonished, glowering over at the now ashen young man. Noting the pale complexion of their guest, James added, "You had better not empty the contents of your stomach on any part of this house again or I shall skin you!"

"James! Your language! And on Christmas Eve!" Mary admonished her raging husband.

"Well, by thunder, I should like an explanation!"

"James, James! Our daughter was overcome with emotion at, as I deduce, Edward's proposal of marriage coupled with his gift of this absolutely lovely cameo brooch, is that correct Edward?" and Mary turned to Edward, who had been rendered mute by the rage of Emma's father. Edward nodded his assent.

Turning the brooch over in her hand, Mary was prompted to say, "I feel certain that this belonged to someone very special to you, am I correct?" Edward again nodded.

Here Edward found his voice and looking at Emma, who was dazedly sipping her tea, said, "The brooch belonged to my dear departed mother and it was her fondest wish that I should present it to the woman of my dreams as a token of my love and devotion to her even as my father had presented it to my mother on just such an occasion so very long ago."

"How quaint!" commented James.

"Shush!" warned Mary.

Emma reached out her hand to touch Edward lightly on the face and then offered, "I am honored," whereupon she indicated for Mary to hand her the brooch, which she carefully pinned to the collar of her dress at the neck. Edward leaned forward and gave Emma a kiss upon the cheek and then glanced defiantly up at James.

"You young men have a lot to learn about manners! If I had come at Mary with a pin instead of a ring her father would have come at me with his musket!" sputtered James.

"I offered her the best of what I have, sir," replied Edward quietly.

"Perhaps your best is not good enough! Now, I am quite worn out with all this falderal. I am going upstairs to retire for the evening but not before I bid you good-evening, Edward. I shall just see you out before turning into my bed," and here James took Edward's sleeve, pulled him up and escorted him to the front door.

"Good night, my love!" Edward called defiantly past James' face.

"Good night, Edward, and Merry Christmas!"

Once outside the house on the front porch, James warned Edward, "Listen here, boy, you had best remember that this is MY house and no one so much as passes wind without my permission, do you understand me?" Not waiting for a response, James continued, "I supply everything these women need and I am now placed in the unenviable position of supplying your needs also. Good manners would dictate that you ask my permission before you give my daughter a...a...an artifice of betrothal," James stopped just short of losing his composure.

"It was not my purpose to offend you, sir, but only to declare my pure intentions toward your daughter in a form commensurate with my meager purse. I was raised to believe that the sentiment behind the gift should always be far greater than the cost," Edward paused, greatly heartened by his own choice of words, as the look on James' face was softening.

"Yes, well, that is very noble-sounding but let us in the future remember who is in charge of these women and this household around here. You will ask my permission in all matters as they pertain to my daughter, do you understand me, Edward?" asked James cocking a wary eye at the young man who shivered before him.

"Yes sir, I do believe I finally understand. Good-night, Mr. Miller. It has been a truly memorable Christmas Eve, would you not agree?"

"Absolutely unforgettable!" concurred James turning to shut the door firmly in Edward's face.

Shivering with cold, Edward remained standing in front of the closed door. Suddenly his face contorted as a blast of hot air escaped from his trousers. With his red nose dripping, Edward addressed the Christmas wreath where it hung from the front door, just inches from his face, "Please pardon my bad manners, but I believe I just farted without your permission!" and he turned on his heels for the long walk back to the mill.

It soon became apparent that Mary had assumed the role of advocate for Emma and Edward in their deepening relationship which continued to provoke outbursts of temper from James. The issue on which James chose to focus his ire was the food that Edward consumed at his table and his annoying manners while so doing. As James continued to browbeat the younger man for these minor offenses, Emma was frequently reduced to tears, prompting Mary to rise to her feet, "tisk-tisk-tisking" around the table serving up even more food to Edward, all the while explaining to James that Edward needed to build up his strength after his terrible illness and that if he, James, would just not work the boy so hard at the mill, then Edward would not work up such a huge appetite.

When Emma whined to her mother about the ill treatment that Edward received at the hands of her father, Mary would reply, "But, sweet, do you not realize that your father is just like my father was, and his father before him? No one on the face of God's earth will ever be good enough for you where your father is concerned. He would view any suitor for your hand in marriage as unworthy, as my own father viewed your father!" Here the two women would laugh and comfort themselves with the knowledge that all men despised their future sons-in-law.

Initially charmed by Edward's facile tongue and disarming manner, James now abhorred the very sight of the handsome young man. "I can see right through the scoundrel, just as I can see straight through that goldfish bowl over there," barked James one afternoon to Mary after a particularly provoking scene with Edward. As a consequence of his deepening dislike of Emma's fiancé, James delighted in piling the work on Edward at the mill. If the job was dirty, hard and time-consuming, James would bellow, "Give it to Edward to do!" All the mill hands were privy to the rancor that James demonstrated toward Edward causing old Bill to sidle up to James one day and say, "Boss?"

"Yes, Bill, what is it?"

"There's somethin' I believe I really do need to tell you," Bill replied twisting his cap nervously between his fingers.

"Not now Bill. We have no time for stories today," James responded irritably.

"It ain't that kind of a story, Mr. James. It's somethin' I hear'd and I knew straight that you'd want to…need to hear it too."

"Oh? And what might the subject be? Now do not tell me that rascal over across the river is going to make good on his threat to open his own lumber mill!" commented James distractedly.

"Nothin' like that, sir. Somethin' far more serious…as concerns our Emma."

At the mention of his daughter's name, James was suddenly alert, eyes riveted to old Bill's face. "Yes man, get to the bottom of it! Come on, spit it out at once!" James commanded the old storyteller.

"Well sir, I have a cousin, as you know, what lives over in Clarksburg," and Bill gestured at the Southport River. "Him and me likes to spend time together now and again and…" Bill paused to look in the direction he had pointed.

"Yes, yes man! Out with it!"

"Please don't hold this agin me for I'm old and widowed a long time, but my cousin and me we likes to visit the ladies, if you get my meanin'."

"Indeed I get your meaning," responded James impatiently.

"Well, there's this one fine house over yonder," again gesturing toward the river, "where the ladies are truly worth every penny…"

"I am sure they are!" exclaimed James. "And?"

"And them ladies likes to talk an awful lot, so one evening my cousin and me were just luxuriatin' in an enjoyable conversation with two of them gals when one of them asks, 'So, how is Mr. Edward?' Now, my cousin looks and me and I looks at him and we both say at once, 'Who?' and she repeats to me as God is my witness, 'Mr. Edward Richardson.'"

James could feel the blood in his veins freeze. Immediately aware of his surroundings, James looked left and right and then grabbing old Bill by the elbow, ushered him outside where there was less chance that their conversation would be overheard.

"So what did these fine ladies of yours have to say about this Mr. Edward Richardson?" asked James, shamelessly pumping the old man for information.

"They had an earful to tell us!" exclaimed Bill.

"Out with it, Bill, or I will hitch the mules to you and drag it out!" James snapped at the stooped informant, who shivered before him.

"What Flossie...that's my gal's name...told us is that Mr. Edward has a fondness for the drink and the girls over yonder," again gesturing toward the Southport. "Mr. Edward has a fondness for the drink and the girls over on this side of the river too," here accompanied by a gesture up toward the town of Grandview. "In fact, wherever there are ladies and whiskey, you can find Mr. Edward."

Old Bill paused dangerously too long for emphasis to let the words have their full impact upon his listener who grabbed old Bill's coat lapels and hissed, "Have you told anyone else this?"

"No sir. My first duty is to you and Miss Mary 'cause you taken care of me and mine all these years. Should I tell you the rest?"

"Good God! There is more?" moaned James.

"Much, much more!"

"Tell me everything, leaving absolutely nothing out, do you understand, Bill?"

"Indeed sir. But could we move out of the cold as I am half froze!"

"Let me send Emma on an errand up to the house and then you and I shall shut ourselves in the office until we have gotten to the bottom of this matter. Wait here until you see Emma leave and then come in the back way," said James over his shoulder as he walked back toward the mill.

Old Bill drew his meager coat tightly around his thin body, stamping his feet up and down on the frozen earth. At last he spied Emma hurrying out the front entrance of the mill and away up the long slope toward the house on High Point Avenue. Seizing the moment, Bill hurried around to the back of the mill and entered the office to find James pacing up and down in front of the potbellied stove. He motioned to Bill to warm himself by the fire and then said sharply, "Now, I must hear everything about the scoundrel."

"Flossie told me that young Edward was a regular customer of one of the ladies out at Miss Hattie's and this lady just happens to be a friend of Flossie's so naturally, the two of them were talkin' about their gentlemen friends and this gal says to Flossie, 'My favorite customer took sick with the clap and went over to that hospital in your neck of the woods and from that moment on, I never laid eyes or hands on him again.' To which my gal asks, 'What was this customer's name?' And she says, 'A fine and handsome gentleman by the name of Edward Richardson,' which almost makes my gal faint."

"Why, for the love of heaven?" interjected James, now twitching with rage.

"Because my gal knows him too from visits over there," gesturing to the river. "And the last time he was there, my gal says he caused a terrible ruckus. Waltzed into the place like he owned it after his leavin' the hospital and just barely cured of the clap, ordered himself up a big whiskey and a big gal to go with it, if you get my meanin'," and old Bill winked at James.

"I get your meaning, Bill. Please be brief now!"

Bill was looking around for somewhere to spit. Opening up the stove with a rag, Bill spat mightily at the raging fire within, prompting James to comment, "Mind you do not put out that fire!"

"Anyhow," resumed Bill, "Flossie tells me that Mr. Edward enjoyed himself and then did not have the funds to pay for his pleasure. So, the Madam calls in these two men of hers who take Mr. Edward to the barn out back of the house and beat the holy crap out of him. Then they take everything he owns except the clothing on his back and pack him off across the river and you know the ending to the story, as he comes here to work for you and asks Miss Emma to marry him."

"CONNIVING SON OF A BITCH!" bellowed James, pulling at the hair on his head as if he would rip it out by the roots.

"Was I wrong to tell you this, Boss?" asked old Bill timidly.

"You were absolutely right to tell me, Bill! Now, not another word to a living soul about this. It will be our secret, do you agree?"

"Yes sir! I agrees!"

"Then back to work, Bill. You did the right thing by coming to me."

Edward, who had been ensconced in the privy shed up the hill away from the mill had taken in the meeting between old Bill and James through a knothole. He had seen Bill gesturing over toward Clarksburg and then up toward Grandview. Edward had earlier seen Emma just before she departed from the mill office. When Edward asked Emma where she was going, she had responded that her father had instructed her to return to their house and make sure that the fire screen was securely in place before the parlor fireplace since Mary was away on the north side of town delivering a baby.

There were three things Edward knew for a fact. James harbored such a fear of the destructive properties of fire that he unfailingly exercised all the proper safety precautions at his home and at the mill. Any man who milled and sold lumber for a livelihood handled fire with the utmost respect.

The second fact that Edward knew was that old Bill could not keep his mouth shut. His love of an audience prompted him to spue forth everything he knew, embellishing his speech with all the salacious details to keep the attention of his listeners fastened upon himself. Thirdly, Edward knew that Bill's love of whiskey and women was rivaled only by his own. Edward began to sort through these details as he tore off a sheet of the Grandview Courier, crumpled it up, wiped his bottom and hitched up his trousers. Edward shivered as he stood in the privy. It chilled him to realize that old Bill had told on him.

Edward peered through the knothole again to make sure that all hands were still in the mill and then cautiously exited the privy taking the back path up to Grandview. Approaching the clearing where the Millers' house and barn stood, Edward circled around to the rear of the property and looking in the barn through a back window above Onion's stall, determined that the horse was gone which meant that Mary was still away from the house performing her duties as a midwife. Heartened that he could now enter the house undetected, Edward strode boldly for the door to the kitchen of the Millers' home. Quietly he made his entrance at the back of the house, closing both the screen door and the solid oak door carefully so as not to alert Emma to his presence.

Creeping softly down the hallway, Edward approached the front parlor. Peering through the scrollwork at the parlor door, he saw Emma kneeling in front of the fireplace with an armful of wood that she was placing on the embers. He moved silently forward and stood inches from her for several long moments enjoying the arousal brought on by her scent, the sheen of her hair as the firelight played upon the auburn curls, the smallness of her body and her vulnerability.

"My darling," Edward spoke at last, causing Emma to startle, scattering the wood about the hearth. He reached down and pulled her up to him, apologizing as he did, "Forgive me for creeping up behind you but I wanted to make sure that there was no one else in the house with us."

"Goodness, Edward! You did give me a terrible fright!" Emma now laughed. "But why must you make certain that we are alone?"

"I feel a...an urgency to be with you, just you. Each time I enter this house it is only to be for the duration of the evening meal and then your father hurries me back down to that cold, barren mill. I desperately crave your companionship. I see you briefly through the office window as I pass but if I tarry to speak with you, your father pounces on me. In short, the man never allows us time in which to be alone. How can I possibly court you, Emma, with your father always lurking about in the shadows? I have therefore stolen this moment together for the two of us," and he bent his head down to kiss the softness of her cheek and then her neck as he reached up to untie the ribbon that restrained her hair.

Ever so gently, Edward entwined his fingers in her long auburn curls, pulling them down about her shoulders and over her breasts, where his hands caressed the folds of her blouse, slowly freeing it from the waistband of her skirt. Meeting with no resistance, Edward slipped his hands under the back of Emma's blouse and drew her against the focal point of his arousal. He kissed her lips, her face, her neck and was leaning to kiss her exposed bare shoulder when Emma protested.

"Edward, we must not do this!"

"Do what?" Edward feigned innocence.

"Do what you are doing!" exclaimed Emma, pushing away.

"I think the problem," soothed Edward, "is that we have not done enough of this," and he leaned over and kissed her on the mouth again. This time she kissed him back, moving her hands across his shoulders and his chest, before pushing him away again.

Edward reached out, tangling his fingers in her long curls and pulled her to him. He kissed her again full upon the mouth, lifted her in his arms and began walking to the staircase in the front hall. "Where are we going?" Emma asked, her head and her emotions spinning wildly out of control.

"Where we should have gone a long time ago," Edward replied kissing her mouth. "If you keep talking, I shall just have to keep kissing you."

Up the long flight of stairs Edward carried his tiny prize, down the hall and into her bedroom at the front of the house where he set her gently upon the pink and rose covers of her bed. He then shut the door and locked it behind them. Emma lay against the pillows looking up at him as if in a daze. He moved to the pink upholstered chair and removed his suspenders. Sitting on the chair, Edward next removed his shoes and then his socks, whereupon he stood to unbutton his trousers, removing them and his shirt. Edward's tight-fitting union suit left little to the imagination, prompting Emma to exclaim, "Edward, whatever are you carrying there?"

"That is my male member...the uh...the root of my passion for you," he replied moving closer to the bed.

"May I see it?" Emma asked naively.

"Oh, indeed, I intend for you to see it very closely but first we must shed some of your outer garments too," and Edward began to remove Emma's clothing. When he prepared to remove her step-in, Emma balked.

Not wishing to scare her off, Edward suggested, "Come let us hold each other on the bed and share some closeness." He lay down next to her, fondling, kissing, caressing and cajoling Emma until he had stripped off his undergarments and hers also, whereupon he mounted her small body and thrust himself inside her.

"Oh, Edward," she moaned, "you are hurting me! Whatever are you doing?"

"I am giving you pleasure," he gasped as he rose and fell rhythmically over her stiffened body. A spasm lasting several seconds engulfed his body, after which he quickly withdrew from Emma and rolled over onto his back. Looking up at the ceiling, Edward asked, "Was that your first time?"

"Yes," Emma responded meekly.

"And was it to your liking?"

"Hardly," she answered.

Suddenly, Emma and Edward both heard a distinct, "Yoo-hoo!" coming from downstairs. It was Mary!

Galvanized into action, Emma sprang from the bed. "Quickly, Edward!" she whispered. "Gather up your clothing and hide under my bed. Once I have Mama occupied downstairs in the kitchen, you leave by the front door." Pulling on her step-in and unlocking the door, Emma jumped under the covers just as Mary stepped onto the second floor landing.

"Well, there you are, darling. Whatever has prompted you to be abed at this hour of the evening?" Mary asked, reaching to touch the forehead of her daughter. "You are so flushed and you feel warm," whereupon Mary sat on the bed, causing the boards that supported the mattress to bow slightly over Edward's head.

"I do not know what came over me, Mama, but I was putting wood on the fire," Emma lied glibly to her mother, "and in the course of leaning over the hearth, I suddenly felt quite dizzy and unwell, so I took to my bed. Perhaps you would mix a powder for me and we could sit for a bit and have a cup of hot tea in the kitchen. Did the birthing go well this afternoon?" Donning her bathrobe and slippers, Emma trailed her mother down to the kitchen. "Perhaps you could tell me all about it."

From his vantage point under Emma's bed, Edward could see and hear the women's feet as they retreated down the hall to the front staircase. Seizing the moment, he rolled out from under the bed, dressed hurriedly and carrying his shoes, tiptoed down the stairs and out the front door, never stopping to put on his shoes until he reached the edge of the woods. Trembling with cold there in the dark, he looked back at the house and smiled. She was his! All his! He had planted his seed and Edward said a silent prayer that it would be a fertile one. He would not lose the one chance he had been given for a future free from want and deprivation. Emma Miller was Edward's meal ticket. He was not about to let her get away and nothing old Bill said and nothing James did was going to change that.

Edward made repeated physical advances upon Emma. Indeed, their trysts became something of an obsession with him. Waking early by himself at the mill, he would plot a course for the day that always included some ruse to get Emma alone, affording him an opportunity to begin undoing her buttons and ribbons, while she meekly rebuffed and then succumbed to his advances. Mary unwittingly played into Edward's hands by having the traditional "birds and the bees" talk with her daughter that winter which she had attempted to have with Emma the previous summer.

Following her first physical encounter with Edward, Emma approached her mother and in an offhand manner asked, "Mama, do you remember last summer when you wanted to tell me how babies got into the wombs of their mothers?"

"Indeed I do remember," replied Mary kneading a mound of bread dough on her kitchen table. "Sift a little flour over here for me, dear. This batch is threatening to stick. Good girl. Now, as I recall, my words to you were something along the line that since you knew how babies exited their mothers' wombs, it was perhaps time for you to learn how they got in there in the first place, or words to that effect. Am I correct?" asked Mary looking over at Emma who was drawing stick figures on the table in the sifted flour.

"Your memory is infallible, Mama."

"So, are we now interested in this subject?" asked Mary as she wiped her hands on the long white apron.

"I believe it is high time, Mama, for me to know…to understand more about the things that occur between a woman and a man." Emma felt the heat rising in her cheeks and she turned to look out the kitchen window at the falling snow.

"Very well then," Mary responded as she handed the lard pan to Emma, "come to the other side of the table and help me grease these bread tins. Once the loaves are in the oven, we can sit with a cup of tea and talk of such matters."

The two women wiled away the gray winter afternoon, sipping their tea, keeping an eye on the baking bread and talking of men, a subject which, as Mary said, "has confounded, amused and thwarted the ambitions of women since time began." Being a midwife, Mary possessed a keen knowledge of both female and male anatomies which she deftly illustrated for Emma with pencil on paper. Whereas Mary had imparted her wisdom about the female body to Emma when she reached the age of eleven, she had never told her daughter about the male body. Emma was shocked and amused when her mother drew a large, erect phallus. Picking up the paper to examine her mother's drawing at closer range, Emma giggled and then turned crimson. "What a funny looking thing!" she exclaimed.

"You are better off seeing it now," commented Mary. "Which reminds me of an amusing story about one of my young mothers. Do you remember Claire from just north of town?" Emma nodded her head "yes." "And you remember that she had her third child, a boy, just a few weeks ago?" Again a nod "yes."

"Well, I went back to check on Claire last week and do you know what she told me?" Here Mary threw back her head and laughed.

"What?" demanded Emma, seizing on the conspiratorial tone of her mother's voice.

"She told me that..." and Mary began to laugh uncontrollably until the tears rolled down her cheeks and she was short of breath.

"Mama! Stop that and tell me what she said!"

"She told me that she had never seen a male organ before, whereupon I asked her, 'How long have you and Walter been married?' and she says, 'Ten years.'" More laughter.

"Mama, that is not funny!"

"Wait!" Mary gasped, "I am not there yet. Claire's sister is in the room with us and steps forward with her hands on her hips scowling at Claire and says, 'That is such nonsense, Claire! Here you are the mother of three children and you say that you have never seen a male organ. Hogwash!' Claire says, 'I have experienced it, but I have not seen it and that is the God's truth. If it were not for the fact that I have just given birth to a male child, I would not recognize one to this day.' And then the sister says, 'Well, Claire Anne! It beats me how you could ever allow such a thing inside your privates without taking a peek at it first.'" Whereupon both Mary and Emma convulsed with laughter at the kitchen table until James was moved to satisfy his curiosity about the hilarity coming from the women in the kitchen.

"Is someone exercising her funny bone in here unbeknownst to me?" he asked, looking in at the two by the table, whereupon both women instantly sobered and leaped from their seats to check on the loaves browning in the oven. Eyeing Mary's drawings, James added, "Well, I see the subject is rather amusing. Mary, my darling, I had no idea that you possessed such artistic abilities!" Not seeing anything edible lying about, James asked petulantly, "And just how soon might I expect my supper?"

"Soon enough, James Miller! Soon enough!"

James retreated to the sanctuary of the parlor and his newspaper and Mary, suddenly sober, was inspired to add a postscript to her conversation with Emma. "There is one other matter which I must tell you, my dear." At the change in her mother's tone, Emma glanced up from her assigned job of turning out the loaves of bread onto cooling racks. "And that is, never refuse your husband's advances in the bedroom. Do not feign headaches or stomach aches. In short, do not fabricate excuses to avoid fulfilling his needs. Men need to lie with their women more often than the reverse. Failure to recognize and honor this fundamental difference will result in marital upheaval and drive your husband to fulfill his needs elsewhere, like Miss Hattie's. And that is all I am going to say about that subject! Now, be a good girl and pick out a nice big jar of my homemade applesauce from the pantry so that we may feed another one of your father's insatiable appetites!" exclaimed Mary, winking at Emma.

Later that night, as Emma lay under her covers staring at the pale moon drifting by her window, she pondered all the weighty matters that her mother had discussed with her that afternoon. She knew only too well what Edward looked like from stem to stern without his union suit. He had made sure of that. She had never refused him. He had also made sure of that. What terrified and troubled her was that she and Edward, while betrothed to be married, were behaving in a manner only befitting a married couple. Emma attended the Methodist Church on the town square each Sunday with her parents. From listening to the preacher and reading her Bible, Emma knew she and Edward were living in mortal sin.

All of these issues would become moot early one morning when Emma awoke before anyone else and rushed to the water closet, where she became violently ill. She vomited convulsively until there was nothing left. Mary awakened to the sound of Emma heaving dry air. Rushing to the water closet, Mary grabbed a wash rag, wet it in the ice-cold water, wrung it out and applied the rag to Emma's face. She did this over and over again until Emma had gotten control of the gagging.

Once Mary had tucked Emma back into bed, she clucked over her daughter, "Oh, my poor darling child! It must have been the roast goose that we ate last night. I thought it had a slightly rancid taste to it but your father did not agree. I should never have served it." At the mention of rancid goose, Emma leaped out of bed and ran for the water closet to heave more dry air. Mary applied another round of cold compresses and then ushered Emma back into her bed.

"Shush, Mama!" Emma admonished her mother wanly. "No more talk of food, please!" and she turned over to go back to sleep.

Downstairs, Mary regaled James with Emma's illness while she fried fatback and brewed up a pot of coffee on the big black, cast-iron stove. James sat with his nose in the Grandview Courier, ignoring his wife. "James?" no answer. She tried again, poking the paper with her fork, "James!"

"Yes, dear," he responded still hidden behind the paper.

"I need some fresh eggs from the hens. Please go to the barn and get some for me," wheedled Mary.

"Not right now, dear. I am busy reading," responded James ignoring Mary.

"Then please pay attention that the bread does not burn on the toasting iron. Turn it for me and I shall be back in a moment with the eggs. James!"

"Yes, yes, dear. Right!"

Mary grabbed her shawl off the peg by the back door, reached up on the shelf above the coat pegs and got down her egg basket. Convincing her old biddy hens to relinquish their lovely eggs took Mary a bit longer than usual that morning and some ten minutes later when she left the barn, she could see black smoke billowing from the now wide-open kitchen door. Next she saw James walk to the steps that lead down to the yard from the back porch and sling the blackened bread, toasting iron and all, out into the grass.

James, coughing and sputtering, greeted his wife, "Mary! What the devil took you so long?"

"I told you, James, that I required your help turning the bread!" Mary answered defensively.

"And I told you I was busy reading!" James glowered at his wife.

The normally harmonious couple had squared off at each other just outside the back door when Emma appeared, gagging in her nightdress.

"Oh, Mama! The smell is atrocious! I can smell it all the way up in my room."

"Now, see what you have done, Mary!" chided James.

"Me?" shot back Mary. "It was you who were in charge of burning the toast! At least have the decency to air out the house while I take this poor sick child back upstairs to her bed," and she huffed back into the house with Emma.

"Women!" exclaimed James. "No one can understand them!"

It began to dawn on Mary a few days later that Emma's sickness was not the result of eating the roasted goose. Her symptoms persisted but at odd hours of the day and night and seemed to be exacerbated by the smell of certain foods such as coffee and fatback or meat of any kind. When she could stomach the taste of food, Emma preferred vegetables, bread, fruit and only in very small portions.

Days stretched into weeks, and still Emma languished. The lack of appetite accompanied an unusual physical fatigue. Normally ebullient until well past the dinner hour, Emma now complained that she had only enough strength left to climb the stairs to her bedroom before Mary had even so much as taken a knife to the pie for dessert. In the mornings, it was becoming commonplace for Mary to rouse Emma from sleep, cajoling her to take a bath and dress for work at the mill. Then it struck Mary that Emma's symptoms were not at all the symptoms of a lingering illness for Emma was not ill. Emma was pregnant.

CHAPTER 10

─────────────── ▼ ───────────────

Baby Johnny startled, flinging out his tiny arms and emitting little sobs, where-upon Emma realized that she had dozed off in the pink upholstered chair. Lifting the baby gently, she spoke softly to him, "Oh, has my poor little precious had a bad dream? Everything is all right now, sweet Johnny! Your ma is here and soon you will be back on the road to Sleepy Town." Emma moved to the rocking chair where she deftly soothed the baby back to sleep. Everyone else in the house was asleep as Emma tiptoed down hall to the baby's room. Tucking Johnny into his crib, Emma returned to her room, turned off the gaslight and fell into an exhausted heap on top of the rose, pink and white squares of her childhood quilt.

As she drifted off to sleep, Emma reflected upon her decision to enter the school of nursing over in Clarksburg. Had she made the right decision? Could her mother continue to handle her rowdy and rambunctious twin boys? Would Johnny receive enough loving care from the nurses on the children's ward? Would their little family of five be able to hang on financially until she could begin to earn an income as a nurse to support them all? Could she summon the strength to handle so many responsibilities at once? The worries and pressures of providing for a family of five had fallen onto Emma's small shoulders, at a time when women were chattel, creatures without rights whose primary function was to serve men.

Emma rose before dawn the next day, as had become her custom, bathed, fed the baby, dressed, ate a light breakfast alone and departed with Johnny for the ferry which would take her across the river to Water Street and Angel of Mercy Hospital. Her mornings were spent in class with the other thirty-four young women studying human anatomy under the tutelage of Nurse Walker, whose fondness for homework was legendary. Endless reading of assigned chapters from the nursing manual and then making sketches of bones, veins, arteries, organs and all the components of human anatomy kept Emma awake into the wee hours of the morning, knowing full well that at the stroke of nine from the hospital bell tower, she and all the other student nurses must be assembled and prepared for their morning question and answer session with Nurse Walker.

If a student failed to show up on time, Nurse Walker made good on her threat and locked the classroom door. That student would then receive a demerit and be assigned bedpan duty for the rest of the day. As additional discipline, the offending student would be called front and center the next morning to be grilled on the previous day's lesson, which she had missed by virtue of her absence from class. If a student received ten demerits, she was unceremoniously drummed out of the nursing school, with no hope of readmission.

With her wooden pointer, Nurse Walker rapped and banged her way through the morning question and answer sessions. Mistake the pancreas for the liver, and whack! The pointer slapped against the side of a student's desk, accompanied by such expletives as, "Never!" "Under no circumstances!" "Off with the head!" which was Nurse Walker's favorite expression, and frequently punctuated with a direct hit on the top of the offender's desk, dangerously close to the student's fingers. Conversely, if the student could name all the bones of the leg and foot sequentially beginning with the femur, she might earn a, "Brilliant!" or a, "Splendid!" accompanied by a great joyous waving of the pointer, as if Nurse Walker were suddenly conducting an unseen orchestra.

Afternoons were spent learning how to apply compresses, bandages and splints to each other as Nurse Walker barked out hypothetical infirmities, "Fractured ulna!" "Broken tibia!" Whack! "That is the femur, Bennington! To the board! Now sketch the tibia and then the femur and," punctuated by a whack with the pointer, "do not help her class!"

On this particular winter morning, Nurse Walker beamed beatifically at her student nurses. "Class," she began mildly, "I have a surprise in store for you today, a true treat, to be sure," and she paused to let the import of her words sink into the weary minds of her students. "This afternoon you will get to meet our Chief of Staff, Dr. Burris G. McKendrick. This class has been honored to receive a personal invitation from Dr. McKendrick to preside in the surgical theatre while our Chief of Staff resects a patient's gallbladder. Normally, Dr. McKendrick's surgeries are scheduled in the morning, but this particular one has been shifted from tomorrow morning to this afternoon due to the patient's rapidly deteriorating condition."

The students began to buzz with Nurse Walker's news. Whack! "All of which means that we have much to do before you are fit to watch Dr. McKendrick perform the surgery. In lieu of our customary review of the previous night's homework assignment and classroom recitation, we are going to be learning how to scrub for surgery as each and every one of you must be properly scrubbed, gowned and gloved before you so much as poke a nose into the surgical theatre."

More buzzing and another rap with the wooden pointer, this time on the trash can, which sent it and its contents rolling down the center aisle. Laughter erupted causing Nurse Walker to pounce upon Emma. "Richardson! Do you find me amusing?" The smile faded from Emma's lips as she responded, "Absolutely not, Nurse Walker!"

"Did I detect a smile on your face just then?" Nurse Walker pursued her prey. "You did, Nurse Walker!"

"Did I give you permission to smile, Richardson?" pressed Nurse Walker.

"You did not, Nurse Walker!"

"Well, now I am going to give you my permission to smile and I had better see that smile on your face all morning, which means that you are ordered to smile from now until the noon hour. If that smile once slips from your face, you will start all over again with another hour. Do you understand, Richardson?" and Nurse Walker loomed over Emma, wooden pointer waggling from arms crossed at the chest.

"I understand, Nurse Walker!" Emma barked, grinning hugely to demonstrate that she was complying with the order.

"Splendid! Now, let us continue. At this juncture, we have only a little more than two hours before your noon recess. Therefore, we must adjourn to the scrub room just outside surgery and, in anticipation of your instruction there, you may commence rolling up your sleeves. Now follow me, class," whereupon Nurse Walker exited the classroom, followed by her thirty-five protégés up the stairs to the first floor.

Emma and Benni were the last two to leave the classroom. As soon as she felt it was safe and that Nurse Walker's eyes were elsewhere, Emma let the smile slide from her face, looking over at Benni in dismay. Benni indicated by pulling up the corners of her mouth with her fingers that Emma had better put the smile on her face again, pointing to the hall clock which showed that it was only a quarter of ten in the morning. Two hours and fifteen minutes left to keep on grinning, Benni was saying wordlessly. Emma shook her head "no." Benni nodded hers "yes." Emma drew the corners of her mouth down in an exaggerated pout. Benni made a pleading gesture, putting the palms of her hands together in supplication.

Emma was so engrossed in their wordless exchange that she failed to negotiate the final step up to the first floor, tripped and fell.

"What is going on at the rear of the line?" called Nurse Walker hurrying back to see for herself. "Not another fall, Richardson!" she admonished Emma. "I do believe these steps are your nemesis!"

With lightening speed, Emma recovered both her grin and her footing. "Yes, Nurse Walker!"

"Perhaps you should be examined for glasses, Richardson. Remind me to schedule you for an appointment!"

"Yes, Nurse Walker!" Emma responded.

As the line moved on down the long marble corridor, Benni grinned at Emma, who grinned back at her. Heads held high, the two women brought up the rear of the line, arms linked, grinning like a couple of cats who had just swallowed a whole cage full of canaries.

As Nurse Fanella Walker taught her students the intricacies of the proper scrubbing techniques in pairs of two at the double soapstone sinks, Emma dodged behind the others to hide briefly and give her facial muscles, which were beginning to twitch, a rest. Benni functioned as Emma's sentinel, signaling whenever Nurse Walker approached or looked their way so that Emma could don her painful grin once again.

Whack! "You absolutely do not touch anything with those hands, Conrad, once you have scrubbed! Now remove your gown, head covering, mask and scrub again. Griffith! Where is your assigned partner? It is her job to put your gloves on your hands. Do not attempt to do it yourself. Pay attention!"

Emma and Benni, who were among the last four in the class to scrub and therefore had the benefit of witnessing the mistakes of the other thirty-three, performed all the maneuvers flawlessly, prompting Nurse Walker to say, "Now, that was perfect, ladies." Turning to the others she added, "That was a splendid example of why it is so important to pay attention. Remember these words, carve them into your brains: observe, listen and be silent, always during surgery and again at the patient's beside when the attending doctor is present. It is only the voice of the attending doctor and his actions that are crucial. We are there merely to assist the doctor. Let us repeat: observe, listen and be silent. One and two and three," Nurse Walker conducted her orchestra of students who replied in unison, "OBSERVE, LISTEN AND BE SILENT, NURSE WALKER!"

"This class shows much promise! Good work, students and now by the tolling of the bell, I ascertain that it is high noon and you all need to eat. Fail to eat and you will faint. Make no mistake about it, I deal harshly with fainters. I had a student once who keeled over onto an instrument cart just as the doctor was making the initial incision with his scalpel. She sent all the instruments and the cart clattering about the operating theatre, disrupting the surgery to the point that I did not believe I would be able to intercede with the board of physicians to have my students admitted to the operating theatre to observe ever again. We will reconvene here in one hour. Class dismissed," and Nurse Walker waved them off with her wooden baton.

Emma caught Benni's arm as the girls exited the surgical theatre, "Listen, Benni, I must run to nurse Johnny. Where do you and the others think you will take your lunch break today?"

"I am too tired to go very far today, Emma, and fear of being late for Dr. McKendrick's surgery would dictate that we stay close by. Maybe the solarium," Benni replied stifling a yawn.

"Good. I shall see you there in about twenty minutes," and Emma turned to walk briskly back to the caduceus and then upstairs to the children's ward to feed her hungry baby. After Johnny had eaten his fill, Emma burped the baby and handed him back to Nurse Eleanor Tyler.

"Is Johnny being a good little man for you today, Eleanor?" asked Emma as she kissed the baby good-bye.

"He is always good. Look what we have fixed up for him," Eleanor replied pointing to a baby buggy parked by the nurses' station.

Emma turned to look and laughed. Eleanor and the other nurses had suspended three baby rattles from the buggy's sun shade. "What a clever idea!" Emma exclaimed.

"He absolutely adores the rattles. Kicks at them with his feet and reaches out his hands as if he would grab one. This little lad of yours is a smart one. We shall teach him to make rounds with the doctors soon," joked Eleanor. "Now, you run along. I hear that you are going to watch our sainted Dr. McKendrick in surgery this afternoon. Lucky you!" and Eleanor winked at Emma.

"Is it true," laughed Emma in return, "that Dr. McKendrick really does walk on water?"

"Not only does he walk on water," replied Eleanor, "he owns it! He can even part that same body of water with a flick of his scalpel and you had best be ready to follow closely behind. Now go and eat some lunch. Dr. G. does not like fainters!"

"So I have heard, but why do you call him 'Dr. G.?'" Emma asked over her shoulder.

"Just remember that his middle initial stands for," and here Eleanor pointed up to the ceiling.

"Right!"

Emma scurried along the corridors and stairs with her parcel of biscuits and cheese in hand until she reached the solarium. Waving to Benni, Emma quickly took a seat next to her friend.

Benni continued to munch an apple while Lilly Conrad, another nursing chum, picked up the thread of their conversation before Emma entered the solarium. "As I was saying before we were so rudely interrupted," Lilly pointed jokingly at Emma who made a face in return, "I am quite fed up with being treated like a bunch of naughty children, constantly subjected to the whacking and cracking of that infernal baton of hers. It is so...so humiliating!"

"Well, Emma here knows only too well the humiliation of being singled out and punished for a minor offense, and by the way," Benni began to imitate the voice and gestures of Nurse Walker, "just why are you not smiling, Richardson?" Benni barked.

Other students began to gather around the three friends, some calling, "Here! Here! The rack for Richardson!"

Emma finished her biscuit and cheese and took a swallow of cold tea. "You girls are missing the point."

"What point is that?" called out Florence Griffith.

"The point is that Nurse Walker is not only teaching us human anatomy, but personal discipline as well," responded Emma. She continued speaking to the gathering crowd of girls, "When a patient enters this hospital, that patient is ill, injured, or perhaps even dying. If we nurses who are responsible for the care of the patient...this suffering human being, allow ourselves to run around like a bunch of ninnies, just imagine, for a minute, how such behavior might affect the patient."

"Don't you think you're overstating just a bit?" asked one of the girls.

"Not a bit," responded Emma. "It is our duty to inspire confidence in our patients by first taking control of our own actions. We must act like nurses and not like a bunch of schoolchildren." Emma paused to look at the faces of the others. "I was quite wrong in my outburst today and Nurse Walker was quite right to discipline me in front of everyone. Think of how disastrous it would be for a patient entrusted to the care of a nurse who giggled her way through childbirth, for instance.

As the mother of three young, dependent children, I can tell you that the helpless ones look to us to be strong. Children and patients have a lot in common in that respect. They cannot manage their lives so we must step in to manage their lives and their predicaments for them, calmly and with great determination."

"Bravo! Bravo!" came from the back of the room, accompanied by clapping. Everyone craned their necks to see who the speaker was.

"Nurse Walker!" exclaimed several of the students.

"Richardson that was perfect! You have grasped the essence of personal decorum to which all nurses should strive. Let us remember Richardson's words. Now gather around here and take a seat, for I am reminded to forewarn you of a particular eccentricity of Dr. McKendrick's, lest we have any unsolicited questions in the surgery," Nurse Walker paused to give the students a chance to find seats.

"Dr. G., I mean, Dr. McKendrick, is a physician by vocation and a yachtsman by avocation. On lovely sunny days, he and Mrs. McKendrick and their daughter can be seen regularly sailing the waters of the Southport. Because of the doctor's passion for sailing, he tends to use nautical terms while operating, which, I am quite certain, you will hear him do today. Please do not comment or question his use of those terms."

"Exactly what terms are we talking about here?" asked one of the students.

"You must think of Dr. McKendrick's position at the operating table as always the fore position of the boat or the front of the boat. Remember that the operating table, like a boat, has four sides. Therefore, the nurse to his right is starboard. The nurse to his left is port, and the nurse directly in front of him is aft. However, if the nurse is shoulder to shoulder with Dr. McKendrick, then she becomes 'Nurse Fore'. So, if Dr. McKendrick should call out 'Nurse Port, retractor,' what do you imagine that means, Bennington?"

"Um…I would guess that means that the nurse to his left must hand him a retractor," replied Benni alternately looking at her right and left hands.

"CORRECT! Always remember that port and starboard have nothing to do with your left and right but only with Dr. McKendrick's position at the head of the table. With those words to the wise, we must adjourn to prepare to view the resection of a gallbladder," and Nurse Walker with her thirty-five student nurses trailing along in her wake, turned to lead them to the scrub room.

Once properly scrubbed, gowned, gloved and fitted with caps, Nurse Walker's students assembled in a tight group in the cramped surgical theatre to await the arrival of the patient and Dr. McKendrick. The gaslights hissed, casting an eerie glow about the room as the suffused light played off metal tables, instruments, shiny canisters and the white of the nursing students' gowns. The room was warm and close. The students began to shift uneasily in their seats.

A clattering noise just down the hall indicated that a cart was approaching the operating theatre's double doors which were banged loudly apart by two aides, causing the students to jump in unison. Through the open doors a hospital gurney was moved by two aides to be positioned under a cluster of gaslights in the center of the room next to a stationary operating table. Two nurses followed closely behind the patient. On the gurney, and now plainly visible to all the students, rested the body of what appeared to be a man, draped in a white sheet from the top of his head to the soles of his feet, causing the nursing students to look quizzically at each other.

On the count of three, the aides and the nurses lifted the draped body from the gurney and placed it on the operating table, adjusting the sheets and turning up the cluster of overhead gaslights. Then the aides departed and the nurses stood with arms crossed at the chest. Everyone waited in silence. Seconds turned to minutes and still the silence of waiting and expectation filled the room. All eyes were riveted on the draped body lying before them.

A muffled sound from beyond the double doors caused the students to lean forward, craning their necks to see what or who was coming next and as their attention was momentarily diverted, all failed to notice the movement upon the hospital operating table. When the doors did not open and the student nurses turned their attention back to the table at the center of the room, they were greeted by an apparition draped in a white sheet that now sat upright on the operating table. Everyone gasped in unison, while several of the student nurses screamed, two fainted and one was prompted to call out, "Saints preserve us for they have forgotten to sedate the patient!"

Benni dug her nails into Emma's arm. Confused as to why the attending nurses did nothing to restrain the patient, Emma rose from her seat to move toward the specter when the patient unexpectedly tore off his sheet, hopped down from the table and shouted, "GREETINGS STUDENT NURSES AND WELCOME TO YOUR FIRST SURGERY!"

Then with considerably more reserve and a deep bow, he added, "I am Dr. Burris G. McKendrick, at your service!" Laughing hugely at his own warped sense of humor, Dr. McKendrick looked around at the chaos he had created. "It would seem, Nurse Walker, that we need a dose of the salts for some of the ladies. Please be so kind as to revive those two who are supine on the floor over there and since I have your attention, let me say that my little stunt just now was designed to capture not only your interest but to illustrate as well a critical point that I like to make to all my nurses which is, always be prepared for the unexpected! If you allow yourselves the luxury of complacency, you are headed for disaster.

A patient who seems to be recovering nicely one moment can turn stone cold the next. Do not let yourselves doze off at the tiller or you will find yourselves aground on that infernal sandbar that disappears out in midstream for six months of the year, only to reappear for the remaining six. Now that our two fainthearted ones are in their upright positions once again, we shall start the surgery, which I shall be most pleased to narrate for you as it proceeds, but, I do believe I need a patient first. Nurses, please be so kind as to escort our real and very heavily sedated patient front and center."

Compared to his overture, Dr. McKendrick's surgical opus went smoothly, with no one fainting at the sight of blood or the resected gallbladder, which he passed among the student nurses in an enameled pan for inspection. As Dr. McKendrick neared the end of the surgical procedure and prepared to suture the wound, he turned to the student nurses and said through his mask, "Now comes the fun part! Being a surgeon is one of few professions that allow men to wield a needle and thread without fear of being called a 'sissy' for I do love to sew! Mind you all have a close look at how I do this. I wager my fine stitches would put all of yours to shame!" and Dr. McKendrick hummed to himself as he deftly closed the patient's abdomen.

Once the patient had been removed from the operating theatre and safely delivered back to the recovery ward by Dr. McKendrick himself, Nurse Walker congratulated her student nurses for having survived the doctor's infamous initiation into the 'Club of Blood and Guts' as he had named it. As the actual surgery had lasted longer than anticipated due to Dr. McKendrick's shenanigans, Nurse Walker dismissed her girls early, reminding them that they would have a lively discussion of the surgery when they returned from the Christmas recess.

By themselves back in the classroom as they fetched their books and coats, the girls began to buzz with comments about their ordeal. "Well, I thought it just a cheap trick!" exclaimed one girl winding a knitted muffler tightly around her neck.

"Scared the holy piss out of me, he did!" laughed another.

"I'd just as soon resign from the 'Club of Blood and Guts' if that's what we can expect from the great surgeon who walks on water," griped Florence Griffith.

"Yes, but did you notice how skillfully Dr. McKendrick excised that gallbladder? Such minimal blood loss. I personally shall be most anxious to track the patient's progress," countered Emma as she gathered up her possessions.

"What do you want to bet the bugger dies during the night?" wagered Sarah Mayhugh, pointing a gloved finger at Emma.

"Why would the man die? The surgery was flawless and there was a minimal loss of blood, from my humble perspective. My guess is he will be remarkably recovered from his surgery and totally without symptoms after we return from the Christmas recess in a couple of weeks," opined Emma.

"And I say he never walks out of the hospital under his own steam. Is it a bet then?" asked Sarah.

"Of course, but what spoils shall I expect when I am proven correct upon our return to class?" grinned Emma.

"Well, how about the loser must buy the winner a coffee and a cake at the Water Street Bakery?"

"Shall we shake on it?" asked Emma, whereupon Sarah offered her gloved hand to her friend.

As the students began to drift out the door and make their way down the corridor to the caduceus, Emma caught up with Benni.

"Say, Benni, I must run to get Johnny but before I do, I was wondering if you would be inclined to spend some time with me, Mama and the children over the Christmas recess? Since my father's death, Mama dreads the holidays and it will be the first Christmas that my boys can remember without their father," remarked Emma, begging Benni with her eyes to join them at the house on High Point Avenue.

"Why, Emma, how lovely of you to invite me into your home! Of course I shall come! But, what about your poor mother? Might I not be an intrusion upon her grief?"

"It is high time that Mama put her grief away for a while. My children need time to be children again. So much sadness, loss and misfortune have been forced upon my two oldest boys these past two years and with it all has come the terrible yoke of responsibility. I hear myself constantly admonishing them to 'fetch this and do that and help your baby brother and help me and help Nana,' until I remind myself that they are only seven years old. So please, lighten our spirits, dear Benni and come spend the holidays with us! Help us to find the Christmas spirit this season!"

"Of course I shall, dear friend," replied Benni hugging Emma. "Of course I shall!"

The two young women said their farewells and Emma rushed upstairs to retrieve Johnny. Bundling him up against the cold, she began the long walk down Chestnut Street to Water Street and the ferry across to Grandview.

Once on the other side of the river with her back to the wind, Emma unbuttoned her coat and snuggled Johnny inside against her chest as she made her way in the dark up Longmeadow to High Point Avenue. As she approached the house, she could see that already the boys had been helping Mary decorate the little tree out front for her beloved wild creatures. Suet balls and dried ears of corn swayed in the wind from its branches. Inside the front hall, she could hear George patiently helping Will with his primer by the firelight in the parlor. Emma closed the front door against the wind and was immediately engulfed in a slobbering dog-greeting delivered by Brute who had by this time grown to three quarters of his eventual adult size.

"Down, Brute!" Emma ordered the immense, friendly dog. "If I did not know you to be the softie that you are, I should be quite terrorized by you...you enormous galoot!"

"Ma!" shouted Will from the parlor. "Is that you? It's so late and we've been worried about you and Johnny," he added dashing into the front hall to embrace his mother and baby brother.

"Do not let him fool you, Ma!" admonished George, peering around the parlor door scrollwork, primer still in hand. "Will is just looking for an excuse to get out of his homework!"

"Am not!"

"Are too!"

"Come on back in here, Will. We only have half a page left to read," ordered George.

"Be still Georgie! Can't you see that Ma is nearly freezed to death and look how happy 'Baby Cheeks' is to see me." Will took his grinning baby brother from Emma into the parlor to undo his wrappings, warming his little toes and fingers by the fire.

"There is your problem, Willynilly!" scolded George. "You just get so interrupted by everything. You have absolutely got to learn to APPLY YOURSELF, like Nana always says or you are never going to amount to a hill of beans!" and George huffed off to the kitchen to see his grandmother and to tattle on Will.

"Thank you, Will, my darling for your attention to the baby. Whatever would that baby do without a big brother like you? Is Nana back in the kitchen?" Emma asked as she removed her coat. Standing by the fire, Emma rubbed her hands together in front of its warmth and then turned to warm her backside, which had borne the brunt of the cold wind coming up the hill from the river.

"Ma," whispered Will.

"Yes dear?"

"There's somethin' the matter with Nana."

"Oh, really, Will, and what makes you believe that? Does she show signs of being ill?"

"No, nothin' like that, Ma, it's just that she's kinda…sorta…sad. Know what I'm sayin'?"

"Yes I believe I do know," Emma replied.

"When we got back from school this afternoon," offered Will by way of explanation as he jiggled the baby on his knee, "she had all the Christmas stuff all over the floor and she was just sittin' in the middle of all of it…doin' nothin'. So, me and Georgie helped her make the suet balls and hang them on the tree outside with the dried corn for all God's creatures to eat and then she says, 'That's all for today, boys,' and went inside to the kitchen. Here I figured we was goin' to put up all that Christmas stuff, bein' as how she'd got out everything."

Kneeling in front of Will and Johnny, who reached for his mother, Emma said softly, "Your nana is just missing Papa terribly this Christmas season. Christmas was always such fun for the two of them and this year it reminds Nana that Papa is not here with us anymore and that makes her feel so sad."

"But, Ma that's not true! I really do know that Papa is here with us! We talk about him all the time with Nana and you. His clothes are still in the closet and me and George wear them sometimes, even though they are a little too big. And, look over there by the chair…there's Papa's pipe and tobacco. Why, if you pick it up and sniff," which Will did to illustrate his point, "it even smells like Papa."

"I know, I know, Will. What you say is true enough, but it is also the reason she misses him so much…so, I thought the best medicine for Nana and all of us would be to have someone special come and visit us this year for Christmas. What do you think?" asked Emma trying to change the subject.

"Really truly, Ma?" Will asked his face lighting up with a smile. "Who's comin'?"

"A special friend of mine from the nursing school and her name is Louise Bennington, but we all call her 'Benni'," Emma replied stroking Will's hair.

"Can I tell?" asked Will excitedly.

"Yes you may," replied Emma whereupon Will dashed out into the front hall and back to the kitchen.

Will planted himself squarely in front of George who was cutting butter cubes into the hot potatoes that Mary was forcing through her ricer with the green handles. Every other butter cube made its way into George's mouth.

"I know somethin' that you don't!" exclaimed Will.

"Do not!"

"Do too!"

"Should I tell him, Ma, or should I just let him suffer?" Will asked looking back at his mother.

"Put him out of his misery, Will, and give George the news."

At this exchange, Mary looked up from the mashed potatoes in time to see Brute eyeing the meat roll that she had just taken from the oven. "Please put that dog outside while we have dinner and before there is no dinner for the people to eat. Mind the dog has already eaten all the suet balls he could reach from the tree out front and I expect he will be sick during the night so make sure you put him in the barn to keep Onion company."

"But...but, Nana!" protested George. Seeing the look on his grandmother's face he quickly added, "All right, all right, but let me first show Ma Brute's new tricks," and George pulled the dog over in front of Emma. "Now SIT BRUTE!" and Brute sat. "Now SMILE BRUTE!" and Brute raised his upper lip to show his gleaming white teeth, causing Emma to start.

"If I did not know Brute to be the gentleman that he is, I might have mistaken that smile for a snarl," laughed Emma, stroking the dog's enormous head. "Just how did you get Mr. Brute to do these wondrous tricks, George?" Emma asked still laughing as the dog continued to 'smile'.

"Do not be fooled, Emma dear," answered Mary, "for Brute here has been rewarded with pieces of my chocolate cookies to perform his tricks, and unless I miss my guess, he will sit like that for hours until George, our animal trainer, feeds the beast another piece of cookie, am I right, George?"

Before George could reply, Will chimed in, "I was tryin' to tell somethin' special and now George gets all the attention, like always, for bein' so smart and teachin' the dumb dog dumb tricks..."

"Hey! I have an idea! Maybe if I gave old Willy here a chocolate cookie every time we sat down to practice his reading he would pay attention and learn quicker!" retorted George.

"Take that dog to the barn before I box your ears, sir," exhorted Mary, "and here, give Brute his reward, whereupon she handed George a whole chocolate cookie that he broke in half and shared with the slobbering dog before dashing off to the barn with him.

"Criminy! Nobody listens to me," whined Will.

"Come to the table and we shall all listen to you, but only after we have asked for the good Lord's blessing upon us," and the little family bowed their heads to give thanks.

Mary began to slice and distribute the meat roll while Emma dished up the mashed potatoes. Baby Johnny gurgled from his baby buggy which Will had pulled up next to his place at the table. Handing his baby brother a rattle, Will pressed on about his secret. "Do you want to guess what I know that you don't, Georgie?" he taunted his brother who was busily gulping down a glass of milk.

"Easy on the milk, George," Mary reprimanded, "or you will have no room left for dinner!"

"Maybe I already know the secret," replied George wiping his mouth.

"Ma!" wailed Will to Emma, "He can't know because you told me first!"

"Told you first, dear."

"So, what did Ma 'telled' you first?" George needled his brother.

"That we are going to have a visitor for Christmas this year and it's a lady and her name is Benni and…"

"Wait a minute, Dummy. Benny is a boy's name. You know, like B-E-N-J-A-M-I-N. No lady is named Benny, Will!"

"Uh-huh! Is too!" countered Will.

"George, be still dear," commanded Emma. "Do give your brother half a second to talk!"

"As I was sayin'," continued Will sticking out his mashed potato-covered tongue at George, "the lady is called 'B-e-n-n-i' cause her real last name is 'Bennington' and ever since she was a little kid she couldn't say the whole word…"

"Like you!" interrupted George.

"George Miller Richardson! Do you wish to spend the rest of the evening in your room with no dinner?" asked his mother.

"No."

"Then you apologize to your brother this instant!"

"Sorry."

"Sorry what?" asked Mary.

"Sorry, Will."

"What a marvelous idea," mused Mary in an attempt to clear the air between the two boys. Emma, this is the Benni that you have spoken of so fondly to me…the young woman who lives over in Clarksburg?"

"Yes, Mama. She comes from an enormous family and times are hard for them this year so I thought that we could share our holiday celebration with someone less fortunate than we are," Emma offered by way of explanation to her mother.

"By all means! That is the true spirit of Christmas, to share what one has with others!"

The house on High Point Avenue once again took on a festive air as Emma, Mary and the two oldest boys sang Christmas carols while draping the house, the dog and themselves with greenery and their favorite ornaments. Mary hung small glass replicas of Santa Claus from her ears and Emma placed a wreath on top of her head with a red bow that dangled down to her waist. Brute pranced around with sleigh bells tied to his neck, busily attacking the tissue and boxes. George and Will raced to the barn and returned with straw tucked into a basket. Lifting Johnny from his quilt on the floor, they nestled him carefully in the basket in front of the Christmas tree. "Look Ma and Nana!" chorused the boys. "We even have our own baby Jesus!" Right on cue, Johnny grinned and waved his tiny rattle.

In anticipation of their guest's arrival, Mary announced that she was going to make the family's favorite gingerbread cookies with dried fruit. Even Emma was persuaded to chop walnuts and raisins with the dried, sugared fruit peels that Mary had put up earlier in the fall. It was George and Will's responsibility to scoop out the dough onto the greased cookie sheets, while Mary supervised the baking. Little Johnny contentedly gnawed on the wooden icing spoon until Brute spied the baby waving it in the air and decided to have a lick himself.

"Now that's enough of that, silly dog!" admonished Will, whereupon Brute sat and smiled for the group.

Christmas Eve day, Mary stuffed and roasted a turkey, making giblet gravy to go with the mashed potatoes and turnips. "What accompaniment shall we have with the meat?" asked Mary.

"How 'bout chocolate cake?" offered Will.

Going to her pantry and surveying the shelves that were lined with the fruits and vegetables which she had spent the previous summer canning, Mary responded, "Sorry young Will, I do not see any chocolate cake but I do see green beans, lima beans, white beans…"

George interrupted his grandmother to recite, "Beans, beans, that magical fruit! The more you eat, the more you toot! The more you toot, the better you feel! That is why we have beans for every meal!"

"Thank you, George, for that splendid recitation!" laughed his mother from the dining room where she was setting the table for dinner.

"Before I was so rudely interrupted," continued Mary glaring at George, "we also have corn, tomatoes, beets, carrots, baby onions…"

"That's what I want, them creamed baby onions so as I can fart like the horse!" and here Will let out an imitation of the poor horse up in the barn. "Do you think Benni would like a helping of onion farts with her dinner?" Both boys laughed hysterically at their crude talk.

"Well, now that just does it!" Mary intoned reaching for the lye soap on the sink ledge. "Get over here this minute, the two of you!"

"Oh, Nana, have a heart! Please not on Christmas Eve!" wailed George.

"Right now! Here!" said Mary raising her voice.

"Ma! Help! Nana's tryin' to kill us with that bar of soap!"

Paying the boys no heed, Mary took them both by the arm over to the sink and wetting the bar of soap, washed out their mouths. "Let that be a lesson to both of you never to use such language in my presence," she admonished them, wiping her hands on a towel.

"Now, as I was saying, I believe we shall have the green beans. What say you, Emma?" Mary entered the dining room to find her daughter, hands pressed to her mouth trying to stifle her own laughter.

"Oh, so, perhaps you think you are too big for a good mouth-washing, Miss Emma?"

Changing the subject, Emma exclaimed, "Goodness, Mama! Look at the time! The boys and I must wash up and go down to meet the ferry, for Benni will be arriving within the hour. Come along now, George and Will. Follow me upstairs to make ourselves presentable for our house guest," and Emma scooped up Johnny from the baby buggy while planting a kiss on her mother's cheek.

"Thank you, Mama, for your patience! I know that we tax your good soul and your fine intentions to the limit. Please forgive us, for surely you must know that we cannot get along without you. By the way, the Christmas Eve dinner that you have prepared for all of us smells divine. Bless you for all your hard work!"

Emma put the baby down for a nap in his crib, washed the boys' faces and hands, combed their hair and her own before bundling them all up in the front hall against the cold. "Will, please put two more logs on the fire for me and let us hurry on down to the ferry to find Benni. Mittens, George! You cannot go out in this cold without your mittens. Good-bye, Mama!" Emma called back toward the direction of the kitchen. "We shall return shortly with Benni."

The three of them braced themselves against the cold down at the dock, scanning the approaching ferry for their first glimpse of Benni. "There she is!" cried Emma pointing to the figure of a woman with a green muffler wound around her neck who was leaning over the railing in a similar search for the Richardsons. "I see her! I see her!" exclaimed George jumping up and down and waving to Benni.

"Me too!" chimed in Will. "But, I can't see much of her 'cause she's all covered up with that scarf." Will began to jump vertically while shouting, "Hello, friend Benni! It's me, Will!" Turning to his brother, Will admonished George, "Don't you dare lay a hand on her bag, Georgie. I get to carry it, Ma promised!"

"You do the carrying and I shall do the talking," George advised Will.

Benni stepped off the ferry into Emma's embrace.

"Benni, please allow me to introduce my two oldest sons. This is George and this is Will." Each boy removed his hat and stepped forward in turn to shake Benni's hand.

"How ever do you tell the boys apart?" asked Benni glancing from George to Will and back.

"It is really quite easy, Miss Benni," interjected George, "as I am the smart one," whereupon he took a deep bow, cap still in hand.

"Oh, yeah? And just what does that make me?" retorted Will swiping at George with his cap.

"As I was about to say," replied George, "my brother is the strong one who gets to carry your bag." Here George took Benni's bag and placed it in Will's hand, while smiling innocently at everyone.

"Enough of this banter, boys! Benni will freeze down here at the dock before you two decide who is doing what. Come along now, everyone!"

The foursome made their way up Longmeadow to the house on High Point Avenue with Will leading the way at a steady gallop, bag in hand. George offered his arm to Benni and was prompted to remark, "You can lean on me, Miss Benni. This hill up to our house is really steep."

More enthusiastic greetings met them inside the front door as Mary hugged Benni for the first time. At the sight of Benni's long blond hair cascading out from underneath her knitted hat and muffler, both boys were moved to hug Benni again themselves. "Say, Miss Benni," offered Will on a cordial note as he took her muffler to hang it up in the front hall, "did you know that green's my favorite color?"

"And it is mine too, Will. Think of that!" Benni smiled down at the boy. Will grinned back.

"Come over to the fireplace, Benni, and warm yourself a bit before supper," said Mary, "for I am sure the trip over on the ferry was a cold one indeed."

"Your home is so very comfortable and inviting, Mrs. Miller," remarked Benni looking around at the front parlor with its velvet drapes and dark, carved wood furniture, "and so beautifully decorated for Christmas." Benni turned to look up at the tree.

"We sure did work hard on the decoratin' this year," added Will approaching their guest and reaching out a hand behind her back to touch the spun sugar hair that fell to her waist. George stepped forward and knocked his brother's hand away, unbeknownst to Benni, while glaring at Will through narrowed eyes.

"I feel certain that our guest would probably like to wash up before dinner and you boys go to the kitchen sink to do likewise," admonished Emma. "Come upstairs with me, Benni, and I shall show you to my room. Then we shall take a peak in at Johnny and see if he is ready for his supper also."

Dinner was a lively affair with both George and Will vying for the attentions of Louise Bennington. Johnny did his best to add to the live entertainment, cooing and drooling incessantly for their guest, prompting Emma to remark as she began to clear the table, "I am afraid it has been a while since we had any company to dinner in this house and everyone is taking tremendous advantage of the opportunity. I fear that we have quite exhausted you."

"Nonsense, Emma! You forget that I am from a big family and very much used to all the merriment and the high jinks that accompany a crowd at the dinner table."

"I would suggest," said Mary commencing to remove the dishes from the table, "that you two friends sit by the fire in the parlor while George and Will help me clear the table and wash the dishes."

"Oh, not tonight!" protested George. "I helped you last night!"

"Me too!" groaned Will.

"Right now, please, boys! Clear these dishes to the kitchen. Let us show our guest what fine helpers you can be," and Mary smiled at Benni, who winked at George and Will, which was all it took to galvanize the twins into action.

Emma picked Johnny up from his baby buggy and ushered Benni into the front parlor. Placing a quilt on the floor, she laid the baby on his stomach with some of his toys and then sat next to him on the quilt prompting Benni to do likewise.

"What a fine family you have!" commented Benni. "And such beautiful children!"

"They are on their best behavior with you here this evening but I confess to you that the three of them are a handful for me and my mother," answered Emma.

"Undoubtedly they are." Benni gazed into the fire for several long moments. "Emma, I do not mean to pry, but why on earth would any man give up all this?" and Benni looked from Johnny to Emma to the Christmas tree and back to Emma.

"It is a long story my friend," Emma said quietly.

"Perhaps it is time that you told this long story to someone, Emma. I sense that you have been keeping a great sadness bottled up inside of you. Perhaps it is time for you to remove the stopper and let that long, sad story out of its bottle." Benni reached out to Emma, grasped her small hand and looked into her friend's eyes for a moment.

"Perhaps it is time," sighed Emma just as Will and George came running into the parlor.

"Nana says it's time to read the Christmas story and hang up our stockings. Then we've got to go right upstairs and take our baths 'cause she says Santa won't come to visit if he sees that we're dirty," complained Will.

"Well, then, run and fetch three stockings from your room and remind Nana to bring the tacks," said Emma.

"Three stockings?" parroted George. "Who gets the third one?"

"Your baby brother," replied Emma pointing to the baby who had rolled over on the quilt and was now playing with his toes.

Mary carried in the family's Bible and read the Christmas story by the firelight to a hushed audience. In conclusion Mary added, "Let us each remember that Christmas is not about presents under the tree," and here she looked squarely at Will and George, "but about the birth of our dear Savior, Jesus Christ. And now boys, do bid your mother, Benni and Johnny good-night and come with me," concluded Mary.

Stalling for more time, Will piped up, "But what 'bout the cookies and milk for Santa? You always say that Santa gets terrible hungry from all his hard work."

"You are right, Will," replied Emma. "Quickly! To the kitchen boys and let us fetch a nice glass of cold milk and a plate of Nana's gingerbread cookies."

After the boys had placed Santa's treats on the hearth, George withdrew a folded sheet of paper from his pants' pocket. "I wrote a letter for Santa, Ma," and he handed the note to his mother.

Smoothing out the folds of the paper, Emma read aloud the neatly penciled message:

"Dear Santa Claus,

Will and I are good boys this year baby John is good this year and here is what we did we brushed our teeth we got firewood for Nana we took care of our baby we feed horse and a dog Will worked hard on his reading we wish this Christmas for Pa to come home when you see him please tell Pa also that we wish for him to come home now we love him.

Your friends

George Will and John"

The only sound in the room was the hissing of the gaslights.

"What a fine letter, boys," Emma finally managed to say. "Let us put it just here by the cookies where Santa will see it first thing. Now, I believe that Nana wants you two upstairs for a bath," Emma said reaching to kiss both of her sons.

"Good-night, Ma," chorused the boys, who shook Benni's hand and kissed Johnny before running up the stairs while complaining to their grandmother, "Please no lye soap tonight. How about that lavender stuff that you and Ma use?"

Benni smiled after the fast disappearing twins and then turned to look at Emma. who sighed audibly and dabbed at her eyes with her fingers.

"This whole mess has been so very difficult for my boys. It seems like such a long time ago that Edward left and then something happens like George reading his letter tonight and I am instantly reminded of the night the boys' father left. It seems like just yesterday that I first laid eyes on Edward. Let me think a moment," Emma mused while turning the baby over onto his stomach again. "Yes, it was the summer of 1881 and I was twenty-one. You must understand that I was a very young and a very immature twenty-one, Benni. You at nineteen possess a certain knowledge…a certain sophistication about people and men that I totally lacked back then."

"Probably because I am from such a large family where there are no secrets, Emma. When you live so closely with nine other people, it is impossible not to know the most intimate details of everyone's lives. Please continue," said Benni playing with the baby.

Emma sighed. "Unfortunately, I had no such intimacy with older or younger siblings to teach me about life. Papa preferred to ignore my budding womanhood and Mama was forever trying to educate me about the intricacies of male and female relationships but would I listen? Not I! I was far too preoccupied with life to listen to Mama. That is until…until I became pregnant out of wedlock." Emma paused to assess the effect her revelation was having on Benni.

"I see. Am I to assume that Edward was responsible for this?"

"Indeed it was Edward who seduced me. I was reluctant but he was persistent. He was so handsome and so courtly at first, and I have to admit that while a part of me resisted his seductive ways, a part of me willingly gave in to them, much to my shame. I longed to know what this enormous secret thing was that occurred between a man and a woman behind closed doors. All the whisperings of the ladies at Hummel's and at parties aroused my baser instincts to the point that I was willing to sacrifice my virginity to his passion in order to satisfy my curiosity." Emma moved to the front windows to close the velvet drapes against the cold night air.

"Did you...did you enjoy it?" asked Benni, engrossed in Emma's story.

"No. There was little to enjoy as Edward was a totally selfish husband, taking but never giving. It was always on his terms and at the most inconvenient times. He put absolutely no thought into his actions which I would liken to a primitive man dragging his mate off by the hair to some hole in the side of a rock for procreation.

I can still hear the bastard now. He would enter the house from the mill around five-thirty in the evening and the first words out of his mouth were always, 'Where is my supper?' Which was usually delivered with a squeeze to my breasts or buttocks. After he had eaten his fill, he commanded me to put the boys to bed and then lie with him in a variety of places that pleased him."

"Whatever do you mean, Emma?" asked Benni.

"I mean that Edward was not content to lie upon our bed to have relations, but instead commanded me to lie with him on the floor, on tables and in short, all over the house, both inside and outside. He even insisted one time that I had to sit upon him in the privy house. It was all so humiliating," blushed Emma at the recollection.

"Poor dear!" soothed Benni.

"I was haggard and tired from caring for the twin boys, the house, our horse, his stall, the laundry, the marketing, the cooking, the dishwashing, the mending, the ironing...it was all so endless, so confounding and so repetitive. I no sooner finished those chores than it was time to begin them anew and I excelled at none of them, much to Edward's keen disapproval. That is when the 'spankings' began."

"The what?" asked Benni.

"The spankings," repeated Emma. "If I failed to produced a perfectly ironed shirt or if I burned a pie, Edward would strip me down and spank my naked bottom hard with his hand until he left my flesh covered with red welts. This punishment always seemed to rouse Edward's passions and he would then require me to lie with him."

"He sounds like a terrible beast!" commented Benni.

"Worse!" said Emma. "For a beast does not act from conscious thought, whereas a man possesses the ability to formulate and deliberate his actions. A beast does not knowingly inflict pain but a man always knows when he is hurting another."

"When did this other side of Edward begin to show itself?" asked Benni picking up Johnny and holding him upright on her lap.

"Edward's dark side began to emerge as his consumption of whiskey increased and that was almost from the very beginning. Initially Edward worked as a mill hand for my father, however after the two of us were married, Papa elevated him to foreman, paying him an inflated salary but only because he was family. Edward had trouble assimilating his new duties at the mill and the pressures that went with the job.

He truly abhorred physical labor and my father, knowing this, made sure that Edward received more than his share of hard, abysmal work. As foreman he not only continued to do the menial dirty work but he was also required to manage the mill hands, a truly difficult task for Edward as he possessed absolutely no ability to take control over men, unlike his keen ability to infatuate women. The men saw straight through him." Emma paused, reaching for the baby who had begun to cry. "This little boy needs to go to bed. I shall just take him upstairs to Mama and return in a moment."

When Emma came back downstairs, she paused at the parlor door and asked Benni, "May I get you a cup of tea from the kitchen?"

"No thank you, Emma. I am still so full of that marvelous dinner that your mother made for all of us. Please come back and finish telling me about Edward," and Benni stood up, smoothing her skirts before settling into the velvet upholstered chair near the fire.

"Where was I?" asked Emma, removing the green satin ribbon from her hair and retying the stray curls back from her face.

"You were telling me that Edward disliked the work at the mill and that he began to drink in earnest when your father promoted him to foreman of the mill hands," responded Benni.

"Oh, yes. It became quite apparent to me that most evenings Edward had begun drinking on his way home from the mill, as I could smell whiskey on his breath the moment he entered the house," Emma continued as she paced the perimeter of the Aubusson rug.

"Once at home, Edward invariably removed his bottle of whiskey from the kitchen cupboard and poured himself a straight shot that he drank down in a single gulp before sitting down to the evening meal. That routine was repeated after dinner so that by the time the boys were headed for bed, their father was in a thoroughly disagreeable frame of mind. Then, as I said, once the boys were abed, Edward's assaults began upon me. But, please understand, he never abused his children. He absolutely adored…"

"Excuse me for interrupting, Emma," said Benni rising from her chair, "but you have just contradicted yourself."

"I have?" asked Emma.

"Yes you have. Any man who drinks himself into a rage and then beats his wife is guilty of abusing the entire family, children included. You cannot tell me that those precious boys of yours failed to notice that their father was an abusive drunkard, Emma. That knowledge alone caused terrible harm to both Will and George, regardless of whether or not Edward ever raised a hand to his sons," concluded Benni.

"Perhaps you are right in your assessment of the damage done, Benni. I never before really saw it that way as I was too intent on surviving Edward's assaults after dark." Emma paused. "I get so upset just recounting the details that I would like to take the sledge hammer from the barn and absolutely beat the daylights out of something...anything..."

"Or someone...by the name of Edward," interjected Benni.

Emma actually laughed. "Yes by all means, Edward! And others...namely the legions of faceless whores that he frequented."

"Oh, surely not!" gasped Benni.

"Oh, surely yes!" retorted Emma.

"When did all of that start," Benni asked, "and how did you know?"

"He began consorting with whores not long after we were married. It was a vicious cycle. His excessive drinking led to carousing and carousing led to more drinking. I always knew when he had been with other women as I could detect their foul scent upon him the moment he walked in the house. He absolutely stank! No quantity of lye soap, water or time could ever eradicate their stench from his body. I remember their nauseating odor to this day," and Emma shivered in disgust.

"But what was it that finally led to Edward's departure from the family?" pressed Benni.

Emma stopped her pacing and stood in front of the fire with her back to the embers. "The final straw actually occurred in the parlor of our little home on Locust Street, late one night last April, when I was in my sixth month with Johnny. After bathing the twins and tucking them into bed with their prayers, I came downstairs to bid Edward good-night. He was inebriated, as usual, and making demands upon me for my favors. I was standing in a spot similar to this one where I am now," whereupon Emma indicated a position in front of and to the right of the fireplace.

"Edward stood over there on the left, just inside the parlor door of our home on Locust Street. I had moved over here by our mantle to make sure that the fire screen was properly in place before retiring. Edward commanded me to strip off

Joan Cox   133

my clothing to the waist," said Emma gesturing toward Edward's imaginary position on the carpet.

"What did you do?" asked Benni looking suddenly ashen.

"I refused," said Emma flatly.

"And then what?"

"And then Edward ordered me to remove my clothing to the waist again or..."

"Or what?"

"Or he was going to shove me into the fire." Tears began to stream down Emma's face.

"I know this is painful, Emma dear," soothed Benni now by Emma's side, "but you must rid yourself of this pain. You must finish with it!"

Wiping the tears away with her hand, Emma continued, "And then I began to do as he told me but all the while I was removing my blouse and my undergarment, I began to tremble, and then to shake with a terrible rage that had been building up inside of me for so very many years. Can you understand that, Benni?" Emma turned suddenly toward her friend who scarcely recognized the contorted features of the young woman who stood before her.

Not waiting for an answer, Emma continued. "When I shrank back from him in fear, Edward moved into the front hallway of our home and just there by the door, he picked up his riding crop where it hung from the coat rack. He began advancing upon me with the crop raised like this," and Emma raised her right hand high above her head as if she were wielding the riding crop herself. "I turned my back to him in order to shield my unborn child from the beating that I knew was coming." Emma shook uncontrollably as Benni watched in horror.

"Edward lashed the riding crop down and across my bare back several times with all of the force he could muster, like this," demonstrated Emma with her phantom crop, "which sent me falling to my knees. It was a pain like no other I have ever felt. As I began to rise to my feet, my eyes fastened upon the brass poker for the fire, similar to the one you see here," said Emma picking up the brass object, now totally immersed in reliving the events of that night.

"When I turned to face Edward, I swung the poker and hit him square across the face, causing him to fall backward into an unconscious heap about here," pointing to a space between two chairs. "I used that chance to escape, running upstairs and locking myself in our bedroom."

"Did he pursue you?" asked Benni looking terrified.

"No. That was the last I ever saw of Edward Richardson. He must have regained consciousness some time during the night and when he did, Edward took all of our money, except for a few dollars that I had hidden under some floorboards in a closet. He rode off on our horse…vanishing into the night…never to return." Emma turned to Benni with a look of total exhaustion on her face.

"Such a coward!" exclaimed Benni.

"And good riddance to the bugger, I have always told her," added Mary from the foot of the staircase.

Both young women were startled by Mary's appearance at such a late hour, so engrossed had they been in reliving Emma's final ordeal with Edward.

"Oh my! I have lost track of the hour, Mama. Did I awaken you?" apologized Emma as she regained her composure.

"Not at all dear. I awakened feeling thirsty and when I walked to the bathroom for a drink, I noticed the light on in the parlor and thought I should investigate." Looking at Benni, Mary added, "I am so grateful that you were able to drag all of the details out of my daughter, as I have tried unsuccessfully for months to do just that. Perhaps it is my age which acts as a barrier between my daughter and me. The simple fact that I am her mother seems to cast me in another realm where Emma thinks I exist deaf, dumb and blind to the problems besieging the young women of today."

"My own dear mother admonishes me in a similar fashion, Mrs. Miller!" exclaimed Benni placing an arm around Emma. Looking into her friend's face, Benni added, "We young women like to think that we invented the world as we know it and that you older women are allowed to continue your walk upon this sphere only with our permission. Is that not so, Emma?"

"It would seem to be the prevailing attitude of the young," admitted Emma. "Yet I would honestly say that my mother has been the cornerstone of my survival…my refuge from the storm and without her, our four lives would surely have been lost long ago." Emma moved to embrace her mother, weeping uncontrollably against her cheek.

"There, there my darling!" soothed Mary as she steadied her sobbing daughter. "It has been a long and terrible journey for you but finally, our friend Benni has gotten you to talk about it and…"

"And I feel a tremendous relief to have unburdened myself." Emma took the handkerchief that Mary offered to her and blew her nose. "I feel that Edward is truly gone and that I am now free to go on with my life. I no longer have to look over my shoulder."

CHAPTER 11

▼

The next morning, Christmas Day, Emma was snoring peacefully in the spare bed next to the windows in Johnny's room when suddenly, the bedroom door banged violently against the wall by her head and the twins shouted in unison, "Merry Christmas, Ma! Wake up! Santa has been here!"

"Merry Christmas," mumbled Emma as she peeked out from under her covers. Glancing over at the windows, she could barely discern the faintest fingers of pink gripping the top of the darkened tree line to the east of the river. "What time is it?" asked Emma as she eased the covers back and moved to an upright position.

"I dunno," responded Will.

"It is Christmas time!" announced George.

"Yeah, and it's time to get up!" chimed in Will, hopping over to the windows on one leg to look outside. "Guess what, everybody?" Will turned to look at his dazed mother. "It's snowing!"

Johnny rolled over in his crib and began to wail at all the commotion in his bedroom.

"Let me see too, Willy," said George nudging his brother out of the way. "Ma! It really is snowing!"

"I believe you, boys. Will, what is the matter with your leg that causes you to hold it up like that?" asked Emma, stretching and feeling with her toes for the slippers under her bed.

"I'm just practicin' bein' a pirate, Ma, 'cause Nana read us this story last night 'bout a pirate that had a wooden leg and he had that thing fastened to his knee and he went thump, thump, thumpin' all over the place, makin' a bunch of noise. Do you think old Bill would make me a thumper like that?" Will asked his mother who combed her hair and wound an old bathrobe around her slender frame before picking up Johnny.

"Peg leg, Will. It is called a peg leg," announced George. "And no, you cannot have one unless you get that Dr. McKendrick cut off your leg at the knee."

"Why do I have to get my leg cut off?" gasped Will preparing to jump up and down on the spare bed.

"Because you are dumb!" exclaimed George jumping up and down on the bed with his brother.

"Boys! It is Christmas and it is very early on Christmas! Much too early for this nonsense. Now come along, let us look in on the others to see if they are ready to join us downstairs."

Will and George charged down the hall, banging on the closed bedroom doors, all the while yelling at the tops of their lungs, "Christmas is here, everyone! Christmas is here!" Whereupon, Johnny began to wail again from his mother's arms and Nana called out, "Shush, boys before you wake Benni!"

"That is quite all right!" exclaimed Benni flinging open the door to the water closet. "The last one down the stairs to the tree is a rotten egg!" and Benni took off running in her bare feet down the hall, pushing the boys aside, bathrobe and golden hair flying behind.

"Oh, no you don't!" challenged Will in hot pursuit.

"Cheaters!' squealed George, sliding down the banister.

Choruses of, "I won! I won!" and, "You're a rotten egg!" and, "You are two rotten eggs!" drifted up the stairwell to Emma and Mary, who just looked at each other, shook their heads and laughed.

"It obviously is the Christmas Spirit which has taken possession of all three of them," called Emma through cupped hands down the stairwell. "You had best not begin opening the gifts until Nana, Johnny and I get down there!" she called to the sprinters as she changed Johnny's diaper.

"Look, Ma!" yelled Will as Emma entered the parlor. "Santa brung me a sled!"

"And he brought me a red wagon," echoed George pulling the wooden wagon over for his mother to see. "How about we put little John in the wagon and I give him a ride?" offered George.

"Let me tie the baby to the slats so he does not fall face down," said Emma placing Johnny upright on his blanket at the back of the wagon. Removing the belt to her robe, she fashioned a harness to keep the baby secured. George took off at top speed with the baby prompting Emma to remind him, "Slowly please or you will scare your brother. Do not tip him over going around the corners!

Now where did Will and Benni go?" asked Emma of her mother turning back to the tree.

"The last I saw of them, they were headed to the front door," said Mary following George and the baby back toward the kitchen.

Stepping into the foyer, Emma caught sight of Benni through the windows on either side of the front door dressed in her bathrobe and a pair of the boys' galoshes pushing Will, clad in pajamas, sweater and galoshes, down the hill on his new sled. "Would you look at those two!" laughed Emma. "I do not know which one is the child and which one is the adult!"

Just then George came careening around the dining room door, nearly knocking down his mother as baby Johnny squealed with delight. "Come, come now, George! Let us round up the other two and commence opening our gifts." Emma handed the baby a rattle, raked up the embers in the fireplace, putting several logs on top and then pushed aside the velvet draperies, allowing the first light of dawn to seep into the cozy parlor.

The front door blew open and in raced Benni and Will, shaking and stomping off the snow onto the rug as they removed their galoshes. "It's freezing out there!" yelled Will.

"I would expect so," said Mary appearing with a pot of hot chocolate and a plate of gingerbread cookies.

"My new sled is really fast," added Will helping himself to a handful of cookies. Mary shook her head "no" and removed three of the cookies from her grandson's hand.

"It will be even faster," commented Benni taking a cookie and a cup of chocolate, "after we rub the runners with some lye soap."

"Yecch!" Will made a face. "Just so's you don't try to put any of that stuff in my mouth. I definitely don't like the taste of lye soap."

"Well, would you look at this!" exclaimed George standing over by the hearth. "Santa ate every last one of those cookies and drank all the milk that we left for him! He must have been so hungry!"

"Yeah! He ate twelve cookies all by himself 'cause I counted them before I went to bed," and Will looked over at his grandmother. "How come he gets to take so many and I only get two?"

"Because Santa is a grown-up and he had a very late night," smiled Mary looking at Emma and Benni.

"Santa really must have thought we were extra special good this year," commented Will to George. "Just look at all these presents under the tree!"

George was still examining the spot on the hearth where the empty milk glass rested on the crumb-littered plate. "Yeah, but I was hoping that Santa would leave word for me from Pa," said George frowning.

"Oh, George, you know how Santa is!" exclaimed Benni. "That jolly man is getting old and fat and…and it is getting to be such hard work for him to keep track of all the children around the world. Santa cannot possibly be expected to keep track of all the fathers too!"

The burgundy, cream, rose and navy blue patterns of the Aubusson rug were soon littered with crumpled tissue and wrapping papers, yards of red and green ribbons, cookie crumbs, hand-knitted scarves with matching mittens, pull toys, drums, books, stick candies, rattles, stuffed animals and sticky chocolate. As was their custom, the adults did not exchange gifts. Christmas was for children.

"Please excuse me for a bit," said Mary rising to gather up the remnants of cookies and cups, "I am quite hungry after all that fun. Is anyone else?"

"Me!" shouted George.

"Me too!" echoed Will.

"Good. Then it is settled. We all are in need of breakfast," and Mary hummed to herself as she bustled around the kitchen preparing their traditional Christmas morning breakfast of sausage, egg and bread pudding and two loaves of her freshly baked dried apple and nut bread, accompanied by a large steaming bowl of cooked oatmeal, topped with raisins, butter, brown sugar and cream.

"A feast fit for a king!" exclaimed George, strutting around the dining room table.

"Yes, and his queen!" curtsied Benni.

"I get to sit next to Queen Benni!" shouted Will.

"She is my queen and not yours!" intoned George

"How about if I sit between both of you? Would that be fair enough, boys?" asked Benni already pulling out the middle chair on one side of the table.

"Any excuse to argue!" commented Mary slicing the fruit bread. "I would expect that some day Will and George might become famous barristers, renowned for persuading courtrooms packed full of jurors, spectators and judges that angels have green wings instead of white ones and that little boys can have ten cookies instead of two."

Will contemplated his grandmother's words for several long moments while busily smearing a slice of apple bread with butter. "Are those bear stars like the ones up in the sky that we see at night?" he asked stuffing the carefully prepared bread into his mouth.

"Bear stars? What bear stars?" mocked George.

"Am I talkin' to you?" asked Will leaning over in front of Benni to point the butter knife at George. Not waiting for George to answer, Will continued, "No! I'm talkin' to Nana," and Will pointed his finger in the opposite direction, "down there at the end of the table. So, what are bear stars anyhow?"

"Barristers, darling Will. I was saying that you and George might become barristers. A barrister is a lawyer."

"Well, I can tell you right now I ain't goin' to be no lawyer...no how...never," declared Will with his mouth full of eggs, sausage and bread.

"But Will," intervened Benni, "in order to become a lawyer, you must be very smart and study hard. You must also be concerned about the welfare of other people and you possess all of those qualities, Will dear."

"Yeah, I know...but there's one thing that lawyers have to do that I would never do," proclaimed Will.

"Oh, really? And what is that one thing?" asked Emma.

"They wear wigs!" exclaimed Will.

The adults began to laugh behind their napkins. Regaining her composure, Emma asked, "Just how do you know that lawyers wear wigs?"

"George over there," said Will stabbing the air with his fork in the direction of his brother, "thinks I don't pay no attention in class...always sayin' how I ignore Miss Rita. Well, smarty-pants, let this be a lesson to you 'cause I looked at that picture real good the other day when Miss Rita was readin' us a story 'bout that lawyer over in England who sent them crooks to jail and that lawyer was wearin' A WIG! Wearin' a wig is sissy stuff and I ain't no sissy!" declared Will.

"Indeed you are not a sissy!" smiled Mary and everyone began to laugh, including Will.

After their breakfast, Benni took the lead in suggesting a snowball fight on the front lawn, "But first, I want to see this dog of yours that I have heard so much about from the two of you. Where do you keep the beast?"

"In the barn," replied George looking sourly at his grandmother, "but he is not a 'beast' at all. Nana is just afraid that Brute will pee on her carpets and steal the food off the table but what Nana does not understand is that I have trained my dog not to do any of those bad things," George bragged to Benni.

"Well then, let us have a look at this highly trained Brute of yours, Georgie," laughed Benni as she playfully boxed his ears. So, Benni and the boys bundled up against the cold and made their way up the hill at the back of the house. As the trio approached the barn, they could hear Brute excitedly barking and scratching at the door.

"Now stand back, Benni, 'cause old Brute is gonna roar outta that door like a t-i-g-e-r," Will spelled the word and then stuck out his tongue at George.

True to form, Brute came bounding out through the barn door, barking, jumping and running in circles around Benni, Will and George. Benni sank to her knees in the snow, inviting the dog to come closer. An ever-obliging Brute responded by flattening Benni into the drifted snow. Standing on Benni's chest, the enormous dog delivered his ultimate welcome by licking the helplessly giggling young woman's face.

"Brute, sit!" commanded George. Whereupon Brute promptly sat upon Benni and grinned down at her face.

"See how well trained he is!" exclaimed George proudly.

"Indeed I do," gasped Benni, "but perhaps he could be asked to relocate his hind quarters over there," she laughed fanning the snow off to her side with a gloved hand.

"Brute, off!" again commanded George, and Brute moved aside, wildly thumping his tail against their legs.

Brushing the snow from her long coat and shaking out her knitted hat, Benni reached down to stroke the dog. "He is truly a magnificent dog, Georgie...so powerfully built and with such a massive head. His paws are enormous!" commented Benni rubbing her chest where Brute had stood. "I would wager this dog weighs more than I do!"

Will came out of the barn where he had been feeding Onion his breakfast, "George, we're gonna hafto muck out Onion's stall today. It really stinks in there!" announced Will wrinkling his nose.

"The deal was, Willynilly, that you would muck out the stall if I helped you with your studies. I have been holding up my end of the bargain and you have to hold up your end too," George reminded his brother.

"But I don't like to shovel all those horse turds!" complained Will.

"Me neither, but a deal is a deal...and we shook on it too!" George reminded Will again.

Just then a snowball went whizzing past Will's head and splattered against the side of the barn.

"Ha-ha on you!" called Benni preparing a second snowball to throw at George.

Benni and the boys began a snowball free-for-all around the barn and up the hill to the edge of the stand of white pines with Brute in hot pursuit of each snowball that was thrown. Jumping high into the air the dog caught his fair share of snowballs before they reached their intended targets. So intent upon their game were they, that the three humans and one dog failed to notice that a fifth pair of eyes was watching from the woods.

From his perch high and inside a towering pine tree, a bobcat took in the playful scene below with his large yellow eyes. Motionless except for his dilating pupils, the big cat crouched silently in the tree, shrouded in pine needles and snow. Just then, Emma stepped out the back door to ring the "summoning bell", as she called it, for the three to return to the warmth of the house.

"We'd better get back home. That's Ma and Nana wantin' to see us right away," Will explained to Benni.

"And just in time too as I am nearly frozen," laughed Benni.

Brute, heeding the call of the bell, took the lead racing down the hill. Benni grabbed George by his muffler and began to drag him playfully along with her through the deepening snow. Will started toward the other two and then called, "I'll be there in a minute. I have to find my other mitten," and he began poking in the snow around the area where they had been playing moments earlier. The child's search took him to the perimeter of the ancient pine with its limb on which the bobcat waited. As the boy flailed around in the snow looking for his mitten, the bobcat perceived that helpless prey was just underfoot.

With muscles tensing along his lean torso, the big cat silently contracted his body into a crouch. When the unsuspecting boy bent down to retrieve the lost green mitten from the snow where it had fallen earlier, the cat recognized his moment for a strike had arrived. Wasting no time, the bobcat sprang, making his silent descent through the air and onto the back of the child.

The air was split with a bloodcurdling scream as Will was pounded into the drifting snow by the full weight of the cat upon his back. Down at the house, Brute raised his great head. With a terrifying howl exploding from his chest, the massive dog raced through the snow back up the hill to the woods behind the barn.

Will lay motionless, face down in the snow with the menacing cat poised upon his back when Brute rounded the barn. The giant dog hurtled faster through the deep snow, slowing only the last few yards to lower himself for the kill. Viciously snarling and displaying a daunting array of fangs, the dog sprang at the bobcat, grabbing him low, just under the head. The bobcat flailed helplessly against the mighty dog who held him fast in the death grip of his massive jaws. Brute bit into the cat's throat, ripped it out and then shook him like a rag doll.

Benni was the first one to reach Will. Cautiously she knelt in the blood-spattered snow beside the motionless child. Turning Will over onto his back, Benni wiped the snow from the boy's face, checking to see that he was breathing. Next she checked the child's pulses before commanding George, "Run and fetch your mother, for I cannot carry your brother back down the hill through the snow alone."

"Is he dead?" asked George on the verge of tears.

"Not by a long shot! Now, run!" commanded Benni cradling Will against her body to warm him.

Removing her knitted muffler and hat, Benni layered each over the unconscious child to ward off the cold. As she watched George disappear down the hill and around the barn, Benni looked over at Brute who was covered in blood and standing guard over the lifeless bobcat.

"What a magnificent animal you are, Brute! For you surely saved young Will's life today!"

Benni caught sight of Emma and George plowing through the snow toward their position by the pines. Emma's hair flowed wildly about her shoulders and she had lifted her skirts, tucking them into her waistband in order to negotiate the snow in her high button shoes. Breathlessly, the two approached the gory scene.

"Will!" cried Emma, falling to her knees in the red and white snow beside Benni and her son. "Can you hear me, Will?"

"He has lost consciousness, Emma. We must move him to the house in all haste, warm him and apply the salts. You take his head and I shall carry his feet. Carefully now!" Benni ordered.

"But what about Brute and this...this...this murderer?" wailed George.

"Calm down, George," Emma said struggling to her feet with a firm grasp of Will's head and shoulders. "Your brother has not been murdered, only rendered unconscious. Bring Brute with you down to the house. The dog just saved your brother's life and deserves to be looked after himself."

Mary was waiting for the group on the back porch watching their progress down the hill. At their approach, she held open the door to the kitchen, instructing the two women to place Will on the kitchen table, where the three of them began to remove the layers of clothing that had protected the child from the bobcat's assault. Once he was stripped to his underclothes, the women wrapped Will in layers of blankets and Mary applied the salts under his nose.

"George! Take off those cold, wet clothes and put on some dry things!" Emma ordered the boy who wept uncontrollably at the foot of the table.

"Come with me, George," offered Benni. "We shall put you to rights in no time," and she placed a comforting arm around the shivering, distraught boy's shoulders as she guided him upstairs to change his clothing.

"Hold Will upright, Emma and let me apply the salts again." Mary waved the vial of smelling salts vigorously under Will's nose causing him to jerk his head aside.

"Pee-yew! That stuff stinks!" and Will was conscious again.

"I am going to add more wood to the stove to warm some broth for him, Mama, but first, I think perhaps we should move Will upstairs to his bed. Would you prefer that I ask Benni to assist me in carrying the child upstairs?"

"No, she has her hands full with George right now. We can do this." Mary turned to look at the dog who was patiently sitting by the table, keeping his vigil over Will. "You are a splendid beast! And I shall tend to you momentarily but in the meanwhile, lie here upon this blanket by the stove and warm yourself, dear Brute. You have done well this day. To be sure, you have done well." Mary patted the air above the dog's massive head, still covered with blood, before turning to help Emma carry Will upstairs to his bedroom.

"We need to wash the boy thoroughly," said Emma to her mother as they carried him up the stairs to the second floor. "Will got sprayed with blood from the bobcat when Brute ripped out the animal's throat," added Emma matter-of-factly.

Mary stifled a gasp. "So, his attacker was a large cat then?"

"Yes. Apparently the cat had been poised up on a pine bough unbeknownst to Benni, George and Will. I guess even Brute was unaware of the danger. The three of them were playing in the snow and throwing snowballs when I rang the summoning bell. That is when Will decided to remain behind to look for his lost mitten and I guess the big cat saw a meal underfoot," explained Emma to her mother as she helped Will into the steaming water in the copper tub.

"Good thing Brute saved me, huh, Ma! Else I might have been that cat's dinner!" and Will laughed weakly for the first time since his ordeal. "Oh, Ma, please not the lye soap," fretted Will. "Can't I just have you wash me with some of that good smellin' stuff?"

"But of course, dear. I think you have earned the privilege of a scrubbing with the good stuff today. What do you say, Nana?" smiled Emma looking up at her mother from where she knelt on the floor beside the tub.

"Absolutely. I was just about to suggest that the child would benefit greatly from the application of some of our fine lavender soap today," and Mary handed the large cake to Emma who began a vigorous lathering of the small boy in the tub.

Just then, George stuck his head in the bathroom. "How are you feeling, Will?" he asked solicitously of his brother.

"Like a horse been steppin' all over me," deadpanned Will, now surrounded in the copper tub by a ring of admirers.

"That cannot feel very good, eh young master Will?" asked Benni reaching for a large towel which she handed to Emma. Turning to Mary and George, Benni said quietly, "Now, when we get Will into bed, Emma and I are going to do a thorough examination of him as we have been trained to do by Nurse Walker and I was wondering if we could count on the two of you to fetch that hot broth from the kitchen that Emma mentioned earlier?"

"You can count on us. Right, Nana?"

"Right, George. To the kitchen my fine lad," said Mary turning George around by his shoulders. "Please let me know when you are ready for Will's broth, ladies."

As the two left the confines of the small bathroom, George reminded his grandmother that the true hero of the day lay blood-covered by the kitchen stove. "Seeing as how it was Brute who killed that old bobcat before he ate Will for dinner, do you think you could find it in your heart to let him sleep inside now? I mean...what if another sneaky old cat climbed in through the window and grabbed BOTH Will and me?" wheedled George, adding, "I know that Brute does not even like to pee on the carpets because I see him use the fence posts, your lilac bushes and the corner of the house all the time."

Mary laughed at her own acquiescence as much as at the logic of her grandson. "It is only fitting that a hero such as Brute be allowed the comfort of our home at night. After all, he most certainly did save Will's life!"

"Does that mean yes?" grinned George enthusiastically in anticipation of the answer.

"That means 'yes'!" proclaimed Mary.

"Yippee! Do you hear that, Brute boy? Nana has finally given in! You can sleep in my room at night."

Foraging through the icebox, Mary produced two cold chicken drumsticks that she handed to George. "I would wager that our hero down there is hungry."

"You are really in Nana's favor now, Brute. She is feeding you our chicken," giggled George handing the chicken legs one at a time to the dog.

Mary pulled out a jar of cold, jellied broth and placed it in a pan to warm on the stove. "George dear, Brute is quite filthy from his ordeal and so we are going to have to bathe him if the dog is to stay in the house with us humans," said Mary stirring the melting jellied broth.

"But how can we wash him, Nana? The snow is real deep outside and the water would freeze on Brute before we could get him clean," puzzled George.

"I was thinking that we might wash him in the tub upstairs," Mary replied with measured insouciance.

George's lower jaw dropped, "What are you saying, Nana?"

"I am saying that we shall take the dog upstairs and bathe him in the copper tub, just like we do you and Will, only with the lye soap! I draw the line at using our fine lavender soap on Brute!"

"Wait until Will hears this! He might just think that he has died and gone to heaven after all!" exclaimed George, taking the plate of soda crackers that Mary handed to him.

"Take those upstairs to your room and I shall follow with a cup of hot broth for everyone. We shall have a picnic lunch upon Will's bed today. Do you think a picnic would lift Will's spirits?"

"Definitely," answered George setting off at a trot.

George fairly ran up the stairs to their back corner bedroom where Emma and Benni were tending to Will. "You cannot possibly guess what I know, Will!" exclaimed George to his brother who lay snuggled in the far twin bed with blankets and quilts piled up under his chin, pale face barely visible.

"This better be good news," groaned Will melodramatically, "'cause I've had far too much bad news for today."

"It is the best of news!" cried George, pausing to set down the plate of crackers. "Nana has decided to let Brute sleep up here in our room! And...and...we are going to give Brute a bath in OUR VERY OWN BATHTUB today!"

Will eyed his brother suspiciously, "Are you lyin' to me, Georgie? Nana would never say such a thing."

"Cross my heart and hope to die," and George traced an X over this heart with his right hand.

"My goodness...Nana is just becoming an old softie!" laughed Emma as Mary appeared with a tray of steaming broth.

"Oh, twaddle!" scoffed Mary at the notion that she was being manipulated. "The dog is a hero after all and has a right to be treated with some deference, even as this old woman should be," which was delivered with a raised eyebrow at her daughter.

After their picnic lunch of broth and crackers, both boys begged incessantly to wash the dog so it was agreed that Emma and George would cajole Brute up the stairs while Benni, Mary and Will filled the tub with warm, soapy water.

"Come, Brute!" commanded George clapping his hands before the exhausted dog where he still lay by Mary's warm stove. Eager to oblige, the immense dog raised himself, stretched stiffly and sat on his haunches in front of George. "Fine

dog. Now come!" and Brute followed Emma and George to the foot of the staircase in the front hall.

"Now Ma," instructed George, "you go up about halfway and clap your
hands." Emma took up her assigned station and George turned back to the dog
who was intently watching the two with his head cocked to one side. "Come!"
George again commanded Brute clapping his hands and moving slowly backward
up the stairs while Emma clapped her hands in unison with George.

Brute cautiously placed a paw on the first step, toes splayed out as if to gain a
firm grip on the oak riser. Then he placed another paw, toes similarly splayed.
Shaking his great head, Brute sprayed blood and slobber on the woodwork.
Momentarily hesitating, the dog raised a hind leg as if to place it on the step with
his front legs, thought better of it and whimpering, made his escape back to the
warmth of the blanket by the kitchen stove.

Again and again, Emma and George tried to coax the big dog up the formidable staircase, prompting Benni to call down to them, "What is the delay? We
have Brute's water drawn and ready."

"Just a mild case of stair fright," Emma laughingly replied. "We shall prevail
here any second."

"I have an idea," George said to his mother. Tilting to one side of Emma,
George asked his grandmother standing at the top of the stairs, "Nana, what
stinky old leftovers do you have in the icebox that I could feed to Brute?"

"I believe that I just might have some rancid fatback," Mary replied holding
on to the railing and making her way down the stairs. She and her grandson went
back to the kitchen and George reappeared waving a piece of greasy fatback.
Catching a whiff of the meat, Brute was instantly alert and followed the boy to
the foot of the stairs.

"Now," said George waving the fatback up the stairs and just out of reach of
the huge dog, "if you want this…you will just have to come and get it." Whereupon, the boy began climbing the stairs one at a time backward with Brute sali-
vating and following, cautiously gripping each riser with his toenails as if the
whole staircase was in danger of collapsing beneath him.

Brute reached the top step to much applause but still no fatback, as George
kept walking backward to the tub, dangling the dog's prize just out of reach.
There he placed the strip of meat on the opposite lip of the tub against the wall.
When Brute jumped into the tub without hesitation to retrieve the meat, Will
slammed the door shut. Benni, George and Emma formed a barricade around the
dog in the tub and proceeded to scrub his coat, pausing every few minutes to

shield themselves from the great drenching the three of them experienced each time Brute shook violently to rid himself of all the soap and water.

Once out of the copper tub and reasonably towel-dried, Brute raced from one bedroom to the next, excitedly rubbing his damp fur on each of the rugs. The dog's antics reduced the twins to hysterics and they too were inspired to roll around with the dog on the rugs, causing the adults to lend their laughter to the melee. From his vantage point in Nana's arms, even baby Johnny seemed genuinely delighted by all the unusual drama.

Finally, Mary put a stop to the nonsense. "All right now, boys! Enough of this! You too, Brute!" and she shook her finger at all of them. Brute slunk off into the twins' room and collapsed in an exhausted heap on top of George's bed, assiduously licking his front paws.

"Emma, dear, please take Johnny while Benni and I clean up this frightful mess in the bathroom. Then we shall join all of you downstairs for some quiet time before supper. So much commotion is not good for the digestion." Turning to Benni, she added, "I am grateful that my late husband did not live to see such a spectacle in his home. You know he quite adored his soaks in the tub and had he been witness to the sight of a slobbering animal spoiling his beloved bathroom, James would have turned us all out into the cold." Mary smiled at the thought.

"Oh, fiddle, Mama!" Emma countered. "Papa would have constructed Brute his very own bathroom and tub out of gratitude for the dog's heroic deeds today. He loved Will far better than any old tub!"

Changing the subject, Mary reminded Emma, "We need to store the bobcat's carcass in the chicken coop over night and then tomorrow, we must notify the knacker and the constable that we have a dead wild animal on the premises."

"Yeah…and maybe I'll become famous," Will called over his shoulder as he descended the stairs. "The mayor might even want to shake my hand."

"Not likely, Willynilly, seeing as how it is the dog that is the hero, not you!" George reminded his brother.

"Is not!"

"Is too!"

"Boys, please do settle down and play quietly with your Christmas toys for a bit so that we may all catch our breath," begged Emma.

George pulled his red wagon to the hearth. Draping one of his grandmother's brightly colored quilts in the wagon, he settled against its slats to read a new storybook. Will sat in front of the Christmas tree and began to construct a large wooden edifice out of building blocks when he spied Johnny's cricket pull toy under the tree. Will failed to notice that the cord to the cricket's head was tangled in a branch of the tree as he began to tug on the green wooden toy. Suddenly, the Christmas tree toppled over with a thud, ensnaring Will in its branches. The stunned child just sat there, peeking out from the tree branches, tinsel and ornaments gone awry.

George looked up from his book in disbelief and at the same moment, Emma called from the kitchen, "What was that noise?"

"Just Will," answered George non-plussed, "again."

Benni was dispatched from the kitchen to check on the boys and when she entered the parlor, she paused, shaking her head. "Will Richardson! Whatever are we to do with you?"

Still seated in his wagon, George piped up, "I think we should have just let the bobcat eat him!"

"That's not nice, Georgie," sniffed Will. "I don't say mean stuff like that to you!"

George smiled at Benni, "Maybe it is not too late to invite another live bobcat down from the woods to feast on Will's meat for Christmas dinner," and turning to his ghostly white brother added, "you know how much Nana loves to feed God's wild creatures at this time of year!"

"Be careful there," Benni cautioned George, "for Will has been through quite enough today. Any more excitement and I fear we shall have to admit him to the hospital. Let us just extricate Will and set up the tree again and keep this a secret between the three of us. Agreed?"

"Okay by me," responded Will immediately.

"George?"

"Maybe."

"George?"

"Oh, all right but the next dumb thing he does and I am telling!" warned George.

Christmas dinner was a rather subdued affair as everyone was exhausted from all the excitement earlier in the day. The little family and their friend, Benni, dined on Mary's baked ham, peas, fried potatoes, corn bread and peach cobbler. It was all they could manage to wash up the dishes and retire early to bed that evening. Even the dog refused to budge from his exalted station atop George's bed.

Everyone slept late the next morning and after a light breakfast, Mary reminded Emma, "We must notify the Constable of the dead bobcat and then I need you go to the knacker's and ask him to retrieve the carcass from our chicken coop."

"Of course, Mama." Then Emma added, "Benni, maybe you and I can ride into town together on Onion."

"I want to go too," piped up George.

"Me too," chimed in Will.

"Not this trip, boys. You have a parlor full of toys to keep you busy while Benni and I are away and from the looks of it, Johnny is in need of a good nap already this morning. So, we shall go into town alone."

The two young women cleared the table for Mary and washed up their breakfast dishes, then bundling up against the cold, made their way through the snow up to the barn to saddle Onion. The horse was frisky and clearly enjoying a sojourn away from the confines of his stall. Benni and Emma laughed and chatted amicably as they both sat astride Onion's broad back. Emma had convinced Benni to wear a pair of her father's trousers cinched in at the waist with a sash and she was dressed in a pair of Will's knickers and long wool socks with warm coats, mufflers and hats pulled down tightly over their ears against the cold and the wind off the Southport.

The journey over to town was slow as there was no discernable path to follow through the drifting snow. Emma reined in Onion at the front of the constable's jail, positioning the horse parallel to the boardwalk so that she and Benni could dismount without falling. After Emma tied the horse's reins to the hitching post, both women entered the gray wooden building to find the constable, feet propped up on the stove, drinking coffee.

"Good morning, Constable Crawford. I see from the empty cells that you have experienced a rather dull Christmas," joked Emma.

"Well, good morning, Miss Emma. Actually, I got soft on Christmas and turned both of my prisoners loose after I was sure they had slept off the effects of too much celebrating." Turning to Emma's companion, Luke Crawford asked, "And who do we have here?"

"This is my friend, Louise Bennington. Louise and I are student nurses together over at Angel of Mercy Hospital in Clarksburg."

"You don't say," responded the constable, eyeing Benni's lovely, long blond hair as she removed her hat and muffler. Constable Crawford was a young single man in his thirties with a flame red mustache, matching hair, blue eyes and at six feet five inches in height, a giant among the men of Grandview. Lean and well muscled, Crawford's prowess with firearms was legendary. To be chased on horseback by Luke Crawford brandishing a pistol was like trying to escape the devil himself. "Please call me Luke, Miss Bennington," he smiled broadly at Benni, totally ignoring Emma. "May I interest you in a cup of my superb coffee this wintry day?" and Luke pulled out a chair for Benni by the stove.

"WE could both use a cup of your good coffee, Constable," answered Emma, "and a chair by the stove."

"Oh, forgive me Miss Emma," and Luke pulled up a third chair then poured generous cups of coffee for both women. "Now what in tarnation has brought two such lovely ladies to my jail the day after Christmas in all this snow?"

"My son Will had a nasty run-in with a bobcat out at our place yesterday afternoon," replied Emma sipping the steaming coffee.

"You don't say! I hope the boy wasn't hurt, Miss Emma. Are you needing me to track down the varmint and kill it for you?" asked Luke Crawford reaching for his holster.

"No, Luke. Actually, our dog killed the wild beast after it jumped down out of a pine tree and knocked Will flat in the snow. Will was rendered unconscious or fainted from sheer fright, I have not determined which, but the child did not have a mark on him."

"You were very lucky that cat didn't inflict serious wounds upon young Will with those fangs and claws of his. Did you say you have a dog that felled the cat?"

Emma laughed, "I guess it has been a while since you have been over to our place because anyone who comes to visit our house on High Point Avenue receives a very warm welcome from Brute."

"A very warm trouncing is more like it," Benni smiled at Luke.

"This is one dog I should very much like to see for myself! Of course, I must also document the size and condition of the bobcat and I will want to backtrack him for a while to try to determine his origins. I trust you didn't leave the cat's body out in the open overnight for scavengers, Miss Emma."

"No. Benni and I went up behind the barn after supper last night and dragged the animal into one of Mama's old discarded outdoor chicken coops…"

"Benny? Who's Benny?" Luke asked with a puzzled look.

Emma laughed and pointed to Benni.

"You're Benny?" Luke asked again looking at her long blond hair, more puzzled than ever.

"Please tell Luke how you got that name while I ride up to Hummel's and make a few purchases for my mother. I shall return shortly for you, Benni. Constable, could you do me a favor and get word to the knacker that we have a carcass for him to retrieve? Right now it is not too bad because of the cold but the carcass will soon start to spoil and I do not relish the thought of my boys playing outside with that foul thing deteriorating behind the barn."

"Quite right, Miss Emma. I'll ride out to Knacker Tom's when you return from Hummel's and tell the old boy that we have a wild animal for him. Then I'll hurry on over to your place so I can backtrack the cat in daylight."

"Perhaps you would consider staying for supper this evening, Constable?" offered Emma looking over at Benni whose gaze was riveted upon Luke Crawford.

"It would be my pleasure to stay for supper, provided that it won't inconvenience your fine mother."

Rising to put on her coat, hat and muffler Emma replied, "We shall all look forward to your company at our table," and addressing Benni, she added, "I shall make my purchases quickly and return for you shortly. Thank you again, Luke, for your hospitality," Emma called as she left the jail.

As the two women once again braved the cold head-on to ride Onion down Longmeadow toward the river, Emma joked over her shoulder to the young woman glued to her back for warmth, "If this cold spell continues, Benni, you might have to ice-skate home across the river."

Teeth chattering into the wind, Benni replied, "You are not funny, Emma Richardson! If that river freezes with me on the Grandview side, you can just carry me across the ice." Both women laughed at the silly mental picture of the petite Emma struggling to carry Benni, easily five inches taller, across the frozen river on her shoulders.

When the women turned onto High Point Avenue, Brute spied them first and came bounding across the snow from the front yard where he had been chasing the twins as they whooped and hollered their way down the slope on Will's new sled. "Easy does it Brute," admonished Emma, "All that barking makes Onion nervous. Hello, boys!" Emma called waving a gloved hand while Benni secretly made horns out of her fingers behind Emma's head as they approached causing the twins to collapse with laughter in the snow.

"Just what is so hilarious, you two?" she demanded.

"You, Ma!" chuckled George. "You are very funny!"

"He's talkin' 'bout them horns you sprouted while you was away in town," giggled Will pointing to Emma's head.

Realizing Benni's trickery, Emma swatted backward with her hand. "This is the thanks I get for taking the likes of you to town to meet the very handsome AND very eligible, Constable Luke Crawford," Emma teased.

"Benni's sweet on Constable Lu-uke...Benni's sweet on Constable Lu-uke," sang Will.

"And she is going to mar-ry him and she is going to mar-ry him," sang George in response.

Dismounting up at the barn onto the wooden box, Benni was forced to defend herself, "I declare! A girl cannot even drink a cup of coffee with a man these days without certain people hearing wedding bells," and she reached out to yank the boys by their scarves to her in a bear hug.

As Emma dismounted, she said, "I see that you did fine work on Onion's stall, Will. I am very pleased that you cleaned it out and give him fresh straw. How many bales do we have left up in the loft?" Emma asked removing Onion's saddle while Will held the reins.

"'Bout ten I reckon," answered Will.

"By my count," interjected George frowning at his brother, "there are exactly twelve."

"There he goes again," protested Will, "always gotta know more than me!"

"Never mind, Will. You were close enough. Now please lead Onion into his stall, take off his bridle and bit and give him a good dinner. George, you and Benni go on down to the house and tell Nana that we shall have one more for supper this evening," ordered Emma.

"Who's comin', Ma?"

"Yeah, exactly who is the one more?" asked George.

"Why none other than Benni's future husband, Constable Luke!" replied Emma grinning at Benni.

"Okay, that does it! How about we get her with snowballs for that, boys!" yelled Benni running for the barn door.

Emma emerged from the barn to a barrage of snowballs. Picking up a handful of snow she yelled to Brute, "All right now, Brute, fetch!" Whereupon the immense dog sprang forward to field the snowballs before they could reach Emma, who used his huge body as a shield as she made her way down to the house while the three attackers continued to try to pelt her with snow.

Shaking and brushing off their snow-clad clothing on the back porch, the four humans and one dog entered Mary's warm kitchen where they were immediately enveloped in the aroma of roasting chickens and blackberry cobbler. "Oh, boy!" exclaimed Will. "Constable Luke's really gonna like this dinner!"

"Are we having company and no one told me?" asked Mary looking up from the pan of fatback and onions that she was frying for the green beans.

"It was a spur of the moment invitation, Mama. I hope that you do not object. Constable Luke is coming out on cat business and since he is coming so far in such dreadful weather, I thought…"

"Benni's goin' to marry him," giggled Will to his grandmother.

"La, la, la, you do not say!" trilled Mary looking at the blushing Benni and perceiving the joke. "That little baby of yours needs to be fed, Emma, and I feel certain that he has just filled his diaper," she added while pouring the beans and water in to the kettle to cook with the fatback and onions.

The twins busied themselves in the parlor with their new Christmas toys while Emma tended to baby Johnny. Benni offered to set the dining room table for six while Mary began peeling potatoes. Brute collapsed in a heap by the stove and was soon fast asleep.

Suddenly, the dog raised his great head looking at the door from the kitchen to the front hall.

"What do you hear, boy?" asked Mary absently, cutting up the potatoes into chunks in a pan. The dog stood at attention for a few seconds and then moved silently through the kitchen door, down the hall, pausing by the front door, where he pressed his black nose to the sidelight, growling.

"What ever is it, Brute?" asked Mary wiping her hands on the long white apron while approaching the furious dog. "What is it that you see or hear?" and Mary strained to see what unnamed assailant so agitated the dog from his vigil at the window. She remained there looking for several minutes while the dog continued to sound a warning.

All at once, Brute threw back his head and let out a terrifying and protracted howl. Mary jumped as did Will and George who came running to the front door. "What's goin' on out there, Nana?" asked Will straining for a look out the other sidelight. Benni too crowded around the little knot at the front door.

"It would appear to be a…a posse approaching the house," said Mary.

"Oh, boy! Guns and horses! Whoopee!" cried Will, running to fetch his new popgun from the parlor settee. Waving his new toy gun in the air, Will raced back to the front hall, exclaiming, "Okay, I'm ready. Me and Brute will bring him back dead or alive."

"Just exactly who or what are you planning on bringing back?" scoffed George.

"I dunno but I reckon Constable Luke can answer your question, Mr. Smart Britches," responded Will flinging open the front door.

"Will, get back inside here!" admonished Mary, grabbing the child's collar and tugging him backward as he prepared to step outside onto the porch. Too late she felt the great dog heave himself past her and out the door. Hackles raised and teeth bared, Brute stood on the front porch snarling at the approaching riders.

"Let me through, Nana," commanded George, "before Brute does serious harm to those men." Moving to the dog's side, George grabbed the nape of his neck and called out, "Sit, Brute!" But Brute did not sit. Instead, he again threw back his head, emitting another terrifying howl.

Constable Crawford, plainly recognizable now, indicated to the riders that they were to slow their horses to a walk, while George continued to hang on to the dog's neck. Motioning for the posse to stop, Constable Crawford approached the house, stopping several yards out from the front porch and the snarling dog. Sitting motionlessly astride the big bay, Luke Crawford studied the enraged animal and the trembling child that clung to its neck.

In a calm voice, Luke called, "Hannibal, is that you, boy?"

The immense black and brown dog fell silent, cocking his head to one side.

"Hannibal, boy…it's me…your old friend, Luke!" Freeing his left foot from the stirrup and throwing his right leg over the saddle, Luke slid down off the horse, never taking his eyes from the dog. "It's me, Hannibal old boy," Luke spoke reassuringly to the dog, who now cocked his head to the other side.

Slowly, Constable Crawford sank into the snow on one knee as everyone on the front porch let out an audible gasp. "Better not do that, sir," admonished George, straining to hold back the immense dog.

Paying George no heed, Luke called, "Come Hannibal! Come boy!" When the dog still did not move, Luke said, "Release him, son. It's all right. The dog and I know each other."

Hesitatingly, the dog moved toward Luke Crawford, head high, sniffing the wind as it blew toward him from behind the man kneeling in the snow. All at once Brute charged the Constable, knocking him backward into the snow. Standing on Luke's chest, Brute covered man's entire face with wet, dog-slobbered kisses.

"Well, I'll be!" exclaimed Tom the knacker, removing his hat and scratching his head with the same hand.

"Amen!" echoed a member of the posse.

"Brute, sit!" commanded George, starting down the front steps. As instructed, Brute sat on Constable Luke's chest, grinning down into his face. "Brute, off!" George again commanded the obliging dog who wagged his tail furiously. "How is it that you know my dog, sir?" asked George.

"Well, son, it goes about like this. Your dog here once belonged to my parents on the outskirts of town," explained Luke dusting the snow from his clothing with his hat and wiping dog slobber from his face and mustache with a sleeve. "Before Hannibal, er, I mean, Brute here was full grown, he took off one evening after a raccoon that was raiding our henhouse and never returned. We combed the hills around our place looking for the young rascal and found nary a trace of him. And that's the long and the short of it," Luke explained to George towering above the boy, who crouched in the snow next to the big dog.

"I believe you because you are the constable and constables do not tell lies, but," and here George stood and drew himself up as tall as he could manage, "you cannot take my dog, sir! I feed my dog every day and I make sure that he does not pee on Nana's rugs and I train him to do tricks and he gets to sleep on my bed at night because he is a hero and he saved my brother's life," George turned toward the porch to indicate Will who, unsolicited, piped up, "Yep...it's true!"

"Besides," continued George in a strangled voice, "I love my dog!"

Clearing his throat, Constable Crawford reassured the quaking boy, "I have not come to take your dog from you, son. Knacker Tom here has come to take the bobcat from the henhouse." Looking up at Emma who had appeared on the front porch with the others, Luke addressed her, "Miss Emma, my men and I are needing to backtrack that bobcat now before we lose any more daylight. I need to determine if we have a problem hereabouts with cats since I've received several reports of dead chickens and geese from folks living just to the west of you. This is, however, the only case that I've had so far of a bobcat attacking a human."

"Now, if you'll excuse us, ladies," said Luke doffing his hat to the women, "we need to ride." With one fluid motion, Luke was astride the bay, neck reining him sharply to the left and making a forward motion through the air with his right arm.

"Phew!" exclaimed George turning to his mother and releasing his grip on Brute's neck as the posse rode out of sight. "For a minute there I thought old Brute was a goner!"

"Now, you do not really think that the constable would ride all the way over here in the snow just to stake a claim on some old flea-bitten dog, do you George?" teased Emma. "Come on inside now, everyone. It is much too cold standing out here on the porch with the wind blowing like this," and Emma walked back into the house with baby Johnny straddling her hip.

The children resumed their play in the parlor, the women returned to the kitchen to continue dinner preparations and gossip about the day's events while Brute took up his station once again by Mary's stove, when suddenly there came a loud rapping upon the front door. Brute was again galvanized into action, scrambling to the front door and barking loudly. Terrified by the sudden noise, Johnny began to wail from his baby buggy in the kitchen.

"Good heaven! Now what?" exclaimed Emma in an exasperated tone. "Here, Benni, take Johnny while I get to the bottom of this," and Emma marched up behind the barking dog at the front door. Peering through a sidelight Emma saw a young man she did not recognize. Upon seeing Emma, the young man removed his cap and flashed a toothy smile at her. Not waiting to be admitted and despite the guttural warnings from Brute, the young man opened the door himself, stepped boldly inside the foyer and handed Emma a card saying, "Good afternoon, ma'am. The name's Angus. Angus O'Malley, reporter for the Grandview Courier here to do ask a few questions pertaining to the wild animal which attacked a child hereabouts," delivered with another toothy smile.

"Yes, well…"

"Good doggie! Good doggie!" crooned the reporter patting the air about shoulder high above Brute's head. Taking out a pad of paper and a pencil, Angus O'Malley flipped over several pages until he came to an unmarked one and commented, "This must be the fine animal that dispatched the demon bobcat to meet its Maker, am I correct?" and he was already scribbling furiously onto his notepad.

"Well…yes…"

Looking beyond Emma and ignoring the snarling dog, Angus O'Malley spotted the boys on the rug by the hearth. "And just what have we here?" he shouted, brushing past Emma and the dog. "Could one of you be the intended victim? But, oh my goodness! Which one? For I surely must be seeing double! Twins, unless my eyes deceive me?" he asked in Emma's direction.

"Twins…"

"Should I say, 'Eeney, meeney, miney mo' or will the true little hero step forward?" delivered with a large, white smile at George and Will, as Angus O'Malley wagged his finger back and forth between the two boys. Brute approached the reporter from behind and shoved his nose between the split in the back of the man's coat, sniffing loudly.

"How rude, doggie!" exclaimed Angus, brushing the dog's nose away while keeping his eyes fixed upon the twins.

Will found his tongue first, "I'm the one you want to see, Mr. O'Key-dokey. It's me, Will, the hero."

"His name is O'Malley, Will, and you are definitely NOT a hero," added George elbowing his way past Will to peer at the reporter's notepad. "Better take this down," said George looking into O'Malley's face. "I am the dog's trainer and that dog over there by my mother is the only hero in this room because he saved my little brother's life."

Looking confused, the reporter turned to Emma, "But I thought you said they were twins?"

"We are twins, but I am fourteen minutes older," insisted George, "which makes me the big, older brother."

"I see," said the reporter scribbling on his notepad. "And your name is?"

"George Miller Richardson."

"And he is?" poking the pencil in the direction of Will.

"William James Richardson."

"And she is?" pointing the pencil over his shoulder at Emma without turning.

"Emma Miller Richardson."

Brute barked. "Oh, of course, dear doggie, and you are?"

"Brute," replied Emma, "and I think perhaps…"

"Just a fabulous cast of characters! Oh, this is going to be sensational news on the front page of the Courier tomorrow morning!"

Will jumped up shouting, "Front page! Did you hear that, Ma? Me and Brute are gonna be on the front page of the newspaper!" Turning to George he boasted, "I told you I'd be famous!"

"And that's not all, friend Will!" exclaimed Angus at the beaming face of Will. "For I have also brought an illustrator from the paper with me, who, unless I miss my guess, is sketching Knacker Tom and the dead bobcat right about now. I know that he wants to sketch you and Brute here also. What say you, Mrs. Richardson, to a headline in your morning paper the likes of, DOG SAVES BOY FROM JAWS OF DEATH?" and he blocked out the headline with his hands in mid-air.

"A little melodramatic, do you not think, Mr. O'Malley?" responded Emma.

Turning back to Will, the reporter scribbled furiously again, "I think it is absolutely perfect! What do you think, young Will, Hero of Grandview?"

"Sounds perfect to me too," giggled Will.

Sticking the pencil behind his right ear and slipping the notepad in a pocket, the reporter said, "Fabulous! Then I shall just fetch the illustrator and we shall get down to business. Be back in a second!" and O'Malley turned to the front door, whereupon Brute repeated his private greeting of the reporter. "No, no, doggie! That is definitely not nice! We need to work on our manners," and he was gone out the front door.

George scratched his head, "Now how come Brute did not attack that reporter, Ma?"

"Well, I think Brute sensed that he is...that he is not a threat," whereupon Emma walked back to the kitchen to inform the others that they were about to receive company.

"Fabulous! Did you hear that, Georgie? Reporter O'Malley called me 'fabulous'!"

"He was not talking about you, Dummy!" admonished George. "He was saying it is fabulous that he is going to write the front page story for tomorrow's paper."

"Oh, yeah?"

"Definitely oh yeah!"

True to his word, Reporter Angus O'Malley returned with the paper's illustrator, who had a large sketchpad and several sticks of charcoal which he placed on the parlor table while he removed his scarf and coat. O'Malley likewise removed his coat and cap and both young men made themselves right at home by the fire, peppering the family with questions and sketching furiously. Brute had been barricaded into the kitchen and was whining loudly to join the gathering in the front room.

All at once, the front door burst open and in stomped Knacker Tom, leaving snow tracks all over the wooden floors in the foyer and the Aubusson rug in the parlor. "I sure could use a drink of something hot as I am half froze to death!"

Benni could hold her tongue no longer and looking at Emma, commented, "Perhaps we should station George just outside the front door to sell tickets? I believe you could clear enough to pay for your nursing school tuition!"

Wheeling around, Angus O'Malley stood with pencil poised in midair, "What was that I heard? Just who is it that is enrolled in nursing school? This lovely lady cradling the precious child?" Whereupon Johnny spit up all down the front of Benni's blouse from the excitement.

"Yes, well...perhaps that should be a story for another day," said Angus, moving away from Benni and Johnny, while checking his shirt front for traces of baby spittle.

Angus O'Malley and the illustrator for the Grandview Courier spent the next hour sipping hot tea and eating Mary's chocolate cookies by the fire, all the while scribbling notes and making sketches of everyone, including Brute on the other side of his kitchen barricade. Then, just as suddenly as he had appeared and with no further fanfare, the reporter stood and said, "Thank you ladies and gentlemen for your most kind assistance in providing us with the information necessary to do a fabulous piece for the newspaper. I am sure Master Richardson here will be quite famous by this time tomorrow as will the dear doggie in the kitchen. We must now bid you adieu and ta-ta!" The two young men were gone in a swirl of papers, pencils, charcoal sticks, coats, caps and scarves...out the door and into the twilight, making their way back to town as fast as they could manage on foot through the snow in order to meet the paper's deadline.

"Wow!" shouted Will. "I'm fabulous famous!"

"You are nothing of the sort!" snorted George. Dismantling Brute's barricade of chairs and putting on his coat, George said, "I am taking this fabulous famous dog of mine outside to pee before dinner."

Still clutching a charcoal sketch of himself that the young illustrator had given to him, Will skipped through the front hall and back to the kitchen. "I am so hungry," he declared that I could eat a..."

"Bobcat," supplied Benni. Everyone was still enjoying a good laugh when George came running into the kitchen, preceded by Brute.

"Constable Crawford is here! Constable Crawford is here!" he announced.

"Evenin' ladies," said Luke, removing his wide brimmed hat.

"Hand me your hat and coat, Constable, and I shall just hang them here by the back door," offered Mary.

"It surely does smell mighty fine in your kitchen, ma'am, and I don't mind tellin' you that I am possessed of a terrible hunger."

"Well, then, Constable, you have come to just the right place. Let us all repair to the dining room, shall we?" said Mary moving everyone along.

Dinner that evening was a lively affair with much recounting of the events of the last two days. Children and adults alike lingered at the table enjoying the merry and agreeable company of others, along with Mary's fine cooking. Fare-wells came late that night and bedtime even later for Emma's two oldest boys, who were wound tighter than tops. The house on High Point Avenue fairly rang with laughter that evening. It had been a long time since the grand home had sparkled so brightly.

True to Angus O'Malley's words, the headline emblazoned across the Grand-view Courier the next morning read, DOG SAVES BOY FROM JAWS OF DEATH, accompanied by two detailed sketches. One was a composite of Will and Brute and the other was of Knacker Tom holding the dead bobcat upside down by his hind legs. Will became the center of everyone's attention and was quite taken with his new-found fame, prompting George to complain to his mother, "This is not fair! That reporter guy did not mention me once in the newspaper and it is MY DOG!"

Emma's response was, "Perhaps you now realize how your brother feels when you grab most of the attention away from him."

Too soon the Christmas recess drew to a close, melting away with the holiday snow, and it was time to see Benni off to her family in Clarksburg, then the boys to Miss Rita and finally, Emma to Nurse Fanella Walker.

CHAPTER 12

▼

On the boys' first day back at school, Will insisted upon taking Brute for Show and Tell along with a copy of the Grandview Courier. "Now, if Miss Rita does not allow Brute to remain in the schoolhouse for the day, you boys will have to walk him back home. Do you understand, George and Will?"

"I understand that I am not going to help Will show off with my dog one lick," huffed George.

"There, there George! Smooth those ruffled feathers of yours. This will all blow over soon enough," and kissing their heads, Emma stood waving to her sons as they headed across the avenue into town with the great dog frisking around their legs.

Then turning south toward the river, she adjusted Johnny upon her hip, took up the leather valise and made her way down to the ferry, just as a light rain began to fall. On the other side of the Southport, the roads were slushy and Emma had to lift her skirts, the valise and grip the baby while trying to maintain her footing on the slick boardwalks up through town to Angel of Mercy Hospital.

Nurse Walker had magnanimously agreed to forego any homework assignments over the Christmas recess and Emma had relished the free time with her children, her mother and friends. Once again Emma's misgivings beset her as she struggled to reach the hospital through the inclement weather.

She worried about her flagging strength that morning as she walked past the usual storefronts still hung with the red and green of Christmas. As long as she kept herself in motion, caring for her patients, playing with the boys, making beds, washing dishes, tending the baby, walking into town, Emma summoned the ability to grind away at the heavy dose of responsibility which she had shouldered. "This is all my own doing," she reminded herself silently as she picked her way along Chestnut Street, feeling that her arms would drop off at any second.

Emma had noticed a disquieting tendency in herself in recent weeks to doze off whenever she sat down to complete a task, such as mending or reading lessons for the next day's class. The boys would frequently nudge her shoulders saying, "You're asleep again, Ma," as she nodded over the sock she was darning by the fire, or the chapter in her nursing manual that she needed to read.

Emma was just about to turn into the gates of Mercy Hospital when her gaze came to rest on the stone church across the street. Looking up at the clock in the hospital bell tower, Emma realized that she had some time before class began. Gripping Johnny, the valise and her skirts ever tighter, Emma minced her way across Chestnut Street to the church. Pulling open one great wooden door by its black iron handle, Emma entered the hushed interior of the church.

Passing the font of holy water, she made her way slowly to the front of the sanctuary where an imposing statue of Jesus on the cross dominated the wall behind the altar. Candles glowed softly from glass cups on the altar and on a table off to one side. Emma slid into the second pew off the center aisle and placed Johnny, who was dozing, on the wooden bench along with her valise. Kneeling on the riser in front of her with her hands folded on the back of the first pew, Emma took in the beauty of the stations of the cross as depicted in stained glass that lined both sides of the sanctuary. Once again her gaze came to rest upon the statue of Jesus and she began to weep uncontrollably.

Bowing her head, she prayed haltingly, "Oh Heavenly Father, I am unworthy to come before You this morning! Forgive me please, for I have no where else to go! You are my strength and my salvation and therefore it is to You that I turn for help in my hour of need." She paused to take out her handkerchief, struggling to regain her composure.

Looking up at Christ where He hung before her on the cross, Emma continued her silent prayer, "I beg You, Lord Jesus, You who suffered and endured so much for us all, please help me now for I do not know if I possess the strength to carry on..." and she resumed her weeping. "Forgive me for these tears of self-pity," she continued praying, wiping her eyes, "but I feel overwhelmed and sorely in need of Your help as I do not intend to...I must not fail my children or my mother. I am weak but You are strong and I humbly beseech You to grant me Your strength to carry on for my family. With You to guide me, I shall not fail! Amen."

Emma wiped away her tears, gathered up her sleeping child once again along with the valise and left the calm of the church to face the life she had chosen for herself.

A man and his muddy horse were slogging down Chestnut Street in the rain pulling a load of supplies covered with canvas in the back of a buckboard. Emma stood under the overhanging eave at the entrance to the church until the buckboard had passed and with it, the threat of spraying mud. As quickly as she could safely manage, Emma picked her way across the street and along the boardwalk to the gates of Angel of Mercy.

Once inside the hospital, she climbed the long flight of stairs up to the second floor to find Eleanor Tyler in the children's ward. As the nurse looked up from her paperwork, Emma greeted her, "Hello, Eleanor. Did you have a happy holiday?"

"I did indeed and how about yourself?" asked Eleanor in return, taking Johnny, still sleeping, from his mother's arms.

"It was most eventful, thank you for asking, but entirely too short."

"Is that not always the case?" Eleanor sighed. "Shall we see you around noon?"

"Of course," replied Emma kissing the dozing child. With her fingers still lightly touching Johnny, Emma paused for several long seconds to look at her child in the arms of Eleanor before turning to resume her studies with Nurse Walker in the basement of the building.

Her fellow nursing students all seemed to be echoing her sentiments when Emma entered the classroom. It was hard to return to the grind but for Emma, the decision to return was made even harder with each departure from her three children. Each day was like the first…filled with a silent intensity of emotion as she looked into their faces and it was never to get any better. With each new day, Emma had to shore up her resolve to walk her chosen path anew.

"Hello, Emma!" called Sarah Mayhugh from across the room. "Today is the day," she warned Emma who waved at her friend but with a vacant expression. "Surely you must remember, Emma? This is the day that we find out if Dr. McKendrick's gallbladder patient survived his surgery."

"Well, how could I forget, Sarah, with you to remind me?" laughed Emma.

Emma yawned her way through class and, making herself as small and inconspicuous as possible behind the girls in front, she managed to escape Nurse Walker's attention and the dreaded work at the board. Just before noon, Nurse Fanella Walker told her students that they would be making rounds with several of the doctors in the afternoon following the lunch break. Nurse Walker admonished the women to take copious notes on the patients' progress, vital statistics and any additional treatments ordered by the attending physicians, all of which would be topics for discussion the next day. Just as the student nurses were exiting the classroom, Nurse Walker approached Emma.

"Did you and the children and Mary enjoy the holidays?"

"We certainly did and how about yourself, Nurse Walker?"

"Lovely, simply lovely and thank you for asking. Now Richardson, in regard to your tuition. I was hoping that you might begin to assist the other nurses with their chores for a few hours each day in order to subsidize your tuition requirement as we discussed that day over in Grandview. I trust you remember the arrangement?" Fanella Walker looked over the top of her pince-nez glasses at Emma.

"But of course I remember. I am eager to meet my financial obligation to the hospital for taking me on as a student at half the cost."

"Splendid. I envision that you will change and make beds, give bed baths, empty bedpans, feed patients, clean up the lab for the interns and generally be available to assist where needed. I know that most of the duties which I have outlined usually come during the second year as a student begins her practical experience but your class work, your grades, your homework and your overall abilities would suggest that an accelerated curriculum might be more suited to your needs. Your level of academic achievement combined with your personal maturity indicate to me that I must move you along more rapidly than the others. I can honestly say that I believe you to be one of the most gifted students that our hospital has ever seen."

Emma looked wanly at Nurse Walker and made no response but mentally wondered how she was going to manage all of these new duties on top of her existing program of studies.

Seeing the look on Emma's face, Nurse Walker hastened to add, "Of course, in order to fulfill these duties you would be excused from most of the classroom work, but not homework, tests or papers." She paused to scrutinize Emma's features, looking for any hint of vacillation. "Can you meet the demands of an altered schedule?"

Without hesitation, Emma replied simply, "But of course."

"Excellent, Emma. I knew I could count on you. This afternoon, I want you to tag along after Dr. McKendrick with six other student nurses. Here is the duty sheet with everyone divided up into groups of seven. After the noon recess, I want you to make sure that each girl knows who her assigned doctor is and stress to everyone the importance of taking notes for tomorrow's class. Now, you and I need to go up two flights to the women's ward where I shall brief you on the patients that you will be tending in the morning in lieu of class. Any questions so far?" and Nurse Walker again scrutinized Emma's face.

"No Nurse Walker. I am ready to begin."

"Do watch yourself on these stairs, Richardson," said Nurse Walker smiling and indicating to Emma that she should grip the handrail. "Rule number one is always remain vertical!"

When the two women reached the second floor, Nurse Walker pointed to the Women's Ward sign, "Of course, I realize that since you have Johnny around the corner there in the Children's Ward," pointing to the right, "you are more than a bit familiar with this floor already. Through that large door to the left are your patients who, as you can see, are divided in beds along the outer walls." Fanella paused at the nurses' station, "Nurse Stewart, this is Richardson, the student that I told you about earlier today."

Nurse Stewart came out from behind the cubicle to greet Emma. "I'm pleased to meet you Richardson." Turning to Fanella Walker she asked, "Do you want me to brief her about our patients' case histories or do you intend to do that?" Nurse Stewart asked.

"I shall maintain control of the reins as Emma is still technically my student and must report to me directly. Her duties will be as we discussed. Remember, under no circumstances is Richardson permitted to mix or dispense medications." Turning sharply to Emma, Fanella further admonished her, "If I so much as catch a glimpse of you standing in front of the locked medicine cabinet over there, I shall expel you from the program. Understood?"

"Understood, Nurse Walker," replied Emma.

"Good. Then, let me tell you about our patients," and Nurse Walker strode up and down between the double row of white metal beds reciting case histories without so much as a glance at the charts which hung at the foot of each bed. "Remember to put up the privacy screen when bathing patients or assisting them with bedpans or anything of a similarly sensitive nature. These are human beings who are placed in our care and we shall treat them with respect. They all deserve to leave here with their dignity intact. Do you understand me, Richardson?"

"Absolutely, I do," responded Emma.

"Just so! Now, I believe you must hurry across the hall to feed your Johnny before you meet with your fellow student nurses at one o'clock. Good luck, Richardson," and she stuck out her hand to Emma, who was surprised both by the unfamiliar gesture and the strength of Nurse Walker's grip.

As the clock in the bell tower struck one, Emma entered the classroom and walked to the podium to address her classmates. Everyone turned around to look for Nurse Walker and not seeing her, turned again toward Emma.

"Ladies, I have been appointed by Nurse Walker to hand out duty assignments this afternoon. We are to be divided into groups of seven and each group will then proceed to make rounds with one of five doctors. This is an exercise that has been arranged especially for us so please remember what Nurse Walker would say if she were here: 'Observe, listen and be silent', to which I would add a fourth admonition and that is, 'Take detailed notes.'" All the girls snickered.

"I am going to divide everyone into five teams with captains for each team and then I shall give you the name of your doctor for this afternoon. For example, I am team captain for group number one, with Dr. McKendrick, and the members of my group are: Conrad, Mayhugh, Bennington, Griffith, Lawrence and Sellers. Please line up over here to my right."

As Emma proceeded to organize the rest of the class into teams, one student was prompted to call out, "I don't see why you are so high and mighty all of a sudden, Emma."

"Because of my advanced years," Emma responded wryly, to much laughter.

"Yes," called out another girl, "age before beauty," and everyone again laughed.

"All right now teams, let us proceed to our assigned duty stations," Emma announced and then to her own team said, "We are to meet Dr. McKendrick in the solarium so let us be on our way now, single file please and no talking."

Quietly Emma and her team filed up the stairs to the marble caduceus and then right toward the solarium where she could see Dr. McKendrick already impatiently pacing back and forth.

"Ahoy, ladies," he greeted the team of seven student nurses when he caught sight of them coming down the hall. "Gather around here and let me tell you briefly what you will be seeing this afternoon. First stop will be the Men's Ward where I shall check on a recent below the knee amputation and a gallbladder surgery from two weeks ago."

Emma shot an I-told-you-so look at Sarah Mayhugh, who ignored the smirks, raised eyebrows and nudges of her compatriots.

"From there," continued Dr. McKendrick, "we shall visit the Surgical Ward to check on my goiter surgery from this morning, then..." scratching his bald head, "let me think. Ah yes, a visit to the Maternity Ward where we shall check on a patient who is due to have her eighth baby shortly and mind you, she never should have had the first seven. Then to the Women's Ward where you will all meet the beloved and elderly Mrs. Ford who is a permanent resident of Angel of Mercy and whatever else strikes my fancy as we go along. Are we ready, Mates?" he called out to the students.

"Aye, aye, Captain," said Emma with a crisp salute of her hand.

Dr. McKendrick looked at Emma in astonishment as did the other six student nurses. "Well, uh, Richardson," Dr. McKendrick said reading her name tag. "Nurse Walker failed to tell me that we had a sailor on board. What a pleasure, what a pleasure," and he wrung Emma's hand for several long seconds.

Emma and her team followed briskly in the wake of Dr. McKendrick's long, flapping white coat as they made their way onto the Men's Ward. Their leader stopped at the third bed on the left where Dr. McKendrick greeted the dozing patient, "Joseph, how are you feeling today, my boy?"

Whereupon, Joseph opened his eyes and answered, "I'm feeling plum poorly today, sir."

"Oh, and why is that?" asked Dr. McKendrick, pulling back the man's sheet and blanket to expose the stump of his right leg which was heavily bandaged and seeping blood. Irene Sellers gasped.

"Silence!" ordered Dr. McKendrick.

Emma glared at Irene.

"Let us take a closer look at that leg, son," and Dr. McKendrick began unwinding the blood-soaked bandages, "but do go on and tell me why you are feeling poorly. Does the leg pain you?"

"No sir, it isn't that. It's just...it's just that I don't know what I'm going to do with only half a leg. I've a wife and four children..." and his voice faded.

"Joseph, son, take a look at yourself from the waist on down and tell me what you see."

"What I see, sir, is a man with half a leg."

"Perhaps you should count again, Joseph, for I count one and a half legs." Dr. McKendrick paused dramatically to let his words penetrate the man's head while he continued to unwrap and examine the sutured stump. "What did you say your trade is, son?"

"I didn't say, sir, but I'm a gunsmith."

"Now there is a trade worth knowing, would you agree, Richardson?" asked Dr. McKendrick turning to Emma for affirmation.

"Absolutely, sir," replied Emma taking the bloody bandages off the bed and placing them in a bin marked, 'Contaminated'.

Dr. McKendrick began to wash his hands in alcohol in a basin and motioned to Emma that she was to do likewise. "Slip a fresh towel under here," Dr. McKendrick indicated the man's stump.

Emma gently lifted the upper half of Joseph's right leg and slid a clean towel underneath, all the while keeping her eyes fastened on Joseph's eyes to ascertain his level of discomfort. He winced as Dr. McKendrick began to probe the wound.

"Now as I was saying, a reputable gunsmith is vital to our community and I assure you, my young friend, that we here in Clarksburg would be in dire straits without your considerable skills. Surely it is not your intention to give up your trade over an insignificant loss such as this?" he asked pointing to the non-existent lower portion of the man's leg.

"But how can I carry on like this?" asked Joseph sorrowfully.

"Richardson, he asks me how he can carry on! Please give him the answer while I hunt up some fresh bandages," and Dr. McKendrick abandoned his patient and his student nurses to rummage through the supply closet.

Everyone's eyes were riveted on Emma, waiting for her response to the question that still hung in the fetid air. Emma cleared her throat, "Joseph, you do not have the luxury of choice, for the decision to carry on has already been made for you."

When Joseph looked puzzled, Emma reached over to his bedside table and picked up a tintype of the young man's family. "Your wife and four children have already made the decision for you. You must carry on for them, with twelve legs or with no legs at all. Would you abandon your loved ones to such a cruel fate as life without you to provide for them? Would you inflict suffering on them forever because you have lost half of one leg, Joseph? Consider the needs of others, Joseph. Consider these five lives," and she handed the tintype to the young patient.

Several of the student nurses dabbed at their eyes with handkerchiefs and all stood silently waiting for Dr. McKendrick to return. "Well, now, where were we? Ah, yes, that stump needs a fresh dressing and I have just the ticket here," said Dr. McKendrick waiving a bandage roll. The great surgeon had seemingly failed to grasp what truly needed his healing touch.

Finishing at Joseph's bedside, Dr. McKendrick moved the little group down several beds to his gallbladder patient. "Look who we have here, ladies, and better than new, I might add," Dr. McKendrick boasted. Turning to the patient, the surgeon addressed him, "Now, sir, what you may not realize is that all these lovely student nurses here are intimately acquainted with your gallbladder. Is that not so, students?"

"Aye, aye sir," they all chorused on cue from Emma.

With an audible harrumph, Dr. McKendrick turned back to his patient and said, "Now, sir we are going to just have a peek at that incision of yours," whereupon the doctor pulled down the sheet to the man's groin area and lifted the hospital nightshirt. "Absolutely beautiful, would you not agree, ladies?" asked Dr. McKendrick admiring his own handiwork.

"Total perfection," Emma answered for her charges.

"You will note that I removed the man's stitches some two days ago and the wound is completely healed." Turning back to the man in the bed, Dr. McKendrick asked, "Have you been up and about today, sir?"

"Yes, I have left my bed to pee and wash up a bit."

"Good work, good work," answered Dr. McKendrick and with his back still to the students continued to address the patient. "I must tell you sir that it has come to my attention that two of our student nurses here today actually engaged in a bet following your surgery. It would seem that one of the students bet that you would leave this fine hospital in a pine box and the other student had the good sense to bet that you would fully recover from your surgery and walk out on your own two legs. So that there may be absolutely no doubt as to which victor go the spoils, would you do me the honor of leaving your hospital bed and walking around a bit?"

Smirking at the student nurses and folding his arms across his chest, Dr. McKendrick moved to one side to allow his patient to demonstrate that he was now fully ambulatory. "Fine job, lad! Fine job! I should think that by this time tomorrow, you might just leave us and rejoin your family. How does that sound to you?"

"I was hoping you might release me today, doctor," said the disappointed man.

"One more day of hospital food should put the finishing touches on your recovery and speaking of food," Dr. McKendrick turned to look squarely at Sarah Mayhugh, "I now declare that you owe both Richardson and me coffee with cake this afternoon at the Water Street Bakery."

Sarah's mouth dropped open in utter amazement. "Now we shall move to the Surgical Ward, ladies," announced Dr. McKendrick. Humming to himself, he retraced his steps to the front of the Men's Ward and down the hall to the recovery ward for new surgical patients. The doctor stopped at the nurses' station and asked, "How is my goiter patient progressing?"

"Not as well as expected, I am afraid, Dr. McKendrick," was the reply.

"Really? And just why not?"

"Well, it would seem that our patient fibbed about not eating after six o'clock last night and she has been violently ill, throwing up food everywhere. I thought to summon you as I am terribly concerned that she may rip out her sutures with all the violent heaving."

"Damnation! Why is it that the patients conspire against me? I tell them no food after six o'clock in the evening before their surgery that is scheduled for the next morning and they deliberately eat all manner of disgusting foods that would make a goat puke."

Dr. McKendrick strode over to the patient's bed where she was being cleaned up by a nurse after retching into an enamel basin. Grabbing the basin from the nurse, Dr. McKendrick shoved it under his patient's nose. "Just what in tarnation is this? Last night's dinner eaten at nine o'clock, today's breakfast consumed at one o'clock in the morning and high tea three hours later? Did you think my intention was to starve you to death? I explained to you that you might become ill from the ether."

Turning to the student nurses, Dr. McKendrick explained in a tone rife with disdain, "The more a patient has in her stomach, the more vomiting...the more vomiting, the more damage is done to sutures, especially when a goiter in the neck has been removed and then all my fine work is for naught...to say nothing of the imminent danger of death due to the aspiration of vomitus."

"Keep me informed of her progress but it is quite apparent to me that she is in for a rough time of it," and he turned back to the students. "Upstairs, ladies to the Women's Ward."

Again Emma and the other six dutifully trudged behind Dr. McKendrick in silence. Upstairs at the nurses' station of the Women's Ward, Dr. McKendrick paused at the desk behind the long wooden counter and not finding Nurse Stewart, rapped loudly upon the counter with his knuckles. "Nurse Stewart, are you hiding from me? Come out, come out wherever you are!" he admonished the air behind the counter.

Nurse Stewart came hurrying down the aisle between the double row of beds, wiping her hands on a towel. "Please pardon me sir, as I was just completing a bed bath and I could not leave my damp patient to become chilled."

"Excuses, excuses! How I detest excuses! Where in thunder is Valeda's chart? I can see quite clearly from here that it is not where it should be at the foot of her bed," said Dr. McKendrick accusingly, jabbing his finger in the direction of the fourth bed on the right.

"Yes, sir. That is correct. The chart is out of place, just here," and Nurse Stewart reached over the counter to retrieve the patient's chart from a shelf, "as I had intended to make some notes…"

"The rule is always keep the chart with the patient so that I may find the chart immediately. It is such a total waste of my time to be running around looking for a chart. Do you understand?" he asked grabbing the chart from her hand.

"Of course, sir. I apologize."

"Just see that it does not happen again," and Dr. McKendrick brushed past Nurse Stewart to bed four on the right. "And here, ladies, we have Mrs. Valeda Suggs, one of my favorite patients and mother of eight children, all girls. How are you feeling, my dear? Have you nursed that baby of yours yet?" Dr. McKendrick busily flipped through the pages of Valeda's chart to read the progress notes of the nurses.

"I'm feelin' fit as a fiddle, doc, and yes, my milk done come in and that babe of mine is a real good feeder."

"Just the sort of news I wanted to hear," responded the doctor. "But Valeda my dear, this must be absolutely the last child of yours that I deliver as I fear one more may kill you. You and that fine virile husband of yours have enough mouths to feed. Your family alone accounts for half the population of our county," and Dr. McKendrick laughed at his own bad joke while Emma and the other students exchanged glances. "Have you thought of sleeping in separate beds?" persisted the doctor.

"Indeed I have, doc, but it don't make no difference no how 'cause Calvin just hunts me down and next thing I know he's havin' a poke," and she grinned at the student nurses showing a mouthful of rotten teeth with several already missing.

"Perhaps more drastic measures would be appropriate, Valeda. After you are healed from the birthing of this child, I want you to come and talk to me about a surgery I can perform for you that will eliminate any further pregnancies. In the mean time, keep nursing that baby so that you do not conceive a ninth child. I shall check on you tomorrow."

"Thank you, doc, and thank you ladies for listenin' too," and Valeda flashed her rotten, toothy smile again.

As Burris McKendrick moved on down the ward between the double row of beds, he commented to the student nurses, "And now ladies, you are going to meet my favorite patient, Edna Ford, blind from birth and since crippling arthritis set in some years ago, a permanent resident of this hospital."

"Edna, my dear, it is old Burr come to aggravate you on an otherwise peaceful winter afternoon. How is my favorite girl today?" and he reached out, touching the wizened old women lightly on her arm.

Edna responded by turning her head toward the sound of his voice, "Well, you old bastard, how the hell do you think I am?" and she smiled in his direction while her opaque, sightless eyes wandered aimlessly back and forth under a fringe of short, salt and pepper colored hair.

"I have brought some company for you today, Dame Edna." Turning to the student nurses, Burris became positively cordial, "Permit me to introduce Emma Richardson, Louise Bennington, Sarah Mayhugh, Ruby Lawrence, Irene Sellers, Lilly Conrad and Florence Griffith, all fine first year nursing students here at Angel of Mercy." The women looked at each other in amazement as Dr. McKendrick correctly recited all their names.

Edna Ford responded by lifting her gnarled right hand out in front of her. Emma edged over to the side of the woman's bed and gently took the hand that had been offered in greeting. "Which one do we have here?" asked Edna.

"I am Emma Richardson, Mrs. Ford."

"What a lovely soft touch you have my dear," commented Edna. She turned her head toward Burris and added, "Unlike that old bastard over there who delights in tormenting my flesh and my joints with those callused paws of his!" Surprised by the salty language, the girls tittered.

"Go easy on the girls, Edna, for my sake as I do not relish the thought of being called 'the old bastard' behind my back in their class tomorrow."

"Trust me, Burr, you are called far worse behind your back. I may be blind but my hearing is still splendidly intact."

Turning her head back in the direction of the student nurses, Edna was prompted to add, "You know, whenever I hear someone slandering old Burr, I always encourage them to slander him to his face. Knowing what others really think about him helps keep our divine physician humble. But say…can you guess why I call him 'Burr'?" asked Mrs. Ford of her audience.

"Would it be a derivative of his given name of 'Burris'?" asked Benni.

"Good guess, but actually I call him 'Burr' because he is such a damned bur under my saddle…always there to irritate me!"

"Coming from a woman who has never sat astride a horse in all of her seventy years!" added Burris joining in the laughter.

Edna began to cough from so much laughing so Emma offered her a sip of water from the blue enamel pitcher and cup by her bedside. "Thank you my dear.

Burr always has such an effect on me! Now, you old rascal, did you bring my tobacco and cigarette papers?"

"Surely your nose can tell you that I have indeed remembered your tobacco," admonished the doctor waving a cloth bag in front of Edna's face. "You who can smell a fart all the way downstairs, out the front door and down by the waterfront!"

"Well, then damn it, roll and light one for me as these nurses of yours are such cowards, afraid to put a cigarette to their lips by day but by night, they can scarcely wait to put their lips upon their husbands'…"

"Edna…Edna, my dear!" admonished Burris. "Let us remember not to embarrass my young students! Soon enough they will become hardened to your tongue, but not just yet, my sweet."

With that, Burris took out a small clip of cigarette papers and removing one thin white sheet, placed a bit of tobacco in the center. Deftly he rolled it to the edge which he then moistened with his tongue before sealing the cigarette. Placing the finished cigarette in his mouth, he struck a match, lit it, took a drag, exhaled and then placed it in Edna's mouth.

All seven women had been totally riveted by this long exchange between doctor and patient and now they turned to look in disbelief at one another. Edna inhaled deeply, savoring the smoke before letting it out in rings that floated around her head like miniature haloes. With the slender cigarette balanced precariously between the gnarled thumb and third finger of her right hand, Edna inhaled and exhaled its smoke in silence for several long seconds.

To her stunned audience, Edna explained, "I know what you are thinking, 'Why is the old bastard encouraging his patient to smoke…and a woman at that?' Am I right?"

"Yes, ma'am," chorused the horrified student nurses.

"Well, ladies, take a close look at me and what you will see is a woman of seventy, blind since birth, completely crippled up for these last several years and in terrible pain," Edna said unflinchingly. "The sainted old bastard here knows that one of the few measures he can exercise to alleviate my pain is a smoke of this fine tobacco and so he indulges me and I absolutely love the man for it. Burr is the roughest cut of diamond anywhere on the face of the earth but he out sparkles the rest."

Each of the seven student nurses swallowed hard.

"Oh, tut, tut, my dear!" admonished Dr. McKendrick in response. "One could imagine whole legions of women lined up for miles just to have me roll them a smoke if you persist with this sweet talk of yours."

"Well, perhaps the legions of ladies should not line up for one of your badly rolled cigarettes but I would surely advise them to line up in rain, sleet, snow or draught in order to be the recipients of your considerable healing powers," and Edna Ford beamed in the direction of Dr. McKendrick.

"Edna, my dear, you positively make me blush with all your inane ravings."

Edna turned her head in the direction of Emma, "Is he blushing child? Tell me quickly."

"Even his toes are bright red," responded Emma.

Leaning back into her pillows Edna sighed dramatically. "Just as I thought. He really does love me." After a long pause to puff on her cigarette, she added smiling, "Now, get your ugly ass out of here, Burr, as I am quite worn out with all your arduous courting."

Burris McKendrick leaned over the old woman and kissed her lightly upon the forehead, "Until tomorrow, my sweet," and the doctor turned to leave.

"See what I mean, girls? The man cannot leave me alone," and Edna Ford resumed her puffing.

Out in the corridor beyond the door to the Women's Ward, Burris McKendrick turned to his student nurses, "Say, I have just had a splendid notion. Since we have finished my rounds early and Sarah here owes Emma a cake and coffee, how about if we repair to the Water Street Bakery right this very minute? I feel absolutely obligated to ascertain for myself that Sarah pays dearly for daring to question my skills as a surgeon. I insist that all of you run along, fetch your wraps and meet me at the caduceus in ten minutes," then with a flurry of white coat-tails, Burris was gone.

"I don't know what to make of that man," Florence finally broke the silence as they all stood motionless watching Dr. McKendrick disappear down the staircase. "One minute he is badgering and bullying and the next, he is rolling cigarettes for a sightless, crippled old lady."

"Yes," chimed in Lilly, "one minute I am Student Nurse Peon and the next minute he can recite my name and all of yours and wants to have coffee with us," she said shaking her head in amazement.

"Well, if you ask me," added Irene, "the man is just an old eccentric who has been sniffing ether from the canisters too long."

"Perhaps," remarked Emma from the back of the group still peering down the stairs, "the man is a genius. Difficult and brilliant at the same time. I say we get to know the man before we pass judgment upon him. Obviously today is just the beginning of our odyssey with Dr. McKendrick and lest you forget, I could cer-tainly use a good cup of coffee with cream and one of those little chocolate cakes with frosting right about now, eh, Sarah?" Whereupon Emma grinned at her friend and poked her in the ribs as she began to descend the stairs.

As the doctor and his student nurses emerged from the entrance to Mercy, a light rain was still falling. "Did any one remember to bring her bumbershoot?" asked Burris McKendrick.

"I did," responded Ruby Lawrence, offering to share her umbrella with the doctor.

The rest of the girls pulled hoods or scarves over their heads and cautiously picked their way across Chestnut Street which was rapidly becoming a quagmire of mud. Skirts held high, they all made it to the other side without falling. Dr. McKendrick called back to them over his shoulder, "I would place my coat in the street to make the crossing easier for all of you, but I must address a group of 'greenies' this evening and having their Chief of Staff appear before them in a mud-spattered coat would not inspire the necessary level of confidence or the reverence which I require, would you agree?"

"What will inspire their confidence and reverence, sir," responded Emma shielding her head and shoulders from the rain, "is not the condition of the surgeon's garment. For I daresay that once you begin to address these residents, they will little note or care about the condition of your clothing, focusing instead on the import of your words. I for one would volunteer, therefore, to use your coat as a bridge!"

Everyone was laughing at Emma's remark when they entered the Water Street Bakery and stood looking at the delicious array of cakes, cookies and tarts in the glass case that spanned the width of the store. The young clerk that Emma knew by sight came forward to ask, "May I offer anyone a fresh cookie this afternoon? We have some pumpkin and molasses ones just out of the oven here on this tray," and she took up a spatula in preparation for serving up their selections.

"Indeed," spoke up Dr. McKendrick, I shall take a dozen of those cookies wrapped up for my family and then I then I should like to have a cup of black coffee and one of those marvelous looking items over there. What are those?"

"Eclairs, sir," responded the clerk.

"Yes, a yummy eclair for me, and by the by, I am paying for my seven hungry young friends here also, so do not take a cent of their hard-earned money."

Surprised, Sarah looked over at Emma who put an index finger to her lips, indicating silence. Emma was last and after she had received her cup of coffee with cream and a delectable looking chocolate iced cake, the clerk asked her quietly, "Do you remember when you came into the bakery with your baby son and I told you that I also have a baby his age?"

"Yes, of course, I remember," answered Emma smiling. "How is your baby?" she asked taking a sip of the hot coffee.

"Not well, I am afraid," responded the clerk with a frown.

"I am sorry to hear that. What seems to be the trouble?" asked Emma.

"We are uncertain as to the trouble, Student Nurse Richardson. My baby is so very thin and cries all the time."

"Really?" asked Emma biting into her cake.

"Come sit with us!" called Lilly to Emma, gesturing with her hand to a place next to her at the table.

"I shall be right there." Turning back to the clerk, Emma asked, "Have you taken the baby to see a doctor?"

"No," was the answer. "I can't afford one."

"I see. Well, then, perhaps you could bring the baby to me at the hospital and I could arrange for a free examination by a nurse. Would that help?"

"Oh, yes, Student Nurse..."

"Please, do call me 'Emma'. What time could you bring the baby to the hospital tomorrow?"

"Around nine o'clock, if that's all right," answered the clerk.

"Good. Please bring him...what did you say his name is?"

"Daniel. Danny, I call him."

"Please bring Danny and yourself to the Women's Ward tomorrow morning at nine o'clock," said Emma turning to join the others at the table.

"I'm afraid you didn't understand. I must bring the baby at nine o'clock at night," the clerk called after Emma.

Turning sharply back to the clerk, a startled Emma repeated, "Nine o'clock at night? Why at that hour?"

"Because I work until five o'clock each evening and then it takes me another two hours to clean up the store and kitchen. Then I must walk south of here where Danny and I live with my mother, pick him up and walk back to the hospital."

"How far south of town is your mother's house?" persisted Emma.

"Almost two miles."

"Well, we cannot have that," frowned Emma and she was silent a moment. "Instead, how about if I come to you?"

"You are most kind, Emma, and I gladly accept your offer."

"Of course. Now give me directions to your mother's house and oh, by the way, what did you say your name is?"

"Rachel," responded the young clerk. "Rachel Johnson."

"All right then, Rachel, until tomorrow night at nine o'clock," and Emma joined the others.

"You're missing out on all the fun," chided Florence. "We've just been telling Dr. McKendrick here all about ourselves."

"Lying, mostly," laughed Benni, leaning forward to point her half-eaten cookie at Irene. "That one over there had the audacity to tell Dr. McKendrick that she was a princess from a faraway land and lived in a castle guarded by dragons."

Taking her seat, Emma joined in the merriment, "Sounds to me, Irene, as if you have been reading from the same book of fairy tales as Will and George!"

"Perhaps our most serious student, Emma Richardson, would tell me a bit about herself," suggested Dr. McKendrick. "It is your turn, after all," and he settled back to sip his cup of coffee while the rain tapped at the windows of the Water Street Bakery.

"Why, Dr. McKendrick, there really is nothing to tell. Just ask any of the girls here for they all know me to be an empty-headed twit, completely devoid of any useful scrap of information."

The doctor looked over the top of his glasses at Emma, "Are you fibbing to me, young woman?"

"Yes, she is fibbing. The truth of the matter is that Emma's life story would make a juicy novel pale by comparison," tattled Ruby.

"Very well, then. Out with it!" commanded Dr. McKendrick.

"Only on one condition," countered Emma.

"Which is?" he asked.

"That when I am finished, you too must take a turn at telling your life story."

"What could an old man like me have of interest to say to such a gathering of beauty and brains? Unless, of course, you would enjoy hearing a review of my technique for the removal of a gallbladder?"

"No, please!" groaned Sarah.

Emma nibbled at her cake and, sizing up the doctor, said, "I sense that there is some great sadness lurking just beneath your surface...a sadness that few are permitted to share."

"Oh, balderdash! I shall agree to tell you some personal tidbits but only after you go first."

All the other women at the table put down their pastries and their coffee cups and turned to look at Emma. Returning the gaze of each, Emma finally began, "Once upon a time on a cold and wintry morning one hundred years ago, a girl-child was born to goblins high in the mountains that ringed the little village of Neverwas…"

"Oh, Emma…do be serious!" admonished Benni.

"Who's telling lies now?" asked Lilly.

"Did I question the veracity of your origins when you were talking?" Emma asked of Lilly with a sly grin. "As I was saying before I was so rudely interrupted, the goblin parents were in a quandary about the unorthodox and unexpected arrival of this girl-child.

Now, it was well-known fact that goblins do not give birth to live offspring. Instead, it was customary for goblin parents to make a pilgrimage down the mountains and into the village of Neverwas in order to request an audience with their great and powerful leader, Behold. Once in front of the great Behold, the goblins were humble, bowing low and requesting an egg-child in polite voices."

"Emma, you have completely lost your mind! The pressures of going school and raising three children have obviously proven to be too great!" laughed Lilly.

"Shush, Lilly!" warned Dr. McKendrick. "Do go on, Emma. This is absolutely fascinating."

"But on this particular winter day, the goblin parents had decided to make their pilgrimage down the mountain and into the village of Neverwas to seek the wise counsel of their leader, Behold, for they did not know what to do with this girl-child that was not an egg-child.

Embarrassed to be seen with a girl-child that was not an egg-child, the goblin parents stuffed her into a basket and left her by the fireplace until their return from Neverwas. All the way down the mountain the goblin parents could hear the girl-child calling, 'Take me too! Take me too!' So, the goblins trudged back up the hill to their house and retrieved the basket which the goblin parents hid behind their backs as again they made their way down the mountain and into Neverwas."

Everyone around the table was silent, eyes riveted on Emma. "What happened next?" asked Florence, wide-eyed, coffee cup in midair.

"The goblin parents were granted a brief audience with their leader, Behold, but thinking to avoid the embarrassment of getting caught with a girl-child, the parents again tried to leave the basket behind, whereupon the girl-child began to wail, 'Take me too! Take me too!' Well, when the great Behold heard the cries of the girl-child, he commanded the goblin parents to bring him this thing called, 'Takemetoo'. But when the goblin parents opened the basket for Behold…Takemetoo Neverwas!"

At the conclusion of her tale, Emma collapsed in hysterics on the table, nearly spilling her coffee. Everyone looked around, momentarily uncomprehending until, one by one, the girls and Dr. McKendrick caught on to Emma's joke and joined in the laughter.

"Never saw it coming," guffawed Dr. McKendrick.

Irene began to hiccup uncontrollably from laughing so violently. "Sarah, hold her arms straight up over her head, like this," ordered Dr. McKendrick, demonstrating with his own arms, "and you, Ruby, make her drink from her coffee cup."

After the laughter and the hiccupping had subsided, the young women began to say their farewells until the only two remaining at the table in the Water Street Bakery were Emma and the doctor. Rachel bustled around them for a few moments picking up the empty coffee cups and plates edged with yellow and blue. Wiping the table clean of crumbs she asked, "Is there anything more that I can get for the two of you?"

"Oh, no thank you, Rachel," and turning to Dr. McKendrick, Emma added, "That was a lovely gesture for you to make. I mean paying for all of us to enjoy coffee and pastries. At the very least, you should have insisted that Sarah pay for mine, since she clearly lost the bet."

"I wanted to make the point that I am not really the old son of a bitch that our beloved Mrs. Ford tries to make me out to be for I do have a heart," and he tapped lightly upon the left side of his chest, smiling at Emma.

"We all now know you possess a very large and grand heart, Dr. McKendrick," Emma smiled back across the table. "But, I still think you are holding some dark secret locked away in that heart of yours. Perhaps you could tell me now that we are alone."

Burris McKendrick traced imaginary circles on the dark wood of the table with his right index finger. Shifting his gaze beyond the glass storefront window with its display of pastries, he remarked aimlessly, "All this rain has been absolutely diabolical. Makes it almost impossible to get around. As you can see just outside the window, the streets are nearly empty. Guess no one relishes the thought of a mud bath this evening."

Emma persisted, "You were going to share that secret with me...the one that causes you to be so ebullient one moment and so morose the next."

"But, my dear, as you can plainly see," and here the doctor rubbed the top of his bald head, "there is not one thing up here to share."

"Actually, Dr. McKendrick, I was referring to what is in here," and Emma traced a heart on the left side of her blouse.

Dr. McKendrick was silent, staring out the window at the muddy street. "Did I understand Fanella to say that you have three small sons?"

"Yes, that is correct. They are George and William, age seven, and Johnny age six months."

Looking at a point somewhere outside the bakery window, the doctor paused for a long while before stating flatly, "I have a daughter, Polly, age nine. Do you ever worry, Emma, about the fate of your children should something happen to you?" asked Dr. McKendrick shifting his gaze to examine her face.

"Indeed I do worry about that very situation, weekly, daily, hourly. I find myself in a constant state of worrying about the 'what-ifs', as my mother calls them," Emma answered honestly. "And you, Dr. McKendrick? Do you also worry about the 'what-ifs' for your Polly?"

"Incessantly," he replied bluntly. "Alas, it has become a most unhealthy preoccupation of mine and I do not know how to rid myself of this obsessive worry." The doctor paused, shaking his head sadly before continuing, "Can you pinpoint when your worries began?" he asked Emma searching her face.

"The night my husband ran away and left me with two children and a third who had yet to be born," was Emma's honest reply.

"I did not know such a torment existed in your young life!" exclaimed Dr. McKendrick.

"And you sir? When did your worries about Polly begin?"

"After I realized...when she...after she was several months old and I perceived that she was not normal. That is when the nightmare of worry began. I mean look at me, I am a man of fifty now, so when Polly was conceived I was forty and my wife was thirty five. It was too late, much too late to begin a family," said Dr. McKendrick shaking his head sadly. "But, as you might imagine, I was so engrossed in medicine and surgery, training all my young doctors and nurses that I just lost track of time...my personal time, that is.

In addition to all that, the right woman had not yet materialized. You know, the one who could understand that she would have to share me with my first mistress, medicine, and all my lesser but included whores, such as long hours away from home, incessant rappings upon my door in the middle of the night, picnics spoiled by tuberculosis-riddled lungs, amputations that could not wait for dinner, budgets to prepare for scrutiny by the hospital board, mounds of paperwork that forced me to wear glasses, et cetera, et cetera, et cetera. Do you see that it was all just too impossible to consider...even to contemplate a private life for myself?"

"Yes, I see," responded Emma simply. "But what does all of that have to do with Polly?"

"She was a baby delayed too long, both in the planning and in the birthing. Once again I was away catering to my first love on the very day that my wife needed me the most."

Emma thought to change the subject for Dr. McKendrick looked as if he were on the verge of weeping. Hardly pausing, however, the doctor reached across the table and squeezed Emma's hand as he said, "It was my fault that Polly was born palsied."

"How can you possibly fault yourself for an event that was an act of nature, completely beyond your control?" and Emma squeezed his hand back.

"But, you do not understand, my dear. I was away from my darling Cordy…Cordelia, when she went into labor. It was her…our first and we lived on the far outskirts of town at that time so there was no way for my wife to summon me. The baby was not due for two more weeks. So, when I departed our house that morning around five o'clock to tend to a man who had been seriously shot the previous day and would require six hours of surgery to repair the nasty wounds, I felt confident that Cordy would spend the day resting."

Burris McKendrick again looked past Emma out the window at the now empty street, once more lost in his private thoughts. "Well, look there!" he exclaimed suddenly, causing Emma to turn and peer out the window into the gloom of early evening.

"What is it, doctor?"

"It has stopped raining," he stated flatly.

"Yes, it surely has," responded Emma.

"Did you know it was raining the morning that I left her alone?" Dr. McKendrick barely paused before adding, "Cordy went into labor within an hour of my leave-taking and by mid-morning was giving birth alone. The poor dear woman had no idea what to do. She just lay upon our bed, fighting each contraction, each pain, in a state of total panic, blood and fluids everywhere," and tears began to well up in his eyes.

"You see, I had planned to be with her in two weeks…I had planned to take time off so that I could deliver the baby myself," and the tears spilled down his cheeks.

"Tell me exactly what happened to Cordelia and the baby," said Emma releasing her hold upon his hand.

Wiping his face with a handkerchief that he had removed from his breast pocket, Burris continued, "The baby was lodged in the birth canal too long and thus deprived of oxygen so that she suffered damage to her brain. When I arrived home, nearly an hour after Cordy had given birth, she and the baby were nearly dead. And damn it! I am a doctor! I have devoted my whole life to saving people! This should not have happened to me!"

Dr. McKendrick's sudden verbal explosion caught Emma off guard and she briefly drew back before responding, "Did you think that being a physician somehow would exempt you and your family from experiencing the same trage-dies as the rest of us?"

"Yes, by all that is holy, I did think just those very thoughts! I absolutely knew that I had been chosen...that if I lived an exemplary life, I would be spared some of life's harsher moments. It is all so unfair, do you see? I mean, why in heaven's name would the Almighty punish an innocent...a newborn baby? Punish me, yes, but please do not punish my child!"

Burris McKendrick lowered his bald head onto folded arms and wept uncon-trollably. Rachel, who had been busying herself cleaning up behind the counter, started around the end of the display case as if to offer assistance, but Emma waved her away. Rising from her chair across from the doctor, Emma moved to the bakery door where she turned over the paper sign to read "Closed". Pulling down the green shade behind the sign, Emma then went to the counter and qui-etly asked Rachel for two fresh cups of coffee.

Resuming her seat across from Dr. McKendrick, Emma cleared her throat and began speaking in a hushed voice, "Is this the first time that you have unbur-dened yourself to anyone?"

"Yes," answered Dr. McKendrick, "and I am feeling mighty ashamed of myself for having done so for I never, absolutely never, ever bother others with my problems because I know others look to me as one who is meant to solve their problems. Not the other way around."

Emma permitted herself a fleeting smile before she said, "Aye, there is the crux of your problem, doctor."

"What are you talking about?" Dr. McKendrick asked wiping his face and loudly blowing his reddened nose.

"You remind me of my sons with your logic, Dr. McKendrick, for you insist on scrambling up the facts to fit inside your head instead of seeing the truth of the matter."

Burris scowled at Emma over his fresh cup of coffee. "Harrumph! Is that so?" he responded, taking a big drink of the steaming hot coffee.

"Yes, it is quite so, dear doctor," and Emma eyed him owlishly over her cup of coffee. "It is abundantly clear to me that in your mind you have worked over this series of events, meaning your work habits, your marriage late in life, the early arrival of your child, the child's palsy and every other misfortune, mixed them all up in your head until you reached the absurd conclusion that your child has been punished for your so-called misdeeds.

Then, instead of talking about all these demons that you have conjured up in your head, you bid them to stay put for nine long years. Trust me," counseled Emma wagging a finger at the doctor, "I am eminently qualified to make such a diagnosis, seeing as how I made the very same mistake concerning personal difficulties in my own life. Perhaps it is just time for you to face the truth, doctor."

"Oh, really? And just what might be the truth according to Student Nurse Emma Richardson? Who, by the way, is more than just a tad bit uppity to address me thus!" he scolded her.

"The truth is that you need some help with your own problems, doctor, especially since you influence so many others, like Polly."

"Polly? She is being looked after very capably by my wife," said Dr. McKendrick defensively.

"Well, then let us start there. You said Polly is nine. Is she in school?"

"No. A child like Polly cannot possibly go to school," snorted Burris.

"A child like Polly?" asked Emma. "Very well, then. Let us start by having you tell me what Polly is like."

"Oh, nonsense."

"Tell me," she said again, leaning forward to look him in the eyes.

Drawing back slightly, Burris rubbed his bald head before answering, "All right…all right! She has a pronounced limp because her right leg is affected," and he looked past Emma at the street.

"Is that all?" she persisted.

"No, that is not all."

"Well, I am waiting! Honestly, Burris, trying to get you to talk is about like trying to pry the meat out of a mussel and you know the best way to do that is to steam it first, so shall I light a fire under you?" she grinned over at the startled doctor.

"Just who in tarnation gave you permission to call me 'Burris'?" he grinned back at Emma.

"I did," she responded sipping her coffee.

"You are surely one uppity young woman, but I like your style, Emma."

"I know you do and I like yours so get on with the answer to my question about Polly."

"Polly's right arm was also affected to the extent that it is drawn up in an 'L' shape," he answered, demonstrating the shape with his own right arm.

"Does she have friends...other children with whom she plays?" Emma persisted in her questioning of Burris.

"Oh, heavens, no. She is too different from the others. I fear they would scorn her. Children can be so cruel, you know."

"Yes, I do know," agreed Emma. "Does Polly read or write?"

"Cordy has been working diligently with her but to little avail, I am afraid."

"Do you recall that we began this conversation when you asked me if I ever worried about the fate of my children should anything happen to me?"

Burris nodded his head.

"I told you that I worry constantly, but that worry is tempered with a healthy dose of preparation for their futures. For example, when my husband ran off and left me, I went to a lawyer friend of ours over in Grandview and had him draw up my will in which I asked him to insert a paragraph stating that in the event of my demise, it is my wish that my mother raise my three sons. Have you made any such preparations for Polly?"

Burris looked surprised, "No. I confess I never thought to do such a thing. I figured I would be here for her..." his voice trailed off. "Or Cordy would always be here for Polly since she is younger than I."

"That is a false assumption to make, dear sir, just as false as the one that I made when I believed that Edward could be counted on to support me and the three children. Preparation for the 'what-ifs' becomes crucial when looked at from that perspective, would you agree, Burris?"

"I can see that now," he responded slowly.

"In my most humble opinion," Emma continued, "Polly lacks the interaction with adults and children outside her own family which is so crucial for her successful development. Look Burris, I have these two boys who are around Polly's age. How about if you and your family come to my home for tea this weekend, giving your daughter an opportunity to play with children her own age?"

Burris was silent a long while before answering, "I fear it would be disastrous."

"We should not shut children away in the house because we perceive them to be different. We must prepare them for our eventual leave-taking and what better way than to install them into the community where they live, surrounded not only by family but by caring friends as well?"

Just then, Emma heard the clock in the hospital bell tower strike five o'clock. "Oh, dear," she exclaimed rising from her chair. "I had no idea it was so late. I must be picking up Johnny from the children's ward and returning home across the river for dinner with my family. So, may we expect you, Cordelia and Polly this next Saturday around three?" she asked gathering up the coffee cups to hand to Rachel who was washing down the display cases.

"You are too kind, my dear," was the response she received.

"Would that be a 'yes' or a 'no', doctor?"

"Has anyone told you how exasperating you are, Emma?"

"Yes, many times. Now which is it?"

"Yes. Yes we shall all be most honored to take tea at your home across the river this coming Saturday. Please drop off directions with my secretary tomorrow. Now let me see if I can get the two of us back to the hospital unscathed with all this mud about the streets and then I shall personally escort you and the baby down to the ferry."

Later that night, after Emma tucked the three boys into bed, she sat reading a text by the fire while Mary darned socks across from her on the settee. "Mama?" began Emma.

"Yes, dear," answered Mary not looking up from her darning.

"I may have overstepped the boundaries today."

"What boundaries are those, Emma?" asked Mary pausing to peer at her daughter over the wire rimmed glasses that hung low on her nose.

"I have agreed to meet a young woman at her home tomorrow evening at nine o'clock to take a look at her baby who is about Johnny's age because the woman is concerned that her baby does not seem to be thriving. Since Rachel, that is her name, lives across the river on the south side of Clarksburg, it will mean that I must leave here right after I put the children to bed and that I shall be gone for several hours, depending upon the weather," said Emma not taking her eyes off her mother's face.

"Mmm," was all that Mary uttered in reply.

"I suppose that for safety and speed, I had better take Onion. What do you think?"

"Of course, you must take Onion. Do you know where this young woman resides? It could be quite tricky trying to find her house in the dark, especially if it begins to rain again," fretted Mary setting her darning aside.

"Since it is a straight shot from the river, up Water Street and then out to her house, I doubt that I shall encounter any trouble finding it. I dislike the notion of leaving you here all alone after dark with the three boys but I feel compelled to assist Rachel. She has an utterly miserable life and cannot afford to have a doctor look at the baby. She works long hours, not finishing at the bakery until seven o'clock at night, at which time she must walk two miles south to her house," fretted Emma.

"Well, we cannot have that, now can we?" commiserated Mary.

"There is more, I am afraid," answered Emma looking sheepishly over at her mother.

"Out with it, dear!"

"Oh, Mama!" exclaimed Emma rising to move to her mother's side. "I feel so guilty already for having placed my burdens squarely upon your shoulders and then I deliberately place an additional load there as well."

"Emma, please tell me what else you have committed me to do. Is it just possible that you think me incapable of helping you with it? What is it?" Mary asked in an exasperated tone.

"I have invited Dr. McKendrick, his wife, Cordelia, and their daughter, Polly, to come for tea this Saturday at three o'clock in the afternoon," answered Emma apologetically.

"Is that all?" asked Mary, looking relieved. "Here I thought you might have committed me to cooking dinner for everyone in that hospital of yours," smiled Mary. "Please do stop your fretting, darling. Yes, I can handle the three boys while you are gone to tend to Rachel's infant and yes, I can prepare tea for the McKendricks. It will be my very great pleasure to be of assistance. How miserably sad my life would be these days now that your father is gone if no one needed me any longer!" and she resumed her darning.

"Mama, what would I do without you?" asked Emma, kissing her mother's cheek.

"You would survive, my darling," Mary responded quietly.

The next day, Friday, dawned bright, clear and cold. Emma rose early and proceeded with the routines that she had firmly established in order to care for her twins and the baby. She handed in her written homework to Fanella Walker before busying herself emptying bed pans, giving bed baths, making beds and feeding the more dependent patients. Just after Johnny's noon feeding and after a slice of cold meat and bread for herself, Emma made her way to Dr. McKendrick's outer office and waving to his secretary, rapped lightly upon the frosted glass in the door to his inner sanctum.

She heard Burris bellow, "Enter at your own peril!"

"Are we grumpy today, sir?" she asked cheerfully, standing by the corner of his desk while the doctor poured over the stack of paperwork in front of him.

"You are damn right I am grumpy today! Just look at this...this...utter nonsense that I must fiddle with in order to practice medicine. I no sooner approve, reject or sign each blessed piece of paper in the lot than another ten thousand pieces of paper appear on my desk. Just who is responsible for this diabolical conspiracy? You? Yes, it has to be you, Student Nurse Richardson!" and Dr. McKendrick managed to laugh at his own display of temper.

"I see that you have made great strides since our little chat yesterday, doctor, for you have actually remembered that laughter is the cure of choice for what ails you," and they both laughed again.

"Now, what brings you to my office, Student Nurse Uppity?"

"I have been thinking about your patient, Joseph, the amputee."

"Oh, save us! The woman has been thinking," and Burris smacked his forehead with the palm of his hand.

"I am a bit concerned about Joseph's reluctance to have his wife and children visit him. Would you not agree that we should solicit the aid of the entire family in Joseph's recovery?"

"To what end?" Burris asked irritably.

"To the end that this man is going to have to return and live among those five people as husband and father and the sooner his wife and children see him the sooner they will begin to accept him with one and a half legs," snapped Emma, "and furthermore, the sooner Joseph will begin to realize that the five of them desperately need him to return home to them."

"Now who is the grumpy one?" Burris shot back at Emma, adding, "So what do you propose, Uppity?"

"I would propose that you arrange to contact the man's wife and insist that she and the children maintain regular visits to Joseph for the duration of his stay here at Mercy."

"Consider it a fait accompli. Now be gone and take this mess with you," and Burris waved the pile of papers at her.

"Sorry, sir, I cannot help you there," whereupon she turned on her heel and left the doctor still fuming over his pile of paperwork.

Emma arrived back at the house on High Point Avenue shortly before six o'clock that evening to have dinner with Mary and the boys. After their meal, Emma rolled up her sleeves and washed the dishes for her mother in the large, soapstone sink as was her custom. Will busied himself around his mother's feet filling a toy truck with marbles while George read to his grandmother in the parlor.

"Ma!" exclaimed Will, pointing to baby Johnny. "Would you look at Baby Cheeks!"

Emma turned from the sink to see that Johnny had almost rolled himself off the quilt where he was playing with rattles and chewing on wooden blocks. "You know, Will, I think we need to have Johnny practice sitting upright. What do you think?" and she stooped to gather the baby into a sitting position, moving his little legs apart for balance and supporting his head from behind at the neck.

"You must always support the baby, Will, for he is apt to tumble over and hurt himself," she cautioned her son. "He is going to be a bit wobbly for a while until he builds up the strength in those back and neck muscles of his to hold up his fuzzy little head. Now, you come here and try it."

Will sat by the baby and carefully moved his hand to support the baby's head. "Look! He likes it," exclaimed Will.

"Of course he does," answered Emma, wiping her hands on a flour sack towel. "Johnny wants to be like the rest of us and see the world from an upright position, instead of from the floor on his back."

At this, Will gently returned the baby to his back on the quilt and lay down beside him looking up at the ceiling. "Yeah, I see what ya mean. This ain't much fun down here."

Brute rose from his corner by the warm stove and seized his opportunity to lick Will's face clean of the telltale signs of dinner. "Oh, yecch! Get away!" Will commanded the big dog, sitting upright and wiping his face with the back of his sleeve. "I hate dog slobber!" Undeterred, Brute wagged his tail in response and moved to lick Will's ears. Will cupped his hands to his mouth and called in the direction of the parlor, "Georgie! Come get this dog of yours!"

George appeared at the kitchen door, "Oh, now the dog is mine again? Get up off the floor, Willynilly, if you do not want the dog to lick you."

"I can't right now 'cause I'm in the middle of a spearment," answered Will, resuming his prone position next to Johnny on the quilt.

"A what?" asked George.

"A SPEARMENT," responded Will loudly.

"I think you mean 'experiment'," coached Emma.

"Zactly," sniffed Will at his brother.

"You are not!"

"Am too!"

"You are just being lazy, lying around under Ma's feet!"

"Boys!" admonished Emma. "George, take Brute into the parlor and finish reading to your grandmother."

Emma lathered up the rag again with lye soap and resumed her dishwashing. "Tell me about your experiment, Will."

"I'm tryin' to see what Johnny sees and I can tell you right now, it ain't much."

"It is not much," corrected Emma.

"So you tried doin' this too, Ma?"

"Not exactly, dear. What can Johnny see from down there?"

"Shoes, mostly, and table legs. The ceiling and that big black spider over there in the corner."

Emma looked in the direction where Will was pointing and seeing nothing turned to look at her sons on the floor, "What spider?" she asked.

"Ha-ha! Made you look! You're the dirty crook that stoled your mama's pocketbook!"

"Very funny, Will. What else can Johnny and you see from down there?" she asked.

"Dust under the stove and the sink and up your skirts…"

"Will Richardson! I shall have to wash out your mouth tonight if you are not careful!" Emma admonished turning to glare at her son.

"Sorry, Ma. It's just a joke."

"Now then, tell me what you cannot see from down there," she said reaching for the flour sack towel to dry the dishes.

Will thought a bit, "Well," he said finally, "I can't see the boats on the river. I can't see Nana's pie on the table and I can't see Pa when he comes walking up High Point to live with us again."

Emma placed the blue and white dish that she was drying on the kitchen table and drawing up a chair, sat down to face Will. "How does lying on the floor make you feel?" she asked looking into his large brown eyes.

"Different," was Will's response.

"Do you like feeling different?" asked Emma.

"Not really. I like bein' like everbody else. You know…be able to stand up and walk and have a father."

"Yes, I do know," answered Emma quietly. "It is very important to all of us to be alike instead of different. Do you know why?"

"Sure. 'Cause you get teased if you're different, like me and Georgie get teased all the time 'bout bein' 'the bastard twins'."

"What do you do or say when you are teased about such things?" Emma asked her son.

"I always say, 'Sticks and stones will break my bones but names will never hurt me' and if that don't work, then I just break their bones with these," and Will held up his fists, grinning at his mother. Warming to the conversation, Will was prompted to add, "Like yesterday at school. I had to teach Caleb a lesson 'cause he kept callin' me a bastard and a dumb orphan. So, I just knocked the snot outta him," and Will made vicious jabbing motions in the air. "Caleb will never be calling me and Georgie names no more," beamed Will.

"But what if you were not a big strong boy like yourself and people teased you? What if you could not fight back to protect yourself? What would you do then?"

"I guess I'd have to find me a second to beat up on Caleb, like…" and Will thought a long time before answering, "like Brute. Old Brute could whup Caleb in a minute," triumphed Will snapping his fingers.

"Will, I need to talk to you about someone who needs a second," Emma said suddenly serious.

"Oh, yeah? Who is it?"

"You have not met her yet but tomorrow afternoon at three o'clock, this girl is coming here to tea at the house," Emma paused to gauge the effect of her words on Will.

"A girl! What girl?" asked Will looking horrified at the idea.

"Her name is Polly McKendrick."

"Isn't that the same name as that doc at the hospital?" asked Will.

"Yes and little Polly is his daughter."

"But, why do we have to gave some little girl come to tea?" complained Will. "Why not a boy so's me and Georgie have somebody to play with?"

"Because this girl has no playmates."

"Oh, yeah? How come?"

"Because she is different."

"You mean she's a bastard orphan kid too?"

"No. Polly has two parents."

"Well, what makes her so different?"

"Polly is crippled. She cannot use her right arm and leg like you and I can," responded Emma honestly.

"Boy, I bet she really gets teased 'bout that one!" exclaimed Will, shaking his head. "But, I don't see why I have to play with her," whined Will.

"Because you are going to be her second, my darling."

Later that evening, after the three children were in bed, Emma readied herself for the trip across the Southport River, through the center of Clarksburg and southward to the home of Rachel Johnson.

With her mother's assistance, Emma packed the leather valise with supplies. As she tucked her stethoscope in among swabs, bandages, bottles of thimerosal and alcohol, thermometers, a jar of ointment, tongue depressors, syringes and a half dozen of Johnny's diapers, she turned to Mary and said, "You know, Mama, just to be on the safe side, I think I had better pack two or three cans of milk and some brown sugar in a jar along with a couple of our baby bottles and nipples that we always keep on hand. What do you think?"

"Better safe than sorry, as I always say," responded Mary.

"I would hate to reach Rachel's house on the other side of Clarksburg at this time of night only to find that the child lacks proper nutrition," added Emma, while Mary unhooked the pantry door to fetch the items to place in Emma's valise.

"While you do that, Mama, I am going upstairs to dress in some of the boys' clothing that I placed in my bedroom earlier."

Mary stuck her head out of the pantry door to ask, "You are what?"

"Mama! It is the dead of night! You do not expect me to ride through the countryside dressed in a skirt, petticoat, high button shoes and stockings, now do you?"

"Well, what will people think?" asked Mary sourly. "I mean after all, you are a woman and a student nurse at Angel of Mercy Hospital."

"I want passersby to think I am a boy so that my journey over and back after dark will be less hazardous."

"Very well then, you had better tuck that auburn hair of yours under Will's green cap in order to complete your disguise, as I think those long curls of yours might just arouse suspicion," Mary added rummaging around in the pantry.

Emma tiptoed upstairs to dress in a cotton shirt, woolen trousers, vest, socks and leather shoes all belonging to her twins, Will and George. Standing before the long oval mirror, Emma studied the effect of her transformation. "Good," she said to her image. Then, pulling Will's green cap down over her hair she carefully stuffed the unruly auburn curls up inside. Next, she flattened the cap full of hair on top of her head with both hands. "Better," she said to her image. George's wool coat with Will's green scarf and mittens completed her ensemble.

Back in the kitchen, Emma walked up behind her mother, "Howdy, ma'am. Are you the little woman of the household?" she teased, deepening her voice.

"Oh, Emma! You gave me a start!" Mary stood surveying Emma's transformation for several long seconds before adding, "Yes, I believe you could pass for a young lad in the dark but just in case you encounter trouble, I think it prudent for you to take my pistol," and Mary offered her pearl-handled pistol to Emma.

"I have loaded it, so do be careful. Keep it in your coat pocket. Do you remember what Papa taught you about shooting this firearm?"

"Like it was yesterday," answered Emma taking a long look at the pistol before placing it carefully in the right pocket of George's coat.

"I have the lantern filled for you and I shall just light the wick," said Mary drawing a match across the striking stone. "Take it with you to the barn while you saddle Onion and then stop out front. When I see the light of the lantern again, I shall come out onto the porch and hand the valise to you. Now go quickly for you do not want to miss the ferry."

Emma strode up the hill to the barn across ground that crunched underfoot. While the rain had ceased earlier in the day, a west wind was rapidly coating the terrain with a crust of ice. Emma rapidly saddled the horse, retrieved her valise from Mary and made her way down to the river. Dismounting at the foot of the meadow, she walked Onion to the landing, searching for the lights of the inbound ferry. Shortly after eight o'clock, Emma recognized the noise of the paddle wheel ferry before she saw the two lanterns that swung port and starboard of the wheelhouse.

She had maintained her distance from the other travelers who lined the landing waiting for the same ferry over to Clarksburg, and she was relieved to see that she was the only one who would be boarding with a horse, as Onion was notoriously antagonistic to other equines. Pulling the collar of George's coat up around her ears and winding Will's heavy green muffler around the lower portion of her face, Emma moved forward to the ramp, holding tightly to Onion's reins.

Approaching the captain's mate who stood at the helm taking fares, Emma held out a penny in her mitten-covered hand. "Boy!" called the mate after Emma as she guided Onion up the gangplank. Emma froze in her tracks. "Boy!" he again called, "Mind I've been shoveling up horse turds from this ferry all day long and if that horse of yours shits on this here ferry tonight, I'll throw you and the bugger overboard. Do ya hear me?"

Turning stiffly to the voice, Emma touched the brim of Will's cap in recognition that she had indeed heard the mate's warning. Uttering a silent prayer that Onion would control his intestines for the journey south across the river, Emma deftly guided the big bay port side as the other passengers were all huddled in the lea of the wheelhouse and away from the direct flow of cold air from the west. For the journey across the river, Emma stood shivering next to the big horse, using his thick body as a shield against the increasingly cold flow of air created by the movement of the ferry.

Once the boat docked at the far shore, Emma retraced her steps with Onion down the gangplank and walked the big horse up into town until she came to some steps in front of a closed store. Climbing the wooden steps up to the board-walk, Emma was then tall enough to place her left foot in the left stirrup and throw her right leg over Onion's saddle and into the right stirrup. Gathering the reins in her right hand, Emma anchored the handles of the valise over the pommel of Onion's saddle. Then holding the lantern in her left hand, Emma made her way slowly up through the center of town.

Water Street up through the middle of Clarksburg was navigable without the aid of her lantern as lights shone down into the street from the dwellings above each storefront. She had memorized the directions written out for her by Rachel, "one mile frum water st and center av—past ole barn lft—big white house rt—barn horses and fence rt—big oak tree down lft—big rocks rt—creek lft to our house." Emma hoped that she could pick out the designated markers in the dark as she did not relish trying to ride along holding a lantern aloft and the horse's reins at the same time.

Onion's gait was sure-footed in spite of the gloom and unfamiliar terrain. As Emma approached what she assumed to be a horse farm from Rachel's description, she noticed a faint light near a horse corral off to her right. As she drew closer to the corral, she could see a small herd of horses moving about nervously. Onion saw them too and began to nicker, throwing his head up and down, making it difficult for Emma to keep him under control. "Stop that!" she hissed into Onion's ears, "Or, I shall let that mate throw you into the water on our way back home!"

Emma reined Onion over to the far left side of the road and just as she came abreast of the corral, a man strode out of the darkness to grab Onion's bridle. The horse reared and Emma hung on but the man retained his grip on the horse's bridle. "Jest where do ya think you're goin' at this time of night, sonny, on that fine horse there?" Emma was momentarily paralyzed at the sound of the man's voice, for she recognized it to be Cletus Donohue's. "You best be a slidin' down offa that fine specimen of horseflesh 'cause as of this very minute, sonny, that horse there belongs to me."

Emma slung the lantern at Cletus, hitting him square in the face. Startled, Cletus dropped the horse's reins. Onion reared, snorting loudly. Emma grabbed the horse's mane tightening her grip around Onion's belly with her legs. Onion reared a second time, moving Cletus backward and Emma regained her grip on the reins.

Startled and rubbing his shaggy head, Cletus swore, "Damn your ass, sonny, you're gonna pay for that. Now climb down offa that there horse!" Before Cletus uttered the last half dozen words, Emma yanked Will's green mitten off with her teeth, reached into the right hand pocket of George's coat and withdrew Mary's pearl-handled pistol.

"Never!" she said calmly, cocking the pistol and pointing it at her attacker's face.

"Just who in hell are you anyways, boy? No need to git so riled…now, now! I was jest funin' with ya," Cletus added backing up several steps.

"You mean you have forgotten me?" asked Emma sardonically. "Let me refresh your memory," whereupon Emma tore off Will's green muffler and cap so that her auburn curls tumbled down about her shoulders.

"Sweet Jesus, Almighty…help me!" swore Cletus as he recognized his victim. Dropping to his knees, Cletus begged Emma, "Please don't shoot me! I've repented! I've repented!"

Emma fired the pistol over her attacker's shoulder. Cletus flattened himself on the ground, while Emma cocked the pistol again. This time she shot into the air, high above the prone body of her attacker. Lights began to waver toward them from the large white house she had passed before coming abreast of the barn with its corral of horses. Barking dogs ran ahead of the lights.

"Horse thief!" shouted Emma at the top of her lungs in the direction of the oncoming lights.

The sound of male voices drew nearer as did the barking dogs. Emma sat rigidly astride her horse, pistol pointed at the recumbent torso of Cletus Donohue. "Horse thief over this way," Emma shouted again above the approaching din.

All at once, Emma, the horse and Cletus were surrounded by a swarm of barking hounds and a trio of men with lanterns. Onion began to rear and snort nervously. "Whoa, there boy," said Emma trying to calm her agitated horse, adding, "Kindly get those dogs back before I am thrown from my horse." Cletus, face down in the dirt, covered his exposed head with his arms to fend off the hounds.

"What have we here?" demanded a gray haired man in shirtsleeves holding the lantern up to Emma.

"What we have here, sir," responded Emma pointing to Cletus where he lay shivering on the ground, "is a cowardly devil that was attempting to steal not only your horses in the corral over there but my horse as well. You can see that the thief brought along his own lantern which he hung over there on your fence post," and Emma gestured across the road with the pistol.

"Easy does it, miss. You can put your pistol away now as my boys, Heath and Payne, are armed," responded the man pointing to his full grown sons busily pulling the hounds off Cletus. "What, may I ask, is a young woman such as yourself doing after dark on the highway from town headed south?" Then eyeing her from head to toe, he added, "Dressed as a boy?"

"I, sir, am on my way to the home of Rachel Johnson to tend to her sick child, Daniel," Emma stated putting Mary's pistol back into George's coat pocket. "I dressed as a boy thinking to avoid this very sort of an encounter on my journey."

"What would your name be, miss?"

"I am Emma Richardson, and you are?"

"Forgive my manners, miss. I am Adam Hamilton, the Mayor of Clarksburg, at your service." Adam walked around the skittish horse and with his boot, rolled Cletus over on to his back, hanging the lantern down into the man's face for a better look. "And as for this good-for-nothing scoundrel, who the blazes are you?"

"I ain't done nothin'," wailed Cletus, shivering uncontrollably.

"I know what you were trying to do, now tell me your name!" Adam Hamilton prodded the man's shoulder with his boot.

"His name is Cletus Donohue," responded Emma, "from across the river in Grandview."

"So you know this person?" asked Adam turning the lantern toward Emma.

"Unfortunately, I do, and what I know is not good."

Turning the lantern light once again upon Cletus, the mayor bellowed, "Do you know what we do to a horse thief over here in Clarksburg?"

"No," whimpered Cletus.

"We hang the son of a bitch!" shouted Mayor Hamilton.

"Oh, please don't hang me!" cried Cletus, wrapping his arms around the legs of the mayor. "I ain't done nothin' worthy of hangin'!"

"Liar!" shouted Emma. "I should personally like to be the one to stretch that filthy neck of yours until it snaps!"

Adam Hamilton seemed surprised by Emma's venomous words. "Easy does it, miss. Do not concern yourself with this. We men shall take care of the matter," and he turned to the strapping young man at his side, "Payne, tie the thief's hands behind his back and march him to the constable's jail for the remainder of the night. We shall deal with him in the morning but we need to rid our streets of this vermin directly."

Payne, as he had been instructed, reached down and yanked Cletus up by the back of his coat. Once he had Cletus in an upright position, Payne began binding Cletus' hands together.

"You're hurtin' me," hollered Cletus. "Them dogs of yours pretty near bit off ma fingers and now you'd be tryin' to cut off ma hands."

"Hold your tongue, man," admonished Payne, "before I cut that off too."

"Miss Richardson," began Adam Hamilton, "I cannot let you continue on your way unescorted to the Johnson house at this time of night. Therefore, I am going to ask my son, Heath, to accompany you. And mind you, Heath, take the young woman back home after she is through at the Johnsons'. Where did you say home is, miss?"

"I live in Grandview sir, on High Point Avenue."

"Really? I knew a fine gentleman that lived on High Point Avenue, although he has been gone for a couple of years now. Owned the lumber mill thereabouts," mused the mayor.

"You knew my father, sir?" asked Emma startled.

"Was your father James Miller?"

"He was indeed, sir."

"Well, now, it is a small world," smiled Adam Hamilton for the first time. Turning to his sons he admonished them, "Payne, get that rat out of here and Heath, put up the dogs and then return quickly to get Emma here on her way to Miss Johnson's sick baby."

Looking back up at Emma he asked, "Will you be all right to proceed Miss Emma? That bugger had to have scared the daylights out of you. My missus could give you some hot tea or a bed if you cannot go on," he offered kindly.

"You are most gracious, Mr. Mayor, but I absolutely must tend to this child of Rachel's tonight and if I may impose upon your son, Heath, I know that the remainder of my journey will be safe."

Heath appeared out of the gloom, carrying a lantern and riding an imposing palomino. "Son," admonished Adam Hamilton, "this is the daughter of a late friend of mine from across the river. I expect you to see her safely to the Johnsons' house and then back to her own. Do you understand, Heath? No harm must come to Emma Richardson."

"I shall follow your orders to the letter, sir. Miss Emma has nothing to fear now," responded Heath urging his horse forward along the dirt highway.

"Hold up a second, Heath," called Adam Hamilton waving Will's green mitten in the air after them. "Miss Emma lost this."

"Thank you again, sir, for rescuing me and my mitten," smiled Emma down at the mayor from high atop Onion's back.

"I did not rescue you, my dear," responded Adam. "You have got it backward, as you were actually the one who rescued my fine herd of horses over there. I am forever in your debt," and he bowed low before waving Emma and Heath off into the night.

The two rode on in silence into the darkness. By the light of young Heath's lantern, she sighted the giant fallen oak to their left, the next of Rachel's markers. Shortly thereafter, they came upon an enormous outcropping of limestone to the right and presently, Emma heard, off to her left, the distinctive sound of a creek rushing along to join the Southport River.

"The house is just ahead, Miss Emma, there on our left," gestured Heath with the coal oil lantern.

"Yes, I see it now," responded Emma. She could also smell the fragrant smoke from a hardwood fire in the clean, cold night air as they approached.

The two rode directly up to the front porch where Heath dismounted first. Tying his horse to a hitching post out front, he laced his fingers together to give Emma a footing for her dismount. Heath unhooked the leather valise from the pommel of Emma's saddle, tied up Onion at the far end of the hitching post and accompanied Emma to the front door where he rapped loudly with his knuckles upon the plain wooden planks.

"Who's there?" came a woman's voice from the other side of the door.

"Student Nurse Emma Richardson, here to see Rachel Johnson and Daniel."

An older woman opened the door a crack to peer out at her visitors, "And who's that with you?"

"This," replied Emma, drawing her traveling companion up closer to the light coming from inside the house, "is Heath Hamilton, the Mayor's son."

"Oh, for pity's sake! I didn't realize that we were going to have company tonight. I'm afraid I'm not prepared..."

"No need to worry yourself, ma'am," responded Heath removing his wide brimmed hat. "I am just here to protect Miss Emma at the instructions of my father, the mayor."

"I see, I see," said the woman, throwing wide the door to admit the two travelers. "Rachel," she called loudly, "Emma Richardson's here and so is the mayor's son!"

Emma and Heath stepped into the small, tidy log house with its large stone fireplace and sparse furnishings. Rachel appeared from a room behind the gathering room where it was obvious that all the daily activities took place, such as cooking, eating and washing. A large wooden spinning wheel dominated one corner of the cozy room next to a basket of sheep's wool. From the back room, Emma could hear the thin, reedy cries of an infant as Rachel emerged to greet her visitors.

"Emma!" Rachel greeted her warmly, "Thank you so much for making the journey across the river to see Danny!" Turning to Heath, she added, "To think you have also brought the mayor's son with you! It is an unexpected honor, to be sure sir!" Whereupon, Rachel gave a little bob of a curtsey in the direction of Heath.

"May I see the baby?" asked Emma getting down to the point of her visit.

"Of course, at once. Mother, please offer the mayor's son…"

"Just call me 'Heath', Miss Rachel."

"Mother, please offer Heath," she corrected herself, "a cup of coffee while Emma and I tend to Danny in the back room."

Emma placed her valise on the first of two quilt-covered beds when she entered the large back room. Next, she removed her wrappings and laid them at the foot of the same bed. From a wooden dresser drawer on the opposite bed came sucking noises from an infant where he lay chewing on his fists.

"This must be our little Danny," murmured Emma soothingly as she approached the baby. Carefully she lifted the baby from his wooden dresser drawer bed and placed him on the quilt, still wrapped in a blanket. "Can you please remove his…bed?" asked Emma, turning to Rachel.

Carefully and slowly, Emma began to unwrap the baby, observing him closely as she went. She spoke quietly to him, "What a fine boy you are, little Danny. So sweet and ever so adorable. I do believe you favor your mother's side of the family." Danny began to coo and smile back at Emma as she proceeded.

When she had the baby's body fully exposed for examination, Emma was startled to see how small and thin the child was. "How old did you say Danny is again?"

"He was born seven months ago," replied Rachel.

"Is this your only child?" asked Emma, hefting the baby briefly.

"It is."

"Did you carry this baby for the full nine months or was he born early?" she questioned the young mother, pulling out her stethoscope from the leather valise and handing a tongue depressor to the baby to hold.

"Yes, I carried him the whole nine months," was the reply.

"Have you experienced any difficulties either during or since his birth?"

"Yes, I have."

"Tell me about those difficulties," said Emma listening to the baby's heart and lungs.

"Well," began Rachel haltingly, "I'm not proud to say these things to you Emma…"

"You can trust me not to reveal your confidences, Rachel."

"Danny's father refused to marry me after he found out that I was with child so my poor mother, whom you met just now, was our sole source of support for many months. She spins wool into yarn for some of the merchants in town. She's the best spinner in these parts," Rachel added proudly. "But, even with Mother spinning day and night, I soon had to find work myself and, as you know, I was fortunate to be hired as a clerk at the Water Street Bakery."

"I see," said Emma as she continued her examination of the baby. "Tell me about any difficulties with your pregnancy which you may have experienced during the nine months that you carried young Danny."

"No difficulties at all. Mother used to say I was meant to have children because I made it look so easy, even the birthing."

"Who delivered your child, Rachel?"

"A midwife around these parts. She's delivered just about everybody south of Clarksburg for miles around. Nobody hereabouts holds any secrets from old Clarine. She's the midwife and she doesn't take any sass from any of her kids! Old Clarine's pretty quick to remind us that since she brought us into the world, she can take us right back out again!" laughed Rachel.

Emma smiled. "How long ago did you start to work at the Water Street Bakery?"

"Well, let's see, it was probably last October."

"So, about four months after the birth of Danny," figured Emma as she carefully dressed and wrapped the baby again.

"Who cares for Danny during your absences from home while you work?"

"My mother."

"And how does Mrs. Johnson feed the baby?"

"She doesn't."

Frowning, Emma turned abruptly toward Rachel and repeated, "She does not?"

"No, a wet nurse feeds him," was the response.

"Do you not have enough milk of your own to feed Danny?" Emma asked looking at Rachel's thin chest.

"I never have since I began working at the bakery."

"This wet nurse," continued Emma picking up Danny to hold him over her shoulder, "how did you know to hire her?"

"She's well known around here. Feeds babies all the time and doesn't charge too awful much for her milk."

"How long ago did this wet nurse have a baby of her own?" asked Emma.

Scratching her head Rachel thought, "Oh, probably three or four years ago."

Trying to control her facial features, Emma asked, "How much does she charge to feed Danny each week?"

"Fourteen cents."

Emma carefully placed the baby back in his dresser drawer bed and opened her valise again to remove the cans of milk, the jar of brown sugar, bottles and nipples.

"What do you think is wrong with Danny?"

"I think," responded Emma quietly, turning to face Rachel again, "that your baby is being starved to death."

"No!" gasped Rachel.

"Yes," repeated Emma, "Danny is being slowly starved to death by the woman you have hired to nurse him."

"How can that be?" asked Rachel horrified. "I pay the wet nurse good money each week to feed my baby and..."

"We nurses and students nurses at Angel of Mercy Hospital are seeing more and more cases like Danny's each month. Unfortunately, there are those who have contrived to earn a living by selling their milk to women such as yourself who cannot, for one reason or another, nurse their own babies. These unscrupulous women put the child only to one breast, pretend to have satisfied the hunger of the infant and then move on to another infant, all the while extracting money from the babies' mothers for non-existent feedings or half feedings."

Emma paused to examine Rachel's contorted features. "Do you understand what I have told you?"

"Yes, but our wet nurse wouldn't do that!" cried Rachel.

"Sadly, I am quite afraid that she has. Our poor little Danny here is living proof of her deception."

Collapsing in a heap in a rocking chair at the foot of the bed, Rachel wailed, "But what am I going to do? I have no milk of my own any longer!"

"I am going to make several bottles of formula for Danny right now. Then, I am going to feed him as soon as I am able cool one bottle down to the point that he can ingest...suck it."

Handing the glass bottles to Rachel and cradling the rest of her supplies, Emma indicated to Rachel to open the door, "You come with me and learn how to make formula."

Entering the gathering room again, Emma found Heath by the fire still drinking coffee with Mrs. Johnson. "What is your water source?" asked Emma looking at Rachel's mother.

"Why, the creek out back."

"Heath, take that pail hanging there by the cookstove and fetch water for me from the creek," ordered Emma pointing to the stove that stood in the corner opposite the spinning wheel.

"Mrs. Johnson," continued Emma, "I need a large pot in which to boil these bottles and nipples. Rachel, I need a measuring cup and spoons," added Emma clearing a space on the eating table and lining up her supplies on its worn surface.

"Put extra firewood in the stove, Rachel," instructed Emma, "and now where is that boiling pot?"

Mrs. Johnson produced a large metal pot with a lid. "Good," said Emma just as Heath entered the house with a full pail of cold creek water. "Now, Heath, pour all of the water over these bottles and nipples that I am placing in the pot. Do not remove the cover to look at the contents," Emma admonished her audience superstitiously, "As we all know that a watched pot will never boil."

Emma then patiently instructed Rachel in the measuring out of canned milk, boiled water and brown sugar as she prepared a nourishing formula for baby Danny. Once the bottles and nipples were clean, she showed Rachel how to fill and then sterilize the bottles of formula in a boiling water bath.

"Now," said Emma, "we must cool one bottle down quickly so that little Danny can have his first good meal in many months. "Heath, please take this bottle out back and cool it in the creek so that when you pinch the nipple here," and Emma demonstrated the technique for Heath, "and express a bit of the formula just so, it feels warm to the wrist."

For the first time during the evening, Emma locked eyes with Heath and she realized that his were blue. Self-consciously, Emma reached up to smooth her tangled curls before turning to clear Mrs. Johnson's table of the baby formula utensils. Sitting in a chair by the hearth, she asked Rachel to bring the baby to her with a diaper from her valise. Presently, Heath returned and handed the bottle of formula to Emma who then tested it upon her own wrist. "Perfect!" she smiled up at Heath who took a seat by the eating table.

All eyes were on Emma and Danny as she offered the baby his first bottle. At first, Danny nibbled at the rubber nipple unsure what to do with it until he got a squirt of the formula in his mouth. Drawing the brown nipple into his mouth, Danny sucked down half the bottle before Emma tugged it from his mouth. "There, there, little one. We must get up a burp now."

Danny began to fret and reach for the bottle. Deftly, Emma placed the baby over her shoulder and patted his back until this produced a burp, whereupon Danny began turning his head in search of the bottle. "Now you try, Rachel," said Emma handing Danny to his mother.

Everyone watched transfixed as baby Danny sucked down the rest of his formula and burped for his mother on cue. "You may find, Rachel, that it is necessary to feed this child of yours every three hours as if he were a newborn in order to get enough nourishment into his little system quickly. At any rate, I believe that young Daniel here will make good progress now but just to be sure, I would like you to drop off the baby at the hospital on Monday morning so that I can have Dr. McKendrick take a look at him. We can keep him there in the children's ward for the day and give him his formula until you are ready to return home and then I am going to ask Heath to escort you and the baby back here to your home."

Turning to look Heath in the eyes again and placing a hand lightly on his arm, Emma asked, "May I impose upon your kindness once more Heath for such a favor?"

"It would be my very great pleasure to be of assistance to Miss Rachel and her young son, Emma," Heath answered flashing a smile back.

"Good. It is settled then," responded Emma preparing to gather up her valise and wraps to make the long trip back home across the river.

"Must you go so soon?" asked Rachel. "Please let us offer you our hospitality first."

"Thank you kindly, Rachel, but Heath and I must leave now in order to catch the ferry across to Grandview. I shall see the two of you next Monday." Kissing the baby lightly upon his forehead, Emma murmured to him, "Good night, little one. Sleep tight tonight."

The small group bid each other farewell. Heath untied Onion's reins and after securing the valise to the pommel again, he helped Emma up into her saddle before mounting the palomino. "I suggest we move swiftly, Miss Emma. Please follow me," whereupon he neck reined his horse around and took off at a gallop north for the town of Clarksburg and the ferry across to Grandview.

Once on board the ferry, Heath tied their horses to the railing. Looking down at Emma, he realized that she was shivering uncontrollably in the cold wind and promptly removed his coat, offering it to her. "Oh, no, Heath," demurred

Emma, "I could not possibly take your coat from you on a night such as this," she replied handing the sheepskin coat back to him.

"I insist, Miss Emma, and furthermore, I am bigger than you," he smiled down at her wrapping the huge coat nearly twice around her small frame.

"Does your size imply that I am to do as you say?" she laughed up at him, imprisoned in his huge warm coat.

"No ma'am. It only implies that I have more heat in me than you do and that heat stays with me longer. Which do you expect would freeze first, a bird or a horse?" his blue eyes crinkled at the edges.

"Yes. I quite see your point. Thank you, Heath, for your coat. It is just that I am not used to such…such kindness from men," Emma said peering off into the darkness.

"Why is that?" asked Heath, studying Emma's profile by lantern light.

"Oh, it is a long and tedious story to be sure, Heath, and one that I am much too exhausted to relate this evening," she replied but, catching a look of disappointment on his face, Emma was quick to add, "perhaps some time when you are in a particularly morose frame of mind the two of us can exchange our sad stories and both enjoy a good cry."

"Well, I for one have not got a sad story to tell but perhaps I could make one up for you. Mmmm, let me think," he said removing his large brimmed hat and smoothing the long, unruly blond curls back from his forehead.

"Ah, yes, I have one now. Once upon a time, Payne and I were stringing barbed wire around the entire state when a herd of wild horses appeared on the horizon. Now, you may not know this about me, but I am a horse breeder by trade, and I saw within that herd some fine specimens that I wanted to introduce into my own herd so I took off running after them. Well, I caught the stallion at the head of the herd with my lasso," and Heath reached over to touch the rope that hung coiled from the palomino's saddle.

"I looked that horse dead in the eye and cast a spell on him so that I could ride him in pursuit of the others. When the rest of that herd of wild horses got a look at me and the stallion coming up behind them, they plunged over a cliff to avoid being captured. The stallion stopped just short of the edge of the cliff but I kept on going, right over his head.

I tumbled and bumped down those rocks so hard I broke every bone in my body and came to rest on a pile of rattle snakes whe…"

At this point, Emma was laughing. "Hey, now! You are supposed to be crying at my sad story! I mean all my broken bones and all those snakes!"

"Heath Hamilton, you are a mess!" giggled Emma.

"Anything for a laugh from you, ma'am," he smiled down at her and tipped his hat.

After the two disembarked at the Grandview landing, Emma turned to Heath and said, "You know of course, this was the last ferry across the river this evening. You must stay in our home for the night."

"Is that an order or an invitation, Miss Emma?"

"That would be an order, unless you think you could get away from me by swimming back across with that horse of yours," she teased.

"Well, since you put it that way, lead on," and the two made their way slowly up Longmeadow to High Point Avenue.

After they had stabled the horses in the barn for the night, Emma and Heath entered the darkened house. "You must sleep in my room, as the others are filled," she again ordered.

"But I could not possibly take your bed, Emma. I noticed that there was a lot of nice straw in that barn of yours. With a blanket from you, I can make do for the night quite comfortably."

"Nonsense. I shall not hear of it," responded Emma pulling Heath along the front hall and up the stairs by his arm.

"But where will you sleep?" he whispered.

"In the spare bed in Johnny's room. Now go!" and she pushed him into her bedroom.

Will awakened early the next morning to the smell of frying fatback. Jumping out of bed and rubbing his eyes, the boy stumbled down the stairs, still half asleep, to the foyer. "Nana!" the child called as he padded barefooted and yawning down the long hall to the big kitchen. "Watchya doin' makin' breakfast so early in the mornin' for? It ain't even light out and it's Saturday. Did you forg…"

Will froze at the sight that greeted him in the kitchen. There at his grandmother's cookstove was a big man wearing a cowboy hat and his grandmother's apron, frying fatback in his bare feet.

"Hey, mister! Who are you and why are you cookin' on my Nana's stove?" Will demanded imperiously, looking Heath over suspiciously.

"Howdy, Half Pint," Heath greeted the boy and turned to smile at him. "The name is Heath. How do you like your eggs? Over easy or sunny side up?" he asked in a friendly tone.

"I don't like no fried eggs…not down or up. I like mine scrambled and my name ain't 'Half Pint'. My name's Will."

"Okay, Will…scrambled eggs it is," and Heath turned to busy himself at the stove again.

Will ran back down the hall yelling, "Maaa! Maaa! Better come quick! Some cowboy with no shoes on is cookin' breakfast in Nana's kitchen!" As an afterthought, Will bellowed up the stairwell, "And he's wearin' her apron!"

Just then, Brute came lumbering down the front stairs and ambled back to the kitchen. Stopping just inside the door, the huge dog began to growl at the unfamiliar scent of Heath.

Heath turned nonchalantly to the dog, "Easy there, big fella. No need to get yourself all riled up over the menu. I have prepared some breakfast for you too," whereupon Heath scooped up the fatback rinds that he had cut off and fried separately from the rest of the bacon and slipped the rinds into the dog's dish by the stove.

Brute forgot his antagonism at finding a stranger in his kitchen and happily crunched away on the crispy tidbits in his bowl. Licking his jowls, the big dog moved up behind Heath and delivered his customary greeting, shoving his nose where it did not belong.

"Okay, boy. Did I pass the test?" Heath laughingly asked, reaching down to scratch the big dog on his head. "Bet you need to piss, so how about we just let you outside for a bit?" and Heath opened the back door and the porch door to let Brute out into the yard.

Will and George were both poised at the entrance to the kitchen when Heath returned.

"See! There he is…just like I telled you!" Will exclaimed, pointing an accusing finger at Heath.

Heath grinned. "I must have slept wrong last night because I would swear there are two of you, Will!" he exclaimed. Looking from one boy to the next he was prompted to add, "And I guess that instead of a half pint, we now have a full pint here!" Heath laughed out loud at the scowls that greeted his humor.

Turning back to the stove where the cast-iron fry pan sizzled with the crisp bacon and eggs, Heath asked nonchalantly over his shoulder, "How does this second half pint like his eggs? And while we are at it, just how does that sister of yours like her eggs, Will?"

Quizzically, Will looked at George before answering, "We ain't got no sisters 'round here, mister. Only brothers…three of 'em."

Then it was Heath's turn to register surprise just as Emma walked into the kitchen holding Johnny on her hip. "Well, would you look at Nana!" laughed Emma.

Heath blushed at the reference and self-consciously began to untie Mary's apron from his waist.

"Oh, no, Heath!" Emma commenced to apologize. "Please pay no attention to my silly jokes."

Flushing pink, Heath explained, "It is just that my mother taught me to cook and she always required me to wear an apron so as not to soil my clothing."

"And mine did likewise," responded Emma placing Johnny on a folded quilt.

"Just look at them toes!" admonished Will. "Somebody shoulda taught Mister Heath here to wear socks so's not to get his toes dirty neither."

"Actually," said Heath flipping eggs, "there is a good reason why I am bare-footed this morning. Know why?"

"Yep," said George. "I just bet Brute stole your shoes while you were asleep last night. That dog is all the time taking our shoes, chewing on them and then hiding them all over the house." For the first time George smiled at Heath.

"Good answer, but the truth is that when I was a small boy, like yourself uh…"

"George. My name is George Miller Richardson," said the boy drawing himself up tall.

"Yes, George. When I was a boy like you," continued Heath, "my mother also taught me to remove my muddy boots and socks before I entered the house as it was her responsibility to oversee the cleaning of the floors and carpets and I was instructed not to make more work for the servants by tracking up the place. Did your mother teach you that too?"

"Yes sir, she sure did," responded George.

"Speaking of your mother, do you think she will be joining us for breakfast this morning?" asked Heath serving up eggs, fried fatback and toast.

The twins cocked their heads at each other and began to laugh. Turning to Emma, George pointed his finger at Emma and said, "Maybe you should ask her?"

"Oh, of course. Emma, do you think your mother will be joining us for breakfast this morning?" Heath asked innocently, falling into the verbal trap.

The twins laughed even harder until Will was reduced to tears.

"Did I say something humorous?" asked Heath, pouring two cups of coffee.

Emma interceded saying, "I think it is time that I explained something, Heath. These three boys that you see before you are my sons."

"Your what?" asked Heath, his jaw dropping in surprise.

"Her sons," chimed in George and Will pointing to each other and Johnny.

"Now how did that happen?" blurted out Heath.

"Mister Heath, didn't that mother of yours teach you nothin' 'bout the stork when you was growin' up?"

"What my dumb brother means is," explained George while taking his seat with a plate of bacon and eggs, "is that my mother here had a husband and we had a father and then one day he just upped and vanished on us and we have never seen him since. But, Ma, Nana, Will, Johnny and I are a family, just like everybody else."

"I see," said Heath slowly looking over at Emma. "What a surprise."

"Surprised us too," added Will cramming his mouth full of the scrambled eggs that Heath had prepared for him. "Only thing is…it was one of them bad surprises and not the good kind. Know what I mean, Mister Heath?"

"Yes, Will. I believe I do know what you mean."

Just then, Mary appeared at the kitchen door to appraise the jovial gathering in her kitchen. "Have I been replaced and no one bothered to tell me?" she smiled at everyone.

"Oh, Mama, do forgive me," apologized Emma. "This is Heath Hamilton, the mayor of Clarksburg's son, and it was he who saved me from certain peril last night and then escorted me back here across the river to our house."

"Do tell!" exclaimed Mary resting her hand on Heath's arm and smiling warmly into his face, adding, "You know Heath, I believe my late husband, James Miller, was a friend of your father's. Is his name Adam?"

"Yes ma'am and I had the pleasure of making the acquaintance of your late husband, Mr. Miller…fine man too."

For the next hour while the family enjoyed Heath's carefully prepared breakfast, Emma and Heath regaled their little audience with a reenactment of their adventures the previous evening while Emma scrupulously avoided any reference to her initial and traumatic encounter with Cletus Donohue.

Will and George sat transfixed at the end of their mother's narrative of the previous night's events. Usually eager to vacate the table as soon as their appetites had been satisfied, both boys remained in their chairs staring admiringly over at Heath.

George spoke first, "I guess that makes you our hero, Mr. Heath. You know…kind of like the ones we read about in books all the time."

"Yeah," agreed Will. "He's just 'bout like Abraham Lincoln."

"There you go again, Will," admonished George turning to his brother. "Did you not hear that he is the son of the MAYOR of Clarksburg, not the PRESIDENT of the United States of America?"

"Well, I ain't met no one famous before so…" Will thought long and hard, "maybe he's more like Wild Bill Hiccup."

"Wild Bill Hickok," corrected Emma. "And yes, Will, I think that is an excellent description of Heath Hamilton."

"Thank you for the compliment, son," responded Heath, rising to clear the table.

"Oh, la-la-la, Mister Heath! Do not touch another plate! I am not accustomed to being waited on by my houseguests," said Mary moving to the soapstone sink to clean up their breakfast.

"What do you boys say to Heath?" asked Emma, scooping up Johnny.

"Will you tell us more stories?" asked George, wide-eyed.

"You bet," responded Heath reaching out to tousle George's dark hair.

"That is not exactly what I had in mind," glared Emma at her sons. "Manners," she prompted.

"Thank you, Mister Heath, for fixing our breakfast this morning," began George, while adding, "We have never eaten food cooked by a man before, especially a cowboy man."

"Yeah," seconded Will. "I didn't even think men knew how to cook."

"Oh, piffle!" snorted Mary turning to point a wooden spoon at the boys. "Just who has been cutting out biscuits, icing cakes and scooping butter for the mashed potatoes all these many years for their Nana?"

"We have," chorused George and Will.

"And who will continue to cook when they are grown up because everyone needs to learn to fend for themselves?" Mary asked again.

"We will," came the duplicate response.

"Smart boys, would you agree?" asked Mary turning to Heath.

"Absolutely the smartest it has been my privilege to meet in a long while," grinned Heath at Will and George.

After a second cup of coffee, Heath told Emma that he needed to return to Clarksburg in order to help Payne deliver three of their horses to a wealthy businessman on the west side of town. "Very well, then, I shall accompany you down to the ferry," and looking at her father's timepiece which she kept tucked into the side pocket of her skirt, she added, "We still have an hour before the ferry arrives."

Emma changed from her skirt into a pair of the boys' wool trousers and then walked to the barn with Heath to saddle his palomino. Heath mounted first and then offering her his arm, pulled Emma into the saddle behind him for the ride down to the landing at the foot of Longmeadow.

Remembering her tendency to become chilled by the wind off the river, Heath positioned himself as her buffer against the cold. Standing close to Emma he looked down at her long auburn curls that bounced about her face in the breeze. "Emma," he began, "I did not realize that you had been married…" he began.

"Am still married," she corrected.

"So, there was never a divorce?" Heath asked. "I thought abandonment of a wife and children was surely grounds for divorce…" and his voice faded into the wind.

"If I could find the…Edward, I would file for divorce faster than you can blink your eye, but the truth is, I have absolutely no idea where the man is."

"Did you make inquiries?"

"No. I was too ashamed to ask a soul," responded Emma sadly, averting her gaze.

"Well, then, I shall make some discreet inquiries for you. That is, if you agree?" offered Heath taking her chin in his hand and turning her face back to look at him.

"Why would you do that for me?" she asked.

"Because I slept in your bed last night!" teased Heath, smiling down into her upturned face.

"Do be serious with me, Heath, just for an instant."

"I am being just as serious as a stampede of wild horses," he responded, not releasing her chin.

"Heath, I believe that you are laboring under a false impression, which I gathered from our silly talk with the boys earlier this morning in my mother's kitchen."

"Really? Just what false impression is that?" he asked moving his hand to brush the curls out of her face.

Pushing his hand away, she asked, "Just how old do you think I am, Heath?"

"I would guess you to be my age, Emma, which is twenty-five," he calculated.

"Heath, I shall turn thirty this year which means that you are much too young…"

"That old!" he mocked her. "Shall I carve a walking stick for you for your thirtieth birthday?" he continued laughing. "Would you like that walking stick made out of oak or sycamore?"

"And, not only am I turning thirty," she persisted, ignoring his attempt at humor, "but I am turning thirty with three young children and a growing mountain of expenses."

"Well, then, we are well suited for each other, as I see it, because your boys need a man to tell them stories and you need someone to help you with expenses.

Remember that at twenty-five, I am already a very successful breeder of fine horses."

"Yes, but what could you possibly want from me? I mean what do I possess that you lack?"

"I lack an intelligent, strong-spirited and beautiful woman to love me. One who needs me to love her back," Heath stated simply.

Overwhelmed by his directness, Emma rested her head against his chest and Heath encircled her with his arms, drawing her closer to his body. "What a shame that you had to come along now!" lamented Emma. "Why could you not have come into my life first…all those years ago before I made such a stupid mistake?"

"As I see it," responded Heath, continuing to hold her in his embrace, "you have not made any mistakes so far, for without the marriage, you would not have been able to produce Will, George and Johnny. Surely you do not consider them to be mistakes, do you?"

"No, I do not consider my sons to be mistakes. I cannot imagine life without them," she answered decisively.

"Good!" was his answer. "Just promise me this," and Heath tilted her head back so that she could see into the depths of his blue eyes. "Promise me that you will never again imagine a life without me in it either."

"But remember that I am a married woman, Heath!" Emma admonished him. "People will talk."

"Well, if people are going to talk, then I suggest we give them something really solid to grind up in that old gossip mill. What do you say to that, Miss Emma?"

She gazed longingly up into the blue of his eyes and at the long, unruly light hair that framed his face covered with blond stubble. Heath removed the well-worn cowboy hat as if on cue to afford her a better look at him. It was part of his strategy as a purveyor of horseflesh. He always let the customers see and feel what they were buying.

Emma's eyes feasted upon the square cut of his jaw and then the thick muscled neck. Daring to look no further, Emma averted her gaze, suddenly ashamed to be so desirous of a man again. Wanting to feel her skin upon his, Heath reached for her hand and placed its open palm against the side of his face.

Emma was feeling faint when she heard the unmistakable sound of the ferry as it approached land. Jolted back to reality, Emma pulled from Heath's embrace.

"Before I leave, I would like an answer to my question," persisted Heath.

"Well, I have quite forgotten your question but I am certain that it was impertinent, just like you," laughed Emma, struggling to regain her equilibrium.

"My question was, shall we give the gossip mill something to grind?" repeated Heath.

"Absolutely!" replied Emma without hesitation.

CHAPTER 13

▼

Walking up the front steps to the house on High Point Avenue, Emma turned once more to look back down the vast expanse of sloping lawn, past the landing and on beyond to the river where she could see the ferry coursing slowly to the far side. She could just make out the figures of Heath and his palomino horse. As she stood taking one long, last look, Heath removed his battered cowboy hat and waved it high in the wind to her. Emma removed Will's green muffler and unfurled it back to him in the breeze.

Once inside the warm house, Emma walked back to the kitchen to watch her mother who was drying dishes and trading kitchen spoons of varying sizes with Johnny to keep him occupied. "Here is a spoon for the baby," she said offering Johnny a large wooden mixing spoon. "Now, you hand it back to Nana. What a bright boy, you are, John! And here," added Mary placing a pan upside down in front of the baby, "is a pan to beat upon with your spoon, like this," and she demonstrated the rudimentary drum for Johnny, much to his delight.

"Thank you, Mama, for your kindness to Heath. I do not know what I should have done last night without his help," Emma began.

"Heath certainly is a handsome young man and would appear to have a temperament to match his good looks," answered Mary.

"Where are George and Will?" asked Emma.

"Oh, I sent them up to the barn to muck out Onion's stall," Mary replied drying her hands on the flour sack towel.

"I shall need to scrub both of them before the McKendricks arrive at three," Emma reminded her mother.

"Do you have any special requests for our tea this afternoon, dear?"

"I noticed that you have made persimmon cookies, Mama. Would you share some of those with the McKendricks this afternoon?"

"Of course, but we shall require more than cookies. Some little sandwiches with the crusts removed?" suggested Mary.

"How about those lovely ones that you do with butter, chopped eggs, thin country ham and sliced pickles? Cut in quarters?"

"Yes, that is a good choice too," mused Mary walking to her pantry. "And we should probably offer them some of my toasted, salted pecans," she added removing a large glass jar from one of the shelves. "Then, I guess, I had better have some butter and jelly sandwich quarters, as I know for certain that Will and George will not touch the other ones."

The two women spent time together preparing afternoon tea for the McKendricks and then Emma rounded up the twins for their scrubbing in the copper tub. Johnny was placed in his crib for a nap shortly thereafter and at the stroke of three from the grandfather clock in the parlor, the brass knocker thudded noisily against the front door.

Smoothing the curls from around her face, Emma flipped her long braid over a shoulder and down her back as she hurried to the foyer. Through the sidelights, she could see Dr. McKendrick, with a tall, thin woman and a young girl, all bundled up against the chill of January.

Will and George, who had been reading their story books by the fire, rose with trepidation as their mother made hand signals for them to follow her. Keeping a healthy distance behind their mother, the boys each placed a picture book in front of their faces and hid, hoping to go unnoticed by the McKendricks and specifically, the girl that accompanied them.

Emma greeted the three of them warmly, as did Mary, then turned to usher her guests into the parlor, when she spied George and Will hiding their faces behind the picture books. Emma snatched the books from them and propelled the twins forward to meet the McKendricks. The three children, Polly, George and Will stood wordlessly glaring at each other. "Do I have to do this?" wailed Polly to her mother. "Shush!" was Cordelia McKendrick's response to her daughter.

Ignoring the children, Emma invited everyone into the parlor. "Please remove your wraps and hand them to George and Will. I know the boys will be delighted to hang them up for you," said Emma turning to squint a warning at her sons.

"I can't get mine off," whined Polly to no one in particular. "This coat's too heavy!" she complained.

"Help her please, Will!" ordered Emma.

Will sidled over to Polly and put out his hand to help whereupon Polly responded by jerking her arm away. "Don't touch me!" she warned Will.

"You silly girl!" responded Will in an exasperated tone, "I wasn't tryin' to touch you. I'm just gonna touch your coat," and undeterred, Will slid the coat down off Polly's narrow shoulders.

"How 'bout that scarf around your head too?" asked Will starting to tug at the wrapping. Before she could protest anew, Polly's long, silky, pale hair was cascading down her back. Will stood speechless looking at Polly. "You've got hair just like our friend, Benni," Will finally found his tongue. "Can I touch it and see what it feels like?" he asked moving toward his intended with outstretched hand.

"No you can't, you dumb boy!" Polly responded slapping Will's hand away.

The adults who had been busy chatting missed the exchange between the children. As their guests took seats in the parlor, George and Will busied themselves hanging up the coats, scarves and hats in the front hall. Leaning over to George, Will whispered, "Wanna make a bet?"

"Depends on how much money," answered George.

"A penny," responded Will.

"This had better be good," warned George.

"It's real good! I bet before they leave," and Will jerked his head in the direction of the parlor, "I get to touch her hair," and he grinned at his brother.

"Will, you are crazy! I do not care if you touch her hair or not!" George admonished his brother.

"Well, I care. It ain't gonna be an easy touch neither 'cause she's already told me not to so I'm gonna have to be real secret like and sneak up on her. Maybe the bet should be two pennies," added Will, contemplating the difficulty of his task.

"Where are you going to get one penny, Will, let alone two pennies?" asked George.

"I ain't gonna be worryin' 'bout gettin' no pennies, Georgie, 'cause it's gonna be you coughin' up the money when I win the bet."

George thought a minute. "Here is the final bet. Two pennies and you have to cut off a piece of her hair and give it to me."

"Two pennies," countered Will, "and I get to keep her hair. Bet?" Will stuck out his hand.

"Bet!" said George shaking Will's hand.

The January afternoon was windy, cold and gray and the McKendricks warmed easily to the comforts of Mary's hearth and home.

"You know," began Burris McKendrick, "I have often noticed this grand home from my sailboat on the weekends when Cordy, Polly and I are traversing the Southport during the warmer months. I always wondered who lived here," mused Burris reaching for one of Mary's sandwiches to go with his cup of tea. "Thank you kindly Mrs. Miller. But I never dreamed that one of its occupants might be a student of mine."

"Yes," seconded Cordelia, "I have especially admired the wonderful, stately old trees that grace your property. We live in the center of Clarksburg now in a lovely home but with few trees and none so magnificent as yours," said Cordy smiling over at Emma.

"There is in interesting story that goes with this old house," commented Emma. "Cream and sugar, Dr. McKendrick?" asked Emma passing the silver tray.

"Yes, thank you. Well, do not keep us hanging about, Emma. Tell us the story!" he laughed, leaning forward in his chair by the fireplace.

"My late father always used to tell this story and whether it is true or not has long been a subject of great family debate and speculation. Anyway, the house here on High Point Avenue had been commissioned by a prominent citizen of Grandview for his family and the house was nearing completion in 1861, when the Civil War erupted. Fearing that the Confederates would cross the river and seize his beautiful new home as their headquarters, this wealthy judge ordered that the house be completely dismantled and its timbers and bricks hidden.

"Fascinating," commented Burris, reaching for another sandwich. "Do go on, Emma."

"One chilly October night, the judge returned under the cover of darkness to the site where his grand but unfinished house had stood, only to find an encampment of Confederate soldiers here, warming themselves by a fire that they had quite obviously built with unearthed timbers from the original house. In a blind rage, the judge charged the soldiers with his sword drawn. The soldiers immediately opened fire upon him and the judge lay mortally wounded in a matter of seconds, but not before he ran a young Confederate lad through the heart with his sword.

As the judge lay dying in a pool of his own blood, he was approached by a soldier who knelt by his side to ask if he had any last requests. The judge said that he had but one and that was to be buried where he had fallen. Accordingly, the Confederate soldiers honored the last request of the judge and buried him just about here," whereupon Emma rose and moved to the front hall.

Spellbound, Emma's audience rose to follow her into the foyer, where she gestured to a spot now occupied by a table on which rested a worn wooden cross. "Under the house, right about here is where the judge is rumored to have been buried. And this," said Emma lifting the cross, "is the marker which the soldiers supposedly placed upon his crude grave that night."

Emma's guests gasped. "May I see that cross, please Emma," said Burris reaching out his hand.

"Let me see it too," added Polly pushing forward for a better view.

"But the story does not end there," continued Emma moving back into the parlor and resuming her seat. Burris followed her, still holding the cross.

"What happened next?" asked Cordy.

"Some of the residents of Grandview began to report sightings here on the property," answered Emma.

"What kind of sightings?" asked Polly scarcely above a whisper.

"Well, the townspeople began to report that they had seen the judge walking around his property late at night holding the wooden grave marker out in front of him like this," and Emma took the wooden cross from Burris and demonstrated for her guests.

"Then, too, people began to report that not only had they seen the judge but that they had heard him as well," Emma added.

"What did he say?" asked Polly breathlessly.

"BOO!" yelled Will impulsively at this point.

Startled at the unexpected outburst, everyone turned to look at Will.

"Now look what you have done, Will Richardson! You have scared our visitors half to death!" admonished Mary placing her teacup on the tray and reaching out to grab Will by his shirtsleeve.

"I was only havin' some fun!" wailed Will.

Looking askance at Will over the top of his round wire glasses, Burris turned back to Emma and asked, "I am assuming that the good judge did not say 'boo', so pray tell, what did he say?"

"Each time that the judge was sighted here, it was reported that he whispered the same words into the wind off the river," Emma answered pausing to sip her tea.

"Good heavens, Emma! The suspense is killing me! Do tell, what did the judge whisper?" asked Burris.

Clearing her throat and lowering her voice, Emma began dramatically, "'My restless soul is forever doomed to wander the meadow among the trees until my house has been rebuilt. Rebuild my house and set my soul free.'" At the end of Emma's recitation, the only sounds in the room were the crackling of the fire on its grate, the hissing of the gaslights on either side of the fireplace and the sonorous ticking of the grandfather clock from its corner of the parlor.

Finally, Burris broke the spell. "Who finally rebuilt this grand house?"

"My father did," answered Emma. "Everyone else in town was too fearful of the ghost of the judge to chance building upon the site where the man had allegedly died and been buried."

"You say the judge had 'allegedly' been buried here. Was his gravesite never authenticated?" Burris grilled Emma.

"No. The cross was here, we know that for a fact, but the earth beneath the marker was devoid of any human remains. When my father determined that there was not a gravesite on the property, he purchased the land when I was about four or five and commenced the task of unearthing as many of the original building materials as he could find. He salvaged what materials he could and used them whenever possible, as in the brick fireplace," said Emma pointing to the crackling fire.

"Your father never saw a trace of the judge?" pursued Burris.

"Whereas my father never mentioned that he had seen the judge's ghost, he did claim to have heard the judge on several occasions," responded Emma, passing Mary's salted pecans around to their guests.

"Did your daddy tell you what the judge said to him?" asked Polly, white as paste.

"Yes, as a matter of fact he did, many times. When I was about your age, Polly, my father and I always used to retire to the porch after supper and swing together. Frequently, during the month of October, my father would cup his hand to his ear, like this," and Emma demonstrated by placing her right hand behind her right ear, "and he would say, 'Hark! Can you hear him?' and I would be very still, stopping the swing so that we could hear above its creaking.

I never heard the judge's voice but my father always insisted that the judge was saying, 'Thank you for rebuilding my house.' I always thought it sounded more like the wind sighing through the pine trees but my father swore it was the judge whispering 'thank you'. That is why my father named our home, 'Whispering House'. Did you know that, Polly?"

Polly sat transfixed, butter and jam at the corners of her mouth, glass of milk poised in midair.

"Oh, heck, Ma! I've heard that old story a thousand million times," broke in Will.

Polly glanced disdainfully over at Will. "What do you know? You're just a boy!"

"I have an idea," said George brightly. "How about if we sit on the swing and listen for the old judge right now. Who knows? We might just get lucky. What do you say, Will?" and George turned to wink at his brother.

"Oh, yeah, Polly. That's a real good idea but 'scuse me for a minute first 'cause I got to pee," and Will ran up the front stairs two at a time. Once on the top landing, Will tiptoed past the bathroom and Johnny's bedroom, going instead straight back to Mary's bedroom. Quietly so as not to awaken the sleeping baby in the next room, Will began to look around for Mary's basket of quilting supplies. Carefully he lifted her scissors from the basket and placed them in his trouser pocket before pulling the chain that hung from the toilet and going back downstairs.

As the trio made their way to the front door, Emma called after them, "Put your coats on this minute boys! It is too cold to sit out there without wraps and help Polly on with hers too."

Reluctantly, the three children did as they were told. Once on the porch, the trio then argued about who was to sit where on the swing. "Don't get any part of yourself near me," ordered Polly, pointing an accusing finger at Will.

"Since it was my idea in the first place," began George logically, "I get to assign seats."

"Oh, yeah? Who says a boy gets to decide where I'm going to sit?" railed Polly.

"I do because this is my house and my swing," George responded decisively.

Mollified by his logic, Polly sat where George pointed, to a spot in the middle of the swing. The twins then took their seats on either side of their visitor, Will to her right and George to her left. Polly responded by drawing herself inward, tightly hugging her body with folded arms so as not to have any part of herself touch Will or George.

"Now what do we do?" asked Polly, turning from one boy to the other.

"We listen," George replied simply.

After several long seconds of sitting in silence, Polly said impatiently, "Well, all I can hear is the foghorn from the barge down on the river and the train going past."

"Wait another minute!" admonished Will, slipping his right hand into his pants' pocket.

"Maybe," suggested George, "if we cup our hands to our ears, like my grandfather used to do, we can hear the old judge better," whereupon all three simultaneously placed a hand behind an ear.

"No, no, not like that!" scoffed George. "You need to get that hair out of the way. You cannot hear the judge whispering with all that hair covering up your ears like that," and George reached up to extricate Polly's long blond hair from inside the collar of her heavy winter coat.

"You lay a hand on me again, George Richardson, and I'll smack you," was Polly's response, as she yanked her hair away from George and inadvertently into the face of Will who sat poised with Mary's quilting scissors.

Seizing the opportunity, Will snipped at Polly's hair with the scissors just as his accomplice on the other side of the swing yelled at the top of his lungs, "I can hear him! I can hear him!"

Momentarily stunned by the large chunk of hair that fell away onto Polly's shoulder, Will recovered quickly, pocketing both the hair and the scissors, to yell back, "Yeah, me too!" Then Will leaned forward and grinned broadly at his brother.

"Well, I didn't hear a thing," complained Polly.

"That's because you're a dumb old girl!" exclaimed Will jumping down from the swing and running to the front door, followed closely by George.

"Hey! Wait for me!" wailed Polly. "I don't want to be left out here alone with the ghost of that dead judge," and she scuttled after the boys.

Once inside, the trio removed their coats while the twins surreptitiously admired Will's handiwork behind Polly's back. A chunk of Polly's hair, measuring approximately six inches in length, was noticeably missing from the back of her head. Unaware of the damage to her tresses, Polly entered the parlor to announce, "Will and George are liars. They said they heard the judge whispering but I was real quiet and all I could hear was the train and that old barge."

"Perhaps another time, under more favorable conditions," Emma glared at George and Will, "you might be able to hear the judge whispering."

As Polly turned from her mother and Emma to take another butter and jelly sandwich, Cordelia was prompted to remark, "Why, Polly dear, whatever have you done to your hair? Do not tell me that you have been cutting it again after I explicitly forbade you to do so."

"No, ma'am, I didn't cut my hair," Polly responded defensively, stuffing her mouth with the sandwich.

"Well, just go look at yourself in the hall mirror," huffed Cordelia.

"My hair!" yelled Polly from the foyer. "Somebody cut my hair!"

"Do you boys know anything about this?" Emma glared at Will and George.

"Nope," responded Will, chewing a handful of pecans.

"Do I look like I have scissors on me?" asked George with great disdain pulling out the pockets from his pants to demonstrate that they were empty.

"Musta been them moths," opined Will, still chewing.

"Moths?" screeched Polly, looking horror stricken.

"Yeah, we've had a big problem with moths around here. You know, those things'll eat anything. Just ask Nana. She's always findin' stuff with holes chewed right through. Isn't that right, Nana?" Will looked over at his grandmother for verification of his hypothesis about the missing length of hair.

"Will, I seriously doubt…" began Mary only to be interrupted by Burris.

"Never mind. I say it is a blessing in disguise as I have been trying to convince both my wife and my daughter for many months that Polly's hair would be so much easier for her to take care of by herself if it were several inches shorter. But do these women listen to me?" scoffed Burris, laughing at his family. "I say we even it up right here and now. What say boys?" and he winked over at the twins, who hovered apprehensively just inside the entrance to the parlor.

George and Will exchanged looks of disbelief as Burris continued. "Now, run and fetch me a pair of sharp scissors, boys, and we shall just even up that hair of young Polly's. May we use your kitchen for cutting hair, Mrs. Miller?" asked Burris turning to the startled looks of the three women.

"Burris!" exclaimed Cordelia.

"Daddy!" cried Polly.

"Come with me, my sweet," said Burris taking Polly's arm.

"May we borrow your kitchen, Mrs. Miller?" asked Burris again, ignoring the protestations of his wife and daughter.

"By all means," replied Mary. Turning to her grandsons who stared at Dr. McKendrick in disbelief, she ordered, "George, pull a stool to the center of the kitchen by the table and you, Will, go upstairs and get my quilting scissors from the basket on the far table in my bedroom. Oh, and also bring down a comb from my dresser."

Cordelia interrupted these preparations, addressing her husband, "Burris! I simply cannot believe that you mean to carry through with such a thing as cutting poor Polly's hair here in front of everyone."

"All right, then, everyone can stay out of the kitchen so 'poor Polly' can avoid having others watch us while I cut her hair. I would expect normal children have legions of others hanging about and watching as their hair falls to the ground. Is that not true, Mrs. Miller? I mean, when was the last time that you cut the boys' hair in privacy? Is there not someone always watching everybody in this household while they bathe, have haircuts, eat, sleep…in short, live normal lives?" Dr. McKendrick had worked himself up into a frenzy.

"Emma, was that not your expressed intent which accompanied today's invitation? As I recall, it was your idea that Polly have an opportunity to be around other children so that she could learn to feel 'normal'. Am I right?" he asked brusquely, jabbing an index finger at Emma.

"Quite so, Dr. McKendrick," agreed Emma.

"Daddy…" wailed Polly.

"Stop your whining, child, and come with me to the kitchen," snapped Burris.

"At least," said Cordelia in an attempt to intervene, "allow me to do the cutting."

Burris stopped dead in his tracks and turned to face his wife, "Just who is the surgeon here? Who is it that makes his living cutting with these hands nearly seven days a week?" he asked holding up his hands in front of his wife's face. "Forgive the conceit dearest, but it is I who am eminently more qualified than anyone else on the premises to cut my own child's hair. Now, stop the histrionics, please," and Burris took Polly firmly by the arm back to the kitchen.

George was poised next to the wooden stool and at his elbow stood Will, with the infamous quilting scissors. Burris lifted Polly onto the stool and then from habit, turned to the sink to scrub his hands. "I need a drape of some sort," he said to Will who obligingly produced a clean flour sack towel from his grandmother's pantry. "Splendid! You, George, be prepared to catch our patient should she faint, and you, Will, are in charge of the instruments, meaning the comb and scissors. Is everyone clear about what they are doing?"

"Yes sir," the twins chorused in unison.

"Very well, then, let us begin. Comb!" Dr. McKendrick called whereupon Will fumbled the comb into the doctor's outstretched hand. "No, no, boy! Not like that! Like this," and he opened up Will's hand, smacking the comb briskly into its palm. "I do not want to have to take my eyes from the patient to look and see if you have handed me the correct instrument. I want to feel it…not see it. Feel it! Do you understand?"

"Yes sir, I do," grinned Will. "I can do that real good, doc," whereupon Will hauled off and slapped the comb against Dr. McKendrick's waiting palm.

"You show a lot of promise, son," Burris grinned back at the child.

For the next thirty minutes, Burris McKendrick enthralled his young assistants as he deftly cut six inches off his daughter's hair in order to achieve a symmetrical look to Polly's tresses following the unacknowledged damage inflicted by Will earlier. Standing back to survey the results of his handiwork, Dr. McKendrick announced, "I predict that the patient is going to make a full and complete recovery from her surgery. What do you think, assistants, Will and George?"

"I dunno," replied Will scratching his head.

"What do you mean, sir, 'I dunno?'" intoned Burris.

"Well, I'll betcha she has one of them re…relaxes and needs to have it cut again!" he crowed.

"RELAPSES!" shouted George.

"Yeah, one of them."

"Yes, I see your point, young master Will. Therefore, I shall prescribe one haircut every four weeks until the patient has reached the age of…let us say, twenty-one."

"Holy horse turds! By then she'll have lost all her hair and won't need no hair-cuts no more!" commented Will, enjoying their verbal banter hugely.

Polly, who had sat quietly sulking on her stool during the whole procedure, began to laugh too.

"Run and fetch a mirror for our patient here, George, so that she may admire the work of a genius," and they all laughed again, including Polly.

Meanwhile, in the parlor, Cordelia had been prompted to confide in Mary and Emma, "I really do not know what has gotten into Burris lately, but he has embarked upon another path, one that I am not familiar with and I shall tell you, I am having a difficult time of it…trying to find my way along this new path of his."

"Perhaps," offered Emma, "you might consider embarking upon your own path instead of trying to follow his."

Cordelia gazed uncomprehendingly at Emma, prompting her to add, "As for example, my dear mother seated here next to me, who was married to a very…shall we say, successful and busy man. James Miller had an opinion on every subject, which he freely shared. After I began my formal schooling, Mama decided to become a midwife and has become highly skilled at birthing babies. Everyone on this side of the river wants Mary Miller to deliver their children!"

"But I cannot go out into the world and become a midwife or a nurse at my age. My path is to follow behind my husband, raising our child, cooking, clean-ing, sewing and the like," Cordelia parroted looking from Mary to Emma and back again.

"Your path will be what you decide it should be," Emma reassured Cordy, patting her hand. "We women all have dominion over this," and Emma tapped at her temple with an index finger.

"Sounds like heresy to me! What do you think, Cordy?" laughed Mary. "Is that what they are teaching you across the river at that fine hospital of yours, Emma?"

"No, Mama dear. It is what I learned from you when no higher than your knee," Emma responded, smiling at her mother.

Just then, Polly entered the parlor followed by George. The flour sack had been removed and her hair neatly combed. "How do you like it?" asked Polly turning in front of her mother.

"Well…it is different…to be sure." Cordelia's response was devoid of enthusiasm.

"I think it quite beautiful, Polly, and I would expect that before too long, all the ladies over in Clarksburg will be imitating your haircut," Emma said admiringly.

"You do?" asked Polly incredulously.

"You bet I do."

"Polly said Will and I can keep a lock of her hair, too," George announced.

In the kitchen, Burris and Will were sweeping up the floor. Will stooped to gather up a handful of Polly's long pale hair. Carefully he smoothed out the strands of hair so that he had a neat little bundle of gold.

"You know what, Will?" began Burris.

"What's that sir?"

"Once upon a time when I was about your age, there was this little girl in my neighborhood and I really took a shine to her. Know what I mean?"

"Yep," answered Will as he continued to tidy up his grandmother's kitchen.

"That girl had the most beautiful long red hair. Well, I made up my mind that it would bring me good luck if I could cut off a strand of her hair and sleep with it under my pillow at night. So, one day while we were sitting in the schoolhouse, I reached up behind her and chopped off a piece of her hair," Burris laughed at the recollection.

"That red haired girl fussed and yelled so loud that the teacher made me spend the rest of the day sitting on a stool in the corner with a dunce cap perched on my head…but I held onto her hair."

"Is that a true story?" Will squinted at Dr. McKendrick.

"Cross my heart," and he made an X across his stomach while pausing to look seriously at Will, and then laughingly, made another X across the left side of his chest.

"I slept with that piece of hair rolled up in my handkerchief until I was a grown man and if you tell another living soul that story, I shall deny it," joked Dr. McKendrick.

"You can trust me," Will replied somberly. "I can really keep a secret. But what happened to the hair?"

"My darling Cordelia made me throw it into the river the day she discovered my good-luck parcel at the back of a dresser drawer in our home," Burris sighed, lost in remembering. Snapping back to the present, he added, "But let me tell you a funny thing about windows, my young friend."

Will looked confused so Burris pointed to the windows at the front of the house. Leaning down to place his lips next to the child's ear he whispered, "Remember lad, those windows allow you to see two ways…inside the house and outside the house!"

The following Monday, Heath Hamilton, true to his word, brought Rachel and baby Danny to Angel of Mercy Hospital for an examination by Dr. McKendrick. As Burris gently examined the small infant, Danny kept up a steady wail until he was handed a stethoscope. While Heath waited just outside the doctor's office, Dr. McKendrick spoke to both Emma and Rachel.

"I am appalled at the condition of this child and I can only attribute the baby's sad condition to your total ignorance," Burris intoned harshly, looking at Rachel.

"Yes sir," she responded meekly.

"This child should weigh twice what he weighs by now and…"

Emma intervened, "Dr. McKendrick, Rachel thought that she was providing the best for her baby by paying a wet nurse to feed Danny. She could not possibly have known that the wet nurse was cheating her by either failing to feed Danny all together or by only offering him one breast in order to double her income by doubling her customers. If anyone is to blame, it is the wet nurse and I for one believe that she should be stopped from this practice before she does additional harm to those babies that she has been hired to feed."

"Absolutely so and as soon as we are finished here, I want Heath Hamilton to take you to the constable's office where you will supply him with the name and whereabouts of this villainous woman. Do you agree, Rachel?" asked Dr. McKendrick sternly.

"Yes sir."

"In the meanwhile, I quite agree with the formula that Emma had the sense to prescribe for Danny. Did I hear you say that Danny has also begun to sleep the night since last Friday?"

"Yes sir. He's much less fretful now that his little stomach is full when I put him to bed at night with his last bottle."

"Splendid. Then in another week, I want you and Danny to return to me for a check up. Is that clear?" the doctor asked, scribbling some notes in the baby's chart.

"But sir, I can't afford the services of a doctor for…"

"Nonsense, woman. Who said anything about money? I do not intend to charge you a cent for my services. Now, do go on to the constable's office and help him to get this dreadful woman off the streets lest she continue lopping out those teats of hers all over town," and Burris turned to smile at Emma, whispering quietly, "Good work, Student Nurse Uppity!"

Emma hummed to herself the rest of the day as she checked on her patients, feeding and bathing them, changing their beds and their bandages, emptying bedpans and writing notes in their charts. It was an exhilarating experience to realize that she had helped to save a life, especially since it was such a helpless little life. "Danny deserves a chance at life," thought Emma to herself, "and I have helped to secure that chance for him."

Emma completed her day at the hospital and, gathering up her own small son, walked wearily out the front door to find Heath waiting for her on the front steps.

"Heath!" she exclaimed. "Whatever is the matter? Did something happen to Rachel and Danny?"

"Absolutely nothing is the matter," smiled Heath, reaching to take Johnny and the valise from Emma.

"What are you doing, Heath?" Emma asked, too tired to comprehend.

"I am going to escort you and the baby home tonight and," continued Heath while offering his free arm to Emma for support, "tomorrow morning, I shall reverse the process."

"Heath," Emma stopped dead in her tracks to turn and look at him, "what are you doing?" she repeated.

"I have thought of nothing else but you and your children this weekend and the near mishap of last Friday night as you rode past our place in search of Rachel's house. Come on now," he urged Emma, tugging at her arm, "we must walk if we are to make the ferry."

"But..."

"Emma, I am a big, strong man and I cannot stomach the thought of a woman struggling alone each and every day...back and forth...back and forth across that dang river with this baby and this heavy valise," Heath paused. "It is absolutely brutal...criminal...unheard of..." Heath groped for the right word. "What the heck...I have been sleepless over you and your kids and your...your...life all weekend. It absolutely makes me sick to think of the risks that you are taking to provide for your family," Heath said to Emma who studied his profile as they walked down Water Street.

"Why should you care about what happens to us?" asked Emma, surprised. "I mean the children and I and our struggles are really no concern of yours, are they?"

"I intend to make them my concern, do you hear me?" and he cranked his head around to glare down at her.

"Why?" Emma looked up at the unruly blond hair and stubble of his beard.

"Because…well…because…I have lost my heart to you and your three boys," and with a smile on his face, Heath delivered these words to baby Johnny who promptly reached out his tiny hand to squeeze Heath's nose. "There! You see, little John approves of me," joked Heath turning to look at Emma again.

Emma fell silent for the remainder of the walk down Water Street to the ferry. Clearly, she was too exhausted to engage in conversation so Heath, respecting her silence, continued to hold the baby and to allow Emma to lean on him as they navigated the waters of the Southport by ferry across to Grandview in the darkness.

Once on the far shore, Emma began, "Heath, would you accompany Johnny and me to the house and take supper with us? Perhaps after a bite to eat I can gather my strength and my wits about me again and we can talk. Will you do this for me?"

"For you, I would do anything," and Heath briefly hugged Emma to him.

"Nana! Nana! Look who's here, would you! It's that cowboy…Heath and Ma and Johnny!" yelled Will running back in the direction of the kitchen.

Mary greeted Heath warmly while Will scrambled around taking his hat and sheepskin coat. Pointing to Heath's boots, Will asked, "Did you forget the rule?"

Laughing, Heath sat down on the stairs in the foyer and bid Will to tug off his big leather boots. The removal of Heath's right boot sent Will flying backward onto the rug. Not wishing to be left out, George said, "Here, let me show you how to do this," delivered with his usual air of superiority as he wedged himself between Will and Heath's left boot. George yanked hard and nothing happened. George yanked again and he too went flying backward into a heap on the rug.

"Pick yourself up and dust yourself off, pardner," joked Heath placing his cowboy hat on George's head. Inspired to look like Heath himself, Will stuck his feet into the big man's boots, which reached up above his knees. Both boys postured around in front of Heath, strutting like they envisioned cowboys might, when Heath grabbed each boy around the waist and hoisted the two of them as he stood up from the stairs in the front hall. "And just for that, I am going to dunk you two horse rustlers in the river," which he delivered to the delighted squeals of the twins, dangling from his waist."

At that same moment, Emma appeared in the foyer, hands on hips, "What is all this noise in here? And who is making more noise, the children or the cowboy?" laughed Emma.

Heath set the boys on the stairs at eye level with himself and then grinning at the two of them, asked, "What say we get the little woman, pardners?"

"On the count of three!" commanded George.

"Oh, yeah!" shrieked Will.

"One..." began George slowly, as Emma began to back away from the boys and Heath.

Arms extended in front of her, palms vertical in a halting signal, Emma continued her retreat. "No, no!" she admonished the three as they continued to advance upon her.

"Two..." hollered Will.

"Get her, boys!" yelled Heath.

As she turned to run back to the kitchen, Heath reached out and scooped Emma up around the waist, even as he had hoisted the boys. While the captive flailed her arms and legs, Heath looked around at the boys, "What shall we do with her now, gents?"

"Throw her in the river!" yelled George.

"I know!" chimed in Will. "Let's tie her to the stake!"

Whereupon, Heath removed his belt with one hand, braced Emma against the newel post at the foot of the front stairs and with his belt, fastened her to it.

"Heath Hamilton!" fussed Emma. "This is not funny! You let me loose this instant!"

"That was worse than roping a wild mustang!" declared Heath to his cohorts, wiping his forehead with the red bandana in mock exhaustion while all three of them ignored Emma's threats.

"Now, I do not know about you men, but I have worked up a mighty large appetite. What say we mosey on back to Nana's chuck wagon and rustle us up some of her fine grub?" asked Heath, warming to the role of cowboy on the range.

"Good idea, pardner," George responded imitating Heath.

"Yep, sounds good, partner," added Will.

"PARDNER," yelled George. "Not PARTNER."

"You cannot just leave me here! I am the mother!" sputtered Emma.

Cupping a hand to his ear, Heath paused midway down the hall and asked, "Boys, did you just hear something?"

"Nope," responded Will.

"Probably just the wind," chuckled George.

"Thought so," said Heath and the three left Emma strapped to the newel post in the foyer.

Emma waited and then yelled, "Mama! Please come undo Heath's belt!" Emma could hear them all back in the kitchen serving up their plates. "I am starving!" she yelled again.

Then she heard Heath's voice, "Just let me handle this one, lady and gents," and the sound of his bare feet as he walked toward her.

Walking around in front of Emma, Heath addressed his captive, "You will have to pay the fine before I can turn you loose, ma'am."

Emma played along this time as if infected by the same delirium. "Well, then, at least tell me what my crime is…the uh, charges…you know?"

"Emma Richardson, you are hereby charged with disturbing the peace," announced Heath seriously.

"And just what might the fine for that be?" asked Emma, imitating his serious tone.

Leaning down to her face, he whispered, "This is the fine," and he kissed her full upon the lips. "Actually, you are going to have to pay a double fine because you are also charged with trespassing," Heath shouted back in the direction of the kitchen, while leaning down to kiss Emma again.

Suddenly, Emma went limp, hanging out away from the newel post, head dangling down upon her chest.

Alarmed, Heath raised her head with his hand and looking at her closed eyes, asked, "Emma, are you all right?"

"Relax, cowboy. Do you not recognize a swoon when you see one?" she whispered to him, eyes still closed. "Now, get me out of here before I starve to death and you deservedly end up in jail for murder," and Emma commenced to giggle as Heath carried her back to the kitchen.

The boys and Mary began to laugh hysterically at the sight of Heath carrying Emma into the kitchen like a sack of potatoes over his shoulder. "Look what I found out yonder on the prairie, boys. Should we fry it up for dinner?"

"Yecch!" commented Will.

"The thought of fried mother meat makes me want to puke!" George delivered with a look of disgust.

For two hours the family lingered around Mary's table, enjoying the meal, the laughter and each other's company. Finally, at eight o'clock, Emma rounded up the boys for their baths while Heath washed and dried the dishes with Mary. At nine o'clock, Mary bid Emma and Heath good-night and the house was blissfully quiet.

Heath stoked the fire in the parlor fireplace, adding logs for the long, cold night. Emma sat quietly watching him as she sipped one final cup of coffee. Taking a seat across from her, Heath gazed contentedly back at Emma. Placing the ankle of his right leg on the knee of his left leg, Heath wiggled his elevated toes at her.

"Heath, stop that! I cannot laugh any more this night or I shall be ill right here in the parlor," she warned him.

"How long has it been since you laughed like that, Emma?" asked Heath, the smile fading from his lips.

"Long enough that I have forgotten the last time," and her voice trailed off as she looked into the fire. Turning back to him she added, "Thank you, Heath, for such a memorable evening. My boys so deserve to laugh and have fun!

Their poor little lives have been turned upside down and I regret that so many burdens have been placed upon their small shoulders so soon in life. I always wanted my children to experience the wonderful kind of carefree existence that I knew as a child," she added wistfully.

"I cannot adequately express to you the rage that I feel when I contemplate these boys of mine and their lost innocence…these three angels who suffer so undeservedly as a result of their mother's monumental stupidity," she spit out the words.

"So…now you would shoulder all the blame for Edward's disappearance?" Heath demanded leaning forward. "What are we going to do about this untenable situation, Emma?" asked Heath.

"I do not know," said Emma slowly shaking her head. "I have been able to chart a course for my professional life but not for my personal life. Do you know what I mean?" she asked Heath sadly.

Without waiting for a reply, Emma continued bitterly, "Edward made sure that each and every one of us would feel the cruel thrust of his hatred. Edward's neglect and abandonment of his three children is criminal and unconscionable. Leaving me to wonder about my destiny as a woman is the edge of the huge sword that he sharpened just for me. It is Edward's daily curse upon me. Am I married? Am I widowed? Am I divorced? Am I slave or am I free? Never…never to have the answer!" Emma began to weep. "Edward has left me in this ambiguous space…this limbo of his, created just for me and designed to last an eternity. I fear I have been sentenced for life to this prison that Edward built for me," groaned Emma burying her face in her hands.

"Then I say we defy the abusive bastard and this life sentence unfairly imposed upon you and the children," whereupon Heath pounded his fist into the chair cushion.

Wiping her eyes with the napkin from under her coffee cup, Emma looked sorrowfully over at Heath's handsome, distraught face. "So, instead of four lives being ruined, we should now endeavor to ruin a fifth life as well? Your life? The smartest move you could make right about now, Heath Hamilton, is to pull on those big boots of yours and let them carry you down to that ferry, across the river and into the arms of some young woman who is free to marry you and have your children," and Emma began to weep again.

Heath rose, picked Emma up like a doll and sat down with her on his lap, gently stroking her hair and softly kissing her cheek. "Stop that crying, now, or you will have me in tears soon, and cowboys are definitely not supposed to cry!"

Emma smiled through her tears. "Dear Heath! Why did I have to meet Edward instead of you all those years ago?"

"You asked me that question before," responded Heath, "and I have thought long and hard about an answer. I do not believe in destiny or fate," began Heath. "I believe that over the course of our lives we are given the ability to make changes…to shuffle the cards and deal ourselves a new hand. Do you understand my meaning, Emma? You do not have to play this hand out the way Edward dealt it to you."

Emma looked up at Heath, her face contorted, eyes swollen, "I understand your meaning," she sniffled, "but how do I shuffle my cards again?"

"Just the way you did when you entered nursing school, with courage and conviction," he replied calmly.

"But I was not in danger of being labeled a scarlet woman or a bigamist, or even worse, a whore, by entering nursing school!" she exclaimed in return.

"Labels that others stick on you can always be peeled off," soothed Heath, wiping her face with his bandana. "I am not suggesting that we resort to bigamy. All I am suggesting is this…let me love you and the children. Let me help provide for you and the children and Mary. Let me spend the rest of my days with you."

"Aye that will be the trick of the century since we can never marry!" said Emma standing on her own two feet and moving to the opposite side of the parlor. Parting the velvet drapes, she looked beyond the scalloped edges of the lace curtains out into the darkness.

"I understand that we cannot marry. I understand that you must continue with your nursing school training even as I must continue to breed, raise and sell my horses. I understand that you live in his house," and Heath pointed to the floor, "and that I live in the one across the river. But, what I do not understand is why any of that should prohibit us from loving each other and being together. Why should that prohibit us from raising your three sons together?"

"It will be a rather unconventional liaison," mused Emma, feeling the cold of the windowpane with her fingertips.

"Well, to hell with convention! We are just going to reshuffle these damned cards until we get a winning hand. Are you in this game with me or not?" asked Heath, extending his hand to her.

Emma approached Heath slowly. Taking his outstretched hand, she kissed it lightly with her lips and whispered, "Oh, Heath! I need you so desperately!"

"Not half as much as I need you," Heath responded as he rose to lift Emma in his arms and carry her quietly up the long flight of stairs.

CHAPTER 14

▼

Over the course of the last remaining weeks of winter and on into the spring of 1890, Emma and Heath slipped into a quiet routine of tending to their work during the day while spending evenings and weekends with the three boys and Mary at the house on High Point Avenue. Heath slept in Emma's bed and Emma slept in the spare bed in Johnny's room, prompting Heath to remark, "I am probably the only man alive that sleeps in a woman's bed without the benefit of the woman!"

Reluctant at first about the unconventional relationship, Mary acquiesced as she began to witness the changes that Heath's presence brought to the lives of her daughter and three grandchildren. Heath worshipped Emma and plainly adored all three boys, who adored him back.

Frequent visitors to the house on High Point Avenue were the McKendricks and Polly, who had come to regard the Richardson boys as friends and accomplices in mischief. Likewise, Emma received a standing invitation to bring her boys across the river to the McKendrick household. Both Cordelia and Burris resisted the temptation to pass judgment upon Emma and Heath's unconventional arrangement, having been privy to the details of the tragedy which had forged their union.

To be sure, not all those who knew Emma accepted her new relationship with such equanimity. Hummel's seethed with salty gossip about Emma and Heath and some in the town of Grandview snubbed the family. To which Mary replied in her customary fashion, "Good riddance to bad rubbish!"

Emma and Mary were fortunate to count among their friends Constable Luke Crawford, who, because of his frequent stops to see the family on his way across the river to court Louise Bennington, formed a friendship with Heath Hamilton. Luke frequently made the trip across the river and back with Benni in order to spend weekends with her at the house on High Point Avenue. Emma, Heath, Benni and Luke soon became fast friends.

Not everyone in the family took such a sympathetic and supportive attitude toward the pair, however. Heath's father, the Mayor of Clarksburg, was vocal in his denunciation of Emma. Initially cordial to Emma, Adam Hamilton grew increasingly contemptuous of her as the details of Emma's past were revealed to him. Adam was determined that his son not become entangled with this married woman who was the talk of Grandview and rapidly acquiring notoriety on the Clarksburg side of the river as well. "Just as an example," Adam Hamilton cautioned Heath, "while I was eating my lunch at the Foggy Bend Hotel this noon, I was advised by a friend that this woman of yours has actually been seen smoking bedside in the hospital.

As if that were not scandalous enough, I beheld her dressed in male attire with my very own eyes the night she came riding through Clarksburg. An associate of mine further assures me that it is not unusual to see her galloping the fields of Grandview dressed in trousers."

Adam was careful never to call Emma by name, preferring instead to refer to her as "that woman of yours", "her" or "she" to Heath's face. Behind his son's back, however, Adam called Emma, "the trollop whom men love to gallop", accompanied by his pantomime of riding a horse.

When Heath ignored his father's narration of petty town gossip, Adam changed tactics. "I have it on good authority," he began somberly one day in early spring, "that she was with child before...before mind you, she married that bugger. It would behoove you to ascertain the veracity of that charge, would you not agree, Heath? I mean, think of it! She was sullied before her marriage!"

Heath continued cleaning out the hoof of his palomino, bent low over his work. From that angle, Adam could not see the emotion that registered on his son's face. While Heath's hands never paused, his heart all but stopped in his chest at Adam's latest charge.

Several days later, the weather warmed enough for Emma and Heath to sit together in the swing on the front porch. A heavy fog drifted through the Southport River Valley carrying with it muffled warnings from the barges that slowly navigated the obscured waters.

"I can barely see beyond the front steps," commented Emma to Heath as he read the Grandview Courier and haltingly guided the swing back and forth with the heels of his boots. As her attempt at conversation produced no results, she persisted, "You certainly are engrossed in what you are reading. In fact, you have been strangely silent most of the day. Are you hiding from me behind that paper there, sir?" Emma teased, rattling his paper with a twig that the previous night's storm had deposited on the porch.

With his face still behind the paper, Heath replied, "I believe you have got it backward. It appears to me that you are the one hiding from me on the other side of this paper."

Emma's smile faded as jokingly she snatched his paper away and saw the look on Heath's face.

"Why, whatever is the matter, Heath?" Emma worried.

Heath slowly and deliberately picked up the newspaper to fold it before responding. "All these weeks I have turned a deaf ear to the gossip, the innuendoes and the insinuations that others have hurled at us, even as I have urged you to do. But…"

"But what, Heath?

"But there is one particularly vicious piece of tripe that I cannot rid myself of no matter how hard I try," and his speech faltered as Heath averted his gaze out into the fog.

"Tell me what you have heard that so troubles you, my dear," soothed Emma placing her hand upon his.

Withdrawing his hand abruptly, Heath stood up from the swing and took several long strides away from Emma before responding. With his back still to her, Heath said, "I have heard that you…were…sullied before your marriage to Edward."

Emma flushed to the roots of her hair as Heath turned sharply to face her, "Is that true?"

Trembling, Emma sat mute, stunned to hear her sin put into such harsh words. All these years she had hidden from the truth herself. Emma had naively believed that only two others knew. Complicit in the grand deception had been Edward and Mary.

Emma found her voice and though barely audible, replied, "It devastates me anew to have you of all people hurl my sins at my face," and she gripped the arm of the swing to keep herself upright.

"Is it true?" he asked again.

"It is true, I confess it." Whereupon Emma began to weep.

"Why?" Heath asked simply.

"Why did it happen? Or why did I lie about it?"

"Both, I suppose."

"Just when I was beginning to trust you...just when I thought I had found a safe haven from all the misery and torment inflicted upon me by Edward...you now seize this moment to wound me also. What is it about you men that you are so driven to destroy the women whom you profess to love?

You hold the sweet little butterfly in the palm of your hand, enjoying its rare beauty," and Emma extended the open palm of her hand, "and then you insist on closing your fingers over its glorious colors until you have squeezed the very life out of it," she added closing her hand to make a fist.

"You trounce me falsely!" thundered Heath in response to Emma's accusations.

Emma sat weeping uncontrollably from her perch on the swing, legs tucked beneath her long skirt. Heath approached her, removed a fresh red bandana from his pocket and wordlessly handed it over to her. Turning abruptly from Emma's display of sorrow, he strode to the far railing and leaned out into the fog, inhaling deeply.

"I guess you had best be going," sniffled Emma, still wiping her nose and face.

"Not on your life!" Heath replied.

"What? Stay with a woman who lost her virginity before her marriage almost nine years ago?" Emma asked derisively. "I want you to turn and look at me, Heath Hamilton, and I want you to answer a question of mine," whereupon Emma clapped her hands together for emphasis.

"Which question would that be?" he responded with a question of his own, looking across the porch at her.

"I want to know if you partook of the pleasures of the flesh before you met me?"

"Indeed I did not!" exclaimed Heath moving to sit beside her once again on the swing. "You are quite missing the point here, Emma," he said in an exasperated tone.

"Oh no! I think I quite get the point! Your holier than thou demeanor has made it plain..."

"Be still," he commanded, "and listen to me for once!"

Emma blew her nose loudly while Heath waited for her silence. "Now may I say what is in my heart and on my mind?" he asked in a quieter tone.

"Proceed," she responded contritely.

"It matters little to me that you chose to lie with Edward before your marriage. After all, what is it that I have done with you? We are not married and probably never will be unless someone can put a bullet through the bastard's hide and drag it back to Grandview as proof that you are free to marry me.

What does matter to me is that you did not disclose the full extent of your relationship with Edward to me. I have told you absolutely everything about myself but you deliberately hid this part of yourself away from me and that causes me pain. It tells me that you do not trust me with your innermost sorrowful emotions. Do you really think me untrustworthy?" Heath looked across at Emma with eyes suddenly the color of slate.

"I feared your reaction to the truth. I feared I would lose you if you knew…" Emma stammered to Heath.

"There can be no secrets between us, Emma. It is not what you did but that you hid it from me that hurts me so terribly."

"Heath, please try to understand my perspective. I was just shy of my twenty-first birthday and unmarried when the twins were conceived," she began haltingly. "At first, Mama and I both thought I was ill but my illness persisted until finally one morning, it dawned on Mama that I might be with child. She is an experienced midwife, after all."

Emma drew a deep breath before continuing. "When Mama approached me with her fears about my condition, I reluctantly admitted that it was probably true. Mama's first thoughts were for me, my baby and then my reputation in the community. I say 'baby' because we did not then know that I carried twins."

Blowing her nose again into Heath's bandana, Emma continued, "Mama did not want the child born out of wedlock, thereby forever having the stigma of 'bastard child' attached to it. So, she approached Edward secretly and advised him of the turn of events to gauge his reaction. Not surprisingly, Edward was delighted at the prospect of bettering his lot and insisted upon marrying me immediately. Mama swore the two of us to secrecy and never told Papa."

"How then did you get your father to acquiesce to such a hasty marriage between the two of you?" Heath asked. "You have often told me of your father's hatred of Edward and it does seem unfathomable…"

"That was fairly easy," Emma laughed for the first time. "Again it was my mother who did the talking. She told Papa that my illness was a direct result of acute melancholia brought on by my unhealthy preoccupation with Edward's prolonged disappearance from my life. She convinced Papa that I so feared the loss of Edward again that it was making me ill. Mama reasoned that the only way to ensure the return of my health was to arrange for the two of us to be married at once."

Heath looked dumbfounded, "And your father accepted this fabrication?"

"He never questioned her diagnosis of what ailed me or the suggested cure, to my knowledge," replied Emma adding, "My mother could have convinced Papa that the moon was made of cheese."

"But, how then did you explain the fact that your boys arrived less than nine months after you married Edward?" persisted Heath in his questioning of Emma.

"Mama, once more, came to my rescue, proclaiming that since there were two babies they had obviously been born prematurely. She would not let anyone outside our immediate family see them, proclaiming the boys were 'too delicate' for many months. Papa was never allowed to see them unwrapped. Mama would always say to him, 'Oh, James, just look at how tiny and helpless they are!' My father saw exactly what Mama suggested that he see."

"On second thought, a bullet is too good for that bugger. The Indians have a way of dealing with his kind. Perhaps someone should turn him over to the Apaches!" exclaimed Heath.

Blowing her nose again, Emma looked uncomprehendingly at Heath, "What would they do?"

"They have been known to strip a man down, bind his ankles and wrists together and then sling him across a horse before riding out into the desert with him. Next they pound four stakes into the ground, one for each hand and foot and these stakes are placed further apart than his arms can reach or his legs can stretch. Do you know what rawhide does as it dries after having been soaked in water?" Heath asked, turning to Emma to make sure that she grasped the full import of what he was about to describe.

"I have no idea," replied Emma.

"It shrinks," Heath paused.

"Well?"

"Well, what?"

"Heath, you know very well what...what would the Apaches do to Edward next?"

"Oh that?" laughed Heath. "You mean you actually want to hear the gruesome details of Edward's torture at the hands of some of the fiercest fighters in the entire West?"

"You bet I do," replied Emma forgetting her troubles as she began eagerly to anticipate Edward's demise at the hands of the Apaches.

"You might faint if I tell you," warned Heath.

"You might faint if I told you about some of the surgeries that I have witnessed old Burr perform so do get on with it!" she countered.

"Very well then. Where was I?" asked Heath scratching his head.

"You were at the point where the Apaches were driving the stakes into the ground and using strips of rawhide," she reminded him.

"Yes. So, the Apaches pound these stakes into the ground far away from where his hands and feet can reach with him lying on his back in the hot sun," continued Heath as he rose from the swing to lie spread-eagle on the porch floor in front of Emma. "Next they attach a strip of wet rawhide to each wrist and each ankle and then to the corresponding stake so that there is very little play in the rawhide. Are you following me so far?" he asked, rising from the floor.

"I believe I may actually be ahead of you," responded Emma, warming to the hypothetical plan for torturing Edward. "Then the rawhide shrinks as it dries. Am I right?" she asked.

"Exactly, so that eventually, but very slowly and very painfully, his arms and legs are dislocated."

"Is that all?" Emma asked, clearly disappointed.

"Well, the Apaches have also been known to sever the testicles after the culprit has been staked out, causing him to bleed profusely. Once the odor of blood permeates the desert air, it is sort of like ringing the dinner bell. That smell is sure to draw a large gathering of hungry scavengers."

"Just what kind of scavengers?" asked Emma, eyes riveted upon Heath.

"Oh, the usual kind," he stalled.

"What is the usual kind?" she prodded.

"You know...like buzzards, coyotes, pumas...all the usual meat eaters. Oh, and I forgot one additional detail," Heath added nonchalantly.

"What detail?" Emma shivered on the edge of the swing.

"The Apaches favor the use of slivers of wood inserted through the eyelids and up through the skin of the forehead to keep the varmint's eyes open in the broiling sun."

"Mmmm...sounds too good to be true!" laughed Emma, feeling that Heath's narrative was all a ruse to get her mind off her problems. "But, I think it makes a good story and I must confess, I rather enjoy the notion of Edward suffering...even if only imaginary tortures!"

"I can assure you that what I have just told you is not a figment of my imagination," said Heath flatly.

"Oh, do be serious, Heath!" she admonished him.

"Well, just let me put it to you this way. If I were Edward right about now, I would definitely not choose to hide out West without the benefit of a full military escort."

"We are not at war with the Apaches!" exclaimed Emma, adding, "Are we?"

"At war? No." Heath walked to the front steps. Leaning against the porch column, he asked casually, "Did I ever mention to you that I have friends among the Apaches?"

Picking up one of the small cushions from the swing, Emma hurled it at Heath's back. "You are the biggest storyteller for miles around, Heath Hamilton!"

"Am I now?" he asked turning to her.

Emma realized that Heath was no longer smiling.

As the first year of her formal training to be a nurse drew to a close and final examinations loomed on the horizon, Emma told Heath that he would have to curtail his visits to the house on High Point Avenue until she had completed her studies.

"What about the boys? Do you expect me to vanish just like Edward from their lives so that you can study for your final examinations? It has suddenly become inconvenient for you to have me around so now you seek to dismiss me. How absurd, Emma!

I have become just like one of your modern conveniences...like water from a spigot or gas to a wall lamp. You expect to flip a lever and I am here! Flip it the other way and I am gone! How handy for you!" said Heath sarcastically as he glared at Emma over the top of Onion's stall where he was busy cleaning out the horse's hooves.

"My nursing certificate represents a secure future for me and my children," she began clumsily.

"Oh, and I suppose I represent a threat to that secure little future of yours by accommodating your every whim? Just how many times have I offered to give you a stipend for your living expenses? How many times have I offered to pay off your nursing school indebtedness? And how many times have you turned me down?" he asked wiping his hands on the worn leather apron while shutting the door to Onion's stall.

"How many times have I showed up at your front door with a wagonload of coal or a box full of groceries? How many cords of wood have I cut, split and stacked for your mother's cookstove and the parlor fireplace? How many hours have I spent on the roof of this house replacing its battered old shingles? Why do you insist that I am trying to deprive you of a secure future instead of understanding that I am doing my level best to provide for you and the boys? But always I am met with this...this nonsensical discourse of yours," Heath paused, angrily jerking off the apron and throwing it onto the straw-littered barn floor.

"Heath, what can I say to clarify my position for you? How can I make you see the world with my eyes?" Emma moved over to Onion's stall and reached out a hand to stroke the long white blaze that ran from the horse's forelock down to his nostrils.

"Whatever it is, it had better be good!" exclaimed Heath in his exasperation at Emma. "We just seem to argue constantly about nothing these days," he added shaking his head. "I wish I possessed one of those crystal balls. You know, like the ones the traveling carnival gypsies always have? So that I could look deep inside your mind and see what in hell is going on in there!" he fumed.

"You might not like what you see," replied Emma, turning to walk away from him.

Reaching out a sinewy arm, Heath grabbed the back of her long skirt and dragged her back to him, while simultaneously turning Emma around to face him. "Then maybe it is high time I be allowed to look inside and decide for myself whether I like what I see or not!" Whereupon, Heath kissed her full upon the mouth.

"Heath Hamilton! I cannot stay angry at you when you behave like this!" Emma scolded him.

"But do you not see, Emma, that I have done nothing to offend you? I have done nothing to incur your wrath. It was Edward, not I, who abandoned you and the boys. He beat and tormented you...not I. You have somehow connected the two of us...like Siamese twins, inside here," and Heath touched the curls above her forehead. "You are punishing me for what Edward did to you and if I may say so, you are doing a damned good job of it too!"

Moving away from Heath's embrace to a rough-hewn bench along one of the barn walls, Emma sat down and motioned for him to do likewise. "Let me see if I can explain my position to you," she began before being interrupted by Heath.

"Just let me say one final thing before you begin bending my ear. Any other woman would be happy to have a man who worships the ground she walks on, loves her children from a previous union, makes a good, decent living and wants to give her the sun, the moon and all the stars in the heavens. There, now you can talk," and Heath reached out to tweak Emma's nose, leaving it smudged with dirt.

"Well first, let me begin by reminding you that I am not like any other woman," huffed Emma, "and second, what is given can also be taken away!" she announced triumphantly.

"Well, just how idiotic is that! I mean, we are given life and then the Almighty takes it away when He decides that our time on earth is through. Are you angry with Him too?" In mock despair, Heath raised his gaze to the cobweb-festooned rafters above their heads, cupped his hands to his mouth and called, "God, what are we to do with this woman? Please tell me!" he implored the dusty air.

"Just like a man! Always missing the point!" admonished Emma, trying to push Heath off the bench. Heath responded by playfully shoving Emma back, causing her to tumble off the bench into the straw and dirt.

"How dare you, Heath Hamilton!" she sputtered.

"It is my recollection, Emma Richardson," he responded grinning down at her, "that you began this shoving match and I suggest that you are a very poor loser. Furthermore, I say to the victor go the spoils," and Heath rose, slung Emma over his shoulder, climbed the ladder to the hayloft and pulled the ladder up behind them.

Still brushing dust from her skirts and picking telltale bits of straw from her auburn ringlets, Emma remarked to Heath as they emerged from the barn, "You of course realize that settled nothing."

"It did for me," and Heath reached down to bite her ear lobe.

"Oh, please be serious for half a second, Heath," Emma implored him, pausing to lean up against the trunk of a massive oak.

"But I am serious!" he protested. "Serious in all that I say to you…serious in all that I do for you…what more can…"

"Stop!" she commanded him. "I never did have a moment to complete my train of thought with you before I was so rudely…well, you know."

"No, I do not know. Before you were so rudely what?" Heath grinned at her.

"Before I was so rudely swept off my feet!" she laughed. "Let me say this…just once, please! All right?"

"Say it, but only once because you know how I dislike having you lecture me over and over again about the same subject like I am some deaf, imbecilic, snot-nosed five-year old," he warned her.

"All right then, here it is. My biggest fear in life is not being able to provide for myself, my children and my mother. Edward ran off with nearly every cent we had along with our horse, leaving me with a little row house, two boys and a third on the way.

Notwithstanding his abuse of me, Edward did work the mill after my father's death with the help of Lowell and old Bill, earning a living for the four of us and my mother. Immediately after Edward's departure, I came to the shocking realization that I did not possess the means, the education or the wherewithal to support my family. It was then that I decided to take control of the reins of my runaway life.

I charted a course that included education, hard work and the help of my angel of a mother. If the five of us could just hang on for two years, I reasoned, I could earn my nursing certificate and then no man could ever again take away that which I had earned…that which was not his.

So you see, my darling Heath," Emma concluded, reaching up to touch his face lightly, "if I were to allow you to step in and rescue us, to provide for us, to wrap us in a cocoon of financial, marital and familial bliss, you might one day decide, like Edward, to take it all away from me, from us. In a heartbeat, everything would be gone again."

Aimlessly, Heath picked patches of lichen from the trunk of the giant oak and hurled them into the spring breeze. Exasperated, Emma snapped, "Have you heard anything that I just said?"

"Why is it that you women always equate silence with deafness? Yes, I heard every word and I am thinking. You think with your mouth open and I think with mine shut."

Whereupon, Emma turned on her heel to leave.

"Hold on there a second. I am just damned sick of the sight of your bustle every time I say something that you deem to be offensive. We are never going to resolve these issues between us if you run off every time I open my mouth. You demand an answer from me, I start to give you one and bang! You are off and running again because I have dared to ruffle your feathers."

Emma stopped in her tracks and turned toward Heath, "Very well, then. I shall be quiet and you can do the talking."

"Emma, I am not attempting to tread on your independence. I am not trying to break you to a saddle like one of my yearlings. I do not own you. You are married to another man, so that for the time, at least, I cannot contemplate asking you to be my wife, although I fervently wish I could legitimize our relationship.

Given those circumstances, I have asked only that you allow me to love you and provide for you. Where is the harm in either of those requests? How do I demean you with either? I am not seeking to enslave you when I deliver a wagonload of coal to your doorstep. I am trying to provide for you, the children and Mary as a way of easing your burdens. Is that not what a decent man is supposed to do these days? Provide for the ones that he loves?"

Softening, Emma replied, "Of course, you are right, Heath, and I apologize for being so harsh. I realize that I carry a very large axe over my shoulder, just waiting for a chance to imbed it in some man's head."

"Yes," interrupted Heath, "and since Edward is not here, my head will do nicely, eh?" His blue eyes lightened.

Such debates would continue to permeate their relationship. Emma's quest to be self-sufficient and independent of all men would constantly thwart Heath's best efforts to provide material comforts for her and her family. She would not give in and he would not give up and it was that mutual stubbornness which made the two of them so ideally suited for each other.

Sequestered in the pink and rose-festooned bedroom of her childhood, Emma studied diligently for her written examinations that spring of 1890, ignoring the shouts and laughter that drifted up through the lace curtains from the front lawn where Heath played with her sons in the evenings and on weekends. Every so often, Emma would detect a faint scraping of paper under her door. Rising she would retrieve the handwritten note which usually read something to the effect that, "The pleasure of your company is requested at dinner in thirty minutes. Cowboy stew, prepared by Heath and company." Signed, "Love, the Cowboy, Will, George and John."

Or Emma's favorite, "Hey, diddle diddle! Hot off the griddle! Pancakes and sausages in fifteen minutes and coffee so strong IT CAN WHUP HEATH (compliments of Will)."

It was during this intense period of study that Emma decided to wean Johnny. At ten months of age, the child possessed enough teeth to chew soft food and, Emma reasoned, the ability to drink from a cup. The weaning process was facilitated by the fact that John was clearly intent on imitating his two older brothers. Whatever George and Will were eating or drinking, John likewise had to have. Mary at first balked at Emma's decision to fly in the face of conventional wisdom which decreed that a child should be breast-fed for at least twelve months and preferably longer. "By that time, Mama," she quipped, "Johnny will have chewed me to bits trying to get enough to eat!"

Emma's decision to wean John also meant that she would not have to take him back and forth across the river with her to the hospital five days a week. John could now remain at home with Mary, thus lightening the workload for Emma. However, with school soon to recess for the summer, Mary was faced with caring for three grandchildren by herself during the week, until Heath stepped in and announced that he would be taking George and Will with him to work on his horse farm just south of Clarksburg each day.

"Providing," added Heath wryly, "that having the two older boys with me all day does not pose a threat to your independence." Emma ignored him.

Fanella Walker's final written examination for the nursing students took one whole Friday to complete. The young women wrote furiously for three hours in the morning with Nurse Walker incessantly pacing the aisles between her students' tables, wooden pointer poised to rap a cheater or a talker. At noon, the class was allowed to break for lunch and the women fled en masse to the Water Street Bakery.

"I for one must have a large slice of chocolate cake for my lunch or I shall not make it through the next three hour session," complained Benni to Emma. "Could you figure out the answer to number four? All that stuff about so many ounces of liquid per so many pounds of body weight. I just know I calculated the answer incorrectly," she moaned.

After a hasty lunch of sweets and strong coffee, the nursing students returned for their final onslaught upon Fanella Walker's difficult questions, neatly handwritten on the blackboard. "We should have thought to bring the old girl some lunch," whispered Emma to Benni as they took their seats. "She obviously spent her lunch hour erasing the whole board and writing the rest of our exam."

At the close of the day, Nurse Fanella Walker gathered up her students' written answers to her final examination questions. "Student Nurses," Fanella addressed the group, "I fervently hope that each and every one of you has had the good sense to pass your written examination!" Waving the sheaf of exam papers at them, she continued, "As I might have to resort to severe and inhuman forms of punishment for anyone who fails," whereupon Nurse Walker smiled at the bedraggled young women.

"Yes, Nurse Walker," chorused the class.

"Yes, what?" asked Fanella. "Yes, you passed or yes, you failed?"

"Yes, we passed, Nurse Walker."

"Splendid! I like my nurses to adopt a positive way of thinking. We shall meet back here on Monday morning to receive our test scores and also to receive job assignments within the hospital for the next two weeks. Class dismissed and," she added grinning, "enjoy your weekend!"

Emma picked up Johnny from the children's ward for the last time and wearily handed the child over to Heath as she walked out of the hospital and into the beautiful spring evening.

"How did it go?" Heath asked solicitously, tossing Johnny onto his shoulders for the walk down Water Street to the ferry.

"About as I expected," she replied, reaching up to pull her long hair from the baby's grasp.

"What does that mean?"

"It means," she replied tersely, "that it was hard as hell."

"Oh," replied Heath quietly, sensing that to say more was to invite an outburst. Instead, he strolled along in silence while Johnny kept up a steady stream of babble from high atop Heath's shoulders.

Once settled on the ferry, Heath held the squirming baby with one arm and, reaching out with the other, encircled Emma and bent low to whisper into her ear, "Have I told you recently how much I love you and how very proud I am of you?"

"Heath Hamilton, you are the sweetest talking man I ever did meet! You do know what I need to hear and when I need to hear it!" she replied wearily.

That weekend, Emma was uncharacteristically tense, tired and just generally out of sorts, prompting Heath to say little and do as much as he could to help Mary with the boys and the cooking.

After a session with Heath in Mary's kitchen Saturday afternoon, Will came running to his mother who lay dozing in the swing while Mary sat in a wicker chair mending a pair of the boys' trousers.

"Hey, Ma!" he yelled, placing his mouth about three inches from Emma's ear.

"Oh, Will! Not so loud!" she exclaimed, sitting upright, rubbing her ear. "Has the kitchen caught fire?" she feigned a joke.

"Nope. Guess again."

"Well, let me see…Brute ate our dinner?"

"Nope. Guess again."

"We are going to have alligators and sausages for supper tonight?" she asked, poking a finger at his navel.

"Wrong again! Georgie and me…we made sugar stick bread all by ourselves to have with the fried meat and potatoes that Heath cooked up," Will announced triumphantly.

"That sounds…special, Will. I can hardly wait to taste it," whereupon Emma rose wearily from the swing and allowed herself to be led by her son back to the kitchen.

In Mary's kitchen, Emma found George busily heaping a platter with the freshly baked sugar stick bread while Heath served up the meat and potatoes. "It would seem as though someone has been exceedingly…busy in here," was all that Emma could manage as she surveyed the mess in the kitchen. Grease, flour, sugar, butter and potato peels were combined into a nauseating stew on every flat surface, including the floor.

"Would you like to try some of our bread?" George asked proudly, shoving the platter under his mother's nose.

Stifling the urge to gag and swallowing hard, Emma responded politely, "Not right now, dear. I think I shall save that treat for dinner."

Mary appeared in the door from the dining room and managed an, "Oh my!"

"Well, then, we should all take our plates to the table," suggested Emma, smiling gamely at Heath.

"Boys did a fine job of cooking tonight," bragged Heath. "Fixing the meal themselves was all their own idea. Knowing how tired you are, Emma," he grinned, "George and Will wanted to do something really special for you."

"And they surely have," Emma smiled wanly at the twins. "Yes indeed...they surely have done something special," Emma repeated for emphasis, nodding her head and looking around in disbelief.

After the blessing, Emma began mashing up some of the fried potatoes for Johnny, while cutting bits of carrot into tiny pieces for him to eat. Emma spent an inordinate amount of time at this endeavor which did not escape the notice of her twins. "Ma, you haven't even started your dinner and I'm nearly through with mine," fussed Will, looking askance at her untouched plate.

"What you need," remarked George, "is a piece of our yummy sugar stick bread," and he placed one of the charred pieces on her plate. "Try it," he urged.

"Pass the butter, please Will," said Emma as she broke open the piece of bread. "My...what an unusual color," she commented examining the interior. "It appears to be...gray and...what are all these little specks inside? Seeds of some sort?"

"Oh, that...well, Georgie, he was kneeing the bread and..."

"KNEADING THE BREAD, Will. With my fingers, not my knees!" admonished George.

"As I was sayin', George was KNEADING the bread and it dropped on the floor. Me and him tried to get all that grit out but Heath said," and Will waved his fork of fried potatoes in the direction of Heath, "that it was okay because everybody has to eat a peck of dirt before they die anyways."

"Ah...that explains it," blanched Emma. "But what about the lovely gray color? Just how was that achieved?" she asked turning to cock an eyebrow at Heath.

"I was wondering about that too," commented George, "so I asked Heath because Nana's bread is never that color."

"Pray tell George, what did Heath say?" asked Emma, still looking at Heath.

"Well," answered George, "he said that the color came off our dirty hands because we forgot to wash them before we did the kneading and we had to knead that dough a bunch of times."

Heath grinned at Emma. Johnny slung potatoes onto Will's head. Mary sat quietly at the head of the table, chewing. George dipped his bread into a glass of milk. Emma began to gag.

Rising swiftly from the table, Emma managed to say, "Please excuse me." She ran through kitchen and out the back door from the porch, pausing to retch violently in the grass.

Looking around at those who remained seated at the dinner table, George asked, "Did I say something wrong?"

"Guess I shoulda told her they was seeds," sighed Will with his mouth full of greasy fried meat.

As Emma was too ill to get out of the spare bed in Johnny's room the next morning, Heath changed the bed linens on her bed where he had been sleeping and then carried Emma into her front bedroom overlooking the vast expanse of lawn that sloped down to the river. He laid her gently on the fresh sheet, draping a quilt over top of her. "But where will you sleep?" she protested.

"Stop your fretting," he ordered her. "I shall be quite content to share a room with Johnny."

Mary entered Emma's childhood room, raised her eyebrows at Heath and commented, "We seem to be playing musical bedrooms." Then producing a glass filled with murky water in which black bits floated, Mary announced, "Here Emma, you must drink all of this at once."

"Oh, Mama! I shall surely vomit if I even smell that horrible concoction!" groaned Emma, turning away from her mother.

"You must, dear, as it is the tried and true remedy for an upset stomach...which you know only too well having given it to your own children many times," said Mary handing the glass to Emma.

"Well, fixing it for the boys to drink is one thing, but actually having to drink it myself..." and Emma grimaced.

"Let me smell that," said Heath bending down to take a whiff of the foul looking liquid. "What in the name of horsesh...I mean...what is that stuff?"

"Why Heath dear, have you never had charcoal tonic?" Mary laughed. "And here I thought its medicinal powers were widely known on both sides of the river! To prepare this, you must first blacken a slice of bread over the fire. When the toast has cooled sufficiently, you then scrape all the charcoal from it into about a half glass of water. You must scrape both sides of the burned toast. Then you mix with a spoon and have your patient drink it up. Works like a charm every time."

"That is," added Emma, "if you can get it past your nose!"

"Stop stalling, Emma!" commanded her mother. "Bottoms up, now!"

"Hold your nose like I do," George helpfully demonstrated by pinching his nostrils together as he walked into his mother's room to sit on the foot of her bed.

"For someone who is such a wonderful nurse, you sure do make a lousy patient!" admonished Heath taking the charcoal tonic from Mary. Holding the glass to Emma's lips, Heath admonished her, "Now drink this before the boys and I have to take drastic action."

"I have always heard that you can lead a horse to water, but you cannot make it drink," stalled Emma.

"Do not bet on it," Heath cautioned.

"Ma, just tell yourself it's a necktie for Jesus!" exclaimed Will pulling Johnny around his mother's room in the wooden wagon.

"A what, Will?"

"A necktie for Jesus," the child repeated.

"Now what in the heck is that, Willynilly?" asked George in an exasperated tone of voice.

"You know…like when Heath drinks beer sometimes and says it tastes like a necktie for Jesus," Will beamed at his mother.

"I think what the lad means," intervened Heath, "is that it tastes like nectar for the gods."

"Cheers!" said Emma as she downed the charcoal tonic.

Emma kept the tonic down but was too ill to get out of bed the rest of the weekend. By Monday, Emma was still feverish and weak so Heath decided to cross the river over into Clarksburg and ask Nurse Fanella Walker to come have a look at her.

"But Heath," protested Emma, "I must go to the hospital today and get my final examination score and my duty assignment for the next two weeks."

"You can do no such thing. You must stay put and let Nurse Walker come here."

Around noon, Fanella Walker rapped loudly on Mary's front door. Brute gave Fanella his customary intimate greeting when Mary admitted her to the foyer, causing Nurse Walker to fume, "Mary, that dog is so obnoxiously intrusive! You really must do something about him!"

"Outside, Brute!" ordered Mary holding the front door wide for Brute to exit the premises. "Please accept my apology, Fanella. He really means no harm."

"I realize that dear, but that huge, wet, black nose of his is unsettling to say the least," and after adjusting her skirts, Fanella marched straight up the staircase.

"Where is my patient?" Fanella began to call midway up the long flight of stairs.

"She's back here, Nurse Fannie," answered Will careening around the corner with Johnny in the wagon.

"Good heavens!" exclaimed Fanella. "Who are these fine big boys that I see before me? Is it George or Will with John?" she asked, pausing at the top of the stairs to greet them.

"It's me, Will. Hey, you wanna take a ride in the wagon, Fannie? Hop in and I'll pull you on back to Ma's room."

Without further ado, Fanella sat in the wagon, "You know Will, I was hoping that some kind soul would offer me a ride today. What I would not give for a fine big boy like you to pull me around that hospital all day long in such a stylish wagon," she told the boy who struggled down the corridor to Emma's room. "It is a rare treat, Will dear, to be able to raise these tired old feet off the floor at this time of day.

Emma? Are you dozing? If so, you must wake up and witness the arrival of Head Nurse Fanella Walker in her red chariot. George! Hello! Sound the trumpet as I make my graceful entrance," and George pretended to make trumpet noises by blowing through his cupped hands.

"It would appear that entering my chariot was easier than exiting it. Will, pull me over to the bedpost," and grabbing hold, Fanella hoisted herself to an upright position.

"Well done, boys! I am once again properly vertical," Fanella praised the children, reaching to clip her pince-nez glasses firmly to the center of her nose before turning her attention to Emma. "Now, Student Nurse Richardson, which would you like first, a taste of my thermometer or," and she reached into her black bag to produce Emma's test papers, "knowledge of your test score?"

"Will the latter make me feel better or worse?" Emma asked, timidly peeking out from under the covers.

"A great deal better I should wager," beamed Fanella.

"Very well, then...tell me," said Emma, propping herself up on the pillows.

"Sound the trumpet again, please George, as I am pleased to announce that Student Nurse Emma Richardson was the only one in her class to receive a mark of..."

George blew loudly through his cupped hands again.

"One hundred percent!" exclaimed Fanella above the noise.

With that, Will took off running downstairs to his grandmother and breathlessly exclaimed, "Nana, Nana! Guess what? Ma got one hundred pennies for her test!"

"She got what?" Mary asked, looking confused at Will.

"One hundred pennies!" he exclaimed again.

"We shall just have to go upstairs for a translation of that, I would expect," mused Mary, following Will down the front hall to the foyer, up the staircase and back down the corridor to Emma's room, where everyone seemed to be suddenly in a celebratory mood.

"Ah, Mary, have you heard the marvelous news?" asked Fanella, beaming.

"I have heard Will's version of the news and…"

Without waiting for her mother to elaborate, Emma interjected, "Fanella has told me that I received the highest mark in our class on the final examination."

"Oh, splendid, my darling. I just knew you would do well."

"Emma here did not miss a single answer to any of the questions," added Fanella, "and, I might add, she was the only student to get one hundred percent!"

"That explains the one hundred pennies!" laughed Mary.

"Whatever do you mean, Mama?"

"Oh, nothing. I shall tell you later, but how very kind of you, Fanella, to come all this way to share the good news with Emma and the rest of us. It was just the sort of news that Emma needed to revive her spirits."

"Well, since my examination of Emma's nursing skills has been successfully concluded, I must now ask all of you to leave the room while I administer a different sort of examination," and Fanella ushered Mary and the children out of the bedroom.

"Does this mean that we can have chocolate cake?" asked George, leaving Emma's bedroom.

"And can Nurse Fannie eat it with us?" chimed in Will as they walked down the hall.

"Absolutely yes, on both counts," Mary responded lifting John onto her hip, "but this time, I shall do the baking!"

Fanella sat on the edge of Emma's bed, stethoscope dangling from around her neck at the conclusion of her examination of the patient.

"What are your findings, Fannie?" asked Emma apprehensively.

"The truth of the matter, as I see it, is that you have been burning a very short candle at both ends. You must understand that I am totally supportive of your goal to become a nurse but…"

"But what?" asked Emma again, the worry evident upon her face.

"But I think you must learn to take better care of yourself, my dear, before you wind up in our hospital as a patient, instead of as a nurse." Smoothing Emma's sheets, Fanella continued, "Trust me the worst is over as there will be no more late nights and weekends spent burning the midnight oil to complete your studies.

Frankly, I do not know how you managed to avoid collapsing long ago with three children and one of them a babe at the breast for much of your first year. Then too, that whole ugly mess with Edward would have done in a lesser woman long ago. You are surely a marvel, Emma, and an inspiration to us all."

"Oh, please, Fannie...you bestow credit where none is due," protested Emma modestly. "My mother has shouldered the burden of the older two boys, your fine nurses have cared for Johnny and Heath Hamilton has ensconced himself in our lives as our protector, so I have had the very best of help from so many, not to mention yourself and Burris McKendrick. How could I have made it this far without all of you?"

"True, we have lent you our support, but what I am trying to say, and rather poorly to be sure, is that your attitude toward this heroic struggle is what renders us all so besotted with you. You have not faltered, not waived an inch from your chosen path, no matter what the obstacles, and I have yet to hear a single complaint from you.

Having said all that, let me now return to the point which is this...this stubbornness...this single-mindedness of yours that has exacted its price...has taken its toll upon you. You must now take a leave of absence..."

"But..." Emma began in protest.

"No buts, my dear. You simply must take some time off to rest and recuperate. In addition, it has not escaped my attention or that of your classmates that you eat like a bird and by my calculations, you appear to have lost a considerable amount of weight. Would you agree?"

"Yes, Nurse Walker," Emma replied as if she were in class.

"Then what I want you to do is to take the next two weeks off, eat Mary's good cooking, sit outdoors and breathe the wonderful, fresh spring air, go for long walks every day and sleep, sleep, sleep! In addition, you must take one tablespoonful of molasses and one of cod liver oil three times each day. Here is the cod liver oil and I assume that Mary has molasses in the pantry," said Fanella looking over her pince-nez glasses at Emma.

Emma made a face at her. "Be careful, Uppity, or I shall require you to swallow two of each for a total of twelve daily," Fanella chided her, smiling.

"Oh, no! Not you too!" complained Emma.

"Me too what?" asked Fanella, busily packing the black leather bag with her nursing apparatus and supplies.

"It is bad enough that Burris calls me Student Nurse Uppity, but now you are doing it also," Emma again complained.

"Well, we call you that my dear, because you are uppity and the name suits you. Also, we seek to keep you humble because you are just too bright for your own good. Conceit would not sit well upon those skinny shoulders of yours.

Now I must be off, my dear, to catch that blasted ferry. I do so wish someone would construct a bridge across that river! The mere thought of sailing on the ferry makes me seasick. What a charming sight that would be! Head Nurse Fanella Walker from Angel of Mercy Hospital leaning over the railing, retching up her lunch.

Any last messages for me to deliver to your friends at the hospital?"

"Yes, please do tell Benni that I would so love to have a visit from her and any of the others that want to make the perilous journey by water over here to see me. Do caution them to take the ferry on an empty stomach, however," Emma teased Fanella. "Oh, and be sure to tell Edna Ford that I shall miss our daily rendezvous for the next two weeks."

"I shall do it," said Fanella, allowing her pince-nez glasses to dangle once again from the black ribbon that punctuated the front of her white blouse like an exclamation point.

"One more favor, well actually, several favors," Emma called as Fanella began her retreat.

"Yes?" Fanella turned back toward her patient.

"I should like to know when Joseph is due to be discharged as the others and I were tentatively planning a 'going home' party for him. He is the amputee, you know. Then, I should like to have word about the woman who just gave birth to twin boys. I assisted with that birth. I need to know how the mother is progressing and how much the babies now weigh. They were such tiny babies and I am wondering if their mother has enough milk to nurse them or if they are going to have to be placed on formula. Please ask Burr if he will examine Daniel Johnson for me during my absence. I want to make sure that child is continuing to gain weight on his formula. And, I really think that Rachel, the child's mother, needs to be seen by Burr as she is looking anemic to me. Then, I would like to know if Burr plans to carry through with his suggestion to render Valeda Suggs infertile as I feel quite certain she will turn up pregnant based on my lengthy conversations with her in the hospital and by my calculations it is nearing the time to assist her with that decision. Then..."

"Emma! Do pause for air!" laughed Fanella. "I still have nurses on staff to cover for your absence! I know that you take an unparalleled interest in each and every patient assigned to you in addition to the strays that you acquire, like Danny and his mother, but you simply must stop for a bit," Fanella admonished Emma, standing once again at the side of her bed.

"I promise that I shall relay all of your concerns to Benni and ask her to come prepared to undergo a rigorous examination as to the condition of each and every patient of yours. How does that sound?"

"Thank you, Fannie. I should be most grateful for news of my patients. They haunt my dreams at night."

"I know they do, dear. That is why you are going to make such a fine nurse. If it is of any consolation to you, both my patients and my student nurses haunt mine as well. Now get some rest!"

Emma did as she had been instructed. For the remainder of the week, Emma adhered to all of Nurse Fannie's instructions but by Friday, she was feeling bored which, as Mary commented, was a good sign. It meant that Emma was almost well.

"Mama, I have an idea," Emma announced at the supper table Friday evening, as she ate her milk toast.

"Heath! Close the shutters and lock the doors! We must not let word of this idea escape the premises!" chuckled Mary.

"I quite agree, Mary. I know only too well the hazards and pitfalls associated with Emma's ideas," Heath winked across the table.

"Tell us! Tell us!" chanted the twins, sensing that their mother was hatching a plan that included them.

"Well, how would it be," she responded casually, "if we invited Benni, Luke, the McKendricks and Polly to go on a picnic with all of us, say, this Sunday?"

"Oh, boy!" shouted Will. "We ain't never been on a picnic before!"

"We have too," corrected George.

"Have not!" shouted Will.

"Dummy, we go to the church picnics all the time," elaborated George, picking up Mary's homemade noodles with his fingers.

"Use your fork, George!" admonished Emma.

"Just where is this picnic to take place?" asked Mary.

"Well, I was thinking that we might ask Luke to hitch up his buckboard and we could hitch up the carriage and then we could all travel to River Bluffs for the day. How does that sound?" Emma asked looking around expectantly at every-one.

"Sounds like one of the greatest ideas you ever had, Ma!" exclaimed George.

"Yeah!" seconded Will.

"Yes, and I could fry up some chickens and make that chocolate layer cake that all of you profess to like so much," enthused Mary already mentally preparing the meal to feed the picnickers.

"I had better bring along Grit," added Heath lost in thought.

"Do you really think that we would have need of a third horse, Heath? I mean, Luke has one and we have Onion," Emma said.

"You are talking about a lot of hard pulling for those two older horses so I need to have one in reserve to take over if one or the other of them pulls up lame," explained Heath.

"I shall leave those details to you," Emma responded blithely waving a hand in Heath's direction. "But, more importantly, who is going to extend our invitation to the McKendricks in time for Sunday?" she asked looking around the table.

Pointing to Will and George, Heath responded, "I believe that honor falls to me and the boys. Right boys?"

"Right, Heath," they chorused.

"Tomorrow, after breakfast, George, Will and I shall hunt up Luke Crawford before going across the river to work at the farm. Luke can then invite Benni. Since the boys and I pass right by the McKendricks' house on our way to the farm, we shall stop off and issue the invitation to them too. Good idea?" Heath asked turning to Emma for her approval.

"Splendid," responded Emma, who turned to her mother and asked, "what do you think, Mama?"

"I think I had better get busy cooking," laughed Mary.

"Whoopee!" shouted Will, suddenly moved to jump up from supper to dance around the table.

"Appears to me that Willy has ants in his pants, Ma. I better get the fly swatter," said George leaving the table for the kitchen. Waving the fly swatter wildly in the air, George returned to chase Will around the dining room table. The idea of a picnic on Sunday had elevated everyone's spirits so that the boys' high jinks produced laughter instead of the customary reprimands.

Sunday morning after church, the tightly knit group of friends began to gather at Mary's house. As Luke Crawford pulled up in the front yard seated atop his straw-filled buckboard, George and Will raced out of the house to admire Luke's draft horse, a black gelding with a white star emblazoned in the middle of his forehead.

"Boy, this here's the biggest horse I ever did see!" exclaimed Will fully extending his arm upward in order to stroke the horse's thick neck. "Whadya call him?"

"This, my young friends, is Thunder," responded Luke, tying the horse's reins to a column at the far end of the front porch.

"How tall do you suppose Thunder is?" asked George trying to measure the horse's height with his hands.

"Well, he's about seventeen of my hands," laughed Luke looking at George, adding, "but I reckon he's about thirty four of yours."

"More like a hundred of mine!" exclaimed George in awe of the enormous black horse.

"Why do you call him Thunder, Constable Luke?" asked Will continuing to stroke the horse.

"Because when this big boy takes off at a gallop," answered Luke, "it sounds like the thunder that warns of a summer storm."

"Can we ride with you and Thunder to River Bluffs?" asked George bouncing a large rubber ball on the porch at eye level with Thunder where he stood tied to the column.

Thunder responded nervously to the thud-thud-thud of the rubber ball, jerking his head up and down and snorting.

"Easy there with that ball, George," cautioned Luke. "Yes, you two rascals can keep me and Thunder company."

Mary appeared on the porch with her last basket of picnic provisions to say, "I can see the ferry approaching our side of the river, Luke, so perhaps you and Heath would be so kind as to fetch the McKendricks and Benni for me. Please take our carriage down to meet them," instructed Mary.

Heath brought Onion and the carriage around from the back of the house where he had tied Onion to the back porch, remembering his skittish behavior around other horses. Grit had been saddled and led from his stall at the opposite end of the barn from Onion to be tied to a column at the far end of the porch, away from Thunder. As Luke and Heath took the carriage down to the landing, Mary called up the stairs, "Emma, are you and the baby just about ready?"

"We shall be down directly," Emma called from the baby's room.

Warmed by the early morning sun, a light spring breeze played with the young leaves newly arrived on the army of huge oaks and maples that lined High Point Avenue and surrounded Mary's house. Two tiny wrens were waging war upon Brute where he lay soaking up the sun on the front porch. The birds took turns scolding the big dog unmercifully for his proximity to the nest they were tucking into a corner of the porch roof, high atop the lazy dog's head.

Heath and Luke returned with the McKendricks and Benni. "Ahoy, mateys!" called Burris. "Fine weather you ordered up for this picnic!"

"Cordelia! Burris! Polly! Benni!" exclaimed Mary as she gave a welcoming hug to each of her friends. "We are so delighted that you could all join us today."

"Wild horses could not have kept us from enjoying an afternoon in your splendid company, my dear," responded Burris as he presented a bouquet of mock orange blossoms to Mary.

Will scampered about the carriage while George bounced the ball on the front steps. "George!" admonished Emma, "Stop that at once. I heard Luke tell you it makes Thunder nervous," and holding John with one arm on her hip, she deftly intercepted the ball with her free hand.

"Hi, Polly!" called Will, running up to embrace his friend.

"Will Richardson, you just get off me this minute," and then catching a warning look from her mother, Polly extended her hand in greeting to Will. It was an obvious compromise arrived at between mother and daughter to be delivered to the ever-ardent Will, who took the hand she offered and kissed it. Whereupon, Polly promptly, and not too discreetly, wiped it upon her skirts. Will just flashed a lopsided grin.

George fiddled with Onion's traces, pretending to ignore Polly and Will. Cordelia returned Mary's hug and began to assist her with the placement of picnic provisions in the carriage. Benni reached to take Johnny from Emma, exclaiming at the baby's growth and all his newly acquired teeth. Heath leaned down to George and whispered an invitation for the boy to join him atop the carriage, with the implication that he might be allowed to handle the reins of the carriage. "Sorry Heath," responded George," but I intend to ride with Thunder."

"So, who else is going to ride with me today?" asked Luke.

"Me!" shouted Polly.

"Me too!" echoed Will.

"Okay, Will, but just don't you try any funny stuff…like cutting my hair, or so help me, I'll slap the poop out of you!" warned Polly, tossing her short hair as she turned to climb into the buckboard.

"How come it is that just as soon as Polly appears, Will forgets that he is supposed to help with the horses?" complained George handing Grit's reins over to Heath who tied the palomino to the rear of the buckboard and then climbed aboard the carriage, holding Johnny and pulling Emma up next to him.

Luke helped Benni up onto the buckboard seat next to him, while Will and George scrambled up next to Polly in the straw behind them. Burris, Cordelia and Mary were the last ones to seat themselves in the carriage before the group set off for River Bluffs, some two miles west of Grandview for their Sunday picnic.

"Did you remember the fishing poles?" Emma called back to George who was pretending to ignore Will and Polly, preferring instead to watch Grit as he trailed the buckboard.

"I remembered, Ma," called George.

"And I remembered to bring some nice fat worms just for your hook, Polly," said Will looking adoringly at her shiny gold hair.

"Do you really think I'm going to touch those horrible worms?" shrieked Polly.

"Nope. I'm not that dumb," answered Will. "I have it all planned to put the worms on for you," he stated with an air of superiority.

Johnny bounced along on his mother's lap next to Heath. Mary, Cordelia and Burris rode in the interior of the carriage, passing the time chatting pleasantly, commenting about the changing scenery and singing songs to entertain themselves.

River Bluffs had long been popular among the locals as a favorite fishing and picnicking spot. Part of the challenge to catching catfish from the river was the descent one had to make from the higher elevation of the bluffs to the flat rocks that lined the shore of the river. It took courage and skill to descend the enormous rocks that lay between the bluffs and the water.

As legend had it, there was an old and especially cantankerous river catfish that everyone thereabouts referred to as "Slippery Pete" who had been sighted but never caught. And of course, like all fish tales, Slippery Pete grew to monstrous proportions with the telling of each alleged sighting, until it was rumored that the fish was longer than a man was tall, which both frightened and challenged the twins.

"I'm gonna be the one to catch Slippery Pete today. You just watch," bragged Will to Polly as they reached their destination and ran about, helping to unload picnic provisions, fishing poles, toys, quilts and Will's jar of worms.

"Slippery Pete is going to take one look at you," warned George, "and have you for his picnic lunch today." Pointing to Polly, he added, "Then that big, old fish is going have you for his dessert. Yummy!" and George rubbed his stomach.

"Well that settles it! I'm not going down those rocks to that river," Polly announced, horrified at the thought of being ingested by a fish bigger than her father.

Cautiously, George approached the edge of the bluff, cupped his hands to his mouth and leaned out shouting, "Did you hear that Slippery Pete? No dessert today!"

The adults laughed but Polly grabbed her mother's skirts in horror. "You are definitely not nice, George Richardson. Stay away from me," she ordered, suddenly confronted with an imaginary picture of George shoving her off the bluff.

Emma sat baby John upright on a quilt under the shade of a sycamore tree with a pile of his toys. "Now remember everyone," she cautioned the adults as well as the children, "we must all keep a sharp eye on John so that he does not crawl out onto the rocks."

"Well, perhaps the best contribution I can make right now," offered Cordelia, "is to sit and play with this precious baby. It is not often that I have such an opportunity these days," and she stationed herself with her back to the rocks, facing John who began delightedly handing his toy soldiers to Cordy. "You know, Emma," she mused, "this child really does favor you with these gorgeous auburn curls and his sweet disposition," and she tousled the baby's hair softly.

"Mama, mama, mama," laughed John, clapping his pudgy hands.

"I declare this is the most adorable baby ever!" cooed Cordelia affectionately to her small charge as she rolled George's rubber ball over to him. "Just look at that!" exclaimed Cordy.

"This clever child rolled the ball straight back!"

"That is because I taught him to do it," George announced proudly. "John and I have been practicing."

"Babies are so dumb," declared Will to Polly.

"Yeah, they really are," she agreed with him.

"They don't do nothin' 'cept poop and pee and spit up all over themselves. That baby over there," and Will waved an accusatory finger over at his brother Johnny, "has pooped, peed and spit up all over me so many darned times that…"

"Hush, Will! Mind your language in front of Polly!" warned Emma.

"Oh, pay him no mind, Ma. Will is just showing off for Polly," concluded George. "I am going down the rocks to see what Heath and Luke and Doc are doing down at the river."

"Be very careful, George. Go slowly!"

"Quit worrying over me, Ma. I am nearly eight years old, you know. Nana?" he called over his shoulder.

"Yes, dear?"

"When are we going to eat that fried chicken?"

"Soon. As you can see, your mother, Benni and I are getting everything ready. Now, go down there and check on the whereabouts of Slippery Pete," suggested Mary.

George picked his way cautiously over the boulders, peering into all of the crevices formed by the mismatched union of two or more of the gray monoliths. Every so often, acting on a hunch, George would make a wide detour around an especially deep and dark crevice.

"Whatever are you looking for lad?" called Burris.

"Snakes," came the swift reply.

"Have you seen any?" Burris called back.

"Not yet," answered George arriving at last on the ledge of flat rocks that lined the riverbank.

"That's because all those snakes saw you first. All those king snakes probably got together and said, 'Here comes that human boy. Quick, crawl and hide before he skins us for his picnic!'" Luke teased George.

"Why are they called 'king' snakes?" George asked, turning to scrutinize the route he had just descended.

"Because they're the biggest snakes hereabouts," chuckled Luke taking out his Bowie knife to whittle a piece of driftwood.

"Just how big, do you suppose?" George persisted, standing in front of Luke.

Luke rose, fully extending his arm and the Bowie knife straight above his head. "About this long, I reckon."

George looked at the tip of the knife glinting in the sun high above Luke's head, down the length of his body to the toes of his dusty boots. "That big?" asked George in disbelief.

"Yup. That big!" declared Luke, stroking the flame red mustache that hid his smile.

"Is there another way back up to the top?" asked George weakly.

"Come, lad," offered Burris. "I feel the need for some of that marvelous cold tea that your grandmother makes. Would you help an old man back up to the top of this heap of treacherous rocks? I fear that without your assistance, I cannot make it," and Burris scowled his disapproval at Luke.

After George and Burris had made a wide berth of the boy's original route, they crested the top and waved down at Luke and Heath. "We made it!" George exalted.

"Good for you George! Good for you!" Heath called back.

"What did I say that made Doc so angry?" asked Luke, returning to his whittling.

"The boys are petrified of their own shadows," responded Heath quietly, skipping flat stones over the smooth surface of the water.

"Why?" asked Luke, uncomprehendingly.

"Because they have no father to teach them differently," said Heath, intent on his pile of stones.

"Oh, gosh, I didn't stop to think about that. Me and my big mouth."

"The bastard has been gone for about a year now and still no word to his children. I fancy the notion of strangling that son of a bitch with my bare hands for what he has done to Emma and these kids of his," whereupon Heath whipped off his hat and wrung it.

"Easy does it, pardner," said Luke placing a hand on Heath's shoulder.

"They live in a state of perpetual fear and expectation, always looking up and down High Point Avenue for their damned father. Ever since that bobcat leaped onto Will, the boys are just sure there is something sinister behind every tree, rock and barn in the county…waiting to grab them. And you know what scares them the most?" Heath asked looking over at Luke.

Luke shook his head.

"Those little kids are scared shitless that this unnamed monster is going to come for them and they will have no father to protect them from it!" Heath looked the other way.

"Oh, I didn't know," said Luke quietly. "But," added Luke brightly, "they have you, Heath."

"Yes, they have me and I can tell you that those kids and their mother have come to mean more than the whole world to me, but I am not what they want. Do you…can you understand? They want that horse's ass father of theirs! Does that not beat all?" asked Heath dejectedly.

Not waiting for Luke to respond, Heath continued, "If only Emma were free to marry me…then I could petition to adopt the boys and maybe then…just maybe then they might come to accept me as their father and their protector. Maybe then I could rid their world of these nameless fears…these nightmares that make the boys cry for their father in the middle of the night…" and Heath could not continue.

"Can we round up a posse and find this missing father of theirs?" asked Luke, removing his cowboy hat and wiping his forehead with a bandana.

"I have been thinking those same thoughts myself lately. I even told Emma in a round about way that I could get word to Gray Feather to find the bastard and scalp him for me," Heath chuckled malevolently, taking Luke's Bowie knife to demonstrate a scalping, Apache style.

"We're overlooking something here, Heath. A simpler, easier way."

"And just what might that be?" asked Heath.

"Wanted posters!" declared Luke.

"Now that is all Emma and the boys would have to see plastered around town!"

"No, I don't mean in Grandview or even Clarksburg. I'm talking about St. Louis. Everybody going west of the Mississippi passes through St. Louis and if I have wanted posters made with this bugger's likeness on it, especially if there's a reward, someone, somewhere on the other side of the Big Muddy will give us the whereabouts of this...what's his name anyhow?"

"Edward."

"Yeah, this Edward. Hell, friend, even his own mother would turn him in for the reward!" exclaimed Luke triumphantly slapping Heath on the back.

"Might just work at that," mused Heath.

"It's darn well worth a try, don't you figure? I mean rather than just sitting around here worrying about Emma and the kids and listening to their nightmares, right?"

Heath smiled at Luke, "Right! But not a word to Emma or anyone else, and for sure do not tell Benni, for as much as I like her, that woman cannot keep her mouth shut."

"It'll be just between the two of us and the twenty or so thousand residents of St. Louis, plus or minus a few thousand more who regularly pass through the city," beamed Luke, pleased to have come up with a plan of action for his friend.

"Hey, you two!" called Emma down from the top of the bluff. "If you do not get up here soon, we are all going to starve to death," and she made waving motions for them to climb back up the boulders.

Turning back toward the others, Emma summoned Will to her side, "It appears to me that Thunder is directly in the sun. How about if you and Polly move Luke's horse and buckboard over there to that shady area, away from Onion and Grit," and Emma pointed to a large outcropping of rock next to which grew an enormous oak tree that spread its shade generously around the picnic area.

"But," cautioned Emma, "do not climb up onto the buckboard. Just lead Thunder by his bridle and make sure you tie him carefully to that small dogwood tree just under the oak."

"Ma!" protested Will, "I'm not a baby. I know how to tie up a horse. I mean I've been doin' it all my life," he boasted looking over at Polly.

"Of course you have, dear. Now go, for we all need to eat."

"Come on, Polly, I'll show you how to do this," said Will, swaggering over to the draft horse. Will untied the gelding's reins, holding them tightly in both hands until he had a firm grip on the horse's bridle, then he guided the huge horse, still hitched to the buckboard, over to the protective shade of the giant oak. Will did as his mother had instructed and tied Thunder's reins securely to the small dogwood.

Everyone began to gather around the quilts that Mary, Emma and Benni had set with their picnic fare. "Boy am I hungry!" exclaimed George viewing the sumptuous spread that the women had prepared.

"I second that, my fine young friend," said Burris as he clapped a hand on George's shoulder.

"Then, please, let us all serve our plates and eat lunch before the ants eat it for us," laughed Mary.

With much merriment and teasing, the group of men, women and children settled down to partake of Mary's cold fried chicken, corn pudding, still warm from the oven that morning, green beans cooked with fatback and onions, baked beans, corn bread, canned peaches, cold tea and Mary's pound cake, rich with butter, eggs and sugar. Without exception, the men went back for second helpings.

"I do so love to see people enjoy my cooking. There is nothing I would rather do than cook for my family and my friends," concluded Mary.

"And there is little this particular group of your friends would not give to sit at a feast provided by you," Burris complimented Mary.

As the women began to wrap up the leftovers and repack the carriage, Burris turned to George and Will, saying, "Now how about the three of us go on down to the water and bait our hooks for I rather imagine that old Slippery Pete is hungry for his lunch too. What do you think?"

"That's why I brought all those fat worms, Doc," and Will ran to fetch his jar.

"No, Will. Slippery Pete wants some of what I brought," whereupon George produced a handful of white bread that he had carefully compressed into balls.

"How about if we try a bit of both?" suggested Burris.

"But what about those king snakes?" asked George.

"Yeah, what about 'em?" echoed Will apprehensively looking over the edge of the bluff.

"I have it on good authority that if you sing loudly and warn the snakes of your approach, they will flee. So what say we give it a try?" suggested Burris.

"What song should we sing?" asked George.

"How 'bout Yankee Doodle? And we can sing it real loud too," offered Will.

"Splendid. Now here we go, one, two, three…" and Burris waved a fishing pole like a band leader's baton while they sang, "Yankee Doodle went to town a riding on a pony. Stuck a feather in his hat and called it macaroni," at the tops of their lungs while descending the rocks.

"Guess I'd better go down there with them in case someone falls in the drink and I have to go for a swim," laughed Luke, pulling out his Bowie knife and whittling stick.

"I think Johnny is just about ready for his nap," observed Emma. "Oh, Luke?" she called after him.

"Yes, Emma?"

"Do you mind if I bed Johnny down in your buckboard in the straw? I believe that this wee one will be asleep the moment his head rests on his quilt."

"Be my guest, young Johnny, as there are no finer accommodations to be had," responded Luke, smiling and doffing his cowboy hat at the baby.

"Well, if a bed of straw was good enough for our dearest Baby Jesus, then I guess it will serve baby John well enough," sermonized Mary.

Emma climbed into the buckboard, made a well in the straw directly behind the wooden seat and lined the hollow with Johnny's quilt. Benni then handed the drowsy baby up to Emma who sat lulling him to sleep. Once the baby's eyes were closed, his mother left the buckboard in the shade of the oak to return to assist the other women with the clean up of their picnic remnants and to trade gossip.

Heath excused himself and walked to a heavily wooded area to relieve himself. Only Polly remained at loose ends.

"This is so boring!" exclaimed the young girl. "I just knew there wouldn't be a thing for me to do all the way out here," she complained to deaf ears. Peering over the edge of the bluff, Polly could see George, Will and her father fishing and the flash of sunlight off Luke's knife as he sat on one of the flat rocks whittling. Polly sat down to sulk in a heap, counting out loud the killdees as they stalked the shallows around the flat rocks at the water's edge. "One killdee, two killdees, three killdees, four…" but as no one took notice of her counting, Polly began to toss pebbles down at the fishermen.

"Hey, quit that Polly!" admonished George, finally paying attention to the girl at the top of the bluff.

"Yeah," chimed in Will, "or you'll scare away all the fish," and both boys turned their backs on Polly again.

"Go find something to do, dear," encouraged Burris, waving cheerfully up at his daughter.

As Polly rose and turned around, she caught sight of George's rubber ball. Picking it up with her left hand, she stood for a few moments clumsily trying to imitate the bouncing rhythm that had so impressed her as she watched George earlier in the day. Frustrated by her inability to keep the ball bouncing, Polly tucked it under her apron and called over to her mother, "Look, Mother, I have a baby in here!"

"Oh, I fervently hope not," laughed Cordelia. Looking over at Polly the other women laughed too, before returning once again to their chores punctuated by gossip.

Polly sniffed loudly, removed the ball from under her apron and wandered over to the buckboard. As she attempted to climb up for a peek at Johnny, her mother reprimanded her, "No, Polly! Do not disturb the baby's nap. Now do go and amuse yourself."

Thoroughly put out because everyone was ignoring her, Polly grabbed up George's rubber ball again and walked to the rear of the buckboard where she spied a well-trod path around the outcropping of rock. Slowly, Polly navigated the path around the outcropping and up the gradual incline that led through a profusion of butterfly weed and Queen Anne's lace to the top of the rocks. Having reached the top of the outcropping of rock while cradling George's rubber ball in the crook of her right arm, Polly gingerly crept to the edge of the flat, gray rocks.

Directly below her and still tied to the small dogwood, was Thunder with his cargo of sleeping baby. Polly looked all around to see if anyone was watching and then took aim at Johnny with the big rubber ball. With the ball in her left hand and with all the force that she could muster, Polly hurled the rubber ball down from the rocks. While baby Johnny had been her intended target, the ball hit Thunder on the withers instead.

Startled, the mighty draft horse snorted in alarm, rearing on his hind legs and pawing the air in a panic to be free of the rubber ball that rolled around under his feet. The second time the powerful gelding rose in the air, the small dogwood tree to which Thunder was tethered began to release its hold on the soil. The third time Thunder rose, the dogwood was free and so was the massive horse.

From her perch high above the horse's head, Polly laughed hysterically at the frantic scene that was playing out directly beneath her feet. Emma was loading leftover picnic provisions into the carriage on the other side of the clearing when the commotion began. The moment Emma heard Thunder's alarm, she dropped the pan of cold cornbread and leaped from the carriage. Gathering up her skirts, Emma flew after the retreating draft horse with the buckboard that held her infant son, screaming, "Heath! Heath! The baby!"

Heath rose from the privacy of a fallen tree shrouded in honeysuckle vine to button his trousers. As he left the dense undergrowth and began to make his way back to the clearing, Heath heard the horse before he heard Emma's screams. Racing back in the direction of Grit, Heath knew the black gelding was loose and running. Through his boots, Heath could feel the vibrations of the fleeing draft horse, still hitched to the buckboard.

Thunder and his precious cargo were already out of sight when Heath charged past Emma, who ran straight at him, arms extended, eyes wide with terror. Dodging Emma's panic-stricken clawing, Heath sprinted the last few yards to the palomino. In one fluid motion, Heath placed his hands on the horse's rump, vaulted into the saddle, yanked the reins loose, spun the pale horse around and was off at a gallop. Heath passed Emma as she continued to scream and run after her child and then he too was gone from sight, and still Emma ran.

When the men down at the river heard the ruckus and the women's screams coming from the picnic area, they immediately began the climb back up the boulders. "Watch the boys, Doc! I've got to help Heath!" shouted Luke as he outstripped the other three in his ascent of the bluff. Having crested the top of the boulders, Luke ran for the carriage and swiftly undid Onion's traces. Grabbing Onion's mane, he leaped onto the horse's bare back and galloped off in the direction of Emma's screams.

Benni, Burris and Cordelia fled single file after Luke. George and Will labored up the bluffs. No one noticed that Mary had fainted inside the carriage or that Polly lay cowering atop the rock outcropping under the giant oak.

Luke quickly overtook Emma who was still running but no longer screaming. Barely pausing, Luke reached down and grabbed up the diminutive woman, slinging her up onto the horse in front of him and together they continued their pursuit of Heath, Thunder and Johnny.

Initially, the uprooted dogwood bounced along beside Thunder, increasing the horse's panic, until it tore free along with its moorings just as the animal cleared the wooded area that surrounded the bluffs. Unfettered by the uprooted dogwood tree and the obstacles posed by the vertical growth of the forest, the powerful black horse gathered speed as he raced across a meadow, far from the picnickers.

Having been startled awake by all the commotion, but unable to sit upright due to the violent forward motion of the buckboard, baby Johnny lay awake in his quilted straw cocoon, crying loudly, "Maa-maa! Maa-maa! Maa-maa!" into the wind as Thunder pounded across the meadow, heedless of the baby's distress. A storm of straw engulfed the baby as the buckboard sped away from the river.

Heath cleared the trees and caught sight of the retreating buckboard. Spurring Grit to an even faster gallop, Heath raced across the meadow, closer until he could hear the baby's cries. The golden horse now wore a mantle of lather and flecks of foam blew from the bit in his mouth as the animal labored to catch the fleeing draft horse. As he had been trained to do when Heath rounded up strays on the Hamilton ranch, Grit approached Thunder from the left.

Parallel to the buckboard, Heath could now see its interior where Johnny lay flat, crying loudly for his mother as he was being jostled up and down in the cocoon of straw that Emma had made for him. Heath urged Grit faster yet until he drew parallel to Thunder's head. The noise of the buckboard wheels grinding on their axles, the horses' hooves pounding through the meadow, the animals' laboring and snorting and the baby's wailing reverberated inside Heath's skull as he rode shoulder to shoulder with the panic-stricken black gelding for several long seconds, gauging his next move.

Heath urged Grit to a position just slightly in front of Thunder's head and reaching out with his right arm, took hold of the bridle of the fleeing horse. Thus attached, the three rode on full tilt until Heath shouted the command, "Haw!" Whereupon, Grit began making a wide arc to the left as Heath hung onto the gelding's bridle. As they neared the end of Grit's arc, Heath commanded, "Whoa!" and the palomino began to slow his gait, almost imperceptibly at first until Heath issued the final command to Grit, "Stand!"

Heath felt the skin ripping from his fingers and the palm of his right hand but he tightened his grip on the gelding's bridle as Grit labored to halt Thunder's forward progress. As the din of the chase eased along with the movement of both beasts and the buckboard, Heath called out, "Whoa, boy! Easy does it!" to the agitated and wild-eyed gelding. "Stand!" repeated Heath and the palomino brought them to a stop. Heath slid off the right side of his horse and removed Grit's reins, which he attached to Thunder's bridle, all the while talking reassuringly to both animals and stroking the heavily lathered neck of the draft horse.

Johnny continued to wail from the back of the buckboard but Heath could not risk letting go of Grit's reins that he had attached to Thunder. Instead, he mounted the gelding and holding tightly to the reins, urged the horse forward at a walk. "Follow!" he commanded Grit who took up his position at the rear of the buckboard.

Only then could Heath pay some attention to the crying infant. "Johnny! Johnny!" called Heath over his shoulder. "You are all right, son. Mama is just up ahead. Be my big boy now and stop your crying. You are all right," and Heath continued trying to soothe the terrified child with his voice as they slowly retraced their path back toward the picnic at the bluffs.

Heath removed his hat, waving it in the wind as he caught sight of Emma and Luke who were rapidly bearing down upon him and the sobbing baby in the buckboard. Heath reined in Thunder and came to a complete stop, waiting for Emma and Luke to approach. As soon as Luke slowed Onion, Emma slid from her position in front of Luke and raced to the buckboard where Heath wordlessly hoisted her up and into the straw with her child.

Kneeling in the buckboard, Emma clawed her way through the straw and the quilt to reach her hysterical baby, finally clutching him to her breast. Over and over again, she rocked back and forth with the baby repeating, "Mama is here, precious! Mama is here! You are all right now," until Johnny stopped his sobbing. With a firm grip upon his mother's long curls, hiccupping and sighing, the exhausted baby shut his eyes and buried his tear-stained face in Emma's bosom for the brief ride back to the other picnickers.

"What the hell happened?" Luke asked quietly as he and Heath rode back across the meadow.

"One minute I was taking a crap and the next minute, all hell along with Thunder had broken loose!" exclaimed Heath.

"Who untied Thunder?" asked Luke, eyes darkening.

"No one untied that horse of yours. He tore himself loose...tree and all."

"Are you kidding me?"

"Do I look like I am joking?" Heath frowned at Luke.

Just then, they came abreast of the others running toward them through the woods. "Is the baby all right, Emma?" called Burris, climbing up onto the buckboard.

"He seems to be," she said wearily.

"Here, just let me have a look," added Burris reaching out his arms to take Johnny, whereupon the baby grabbed Emma's neck, refusing to release his hold upon his mother.

"I think," she began, "that the best thing for Johnny right now is just to let me hold him until I can calm him down a bit."

"Quite right, dear," responded Burris and turning to the men he asked, "What in tarnation caused the horse to take off like that anyway?"

"We were both wondering the same thing," replied Heath.

"Did anyone see what happened?" asked Burris.

"No," panted Cordelia, "I had just gone to the edge of the bluff to shake out our picnic quilts and refold them when I heard the commotion and saw the horse charge into the woods."

"I saw it," exclaimed Benni, bent double from running so hard.

"Out with it girl!" commanded Burris.

"Someone threw…the rubber ball at Thunder…the horse panicked…unable to extricate it from under his feet," she replied breathlessly.

"Who?" demanded Burris. "Both boys were with me so I know that neither George nor Will did it." Burris paused, thinking. "Great God! Polly did this!" he roared and he turned to run back to the bluffs.

"Burris!" called Cordelia after him. "Please wait, Burris! We do not know for sure…" her voice trailed off as Burris pivoted to face his ashen wife.

"Like hell I do not know! Of course she did it! Who else could it be? Poor Mary? The child's own grandmother? Not likely. Figure it out, Cordelia! It was our very own daughter and by God she will be punished for this," whereupon he turned his back on his wife and ran through the woods.

"Oh, Burris…please!" Cordy pleaded with her rapidly vanishing husband. "Do not do this! Polly is far too delicate…she cannot withstand…"

When Burris reached the picnic clearing, he shouted, "Polly McKendrick! Front and center right this instant! Do you hear me?"

At the sound of Burris' voice, George stuck his head out of the carriage and called, "Doc, quick! Could you take a look at Nana? She has fainted dead away in here."

"Where are Will and Polly?" Burris demanded as he ran toward the carriage.

"Up there," George pointed to the outcropping of rock.

"I shall deal with Polly later but first, let me relieve you here," and Burris knelt in the bottom of the carriage. Propping Mary upright, he said to George, "Kindly fetch my black bag, son. It should be under the front seat and open the door on the other side of the carriage at once. Mary needs some ventilation in here."

George reappeared with the black bag. "Open it, son." Burris stuck out his palm and commanded, "Stethoscope!" Whereupon George slapped the instrument into the doctor's waiting hand. Next he called, "Salts!" and George slapped the vial into the doctor's upturned palm.

As Mary began to come around, Burris looked across at George and said, "Well done lad! I shall make a doctor out of you yet!"

Burris sat in the bottom of the carriage holding Mary in his arms as the others rode back into the clearing. George ran to his mother, tears streaming down his face as he looked at his baby brother. "There, there, sweet Johnny," George soothed his brother. Tenderly he stroked the baby's back, "It is your big brother, Georgie, come to see you, Baby Cheeks. Everything is all right now. Right Ma?" and he looked apprehensively past the trembling baby at his mother.

"Yes, George, my darling. The baby is fine. Just terribly frightened," Emma reassured her son.

"Then why does he not open his eyes and look at me?" worried George.

"Johnny is totally exhausted after his ordeal and it would be best if we just allow him to rest for a while. Where are Nana and Will?" asked Emma looking around the clearing.

"Well, Nana fainted dead away in the bottom of the carriage and Doc is over there with her and Will...well, I am not sure, but I think he and Polly are hiding out on top of the rocks," George responded pointing to the limestone outcropping under the oak tree.

"Benni!" commanded Burris from the interior of the carriage.

"Yes sir?"

"Come here at once and tend to Mary. I have a spanking to deliver," bellowed Burris.

"Oh Burr...dear...please reconsider..." Cordelia begged her husband.

"Stand back, Mother. This is long overdue," intoned Burris, stomping through the Queen Anne's lace and butterfly weed.

"You are to blame for this, Emma Richardson!" exclaimed Cordelia suddenly pointing an accusatory finger at Emma, still seated in the buckboard with Johnny clinging to her neck and hair. "It was you who planted the notion in my husband's head that our Polly needs to be treated like other children. Well, she is definitely not like other children and she surely cannot withstand physical punishment. She is far too delicate!"

"Shut up, Cordelia!" yelled Burris. "I shall deal with you directly. Polly McKendrick, where are you hiding? Come out at once!" Burris thundered as he strode up to the rocks.

As Burris reached the ledge of limestone that overlooked the upturned faces of the hushed gathering below him, the doctor was confronted by an unexpected sight. There, spread-eagle over the inert girl, was Will. "Up! Off the girl!" commanded Burris, making rising motions with his hand.

"I can't let you do this to her, sir," replied Will. Rising to face the doctor and knotting his fingers into fists, he announced, "Because I am her second." Will stood defiantly between Polly and her father, fists raised, ready to defend the heap of a girl who lay on the rock behind him.

Just then, Heath reached the top of the limestone slab. "Sir, if I may say so, I believe that we have all had entirely too much excitement for one day and it would be my strong recommendation that we all calm down a bit. Exhaustion is fueling our anger at the moment. Let us address the issue of wrong-doing later, with clear heads." Heath reached out a hand and touched the doctor on his shoulder. "Come, let us go back down to the others and prepare to return to Grandview. We can deal with these matters later, sir."

"But, I am incensed to think...outraged to learn that my own..." commenced Burris anew.

"Yes sir, and I share your outrage at what has just transpired, but we should not, nay, we dare not, address punishment in the heat of anger. Would you agree?"

"I suppose you are right," sputtered Burris, allowing Heath to lead him back down the worn path to the clearing.

The gaiety of the afternoon had evaporated. Just before the subdued group departed the clearing for Grandview, George retrieved his rubber ball and walking to the edge of the bluffs, hurled it as far as he could throw. Heath walked to the boy's side and stood with a protective arm around the child's shoulders as the two of them watched the ball bounce down the boulders and then drift away, caught up in the current of the Southport River.

"It is all my fault," George said sadly to Heath.

"It is the fault of no one and it is the fault of everyone, son," Heath said in an attempt to comfort the distressed child.

"Is that supposed to be a riddle?" asked George looking up into Heath's face.

"I guess it is a riddle of sorts. The sort that has no answer. Sometimes in life, there are just riddles that have no answers, no matter how hard you try to find them."

Heath stood with his arm around George, watching the rubber ball disappear down river.

"Do you think my ball will make it all the way to the Mississippi?" asked George somberly.

"I think," replied Heath, "that your ball will make it all the way down to the Gulf of Mexico where it will wash up on one of those fine, white sandy beaches and some little boy, like yourself, will find it."

"Really?"

"Yup."

Over the course of the following week, Emma remained at home ostensibly recovering from her own exhaustion and illness, but in reality tending to her mother and Johnny, both of whom had been severely traumatized by the events at the picnic. Johnny was determined to remain attached to his mother day and night, crying loudly if he lost sight of her for a moment. Emma even relented and took the child into her bed at night to help him through his terror of losing her.

Again, Emma saw the effect of caring for three small children etched into her mother's face and she was once more awash with guilt for putting such a heavy burden upon Mary. With yet another year of nurse's training to go before she would be able to hire on at the hospital, Emma prayed for the power to withstand the pressures of their fight for survival. Emma and Mary had to continue pouring every ounce of their combined strength into earning a living and raising three children. There was no alternative.

A morose and somber mood had descended upon the house on High Point Avenue since the weekend picnic fiasco, added to which were the women's faltering finances. It was Mary who brought up the subject of money first, having recently calculated their fortune as it remained in the blue glass jar high atop the shelf in the cherry armoire of her bedroom.

The mournful wail of the one o'clock train drifted up though the oaks and maples as it clicked and clacked its way along the river. "That sound always makes me think of your father," Mary said dejectedly as she sat uncharacteristically still in the swing with Emma, hands idle in her lap.

"Why is that Mama?"

"For most of every year that we spent together in this house, your father and I always took our lunch together out here on the porch on the weekends and inevitably the train would be passing as it is now," answered Mary removing a handkerchief from her skirt pocket to dab at her eyes. "James would say to me, 'Mary darling, do you know why that train is whistling such a sad tune?'

And, even though I had heard this a thousand times before from your father, I would always respond, 'No, James. Pray tell, why is the train so sad today?' He would always answer, 'Because the train cannot see your beautiful face behind all these enormous trees. If you listen closely, you can make out what the train is saying as it rushes past. "Who is the beauty behind the trees? Who is the beauty behind the trees?" Can you hear it dearest?' Of course, I would blush and kiss him…" Mary's voice faded into her handkerchief.

Regaining her composure, Mary began again, "Speaking of your father, he always told me privately that if anything were to happen to him and I fell into dire financial straits, I should do two things. First, I should sell the mill, which we did last year, and secondly, I should sell off some or all of the wooded property just north of the barn," Mary paused to gauge the impact of her words upon Emma.

"Is our blue glass jar that empty, Mama?"

"It is indeed that empty."

"To whom do you propose we sell some of our acreage?" asked Emma, staring at the painted boards of the porch floor.

"Actually I was approached by both the chairman of the town council last week and Pastor Nesbitt," responded Mary.

"Separately or together?" asked Emma.

"Together."

"Why are those two interested in purchasing the woods behind the barn?"

"It would seem that the little cemetery behind our Methodist church is nearly filled to capacity and so Pastor Nesbitt along with some of the church elders, met with the members of the town council seeking a solution. It was actually the recommendation of Councilman Hummel, I believe, that the church should approach me about the possible purchase of some of our high ground. What do you think of this idea?"

"Is there no other solution?" Emma asked looking off toward the river.

"Well, we could take the money that Heath has been offering..."

"And be marked 'For Sale'? No, I absolutely refuse to take his money, Mama. Do you not see that every time a man hands a woman money, he feels that he is buying another piece of her, until finally the only thing left for sale is her soul? Once he owns her soul, the lout throws her onto the rubbish heap like so much garbage. I shall never, ever again allow a man to have such dominion over me!"

"Not all men are like Edward, my dear. Heath for instance..."

"They are all alike!" proclaimed Emma.

"Well then, I guess I have my answer to the question of our financial dilemma," sighed Mary at her daughter's intractable stance on men. "When I meet with Pastor Nesbitt and the chairman of the town council again, I want to be prepared with some demands of my own. With that in mind, I need you and Heath to assist me in assigning a value to the ground. In addition, I want to request that your dear father be disinterred from his resting place behind the church and reburied in his own ground, where he could overlook our home for all eternity."

Mary paused to blow her nose. "Further, I would request that I bear no expense for having Papa relocated to the property behind the barn and I want the cemetery to be named, 'Miller's Grove Cemetery', in honor of your father. What do you think?"

"I think Papa would approve," said Emma smiling at her mother and squeezing her hand.

Brute interrupted the conversation between the two women by announcing the arrival of someone traveling along High Point Avenue on foot.

"Shush Brute, or you will wake up the baby!" Emma admonished the great dog, grabbing his collar and dragging him inside the front door. Shutting the door behind her and turning toward the figure that strolled up the front lawn, Emma recognized Angus O'Malley, the reporter for the Grandview Courier.

"Ladies! Ladies! Ladies!" Angus began expansively. Coattails and hair aflutter, Angus took the porch steps two at a time. "Just the very ones I had hoped to see this fine afternoon," whereupon he embraced each woman, carefully kissing the air over their shoulders.

"What brings you to our doorstep, Mr. O'Malley?" asked Emma.

"Mr. O'Malley! What? Am I no longer 'Angus' to you Emma?" he chortled in a tone oozing with familiarity. Riffling through the pockets of his jacket and his trousers, Angus looked perplexed as he added, "Now where in heaven do you suppose that pencil of mine is hiding?"

"Behind your right ear," answered Mary helpfully, tapping her own right ear.

"So it is, Miss Mary. What keen eyesight you have, my dear."

Emma and Mary exchanged amused glances. They were in for an interesting afternoon. Angus O'Malley was just the ticket to brighten anyone's day. The first few minutes of O'Malley's visit were spent arranging himself comfortably in the wicker chair adjacent to the swing where the women sat, fiddling with his note pad and pencil and tying his shoelaces tighter. Finally satisfied that he was ready to begin, O'Malley looked over at the women expectantly, pencil poised in mid-air.

"Well?" he addressed the women.

"Well what?" asked Emma.

"Now, now, Miss Emma, do not play that game with me. You both know perfectly well what brings me here!" O'Malley playfully chastised the women.

Emma and Mary looked blankly at each other and then over at the reporter. "Come, come! The baby...the runaway horse...the mayor of Clarksburg's son..." he coached the women, making pulling motions toward his chest with his hands. "Out with the story or I shall faint before your very eyes!" he tried again in exasperation.

"Well, now," responded Mary, "we cannot allow our friend here to faint, Emma, so I shall just fetch some tea and sugar cookies. Would that help, Mr. O'Malley?"

"Oh, dear lady, you have accurately perceived that the quickest route to my heart is through my stomach!" Whereupon O'Malley focused all of his attention on Emma. "And as we were saying..."

"I was saying nothing," came the tart response.

"Have I offended you in some manner, Miss Emma?" the reporter asked sorrowfully, reaching over to touch the arm of the swing.

"It is nothing that you have done, Angus. It is just that the circumstances of my life are difficult right now and everything is further complicated by the fact that I have been ill and…" she turned away abruptly.

"Oh, my dear," said O'Malley solicitously, moving next to Emma on the swing, "I had no idea," and he put an arm around her shoulder, patting her on the back.

Regaining her composure, Emma faced O'Malley with a smile. "Yes, what you have heard is true. Our family and friends had ridden to River Bluffs for a day of picnicking when Luke Crawford's horse became frightened by a child's rubber ball and ran off with the constable's buckboard in which my youngest son, John, was napping," and Emma told O'Malley the story of the runaway horse. She never mentioned Polly, playing up instead the heroism of Heath Hamilton.

"What an absolutely…fabulously divine story, my dear!" exclaimed the reporter, never looking up from his notebook where he had been scribbling incessantly ever since Emma began talking about the events of the previous weekend. "This piece will surely be tomorrow's headline, only I cannot think exactly how to phrase it," he said drawing a long line horizontally through the air with his pencil.

Just then, Mary came through the screen door bearing a tray of hot tea and sugar cookies. "Now that," said O'Malley pointing his pencil at the tray of food, "is precisely what I need to stoke up my brain again. Food is fuel you know," chuckled Angus, taking a handful of cookies and the cup of tea that Mary had poured for him.

"I have it!" O'Malley exclaimed suddenly. With both hands framing an imaginary rectangle out in front of him he shouted: CONSTABLE'S HORSE FLEES WITH BABY—MAYOR'S SON RIDES TO THE RESCUE. What do you think, ladies?" he asked brushing cookie crumbs off his notepad.

"I think you will sell a lot of papers tomorrow with that headline," answered Mary.

"People will definitely sit up and take notice of that one, Angus," smiled Emma.

"Please excuse me, I have some bread to knead and get in the oven for dinner," said Mary rising from the swing. "May I get anything else for either of you?"

"No thank you Mama."

"Oh, Mrs. Miller," trilled O'Malley, "I do so love your hospitality and your cooking. You always make me feel so welcome here. One day soon I must do an article on the virtues of being a splendid cook. I should fancy featuring you and some of your delectable recipes, Miss Mary."

"Oh, la-la-la, how you do go on, Angus!" flushed Mary as she retreated to her kitchen.

Angus O'Malley deliberately closed his notebook and put it along with his nub of a pencil away in a jacket pocket. "There is something else I should like to speak to you about, Miss Emma," he began quietly.

Surprised by his change in tone, Emma looked inquiringly over at O'Malley.

"It has long been a dream of mine to write a book," he began in an uncharacteristically somber tone. "Please do not misconstrue what I am about to say for my job at the paper does put bread on the table for both my mother and me. I am able to earn a decent living as a reporter, but…grinding out sensational, head-line-grabbing stories does not fulfill my artistic sensibilities. Can you understand that, Miss Emma?" he asked timidly.

Caught off guard by O'Malley's personal revelation, Emma did not immediately respond.

"After so many years of covering bobcats, tea parties, weddings, funerals and runaway horses, I feel stifled as a writer. I mean," he continued, "what do people do with yesterday's newspaper? They hang it in the outhouse and wipe their bottoms with it. That is not the way I want to be remembered," the reporter complained.

"I think I understand what you are saying, Angus. I believe that each of us in our heart of hearts wants to be remembered as having done something worthwhile…striving to leave something tangible behind for those who follow in our footsteps. I too would like it recorded that once upon a time I passed this way, and while I was here, I tried to enrich the lives of others."

"That in a nutshell, dear lady, is exactly what I mean," beamed O'Malley.

"What will be your claim to fame?" Emma smiled back at Angus as she sipped her tea.

"My idea," he enthused, "is to write a book. Not just any book, mind you, but one that will continue to sing to generations of readers long after I am gone. A book of carefully crafted prose that never goes out of style and I believe," O'Malley cleared his throat, "that is where you and I enter together…stage right."

"Whatever are you talking about, Angus?" Emma asked raising a suspicious eyebrow at the reporter.

"Well, there you go feigning ignorance again, dear!" O'Malley admonished Emma, wagging a finger at her. Before Emma could respond, O'Malley rose to his feet and began flapping up and down the porch like a caged bird.

"Whatever is it, Angus?" Emma asked again.

"Oh, how to explain this...this dilemma!" Placing his hands on his hips and drawing near to her, O'Malley leaned down close to Emma's face and warned her, "So help me, I shall be compelled to smack the living daylights out of you if you laugh at me or if I see so much as a smirk at the corners of your mouth."

"Angus, please do sit here next to me and calm yourself! I am not laughing at you, am I? I believe I am listening to you. Now come. Sit."

"I am far too agitated to sit down just yet," O'Malley responded, placing the back of his hand against his forehead and continuing his flight up and down the porch.

Emma sat quietly sipping her tea, waiting for O'Malley to settle on the arm of a wicker chair, where he began restlessly to swing his leg back and forth. "I am not like other men," he said softly, gazing across the expanse of green meadow at the dark waters of the Southport. "I have certain...certain proclivities which are unlike those of Heath and Luke," he added looking over at Emma.

"I have long known this," replied Emma, unsmilingly.

"I know that people laugh at me behind my back and call me unsavory names. Just last week, I was covering a funeral and someone in the crowd at the church cemetery called out, 'Hey, look! Here comes old Anus O'Malley! Rub up against him and you can be tomorrow's headline.' Rude comments like that are a personal torment to me."

"Angus, I am so sorry for the pain that you bear as a result of the thoughtless and cruel remarks of others," Emma said frowning and reaching out a hand to O'Malley.

Angus took the hand that she had offered to him, saying forlornly to Emma, "I know what I am but I am just so sick of being called names because I am different from other men. How many times do people have to say things like, 'Look, here comes that silly little fop,' before they run afoul of their own rudeness...their own insensitivity to the suffering of others?"

"I quite agree that people can be insensitive and rude, but what does that have to do with me and the book that you want to write?" Emma sympathized.

Angus offered a circuitous response. "As you can imagine, I shall not be writing about guns, carriages, horses, hay bales or carpetbaggers," laughing at himself O'Malley ticked off the negative subjects on the fingers of one hand.

"Oh, so it is quite all right for you to laugh but not for me to laugh, or may I laugh when you do?" she teased O'Malley. "And since you have told me what the book will most certainly not contain, may I now inquire as to the subject matter that it will contain?"

O'Malley rose from his perch on the arm of the chair and resumed his nervous flight up and down the porch once again.

"Angus, sit!" Emma commanded the reporter as if she were speaking to Brute.

"I should just never have brought up this...this dream of mine in the first place. It is so impossibly absurd," fretted O'Malley.

"Let me be the judge of that. Now, speak!" she commanded him again.

"Very well then, here it is. I envision writing a book about a woman," and Angus O'Malley visibly flinched as he uttered the last word, anticipating a swift rebuke.

Emma finished her tea before reacting to the reporter's news. "Do I know the woman?" Emma asked innocently.

Smiling broadly, Angus replied, "I expect you know her better than anyone for the woman is...YOU!" and he bowed low in front of Emma, making a sweeping motion with his arm in front of her.

"Well, that will surely be one of the shortest books ever published," and she began to laugh. "Yes...I can just imagine the first chapter...she is born. Chapter two...she grows to womanhood. Chapter three...she marries. Chapter four...she bears twins. Chapter five...husband abandons her and his children. Chapter six...she becomes a nurse. Chapter seven...she grows old. Eighth chapter...she dies. Say, how am I doing so far? How many copies have we sold?" and Emma laughed uncontrollably until the tears streamed down her face.

Hands on his hips, O'Malley confronted Emma, "I knew you would laugh at me!"

"Oh, my silly friend! Do you not comprehend," asked Emma pausing to wipe her tears, "that I am laughing at myself...me, the nobody that you would turn into fodder for your book? Surely between the two of us we can come up with someone of noble bearing or at least of noble cause, someone infinitely more deserving of your time and attention? Someone who would grab the attention of your readers?"

"I believe I am the auteur here and it is I who shall determine the subject matter of my own book!" snorted O'Malley defensively, hands on hips. "You just do not get it, Emma!" and he turned on his heel as if to leave.

"Oh, please wait, Angus!" she implored the retreating reporter. "Do come back!"

As if Emma had jerked a cord tied to the middle of his back, Angus returned to sit beside her on the swing. "I really had no intention of leaving," he chortled. "My feigned departure was unabashedly an attempt to get you to beg and grovel for my return and," he crowed, "it worked!"

"You are so transparent!" Emma scolded him. "Now, tell me more about this book of yours and why on earth you think I am the proper subject," she said, curling up like a cat in a corner of the swing.

"Well," began Angus, clearly delighted to have Emma's undivided attention, "I have long been interested in the activities of women, watching them up close and from afar ever since I was a small child. Secretly I envied the way they were able to conduct the business of being…you know…women…so openly.

As a youth, I realized that the only acceptable means by which I could continue living out my fascination with the weaker sex was at the end of a pencil, so to say…as a reporter. In school, I was always the one who interviewed the girls for Miss Rita's weekly newsletter that she posted for parents to read on the schoolhouse door. Everyone used to complain that I wrote longer paragraphs about the girls than I did about the boys. Does she still post the weekly newsletter?" Angus asked.

"Yes, as a matter of fact, she does," responded Emma.

"Well, I am happy to know that the tradition has survived me. Where was I?" asked O'Malley looking over at Emma.

"You were saying that you wrote more about the girls than you did about the boys," offered Emma.

"Yes, and about the same time that I commenced writing for the newsletter, I began to realize that I wanted to…that I rather enjoyed…dressing in my mother's clothing." Angus rose from the swing and with his back to Emma, sighed, "Oh, this is too painful to continue."

"Come back here at once and sit next to me," Emma said quietly, patting the empty cushion.

Heeding her admonition, Angus again sat next to Emma on the swing. Gazing directly into her eyes, O'Malley whispered almost inaudibly, "I realized at very young age that I was actually…a girl locked away inside the body of a boy," before burying his face in a throw pillow, afraid to see the reaction on Emma's face that his revelation produced.

With all the sangfroid she could muster, Emma pulled the pillow from O'Malley's face and soothed, "Your secret is safe with me, my friend. Only you and I shall know these intimacies." Clearing her throat, Emma asked, "But why have you selected me as the subject of your book?"

"Because I view you as a kindred spirit in one respect which is that both you and I have found ourselves in a torment over what men have done to us and what others are saying about us. Would you agree?" he looked expectantly over at Emma.

"Yes, I believe I am beginning to understand now," she replied.

"And in spite of everything," Angus continued, "including the cruel beatings, the unconscionable departure of that womanizing drunkard, Edward, the rank gossiping of our Bible-thumping brethren, et cetera, et cetera, you have stood tall…alone and strong in the face of seemingly insurmountable obstacles," Angus paused to wipe the foam that was collecting at the corners of his mouth.

"More tea?" Emma demurred.

Ignoring her, Angus continued again, "and I admire your resilience…nay, your gutsy strength and if I may be permitted to say so," here O'Malley looked around to make sure that he would not be overheard, "your balls!"

"Of course you realize," said Emma laughing, "that I am totally undeserving of such praise and that I have indeed had help in the persons of my sainted mother and Heath Hamilton?"

"Which brings me to the second reason for choosing you as the subject of my biographical endeavor and that is the way in which you blithely fly in the face of convention…as if you are deaf, dumb and blind to what others around you are saying. I mean, just how many women are daring enough to live openly with their lovers…even though it is 1890? How many of your classmates are over the age of thirty? How many of your classmates have three children? How many of those precious student nurses would dare to venture over the river after dark dressed as a boy to tend to a sick child?" and Angus punctuated each question with a poke at Emma's shoulder.

"A cup of hyperbole, anyone?" joked Emma holding her cup and saucer aloft.

"Oh do shut up…unless of course you are inclined to agree with me," O'Malley scowled at his audience of one. Waxing loquacious, O'Malley rose to his feet and announced, "Emma you have struck me like a bolt of lightening and when I am around you, each and every hair on my head stands on end. You are poised on the brink of something far greater than what we can immediately divine. I positively feel it in my bones! Emma you are the woman that I have longed to be but never shall be. I am consumed at once with a fierce admiration and jealousy of you. If I cannot be you in this lifetime, at least allow me the joy and privilege of being your friend and your biographer," and Angus flopped down in the wicker chair across from Emma, never taking his eyes from her startled face.

Fiddling with the brooch at the neck of her blouse, Emma stammered, "Angus…I hardly…this takes me quite by surprise!"

"I cannot leave here without your answer. To do so would be unbearable torture…far worse than anything I have yet to experience."

"But Angus, I do not comprehend…" she pleaded.

"Oh good heaven dear! Have you not been listening? Here I have been ranting and raving on about my most private thoughts to you and you have not been listening!" he accused her.

"Rest assured, Angus, that I have indeed heard each and every word out of your mouth. However, I do not believe that you have posed the question properly…you know…um…in order that we might enter into a legally binding relationship." Whereupon the corners of Emma's mouth curled upward as she reached for his hand.

Imitating her lighter tone of voice, Angus held onto her hand, looked deeply into her eyes and asked, "Emma Miller Richardson, wilt thou solemnly swear to appoint me alone as thy one true biographer, forsaking all others? And wilt thou promise to love, honor and obey me until death us do part?" O'Malley grinned across at Emma.

The smile faded from Emma's lips with the final question. Pulling her hand from his, Emma rose abruptly from the swing as if she had quite suddenly realized that she was sitting upon a nest of hornets.

"What is it dear?" asked a startled Angus O'Malley. "What have I said?"

Emma leaned upon the porch railing, seemingly distracted by three small sailboats as they plied the calm waters of the Southport River. Keeping her back to Angus, Emma ignored his entreaties.

"Oh, now! This is positively killing me, for I do not know how I have offended you, my darling Emma!" Angus tried again, rising to join her at the railing.

"Have you ever noticed," asked Emma, "how tiny…almost like toys, the boats appear from this distance?"

"I cannot say that I have," responded O'Malley to her non sequitur, never taking his eyes from her profile.

"And have you ever noticed," Emma continued in the same vein, "how charming they appear from a distance…how perfect the toy boats are?"

"No, I have not," was his worried reply. "Emma this has nothing to do with…"

"Ah, but it does, Angus!" she exclaimed, turning to look him full in the face. "From a distance, the boats appear quite perfect but up close…one readily discerns that the hulls are pitted, encrusted with barnacles…the sails are ripped and stained…the teak decks peeling…"

"Emma, have you gone abruptly insane? What in the hell do boats have to do with the thread of our conversation?" Angus asked with growing alarm.

"Absolutely everything!" she answered vehemently.

"Come with me," ordered O'Malley, taking Emma by the elbow and leading her back to the swing. "Now sit down and collect your thoughts."

"But my thoughts are collected…in fact, my thoughts have never been more collected than they are right this very minute," she added, gazing the length of the porch. Speaking to the white columns, Emma soliloquized, "So very many years ago, I met this incredibly perfect-looking man…perfect hair…perfect eyes…perfect teeth…perfect body. It was not until I drew closer to him that I began to perceive the flaws…small ones at first. The white lies that lead to horrific fabrications about his past. The little spankings that escalated into full-fledged beatings. The occasional sip of wine that developed into a raging addiction to alcohol. The courtly nod to other women that belied an obsessive need to possess every whore on both sides of the river."

"Now, now, dear," Angus tried soothing Emma, for he could tell by the tone of her voice and the flush upon her face that she was terribly distraught.

Emma brushed O'Malley's hand from her shoulder as she continued, "Do you know what I said when the preacher asked me if I would promise to love, honor and obey that same man who looked so utterly perfect from a distance…?" she asked rhetorically. "I said, 'I do.'" And Emma convulsed with laughter until she began to sob.

"Oh, my goodness! Oh, my goodness!" Angus O'Malley repeated as he held Emma in his arms.

Withdrawing from O'Malley's embrace, Emma fought to regain her composure, blowing her nose loudly upon a lace handkerchief and dabbing at her eyes. "So you see, my friend," she continued, "some things are better viewed from a distance. Scrutiny at close range is likely to reveal the sordid…the ugly…the naked truth."

"In the name of heaven, what truth are we talking about here?" asked Angus.

"This truth…my truth…that I shall never again promise to love, honor or obey another man so long as I live…even in jest…including you."

CHAPTER 15

▼

Emma resumed her duties at the hospital for the summer of 1890, fulfilling her obligation to pay the balance of her tuition. One afternoon, Fanella Walker called Emma and Benni into her office.

"Ordinarily, I assign my more experienced nurses to the night shift, but since we are in a bit of a bind this summer as a result of staff illnesses, absences, difficulties with family and so forth and so on," began Fanella looking over the top of her pince-nez glasses at the two women, "I must call on the two of you to do night duty tomorrow evening in the men's ward. Can you manage that, Emma...with the children and all?"

"I feel certain that my mother can cover for me at home," Emma replied, forcing a smile and hoping that Nurse Walker did not detect her reluctance to accept the assignment.

"I too can be here for the night shift with Emma," added Benni.

"I knew I could count on my two best students to fill in for me. Please report to the men's ward tomorrow evening at five o'clock to give yourselves enough time for a brief review of your patients' medical histories from the duty nurse. Thank you ladies. You are dismissed," and Fanella Walker resumed reading the chart spread out before her on the dark walnut desk.

As they had been instructed, both Emma and Benni reported to the duty nurse and her assistant promptly at five the next evening. "Anything unusual or out of the ordinary that we might anticipate this evening?" Emma asked as the nurse in charge completed her review of the medical histories for all seven male patients on the ward that night. "I mean, can we anticipate that anybody is going to want to play checkers at two in the morning?" she joked.

"No," responded the nurse, "all of my patients are pretty good boys and sound sleepers, according to my regular night nurses. Once you have them fed and bedded down, I daresay the only request that you will get in the middle of the night is for a urinal. No one on this ward is acutely ill right now, so that should make your work a bit easier this evening."

"Are any of them likely to be rowdy?" asked Benni looking down the expanse of white hospital beds.

"Perhaps Mr. Samuelson over there," laughed the duty nurse pointing a pencil at the third bed on her right, "and only if he cannot find his dentures in time for the evening meal. I have tried in vain to convince the old gentleman that the best place to keep his teeth is in his mouth but Mr. Samuelson insists on playing hide-and-go-seek with his dentures. Just remember to check under his pillow, in the nightstand drawer, in the pockets of his bathrobe and oh yes, even in the waste can."

Emma and Benni exchanged glances prompting the duty nurse to add, "Fear not, ladies. I can almost guarantee that the only excitement you will experience is sunrise tomorrow morning," and she waved good-bye to them both.

Benni located Mr. Samuelson's dentures for him shortly before six o'clock that evening as the two women began to deliver dinner trays to each patient. "Where were they hiding?" Emma whispered to Benni as she leaned into the cart to retrieve another tray. "Under the newspaper on his chair," Benni whispered back.

"Just look at this delicious meal, Mr. Tobin!" exclaimed Emma as she placed a steaming tray of beans, fried fat back, corn bread, stewed tomatoes and hot coffee on the patient's bedside table, carefully tucking a napkin under his chin.

"Well, if it's just so darned all-fired delicious, then why don't you eat it?" groused Mr. Tobin scowling over at the tray. "Hey, Charlie!" Mr. Tobin called over to the man in the bed to his left, "Is this third or fourth straight night in a row that we've had beans for dinner?"

"By my count, it's been more like five straight dinners in a row," responded Mr. Tobin's neighbor.

"Beans are a natural laxative, Mr. Tobin," Emma informed her unhappy patient helpfully.

"Ain't nothin' natural about havin' to shit all day long. Besides, you're the poor gal what gets to wipe my arse every time them natural beans start havin' their way with my intestines."

"That's it, Tobin! Better food, less arse wipin' for the ladies here. Whadya say, Miss Emma? Could you wrangle a deal with the cooks for us?" laughed Charlie.

"Not likely. Now eat up," Emma admonished the two conspirators.

Once their patients had been fed and cleaned up for the night, Emma and Benni wrote notes in the patients' charts, handed out books, newspapers and medicines with cups of water. Bandages were checked and changed. One patient asked Benni to trim his mustache. "Dang thing's so long, I'm chewing it up with my food," he complained. Another patient asked Emma to cut his fingernails.

By nine o'clock, the two women announced that they were turning out the gaslights by all the beds and by nine-thirty, most of the men were asleep. Except for an undercurrent of snoring and an occasional cough, the silence was punctuated only by the sound of air escaping from men who had eaten beans for their fifth supper in a row. At one-thirty in the morning, Mr. Samuelson called for the use of a urinal after which quiet returned once more to the men's ward just down the hall from the caduceus at the entrance to Angel of Mercy Hospital.

At two o'clock in the morning, Emma made the rounds of the ward, checking on each patient, covering an exposed limb here, adjusting a pillow there and tucking in loosened covers. Returning to the nurses' station at the entrance to the ward, Emma realized that Benni had dozed off in her chair behind the counter, head resting on an arm across the desk. Taking a spare blanket from the linen closet, Emma lightly draped Benni's shoulders and then sat down to enter her two o'clock notes in the patients' charts.

Eight years of listening for children's noises during the night had sharpened Emma's hearing to the point that Will and George liked to joke about their mother being able to hear a dove's feather fall from the oak at the front of the house on High Point Avenue while she was inside the kitchen at the back of the house. It was therefore Emma who first became aware of the visitor to the men's ward.

At the sound of the first faint footsteps along the main corridor outside the closed doors to the men's ward, Emma put her charts aside and stood by the desk. As the footsteps continued their slow, deliberate approach, Emma moved forward, listening. Accompanying the footsteps was the faint, but unmistakable sound of jingling, as if there were spurs attached to the boots that approached. The shuffling and jingling grew more distinct until it stopped just on the other side of the double doors.

Emma waited. Nothing. Emma surmised that she was about to take delivery of fresh sheets, towels and gowns, even though it did seem to be a rather odd hour for the laundry to be in operation. But then, what did she know? She had never worked the night shift before and so she resumed her seat behind the desk next to the snoozing Benni.

All at once, both doors banged apart and there stood a young man dressed only in a cowboy hat, leather belt that holstered two six-shooters, boots and spurs. Emma leaped to her feet at the sight of him.

"Evenin' ma'am, or maybe I should say, mornin'," he slurred, tipping his hat to Emma.

"Shush!" she warned him, pressing a finger to her lips. "My…people are sleeping."

"Pardon me, ma'am," he said in a softer tone, "but I was a wonderin' if I might get a meal in this fine establushment?"

"Close the doors first," ordered Emma. "You are letting in a draft." The visitor obligingly turned his naked backside to Emma, taking elaborately exaggerated measures to close both doors quietly.

"What makes you think we are open at this hour of the morning?" asked Emma calmly playing along with the visitor, whose acute alcohol intoxication was unmistakable.

"Door's unlocked…light's on…so, must be open," he concluded with all the logic of a drunk.

"Actually, I was just cleaning up and preparing to leave the premises for the night. Perhaps you could come back tomorrow when we open for…uh, breakfast," offered Emma.

"Nope. I'm hungry now. Went to some damned tavern down yonder and they had the nerve to make me leave without my supper." Removing a six-shooter from its holster and waving it in the direction of the doors he had just closed, the gunslinger walked unsteadily toward Emma. Sticking the gun to her nose, he repeated, "I'm hungry now. Get it?"

"Well, I can see that you are by those ribs of yours that are sticking up…er, I mean, out," she responded, calmly pushing the barrel of the drunk's gun away from her face. Picking up a pencil and a pad of paper, Emma moved slowly and deliberately to a small table stacked with clean urinals and bedpans by the double doors, saying as she walked backward, "I believe your table is waiting just over here," as if she were the maitre d' at the Foggy Bend Hotel restaurant.

Years of experience in dealing with Edward's drunken nighttime rampages had taught Emma that she could significantly reduce the damage that her spouse was likely to inflict upon her if she would just play along with whatever scene he had set for the evening. Coddle, amuse, cajole, agree and reassure were words that automatically filled her head as she stood before the wavering, gun-toting, naked drunk.

"Smile, but not too broadly," Emma silently cautioned herself, "and pretend that this all somehow makes sense."

"Oh, would you look at this!" exclaimed Emma in mock disgust. "The hired help left this evening without remembering to clean off your table," whereupon she whisked the urinals and bedpans from the small table and placed them on an empty bed, noting all the while that her patients and Benni continued to sleep soundly.

"What in the name of hell are we whispering for in this here saloon?" asked the drunk, suddenly agitated and loud again.

"Because, sir," Emma said softly, "a number of our…our patrons have quite obviously been unable to hold their liquor and are sleeping it off in the back."

"Well now, ain't that real thoughtful of this here establushment. What's it called?" the gunslinger looked at Emma with eyes that were not focusing.

"This would be the Big Rise Saloon," Emma responded glibly without pausing.

"Do tell? Well, as I was sayin', this here's a mighty fine and high class saloon to be providin' beds for its customers. I reckon I might be in need of one of them there beds when I finish my vittles. How much do they cost?" fretted the drunk.

"Why, good sir, this is your lucky night! Absolutely everything is on the house! The food, the alcohol and the beds are all compliments of the Big Rise Saloon," responded Emma, pushing a chair behind the tottering man's knees, causing him to sit abruptly.

"Damn, that chair's cold!" he exclaimed in a loud voice. "Shoulda worn pants tonight! Lost 'em somewheres."

Pressing a finger to her lips again, Emma picked up her notepad and pencil saying, "Now what will you have this evening, sir?"

"No menus in this here place?" the drunk slurred up at Emma as he waved his gun around before he placed it on the table.

"Oh, no sir. We have absolutely everything and anything that you could ever want to eat, cooked just the way you like it. So, what will it be?" and she prepared to write on her notepad.

"Now that you put it thata way," said the drunk pushing up his hat and leaning back in the chair, "lemme think on it."

"Take your time sir. We want to get this right and how about a little drink to wash down some of the day's dust while you are deciding what you would like our cook to prepare for you this evening?"

"I'll take a double," he slurred. "Been on the road a long ways."

"Coming right up," Emma responded moving over to the supply closet, where she picked up a bottle of rubbing alcohol from the bottom shelf. Filling a blue enamel cup to just below the rim with alcohol, she returned and handed the man his drink. "Here you are sir, just as you ordered."

The gunslinger took the cup from Emma and moved it to his lips. "Damn and son of a bitch! No wonder all them folks is passed out," he swore, pointing around the room with his drink at the recumbent patients. "This here's the good stuff," and he took another long draft from the enamel cup.

"Are we ready to order, sir?" Emma asked brightly.

The visitor to the men's ward belched. "Believe we is," he responded, noticeably tilting to one side.

His eyes blinked at different intervals as he attempted to place his order with Emma. "Cook...me...stea...lotsa fa...well...an...a...po?"

"Yes absolutely, we shall fry that steak of yours well done with a baked potato on the side," Emma said to her pad of paper as she scribbled furiously the words, "DO NOT MAKE A SOUND DRUNK HAS GUNS GET PAYNE HAMILTON."

Pretending to read the order back to him, Emma said, "Steak fried well done in extra lard with a baked potato. Will you have butter on that potato, sir?" The drunk just looked incoherently up at Emma. "I shall take that to be a yes." Whereupon, Emma ripped the page from the tablet, adding, "Let me take a moment, sir, to deliver this to the cook who will then repair to the kitchen to prepare a most delectable meal for you."

Emma walked over to Benni, still covered with a blanket and her head buried in her arms on the desk behind the nurses' station.

"Oh, cookie!" Emma whispered into Benni's ear while delivering a firm pinch to the woman's arm. Shoving the note under Benni's startled face, Emma returned to her customer.

"How about a refill?" she asked.

Still upright in his chair but leaning precariously to one side, the man blinked twice. Wordlessly, Benni made her escape through one of the double doors from the men's ward, down the long marble corridor, running across the caduceus and out into the chilly night air.

As her inebriated customer was in imminent danger of falling to the floor, Emma seized a sheet from the supply room and tied him to the chair after removing his other gun from the leather holster, still buckled around his naked waist. With the erstwhile gunslinger now out cold and tied to one of the ward's wooden chairs, Emma went around quietly to each of her patients' beds making sure that the men were still asleep. Only Mr. Samuelson coughed and turned over in his sleep as Emma approached. Having ascertained that her patients had not been awakened by the commotion caused by the visiting drunk, Emma returned to resume her vigil over the guest in the men's ward.

Even though the man remained unconscious with his head hanging forward upon his chest, Emma immediately took up the six-shooter from the table where the drunk had set it, cocked the hammer and trained its long barrel on the sagging man before her. The longer she sat, the angrier Emma got. Deprived of sleep, it began to seem to Emma in the wee hours of the morning as if it were Edward before her, instead of the anonymous drunkard. Edward's dark and distorted face wavered before her and Emma fought an almost overwhelming urge to pull the trigger.

The sound of voices and footsteps rapidly approaching on the other side of the double doors to the men's ward shook Emma from her grim musings. Payne entered the doors first, followed by Burris McKendrick, Adam Hamilton and then Benni.

"Jesus, Mary and Joseph!" exploded Burris. "Emma, whatever are you doing? Let go of that weapon at once!" he commanded, holding out his hand to take the gun.

Releasing the hammer and handing over the six-shooter, Emma looked around at the startled faces of the three men before replying quietly, "I am protecting the lives of my patients."

"From what?" asked Burris McKendrick, stooping to examine the man sagging in the chair before him. "From this comatose sack of bones?"

"This comatose sack of bones barged in here stark naked at two-thirty in the morning, drunk as a skunk and stuck a gun in my face," Emma replied hotly.

"How is it that you failed to mention those details, Student Nurse Bennington?" asked Burris in an accusatory tone, jabbing a finger at Benni who quaked timidly behind Adam Hamilton.

"Because…because…" Benni began to stammer. "I was…"

"Because," answered Emma for Benni, "she was on an errand in another part of the hospital, at my direction. Fortunately for us all, Benni returned when she did to deliver my message for help," lied Emma covering for Benni.

"Harrumph!" exclaimed Burris, apparently satisfied with the explanation. Turning back to the drunk, he added, "This man is on the verge of dying from alcohol poisoning. I can barely get a pulse on him. Payne and Adam, I am going to have to rely on the two of you to carry this man to the acute ward for me and…no…no…do not try to untie him. Simply carry him in his chair and follow me," ordered Burris, as he held open the doors for the two burly men, each with a firm grip on the drunk and his chair.

"I shall expect to see you, Emma, in my office first thing this morning," called Burris over his shoulder. "Do not return home, Richardson, without seeing me first," and he was gone down the hall, issuing orders to Payne and Adam.

Benni and Emma stood looking at the retreating trio as they carried their comatose cargo down the marble hall. With a panic-stricken look on her face, Benni turned to Emma and whispered, "Whatever am I to do?"

"Do about what?" Emma asked in return.

"Do about the fact that I fell asleep while on duty!"

"I believe I have already covered that for you," responded Emma icily.

"But that is just the point. I cannot allow you to lie for my mistake. I shall have to confess it tomorrow to Burr...I mean, Dr. McKendrick," whimpered Benni.

"Indeed you shall not!" and Emma spun Benni around by the shoulders. Still grasping Benni's shoulders tightly, Emma said, "We are nurses and we stick together, do you understand?"

Benni nodded her head.

"And this fiasco tonight was not of your doing or mine. It occurred because the members of the hospital board, all of whom are men, have long refused to acknowledge the danger and risk to their night nurses. We nurses are being required to work in an unsupervised, unprotected environment, while the doctors are all at home...asleep in their nice warm little beds. An episode such as the one tonight was bound to happen sooner or later."

Benni again nodded her head in agreement.

"But I am telling you, as God is my witness, I shall be heard on this issue. Neither you nor I, or any of the other nurses are ever going to spend another night working in this hospital without the benefit of armed guards and locks on all the doors."

Brimming over with resolve, Emma made her way to Burris McKendrick's office after the morning nurses had arrived to relieve her on the men's ward. Then, Emma stationed herself in a chair just outside the doctor's locked office door and prepared to wait for his arrival.

Dark smudges of fatigue framed her eyes. The lovely auburn hair was untidy and threatened to collapse from the top of her head. Emma had not slept in the last twenty-six hours. Impatiently, she tapped her black high button shoes on the wooden floor to keep herself awake. When she felt likely to doze off, Emma rose to her feet and paced. Finally, at eight-thirty in the morning, Dr. Burris G. McKendrick came whistling down the hall to his office, keys jangling.

"Hello, there, Emma!" Burris hailed the seething woman who stood rigidly waiting for him, poised to strike. "My, my, my, but you do look a fright," he commented turning his back to her and unlocking the wooden door with its imposing sign, Dr. Burris G. McKendrick, Chief of Staff.

"You too might look a fright without sleep for over twenty-six hours!" she hissed at his back.

"Might as well get used to it," he chuckled, "because sleeplessness is synonymous with the profession of nursing," and he walked past the empty secretary's desk back to the door leading to his private office. There he paused once more to unlock the door, taking a seat behind the massive walnut desk while indicating that she was to sit in the chair which faced his desk. "All my nurses are either wide awake here in the hospital tending to patients or wide awake at home worrying about them," he smiled, oblivious to the ensuing storm.

Unable to contain herself any longer, Emma began to pace. "Now, now, Uppity! Do sit! I understand that you are tired as hell but we simply cannot have our nurses wielding guns in this hospital and force-feeding rubbing alcohol to people, of all things! You must realize…"

Emma spun around to confront the doctor, "Let me tell you what I realize! I realize that each and every night that you allow…nay…that you order us nurses to remain in this hospital unprotected, you are jeopardizing all of our lives, your patients included."

"Listen here, young woman, that has always been the policy of this hospital. We do not require guns and locks. We are a hospital, for heaven's sake! We encourage people to come here, not to stay away!"

"You would lock up these…this pile of papers on your desk," and Emma took her arm and swept the desk clean, sending journals, papers, pencils, charts and notebooks crashing to the floor, "but not lock the doors behind which we nurses are working in order to ensure our safety?" she snarled at him.

Startled by her venomous words, Burris recoiled. "And then there is the issue of the firearms," he tried again.

"Yes, the firearms. Let us address that issue. Who brought the firearms into my ward at two-thirty in the morning anyhow? Did I? Did Bennington? Or did Wild Bill bring the guns…not one, but two, into my ward and stick a loaded one in my face?"

"He was so drunk that you should have ignored…"

"Ignored what?" Emma exploded. "Ignored the loaded six-shooter pointed up my nose? He was so drunk that if the bastard had hiccupped, he would have blown my brains out the back of my head!"

"But you know better than anyone the possible lethal reaction to rubbing alcohol ingested…"

"He had already ingested a potentially lethal dose of alcohol by the time he reached my ward," fumed Emma, still pacing.

"You know very well that we are all sworn to do no harm…" Burris tried in vain.

"Do no harm! What about me? What about my patients? What about my assistant? Are we to be sacrificed to some drunken son of a bitch who has wandered in from the street waving a loaded gun? The man was not my patient. I had no duty to that drunk. I do, however, recognize my duty to the patients entrusted to my care. I must do no intentional harm to my patients and I have sworn to protect them with my very life if necessary, and so help me God, that is exactly what I was doing earlier this morning," whereupon Emma sat down, staring defiantly across the empty desk at the Chief of Staff of Angel of Mercy Hospital.

"Well," began Burris deliberately wiping imaginary dust from his glasses, "since you put it that way I suppose I commence to see your side of the issues but…"

Emma again interrupted the Chief of Staff, "There are no buts about the issues. We simply must have locks and guards installed at once in this hospital or you mark my words, there will be another episode like the one earlier this morning only with tragic consequences."

"I am quite afraid I cannot guarantee the installation of either locks or guards as such decisions fall under the jurisdiction of the Hospital Board. While I am a member of that august body, I cast but a single vote. A two-thirds consensus vote will be required to pass such changes as you suggest and that will take time," Burris paused, picked up his calendar from the floor and thumbed through its pages, "and by my reckoning, the Board does not meet for another month," and he closed his leather-bound calendar decisively.

"Let me put the matter to you in this fashion, Dr. McKendrick," said Emma rising stiffly from her chair, "unless the locks and guards are in position within the next twenty-four hours, we nurses shall all stay away from this hospital, affording you doctors and the orderlies an opportunity to see what conditions are like for yourselves."

"You will what?" stormed Burris G. McKendrick, suddenly purple with rage.

"We shall all remain at home. Just try to run this hospital without your nurses," whereupon Emma turned on her heel to leave the office of the Chief of Staff.

"You, madam, are nothing more than a petty insurgent!" raged Dr. McKendrick, pounding the top of his desk with his fists.

"I, SIR, AM A WOMAN!" shouted Emma over her shoulder at Dr. McKendrick as she slammed the office doors behind her.

Emma's first stop was Fanella Walker's office in the basement of the hospital. Word had already spread throughout the length and breadth of the building of the events that had unfolded in the men's ward earlier the same morning, so Fanella was not in the least surprised when Emma entered her office unannounced.

"My goodness, dear, but you have been through a terrible ordeal!" exclaimed Fanella, rising to greet Emma with a comforting arm around her shoulders. "I am so very proud of the way you handled the situation. I daresay that even some of my more experienced nurses would not have reacted so well to such threatening and dire circumstances. And quite frankly," Fanella chuckled, "I thought the rubbing alcohol was a splendid touch!"

"Apparently our Chief of Staff does not agree with you, Nurse Walker."

"Really? Have you met with him since the episode earlier this morning?"

When Emma nodded her head, Fanella indicated to Emma that she should take a seat, "Now then dear, you must tell me all the details and leave out nothing, but first, you look as though you could use a good cup of coffee. Just let me fetch one for you," and Fanella left the office.

Emma sagged into a chair and might have dozed off except that Fanella returned immediately with a steaming hot cup of black coffee for her. Fanella handed the cup and saucer to her student nurse and then sat on the corner of her desk listening to Emma recount the details of her meeting with Burris McKendrick.

When Emma had finished her recitation at last, Fanella paused before rising to warn the young woman who looked up at her with bleary, reddened eyes, "That was a dangerous threat which you made on behalf of the nursing staff."

"What is far more dangerous, Nurse Walker, are the conditions under which we nurses are expected to work. I could have been shot to death in the wee hours of this morning, along with Benni and my seven patients. No nurse should have to work in conditions where she fears for her life!"

"What exactly do you propose to do now in light of your threat?" asked Fanella, placing her pince-nez glasses on her nose and sitting behind the desk across from Emma.

"I propose to have Benni, you and others assist me in getting the word out to all of our nurses that unless there are proper locks installed on the doors and guards posted at the main entrance to the hospital within the next twenty-four hours, we nurses shall all remain at home over the weekend."

"I can assure you that Burris will call your bluff. There will be no locks or guards," Fanella stated flatly.

"Whether Burris calls our bluff or not is immaterial. We must employ every means available to us in order to prevail in this cause of action…to ensure the safety of each and every one of us, before someone is tragically killed."

"Mmmm, I quite agree," mused Fanella. "But who will care for our patients if we stay at home this weekend?"

"The doctors can care for their own patients. Perhaps a night or two without sleep will convince our illustrious physicians to grant us a few concessions, such as a safer work environment and doctors present in the hospital during the night," and Emma yawned hugely.

Fanella removed her pince-nez glasses and twirled them excitedly from the black ribbon that anchored them to her white blouse. "Yes, yes, by my auntie's bloomers! It is high time for a change in hospital policy! None of us nurses have ever been consulted about any of the details concerning the operation of this hospital, even though we serve here twenty-four hours a day, seven days a week, fifty-two weeks of the year. Can you imagine such an absurd injustice?" seethed Fanella, warming to the plan.

"That is precisely why we must insist on the placement of one or more members of our nursing staff on the Hospital Board. The male doctors make decisions that affect all of us nurses and we have absolutely nothing to say…no voice to be heard. It is time to put a stop to that practice. The slaves have been emancipated, but we have not!" exclaimed Emma heatedly.

"Oh, you are so right my dear! We are treated as mere chattel!" exclaimed Fanella in return, jumping to her feet. Walking around to the front of her desk again, Fanella added more calmly, "Now, Emma, it is quite apparent that you are totally exhausted. You simply cannot be effective in this condition. I suggest that you return home, get some sleep and come back this evening after five, prepared to speak to the nurses. In the meantime, I and a select few shall contact the other nurses and tell them what is afoot. We shall plan on meeting in the solarium around five-thirty this evening to hear speeches, draft a demand letter to the

Board and if our demands are not met, we should all agree to stay home over the weekend. How does that sound?"

"Perfect. I just hope I can make it home without falling asleep on the ferry. Knowing that cantankerous captain's mate as I do, he would probably throw me overboard if he found me sleeping in one of his deck chairs. He is so tremendously fond of going about the boat issuing directives to the passengers concerning what they can and cannot do that I..." but Emma was interrupted by Fanella.

Looking past Emma's right shoulder, Fanella said, "I do not believe anyone will trouble you on the return trip home with two armed bodyguards at your side."

Emma turned to look in the direction that Fanella was pointing and there in the doorway to her office stood Luke Crawford and Heath Hamilton, both wearing side arms. "We have come to fetch you home, Emma," said Heath simply, extending his hand to the exhausted woman. "The news of your ordeal is all over Grandview and Clarksburg. Now, come. Mary and the boys have been worried sick about you."

Before taking his outstretched hand, Emma turned back to Fanella and said, "I shall return by five-thirty this evening for the meeting. Thank you for agreeing to round up the other nurses."

"I am doing this not only for you, Emma, but for myself and the others as well. Now go and get some rest."

The trio left Fanella's office. Once on board the ferry, the men peppered Emma with questions but seeing the wan look on her face and the obvious signs of exhaustion, Heath was prompted to place a warning finger across his lips to signal Luke to be silent. Once on the other side of the Southport, Heath and Luke linked arms with the exhausted woman. Nearly lifting her off the ground, the two men strode with Emma up the sloping lawn to the house on High Point Avenue.

Once inside the front door, down the long hall to the kitchen at the back of the house, Emma spotted Johnny rolling a ball along the hardwood floors and at just the same moment, Johnny caught sight of her. "Mama! Mama!" exclaimed the child, toddling toward her with his arms outstretched. "Oh, Johnny, my darling!" Emma cried as she scooped the child up into her arms. "How I have missed you!" and she showered his little face with kisses.

"Well, I declare, Miss Emma!" exclaimed Elizabeth, coming down the hall with a neat stack of freshly ironed sheets, "I am truly relieved to see you safely on this side of the river again," and turning to Heath and Luke she added, "Did you gents have to shoot anybody to get our Miss Emma back again?"

"I confess, Elizabeth, that I was sorely tempted to put a hole in the bugger where he lay in his hospital bed," Heath replied smiling, "but Luke here possessed a cooler head than mine and convinced me to do otherwise."

"Where is Mama?" asked Emma, sitting at the kitchen table with Johnny on her lap.

"Oh, she got called away about two hours ago to deliver a baby over at Scroggins' farm. When she left she said not to expect her until after dinner. So, Johnny and I have been taking care of the household chores and Will and George are in school."

"I need you to stay on until my mother returns, Elizabeth, because after I bathe and rest, I shall have to return to the hospital for a meeting this evening."

"Is that wise, Miss Emma? I mean after all the trouble earlier in the day?" fretted Elizabeth, still holding the sheets out in front of her.

"I shall be fine and besides," replied Emma pointing to Heath and Luke, "I shall have these two fine bodyguards with me at all times. But, right this very moment, I am going upstairs, draw a bath and then sleep for a few hours. As much as it pains me to have to ask this, Elizabeth, please do not let George and Will disturb my sleep."

"I quite understand, Miss Emma. I can keep those boys plenty busy and out of your hair. Just never you mind about those two!"

Gathering up the long dark folds of her skirt, Emma wearily grasped the banister with her left hand and slowly climbed the stairs to her room. Minutes later, Emma stepped into her father's beloved copper tub, turned on the tap, added some fragrant oil and sank down into the steaming water. Closing her eyes, Emma lay immobile in the tub, arms floating out to her sides, water up to her chin. Beads of sweat were beginning to trickle down her forehead, cheeks and nose when she heard a light taping at the bathroom door.

"Yes? What is it?" she responded almost inaudibly.

"May I come in?" asked Heath.

"No! Go away!"

"But I bring food and drink," he cajoled from the other side of the wooden door.

"What kind of food and drink?" asked Emma cocking a wary eye at the still-closed door.

"Fried possum, stewed swamp rats, bat wing pudding and warm gopher milk. Just the usual favorites," Heath teased.

Emma hurled a hairbrush at the door.

"Was that a yes or a no?" persisted Heath through the door.

"That was a maybe," Emma responded closing her eyes again.

"Maybe what?"

"Maybe I do not care for the menu."

"Maybe I do not care for the menu," Heath parroted back. "Well then, how about a nice cup of hot chamomile tea with honey along with some of Mary's molasses and ginger cookies?"

There was a pause and then, "You may enter."

Slowly and deliberately, Heath opened the door to the small bathroom and stepped inside with a tray of tea and cookies. "Is it safe?" he asked feigning fear as he looked around, "Or is Miss Annie Oakley of Angel of Mercy Hospital going to blow off my head?"

"What I should do with that head of yours is dunk it in this hot water," retorted Emma, reaching for a cookie. "Perhaps a nice, long, hot soaking of all that tangled gray matter of yours would improve your disposition."

"My disposition!" Heath exclaimed with mock annoyance. "Just listen to you! What was it I heard you say to Elizabeth that after a few hours of sleep, you intend to go back to the hospital for a meeting?" Heath asked handing Emma her cup of tea and then adding, "Surely this meeting cannot be worth any additional personal sacrifice!"

Emma sipped her tea, still submerged in the tub, thinking how best to explain the crux of the meeting to him so that he would understand.

"Well?" Heath asked, trying to draw Emma back from her thoughts.

"Well what?"

"Why are you so determined to go back to the hospital for a blasted meeting this evening?"

"Heath, let us suppose for the sake of argument..." she began only to be interrupted at once.

"Oh, here we go with the argument business again. I believe you to be the most argumentative woman I have ever met!"

"Quite true but that is neither here nor there. Now, let us suppose you learned about a whole herd of magnificent wild horses that had been rounded up, taken to a farm and hobbled. Then, let us suppose you saw with your own eyes that those same wild horses with the hobbles in place were being used to work the farm. What would your reaction be?"

"Well, first of all, horses cannot work with hobbles on and second of all, what do wild horses have to do with you going back to that hospital this evening?" he asked looking totally confused.

Emma sat bolt upright in the tub, damp curls framing her face. "We nurses are those wild horses, Heath!" she exclaimed, looking expectantly into his eyes.

"Really?"

"Really."

Not wishing to appear immediately ignorant of the import of her words, Heath deliberately tidied up the tray, wiping cookie crumbs from the tray into Emma's empty tea cup with the linen napkin, which he then refolded and placed carefully next to the saucer. Next, Heath rolled up his sleeves and reached for a large chunk of sea sponge that rested in a wire rack hanging from the side of the tub. Taking the sponge in one hand and a cake of lavender scented soap in the other, Heath painstakingly lathered up the sponge and began to wash Emma's back.

With her back to him, Emma tried again, "Did you understand what I said to you?"

"Not exactly. I mean, wild horses, hobbles and nurses do not seem connected to me."

"What occurred earlier this morning at Angel of Mercy Hospital could easily have been prevented with a proper system of locks and guards in place. We women are at risk in that hospital, night and day, but especially at night, from intruders, such as the one who confronted me. We nurses have no say in the making of hospital policy as we are not permitted to have delegates on the Hospital Board."

"I never really thought about it that way before," mused Heath as he pinned a long curl back up on the top of her head. "So, you nurses are the wild horses and the lack of representation upon the Hospital Board would be the hobbles that you mentioned?"

"Exactly."

"I see."

"So, we nurses and student nurses are going to meet this evening to draft a demand letter to the Hospital Board and if these demands are not met by sundown tomorrow night, we are all going to stay home for the entire weekend," Emma stated triumphantly turning around to face Heath.

Heath sat at the edge of the copper tub on a small stool belonging to George and Will, bent knees reaching nearly up to his chin. "Whew!" he exhaled loudly. "It would seem that Luke and I will have our work cut out for us this evening."

"What work is that?" asked Emma, suddenly confounded by a moment of ignorance herself.

"The work of protecting all you proselytizing nurses from harm. Surely you must realize that each side of the river harbors individuals who do not look kindly upon women crusaders," Heath replied squeezing out the sponge.

"Do you?" Emma asked.

"Do I what?"

"Do you look kindly upon women crusaders?"

"If you are a part of the crusade, then I do because I have boundless respect for you," Heath paused before adding, "and I have something else for you also."

"Oh? And just what is that?" asked Emma wiping the curls back from her forehead.

"First you must turn around with your back to me and close your eyes."

"Why?"

"Just do as I ask."

Obediently, Emma turned her back to Heath and closed her eyes. After several long moments of fumbling with his clothing, Heath announced, "You may now turn around and open your eyes."

Just as Emma turned to look at him, Heath slipped into the tub with her.

"Oh, good heavens, Heath! Not now! Johnny and Elizabeth are downstairs and perhaps even Luke..."

"Luke was going back to the jail, Elizabeth is ironing a mountain of sheets, Johnny cannot yet climb the front stairs, George and Will are in school and Mary is delivering a baby at the Scroggins' farm. Does that account for everyone?" he laughed.

"But I need my rest," she protested feebly.

"Then come over here and allow me to administer a special sleeping potion that I have stirred up just for you," said Heath grinning at her.

Emma flicked water at him.

After a few hours of rest, Emma awoke, dressed and went downstairs to spend time with her children before leaving once again for Clarksburg.

"But why do you have to go back to the hospital now?" complained George, standing beside his mother where she sat at the kitchen table eating cold meat, bread and cheese.

"Because I must give a speech to all the nurses and student nurses at five-thirty this evening in the hospital solarium," Emma replied pulling George onto her lap. "I would much rather stay here with you three boys this evening. However, this weekend I promise I shall not budge from this house unless the three of you are with me. What do you think about that?"

"I guess that will have to do," sulked George.

"Ma, I was wonderin' just what it is you're doin' at that hospital most of the time...I mean now that you don't take no classes no more?" asked Will.

"That is a very good question, Will. I guess I too often assume that you and George know what I do at the hospital. I bathe my patients, change their beds, feed them if they need help with that, change their bandages, write notes about each patient in the charts, help the doctors with..."

"But do you have to wipe their..." and Will pointed to his behind.

"Yes, I must often help my patients with that too."

"Oh, no! It's true, Georgie!" wailed Will. "Every word Benjamin said was true and I beat the holy crap out of him for nothin'!" Will collapsed into a chair at the kitchen table with his head in his hands.

"What exactly was it that Benjamin said, dear?" asked Emma.

"Well, Miss Rita told us we had to write a paragraph about our parents or our grandparents and so I wrote about you," answered Will. "Can I have the rest of that cheese, Ma, if you're not goin' to eat it?"

"Help yourself. Now why did you get into a fight with Benjamin over your paragraph?" persisted Emma.

"Because I wrote about you bein' a nurse and all and how you help the sick peoples and that you study real hard to learn your lessons and that you probably have to read more than the President of the United States of America," answered Will, his mouth full of cheese.

"That is most flattering, dear, but what was the problem that caused you to fight with Benjamin?"

"Benjamin raised his hand after I read my paragraph and said I lied about my mother. He said you ain't no real nurse yet and that you spend all your time wipin' as...behinds and that made me pretty darned mad," Will flushed pink at the recollection.

"It made Miss Rita mad too, Ma," interjected George. "She boxed Benjamin's ears and made him sit in the corner for the rest of the afternoon."

"George, who's tellin' the story about my paragraph, anyhow? You or me?" Will asked angrily.

"Sorry, Will. I was just afraid you were going to leave out the good part," offered George.

"I ain't...I mean, I am not goin' to leave nothin' out!" snorted Will. Turning to his mother again, he added, "And I think the real reason that Miss Rita got so mad was because Benjamin used the bad word in front of the whole class."

"The bad word, dear?"

"You know…A-S-S," spelled Will to lessen the impact of the forbidden word upon his mother.

"Most definitely, that is why she boxed his ears," smiled Emma.

"So, I said to myself that Benjamin is lyin' 'bout my mother and I'm gonna fix him good for it after school. And, I did."

"Will made Benjamin's nose bleed," boasted George of his brother's pugilistic skills.

"Boys, I do occasionally wipe my patients' behinds much as I used to wipe yours when you were babies, or as I do now for Johnny. We nurses and student nurses take an oath to help those who cannot help themselves, young and old alike. It is a very noble calling to be a nurse or a doctor. I am not ashamed of studying and training to become a nurse and you must not be ashamed for me," Emma counseled her two oldest boys. "I am very proud of you for rushing to my defense when Benjamin said unkind and untrue things about me," concluded Emma, hugging Will.

"There is another thing we need to talk about," said George from the other side of the table.

"Oh? And what is that?"

"Heath told us that some crazy man walked into the hospital last night when you were there and scared you half to death with a gun," fretted George.

"Yes, that is true," admitted Emma.

"So, me and Georgie have some stuff we want you to keep with you all the time when you're at the hospital from now on," whereupon Will reached into his pocket and pulled out a large green and black cat's eye marble that he held out for his mother on his upturned palm.

"Go ahead, Ma. Take it," said Will, extending his hand closer to his mother. "It's yours to keep. It's my good luck marble. My favorite color, too. Put it in your pocket so when you're scared, you can just reach in there, feel my marble and don't be afraid no more."

"What a special gift this is!" exclaimed Emma taking Will's green and black cat's eye marble from her son's hand.

"And I have something for you too, Ma," said George pushing Will out of the way. Reaching into his pocket, George produced a small pewter cross that he pressed into his mother's hand alongside Will's marble.

"But, George, this is your cross that Nana gave you to hold when you say your prayers at night and in church."

"I know, but it has special protecting powers and I want you to be protected. Just like…" and George paused.

"Just like what?" asked Emma, holding both the marble and the pewter cross in her upturned hand.

"Well, I know I am not supposed to say his name, but since Nana is not here maybe I can tell you this." George moved closer to his mother, pressed his lips to her ear and whispered, "At night, after you and Nana leave my room, I always hold my cross tight and ask God to protect my Pa no matter where he is…no matter that he ran away…no matter that he is never coming back ever again."

Emma's eyes filled with tears as she hugged her sons to her. "I shall keep your gifts with me always, boys, and I shall never again feel afraid or unprotected!"

The trip back across the Southport later that same afternoon was made in silence. Heath had warned Luke that Emma would in all likelihood be preoccupied with the speech that she was scheduled to make that evening and it would be best for the two of them to remain silent unless Emma chose to engage them in conversation. Both men were heavily armed and wary of the passengers on the ferry.

Luke and Heath had been reminiscing about the tragic case of Sallee Meyers that occurred some ten years earlier. Sallee had been married to a young tobacco farmer in Clarksburg and together with their five young children, they had eked out a living on a parcel of land just south of town. The tiny log house was neat as a pin, whitewashed inside by Sallee herself. When the family came into town, Sallee, her husband and the children were always freshly scrubbed and their clothing carefully mended.

Hard times set in for the little family, however, following the summer of the drought when Sallee's husband harvested a meager crop that fall and died almost immediately thereafter following a brief illness. Sallee grew desperate. The tobacco farmer's widow was to be seen going all around Clarksburg, petitioning town officials for aid for her five children, to no avail. Sallee's attempts to secure financial help for her family were met with warnings that she should go home and stay there. It was unseemly for a woman to be begging for money.

Concerned citizens took food and clothing out to the little log house but when Sallee mounted a soapbox on the corners of Clarksburg and made her plight public, she was met with a barrage of insults and rotten vegetables. "Here, eat this!" yelled one incensed male onlooker as he pelted Sallee with putrid tomatoes.

Sallee grew thin and gaunt, refusing to eat so that her children might have what meager rations the family could scrape together. She continued her campaign in town, adding hand-lettered signs which she tacked to establishments that served or sold food. As winter set in, Sallee redoubled her efforts to secure food for her family. By now a familiar sight on the streets of Clarksburg, Sallee had become a pariah, despised by the men and pitied by the women.

So it was that on a particularly cold and icy afternoon in the dead of winter when Sallee stood on her soapbox just outside the Foggy Bend Hotel exhorting the passersby for aid that a gang of young ruffians made their way up Water Street. "Well, lookee here! If it ain't our favorite little beggar!" the gang's leader snarled. "Ain't there laws about no loiterin' on the town streets? I say we shut her up once and for all." Whereupon the gang of ruffians pelted Sallee with balls of snow, ice and rocks until she fell from her soap box.

Sallee died two days later, leaving her five children to grow up in the county orphanage. While Heath had been a boy of only fifteen at the time, he remembered the familiar sight of Sallee on her soapbox. Several of the Meyers' children had attended school with Heath and he had often heard his parents speak in hushed voices about the plight of Sallee Meyers and her family. Never able to erase the memory of what befell that family from his mind, Heath did not want to see Emma subjected to such cruelty as she embarked upon this crusade. Women were valued for their appearance, their housekeeping and cooking skills, their ability to conceive repeatedly but never for their opinions. Women, like their children, were expected to be seen but never heard.

Having confronted Emma's stubborn streak on numerous memorable occasions, Heath had finally come to respect the beautiful and defiant little woman standing next to him, face to the wind as the ferry churned its way across the Southport River to Clarksburg. Heath felt strangely moved by Emma's determination to be accepted as an equal and he was beginning to comprehend the notion held by Emma and others, that women were treated unjustly by men.

Heath felt fiercely protective of Emma's right to speak out about the issues that concerned her and the other nurses at Angel of Mercy. It took only the episode earlier that same morning to convince Heath that Emma and the others were in danger. He agreed that changes needed to be made in hospital policy for the safety and welfare of Emma and the nursing staff. Even though Emma was at first adamantly opposed to Heath tagging along with Luke to stand guard outside the solarium as the women held their meeting, Emma acquiesced after Heath reminded her of Sallee Meyers' tragic story.

The hospital solarium was already beginning to fill with nurses and student nurses who stood around in small groups discussing the events of the day. The women fell silent as Emma entered the room and then just as suddenly, the solarium began to reverberate with applause. Emma waved modestly to her compatriots and turning to Heath and Luke asked, "Where will the two of you be in case of trouble?"

"Luke and I have been discussing the matter and it is our opinion that one of us should be positioned down the hall by the caduceus and the other one should be positioned here at the entrance to the solarium. What is your preference?"

"I would prefer you to be here by the solarium, Heath, and Luke down by the caduceus with your Constable's badge and side arms clearly visible. Would that be all right with you, Luke?"

"Sounds logical to me," responded Luke preparing to take up his assigned post.

"And one more thing, Luke," Emma added reaching out for Luke's sleeve, "there should be absolutely no reason for any man to be allowed back down this hall until the meeting adjourns."

"Then that is just the way it will be," said Luke, removing his hat and pushing back the long red hair that threatened to gallop about his shoulders, as he strode back down the corridor toward the entrance to Angel of Mercy Hospital.

Fanella Walker arrived, pince-nez glasses dangling from their black ribbon, carrying a large sheaf of papers and her infamous wooden pointer. "Are we ready, Emma? It would appear that just about all of our nurses and student nurses are here and anxious to begin the process of drafting our demand letter."

Emma nodded and together the two women made their way to the front of the room, passing by nurses and student nurses who patted them, smiled and uttered words of encouragement.

Fanella assembled a makeshift podium by stacking one chair on top of another and then, after signaling to Heath to shut the solarium doors, she rapped with her wooden pointer upon the stacked chairs to indicate to the women that they should be seated before beginning, "Nurses and student nurses of Angel of Mercy Hospital, let me start by saying how enormously gratifying it is to see all of us assembled under one roof on such short notice and for such an important cause." Fanella was immediately interrupted by applause.

Fanning the air by her sides as if she would fly, the infamous pointer whistled through the air as Head Nurse Walker continued, "For the record," and she turned to the group's self-appointed secretary who sat taking notes in shorthand on a piece of paper, "just let me state that virtually every orderly on staff here is present in the hospital this evening at my behest to oversee the dinner hour and whatever other hours are necessary with our patients so that we can conduct this meeting and I would urge each and every one of you in the coming days to make a special point of thanking them," which was delivered to more applause.

"Please, ladies, do hold your applause, or rotten eggs, as the case may be, until the end of the proceedings or we shall never finish," joked Fanella to her appreciative audience, while waving her wooden wand over the enthusiastic gathering.

"Most of you know that I called for our assembly this evening in order to draft a demand letter to our Chief of Staff, Dr. Burris G. McKendrick. It is a particularly sad commentary on our times that such a letter is needed at all, but events that occurred in the hospital earlier this morning have made such a letter mandatory.

We nurses have long known that this hospital is not secure. We work at night without the benefit of assistance from our staff doctors and we have no representation on the Angel of Mercy Hospital Board, which Board decides hospital policy for each an every one of us." At this point, Fanella was again interrupted, this time by a nurse who stood up at the back of the room.

"Begging your pardon, Head Nurse Walker, but we are also paid less than the male orderlies and these orderlies do not possess the same level of skills as we nurses."

Thunderous applause engulfed the room and Fanella strode back and forth making her flying-arm motions to quiet the group. "We must not be greedy, ladies!" she exhorted the animated group. "We must be selective in our demands this first time. The crucial demand, and I cannot emphasize this strongly enough, is for representation on the Hospital Board, for therein lies our key to bargain for the future, not only for ourselves, but for those who come after us."

Even as the nurses and student nurses were applauding Fanella Walker, a fracas erupted on the other side of the solarium doors. "Let me through!" yelled a man's voice. "Freedom of the press must prevail! I invoke my Constitutional right to be present at this meeting!" accompanied by the sound of much scuffling.

Emma recognized the voice at once. It was Angus O'Malley. Turning to Fanella Walker, Emma whispered, "That would be Angus. Do let us include O'Malley in our meeting."

When Fanella did not seem to recognize the name, Emma whispered again, "It is Angus O'Malley, my friend who is a reporter for the Grandview Courier. A newspaper report of our meeting this evening might just aid our cause."

"Oh, of course, dear," Fanella whispered back to Emma and then in a louder voice, she called to the nurses at the back of the room, "Open the doors at once ladies and usher in Mr. Angus O'Malley who has come all the way over from Grandview to report upon our meeting for tomorrow's paper."

When the nurses opened the doors, everyone caught a glimpse of a disheveled Angus O'Malley, dangling by his arms and furiously pedaling the air in between

Luke and Heath. "Unhand me at once!" yelled O'Malley. "This is a clear violation of the Constitution of the United States of America," O'Malley continued even louder now that he had an audience. "Freedom of the press!" he screeched.

"Shut up, O'Malley!" warned Luke as he and Heath set the small man back on his feet. "The only thing being violated around here is our eardrums."

O'Malley looked disdainfully back at his captors, before turning dramatically to his audience of women. Tugging his satin waistcoat back down into place and smoothing his hair flat, O'Malley modulated his voice in greeting to the women, "Good evening ladies. Allow me to introduce myself. I am Angus O'Malley, reporter for the Grandview Courier and it is my very great pleasure to have the opportunity to report on this most auspicious of occasions," whereupon he bowed low to the assembly of tittering females.

"Hello to you, Emma dear," Angus called, smiling and waving to Emma.

Emma waved back. "Do have a seat, Angus," she called to her friend, whereupon Angus, oozing congeniality, sat triumphantly between two pretty student nurses. Taking out his notepad and pencil, Angus O'Malley stood once again and addressed Fanella Walker, "Please, madam, feel free to commence when ready and do just forget that I am here." O'Malley sighed hugely, while winking at Emma before resuming his seat.

"Thank you Mr. O'Malley and now to return to the issues at hand, I have asked Emma Richardson to say a few words to you this evening. I really do not believe Student Nurse Uppity needs any further introduction from me," said Fanella pointing with her wooden wand to Emma on her right.

The solarium erupted in laughter, applause and whistling as Emma rose to her feet and moved to the makeshift podium. "I guess my reputation precedes me," laughed Emma with her audience. "Certainly it is a reputation that my mother would tell you I earned at a very tender age. My mother has always described this only child as 'willful, stubborn, determined, obstinate, headstrong' and so forth and so on, which all of you as my friends and co-workers have clearly deduced for yourselves during the nine or so months since we first began working together here at Mercy." More laughter greeted Emma's self-deprecation.

"And tough as nails!" yelled Louise Bennington from the middle of the audience.

"I shall take that as a compliment, Benni," laughed Emma, pointing to her friend.

"I learned very early in life," Emma continued after the laughter and comments had subsided, "that the meek do not inherit the earth," which pronouncement produced a smattering of gasps from her female audience. "To the contrary, only we women who are willful, stubborn, determined, obstinate and headstrong enough to dare to advocate change will inherit that portion of this earth which is rightfully ours!" This last comment brought down the house, prompting Head Nurse Walker to rise to her feet once more and commence fanning the air with her wand.

"I am reminded of an outing that I enjoyed with two of my sons over here on this side of the river about a year ago. My twin sons were seven at the time and upon seeing a handsome, matched pair of horses pulling a carriage, one of them was inclined to comment that the horses probably belonged to the king. The second son corrected the first and reminded him that we have a president instead of a king in this great country of ours, adding that some day he planned to vote for the President of the United States. A chilling thought occurred to me as I stood in the middle of Clarksburg that summer day. Each of my three sons would in due time be able to exercise his right to vote for the President of the United States and I might never…" whereupon the women in the solarium stomped their feet, whistled, clapped and yelled, "Hear! Hear!"

When the women had settled down again, Emma continued, "Unless I was prepared to do something about it!" Her audience cheered loudly and so did Nurse Walker. Angus O'Malley scribbled furiously in his notepad.

"When a naked drunk entered the men's ward in the early hours of this very morning and pointed a loaded pistol at my head, it occurred to me that I had a choice. I could either faint or I could take control of the situation. Do you know which I chose?"

"TAKE CONTROL!" Emma's audience shouted back in unison.

"Yes! I decided to take control!" Emma shouted back to the women, pounding upon the chair in front of her for emphasis.

The group was electrified by such radical words and both Emma and Fanella had a difficult time calling the women to order again. When the noise abated, Emma resumed her comments, "When I first met our Head Nurse Fanella Walker, she jokingly told me after I fell down a flight of stairs that the first rule for her nurses here in the hospital was, 'Remain vertical.' Today, we are adding a second rule, 'Take control.'" Again the room erupted.

Raising her arms to quiet the gathering, Emma concluded her remarks, "Let my ordeal in the men's ward earlier today serve as a catalyst for change in this hospital, for unless we are prepared to take control and effectuate changes, we nurses and student nurses shall continue to be at risk from intruders both day and night. We shall continue to work nights without the benefit of doctors present in the hospital. We shall continue to work without the benefit of representation upon the Hospital Board and," here Emma pointed to the woman in the audience who had stood up earlier to address Fanella Walker, "we shall continue to earn less than the orderlies who are meant to be our assistants." Emma sat down to thunderous applause.

Silence eluded the group for a full ten minutes until Fanella Walker finally stepped to the makeshift podium again. "Ladies, I believe you would concur that we have our work cut out for us this evening as we must prepare and deliver a letter of our demands to Chief of Staff Burris G. McKendrick before midnight this evening. I and the other senior nurses on staff have concluded that unless our demands are met by sundown tomorrow evening, we shall all remain at home over the coming weekend.

We must be unanimous in our decision to remain at home in the event that Dr. McKendrick and the other members of the Hospital Board do not accommodate our demands. If even so much as one of us nurses or student nurses reports for work, we shall fail. Let me see by a show of hands, how many of us are going to TAKE CONTROL!" Fanella shouted.

Virtually everyone in the audience, including Angus O'Malley, raised both hands, and for the next five hours the women worked feverishly writing and rewriting their demand letter to Burris G. McKendrick and the other members of the Hospital Board. At eleven o'clock that night, the letter was ready for delivery to their Chief of Staff. Fanella asked for volunteers to hand deliver the letter to the residence of Dr. McKendrick before midnight and to a woman, all in the room raised a hand, as did Angus O'Malley.

Fanella chose two other nurses and Angus O'Malley in addition to herself to deliver the group's carefully worded missive to the residence of the Chief of Staff. As nurses and student nurses prepared to depart the solarium for their homes and their night shifts in the hospital, Fanella made one final comment to the group, "I shall wager that our dear Dr. McKendrick and all the other staff physicians will spend the remainder of this night tossing and turning about their comfy, cozy little beds. What say all of you?"

"STAY VERTICAL AND TAKE CONTROL!" Angus O'Malley was suddenly moved to shout over the "Hurrahs!" of the assembled women from high atop his chair.

"Quite so, Mr. O'Malley, quite so!" remarked Fanella as the departing women enjoyed one final bit of humor that evening.

Fanella Walker, two of her senior nurses and Angus O'Malley arrived on foot and by lantern light at eleven-thirty that night in front of Burris G. McKendrick's residence in Clarksburg, not far from Mercy Hospital. Fanella opened the iron gate to the front yard and strode up the cobblestone walkway to the front door of the doctor's darkened house. The others stood tightly grouped around Fanella as she rapped loudly with the brass knocker upon the massive walnut door that dominated the front of the federal style house.

Cordelia heard the knocking first and rolled over on her side toward her husband, "Burris!" she said to his profile. The doctor continued to snore. "Burris!" she tried again, nudging his shoulder. "Someone is knocking at the front door!"

"What? Who?" was the response.

"Someone is knocking at our front door," repeated Cordy.

"What hour is it?" he asked.

"I am not sure but it is still pitch black outside," she responded sitting up in bed and peering toward their bedroom curtains which sighed in and out with the summer breeze.

"Well who in thunder would be knocking at my door at this ungodly hour of the night?" asked Burris, rising on the edge of the bed to fumble with the matches and candle on his nightstand.

"I really do not know, dear," replied Cordy pulling the sheet up under her chin as if to ward off the unknown visitors from her bedchamber.

"Damnation! Do people not realize that I need my rest?" Burris groused. With bare toes, the doctor felt clumsily about the hooked rug on the floor by the side of the bed for his slippers before taking up the flickering candle to light his way down the hall to the staircase.

Fanella thudded the knocker rudely against its brass plate again.

"I am coming! I am coming!" announced the doctor in a loud voice as he picked his way down the long flight of stairs to the front door.

Opening the walnut door, Burris thrust his candle out in the darkness to ascertain the identities of the group that stood before him. "Nurse Walker!" he exclaimed. "Ladies and…Angus O'Malley? What the devil are the four of you doing here at my residence at this hour of the night?" he demanded.

"We have come on behalf of the nursing staff at Angel of Mercy Hospital," began Fanella in her most formal tone, "to deliver this letter of demands which letter has been signed by all fifty-one of us staff nurses, retired and active alike, and all of the remaining twenty-two student nurses," she announced shoving the sealed envelope at Dr. McKendrick's chest.

O'Malley stuck his pad of paper into the circle of candlelight and scribbled.

"What in blazes did you say you have?" Burris asked in disbelief.

"A letter of demands," Fanella replied tartly, this time waving the sealed envelope under the doctor's nose.

"Who is it dear?" came Cordelia's voice from the dark interior of the house.

"Go back to bed!" Burris ordered his wife gruffly. Turning back to the little group, Burris snatched the letter from Fanella's grasp and asked, "Well then, am I to read this in your presence or what?"

"If you would prefer to do that, sir," responded Fanella.

"Very well but let me light the gas lamps before you stumble and fall," and the doctor disappeared into the interior with his flickering candle preceding him.

With the front room of the house illuminated, the doctor reappeared at the doorstep to usher his callers into the parlor. Gathering the long, stiffly-starched white nightshirt about him, Burris sat down on an ottoman close to one of the gas lamps and prepared to open the envelope that Fanella had handed to him as she stood outside his front door. "Sit down! Sit down!" he ordered everyone, adjusting his spectacles and preparing to read the letter which he unfolded upon his lap.

"Oh, merciful Jesus!" he shouted midway through the letter. "I do not believe this!"

When Dr. McKendrick finished reading the contents of the handwritten, six-page letter, he stood abruptly and began pacing back and forth in front of the fireplace which still smelled faintly of the final oak log fire of spring. "Just what do you expect me to do with this...this..." and he waved the sheaf of papers angrily above their heads before finding the right word, "crap?"

"We expect," began Fanella in an equally angry tone, "that you will go at once and present our letter of demands to all the members on the Hospital Board at Angel of Mercy Hospital. Please pay careful attention to the paragraph in which we the undersigned have agreed that unless our demands are met by sundown Friday...tomorrow evening...then it is our united intention to stay home for the duration of the weekend, which means that..." and Fanella was interrupted by Dr. McKendrick.

"I know damn well what the meaning is," shouted Burris, clearly purple with rage, even in the dim light of the parlor's gas lamps. "You have no right whatsoever to do this!" and he shook the papers in the faces of his four visitors.

"That is just the point, doctor!" shouted Fanella jumping to her feet, even though the other two nurses attempted to restrain her. "We have no rights, WHATSOEVER! And we are going to terminate these abysmal working conditions once and for all! We bid you good-night, sir!" and Fanella stormed from the house with her entourage following closely at her heels.

"That was splendid! Simply rousing! Magnificent!" crooned O'Malley trotting at the elbow of Fanella Walker as she marched from the doctor's residence out into the darkness.

Only after the group was a full two blocks away from the McKendrick household did Fanella slow her pace and then stop, doubled over with laughter. The other three began to laugh raucously as well.

"Did you see the look of total disbelief on his face?" asked Fanella of her co-conspirators. "That expression alone was worth the trip!"

From a second story window, a leather boot came hurtling through the night air, accompanied by a loud, "SHUT UP DOWN THERE!"

"I feel a bit like old Paul Revere this evening," whispered Fanella, still laughing as she guided the other three away from the McKendricks' neighborhood. "The doctors have been warned!"

The headline in the Grandview Courier the next day read, "THE MIDNIGHT RIDE OF THE NURSES", with a subtitle of, "Angels of Mercy To Show No Mercy."

Emma had gone straight home from the meeting of the nurses at the hospital and collapsed on her bed in an exhausted heap. Luke had bid Emma and Heath farewell at the entrance to the house on High Point Avenue before seeking refuge in his own bed further north of Grandview in the home of his parents. Concerned about possible repercussions due to the events of the last twenty-four hours, Heath insisted upon bedding down in the parlor with his side arms nearby. He was taking no chance that another itinerant drunk would stumble upon the premises seeking to even the score with the infamous little woman crusader, peacefully sleeping upstairs along with her mother and three sons.

The next morning with the first light of day, George and Will awakened to tiptoe into their mother's bedroom. Emma was asleep on her side, facing the east windows. Will padded around the bed and carefully lifted Emma's right eyelid, "Are you waked up yet, Ma?" he whispered.

"I am now," she replied, still motionless on the bed.

Will let go of her eyelid and stood by the bed waiting. At last, Emma rolled onto her right side, where George sat observing his mother.

"Go on!" exhorted Will in a terse whisper to his brother.

"Go on what?" George whispered back across the recumbent figure of his mother.

"Go on and lift her eyelid like I did."

"What for?"

"'Cause that's the only way you'd know if she's dead or passed out. Ma told me if you see just the white part of the eyeball, then you're gonna be dead or passed out," Will added with unfamiliar superiority.

"She just spoke to you, dummy Willy, and she moved too, so I think we can cross 'dead' off the list," George reasoned across his mother's inert body.

"Well, you never know. Just movin' over in the bed could of caused one of them…you know…blood snots that she's always worryin' about with her patients and…"

"It is a blood 'clot', Will, not a blood 'snot'," replied Emma still without opening her eyes.

"SHE'S ALIVE!" yelled Will.

Just then, Emma rose up in bed, grabbed both boys and yelled back, "AND I MIGHT JUST HAVE TO GIVE THE TWO OF YOU A COUPLE OF BLOOD SNOTS IF YOU ARE NOT CAREFUL!"

Whereupon a free-for-all of wrestling, shouting and laughing erupted upon the bed, prompting little Johnny to climb out of his crib and toddle into his mother's room to join in the fun. Will lifted the baby onto the bed and George playfully rolled him over onto his back. Johnny looked startled and sucked in his lower lip as if he would cry.

"Easy does it, boys," cautioned Emma gathering her smallest child to her, "we must remember that Johnny cannot roughhouse quite as handily as the two of you can."

"Ma!" exclaimed Will. "What you don't seem to understand is that Johnny gets away with murdering me and Georgie. He pinches and bites and kicks and we get blamed for it."

"Yeah, nobody ever tells this silly baby 'no'," chimed in George. "Goo-goo baby is spoiled," laughed George jumping up and down on the bed near Johnny in order to make him tumble over onto the covers.

Just then, Heath appeared in the doorway, "Do I have to come in here and restore law and order?" he asked pulling a toy pistol from one of the boy's little holsters that he had strapped to his right thigh.

"Are these critters bothering you, ma'am?" Heath asked in mock seriousness.

"Yes, kind sir, and I feel quite faint with all the commotion. Perhaps you had better seize these varmints and lock them up in the town jail," and Emma swooned back onto the pillows.

"Your wish is my command," laughed Heath. Scooping up all three boys into his huge embrace, Heath carried the yelling boys into the bathroom and deposited them in the copper tub. "And now, gents, for the highlight of my day and yours…A BATH!"

"NO!" all three boys yelled back.

"Reach for the sky, pardners!" ordered Heath, again unsheathing the toy pistol. Six hands shot into the air.

"Very good! Now drop 'em!" Heath ordered pointing with the toy pistol to the boys' pants and Johnny's diaper. But, when the two big boys lowered their hands to comply, Heath chuckled and asked, "Did Simon say 'drop 'em'?"

"But how can we get undressed if we can't use our hands?" wailed Will.

"Use your teeth," Heath deadpanned.

"Is he serious, Will?"

"I dunno, George."

As Heath turned to exit the bathroom, he added, "Oh, and Simon says 'you can use your teeth,' but have those clothes off and on the floor by the time I come back in here."

The boys proceeded to attempt removal of their clothing using only their teeth, amid peals of laughter.

"What is going on in there?" asked Emma from her bed as Heath returned to check on her.

"Nothing much. Just trying to keep the boys occupied and out of your hair so you can get up and get dressed without all the noise. How are you feeling today?" he asked solicitously.

"Just like a quarter-past-ten," she replied smiling at him.

"A quarter-past-ten? What exactly does that mean?" he looked puzzled.

"Like someone tied me to the railroad tracks in front of the ten o'clock train!"

Heath made breakfast for the family that morning while Emma explained about all of the previous day's events to her mother. "Oh, Emma, darling! I am so very proud of you for managing the terrible incident at the hospital with such aplomb," responded Mary as she moved to embrace her daughter in the kitchen while the boys gobbled Heath's scrambled eggs, toast and fried fatback at the table in the dining room.

"But, frankly, I am deeply concerned about the wisdom of the decision by you and others to issue demands to Burris and the Hospital Board, while threatening to stay at home if those demands are not met," Mary worried out loud.

"Mama, the incident with the naked drunk was the straw that broke the camel's back, for me and for all the others as well. We are united in this. We must not behave in the manner of a bunch of ostriches, no matter how unpleasant the consequences," announced Emma while unconsciously straightening her spine.

When Emma reached the hospital that morning for her shift, Ramona Stewart took her aside to say, "I feel I should caution you that Edna Ford has been asking after you all day and her mood is terribly cranky," and Ramona motioned with her head down the long row of beds on the women's ward.

"Well, I guess I had better face her right now," responded Emma brightly.

Even though Emma's heels never touched the floor as she walked down the length of hospital beds, noting as she went that each bed had been carefully made up with crisp white linens complete with the requisite precision hospital corners at each end, Mrs. Ford was instantly alert.

"Who goes there?" demanded the blind woman turning her head in the direction of Emma's footsteps.

"It is I, Mrs. Ford."

"Just the one I have needed to see all day! The little instigator herself has finally arrived!" Edna Ford said unpleasantly.

"Now what on earth has you so riled up so early in the day?" asked Emma innocently, adjusting Mrs. Ford's pillows.

"You!" the old woman snorted.

"Me?"

"Oh please! Spare me the torture of feigning ignorance. The whole damned hospital is awash with talk of your activities over the last couple of days," huffed Edna Ford.

"I thought you of all people might understand the logic of our decision," tried Emma.

"The logic, yes! The reality, no!"

"How could you possibly object?" asked Emma feebly in the face of such opposition from a woman whom she had come to like and admire.

"I can object because I am your patient, or have you conveniently forgotten that one small detail Miss Crusading Uppity?" Edna scolded.

"You can relax, dear," soothed Emma reaching out a hand gently to stroke the woman's withered arm. "Head Nurse Fanella Walker has made arrangements for the orderlies to be on duty around the clock to take care of our patients and then there are always the doctors…"

"Baboons! Absolute baboons, the lot of them!" and Edna moved her arm away from Emma's caress. "In fact, I think I would prefer the ministrations of a red-assed baboon over those from either the orderlies or the doctors!" she complained as her sightless eyes roved agitatedly back and forth in their sunken sockets.

Startled, Emma asked, "How do you know that some baboons have red on their behinds? I mean, you have been blind since birth and you would not know what red is…" stammered Emma.

"Well, I may be blind but I am not deaf. I hear things, you know, and I remember them," she said angrily touching a gnarled hand to her head. "Just like I heard about all the crap that you have been stirring up around here. What am I to do?"

"About what, dear?" Emma tried again.

"About my bath!" wailed Edna Ford.

"The orderlies or the doctors will see to your bath," Emma answered reassuringly.

"Over my dead body they will see to my bath! Do you realize, child, that I have never been married? No man's hands have ever touched the most private parts of my body, not even the hands of our most illustrious surgeon, Burr. You married women act like you enjoy all the fumbling around that goes on under the sheets but I can tell you that for me, the notion of it is sheer torture. I cannot stand the thought of some man touching me on my private areas. If I could only use these hands for something more than hoisting a cigarette to my lips!" she cried mournfully as tears slid from her opaque eyes.

"Oh, Mrs. Ford, forgive me! I did not understand your particular dilemma until just now. How terribly stupid of me!" Emma replied on the verge of tears herself.

"Speaking of cigarettes, Emma, how about rolling one for me?" Edna asked, suddenly mollified. "Actually, make that two cigarettes."

"Why two, Mrs. Ford?"

"One for me and one for you. The way our day has gone, I believe we could both use a good smoke."

Obligingly, Emma took the thin white cigarette papers from Mrs. Ford's bedside table and placing two side by side, carefully placed a pinch of the brown tobacco in the middle of each. Next she rolled the papers and tobacco into neat little cylinders. Dipping her finger into Mrs. Ford's water glass, Emma moistened the exposed edges and sealed them. Twisting the end of each cigarette, she placed both in her mouth at once and touching a lighted match to each, inhaled deeply and promptly began to cough.

Emma carefully placed one cigarette between Edna's lips and the other she kept in her own mouth.

"Ah, nothing quite like a good ciggie!" exclaimed Mrs. Ford, suddenly calmed. "What say you, Emma?"

"You have a point there," responded Emma inhaling briefly before coughing spasms racked her small frame again.

Ramona strode briskly back to where the two women sat puffing on their cigarettes, "Here! Give me that thing!" she hissed, snatching the cigarette from Emma's lips and snubbing it out in Edna's morning coffee cup. "Mrs. Ford has need of her cigarettes, but you, on the other hand, do not!" and Ramona marched back to the nurses' station with the fouled coffee cup and its saucer.

"Sorry, dear. I guess I got you into more trouble," apologized Edna in Emma's direction.

"The cigarette smoke has actually cleared my brain," said Emma in return, "and I have an idea."

"Not another one of your ideas," smiled Mrs. Ford at the space that Emma had just vacated.

"I think that I could persuade my very own mother to come over to the hospital in the guise of a visitor and once here, give you your bath. What do you think of that, Mrs. Ford?" asked Emma beaming at the little gnarled, puffing woman.

"What are her qualifications?" Edna Ford demanded suspiciously.

"She is a highly skilled midwife and has been for many years. She even delivered my twins."

Still unconvinced Edna asked peevishly, "And just how do I know that I can trust her...what did you say her name is?"

"I did not say but my mother's name is Mary Miller. Let me tell you a story about my mother, Mrs. Ford. As I mentioned to you, my mother is a midwife of considerable standing and skills in our community and has been for a very long time. Years ago, our household was awakened in the middle of the night by loud banging upon our front door and that banging brought lights to the windows of all the houses up and down High Point Avenue," laughed Emma at the childhood memory.

"What does that have to do with my bath?" worried Edna Ford.

"I am getting to that. Anyway, my father went down to the front door and found a young man clad only in his nightshirt and exceedingly agitated because his wife was in the first throes of labor. So, Mama dressed quickly while Papa saddled the horse, and taking her black bag, galloped off behind the agitated young husband astride his horse."

Edna puffed away, "Good story, so far."

Emma smiled, "Ten minutes into the ride, the young man suddenly reined in his horse and turning to my mother said, 'Dear God! I have forgotten the way to my own house,' so great was his distress at the impending birth."

Both women laughed at the mental picture the scene presented. "Well, what on earth did your mother do?" asked Edna.

"Mama had the presence of mind to administer a dose of smelling salts to the young husband which seemed to clear his thinking enough to the point that he could guide the two of them back to his modest home. When Mama entered the young man's house, she found a pathetic young girl, barely eighteen years of age, who had been experiencing the first stage of labor for some two hours."

"Yes, yes, and then what?" asked Edna Ford with the cigarette clenched firmly between her teeth.

"To give the young husband something to do, Mama ordered him to boil water and then go outside to sit on the front step and smoke his pipe while she tended to his wife. It was a long and arduous labor because the girl was so young and so small and she fought each successive labor pain as if it were a tiger come to take her life," related Emma.

"Is that customary?" asked Edna, straightening herself in the bed and handing her cigarette butt to Emma for disposal.

"Quite customary until the girl entered the 'if-only' stage," laughed Emma again.

"Well!" snorted Edna Ford, "I am so glad you are enjoying the joke but just what in hell is so funny about that and mind you, I fail to see how those events should convince me of your mother's trustworthiness."

Emma continued, still smiling at the recollection, "As I was saying, when the girl entered the 'if-only' stage and began saying things to my mother like, 'If only you will make the pain go away, I promise to attend church every Sunday' and 'If only you will make the pain go away, I shall promise to love my mother-in-law like my own mother' and so forth and so on until, the young girl suddenly cried out in desperation to my mother, "If only you will make the pain go away, I promise I shall confess to my husband that this baby is not his.'"

"Good gravy, no!" gasped Edna.

"Yes," responded Emma, "and do you know what my mother said?"

"Tell me at once before I fall from this bed trying to wring it out of you!"

"My mother bent low over the girl where she lay writhing in pain and whispered in her ear, 'You will do nothing of the kind, my dear. I have just spent the last fifteen hours tending to you in preparation for the birth of this precious child and for the last nine months, the good Lord has been tending to both you and the child. I shall not allow you to undo all my hard work and that of the Blessed Father in a few careless seconds. Now, be quiet and PUSH!'"

Edna Ford laughed hugely. "What a dandy story! Do make another cigarette for me, Uppity," adding, "unless of course, you think you could salvage the one that Ramona so rudely grabbed away from you," and both women laughed again.

With Edna puffing away, Emma continued, "The point I wish to make in telling you the story about my mother's experience with the young girl is that only twenty years later, as I lay in labor with twins, did Mama reveal the anonymous girl's confidence. So, I believe that you can trust Mary Miller not to relate any of the details concerning your bed bath," she concluded, again touching Edna's arm.

This time, Edna did not withdraw her arm. "Please tell your mother that I shall look forward to meeting her and hearing more of her stories. That is, the stories which would not be considered a breach of her patients' confidences," and Edna puffed contentedly on her second cigarette.

Emma finished the rest of her shift uneventfully and then reported to Fanella Walker's office. Rapping lightly upon the door, Fanella called, "Enter," whereupon Emma realized that Head Nurse Walker's office was filled to overflowing with other nurses and student nurses.

"Ah, Uppity...good timing." Removing her pince-nez glasses from her nose, Fanella handed a letter to Emma.

Emma had only to scan the contents of the paper to realize that the members of the Hospital Board and Dr. Burris G. McKendrick in particular had repudiated all of the nurses' and student nurses' demands. "Well, it seems quite clear to me and probably to all of you," commented Emma, "that each and everyone of us will be spending the coming weekend at home."

"Indeed, none among us shall report for work either tomorrow or the next day. Are we all in agreement on this?" asked Fanella.

"Yes, Head Nurse Walker," the women responded.

"Good. Then, I need all of you to go out and get word to those who are not present that we must remain at home for the entire weekend.

Additionally, I have notified all the orderlies of our decision in light of the response from Dr. McKendrick and I have organized them to take over the daily care of our patients. I took the liberty of drafting, signing and hand-delivering a brief response from us indicating our intention to stay at home for the next two days."

Emma felt both exhilarated and exhausted as she made the trip home to Grandview. Mary, the children and Heath were all in high spirits when she entered the house on High Point Avenue. Will ran to his mother announcing, "Guess what?" Without waiting for a response, Will added, "Heath is going to take us all swimming tomorrow over in Clarksburg at a lake where he used to swim when he was a kid and Nana says we can pack a picnic lunch and…" his voice trailed off as he noticed the look on his mother's face. "Are you feelin' sick, Ma?"

"Sort of," Emma said quietly.

Sizing up her daughter, Mary spoke first, "Would that have anything to do with conditions at the hospital?"

"It would."

"Are you going through with this?" asked Heath cautiously.

"I must. Not only for myself but for the others as well," she answered.

"Then, I reckon it would not be a good idea to swim or picnic over in Clarksburg this weekend," said Heath looking into the stricken, upturned faces of the boys, adding quickly, "but we can sure have fun on this side of the river. Right Will? Right George? Right Johnny?"

"Wrong," grumbled George.

"Heath, I must speak to Mama a bit. Can I ask you to busy the boys in the parlor?" Emma asked, taking a seat at Mary's kitchen table.

While Heath herded the three boys down the hall and into the parlor, Emma remained seated watching her mother fry chicken in the big cast iron skillet. Emma was silent for so long that Mary finally turned around to look at her daughter. "I thought you told Heath that you wanted to speak to me?" she began.

"I do," responded Emma, "but I just do not know where to begin."

"When in doubt," reasoned her mother, "always begin at the beginning."

"Easier said than done," Emma answered, removing raw chicken pieces from a bowl of buttermilk and tossing them in flour, salt and pepper before handing them to her mother to fry in the skillet of smoking lard.

"How did I get here?" Emma asked looking at the chicken leg that she was aimlessly dusting with flour.

"Oh my goodness! When I suggested you should begin at the beginning, I did not realize just how far back this story was going," Mary chuckled.

Seeing the amused look on her mother's face, Emma smiled.

"I have made some really bad decisions in my life, Mama. Have I not?"

Mary took the chicken leg from Emma, dropped it into the sizzling grease and then turned to the soapstone sink to wash her hands before replying, "We are all guilty of making bad decisions, Emma. Each and every one of us." Wiping her hands on the blue and white kitchen towel, Mary added, "I believe that is the best way to learn. You burn yourself once on this old stove and you learn not to burn yourself again."

"Well not me!" exclaimed Emma. "I just keep burning myself over and over and over again. I mean, even Will learns faster than I do."

"Emma, what are we talking about here for pity's sake…learning or burning or what?" asked Mary turning a piece of chicken with the long wooden-handled, two-tined fork.

"I wish I could have perceived all those years ago how just one decision would change the course of my life forever," Emma mused sadly to her mother.

"Oh, Emma darling, you were so very young when you decided to marry Edward, even as I was when I married your father," responded Mary, trying to comfort her distraught daughter.

"But Papa was an excellent choice…a true gem among men, would you agree, Mama?"

"To be sure, your papa was a gem, but at the time of our marriage, I knew little more of him than you did of Edward."

"But you made a wise choice, Mama. Somehow…intuitively…you made a wise choice and I made a very poor choice, one that continues to affect every aspect of my life on a daily basis. Some days, I feel as if I shall never fully recover from that initial terrible decision. Now, I find myself in another kettle of stew because of a decision that I made."

"Which decision is that?" Mary asked, sitting across the table from her daughter.

"My decision to study nursing and most recently, my decision to instigate changes at the hospital. Your chicken is burning, Mama," Emma cautioned.

Mary rose to move the pan of chicken to the back of the stove, turning the crisp pieces again.

"I am rather like your chicken. I no sooner get out of one hot pan of grease than I jump into another," Emma commented mournfully about herself. "Because of my…my impetuous decisions, all of you suffer."

"Emma, we are not suffering. Whatever has put that notion into your head?"

"Just when this ship is about on an even keel, I insist on rocking it, forcing everyone to fall overboard, to phrase my dilemma in terms that old Burr would appreciate," Emma smiled faintly.

Not waiting for a response from her mother, Emma continued, "But, there is a voice inside my head that cries 'foul' when there is an incident such as the one that occurred during my shift the other night at the hospital. I simply cannot slough it off as inconsequential. My conscience screams, 'Fix it! Fix it!' and I unfortunately always decide to listen to my screaming conscience."

"All of us who are privy to the incident at the hospital the other night are outraged by it. I have had so many people approach me to say what a brave and clever woman they believe you to be for reacting so calmly to such a dangerous event," Mary said rising to place the fried chicken pieces on a wire rack over a china platter to drain.

"But I cannot let go of it, you see. I cannot leave it at that. No, I must now crusade for changes so that similar events never happen again," sighed Emma, propping her elbows up on the wooden table and placing her chin in her hands.

"And where is the fault in that?" asked Mary.

"The fault is here," and Emma waved her hand at her surroundings. "Here I have three sons, a mother and a dear friend, but where am I? I am over at that hospital crusading for us nurses," said Emma bitterly.

"You must regain your bearings, my child. Let me attempt to reshape some of those somber thoughts. One, from your travails and your education at that hospital will come the ability to support your family. Two, when you see a wrong, correct it. Your father and I taught you that long ago. Three, stop wasting the time that you have to spend with us worrying about the time that you do not have to spend with us. Four, stop using your decision to marry Edward as a measuring stick for all other decisions. Five, let go of the past because it is a millstone about your neck. Six, embrace each new day with courage and conviction and seven, tell that conscience of yours to be still for a bit because you are worn out with listening to its voice reverberating within your head!"

Mary had been walking up and down the length of her kitchen ticking off her thoughts on her fingers to Emma when Heath appeared in the kitchen door, "And eight, are you two ever going to serve dinner? It seems to me," he grinned, "that a little bit of talking sure turned into a whole lot of talking. The boys and I are half starved!"

Emma wadded up the blue and white kitchen towel and threw it across the room at Heath, "Just like a man!" scolded Emma. "Always worrying about his stomach!"

Emma and her family were still eating their dinner when someone began knocking on the front door, sending Brute trotting down the front hall, hair on end, barking ferociously.

When Emma rose to answer the door, Heath intervened, "Sit down and finish eating your supper. I shall handle this," and with his napkin still tucked under his stubble-covered chin, Heath followed Brute down the front hall to the door. Peering out the side window, Heath saw Luke Crawford, twirling his hat in his hands, red hair flowing wildly about his neck.

As Heath opened the front door to admit Grandview's constable, Luke swatted Brute on the rear end with his hat, "Howdy old boy! You act like I'm some kind of a thief come to run off with Mary's silverware!"

"Luke? Is that you?" called Mary from the dining room rising to greet the constable.

"Yes, ma'am," Luke responded. "Please excuse me for interrupting your dinner."

"Oh, nonsense! We were just finishing and besides, I would bet that you could use a plate of supper yourself. Emma, do go into the kitchen and fix a plate for Luke," instructed Mary.

"Thank you kindly, ma'am, but I don't have time to eat right now. I've come to speak to Miss Emma a moment," replied Luke nodding to the boys. "May I speak with you, Emma?"

"Yes, of course," said Emma rising to join Luke and Heath in the parlor.

"I know this is a bit of an imposition but I really didn't know what else to do," apologized Luke.

"What is the trouble, Luke?" asked Emma.

"Well, I have a prisoner in the jail with a toothache," began Luke, tapping the right side of his own jaw, "and his whole head is swollen and red and the bugger keeps yelling that he's going to die unless I get the doctor to come take a look at him."

"Where is Dr. Abernathy?" asked Emma.

"Apparently he was called away on an emergency. Some kid fell out of an apple tree and broke his arm, so that means the doc won't be back for a while and I don't much cotton to the notion that I have to spend the night in jail listening to all that hollering."

"Where is Benni?" asked Emma.

"She won't budge from the other side of the river until after this weekend because of the problems at the hospital...she's afraid to be seen on the streets of Clarksburg or Grandview," groused Luke.

"Well, I guess that leaves me. Let me get my bag and we shall be off to silence that prisoner of yours," Emma smiled brightly at Luke's sullen face.

When Emma came back downstairs with her bag in hand, Heath told her that he would remain behind with Mary and the children. Therefore, Luke and Emma set off together for the town jail, walking briskly along High Point Avenue to Longmeadow and then to the far end of Elm. When Emma and Luke turned onto Elm, they could hear the prisoner yelling in Luke's jail from a block away.

"See what I mean?" asked Luke, looking over at Emma.

"Yes, it is a bit deafening, even from this distance. That must be some tooth-ache!"

When Luke unlocked the front door and the two of them entered the jail, Emma saw a tall, thin man holding his head in his hands, agitatedly pacing behind a row of steel bars and yelling at the top of his lungs.

"Pipe down, you bastard," yelled Luke back, "before I'm tempted to put you out of your misery." Pulling out his revolver, Luke gestured at the man, "Shut up, I say! This...doctor's assistant is going to have a look at that tooth of yours and if you pull any funny stuff or make any noise again, so help me, I'll pull the trigger. I've been listening to your racket for two hours straight and I've had enough. Do you understand me?" and Luke moved menacingly toward the man's cell with his gun aimed at the man's face which was swollen to the size of a large pumpkin.

"Uh-huh," responded the thin man.

Luke unlocked the door to the man's cell and Emma walked inside, set her leather bag down at one end of the untidy cot and ordered the man to take a seat at the other end of the cot. It was then that she noticed the second jail cell was occupied. "Why is he in here?" asked Emma gesturing to the man who apparently lay sleeping in the next cell in spite of the incessant din of his neighbor.

"Had to arrest him at three o'clock this afternoon because he was drunk as a skunk and pissing on the courthouse steps. Apparently the judge granted the man's wife a divorce from him yesterday and the guy was showing his contempt for the judge's ruling," and for the first time that evening, Luke managed a smile.

"I am going to need a lantern here, Luke, in order to see into his mouth. Sir, what did you say your name is?" asked Emma turning to look at the prisoner.

The man began to yell again and this time, Luke pulled the hammer back and pointed his gun at the prisoner's head. "I'll put a bullet in that miserable brain of yours unless you shut up this instant!"

Turning to Emma with a look of agony on his face, the man uttered an unintelligible sound, "Horskumpfh..."

"Horskumpfh?" repeated Emma.

"Uh-huh," nodded the thin man still cradling his grotesquely swollen face between filthy hands.

"The bastard's name is 'Horstketter'," said Luke returning with a coal oil lantern.

"My goodness! We shall need to shorten that name a bit. Perhaps..." mused Emma when Luke interrupted.

"Just call him 'Horse'. He answers to that most of the time."

Taking the lantern from Luke, Emma quietly advised the prisoner, "Now then uh…Mr. Horse, you are going to have to remove your hands from your face and open your jaw for me as wide as you possibly can so that I may see clearly inside your mouth in order to determine how best to help rid you of this terrible pain. Do you understand?"

Horse shook his head 'no'. "You did not understand me, Mr. Horse?" Emma attempted again, moving closer with the lantern.

"The bugger understands you, Emma, he just isn't going to open his mouth but I have a cure for that. Step aside." Whereupon, Luke grabbed the man who began to yell again and threw him to the floor in front of the iron bars. In one fluid motion, Luke handcuffed the prisoner to the iron bars, "Now, you bastard, see how you like that!"

Next, Luke dashed from the cell, grabbed a length of rope from above his battered wooden desk on the far wall, and lashed the man's legs to the iron bars of the cell. "It does seem a bit brutal," commented Emma weakly.

"It's going to get a lot worse if he doesn't settle down and RIGHT NOW!" yelled Luke into the prisoner's ear.

"Actually, I believe I may have something which will take the edge off of his discomfort and relieve his agitation," said Emma reaching into her bag. Pulling out a bottle of ether, Emma uncorked the bottle, removed her handkerchief from the waistband of her skirt, and dabbed a bit onto the lace. Then, she held the handkerchief to Horse's nostrils for a few seconds.

"Breathe deeply," Emma ordered Horse.

The prisoner struggled briefly and then suddenly, relaxed. "One of modern medicine's little miracles," laughed Emma as Luke stared in disbelief.

"Now, kindly pry his mouth open so that I may have a look," and Emma knelt on the floor of the jail cell with her tongue depressor and lantern. As she bent forward to look into the gaping jaws of Horse the prisoner, Emma was overwhelmed by the stench of the man's putrid breath.

"Phew!" gagged Emma, rocking backward on her knees, tongue depressor and lantern still poised in midair. Undeterred, Emma leaned forward again, and holding her breath, examined the interior of the man's mouth.

Withdrawing the tongue depressor and the lantern, Emma stood up and said, "Well, I can see the problem clearly enough."

"And that is?" asked Luke, also rising to his feet.

"Horse Horstketter here has a badly abscessed molar in the lower right posterior jaw."

"Can you fix it?"

"Do you have a pair of pliers?" asked Emma.

"Somewhere around here, I guess."

"I shall also need you to stoke up the stove to heat water and…I shall need a bottle of whiskey. Did your newly divorced prisoner over there happen to have a bottle on him when you apprehended him upon the courthouse steps?" Emma asked, smiling at Luke.

"You bet he did," and Luke left the cell to produce a brown glass bottle from his desk drawer.

"Now Constable Luke Crawford! You were not intending to drink that stuff on the sly, were you?" teased Emma.

With his face suddenly the color of his hair, Luke replied, "Well, I have to admit the thought did cross my mind," and he handed the bottle over to Emma. "Especially after the first hour of that bugger's caterwauling."

With a clean coffee pot of boiling water at her side, Emma took the pliers that Luke had found and washed them with cold water and lye soap. Next, she tied a bit of rag to the handles of the pliers and lowered them into the pot of freshly boiled water to sterilize the crude dental instrument.

"Luke, you must open his mouth again for me," and Emma pointed to her patient who looked rather like a side of beef, hide on, fully clothed and ready for roasting. Emma saturated another piece of clean rag with the whiskey confiscated from the prisoner in the second cell. With this, she swabbed out Horse's foul mouth.

Next, Emma carefully pulled the pliers out of the hot water and allowed them to cool enough so that she could grasp the handles. Then, she said to Luke, "Steady now with the lantern and keep his head in that position as it exposes the area where I must work." Reaching back into Horse's mouth with the pliers, Emma grasped the abscessed molar with her still warm instrument and yanked. Expecting more resistance, Emma was unprepared for how easily the tooth tore loose of its moorings, which sent her tumbling onto her back.

Never releasing her grip upon the tooth which she held high in the air in the vise of the pliers, Emma declared, "Well, that was one of my greater successes! Would that I could pop out a baby that easily!" she laughed. Luke laughed with her, relieved to have the ordeal over and anxious to have peace and quiet restored to his jail.

Emma finished up by wrapping a bit of rag around her index finger, dipping it in some of the whiskey and cleaning Horse's teeth, giving the area of the abscess a meticulous cleansing. "Mr. Horse really must be instructed to clean his teeth with salt and soda at least twice a day and he should also be instructed to wash his person every day," Emma sniffed, wrinkling her nose before adding, "How is it that Horse came to be arrested anyway?" Emma tidied up from the impromptu procedure while Luke released the man and dragged him up onto the cot before answering.

"Old Horse here has a fondness for taking that which doesn't belong to him. He can be standing right in front of you carrying on a conversation just as nice as you please, and the next minute he's lifting money out of your pocket with a smile and a 'howdy do.' Horse is particularly skilled at removing merchandise from Hummel's," explained Luke.

"Such as?" asked Emma, intrigued to have met her first pickpocket.

"Oh, such as tobacco, snuff, hair oil, that sort of thing. Even ran off with a pair of lady's garters last week. Never figured him for a lady's man though," laughed Luke.

"Well then, how did you catch him?"

"Horse went into the store and stole a packet of Hummel's headache powder because his tooth was beginning to hurt like hell. Only trouble was, Horse tore the paper packet when he lifted it and the powder began to sift about like flour, marking him and his path out the door," again Luke laughed at the recollection. "So he was a real easy one to find."

"Where did you finally catch up with him?"

"Just out front of the saloon, trying to dust that stuff off his trousers. When I took a look through the room that he rents over the livery, I found all kinds of goods that Hummel identified as coming from the store."

"Amazing!"

"Just my job, Miss Emma. Just my job," replied Luke self-effacingly.

The door to the jail suddenly swung open and Heath strode inside. "Emma, your mother got to worrying about you so I just thought I would make sure that you returned home safely."

"That is most thoughtful of you, Heath. Luke and I have just finished here. It was necessary to remove one of Horse's teeth which was badly abscessed," Emma explained.

"Damn, Luke! This place smells like you have been cooking up home-brew!" exclaimed Heath, sniffing the air.

Luke and Emma looked at each other and laughed like a couple of conspirators. "What you smell, Heath dear, is a combination of ether and alcohol, both of which were used for strictly medicinal purposes, I can assure you."

Heath escorted Emma home where she remained for the rest of the weekend with her children but the following Monday, she was up before dawn, dressed and ready to assemble once again in the solarium of the hospital as Fanella Walker had instructed all her nurses and student nurses. The normally sunny room with its cheerful yellow paint was tinged with gray as rain hammered against the large windows that overlooked the spectacular showcase on the side lawn where the early blooming dogwood and redbud trees were showing off their new flowers.

Fanella strode to the makeshift podium, still intact from the group's last meeting and rapped loudly for silence. Clearing her throat and firmly clipping the omnipresent pince-nez glasses to the bridge of her nose, Fanella read from a paper, "I have before me a letter, just received this morning from our illustrious Chief of Staff, Dr. Burris G. McKendrick, and the other members of the Angel of Mercy Hospital Board." Loud whisperings greeted her announcement prompting Fanella to rap again upon the chairs stacked in front of her, "Silence!" she commanded.

Emma was keenly aware of her heart thudding out of control in her chest as Fanella continued, "'For the past forty-eight hours, we, the undersigned staff doctors at Angel of Mercy Hospital, all took charge of those duties and responsibilities normally assumed by the nursing and student nursing staff and, along with the orderlies, ran the hospital by ourselves.'" Fanella paused, looked over the top of her glasses and smirked at her audience.

"'After much deliberation, we have concluded that it is patently untenable for such an arrangement to continue...'" she read before being interrupted by deafening applause and stomping of high button shoes, which produced more rapping by Fanella upon the chairs with her wooden pointer, "'...without jeopardizing the health and well-being of those we have taken an oath to care for and to protect.'"

"Hear, hear!" reverberated throughout the solarium accompanied by prolonged applause while Fanella strode up and down in front of the victorious gathering, conducting the noise with her wand. "'It is therefore our considered opinion,'" Fanella continued above the din, "'that appropriate locks should be installed at all secondary entrances to Angel of Mercy Hospital commencing Monday morning, which locks are not to impede an exodus from said Hospital. A guard will be stationed at the primary entrance to Angel of Mercy Hospital, which guard is to be on duty twenty-four hours a day, seven days a week.'"

More applause ensued but Fanella kept on reading, "'We the undersigned agree that a minimum of three doctors are to be stationed in the hospital during each night shift for the benefit of the nursing staff and our patients, seven nights a week.'" Thunderous applause and stomping accompanied Fanella's flying motions as she finished, "'We agree further to negotiate with the nursing staff for a member of their group to sit upon the Hospital Board...'" but Fanella got no further as pandemonium broke loose in the solarium while the rain and thunder outside echoed the noise that reverberated inside the yellow room.

It was a sweet moment for the nursing staff at Angel of Mercy Hospital and rather than attempt to silence the women, Fanella joined in the celebration of the important concessions that she and the others had won by refusing to report for work over the weekend. Congratulating themselves and laughing now that the nerve-wracking ordeal was over, the women were not immediately aware that Dr. McKendrick was observing their antics from the entrance to the solarium. As an unshaven, haggard and unsmiling Burris McKendrick made his way slowly through the sea of white uniforms, silence followed him.

"Good-day," Burris greeted Fanella Walker, tipping an imaginary hat to her as he stepped up to the podium of chairs. One could have heard a pin drop, so silent was the solarium, save for the rain as it rapped incessantly upon the windows for attention. "Ladies," the doctor greeted the victorious nurses.

Looking briefly at the wall of windows, Dr. McKendrick began, "I must say that the weather matches my mood exactly," and turning back to look at the waiting ranks of nurses he added, "I realize that all of you are pleased to have achieved your objectives. However, I caution each and every one of you to keep in mind that for each success in life, there is a price to pay. Success always exacts its own price. So, even as you are congratulating yourselves for the moment, remember that not all share your celebratory mood. This petty display has angered many on the Hospital Board. I can further assure you that this display of yours has also undermined the confidence that your patients placed in you a mere forty-eight hours ago."

The women looked at one another in disbelief. "You achieved your objectives primarily because I decided discretion to be the better part of valor. I simply could not allow this charade of yours to continue to the detriment of my patients. I hope you are immensely happy with yourselves. I for one take no pleasure from the pain and turmoil that you have caused to me and to this hospital. In my opinion, you have done us all a great disservice," whereupon Dr. McKendrick took leave of the women, abruptly parting the sea of startled and flushed faces as he made his way to the solarium doors.

Disbelief quickly turned to anger as the women commented to themselves about the doctor's dismissive and cavalier attitude that he had taken toward them. Shouts of, "poor loser" and "scoundrel" made it necessary for Fanella to resume her stick-waving antics in order to quiet the group of outraged nurses.

A nurse from within the sea of white shouted at Fanella, "We won fair and square!"

"Indeed we did ladies," agreed Fanella, banging her pointer against the chairs, and then quite uncharacteristically Fanella was moved to shout, "Hallelujah, Sisters! We have prevailed!"

The ramifications of Dr. McKendrick's gloomy forebodings were all too readily apparent over the course of the next week and for a long time thereafter. True to his word, Dr. McKendrick had the necessary locks installed and guards were posted around the clock at a makeshift desk just inside the front door. Fanella was instructed to conduct an ex officio election among her nurses to determine who would be their representative upon the Hospital Board and it came as no surprise that she herself was chosen to serve in that capacity. The entire nursing staff, students and regulars alike, were enthusiastic and energized by the recent turn of events. The future looked brighter than ever for all those women who gave so tirelessly of themselves to the great institution of medicine and specifically, to the hundreds of patients who desperately needed their care each year.

The women soon realized, however, that there were some rather large flies in the ointment. Young and old alike, the doctors felt demeaned to be required to leave the comforts of hearth and home to serve a shift in the hospital, no matter that it amounted to one night a week and only every other week. Usually, they were subtle in the way they showed their contempt for the nurses. Sterilized instruments inexplicably clattered onto unsanitary floors during surgical procedures. Whole trays of food slipped from delivery carts onto hall floors and mysteriously tipped over onto clean hospital beds. Nursing notes were found scattered topsy-turvy about the nurses' stations. Patients with no history of bowel or bladder disturbances returned from bathing to find their sheets soiled with feces and urine. It became readily apparent that the doctors were intent upon sabotaging the nurses' success. Dr. McKendrick had been correct. The nurses were paying dearly for their recent victory. Since the Board would not be meeting for another few weeks, it would be a while before Fanella could stand before the culprits to cry "foul" and "shame".

Emma and the others were required to fetch an ever-increasing list of foodstuffs and supplies for the male doctors. "Get me a cup of coffee and a pastry from the Water Street Bakery," was a frequent order, along with, "Everything in this supply closet is in total disarray!" Or, "Where are the clean bedpans?" which always sent the nurses flying off like dogs to retrieve the required object. "Pick up those sheets and blankets from the floor before someone trips and breaks a bone!" "I did not ask for these bandages. Get rid of them!" Whereas the safety and well-being of the patients was never an issue, the sanity of the nurses was being sorely tested. Chores were endlessly repeated by an exhausted cadre of nurses and student nurses, trained to take pride in the cleanliness of their patients and the hospital facilities.

Since Emma preferred to spend her shift at the hospital caring for patients, cleaning the laboratory was not particularly to her liking but private thoughts had never betrayed her outward performance of duty. Just as zealous with a mop, pail, rags and disinfectant as the next student nurse, Emma dispatched the cleaning and sterilizing of the laboratory sinks, counters, beakers, microscopes, slides, floors and so forth with aplomb. Tackling the laboratory first, she reasoned, got the most unpleasant part of her day out of the way, allowing Emma to devote the remainder of her shift to the patients.

One week after Fanella had stood triumphantly before the nurses and student nurses at Angel of Mercy Hospital, Emma entered the laboratory prepared to wage war upon the customary leavings following a day of hard use by the hospital doctors. What she saw and smelled caused Emma to freeze in her tracks. Every flat surface was covered with either dissected animal carcasses, smeared feces, knotted entrails or broken glass and above it all, swarmed black flies by the hundreds, let in through the open windows. Emma gagged. Confronted by such profound filth and such horrendously unsanitary conditions, Emma closed the door to the laboratory and retreated to the hall outside. Emma leaned her head up against the cool marble wall as she struggled to regain control of the urge to vomit.

Irene Sellers happened by just at that moment and spied Emma leaning against the wall, prompting her to ask, "Are you ill, Emma?"

"Take a look in there for yourself," answered Emma turning her ashen face back to the wall.

"Oh, dear heaven!" exclaimed Irene, quickly shutting the door. "How nauseating!" As she too began to gag, Irene clamped her hands over her mouth to stifle the rising tide within her throat.

"Here, place your face against the cold of the marble. It helps," offered Emma.

The two women stood together as Irene pressed first one side of her face and then the other to the cold marble wall. Finally, Emma spoke, "That has to be the lowest trick yet."

"Unbelievably low!"

"I am going to put a stop to such nonsense once and for all," and Emma marched away down the hall to the caduceus and then down the stairs to Fanella Walker's office.

Fanella was sipping a cup of coffee when Emma knocked upon her office door.

"Enter," she said, never taking her bespectacled gaze from the chart in front of her.

"Nurse Walker," began Emma, "I have something that I wish to show you and Dr. McKendrick up in the laboratory right this minute."

"Whatever is it?" asked Fanella peering over the top of her pince-nez glasses, surprised by the expression on Emma's face.

"You will just have to see and smell this for yourself to believe it," was all that Emma would say and she turned on her heels to retrace her steps, stopping this time at Dr. McKendrick's office, several doors removed from the laboratory.

Fanella caught up with Emma just as she strode past Dr. McKendrick's startled secretary and banged open the door to his private office without knocking.

"What the..." began Burris McKendrick before Emma interrupted him.

"You need to come at once with Head Nurse Walker and me to the laboratory. There is something you must see for yourself," whereupon Emma again turned and strode out into the hall, down to the laboratory. Stationing herself with arms folded across her chest, Emma waited outside the laboratory door with the quaking Irene for Dr. McKendrick and Nurse Walker to catch up with her.

Long white coat flapping, Dr. McKendrick huffed up to Emma, "Now, just what is all this nonsense?"

"There," replied Emma, jabbing a finger at the door to the laboratory.

"There what?" asked Burris McKendrick.

"In there is the nonsense. Go on, open it for yourselves!" ordered Emma, not budging.

Obligingly, Nurse Walker opened the door to admit Dr. McKendrick ahead of herself.

"Sweet Jesus!" exploded Burris.

"How awful!" echoed Fanella, as she retreated, hand covering her nose, before Burris, who shut the door firmly behind them.

"Who did this?" he bellowed and looking directly at Emma added, "You?"

"Do you think if I had done something as atrocious as that, I would actually summon you to see it?" responded Emma hotly.

"Well, who then?" he asked.

"You know all too well who did this…your precious doctors did this!" she fairly yelled into his ashen face. "Just as they have been creating messes all over this hospital for us nurses to clean up ever since we presented our demand letter to you and the Hospital Board. The doctors are seeking reprisal for our success…how did you put it? This is the price we must pay for our success! You, by your very words to us that morning in the solarium a week ago…you put them up to this…you encouraged this outrageous behavior…you fostered it!" Emma accused Dr. McKendrick angrily shaking her finger inches from his nose.

"Simmer down," cautioned Fanella Walker, taking the sputtering Emma by her arm. "Nothing can be resolved out here in the hallway accusing and shouting at one another."

Yanking her arm from Fanella's grasp, Emma hissed, "I refuse to clean up that dung heap of a laboratory…intentionally fabricated at your direction and implemented by your doctors and I shall see to it that none of the other nurses set a hand to cleaning it either if I have to remain planted by this door for the rest of the week," and she stormed down the corridor and out of the hospital for a breath of fresh air.

Burris and Fanella stood staring down the hall at the diminutive retreating figure of Student Nurse Emma Richardson. Irene cowered behind Head Nurse Walker, watching in disbelief as Emma departed.

"That one is nothing but trouble! I should have seen it coming!" ranted Burris.

Fanella turned to him, "Wait just a minute, Burr! 'That one' is all of us! Remember? We nurses and student nurses are all united about the conditions in this hospital. Furthermore, Emma did not create that staggering, putrid mess beyond the door there…your troublesome doctors did that all by themselves just to harass us nurses. So, I suggest you get busy and order the scoundrels to get in here to clean up after themselves for once because I can tell you this, hell will freeze over before I order any of my girls to touch that gory scene," and grabbing Irene by the belt, she marched them down the hall away from their sputtering Chief of Staff.

Burris McKendrick moved swiftly to call a meeting of all the hospital doctors later that afternoon behind the closed and guarded doors of the hospital cafeteria. Stationing doctors by the doors to and from the large room just across from the library and up from the kitchen, Burris paced before the assembled physicians. Chairs were stacked neatly upon the tables above the freshly scrubbed floor in preparation for breakfast and lunch the next day, theretofore, the only two meals eaten by the doctors in the hospital.

With his hands clasped tightly behind his back, Burris wore a path back and forth in front of the double doors to the kitchen area at the rear of the room. His thoughts were interrupted by a young doctor at one of the tables nearest to the Chief of Staff, "Uh, sir? I believe that everyone is here."

"Sir?" he repeated.

Looking around at the faces above a mass of white coats, Burris asked, "Are we missing anyone? I want absolutely every one of my doctors present in this room so as not to miss a word of what I am about to say. If anyone is missing, go and fetch him at once."

Burris waited while the men took a nose count and the same young doctor replied, "We are all accounted for, sir."

"Good. Then I shall begin," and clearing his throat, Burris reached for a glass of water where it rested on a tray of untouched lunch food still set with a napkin and eating utensils on a table by the kitchen door. He raised the glass to his lips as if to drink and then suddenly, hurled the glass and its contents down the center aisle onto the floor, where it shattered, sending water and glass fragments skittering around the feet of the men seated by the center aisle. The doctors closest to the Chief of Staff's missile, jumped up and away from the ensuing mess.

Without hesitating, Burris next picked up the plate of food and a spoon, flinging in rapid succession, mashed potatoes, peas and carrots, meat covered in gravy, applesauce and a caraway seed-covered roll at his horrified audience before bellowing, "DO I HAVE YOUR ATTENTION NOW?"

"Sir!" exclaimed the same young doctor, now on his feet, wiping mashed potatoes out of his hair, "What is the meaning of this?"

"I shall be only too happy to tell each an every one of you what the meaning of this is, but first you will all sit your behinds back in those chairs and BE SILENT," Burris, purple with rage, yelled at them.

Stunned silence prevailed as the doctors surveyed the mess on the floor, tables and each other before turning to watch their Chief of Staff as he slowly and deliberately cleaned his hands upon the linen napkin, which he meticulously refolded and placed back upon the lunch tray.

Shoving his hands deep into the pockets of his white coat, Burris began, "A short while ago, I had the distinct displeasure of being summoned to bear witness to an indescribably nauseating mess in the hospital laboratory, which mess, it has been reported to me, was caused by one or more among you," and he jabbed an accusatory finger at his audience.

"You," he continued, "who are highly trained and skilled doctors…the finest of the best and the elite of the renowned Angel of Mercy Hospital, deliberately sabotaged your own laboratory," and he resumed his pacing in silence. All eyes were riveted upon Burris G. McKendrick as he strode back and forth like a caged lion in the cafeteria.

Stopping abruptly and turning to glare at the doctors, he asked, "How many of you have seen the mess in the hospital laboratory to which I refer?" Cautiously, each man in the room raised a hand in acknowledgement.

"And who among you did this?" he asked next, looking around the room.

Silence and no show of hands was the response.

"I warn you, we shall be here for as long as it takes while I wait for the culprit or the culprits to come forward, AT ONCE!" he again bellowed.

The gathering of white coats began to quarrel, accuse and bicker while Burris calmly took a chair from one of the tables and sat at the head of the center aisle, sipping a cup of cold coffee, from the infamous luncheon tray. Dr. McKendrick was hugely enjoying the spectacle before him and he knew it would not be long before the miscreants were handed over to him. He had only to sip his cold coffee and wait.

A scuffle broke out at the far edge of the cafeteria, signaling to the Chief of Staff that the moment he awaited was nearly at hand.

A group of six dragged two young doctors up to the front of the room and held the men fast in front of Dr. McKendrick.

"Ah-ha! So it was you, Dr. Simmons and Dr. Cleary, who created this mess?" he asked the scarlet faced men still struggling with their captors before him.

"Pray tell, just what was it that prompted the two of you to sabotage your own laboratory?" Burris persisted in his questioning of the two men, still struggling.

"HOLD STILL, DAMN IT, AND ANSWER ME WHEN I SPEAK TO YOU!" thundered Burris at the doctors.

"It was all his idea," Dr. Simmons accused Dr. Cleary with a toss of his once carefully oiled hair that now hung in disarray around his face from the pummeling he had just taken.

Dr. Cleary glowered at his co-conspirator. "I am waiting, Cleary!" hissed Burris.

"Yes...yes! All right! It was my idea," confessed Dr. Cleary through his dark and drooping mustache.

"Why would you suggest such a rampage upon our laboratory and why in the name of heaven would you think to carry out such atrocities?" Burris asked the two men.

"To teach them a lesson," replied Dr. Cleary.

"Them?" Burris feigned ignorance of the intended victims.

"The nurses," interjected Dr. Simmons.

"Exactly what lesson was it that you sought to teach our nurses, Cleary?" Burris asked again.

Pulling his arms loose from his captors, Dr. Simmons replied, "Go on Cleary and tell him since it was your vindictive idea in the first place," and he stood rubbing his arms before Dr. McKendrick and looking belligerently over at Dr. Cleary, still firmly in the grasp of two other doctors.

"Let go of me," whined Dr. Cleary.

"You may let go of him now. He cannot escape," said Burris waiting for the man's response. "Come, come, man! What lesson was it that you intended to teach our nurses by fouling the laboratory?"

"I intended to teach those haughty females their proper place in this hospital," replied Dr. Cleary full of self-righteous hostility.

"Just what is the proper place for our nurses?" pursued Dr. McKendrick.

"On their hands and knees cleaning up the messes that we doctors create," replied Dr. Cleary triumphantly, as the dark mustache blew about his snarling mouth.

"Why is it that you think such low duties should be assigned to our nurses?" asked Dr. McKendrick.

"Because," came Dr. Cleary's well-reasoned response, "we all know that women are inferior to men. They lack the physical strength, mental capacity, balance of character and education that we men possess. In addition to which, women are sullied with menstrual blood each month of their adult lives and those menstrual irregularities of theirs control their lives to such an extent that they concoct fainting spells and the vapors and all manner of aliments designed to get them out of doing their assigned work. Women are unreliable, irritable and generally unsuitable to take on responsibility other than what we assign to them. Furthermore, we men must maintain not only a constant vigil over those assignments which we dole out to the women but over the women themselves and in addition to that…"

"I think that is quite enough of a denouncement of the female gender for one day, Cleary. I do, however, have one remaining question for you," and Burris paused to pace away from the young doctor.

Turning back to face the man from a distance, Dr. McKendrick asked, "Were you born of a man, Cleary, or were you, like the rest of us, born of a woman?"

"I…I…" Cleary stuttered.

"Yes, I feel quite safe in supposing that you too were born of a member of the so-called inferior gender and by the way, when you return home to your mother this evening, do tender my condolences to the poor woman. I am rendered quite sorry for your mother, Cleary, since your scornful assessment of the characters of our nurses here undoubtedly mirrors the contempt and low regard in which you hold your own mother."

Turning to Dr. Simmons, Burris asked the trembling young man, "Do you agree with Cleary that our nurses are meant to be subservient to your every need?"

Smoothing back long oily strands of hair from his forehead, Dr. Simmons replied in haughty tones, "More to the point, Dr. McKendrick, I do not agree with the decision to grant the nurses free election of one of their members to the Hospital Board. I do not agree that we doctors, who are the lifeblood of this venerable institution, should be required to remain in this hospital at night for the benefit of the nurses. We need our rest. We are indispensable and the nurses, quite simply, are not," Dr. Simmons spit out the words.

"Further, I do not agree that the doors should be locked or that a guard needs to be posted. Nurses who flaunt their gender and curry the attentions of male visitors to the hospital are guilty of wanton disregard for potential danger not only to themselves but to their patients as well," Dr. Simmons concluded.

"Sit down, now," intoned Burris to the young doctor still fiddling with his unruly hair. "Fortunately for all of us doctors, nurses and patients at this hospital, you, Simmons, do not make the decisions that govern us. That is why we elect members to the Hospital Board," and Burris indicated to the doctors still guarding the two young men that they should all be seated in front of the assembly.

"Since the guilt of both Cleary and Simmons has been indisputably established in regard to the malicious vandalism of the hospital laboratory, we must now decide as a body if the seriousness of these infractions warrants dismissal from the practice of medicine here at Angel of Mercy Hospital or if the infractions warrant a reprimand only. We on the Hospital Board met earlier today and determined that each and every doctor present in this room must cast a vote either to reprimand or to dismiss Cleary and Simmons."

"Do we concur?" asked Burris of the assembled doctors.

Shouts of "aye" filled the cafeteria.

"Very well then, let us conclude this matter by putting it to a vote, first as to Cleary. All in favor of reprimand, raise your hands," instructed Dr. McKendrick.

Six hands were raised.

"All in favor of dismissal, raise your hands." There was a pause before Burris announced, "It has been unanimously decided that Cleary will be dismissed from Angel of Mercy Hospital."

"Now as to Simmons…"

Without warning, Simmons sprang suddenly from his chair, turning to shout in front of the doctors, "Please, my colleagues! Do not dismiss me! Unlike Cleary, I have a wife and two small children at home who depend upon me. Be merciful! I was not the instigator of the vandalism," which last few words were delivered as Simmons was shoved back down into his chair.

"The time to plead your case has expired," Dr. McKendrick warned the profusely sweating young doctor being held in his chair.

"Now as to Simmons," continued Burris. "All in favor of reprimand, raise your hands."

The cafeteria before Dr. McKendrick filled with hands but as a formality, Burris continued, "And all in favor of dismissal, raise your hands."

Not a single hand was raised.

"Simmons, you are hereby reprimanded for participating in the malicious and unjustifiable vandalism to the hospital laboratory. Your behavior, Simmons, is a most shameful blot upon the medical profession of this fine institution. I am hereby instructing each and every one of you that I do not want any discussion of these events beyond those doors," and Burris gestured toward the cafeteria doors behind the assembled doctors. "Is that understood, colleagues?"

Shouts of "aye" again filled the room.

"There is one remaining matter which I must place before you this evening," continued Burris. "That is the matter of cleaning and restoring the laboratory to its former standard. How shall we proceed?"

A young doctor leaped to his feet, pointed to Simmons and Cleary and shouted, "They must be required to clean the mess which they created."

"Hear, hear!" shouted the assembly.

"Very well then, Simmons and Cleary you must proceed at once to the hospital laboratory and commence the cleansing, sterilization and organization of those premises before you leave this evening and I am to be summoned to inspect the laboratory when all has been completed. Now, who will supervise these two miscreants?" asked Burris scanning his flock.

A flurry of white coats produced three doctors who volunteered to oversee the restoration of the laboratory.

"Fine," he announced preparing to depart the cafeteria, "and when all is in order, please summon me as I shall be in my office. Oh, and one final note of caution to each and every one of you. If I so much as catch a hint of abuse toward our nurses, I shall haul the culprit or culprits in front of this kangaroo court for similar disciplinary measures. You are now all dismissed," and he marched down the center aisle and out the double doors.

The laboratory was put to rights that same night but Emma was not mollified, especially when she and the other members of the nursing staff learned via the hospital grapevine who the culprits were. The next day, Emma went straight to Fanella Walker.

"Have you heard?" Emma asked when she caught up with Fanella at the nurses' station in the women's ward.

"I have not missed a single syllable of the news," she smiled at Emma over the top of her pince-nez glasses.

"Well then, what are we going to do about it?" pressed Emma.

"Do about what, Student Nurse Richardson?"

"Do about the scoundrels who trashed the laboratory," responded Emma.

"As I hear it, the matter has already been concluded. Dr. Cleary has been dismissed from the hospital, Dr. Simmons was reprimanded in front of the entire assembly of doctors and they both were required to straighten up the laboratory. What more could you ask, Emma?"

"Yes...well, Cleary is gone but there still remains the issue of Simmons with his atrocious rhetoric about how he and the others need their sleep at night and we do not and how we, or rather I, enticed that drunk in off the streets..." sputtered Emma angrily.

"Emma, Emma! Calm down," whispered Fanella, "before old Edna down at the other end hears of this and blabs it all over the place."

"Do not worry about me ladies," called Edna Ford cheerfully, "for I have already heard the news and have not yet seen fit to blab a single word of it."

"You are impossible, Mrs. Ford," Fanella laughingly called back.

"I do my best! You know...being impossible requires great skill, finesse, talent, restraint..."

"Listen to her, would you?" chuckled Fanella, enjoying the banter with the sightless old woman. "I agreed with you, Mrs. Ford, up until the 'restraint' part. Few would ever accuse Edna Ford of exercising restraint, would they, Emma?" whereupon Fanella glanced over at Emma who stood rigidly by her side.

"This is not funny," seethed Emma. "I have been falsely accused of pandering to that vulgar drunk who happened into the men's ward that night and I..."

Quietly, Fanella addressed Emma, "You, my dear, are simply going to have to develop a thicker skin about certain issues around here," she began.

"Oh, like ignoring Dr. Simmons' penchant for cornering certain of us in the supply closets in order to satisfy his prurient need to fondle, squeeze, explore and pinch the forbidden parts of our female anatomies? How does one develop a skin so thick as not to feel humiliated by the man's unsolicited touch?"

"I can assure you, Emma, that Dr. Simmons will be a chastened individual from this point forward," whispered Fanella Walker. "He knows that everyone in this hospital is watching and waiting for him to transgress again. Sadly, Simmons' antics in the closet began in earnest when one of our silly little nursing students expressed her pleasure at being violated in a supply closet, encouraging Simmons to assume that all the student nurses would react similarly to his attentions."

"Well, I for one find it quite abhorrent!" hissed Emma, hands on her hips.

"Most do."

"What about the gossip that I enticed the drunk in off the street?" Emma persisted.

"Trust me, not a single nurse or student nurse believes that story. That is just the sort of nonsense that men conjure up in order to obscure their own guilt. Try not to personalize what just happened. Try to step back...remove yourself from the fray and see the victory that has resulted for us...the nursing staff," she admonished Emma.

"What victory?" asked Emma.

"Dr. Cleary was dismissed from the hospital. Dr. Simmons was reprimanded. Both men had to clean up the laboratory. Simmons has been humiliated and put on notice. Dr. Burris G. McKendrick took our part in the fracas. What more could you possibly want?"

"An apology," retorted Emma.

"Not likely," Fanella replied flatly and then added, "Listen Emma, we win in the very tiniest of increments in a man's world, so when we are victorious, my dear, we must all celebrate like hell. Learn to separate the wheat from the chaff because it may be a long time before you wind up with enough wheat to use for baking another loaf of bread."

"Amen!" sang Edna Ford from the far end of the ward.

Emma began to laugh. "She may not be able to see, but she hears better than any of us!"

"And if only you could see what I hear sometimes!" laughed Edna Ford.

CHAPTER 16

▼

Emma could not have anticipated the strife and conflict that would swirl about her as she embarked upon a career in nursing. Naively assuming that once her decision had been made to enter the field of nursing, Emma rationalized that she had only to study and work diligently, which endeavors would be rewarded with the coveted diploma that would afford her the ability to minister to the needs of her patients while supporting her family.

The reality of her circumstances was a far cry from the dream that she had so cherished about becoming a nurse. Emma never set out to be "Uppity the Crusader" but somewhere along the way, probably in part because she was the oldest woman among the student nurses, she took on a position of leadership within the class. Emma was dumfounded by the social and professional injustices toward women that she witnessed each day. Clearly it was not going to satisfy Emma Richardson to receive a mere diploma in nursing. She felt compelled to change the role women were constrained to play within the field of medicine.

Nor could Emma have anticipated the exhaustion that would dog each day of her study and work schedule, leaving so little time for her precious children and the man whom she had come to trust and to love. Emma began to realize that she was often unfit company for those she cherished the most. The events of the day continued to rankle and fester within her mind long after sundown, causing Emma to lie awake at night. Sleep deprivation only served to heighten her irritability.

Over the course of a weekend in the summer of 1890, Emma was fussing at her mother about Lowell, the man who, along with his family, rented the small row house on Locust Street where Emma had initially lived with the boys and

Edward before moving into Mary's house on High Point Avenue. Lowell was behind in paying Emma the rent and Emma had not had the time, inclination or the energy to haggle with Lowell about the money that he owed to her.

"I cannot let this situation go on much longer, Mama," Emma worried to her mother as they sat in the swing on the front porch darning socks together. It was cheaper to buy darning thread than to buy new socks all the time for the four males that lived in the house, reasoned Mary, but she was having trouble keeping up with all the laundry and mending. Even though Emma's skills with a needle and thread were negligible, Mary welcomed her daughter's help.

"How much does Lester owe you?" asked Mary, never looking up from the sock heel that she stretched taught over the blue, wooden darning egg. A brown wren perched on the white porch rail to monitor the progress of the two women and occasionally to dart about their feet picking up snippets of thread to weave into her nest.

"Lowell, Mama. His name is Lowell," Emma reminded her mother.

"Yes, yes. How much does Lowell owe you?"

"Two months' rent," replied Emma pricking herself with the needle. "Ouch!"

"Wear a thimble and that will not happen," Mary chided her daughter. "And how much is that?"

Unbeknownst to Emma and Mary, the two boys, George and Will, were under the porch digging tunnels in the dirt and eavesdropping upon the conversation between their mother and their grandmother.

"He owes me eight dollars now which is soon to be twelve dollars with the first of next month rapidly approaching. I have a mind to start charging him an additional fifty cents of interest for each month that he fails to pay me by the first. Lowell seems to have decided that because he is a man and I, his landlord, am a woman, he no longer owes me the money. He was surly and belligerent the last time I saw him in town and asked him for the rent, which was a month past due at the time," Emma complained to Mary.

"Perhaps you should speak to Heath about collecting the rent money for you," offered Mary, reaching for another sock from the wicker basket that sat on the swing between them.

"Never. That house on Locust Street is mine and I am responsible for collecting the rent money. I must make up my mind to do it. I keep putting it off because I am so tired when I get home and dread the thought of creating a scene with Lowell after all the unpleasantness at the hospital recently. I crave some peace and quiet."

In the cool shadow of the porch floor from above, Will swiveled his head as if to speak to George but was stifled when his brother clamped a dirty hand across his mouth. Pressing a dirty finger to his own lips, George signaled Will that they should creep out from under the porch and around to the back of the house.

"I have an idea!" exclaimed George when they were out of earshot of the two women.

"Not again!" complained Will.

"Come inside with me and wash your face and hands," George instructed Will.

"Are you crazy? Heath is forever makin' us take a bath and I'm not doin' it unless I hafto. Besides, what's wrong with a little dirt?" asked Will surveying his filthy hands.

Taking his brother by the shirt, George began to pull Will to the back door, "Get in here I say!"

Making fists of his dirty hands and shoving them under George's nose, Will asked, "Says who?"

"Says me. Now, look here, Will. You heard Ma say she cannot get Lowell to pay the rent and I have an idea that just might work but first, we have to be clean. Now come on!"

The boys washed diligently at Mary's kitchen sink and then as an after-thought, George dampened the palm of his right hand and slicked Will's hair to the side before doing the same to his own dark hair.

"Where is Brute?" asked George, satisfied with the results of their grooming.

"Asleep in the barn where it's cool, I reckon," answered Will, taking a cookie from the blue and white stoneware jar that sat in Mary's cupboard by the stove.

"Hand me one of those too and come on," instructed George, already halfway out the back door.

Brute rolled over onto his back and pedaled all four legs in the air, vigorously thumping his tail in the dust of the barn floor when the boys ran inside.

"Brute, old boy," announced George addressing the dog, "we are going on a mission to collect the rent for Ma!"

"Oh no we're not!" exclaimed Will, suddenly apprised of the great idea that had struck his brother under the porch.

"You heard Ma. Lowell owes us eight…no make that, twelve dollars and…let me see…uh…another dollar in interest for a total of thirteen whole dollars! And poor Ma is so tired and works so hard! Now you and I and Brute here need to help her out and collect that money. Are you with me or not?" asked George, pressing his face close to Will's.

"I dunno," Will hesitated.

"If you do not go with me and Brute, I swear to tell Ma that it was you who knocked the Christmas tree down last year," threatened George.

"You wouldn't dare!"

"Just try me!"

Will doubled up his fists and threw a punch at George, catching him on the chin and sending him reeling backward.

"Damn, Will!" cursed George, grabbing his chin, "That hurt!"

Still maintaining his boxer's stance, Will threatened, "And if you tell on me, I'm gonna hurt you a whole lot more."

"Okay, okay. Truce?" and still holding his chin with the right hand, George extended his left hand to Will.

"Truce," replied Will, gripping George's fingers with his own, "but only if you swear not to tell Ma on me 'bout the tree. Swear it!"

"I swear."

Satisfied by his brother's pledge of loyalty, Will sat down on a bale of straw, pulled another cookie from his pant's pocket and asked, "So what's the deal with collectin' the rent? I mean, how are we gonna do it? By the way, what was Ma talkin' 'bout when she told Nana that we was gonna be Indian gents?" he asked, munching on his cookie.

George sat astride a straw bale next to Will feeding cookie crumbs to the dog. Squinting over at his brother, he asked, "Have you been smoking grapevines behind the barn again, Will?"

"After Heath tanned our hides the last time he caught us smokin'? I may be dumb but I ain't crazy," announced Will, licking the sugar off his fingers.

"I happen to know that smoking grapevines always make you start talking stupid like that," stated George with an air of superiority.

"When we was under the porch, you and I both heard Nana say plain as day to Ma that if she didn't collect the rent soon from Lowell, we was all gonna be Indian gents," and Will stood up to brush off his pants.

"Will!" exclaimed George, slapping the palm of his hand against his forehead. "Nana was saying we would be INDIGENT. That means we would be poor without the rent money," explained George.

"Oh…well…we sure can't get to bein' poor over Lowell's rent money now, can we? So what was it 'zactly that we was gonna do to get that rent money, Georgie? You want I should beat it out of him?" asked Will making fists again.

"Brute here is going to get it out of Lowell," announced George proudly, stroking the dog's head.

"Okay. I get it," beamed Will.

"Finally!" said George. "But there is one more teeny thing I need you to do," and George leaned over to whisper in Will's ear.

A grin spread across Will's face, "Oh boy! This is gonna be fun!"

The twins set off with their dog for town, making sure to skirt the property at the back of the house so as not to attract the attention of Emma and Mary who were still busy darning the pile of socks on the front porch.

As the boys approached Locust Street, George said, "You know, Will, it seems real strange to be going back to the old house. I feel like maybe Pa will answer the door instead of Lowell. Know what I mean?" and he looked sadly over at his brother.

"Yep, Georgie. I been thinkin' the same thing myself but no matter how much I think on it, nothin' ever changes so I guess maybe you and I just better quit thinkin' that stuff. Besides, we're better off with Heath. He treats all of us real good and Pa…well, he didn't. You know?"

"Yeah, I know."

The twins walked down Locust Street to their old house in silence, remembering.

Two boys and a dog took their positions on the top step in front of 21 Locust Street before George signaled to Will that he should knock on the peeling door.

Will knocked loudly several times before a disheveled and unshaven man in his thirties opened the door, just wide enough for Will to insert his foot. Leather suspenders sagged around his worn trousers and a cigarette drooped from the corner of the man's mouth, wobbling up and down as he spoke to his callers, "Yeah, whadya want?"

"Hello, Mr. Lowell," George began politely. Smiling up at the man, George continued with the introduction, "I am George Richardson and this is my brother, Will Richardson."

Will also flashed a toothy smile while Lowell just glared malevolently at the boys and their dog through the cigarette smoke.

"So?" he snarled.

"So," continued George, "I have come about the rent money that you owe to my mother, Emma Richardson."

"Oh, really? Well now, ain't that a good one!" and Lowell laughed so hard that he began to cough.

"By my calculation, you owe my mother eight dollars in past due rent, four dollars for this month and another dollar in interest for the two months that are past due which makes a total of thirteen dollars that I have come to collect today," George recited confidently.

Whereupon, Lowell angrily thrust aside the front door, "Interest! Nobody said nothin' about no interest!"

Seizing the opportunity that presented itself when Lowell turned his attention upon George, Will slipped unnoticed inside the front door. As the boys had planned, Will then positioned himself on his hands and knees just behind Lowell as George was saying, "Yes sir, that will be twelve dollars and one dollar of interest for a grand total of thirteen dollars today."

"You tryin' to rob me boy?" and the smoking cigarette bobbed angrily up and down in the man's mouth.

"No sir, but I do aim to collect what belongs to my mother. Sit Brute!" George suddenly commanded the dog without taking his eyes from Lowell's face.

The ever-obliging Brute sat and showed his teeth at Lowell, only this time, the dog sensed the danger to the boys and emitted a low growl, which prompted the man to take a step backward, trip over Will and fall flat on his back. Immediately, Brute rushed inside the house to stand on Lowell's chest.

"You were saying, sir?" asked George looking down at Lowell.

"I was sayin' get this bugger offa me afore he crushes my chest! Damn dog weighs a ton!"

Brute leaned down into the man's face and growled again.

"Jesus, boys! Do something afore the devil bites off my nose!" exclaimed Lowell.

"You first, sir. Just reach into your trouser pocket and pull out the thirteen dollars that you owe my mother and I shall call off my dog," bargained George.

"All right, all right, but get the bastard away. He's gettin' slobber all over my face," complained Lowell.

"You need a good bath anyhow," announced Will holding his nose.

George made no move to withdraw Brute from the man's chest. Instead, he shoved his hand in Lowell's face, "Money, sir!"

Under the weight of the dog atop his chest, Lowell fumbled in his trouser pocket for a crumpled wad of bills that he pulled out and tossed over at George.

George counted the bills, "You have here, sir, a total of fifteen dollars but I shall take only what is owed to my mother and give you change of two dollars," and the boy carefully smoothed out two one dollar bills and placed them on a table by the front door.

"Next time sir, I suggest that you pay Emma Richardson on the first of the month to avoid any additional…uh…interest," and grabbing Will by the arm, the boys ran down the front steps of 21 Locust Street.

"Hey! Wait a minute!" called Lowell from the floor with the dog still standing on his chest. "What about your dog?" he yelled after the retreating twins.

When the boys were nearly to the end of Locust Street, George placed two fingers of his right hand between his teeth and let out a shrill whistle. Brute obediently cocked his leg over the recumbent man and then galloped off after the boys, who were running lickety-split for home.

The twins never stopped running until they caught sight of their grandmother's house. "Got to stop a minute," panted Will leaning up against an ancient sycamore tree after they had crossed the railroad tracks at the foot of Longmeadow. "I've got a stitch in my side."

"Yeah, me too!" echoed George, slumping to the base of the tree to catch his breath.

Brute ambled up to the two winded boys. The great dog stood expectantly looking from one flushed face to the other as if waiting for his next assignment.

"It'll be a cold day in hell before that bugger forgets to bring Ma the rent money again, I'll wager," laughed Will, reaching out to stroke the dog's massive neck. Brute responded by licking Will from his chin all the way up and through the boy's dark hair, causing it to stand out at an angle from his head which made Will look a bit like a peacock with half its tail feathers ruffled.

George pulled the paper money from his pocket and laid the bills neatly on the grass by his leg, counting out loud to make sure that he had not lost a single one during their flight from Lowell. "Phew! Every dollar is here!" exclaimed George. "I sure would hate to have to go back down Locust Street and pick up any dropped rent money right about now!" he exclaimed.

"Me too!" chimed in Will. "'Cept it'd be fun just to get a gander at old Lowell with dog piss all over him." Both boys doubled over with laughter at the thought. "Actually," added Will still laughing, "Dog piss might make Lowell smell better," and he fanned his nose with his hand, adding, "Did you get a whiff of him?"

"I was concentrating so hard on what I had to say, I was hardly breathing," joked George.

"Well, Georgie, take it from me…when old Lowell rolled over me there on the floor, the bugger smelled so bad, I thought sure he'd just shit himself!" and the twins laughed raucously again.

"Maybe we had better speak to Heath about tossing Lowell into the river," continued George in the same vein.

"Yeah, and with one of Nana's HUGE cakes of lye soap!" Arm in arm, the boys made a couple of victory laps around the sycamore tree before continuing up to the house on High Point Avenue with Brute in the lead.

Emma and Mary were still seated in the swing, sipping coffee with sugar and cream over ice and chatting on into the summer afternoon with the neat pile of carefully darned socks resting on the slats between them.

"Hi, Ma! Hi, Nana!" the boys called cheerfully as they approached the two women.

"Now what have the two of you been up to?" asked Emma eyeing her sons suspiciously.

George and Will exchanged glances before Will said, "Go ahead, Georgie, tell her," magnanimously adding, "I mean, since it was all your idea in the first place."

Puffing out his chest in an exaggerated fashion, George approached the women with his hands stuffed deep into his pockets. Brute flopped on the porch floor at Mary's feet and drifted off to sleep. The little brown wren hopped agitatedly along the porch railing, loudly scolding the four humans and one dog.

"You have to guess what I have in my pocket, Ma," George said, grinning at his mother.

"What you have in your pocket...mmm," mused Emma. "Oh, that is an easy one since your grandmother and I have found them in each and every pocket of yours all this spring. I would bet that you have fishing worms in your pocket from under the rocks around the well out back."

"Nope. Guess again."

"Let me try," suggested Mary. "You have picked some dandelions for the dining room table tonight."

"Wrong again. Do you give up?" George asked, delighted to have foiled the two women.

Emma looked at Mary who nodded her head in response, "Yes, we give up. Please tell us what you have in that pocket of yours before curiosity kills us," smiled Emma.

George produced the neat stack of dollar bills, which he fanned out in front of Emma for her inspection.

Mary and Emma gasped at the sight of the money. "Where did you get this much money?" asked Emma taking the bills from her son's hand and counting them. "Thirteen dollars?"

"Yep, thirteen dollars 'zactly," Will found his voice.

"So, you know about this too?" asked Emma turning to look at Will for the first time.

"Yep. I was part of the plan," he announced proudly. "And so was old Brute boy."

At the mention of his name, the big dog thumped his tail, but moved nothing else.

"Where did you get this money?" Emma demanded harshly, looking from one boy to the other.

"Well, we got it from Lowell. Will, Brute and I decided to help you and collect the rent money that Lowell owed you from a couple of months ago and…"

"You did what?" screeched Emma, interrupting George.

"We done collected the rent money for you, Ma," answered Will calmly.

"I think I am going to faint!" and Emma looked over at her mother, who sat gazing incredulously at her grandsons.

"Do not look to me dear," warned Mary, "as I have been rendered nearly speechless."

"How…when…what…" stammered Emma before the boys climbed onto the swing, both talking at once, each vying to tell his version of their rent-collecting caper first.

"One at a time, boys," chastised Emma and then for the next half hour, both women sat listening to the escapades of Will and George, aided by Brute, as they regaled their mother and their grandmother with the details of collecting the thirteen dollars which Emma still held like a fan in her lap.

"Unbelievable!" exclaimed Mary when the boys had finally worn themselves out with telling and retelling the details of their Locust Street escapade.

Emma drained the last of the cold coffee from her glass before rising to her feet to pace the length of the porch and back again. Brute opened one eye and then went back to sleep, still at Mary's feet. Pausing in front of the swing where the twins flanked their grandmother, Emma abruptly smacked the stack of paper money against the palm of her hand, "Do you not realize how dangerous it was for you to accost Lowell in his own home? What if the man had a pistol tucked into his trousers? I mean, Lowell is a mill hand, after all, and they are a rough bunch. Your grandfather always used to say his men were like the first cut off a tree…full of splinters waiting to get under your skin," Emma lectured the boys.

"Well, first of all, Ma," began George, "21 Locust Street is not Lowell's own home. It is ours…or yours and he can only stay in that old house if he pays you his four dollars rent money every month."

"Yeah, and second of all," chimed in Will, "me and Georgie decided we was not about to be indigents," whereupon Will folded his arms across his chest and smirked at his brother.

"La, la, Emma, my dear," intervened Mary, "the boys' intentions were admirably pure and just. However, Will and George, your methodology leaves a bit to be desired and quite possibly put you in harm's way, all of which causes both your mother and me great concern," said Mary, dabbing at the tiny beads of perspiration that were forming on her forehead.

"You two are just too old to understand anything, except cooking, working at that hospital and talking. All the time cooking, working and talking blah-blah-blah and nobody is doing anything that needs to be done around here since Pa left," complained George, jumping down off the swing and pointing his finger angrily at his mother and grandmother.

Will jumped down off the swing to stand shoulder to shoulder with George, adding, "Yeah!"

"So Will and I decided it was high time the men in the family had a little talk with Lowell. We figured that with the help of Brute we could persuade him to cough up the money that he owed you, Ma."

"Yeah, Ma. We had a plan all along and it worked too!" crowed Will.

"It worked this time, but next time, Lowell just might pull a gun on the two of you," warned Emma. "Look boys," said Emma pulling her sons to her, "I am grateful for the money that you collected today, for we surely do need it, but the next time the rent money is due, how about if the three of us walk on over to Lowell's...our old house and collect the four dollars?"

"Can we still take Brute?" asked Will.

"We can as long as you keep him on a tight leash and do not allow the dog to relieve himself on my tenant," smiled Emma.

"From now on, I am going to keep track of the money that Lowell owes and what he has paid because somebody in this family needs to do their arithmetic every month," George glared accusingly at his mother.

"All right, all right, George. I quite agree. I have been far too busy with other activities and shame on me too, because I was, after all, the one who kept Papa's books at the mill. So, I guess you inherited that from me," laughed Emma.

The sound of a horse trotting along High Point Avenue in their direction brought the conversation to an abrupt end as Heath appeared with Johnny on Onion's back, clutching a box of groceries under one arm while holding on to the small boy and the horse's reins with his free hand.

"Howdy, howdy, everybody!" Heath greeted them jovially.

Eager to change the subject, Will dashed down the front steps to take Johnny off the horse and George quickly followed his brother to retrieve the groceries.

"I can put the food away for you, Nana. No need to get up," and George disappeared into the house with his brown cardboard box.

"Yeah, and I think old Johnny here needs something cold to drink," and Will too disappeared into the house with his baby brother.

"What got into those two?" asked Heath, sliding down off Onion's back and tying the horse up to the porch railing.

"Heath, dear, for heaven's sake! Do move the horse out of the way of my lovely petunias that I have worked so hard on," fretted Mary grabbing Onion's halter and jerking his head away from the profusion of pink flowers that grew on either side of the front steps.

"Whoops! Sorry, Mary!" apologized Heath. "Come on, Emma, help me take this beast to the barn. As the two of them walked around the house toward the barn, Heath again asked,

"So why were Will and George behaving so strangely?"

"What did you find so strange about their behavior?" asked Emma, pretending innocence.

"George helping with the groceries and Will helping with Johnny, without being told. That is what I find strange."

"Well, just maybe the boys are beginning to grow up and to understand that they have certain...responsibilities in life, just like the rest of us," Emma answered looking up into the beautiful blue of Heath's eyes.

As the two of them continued their leisurely walk to the barn, Heath put his arm around Emma's shoulders and then nonchalantly walked his fingers down the back of her dress, stopping beneath the waistband to her light colored skirt, where he began to feel around with the flat of his hand.

"Did you wear your undergarments like a good girl today?"

Without pausing, Emma deftly flicked Heath's hand away with a backward swipe of her arm, as if dispatching a troublesome black fly, "Not in broad daylight!" she admonished him.

"Oh, how long the list grows!" complained Heath.

"List? What list?" asked Emma, cranking her head around to look at Heath's profile.

"Let me see," began Heath leading Onion into his stall, "as I recollect, the list that starts out something like, 'Not now because I have a headache. Not now because the boys are in the house. Not now because I need a bath. Not now because the bed needs to be changed. Not now because it is daylight outside. Not now because the straw tickles my backside.' Shall I continue?" he teased Emma as he removed Onion's worn saddle and threw it onto a weathered cedar work table on the far side of the barn.

"You are incorrigible!" laughed Emma in response. "We women like to prepare for such encounters and you men are forever..."

"Striking while the iron is hot!" interrupted Heath.

"And your iron seems to be hot most of the time," she giggled, submitting to Heath's embrace.

Just then, George, Will and Johnny came racing into the barn, "As I was saying, Mr. Heath Hamilton, we have company," Emma announced turning to hug her sons. "Do you boys know what Nana has in the oven for our supper this evening?"

"Turkey and stuffing?" guessed George.

"Are you nuts, Georgie? It ain't Thanksgivin' time," and Will scratched his head before shouting, "I know! Liver and onions with mashed 'tatoes and gravy," announced Will, hungrily licking his lips at the thought of his favorite meal.

"How about chicken pie with peas and carrots?" asked Emma.

"Speaking of food, I am reminded, Emma, that my mother has asked you to join her for lunch tomorrow at the ranch over in Clarksburg around twelve-thirty in the afternoon," Heath said nonchalantly as he hung up the rest of Onion's tack.

"Oh, goody! Can we go too, Ma?" asked George.

Ignoring her son, Emma stood stock still looking at Heath, "I have been invited to what?"

"You heard me. My mother has invited you to join her for lunch tomorrow," repeated Heath.

Turning to the boys who were climbing up onto the hay bales and then jumping off into the dust of the barn floor, Emma said, "Run along now, boys, and wash up for supper. Tell Nana that Heath and I are on our way. Shoo!"

As the boys disappeared through the wide expanse of the open barn doors, Emma remarked, "Heath, how long have you and I been keeping company?"

"Forever," joked Heath as he and Emma strolled after the retreating children.

"Never once during that time have either of your parents wanted to meet me. In fact, just the opposite has occurred, for they have gone out of their way to ignore me. Your father, in particular, has been exceedingly scornful of me. So what has suddenly changed your mother's mind?" Emma asked suspiciously.

"I have been asking myself the same question," answered Heath. "My father has gone down south for a few days to look at some new breeding stock and

Mother is alone so maybe she thinks this might be a good time for the two of you to try to get to know one another. I mean, I talk to her about you all the time."

"You do?"

"Sure. How could I refrain from talking about you? You are the most important person in the world to me. It is apparent to everyone in my family how much I love you and the kids. Those are some strong feelings to try to hide from your mother. She sees right through me. I swear the woman, just like you, can read my mind and she always knows when I am pondering about you."

"And what do you tell her about me?" asked Emma.

"Everything that is on my mind and in my heart about you."

"Oh, please tell me that you do not!"

"Emma," Heath paused to take her by the shoulders, "this arrangement is driving me crazy. I have to be able to talk about it to someone. The frustration that I feel, the anger, the sorrow, the…the…it nearly consumes me at times."

"And your mother is sympathetic to our union?" Emma asked cautiously.

Heath let go of Emma's shoulders and looking over the auburn braids coiled about her head, responded, "Mother is certainly sympathetic to how miserable I am rendered by not being able to make our union permanent in the eyes of God, the church, my family and the law."

"I see," responded Emma softly.

Lost in thought and conversation, the two of them strolled past the house and on down the expanse of lawn, crossing High Point Avenue, underneath a canopy of stately maples, oaks and tulip poplars.

"Perhaps, then, it would be best for the two of us to sever this relationship so that you might be free to marry a woman who is likewise free to marry you and bear your children…and…and," Emma began to cry.

Heath took Emma in his arms and kissed the tears upon her cheeks, "What utter nonsense is this you are speaking?" he asked tilting her face up to his. "There can be no one else for me. I cannot even contemplate such foolishness. To leave you would be like cutting off my arm and leaving it behind. Nay, leaving you and the boys behind would be more like cutting off both my arms. I quite simply could not survive without the four of you!"

"Oh, this conversation makes my head and my heart ache because there is never any resolution to the issues of which we speak," Emma complained rubbing her forehead with one hand and touching her chest with the other.

"Which is exactly how I feel," said Heath, "and I believe that my mother finally understands the torment of our dilemma and because she does, Mother is trying to reach out to you in her own fashion and offer you a measure of comfort even as she attempts to offer me a measure of comfort by allowing me to talk to her about you."

"Does your father ever allow you to speak of me?" asked Emma, eyes still shining with tears.

"No," admitted Heath. "I tried once and my father told me I was never to speak of you again in his presence."

"How can that be Heath?" asked Emma, the tears coursing down her cheeks. "What have I ever done to incur the man's wrath? After all, it was I who saved his horses from being stolen by that lout, Cletus. What have I ever done to your father to make him loathe me so?"

"I honestly do not know, my sweet, and I am intensely ashamed of my father's discourteous treatment of you but perhaps, if you visit with my mother she might be able to shed some light on the harsh feelings that my father harbors toward you," Heath offered apologetically.

"I dislike the notion that I must sneak into your parents' home while your father is away on business in order to have a clandestine lunch with your mother," sniffed Emma, blowing her nose on a monogrammed handkerchief.

"But, it is a beginning," offered Heath. "Up until now, we have been met with silence. At least now, Mother is offering you her recognition and breaking her silence. That has to be a good sign, would you not agree?" Heath asked, smiling gamely at Emma.

"I really do not know quite how to interpret her sudden change of heart," murmured Emma.

"And is that not just like a woman? And is it not you who remind me constantly that women have the right to change their minds whenever they choose? So too, my mother, apparently, has changed her mind. Please, Emma, promise me that you will give my mother a chance. She is, after all, reaching out to you. Will you accept the hand that she has offered to you?" asked Heath.

"Frankly, I do not know whether to accept her hand or to bite it!" and Emma smiled.

"Try?" persisted Heath.

"I shall try," responded Emma unconvincingly.

"Thank you," answered Heath, hugging her to him. "But," he added, "I do have one request."

"Oh? And just what might that be?" Emma looked surprised.

"That you remember to wear your undergarments," and Heath slid his hands down her buttocks, cupping her small body to him.

The following morning, Emma rose earlier than usual and took a long, hot bath, carefully washing her hair and her body with the lavender scented soap that her sons so coveted for their own bath. Climbing from the tub, she wrapped one towel around her hair and a second one around her body before spreading a third towel on the floor where she sat to file her toenails.

"It is so ridiculous for me to waste so much time and energy preparing to meet a woman who hates me, sight unseen!" Emma fumed to herself, while sawing back and forth with the metal file on each of her small toenails. "How utterly silly to file my toenails when that woman will not garner a peek at them encased in shoes!" she continued scolding her vanity.

Rising from the bathroom floor, Emma unwound the towel from her hair, rubbing the soggy mass of auburn curls until they glistened. She hung one towel neatly over the edge of her father's copper tub to dry and then tiptoed to her bedroom. At her insistence, Heath now shared a room with Johnny at night for the sake of appearances.

Standing before the oval mirror in a corner of her pink bedroom, Emma let the second towel fall from under her arms and stood surveying herself. Pinching the flesh of her abdomen between a thumb and forefinger, Emma chided the reflection, "Too fat!" And then, "So what! The old crone is not going to view me without my clothing anyhow."

Emma moved to the cherry wardrobe that had been her grandmother's, pulled on fresh step-ins and took out her best navy blue skirt and white blouse which she draped across herself for surveillance in front of the mirror. "Too dark. Too hot," she thought, casting the outfit onto the unmade bed with its jumble of covers.

Next, she selected a white skirt and a second white blouse, just a bit thinner than the first. Swirling around in front of the mirror, Emma again looked critically at the new ensemble. "Too thin. Too revealing," she sighed to herself, tossing the clothing onto the growing heap in the middle of her bed.

Then, out came her best sage green taffeta dress with the puffy sleeves that she loved to wear so much during the Christmas season. "Too fancy. Too swishy," and the dress joined the other discarded garments that lay forlornly atop one another. Similarly, a muslin skirt and blouse all smartly edged in navy blue trim joined the other castoff ensembles because they were, "Too youthful."

Emma's hair was nearly dry and hung irritatingly in her face. Pulling a satin ribbon from the cherry dresser, Emma tied the unruly curls behind her neck, climbed onto the bed and sat amid the discarded jumble of clothing. Then she collapsed back on top of the disarray she had created, completely frustrated by her inability to find an appropriate outfit to wear to lunch with Heath's mother.

"Absolutely nothing to wear!" she huffed, kicking her heels like one of the children in the midst of a tantrum.

"Such a lot of bother," Emma thought to herself as she lay upon her bed gazing out the window toward the river that would soon carry her to meet the woman she feared most. Sitting upright again, Emma pressed the flat of her hand against her forehead, "Yes! I feel it now! I am quite ill with a fever!" she feigned silently. "I am far too ill to go out for lunch today," and she stole over to gaze at herself again in the mirror. Moving close to the glass, she scrutinized her face. "Too rosy to be sick. Maybe a dusting of flour to achieve the right pallor," she thought. "No, Mama would detect the flour in a second," she reminded herself.

"Oh, Emma!" she scolded herself softly. "You are acting like such a ninny...the very quality that you detest in other women!" Emma began to pace around the pink room. "Mrs. Hamilton is just an ordinary woman...no different from Mama. What would Mama like to see me wear? Yes, that is the solution! Ask Mama!"

Quietly opening the door to her bedroom, Emma tiptoed past Johnny's bedroom and then the boys' bedroom until she stood before Mary's door. Rapping lightly with her knuckles but not waiting for a response, Emma entered her mother's bedroom.

"Mama," whispered Emma in her mother's ear.

"What is it dear?" asked Mary, turning to find Emma standing beside the bed just inches from her face.

"I have nothing to wear," Emma whispered to her mother.

"It would appear to me that you are wearing your step-ins," muttered Mary still half asleep as she rolled over to face the wall.

Undeterred, Emma moved around the foot of the bed to the other side where she could once again address her sleeping mother. "You do not understand me, Mama. I have nothing appropriate to wear today."

"I agree. Your step-ins are not appropriate," and Mary began to snore lightly.

Exasperated, Emma climbed onto the bed with her mother and continued, "Please, Mama, do wake up as I must have your advice on an outfit for today. I find that I am quite incapable of making a choice and I must make a good first impression, or rather undo the wrong impression, that Mrs. Hamilton has of me," Emma rattled on to Mary who responded by pulling the covers up over her face.

"Mama! You are hiding from me!" Emma scolded her mother, tugging at the covers.

"Yes I am!" responded Mary, throwing back the covers from her face. "Do you have any idea of the time, my girl?"

"It is about six o'clock," responded Emma sheepishly.

"And do you know what day of the week it is?"

"Sunday."

"You are forever professing to be so worried about my health and my rest and so forth and so on but the one day that I am able to rest an extra hour in the morning, you come rudely into my room and insist that I give you advice on your clothing for the day. What rubbish is this, Emma?" scolded Mary.

"I am just at the end of my wits trying to select an outfit that will create a favorable impression upon Heath's mother and I need your help," repeated Emma.

"Well, the solution is clear," yawned Mary rolling back over and pushing herself up to a sitting position.

"Really, Mama? What is it?" asked Emma scrambling across the bed to sit next to Mary.

"Go jump on Mrs. Hamilton's bed and ask her which outfit she would like to see you in today. I personally would prefer the step-ins with the satin ribbon but who knows what she…"

"Mama! This is serious!"

"And what about my rest on Sunday morning? That is very serious too!" whereupon Mary rose from her bed, took a pillow and buffeted Emma with it. Emma took the other pillow and hurled it at Mary. The two women began to giggle. As the pillow tossing escalated, so did their laughter. Soon, the three boys were standing wide-eyed with disbelief in Mary's room watching their mother and their grandmother have a pillow fight.

Heath arrived bearing additional pillows and soon three adults and three children were embroiled in a raucous pillow fight. The boys climbed onto Mary's bed in order to gain better leverage with their pillows, when suddenly Will's pillow split at the seam, sending a storm of white goose feathers floating down upon the combatants.

"Snow, snow, snow!" sang Will raising his arms to catch the feathers drifting overhead.

"Now see what you have done!" scolded Mary.

"It appeared to me that you were enjoying yourself more than all the rest of us combined," countered Emma, swatting George one more time.

"Watch now, or you will break open another of my pillows!" Mary fussed. "Heath, you and the boys get busy and clean up this mess. Emma and I must retire to her bedroom to pick a suitable outfit for her luncheon today. Then we need to eat and go to church," and Mary clapped her hands.

When Emma came downstairs for breakfast an hour later, Heath whistled his approval. Emma flushed pink and both boys looked up from their pancakes smeared with butter and sorghum to stare at their mother in disbelief.

"Lads, please rise and escort the lovely lady to her seat at the table," instructed Heath as he wiped his hands clean on Mary's apron stretched around his middle. Pulling Emma's chair out for her, Heath flicked off imaginary dust with the kitchen towel before George and Will led their mother to the table.

Folding the kitchen towel neatly across his arm, Heath asked her in French, "Eh bien, Madame, qu'est ce-que vous désirez manger pour votre petit déjèuner ce matin?"

"What's that you're talkin' like?" asked Will looking puzzled at Heath.

"Heath is speaking Greek," announced George importantly.

"Yeah and Ma, you look like one of them Greek goddesses that Miss Rita is always readin' to the class about," Will complimented his mother, looking her over from head to toe.

Emma's hair, now combed clean of goose down feathers, was coiled around her head and held in place with two mother of pearl combs. She wore a muslin blouse of Mary's tied at the neck with a mauve satin ribbon to match her gabardine skirt. Her high button shoes shone with a fresh application of shoe blacking and her stockings were held snugly in place with garters just above each knee but invisible beneath the long, flowing skirt. Emma swished when she walked, causing Heath to wink acknowledgement of the detested undergarments which she wore. Pearl earrings and a pearl necklace completed Emma's ensemble.

A light scent of perfume emanated from Emma as she sat at the dining room table prompting Will to comment, "Ma, what's that you stink like?"

"Ma does not stink, Willy. Stink is when you poop in your drawers, like Johnny. Ma, on the other hand smells like rose perfume," explained George sticking his food-covered tongue out at his brother who obliged George by imitating the gesture.

Emma begged off going to church that morning in order to catch the ferry that would take her across the Southport River to Clarksburg. Heath insisted upon hitching Onion to the carriage so that he could escort Emma through Clarksburg and on out to his mother's house. "I cannot have my fine lady arriving for her lunch in disarray from riding upon the back of a lathered horse!" exclaimed Heath.

Welcoming the company, Emma confided her nervousness to Heath on the journey across the river.

"No need to fret, Emma," soothed Heath, "Mother is just a woman, like yourself. Treat her like you would your own mother and your visit will go well."

"Oh, Heath, you are so impossibly naive when it comes to such matters!" she chided him. "Your mother is not just a woman, she is your father's wife! I must make a good impression upon her so that hopefully she will see fit to condone our relationship and soften up your father a bit. Then, just maybe they can both come to accept us and lessen the strain of censorship upon you and upon me. Censorship by your parents is breaking your heart. Mine is being broken because you are so affected by their scorn," and she reached up to stroke his clean-shaven cheek.

The rest of the trip was made in silence, save for Onion's occasional flatulence. To bolster Emma's resolve, Heath held fast to Emma's hand, while she distracted herself mentally by nervously counting pigs, cows, chickens, horses and the like until the Hamiltons' home loomed into view, large and imposing in the daylight.

Surrounded by whitewashed fences that delineated grazing pastures for the mares and their colts, the white, two-story frame house was wrapped on all sides by a covered porch supported by simple columns. Its cedar shake roof was host to a colony of moss that shimmered green in the summer heat. Two field stone chimneys anchored each end of the residence and dark green shutters at each window were thrown wide open to admit the slightest breeze. A trio of oak rocking chairs close to the front door continued to saw back and forth long after the napping house cats hastily abandoned their favorite perches. Nearby the main house, the distinct baying of coon hounds drifted up from an old abandoned corncrib where the dogs were penned to serve as sentinels for approaching visitors.

Before disappearing into the house to retrieve his mother, Heath suggested to Emma that she remain on the porch until their return. Pausing by one of the rockers, Emma instinctively reached out to touch the worn wood of its ladder back. "How pleasant it would be to rest a bit in such lovely surroundings under different circumstances," Emma mused to herself as she settled onto one of the rocker's cushions, gazing out at the horses, until the creaking of a screen door brought her back to the purpose of the visit.

"I see that you have discovered my favorite perch which I share with Milly, Tilly and Lilly," laughed a woman's voice behind her. "I gather that you have met the Silly Cat Sisters?"

Emma rose so abruptly from the rocking chair that it nearly overturned. "I am quite afraid the cats took one look at me and fled," Emma smiled at the beautiful blond woman who stood before her.

"Mother," began Heath, "I would like you to meet Emma Richardson. Emma, this is my mother, Roselle Hamilton."

"Please call me 'Rose', dear, everyone does," replied Heath's mother, offering Emma her hand.

As Emma took the hand that Rose offered to her, she fought the urge to take a bite of it as she had joked earlier with Heath. Deftly, Rose pulled Emma close and gave her a peck on each cheek before releasing Emma's sweaty grip.

"I am so pleased to meet you after all this time, Emma, and truly delighted that you would journey across the river to join me for lunch on this glorious Sunday afternoon, when I am quite sure you have so many other responsibilities that might justifiably keep you at home," she smiled. "Heath darling, I thank you for assisting Emma on the journey over here. Perhaps it would be wise to take her horse to the trough for a drink. Oh, and dear...the cook has lunch prepared for you in the kitchen," and Rose dismissed her son.

The dreaded moment had finally arrived. Emma and Rose were alone. Both women spent several awkward minutes silently appraising each other. Emma noticed at once that Heath favored his mother. Roselle was tall, slender and blonde with the same azure-colored eyes. Her long hair showed no trace of gray and was fashionably swept back on each side with large tortoise shell combs, adding to her youthful appearance. The skin of her face was pale and unlined and her hands unspotted, indicating a woman who spent little time out of doors. Roselle appeared to wear a hint of powder, further complimenting her natural complexion.

Her dress was of a simple light muslin but edged at the neck, wrists and hem with exquisite lace. In each ear lobe, Roselle wore gold stud earrings circled with the tiniest of diamonds and a magnificent diamond hung from a gold chain around her neck. On her left hand, she wore a plain gold band.

"Do let us sit here in the rockers for just a bit as Cook is putting the finishing touches to our luncheon," Roselle was saying, gesturing to Emma that she should take a seat in one of the rocking chairs. The cats eyed Emma suspiciously from under a large, white wicker table set with fine linens, china and silver at the far end of the porch.

"Meow," fussed a cat as Emma took a seat.

"Just ignore Milly," advised Roselle. "Miss Milly tends to be a bit on the bossy side. She is Mr. Hamilton's favorite and the cat knows it. My husband, over my objections, spoils Miss Milly absolutely rotten, feeding her salted fish from the breakfast table on a silver fork and offering her a splash of cream on the Limoges. Men can be so unreasonable when it comes to their pets," tittered Roselle. "Would you not agree?" she asked Emma amicably, reaching down to stroke the cat who was busily rubbing itself against the lace of her skirt.

"My father simply had no use for household pets and I never had any as a child. Papa simply felt that animals were meant to be beasts of burden, like our horse at home or those at the mill, and cats were meant to catch mice in the barn," Emma replied forcing her facial muscles to relax.

"And what of your husband, dear, was he of like mind? Did he forbid you and his sons to have pets? That is, when he lived with you?" and Roselle's eyes suddenly turned the color of slate.

"Ah," thought Emma to herself as she faced Roselle while managing a smile, "she has cut right to the crux of the matter."

"Actually, Edward would have made every stray in town welcome in our home, but it was I who objected," responded Emma, never taking her eyes off Roselle's face, "much the same way I can detect that you object to Mr. Hamilton's decision to feed the precious kitties at the table." The corners of Emma's mouth remained curled upward.

"Yes, well, we can certainly agree on that then," responded Roselle rising from the rocking chair and bushing off the front of her skirt as if to deflect Emma's remark. "I will just check with the kitchen now and see how much longer until luncheon is served. Excuse me a moment, dear," and with a flurry of lace and muslin, Roselle was gone.

Emma jumped up from the rocking chair as if she had been stung by a bee and stormed over to the railing, digging her nails into the white paint as she pretended interest in the pastoral scene before her. "How stupid I was to agree to have lunch with this woman!" Emma chided herself. "I knew it would turn out this way but I did not realize how quickly she would slash at my jugular. The woman wastes no time," Emma was thinking to herself as she leaned out from the railing, forcing herself to breathe deeply of the freshly cut alfalfa and clover.

Above the squeaking door, she heard the lilting voice of Roselle say, "Cook will be serving our luncheon directly. Do let us take our seats," and Emma turned to follow Heath's mother down the great expanse of porch to the exquisitely prepared table at the far end.

"What gorgeous roses!" exclaimed Emma as she took her seat. "Do you raise them?"

"Yes, I personally instruct the gardener each and every day of the growing season as to the maintenance and care of my rose beds. It is quite a task too, I shall tell you, as this summer we have had an absolute plague of beetles," Roselle announced as she spread the neatly pressed linen napkin upon her lap.

Observing Roselle, Emma had to control a sudden impulse to tuck her napkin in at the chin. Instead, she fanned the generous square of linen and lace across her skirts in perfect imitation of her hostess. "To what do you attribute such an influx of beetles?" asked Emma feigning interest.

"Well, I personally believe that the unusually wet spring combined with too much fertilizer, due to an error on the part of the gardener, has led to the infestation," Roselle declared decisively. "The plants are quite simply too rich, too succulent this season, thus attracting huge numbers of the loathsome pests."

"Undoubtedly true," Emma responded benignly.

"So, you are a gardener too?" asked Roselle, brightening.

"Ah, no, but my mother is possessed of an extraordinarily green thumb. Why her petunias this year have…"

"Yes, yes, to be sure. And now cast your eyes upon the splendid luncheon that Celeste is bringing to the table!" exclaimed Roselle, rudely interrupting Emma.

Just then, the Hamiltons' maid arrived at Roselle's left elbow with a Limoges platter that contained buttermilk biscuits that had been split in two and filled with butter, cucumber, country ham and watercress. The platter of dainty sandwiches was punctuated by the bright pinks, yellows and lavenders of small flowers grown around the ranch. "C'est très bien fait, Celeste. J'aurais deux, merci," whereupon the maid placed two biscuit sandwiches on the porcelain plate in front of Roselle.

Celeste then moved to Emma's left elbow. "J'aurais deux aussi. Merci, Celeste," Emma said in perfect French.

"Why Emma, Heath failed to mention to me that you can speak French," marveled Roselle.

"Shame on that man for forgetting to tell you that my grandmother was French!" exclaimed Emma with more than a hint of sarcasm. "As a child, it was my mother's mother who taught me to speak her native French," Emma smirked to her hostess.

"You are indeed a woman of many talents!" exclaimed Roselle in return, lifting her glass of cold tea and offering a toast. "Here is to the abundance of your talents!"

"And your kind recognition of them!" added Emma, as she lifted her glass, refusing to be outdone.

The two women nibbled politely at their sandwiches in silence for a few moments before Roselle once again addressed Emma. "You may not realize this but my husband, Adam, knew your father back in the days when he owned and operated the lumber mill there in Grandview."

"Yes," responded Emma dabbing at the corners of her mouth with a flurry of lace, "Mayor Hamilton told me that he had known my father the night I was accosted by a horse thief on the road in front of your ranch."

"Oh, me, and what an horrendous experience that was for you, dear!" exclaimed Roselle in reply. "Remind me again how you came to be out on the road by yourself after dark dressed in…in trousers?"

"Here it comes," thought Emma, still smiling serenely. "Yes that was an ordeal," agreed Emma never taking her eyes from Roselle's face. "You see, I had learned that an infant by the name of Daniel Johnson, who lives with his mother and grandmother just down the road a piece from you, was in dire straits and appeared to be suffering from some sort of wasting disease as reported to me by his mother, Rachel."

"Really? Do go on," instructed Roselle stirring sugar into her tea.

"The mother of the child was without sufficient funds to pay a doctor to examine her son so…"

"So you agreed to examine the child free of charge, as I have heard the story," interrupted Roselle. "Which was certainly most noble of you if not a bit fool-hardy and presumptuous. I mean a nurse does not exactly qualify to make a medical diagnosis, does she dear? And then to travel across the river after dark to make the diagnosis? Tisk, tisk!" scolded Roselle.

Emma felt her cheeks flush. "Let me respond to your charges by asking you a question, Mrs. Hamilton. Let us suppose, for the sake of argument, that you are riding down the road and you happen upon a child who is badly injured and bleeding profusely from a leg wound. You have no medical training, either as a doctor or as a nurse. Would you ride on by the child and ignore his suffering? Or, would you stop, dismount, rip a suitable bandage from your petticoat, wrap it tightly about the child's leg and stop the bleeding?" Emma paused to gauge the effect of her words upon Roselle.

Heath's mother averted her head, gazing out at the colts that frolicked about her front lawn. Then turning back to Emma she replied, "Well, since you put it that way, of course, I would stop and assist the child."

"Then why do you find fault with me for doing that very thing?" jabbed Emma.

"Why dear, I was not finding fault. No, no, no. You have totally misunderstood my intentions," Roselle tried to assuage Emma's rising ire. "But why after dark and dressed as a boy?"

"The poor mother of the child works until seven o'clock each evening in town, after which she must walk some two miles before reaching her home. I dressed in my sons' clothing to afford myself a measure of security by successfully passing as a boy until I came upon the detestable Cletus Donohue who was busy stealing your fine horses. Thanks to me, Mayor Hamilton did not suffer the loss of any of his animals that night," Emma reminded Roselle harshly.

"Ah, Emma, my dear, you are a rare bird indeed! I like you!" laughed Roselle.

"Well, I cannot tell you what a relief that is," Emma responded, returning the laughter.

"You see, my dear Emma," continued Roselle, pushing her plate aside, "I am married to a man who reports events to me as he wants me to hear them and not necessarily in the same context or in the same fashion that he heard or saw them himself."

"Yes, I understand, Mrs. Hamilton," sympathized Emma. "In other words, your husband edits heavily his words to you."

"That would be an understatement. Every scrap of news that I get from that man has first been carefully wrung through cheesecloth. I simply had to verify for myself what really occurred the night that you met my husband and my son. I have Heath telling me one thing in this ear," Roselle tugged at a gold and diamond earring, "and Adam telling me something altogether different in this ear," while tugging at the other earring.

Changing the subject for the moment, Roselle lifted a crystal bell which she jangled until Celeste appeared. "Please tell the cook that Miss Emma and I should like to have our fresh strawberries, whipped cream and shortbread cookies now. Oh, and Celeste, we should each like a fresh glass of tea. Thank you."

"Now, where was I, Emma?" Roselle addressed the baffled-looking woman who sat opposite her.

"You were telling me, ma'am, if I have interpreted your words correctly, that you had determined to come right to the source for information about me. Right to the horse's mouth, as my father used to say."

"Quite so, Emma. You see, I have this wonderful, thoughtful, truthful, insightful son by the name of Heath on one side of me. And on the other side of me, I have this impossibly controlling, protective, arrogant and demanding husband. Heath will tell me one thing and Adam will tell a totally different version of the same event. So, I simply had to get at the truth for myself, without either Adam or Heath present. Can you understand that, my dear?"

"I can but what I do not understand, Mrs. Hamilton, is why you have remained with your husband all these years if he exhibits so many characteristics that you find loathsome," Emma commented cheekily.

"Now that is truly the subject for a whole afternoon of conversation!" smiled Roselle.

"Had you not intended for me to spend the whole afternoon with you?" countered Emma.

"Why, of course I had," but just then Celeste entered with a silver tray bearing crystal bowels of bright red berries, a third bowl of whipped cream, a silver sugar shaker, a Limoges plate of shortbread cookies and two glasses of iced tea, which she deftly served to the two women. "I like a generous shaking of sugar on my cream and berries. How about you dear?" asked Roselle.

"Yes, ma'am, I too like sugar on my cream and berries," Emma responded, suddenly feeling quite relieved and very agreeable toward the woman at the other end of the table.

"That will be all, Celeste, and please see to it that Miss Emma and I are not disturbed as we are going to enjoy a delicious visit this afternoon," whereupon Roselle waved off the young woman who made a brief curtsey toward her mistress.

"You know, Emma, I sometimes think that Adam has all these servants and handymen about the premises to report to him about my activities during his absences. I cannot even take control of the carriage by myself to go into town without someone grabbing the reins from me. It is so tiresome!" complained Roselle.

"What exactly is it that the mayor fears you might do?" asked Emma picking up a large red strawberry on her silver spoon, dripping with cream.

"I think he fears that, like a bird, once the door to my gilded cage is thrown open, I should fly away," responded Roselle wistfully looking out over the pastures.

"And would you? Fly away, that is?" asked Emma, reaching for a cookie.

Roselle had not touched her dessert and the cream was beginning to slide off the edges of the crystal bowl. "I would," she said without hesitation, looking directly down the table at Emma.

Startled by the response, Emma asked, "Where would this flight take you?"

"That is a question that I have asked myself a thousand times," said Roselle, shaking her head sadly. "And I do not know the answer, for you see, I am so unqualified to do anything but remain here," and she gestured about at her expansive surroundings. "To plan menus, keep the servants in line and well directed in their tasks about the house, to fix my hair, my nails, to select my garments, to serve my husband and my sons...to, in short, do nothing of any substance."

For a moment, Emma had the distinct impression that Roselle was on the verge of weeping. Emma's first impulse was to rush to the opposite end of the table and embrace the sad, elegant woman who sat before her, but she paused and Roselle continued.

"I so admire you younger women who are, either out of necessity or out of determination, taking control of your lives to seek fulfilling work outside the home. I do so love working with plants but if one freckle dares to appear on my skin, Adam deduces immediately that I have been out in the sun getting dirty and heaven forbid, sweaty!" she laughed out loud causing Emma to join in the laughter.

Pushing the untouched dessert away, Roselle continued in her reflections. "I remember one day I had been enjoying a glorious afternoon working in the rose beds but I had been careless, having forgotten to wear my long leather gloves, so I was badly scratched from the thorns. Adam flew into a rage to see all the scratch marks upon my arms that evening. He actually forbade me to go out in public until the scratches had healed. Each night, he would rub ointment on my arms and wrap bandages about them, nearly cutting off my circulation. In the middle of the night, I would have to rise from my bed and remove the bandages because they were so tight," Roselle related mournfully as she rubbed her arms at the painful memory.

"Why do you think he is so possessive...so controlling?" asked Emma folding her napkin neatly before placing it beside the empty berry bowl.

"I know this may be difficult for you to understand, dear, but it is not so much that Adam seeks to control me as it is that he seeks to preserve his reputation in the community. Does that make sense?" Roselle asked pushing back her chair.

"No. Quite frankly it makes absolutely no sense whatsoever," responded Emma bluntly.

Rising to her feet, Roselle suggested, "Come dear, let us walk around the grounds a bit and I shall try to explain...out of earshot of the servants, lest they report on our conversation to Adam."

The two women linked arms and began a leisurely stroll down the front walk. "My husband," began Rose, "was the son of poor, immigrant parents. His father was a blacksmith and his mother cleaned homes for the wealthy. Adam has recounted to me how his mother used to take him with her when she cleaned. He has so many painful memories of her on her hands and knees scrubbing floors for hours and rubbing the soiled undergarments of the wealthy across a wash board with harsh lye soap, causing her knuckles to bleed and crack."

"Are you sure you want to hear this sordid little tale?" asked Rose suddenly, pausing in the shade of a willow tree, whose long, pliable branches swayed with the breeze.

"I am vitally interested in anything that concerns Heath or that will assist me in understanding him. Please do go on with your story," responded Emma, taking a seat on a white wrought iron bench under the shade of the willow tree.

Roselle sat next to Emma, idly twirling the stem of a four leafed clover between her fingers. "As a result of his impressionable upbringing at the side of his mother, Adam determined that through hard work, determination and the assiduous cultivation of a genteel exterior, he could rise above the poverty and menial tasks that he had watched his parents so routinely performing. Further, Adam decided that the woman he married would never have to sully herself with the chores that he had witnessed his mother laboring to complete."

Heath suddenly appeared on the front steps and called to the two women, "Hello down there! Are the two of you getting along or must I come rescue one or both of you?" he teased.

"We are getting along famously," called his mother back, waving her handkerchief at him.

"Well, you know what they say," Heath persisted, "a white flag is a sign that someone is in need of relief."

"Go away, Heath Hamilton!" Emma called cheerfully. "We are getting along well enough that we do not require your services."

Roselle dismissed her son with a flutter of lace handkerchief.

"Suit yourselves," laughed Heath before striding toward the main barn.

"And as you were saying about the mayor," continued Emma, picking up the thread of their conversation.

"Yes, Adam. Dear, sweet, handsome Adam put me in a gilded cage the day I married him. He had already achieved his fortune when I met him and he could afford to buy this home and staff it with all manner of help so that I did not have to lift a finger, save to wipe my own posterior," and both women laughed out loud.

"Yes, but if you tell him that you are bored and in need of a diversion, surely Adam would understand and concur," offered Emma.

"I have tried on countless occasions," sighed Roselle, "but his response is always the same."

"What exactly is his response?"

"That if I were to weed my own flower beds, scrub the front steps, bake a pie for dinner or take the carriage into town by myself, it would reflect adversely upon him. Adam imagines that people would accuse him of being a sorry provider. He actually believes that if I lift a finger at anything, others will call into question his capabilities as the head of the household and that will have a deleterious effect on all aspects of his business life, from his job as Mayor of Clarksburg to the breeding, raising and selling of fine quarter horses," concluded Roselle.

"How absurd!" exclaimed Emma.

"I quite agree," said Roselle. "But, my husband is not a modern man and no degree of reasoning can change him. Lord knows that I have tried!"

"Why not leave Adam, then?" asked Emma.

"Leave him?" asked a startled Roselle. "And go where? To do what?"

"Go anywhere and do anything of your own choosing," replied Emma.

Roselle reached out to take Emma's hand, which she patted solicitously. "You do not understand, Emma. I love Adam. He treats me very well. He does not abuse me the way Heath tells me that Edward abused you. I cannot...would not leave Adam...ever. Since the age of sixteen this has been my entire existence. It is much too late for me to change," mourned Roselle.

"I see," responded Emma, nodding her head. "What you are saying reminds me very much of a similar conversation I had with another woman about your same age who is married to a doctor here in Clarksburg," and Emma paused to reflect briefly upon her conversation with Cordelia McKendrick.

Gathering her thoughts, Emma continued again, "You have likened your marriage to Adam to the life of a bird in a gilded cage and I would similarly liken my marriage to Edward to that of a bird, but one whose wings were broken. The result for each of us was the loss of independent flight.

Perhaps it was the moment of Edward's departure that sent me soaring again or perhaps it was the moment that I enrolled at the hospital to become a nurse. Having regained my ability to fly, I have resolved never again to relinquish my freedom to any man. I can never go back to being under the thumb of a man again. And forgive me, Mrs. Hamilton, that includes your son."

"So, you mean that even if you could prove, say for example, Edward's demise, you would not choose to marry my Heath?"

"I have asked myself that question repeatedly, Mrs. Hamilton, and I honestly do not feel that marriage suits me," Emma responded firmly.

"But why not?" asked Roselle incredulously.

"Because I refuse to have my wings broken again," Emma answered quietly.

"Heath is definitely not cut of the same cloth as that scoundrel, Edward, I can assure you, Emma," Roselle stated adamantly.

"Probably not, but I cannot risk my freedom again. I have suffered horribly to achieve my independence and I cannot just turn off all the pain and suffering and hard work which I have endured in order to become a nurse," concluded Emma.

"Yes, dear, Heath has explained all of that in the most excruciating detail to me," answered Roselle.

"Why are the details so excruciating?" asked Emma.

"Because Heath is so in love with you and wishes to marry you and serve as a father to your three sons," Roselle replied honestly.

"I am privileged to have the benefit of Heath's companionship...along with his love and support for all those in my family, without marriage. Why should I seek to change the status of our union now?"

"Because your union has not been...is not...sanctified," replied Roselle, a touch of scorn creeping into her voice.

"Ah, there it is...at last out in the open. You are worried about what others think and say," deduced Emma correctly.

"Actually, the person who worries the most is Adam with his constant ranting and raving to me about you and Heath living together in your mother's house. Most people outside our immediate family are too polite to assail me with criticism of my son's illicit...no, that is too harsh. Let us just say 'unconventional' life with you and the children. Adam is just such a bear concerning this subject," Roselle sighed.

"Then tell Mr. Hamilton to speak to me. I would welcome a discourse on the subject. The man keeps me at arm's length, ignores me completely, never makes an effort to get to know me as a person...as a woman. And while I am on that subject, just let me say, Mrs. Hamilton, how truly grateful I am that you would...dare, I think is the appropriate word, to invite me into your home this afternoon, especially in light of Mr. Hamilton's abject rejection of me."

"It has been my very great pleasure to spend this afternoon with you. I feel that you and I together have begun the process of building a bridge over the enormous gap that exists between your household and ours. Whereas Adam is venomous about the arrangement that you and Heath have devised for yourselves across the river in Grandview, I totally condone your liaison."

"Really?" Emma looked surprised.

"Yes."

"Then what remains to be resolved?" asked Emma.

"The issue of whether your...the reprehensible Edward is alive or dead," responded Roselle, narrowing her eyes, "and Heath has measures underway which may shed some light on that issue."

"Oh, he does, does he? And just what measures are we discussing here?" Emma asked, suddenly suspicious.

"I am not at liberty to discuss that with you, dear. You shall just have to pry that information out of Heath," and Roselle stood up from the bench, straightening her skirts.

"Well, how mysterious!" declared Emma, rising also.

"And now, my dear, I think we had best conclude our afternoon and send you home once again to your adorable children. Did you know that since Heath has been bringing Will and George with him to the farm this summer, I have been afforded the rare opportunity of spending a bit of time with your sons? For me, having two small boys here again seems like old times."

"How strange it is to realize that my children have been made welcome here but I have not," commented Emma. "And does Mr. Hamilton share your appreciation of my twins?"

"Adam, I regret to say, largely ignores the boys when they are here, busying himself elsewhere on the property. Then too, Heath seeks to keep them from under his father's feet. My son, however, knows that I have a soft spot in my heart for small boys and he always brings them into the house for cookies and milk or a bite of lunch so that I can talk with George and Will."

"My dear," continued Roselle taking Emma by the shoulders and giving her a peck on each cheek, "you and I shall talk again but I must end our visit now as I am expecting Adam to return soon. Cook is preparing his favorite meal of beef stew baked between layers of her succulent lard crust and Adam, as he is fond of saying, can 'smell the aroma of Cook's meat pie all the way to Tennessee.'" Whereupon, Roselle was gone in a flurry of muslin, lace and laughter.

Emma remained standing under the thin, drooping branches of the willow tree watching Roselle retreat up the cobblestone walk to the porch of her magnificent gilded cage. "Poor woman!" Emma thought to herself. "She is worse off with a husband than I am without one," and she followed the whitewashed perimeter of the pasture fences to the main barn where Heath was still busy assisting the blacksmith.

Worn and discarded horseshoes littered the dirt floor of the barn around a mare who stood patiently between two ropes attached to either side of her halter while the men worked on her feet. An imposing wooden cage, positioned high above the ground just outside the tack room, resonated with melodious cooing sounds.

"Oh, what lovely birds!" exclaimed Emma as she approached the cage and stood on the tips of her toes to admire the dazzling white doves.

With the shank and the hoof of the mare's hind leg still firmly held between his knees and without looking up from pulling nails from the worn out shoe, Heath replied, "Those are Robert's pride and joy. Old Rob here," grunted Heath, head down, struggling with the pliers, "claims his birds are descended from the same pair of doves that Noah took onto the Ark."

Robert swung his hammer down on the red-hot shoe astride the anvil in a rhythmic cadence before thrusting it into a tank of water where it hissed venomously. Pulling the cooled shoe from the water, Robert smiled at Emma, "Beggin' your pardon for all the noise, ma'am, but I gots to strike while the iron's hot."

"Indeed, Robert!" laughed Emma, extending her hand in greeting, "I am no stranger to that strategy."

Robert offered his hand to Emma after he had carefully wiped it on the dark blue cotton apron tied around his thin waist. "Yep, them birds of mine sure do like to raise a ruckus whenever I gets to hammerin'. Kind of inspires 'em to sing loud, like the brethren do on Sundays when that fine big organ starts makin' music," Robert added, holding the mare's new shoe with his tongs.

"Have you been raising the birds very long?" asked Emma, standing by the cage.

"Most of my life, I reckon," replied Robert.

"Robert gets paid by his church for the birds," interrupted Heath.

"Paid by the church?" asked Emma uncomprehendingly.

"Yep. In my church, every time one of the brethren passes on, Pastor says, 'Rob, we be needin' one of your birds.' Get twenty-five cents a bird, I do, 'cause they ain't no finer in the county nowheres," Robert announced proudly.

"What does your pastor do with the birds?" Emma asked, her curiosity mounting.

"Well, I takes one of my finest birds in a cage to the cemetery for every funeral and when Pastor says, 'Lord, God the Almighty! We be a beseechin' you to receive another lost soul on the wings of this here dove into Your eternal embrace'...it's then I open the door to the cage and let my beautiful bird fly up to the heavens," beamed Robert importantly.

"How lovely," said Emma, reaching out to touch the old man on his shoulder as he stood proudly next to his cage of noisy white doves.

"Heath, your mother and I have concluded our visit," said Emma turning back to Heath, who remained bent double. "And Roselle told me that your father would be returning soon," she said with more urgency in her voice.

Heath let go of the mare's foot and slowly began to uncoil himself upward from the waist. "Damn, Rob! One of these days soon I am going to remain permanently bent like a pretzel from trying to keep up with you around here. Say, Emma, did you know that old Rob here is…uh…what are you now, Robert? Seventy or is it seventy-one?" Heath smiled at the old man with the clean-shaven head and face, which gave him the appearance of a freshly laid egg.

"I'd be seventy-two, Mr. Heath. Yes ma'am, I been Mr. Adam's blacksmith nigh thirty years. Since afore this 'un here started out life pissin' his pants," and Rob winked at Emma upon the revelation of that vital statistic.

"Now, now, Rob, Miss Emma does not wish to hear all that rubbish about me," warned Heath.

"Oh, but that is where you are quite mistaken, Heath, for I long to hear every salacious bit of gossip that concerns you," teased Emma.

"And I'm jest the man to tell you all about that there salad gossip too," beamed Rob, attempting to lead Emma off by the arm.

"Not so fast my man!" laughed Heath. "Emma and I have to be returning to Grandview on the next ferry and you, Robert, need to finish up this mare so she can nurse her foal."

"And jest when I was warmin' to the subject! Next time, then, ma'am," said Rob as he bowed low to Emma.

"I shall make a special point of seeking you out next time, Robert, and you can whisper all of Heath's secrets in my ear," waved Emma as she and Heath walked toward the door of the barn.

"It would be my pleasure, ma'am," Rob called after them.

"Do not encourage the old gentleman, Emma, or I promise you," laughed Heath when they were out of earshot of the barn, "you will never get away from Rob. He loves an audience."

"Well, does not everyone love an audience every so often, my dear?" asked Emma, pinching Heath in the side.

"Yes, but old Rob can talk for two days straight without coming up for air!"

Just then, Robert came running after Heath and Emma, waving a small wooden crate at them. "Hold on there a bit, ma'am," he called breathlessly as he approached the pair.

"What have you got there, Robert?" asked Heath, looking at the crate.

"Beggin' your pardon, ma'am," Robert apologized to Emma, ignoring Heath. "But I says to myself, young master Georgie is all the time likin' my birds and them birds has sure taken a shine to him. Them birds let master Georgie hold 'em and everything. So, I says maybe young Georgie could take two of my birds and start hisself his own flock. Whadya think, ma'am?"

"Now, now Robert…" began Heath.

"Shush, Heath!" admonished Emma and then turning to Robert and holding out her hands to take the crate she said, "Why, Robert! What a marvelous idea and such a kind gift! I am sure these beautiful birds will delight George, but may I please pay you for them?"

"No ma'am. They's a gift from me to the boy. I been watchin' master Georgie and I seen that he has the knack…with animals, that is. Ain't many what do. Now, you go on and git before old man Hamilton appears," and Robert pushed lightly against the crate in Emma's hands.

"Thank you, Robert," said Emma as she and Heath turned to walk to the carriage.

"He must be lonely and speaking of such, your mother is a very lonely soul herself," Emma said becoming serious.

"Yes, I know. My father keeps her locked up in this place and I think it is slowly driving her mad," replied Heath untying Onion's reins. "Do you know what she told me the other day?" he asked giving Emma a hand up into the carriage and handing up the crate containing the two doves before taking a seat next to her.

"No, what?"

"Mother told me that if it were not for the visits by your sons to the farm, she might just be tempted to adopt an orphan to keep her company," and Heath urged Onion off at a trot.

"Now that is sad!" exclaimed Emma.

"Yes, Mother is heartbreakingly lonely, which is why I spend so much time talking with her because I know it gives her great comfort."

"What about your brother, Payne?" asked Emma.

"Payne has always been Father's favorite and I have always been Mother's favorite," Heath slapped the reins along Onion's back.

"Mmm," mused Emma.

"So, how did the two of you get along? Since I did not hear any gunfire, I assumed the two of you were doing all right by yourselves," joked Heath.

"We got along quite famously!" exclaimed Emma. "I could not have been more pleasantly surprised by the turn our luncheon took. I began by dreading the visit and the first few minutes of conversation merely confirmed what I had feared and then…" Emma snapped her fingers. "Your mother let down her guard and we were suddenly allies!"

Lifting Emma's hand to his lips, Heath kissed her fingers and said, "I am so pleased that the two women whom I love the most are making an effort to get to know one another. Thank you for your gesture of friendship to my mother," and they rode on in happy silence to the ferry.

As Heath and Emma made their way up the sloped lawn to the house on High Point Avenue, they could see Thunder, Luke's draft horse, tethered to a front column with the buckboard detached and sitting out in the yard.

"Wonder what brings Luke to the house today?" asked Emma, looking up at Heath.

"I have no idea," responded Heath surprised himself to see the big black horse. "Perhaps Mary invited him to dinner. Just let me drop you off by the steps and then I shall take Onion, the carriage and the doves around back to the barn," he added.

"Thank you but do hurry as the boys will have been missing you terribly all afternoon," she smiled at Heath before climbing down from the carriage.

As Emma walked up the front steps, she could hear the animated conversation of children and adults coming from the parlor. Brute greeted Emma noisily at the front door, alerting everyone of her arrival. "Such happy sounds," said Emma as she paused in the entrance to the parlor.

"Ma!" shrieked Will, running to his mother to give her a hug. "Benni and Luke are gonna get hitched! I was right all along! They're sweet on each other," and Will proceeded to dance an impromptu jig around his mother.

Benni stood blushing and clinging to Luke's arm in front of the fireplace. Mary held Johnny on her hip and George was jumping on the settee. "George, darling, get off Nana's furniture at once," Emma scolded her son gently. Turning her attention to the adults, Emma asked, "And when did this marvelous betrothal take place? I surely had no inkling that such excitement was in the offing so soon."

"Luke invited me on a picnic lunch with him today," began Benni, smiling coyly and looking up at Luke, only to be interrupted by George.

"Hurry up, Benni! Tell Ma what he did!" Turning to his mother George added, "Luke did the funniest thing ever."

"Yeah, tell her quick, 'fore she faints away from curiosity," chimed in Will

"Yes, please, someone, do tell me what exactly the Constable of Grandview did when he proposed to our Miss Bennington here," responded Emma.

"Well," began Benni, laughing and blushing, "we were spreading out our picnic lunch on the blue and white pinwheel pattern quilt that I made for Luke…you know the one Emma," stalled Benni.

"Benni, lookit Ma! She's gonna faint if you don't tell her quick or maybe I'll just tell…"

Whereupon, George clamped his hand over Will's mouth, "Shut up, Willy!"

Benni giggled. "As I was saying, I had just set out the fried chicken, biscuits and apple pie on the quilt, when suddenly, Luke fell to the ground under the tree nearby. So, I rushed over, fearing that he might be having a seizure of the heart or some such. I mean his eyes were rolled back in his head and his legs were twitching. I was absolutely terrified," Benni elaborated.

"Yes, yes, then what?" asked Emma, mystified.

"Well, I knelt down beside Luke there on the grass to examine him," responded Benni, "and I could see that his lips commenced to move but there was no sound, so I placed my ear close to his lips and said, 'Luke, I cannot make out your words. Do speak louder, my darling.'"

Unable to contain himself, Will interrupted, "I just love that 'my darlin' part!"

"Shush!" George reprimanded his brother wrapping an arm around Will's neck.

"And then?" asked Emma.

"And then," answered Benni, "Luke opened his eyes, grabbed his chest, looked up at me and whispered, 'It is my heart.'"

Emma scanned the faces around her. All were turned in rapt attention toward Benni and Luke. "Do tell!" exclaimed Emma.

"You can imagine that I was quite convinced that Luke was expiring before my very eyes," Benni continued her narration. "And then he said, 'I have medicine for my heart in the left hand pocket of my shirt. Please remove the medicine so that I may not die' and with that, I pulled out a small paper packet from Luke's shirt pocket, only to discover that it did not contain medicine as he claimed, but this jade ring instead," at which, Benni proudly showed Emma the ring on her left hand.

"Well, how novel," said Emma examining the delicate green circlet.

"But tell her what he said next!" prompted Will.

"Luke then rose to his knees in front of me, slipped the ring onto my finger and said, 'Louise Bennington, I ask for your hand in marriage for without you by my side for the rest of my natural life, I shall surely die of a broken heart,'" and having recited this, Louise promptly began to weep, just as Heath walked into the parlor.

"Has someone died?" asked Heath looking in alarm at the weeping Benni.

"There's gonna be a weddin'!" yelled Will excitedly, jumping up and down in front of Heath.

"Whose?" asked Heath, looking blankly around at the group.

Will ran over to Benni and Luke and holding their hands high above his head, shouted, "Theirs!"

"Luke, old man! Congratulations!" exclaimed Heath, striding over to shake the hand of his friend. "Have you set a date?" he asked pumping Luke's hand.

"We have decided upon October," grinned Luke.

"What splendid news!" Heath added, turning toward Emma, who remained stock-still and unsmiling.

"Yes...well, perhaps Benni and I need to bathe her face with some cold water," and turning toward the entrance to the parlor, Emma commanded, "Come dear."

Obediently, Benni followed Emma up the long flight of stairs as she babbled on about the ring having originally been given to Luke's grandmother by his grandfather when they became betrothed, until Emma shut the bathroom door behind them and said curtly, "Stop this nonsense!"

"Why, whatever do you mean?" asked Benni, the smile fading from her lips. She looked puzzled at Emma through reddened eyes, her cheeks still damp with tears.

"You cannot get married!" Emma hissed at Benni.

"Why not?" asked Benni, looking hurt.

"Because you are going to be a nurse first, that is why not!" and Emma shook her finger in Benni's face.

"Getting married is much more important than becoming a nurse," retorted Benni, leaning over the sink to splash her face with cold water.

"Come into my bedroom at once where the two of us can have more privacy to finish this discussion," said Emma snatching the towel out of Benni's hands and tossing it into the copper tub.

Once the two women were behind the door to Emma's bedroom, she ordered Benni to take a seat upon her bed as she began to pace silently back and forth in front of her friend for several long minutes, trying to formulate her argument against the impending marriage.

"How long have you been studying to become a nurse, Benni?" Emma asked, stopping abruptly in front of her friend where she sat in a dejected heap upon Emma's bed.

"Just as long as you have...since September of 1889," responded Benni.

"And now that you are about to complete your first year of formal studies and begin your second and last year of practical nursing skills, you have decided to ditch your education and a promising career as a nurse for a...a...man?" Emma glared at her friend.

"It is not every day that a man of Luke Crawford's caliber and character comes along, I should like to remind you," Benni responded tartly.

"Have you learned absolutely nothing from my experience with Edward?" Emma asked, her voice brimming with exasperation. "May I remind you that 'haste makes waste' in the truest sense here."

"I fail to see why. Luke is the highly respected Constable of Grandview and as such, quite capable to supporting the two of us. There is absolutely no need for me to continue to throw money away on becoming a nurse. I have no need to support myself, unlike you. I feel terribly sorry for you Emma. News of my engagement must have opened old wounds for you," and Benni stood preparing to leave the room.

"Sit back down this instant," ordered Emma, "or so help me, I shall throw you back down until you have heard all that I intend to say to you. Obviously your own mother does not possess enough sense to have such a talk with you, so it is up to me, your true friend, to explain the facts of life to you.

Benni, you are nothing more than an ignorant girl and you are about to embark on one of the biggest mistakes of your young life," began Emma, walking over to the lace curtains to look out over the sweeping vista of lawn, trees and river.

"I wish I had listened to my mother when she cautioned me about Edward and about the pitfalls of not being prepared to care for myself," Emma said sadly, fastening the curtains aside to let in the summer breeze. "My own dear mother tried in vain to impart her knowledge to me but I chose not to hear her words of wisdom. Each time Mama would attempt to have a serious talk with me about being a woman, marriage and the like, I would wave her off by telling her that I had no need to hear such things. And then suddenly, so suddenly, it was too late. I had to marry Edward."

"But I thought you loved Edward at the time of your marriage," sniffed Benni, curling her legs under her skirts on the pink bed cover.

"What I felt for Edward was a heady combination of lust and love running riot with my sensibilities. There is such a thin line that separates the two and when we women are in the throes of that first intense encounter with a man, especially one who dazzles the senses, we quite often lose the ability to think clearly," Emma paused in front of the mirror to adjust the pins in her hair.

"Is that what happened to you?" asked Benni, never taking her eyes off Emma. "Indeed it is."

"Well, I admit that I feel both love and lust for Luke but I also feel quite certain that he would never abuse me the way Edward abused you," said Benni defensively.

"That is not the point," said Emma, sitting next to Benni on the bed. "There are two potential pitfalls here. First of all, the two of you scarcely know one another. The less knowledge you have of your intended, the greater the potential for some nasty surprises after you say, 'I do', and I can tell you that discovering Edward's fondness for whiskey and whores after our marriage was absolutely devastating. His inability to control his appetite for the two had disastrous consequences for our entire family, and will continue to have consequences for all of us for a very long time to come."

"I know, my poor dear," responded Benni putting a consoling arm around Emma, "but you do not need to worry about Luke. He favors neither drink nor other women," she reassured her friend.

"Life is not that simple, Benni. People begin to change after they get married, sometimes for the better and sometimes for the worse. Traits that have long lain dormant or traits that have been stifled during the courtship, begin to surface once again as the pressures of married life begin to take hold. You will never truly know Luke until after you are married to him. That is why a long engagement is of such benefit to a newly betrothed couple. It affords both of you every opportunity to get to know each other before you rush into a mistake," Emma warned.

"Yes, yes," said Benni impatiently, rising from the bed. "Now that you have spoken your piece, can we return to the others?"

"Not just yet, please," and Emma rose to take a seat in the rocking chair next to the window. "There is a second matter to consider before you rush into this marriage."

"Emma! Your advice is endless!" scolded Benni, plopping back onto the bed.

"Someone needs to fill your ears with sound advice and since no one else seems to be capable, then I feel it is up to me to act as your friend and your advisor. Can you not understand, Benni, that I feel almost a duty to those I love and care about to offer advice in light of my horrible experiences? I cannot sit idly by and watch you, whom I love dearly, enter into this hasty marriage without the benefit of my insights...as an older and more experienced woman."

Sprawled across Emma's bed, Benni propped herself up on her elbows before responding, "Yes, wise Mother. Proceed. I am all ears," and she stuck out her tongue at Emma.

"That is more like it!" laughed Emma. "Now, as I was saying, the second matter that you must take into consideration before entering into this marriage is the issue of what might befall you should Luke leave you high and dry, as Edward left me. Or, God forbid, should Luke depart this earth suddenly due to illness or accident. How would you care for yourself?" asked Emma, leaning forward in the rocking chair.

"Well, I could always do what Rachel did and get a job somewhere like the Water Street Bakery, or the Foggy Bend Hotel or Hummel's or…"

"And what if you have one, two, three or four children to support? Do you really think that you could support, say five people on the pittance that you would be paid to wash dishes twelve hours a day in the kitchen at the Foggy Bend Hotel?" Emma asked scornfully.

"Well, if the children are boys, I could always have them enlist in the United States Army when they turn sixteen and then the girls…"

"Do you hear how ridiculous you sound, Benni? I find it hard to believe that I am listening to the same young woman who received such high marks on her final examinations and is but a year away from obtaining her nursing certificate. With that certification, you could support yourself and your children, come what may. Does that which meant everything to you mean so little to you now that some good-looking man has slipped a jade ring upon your finger? Is the ring so tight that it is squeezing off the flow of blood and oxygen to your brain?" stormed Emma, jumping to her feet.

Flushing bright red and sitting bolt upright on the pink cover, Benni responded sourly, "You have no right to speak to me that way!"

"Do you want to wind up like your mother with dozens of mouths to fill and nothing with which to fill them? How many times have you lamented the plight of your very own mother to me?" Emma reminded Benni.

"But I am in love with Luke!" wailed Benni. "If I do not accept his proposal of marriage now, someone else will and Luke will be lost to me forever."

"Did Luke actually say those words to you?" asked Emma, grasping the cherry footboard of the bed while leaning forward to look Benni squarely in the eye.

Benni looked away, "No, he did not say those words to me."

"So then, you just fabricated all this…this fluff in your head, this nonsense about someone else snatching up Luke if you do not agree to an October wedding?" Emma pursued Benni around the other side of the bed.

"Emma, stop!" begged Benni, holding out her hands to ward off her advancing friend.

Emma seized her friend by the shoulders and then drew her near into a hug. "Oh, Benni, my sweet friend! Sometimes I think I care more for you than you care for yourself!"

Whereupon, Benni began to sob. "A couple of hours ago, I was the happiest woman alive and now I feel that I have lost everything."

"Do not be melodramatic, Benni. You have lost nothing. What you have done is to gain a new perspective of your situation and all I ask is that you reflect upon what I have told you while making your plans for the future. Do keep in mind," cautioned Emma stroking Benni's beautiful blond hair, "that whatever decision you make will be yours and yours alone, as will the consequences of that decision. As I always tell the older boys, for every decision which you beg to make on your own, there will be consequences, some good and some not so good. Be prepared to shoulder those consequences, while forgoing the temptation to blame others when the consequences of your decisions and choices in life turn out to be less than good. And that, dear Benni, is the end of the sermon, so let us all say, 'Amen!'"

"Amen!" smiled Benni through her tears.

"Come now, Benni. Let us again wash away those tears before we present ourselves downstairs for Mama's wonderful dinner, which, unless my nose betrays me, would be baked ham. My favorite Sunday supper, especially since Mama will probably serve it with green beans and sweet potatoes," and Benni followed Emma to the washroom again.

Downstairs, Will galloped up to the two women, "Boy, it sure took two people a long time to wash one face! If I took that long to wash my face, Ma would give me a lickin' with the wooden spoon." Examining Benni's face, Will was prompted to add, "And it looks to me like she's been doin' more cryin'."

"Tears of joy, my dear Will. Tears of joy," explained Emma as she lead the trio into the dining room.

CHAPTER 17

▼

At the hospital the following week and after Fanella Walker had reviewed the current nursing notes in a stack of patient charts, she summoned Emma to return the charts to the women's ward.

"What is all this business I am hearing about Louise Bennington becoming engaged to that dashing constable of yours over there in Grandview this past weekend?" Fanella asked Emma, peering at her over the silver rims of the pince-nez glasses.

"Yes," sighed Emma. "I am quite afraid the gossip is true. Benni and Luke Crawford have announced their engagement."

"Well, how splendid, but you seem a bit disapproving, Emma," commented Fanella.

"Oh, no...uh, not really," stammered Emma, forcing a smile. "I think Luke is a splendid man and will make a fine husband for Benni," and she began to pick up the charts.

"When do they intend to be married?" asked Fanella, removing her glasses.

"Oh...you know, with all the excitement of their announcement, I do not believe I actually heard the date," Emma replied evasively.

"I feel certain it will not be until some time after graduation, so let me see, that would be, by my calculation, in the summer of next year. Oh, how perfect!" exclaimed Nurse Walker clapping her hands together. "Do you not agree that a summer wedding absolutely suits the two of them?"

"Absolutely, I agree," responded Emma, vigorously nodding her assent.

"Well then, we must prevail upon Louise to make plans for a wedding in the summer. What do you say?" Fanella asked Emma, rising to steady the stack of charts on Emma's outstretched arms and open the door for her.

"Yes, we must urge Benni to marry next summer after our graduation," Emma parroted as she turned to flee Nurse Walker's office before the woman could pry any additional information from her.

Emma was struggling up the two long flights of stairs with her unwieldy stack of charts on her way to the women's ward when a male voice said from behind her, "Here. Allow me to carry those for you." She recognized the voice of Burris McKendrick.

"Why thank you, sir," replied Emma, pausing to allow the Chief of Staff to grab her bundle of charts.

"Fanella told me she had sent you up here to the women's ward with these so I set off at a brisk trot to intercept you," puffed Burris. "I am going to need your help at once with a surgery."

"Who is our patient and what is the procedure?" asked Emma.

"A boy of around nine was carried into the hospital within the last hour by his parents and upon completion of a thorough examination of the child, I have determined that he is suffering from an acute attack of appendicitis," responded Burris, setting the stack of charts down on the desk at the nurses' station. "Now, where in hell is Nurse Stewart?"

"Coming, sir," answered Ramona Stewart, appearing from around the corner with an armful of linens. "Oh, Emma, am I glad to see you! Edna Ford has been positively adamant that you must bathe her this morning. No one else will do."

"I am afraid Dame Edna's bath will have to wait," interrupted Burris. "I am here to purloin Student Nurse Richardson from you for the rest of the morning as I have need of her skills administering the ether while I remove a boy's appendix. Can you manage without her for a bit?" asked Burris, reaching out to halt an impending avalanche of charts from the desk. "And get these damned things put away," he barked at Nurse Stewart.

"Come at once, Uppity," and Burris grabbed Emma's arm, briskly retracing their steps. "I have also asked that student nurse...what's-her-name...oh, you know the one," he fished around in his memory pool. "The one that sounds like a gem...Opal?"

"I think you mean Ruby, sir. Ruby Lawrence," responded Emma, gamely taking the stairs two at a time in order to keep up with the doctor.

"You had best slow down a bit, Uppity. Remember that nasty fall you took on the stairs," and Burris held onto Emma's arm again as they descended the rest of the stairs.

At the foot of the staircase, Burris released his grip upon Emma's arm, but never slowed his forward progress. As they crossed the marble caduceus, Burris worried out loud, "I do hope Student Nurse Lawrence is proficient enough to hand instruments to me for the duration of the procedure."

"She will be just fine," Emma reassured the doctor, taking three steps to his one.

"I must speak one final time to the boy's parents so you get back there to the scrub room and get Opal and yourself ready," Burris instructed Emma.

"Ruby, sir," Emma reminded the doctor.

"Yes, yes. Now, all hands on deck!" he ordered, as he outdistanced his student nurse.

Emma found Ruby already lathering up her forearms and hands with a stiff brush and soap at the large sink in the surgical scrub room.

"Oh, Emma! I am so glad you are going in there with me!" fretted Ruby, looking worried. "That man scares me to death. What if I get nervous and hand him the wrong instrument?"

"You will not hand Dr. McKendrick the wrong instrument," responded Emma, unbuttoning her sleeves and rolling them above the elbows to begin vigorously scrubbing her skin. "Remember that exercise in class when Fanella Walker blindfolded us and made us pick out forceps, retractors, scalpels and the rest of the instruments by touch?" laughed Emma, trying to reassure her friend.

"Yes," smiled Ruby, "and I remember that she tricked you by placing a letter opener on the table which you mistook for a scalpel. I can still hear what she said to you, 'Student Nurse Richardson, if you intend to slice with that implement, I suggest that you go to work for the United States Post Office.'"

"Oh, how well I remember that!" laughed Emma.

"I absolutely hate these cumbersome gloves," whined Ruby, struggling to pull on the thick, brown rubber gloves that Dr. McKendrick required of his surgical assistants. "I can hardly feel the instruments through all of this," and she made a snapping noise with the rubber at her wrist.

"I agree with Dr. McKendrick on this issue, Ruby. The latest statistics show that patients receiving surgical care from doctors and nurses who do not use the gloves have a higher degree of post-operative infection than those patients who are operated on by staff wearing the rubber gloves," reasoned Emma, drying her arms and hands.

"If that man gets a whiff of some new technique…some new instrument…some new piece of equipment…he just cannot wait to try it!" complained Ruby, struggling to adjust her long surgical apron with her elbows.

"Here let me help you with that. You should remember next time, dear, to fix your apron and head covering before donning your gloves," Emma gently reminded her friend. "I must say," continued Emma, "I admire old Burr tremendously for precisely the same reason that you find fault with him."

"Now what is that supposed to mean?" asked Ruby as Emma redid the ties to the back of her apron.

"It means that Dr. McKendrick is remarkably knowledgeable and up to date in his field of expertise and that only comes with the constant studying and reading that he does in order to be able to teach the young doctors. So, we are all blessed to have such a man as Dr. McKendrick in our midst…to both teach us his skills and treat aliments. Would you not agree?" Emma asked her friend.

"Yes, I suppose so," agreed Ruby reluctantly, "but just when I get used to doing something one way, old Burr decides it has to be done another way and then we all have to sit through another one of Fanella Walker's infernal teaching sessions."

"Is that not one of the methods by which we achieve excellence? Exposure to new and better information?" asked Emma, adding, "And by the way, is this your first time to scrub for Dr. McKendrick?"

"Yes," Ruby swallowed hard.

"Well, no wonder you are a bunch of nerves. Just breathe deeply and relax. Focus only on Dr. McKendrick's voice and the patient. Ignore everything else," advised Emma.

"I hear the cart. They are bringing the boy now," Ruby announced in a tight little voice.

"Come, then. Let us get the child ready for his surgery," and Emma pushed open the door to the operating room with her hip, arms held at a forty five degree angle from her body.

"Are you going to make it stop hurting?" were the first words out of the boy's mouth as he looked up at Emma. Without waiting for an answer and in rapid succession, he asked, "Are you a bandit? Is that why you are wearing a mask? Where's my mother? How long will it hurt?"

Emma countered by quietly asking the boy a question, "What did you say your name is?"

"Frederick Sampson Filmore," gasped the child, beginning to writhe.

"May I call you 'Freddie'?" Emma asked as she deftly smeared the edges of the ether cone with salve.

"Yep. Freddie's okay with me but I can't hardly stand it anymore," whimpered the boy.

"We are going to play a little game now, Freddie, and this game will take away your pain. Are you ready?" asked Emma with the ether cone poised to the side of the child's face.

"Uh-huh," Freddie grunted.

"Good. Do you remember the story of the Three Little Pigs and the Big Bad Wolf?"

"Sure," responded the boy squirming.

"Remember that the Big Bad Wolf huffs and puffs in order to blow down the little pig's house? I want you to take in a deep breath and then blow it out hard just like the wolf does when he blows down the pig's house and then do it again. All right?" Emma instructed the child.

"Yep."

"And we are going to pretend that my cone here," Emma said showing the ether cone to the boy, "is the little pig's house that you are going to blow down, all right?"

"Yep, but hurry or I might not be able to blow hard enough!"

Gently, Emma placed the ether cone over the child's nose and mouth, and with her dropper of ether poised in the other hand, she instructed the boy, "Get ready to take a deep breath when I count to three. And here we go, one...two...three. Take a deep breath," Emma told the child, while simultaneously dripping ether over the cone and timing the drops with her father's pocket watch that she had placed on the cart by her side.

"Now, Big Bad Wolf, blow the house down. Good! And again, deep breath in and blow the house down. Splendid! And again!" Emma coached the woozy boy.

"All right, Ruby. Freddie is under now and you may begin to prepare the field for Dr. McKendrick," Emma announced looking over at Ruby for the first time since the child had been wheeled into the operating room.

Ruby stood immobile by the boy's side.

"Ruby! Snap out of it! The boy needs to be prepared for Dr. McKendrick, at once!" ordered Emma. "Cleanse and drape the boy's abdomen...RUBY!"

"Oh...yes, yes...right away," stammered Ruby, springing into action.

Emma noticed that Ruby was trembling as she prepared the boy. "Poor girl" thought Emma to herself. "Ruby is more frightened than Freddie!"

Just then, Burris G. McKendrick entered from the scrub room, "Ahoy again, ladies. I see that our patient is now resting comfortably and nicely prepared for the procedure," and he moved to the boy's right side.

"Any problems putting him under?" asked Burris looking at Emma over the top of his mask.

"None, sir," was the reply.

"And my instruments are ready?" he asked turning to look at Ruby.

"Yes sir," she replied.

"And we all understand our relative positions at the table?" Dr. McKendrick asked, looking at both women.

"Yes sir," replied both women.

"Good. Nurse Fore, scalpel," commanded Dr. McKendrick sticking out his gloved right hand, palm upward.

Ruby gave Emma a stricken look and paused, then slapped four scalpels against the doctor's right palm.

"What in the hell is this?" thundered Dr. McKendrick looking down at the jangling cutlery in his right hand.

"Four scalpels, sir," stammered Ruby, visibly shaking.

"Do I look like an octopus to you, Nurse Opal?" thundered the doctor again. "Do you honestly believe that I am going to need four scalpels to make one incision in the child's belly?"

"It is Nurse 'Ruby' and sir, I think she simply misunderstood…" Emma tried to intervene.

Burris ignored Emma. "You know very well that I am the head of the ship and wherever I am standing is FORE. Since you, Opal, are standing here glued to my right side, you are NURSE FORE, and since Emma there is standing at a ninety degree angle to me on my left, she is NURSE PORT. Everyone in this hospital is supposed to know that by now. I run my operating room as I skipper my boat. REMEMBER?" he yelled into the hapless young woman's mask.

"I…I…am so…so…sorry, sir. I…I…forgot. It…it…will not happen again," Ruby stuttered.

"Damn right, it will not happen again or you will never receive your nursing certificate and cap. Now tell me if you can solve this mathematical problem. What is four minus three?" Dr. McKendrick asked sarcastically, his eyes magnified slits through the glasses that perched high up the bridge of his long nose.

"One?" asked Ruby, gingerly selecting a scalpel from the doctor's upturned palm.

"RIGHT YOU ARE!" Whereupon, Burris hurled the remaining three scalpels across the room, where they clattered off the wall and then skittered around the floor.

Ruby jumped and so did Emma.

"If we are through playing charades, then I suggest we get on with the removal of this poor child's appendix. Do we all agree?" asked Dr. McKendrick, suddenly an oasis of calm.

"Absolutely, Skipper. We quite agree," Emma stated firmly for both student nurses. The removal of Frederick Sampson Filmore's appendix went forward with no further hitches.

As Dr. McKendrick tied off the last couple of sutures, he suggested to Emma, "You might consider putting the boy's appendix in a bottle for him to take home and terrorize all his little friends with," chuckled Burris, "but just make sure that you secure the cork with a bit of sealing wax as I would not want the young lad's grossly swollen appendix to make an unexpected appearance in his mother's steak pie!"

Burris G. McKendrick was finished and gone, leaving behind a trail of discarded operating attire, bloody instruments, soiled linens, one snoring nine year old and two exhausted student nurses.

It was past noon and Emma, though famished, remembered that Edna Ford had been asking for her earlier that morning upstairs on the women's ward. After a second scrubbing, Emma tied on a fresh apron and hastily made her way to Edna Ford's bedside.

"How is my favorite patient today?" Emma asked cheerfully.

"What time is it, Ramona?" called Edna in a loud voice, turning her face in the direction of the far end of the ward, sightless eyes roaming agitatedly from side to side.

"Nearly one o'clock, dear," answered Ramona from the nurses' station.

"Do not 'dear' me when you know very well how angry I am!" Turning back in the direction of Emma she added, "And just where have you been for the past three hours? Across the river with that…that…lover of yours I expect. Getting all sweaty between the sheets with him. Eh? I shall have you know that I have been waiting forever for my bath and by now, I must stink like George Washington's outhouse!" fumed Edna, raising her head from the pillow.

"I have been with a very sick nine year old boy all morning, Mrs. Ford," replied Emma calmly.

"What is wrong with your mother that she cannot care for your sick child?" asked Edna sourly.

"Thankfully my own children are all quite well. The sick child to whom I was referring is a patient of Dr. McKendrick's and I have just spent the better part of three hours assisting our brilliant surgeon who removed the boy's appendix," Emma explained, controlling the urge to shout back at the old woman.

"Appendix, eh? Well, as I recall, an 'appendix' is found in a book and not in a boy," Edna made a lame attempt at humor.

"Actually, you have an appendix," said Emma moving aside Edna's sheets, "and it is found just about here," lightly touching the lower right-hand portion of Mrs. Ford's abdomen.

"Oh, that tickles!" giggled Edna.

"Well, I can assure you it was not tickling young Frederick Sampson Filmore when he was wheeled into the operating room. He was one very sick little boy," Emma said firmly.

"So, will young Frederick recover from his surgery?" asked Edna, suddenly ashamed of her unjustified display of temper toward Emma.

"He is well on his way to doing just that," replied Emma quietly, "thanks to the skillful hands of our fine surgeon."

"Yes, they are such skillful hands," agreed Edna, finally smiling at a place just to the left of Emma's face. "And speaking of such, I must tell you that the only reason I request you to bathe me is because you have such a gentle touch, which I assume you inherited from that sainted mother of yours who traveled across the Southport to bathe me during the weekend that you nurses staged that idiotic rampage of yours. Not having my nurses here was a frightening experience and certainly worked a terrible hardship on me," complained Edna reaching out a gnarled hand for Emma to take.

"I understand, dear," replied Emma, cradling the knotted fingers in her own.

"And just let me say this, while I am on the subject. Those other student nurses are dreadfully insensitive and unskilled. They go at my flesh as if they were killing rats, leaving me positively wounded and bleeding. Why, it takes me two whole days to recover from one of their drubbings!" Edna exclaimed.

"If you stop and think about it for a moment, I am the only one in my class who has any children. Do you know how much a baby weighs, Edna, when it is born?" Emma asked the elderly lady as she prepared towels and soap at her bed-side.

"Twenty pounds? Forty pounds? I guess I never really contemplated such a statistic. Do tell, Emma, what does a baby weigh when it is born?"

"Well," responded Emma, carefully removing Edna's soiled gown under the privacy of her top sheet, "my twins weighed less than six pounds each and my third baby weighed less than seven pounds, which is quite small when you consider that I weigh about ninety-five pounds and you probably weigh eighty pounds."

"Umm," responded Edna, attempting to scratch a spot on her left arm with the curled fingers of her right hand.

"I shall apply some ointment to that spot after your bath. Do not keep digging at it!" admonished Emma. "Anyhow, you can imagine that when one handles a fragile infant who only weighs six pounds, one does so with great care and a light touch, which explains why you prefer me to administer your bed bath rather than the others. My colleagues handle you roughly out of ignorance and not by design."

"Umm," Edna responded before falling silent again.

Carefully, Emma placed a folded towel behind Edna's head and upper body. Turning to the enamel wash basin that she had filled with tepid water, Emma lathered up the washcloth and proceeded to cleanse her patient's face, neck and shoulders, pausing to rinse the cloth after each soaping. Gently, she patted Edna's crumpled skin dry with a fresh towel before moving on to the next area to be washed, taking great pains never to expose her patient's body.

Edna had not spoken since Emma had begun her bath and at first, Emma thought perhaps the old lady had fallen asleep, a common occurrence. As Emma began to wash her patient's feet, Edna said quietly, "You know, of course, that I am just rendered incapable of controlling my outbursts occasionally."

"Yes, dear, I have long realized that."

"And I never mean to hurt your feelings."

"Yes, I realize that too."

"It is just that...that..."

"That being imprisoned in a bed twenty-four hours a day, three hundred and sixty-five days of the year for the last decade," answered Emma for the old woman, "has exacted a terrible toll."

"You are reading my mind!" laughed Edna.

"Actually," Emma began to massage ointment into Edna's parchment-like skin, "I was thinking that we might want to try to place you on one of old Burr's tables with wheels that he uses to transport his patients to and from the operating room and then take you outside for a breath of fresh air some afternoon soon. What do you make of that?"

"Oh, for pity's sake! How could I...how would I...?"

"You would just leave the details up to me and several select members of the staff. What say you, Dame Edna? Would you like to live dangerously for an afternoon?" Emma grinned at her sightless charge.

"Hell yes! And now you have me so stirred up that I shall never fall asleep this evening. Best light a ciggie for me and one for yourself also! Are you going to leave me naked under these sheets?" laughed Edna. "Or do I rate a clean hospital gown?"

"Coming right up, Mrs. Ford. Would you prefer the white gown or...the gold gown?"

"I should like the gold one," responded Edna, raising her head and shoulders off the bed, "with all the pearls stitched onto the sleeves."

"The one with rows and rows of ivory-colored lace at the bottom?" joked Emma.

"The more rows the better!" exclaimed Edna jovially. "Just as long as it is stylish. I definitely feel stylish this afternoon."

When Emma returned home to Grandview that evening and began the long walk up from the riverboat landing, she could see Heath playing with her sons on the front lawn. It appeared that they were playing a game and laughing boisterously at Johnny's participation.

"Ma!" yelled George, greeting his mother's arrival. "You must watch Johnny play hide and seek."

"Yeah, Ma!" chimed in Will, "Me and Heath and Georgie been teachin' him to play and he's gettin' real good at it too. Just watch this!"

Johnny was toddling toward his mother, arms outstretched for her embrace. "Hello, my precious," Emma greeted her youngest son, hugging him to her. "Are you going to show your mama how you can play hide and seek?" she smiled at Johnny.

"Set him down, Ma, and we'll show you how he can play," enthused Will.

"All right now, lads," interjected Heath, "remember the rules. The one who is 'it' must hide his eyes on the tree trunk for the count of ten, while the rest of us hide. 'It' must then call out, 'Ready or not, here I come,'" Heath reminded the boys.

"Now here comes the fun part, Ma," giggled George. "Just watch how we taught Johnny to be 'it'.

"Johnny, my boy, come here and hide your eyes," Heath instructed the toddler while placing the child's forehead against the tree," and remember to count with your fingers." Heath winked at Emma as he ordered the older boys to, "Scat!"

Emma was amused to watch one grown man and two small boys hide in plain view of the toddler who was busily placing his fingers one at a time against the bark of the oak tree. As Johnny touched the bark with the last of his ten fingers, he raised his forehead from the tree trunk and babbled in baby talk an unintelligible version of "ready or not here I come" before pausing to look at his mother.

"Go ahead, dear. Go find Heath and the boys," Emma encouraged Johnny.

Whereupon, Johnny ran around in circles for a few seconds before sighting Heath, hidden only from the waist down behind one of Mary's bushes by the front porch. Running over to Heath, Johnny grabbed him by the leg of his trousers, grinning broadly back at his mother.

"Good for you, darling," clapped Emma. "Now, go on and find the boys."

Will was having difficulty stifling his laughter from his perch on the swing and drew Johnny's attention next. Carefully, the toddler picked his way up the front steps on all fours and ran down the length of the porch to throw himself against Will on the wicker swing.

As a result of laughing so hysterically, Will began to hiccup uncontrollably as he said to his mother, "I just...hic...love the...hic...way Johnny...hic...runs," and he pumped his legs up and down in an exaggerated fashion by way of a demonstration.

"Yes," agreed Emma, "once Johnny learns to channel all that upward leg motion into forward leg motion, he will be able to run like the wind."

"Only one to go, Johnny," shouted Heath.

Will carried his brother back down the front steps to level ground and just then, Johnny spied George, hidden behind the gray and white trunk of a sycamore, with one arm sticking out at the side, to indicate his presence. Obligingly, Johnny ran over to where his brother stood and pointed behind the tree while looking back at Heath who stood with his arm around Emma, enjoying the antics of the children.

"You bet, little John! I see him too!" laughed Heath.

Emma shouted, "Bravo! Bravo! Johnny has found everyone! Good for you, my sweet."

"Would you believe," Heath asked looking down at Emma, "that the boys and I taught little John to play like that in less time than is required of Mary to ring the dinner bell? What a smart little lad our John is!"

Heath's use of the word 'our' made Emma beam. She had been noticing similar tendencies in Heath in recent months. Unfailingly kind to the boys from the outset of their relationship, Heath had, that summer, begun to acknowledge his attachment to the three boys and to express great pride in their small accomplishments, which greatly lifted the spirits of both Emma and Mary. Finally, the boys had the father whom they so deserved and more to the point, whom they so desperately needed. Heath was warming to the notion that he would be the one to teach Emma's boys to be men, and the three boys absolutely adored Heath in return.

Just then, Mary appeared at the screen door and seeing the others assembled on the front lawn obviously enjoying themselves, she pushed open the screen door to observe, "What a joy it is to see such a happy family!" Wiping her hands on the long white apron, Mary then announced, "Dinner is ready. Do I have anybody out here who feels inclined to partake of fried catfish, lima beans and corn, grits, sourdough bread and if you finish all that, peach cobbler?"

"Last one to the table is a one-legged centipede!" shouted George making a dash for the front steps.

"Oh, no you don't!" yelled Will, close on his brother's heels.

Heath scooped up John and streaking past Mary in his cowboy boots, he thundered across the oak floor in the front hall, passing the twins. Heath and John reached the dining room table first with Heath shouting, "And the winner is little John!" The baby giggled and clapped his hands.

"It would appear," laughed Mary as she and Emma entered the dining room behind the others, "that we have four very hungry boys this evening."

"Yes," smiled Emma back at her mother, "but if I were you, I would keep my eye on the big one over there," pointing to Heath. "As I have a feeling that he is inclined to eat more than the other three put together."

"Now you are beginning to sound like your dear departed father," joked Mary. "Remember how obsessed he was with how much or how little everyone ate at the table?" she smiled at Emma.

"Yes, and I never really did strike the happy medium in food consumption as far as Papa was concerned," Emma recalled fondly as she tucked a napkin under Johnny's chin.

"I'll just bet that Papa Miller would've given Heath holy hamsters for wearin' them boots to Nana's table," Will pointed out as he forked a crisp, golden catfish onto his plate.

"La-la!" admonished Mary, tapping the back of Will's hand gently with her fingers. "Put that back. We have not yet asked the dear Lord to bless our meal," she reminded her grandson.

Sheepishly, Will returned the catfish, fork still stuck in its middle, to the oval serving platter in front of his grandmother.

"And just for that, sir, I shall choose you to be the one to ask the blessing this evening," Mary reprimanded Will.

"Aw, Nana. Do I hafto?"

"Yes, you do have to. Prayer hands, please," and Mary interlaced her fingers and bowed her head, waiting for Will to begin the blessing.

Will sat with his face pressed against his intertwined fingers for several long seconds, prompting Mary to add, "Any time, Will, you may commence."

"God is great, God is good," began Will, "and we thank Him for our food and while I'm here, God, there's somethin' really 'portant I need to say to You and it ain't 'bout food neither," Will paused to open one eye and look over at Mary. "You think that's okay, Nana?" he asked softly.

"Yes, dear. God is listening," responded Mary, never raising her head.

"Okay God, then here it is. Heath is the bestest dad we ever had and I want to ask You to bless him too. Thanks and Amen," concluded Will, promptly taking his fork loaded with catfish from the serving platter and placing it on his dinner plate once again.

With his first bite of food, Will realized that everyone at the table sat motionless and silent, except for Johnny who was noisily banging the tray of his highchair with a spoon.

Heath cleared his throat and said quietly, "I believe Will is quite right. I had best take my boots off on the front porch before it starts raining hamsters," and he left the table. Emma hurried after him.

Mouth full of catfish and with a look of alarm, Will asked his grandmother, "Did I say somethin' bad, Nana?"

"To the contrary my darling," responded Mary, dabbing at the corners of her eyes with the linen napkin, "you said something very, very good."

"For once in your life!" added George, making a face at his brother.

Back at the hospital later in the week, Emma approached Burris McKendrick about her idea to lift Edna Ford onto a hospital gurney so that the elderly woman could be wheeled outside for a breath of fresh air. Emma rapped lightly upon the doctor's inner office door with her knuckles.

"Enter!" barked Burris from the other side of the door.

"Dr. McKendrick, I…" began Emma as she approached the massive walnut desk awash in a sea of papers, journals, medical books and charts.

"Oh, Jesus, Mary and Joseph! Not you! Not now! Can you not see what a damned mess I have here?" and Burris spread his arms protectively over the untidy flotsam which jammed the top of his desk.

"Calm yourself, sir," Emma smiled reassuringly, "for today I come in peace," and she held her right hand up, palm facing the doctor as if to take an oath.

"That will be the day that Miss Uppity comes in peace!" groused Burris, picking up the medical books and placing them back in their empty slots in the bookcase behind his desk.

"Paperwork always turns you into such a bear, sir. Why do you not just designate one of your subordinates to take care of this for you? You could call in several of your student doctors, for example, and hand one that pile and say, 'Review this correspondence and report back to me,' or hand this stack of charts to another and say, 'Give me an update in writing on all these post-operative patients' or…" Emma was interrupted by the doctor.

"That will be quite enough of your unsolicited advice, Uppity. You clearly lack comprehension of the situation here," he advised Emma.

"On the contrary, sir, I believe I possess an excellent grasp of the situation," Emma countered, hugely enjoying the give-and-take of their exchange, much the same way she used to enjoy engaging her late father, James, in their lively debates. "You are just too set in your ways to realize that times have changed and there are better strategies to put into place for dealing with a mountain of paperwork like this," and she moved nearer to his desk.

Alarmed, Burris threw himself spread-eagle across the top of his desk in a protective posture to safeguard the mess. "Not one step closer!" he warned Emma. "Touch anything…anything at all, and I shall be forced to evict you from my office at once!"

"My we are testy today!" Emma mocked his reaction.

Looking at her owlishly over the top of his glasses Burris said, "I should like to rise up off this infernal mess now but you must first promise not to send so much as a pencil crashing to the floor. Do you promise?"

"I promise," Emma replied with mock disdain, "but I still say that you should avail yourself of some assistance. By involving your students in a few of the administrative duties of your position, you would also be imparting additional valuable knowledge that they too will be required to exercise when those same students become doctors." She paused to gauge his reaction before concluding, "It is, after all, not enough just to know how to remove an appendix or set a broken bone today."

As Burris regained his footing behind the desk and straightened his long, immaculately starched and pressed white coat, Emma could not resist adding, "Just look at it this way, does one truly know anything about horses without having first mucked out a stall? From my observation, it would be therapeutic for your student doctors to have to muck out a stall, so to speak, from time to time."

"Are you quite through now?" Burris asked wearily.

"Yes. At least on that subject but that is not the subject about which I came to speak with you."

"I was afraid of that," he replied peevishly. "For the life of me, Emma, I do not know why I tolerate your impertinence."

"You tolerate and encourage me because I am the only one in this whole entire hospital who does not faint dead away when you yell, 'Boo!'" she laughed.

"Yes, yes, but one of these days I shall be forced to string you up by your thumbs!" Burris finally laughed at her boldness. "So do tell, what brings you here today then?" and he plopped resignedly into the big leather chair.

"I have come on behalf of Edna Ford," began Emma, also seating herself.

"Is something wrong with her of which I am unaware?" Burris leaned forward to ask in a tone of concern.

"No...nothing like that. But, do you realize how old Mrs. Ford is?"

"Of course I do. Dame Edna is seventy," responded Burris matter-of-factly.

"And during the past seventy years, do you know how many times she has been out of doors?" Emma asked again.

"Mmm...well let me think a bit." Burris fell silent for a few seconds tapping a bare spot on the desk with his pencil before responding, "Actually, I have no clue."

"Edna has been outside just three times in her life. Once to attend the burial of her father, once to attend the burial of her mother and once to be brought here to the hospital," stated Emma.

"But how can that be possible, Uppity?" Burris asked incredulously.

"Because it never occurred to anyone that Edna Ford might like to go outside and 'feel' what everyone else is able to see."

"What of her parents...what did her parents do with her as a child?" Burris asked dumbfounded by this new knowledge of his favorite patient.

"According to Mrs. Ford," began Emma, "her parents were very dedicated caretakers. Both her mother and her father made sure that she was carefully washed and dressed each day and received the proper nourishment, morning, noon and night. The two got little Edna out of bed each morning, placing her in a comfortable chair where she remained for the duration of each day. At night, both parents tucked Edna tenderly into bed with her prayers. While her physical care ended there, her parents were admirably cognizant that their daughter required an education.

Since little Edna was blind from birth, she could neither read nor write but that did not keep her parents from educating their daughter. They taught her to say the alphabet and to count. Edna learned to spell hundreds of words and to master the verbal composition of sentences and paragraphs. She acquired basic arithmetic skills by counting with marbles placed in a tray of sand.

And, according to Mrs. Ford, both Mother and Father read volume after volume of the best literature and poetry and even the newspaper to her. But, the child was never offered an opportunity to go out of doors," Emma concluded quietly.

"I had no idea her life had been such a tragedy," Burris shook his head sadly. "And why was it that little Edna never went out of doors?" asked Burris ignorantly.

"Because her parents were ashamed that their daughter had been born blind. They mistakenly mistook their daughter's blindness as evidence that God was punishing them for some unacknowledged sin and so those two, well-meaning, decent people, hid little Edna away from the rest of the world," responded Emma.

"How absolutely abysmal!" exclaimed Burris, checking his pocket watch. "So what is it that you propose again, please?"

"I propose that several times a week, weather permitting, we place Edna on a hospital gurney and wheel her outside," Emma smiled broadly.

"And who is the 'we' in your plan?" he asked, suddenly scowling across the papers at her.

"You, because she trusts you implicitly and I, because I have won her confidence. Honestly, the woman weighs next to nothing. I really do not think it would be a burden upon either of us and I could stay outside with her and you could then go about your business and when it is time to return to the women's ward, I could have you summoned and…"

"Silence! You positively give me a headache," complained Burris rubbing the temples on each side of his forehead. "If I agree, will you promise to leave me in peace, at once?" he asked, narrowing his eyes at Emma.

"I shall leave you in peace but only after you have promised, in return, to meet me at Edna's bedside in say, one hour," she bargained.

"Fine, fine. Now, go! Out with you!" and Burris waved her away from his desk.

"In one hour," Emma reminded him as she turned one final time before closing the office door.

As she passed the secretary's desk, Emma paused to suggest, "You might want to get the doctor a nice cool drink mixed up with a powder. It would seem that our surgeon has a bit of a headache." Out in the corridor, Emma rubbed the palms of her hands together in delight as she hurried to fetch a surgical gurney.

The wooden gurney on wheels creaked and clattered as Emma pushed it down the first floor hall from the surgical supply room. Humming to herself, she positioned the cart at the foot of the stairs up to the second floor. Emma hurried up the steps to find Nurse Ramona Stewart restocking the medicine cabinet on the women's ward.

"Dr. McKendrick has just authorized an airing for Edna Ford," she announced breathlessly.

With her back still to Emma, Nurse Stewart asked, "A what, please?"

"An airing," Emma responded triumphantly.

"You have got to be teasing!" exclaimed Ramona wheeling around to face Emma.

"Not in the least," she beamed.

"And just how are we supposed to accomplish this...this 'airing'?"

"I have already positioned a surgical gurney at the foot of the stairs. All we have to do now is place Edna on a litter and carry her downstairs to the gurney and then wheel her out onto the main veranda," explained Emma enthusiastically.

"Just whose idea was this? Oh, wait! Let me guess! Could it have been Student Nurse Uppity's idea?" Ramona laughed, turning to lock up the contents of the medicine cabinet.

"Then you approve?" asked Emma.

"Would it matter to you if I disapproved? Emma, sometimes you are like a stampede of horses...nothing can long stand in your way!" Ramona exclaimed.

At that moment, Burris McKendrick appeared on the ward carrying a folded canvas litter. "All right ladies, let us get to it. I have a gentleman scheduled in my office for a consultation in fifteen minutes and do you know why?" asked Burris in disbelief. "The fella insists that I must perform a barbaric bloodletting upon him. Seems the man cheats incessantly upon his wife with other women and believes himself to be possessed of the devil. He actually thinks I can drain this proclivity out of him!"

"I can just hear the man speaking to his poor wife now," snorted Ramona, "'But dear, the devil made me to do it!' Well, if I were his wife, I would offer to beat the devil out of him with my old iron skillet and never charge him a red cent for the service," added Ramona, swinging her imaginary frying pan.

"Now that you mention it," joked Burris, striding down the ward to Mrs. Ford's bedside, "I believe that might be the ultimate cure for what ails him."

"What ails whom?" asked Edna Ford, waking from a catnap.

"Nothing to concern yourself with, my dear," Burris greeted Mrs. Ford. "We are here to take care of what ails you this afternoon. As I understand it, your predicament might be likened to a severe case of claustrophobia, such as miners experience when they go underground for the first time."

"Now that is just damned stupid of you, Burr!" Edna shot back, fully awake. "Hell, I have been locked in the dark for seventy years! Only you folks with two good eyes get the jitters looking at how close the walls are."

"Now, now, old girl!" Burris cheerfully admonished Edna, "Do hold that tongue of yours in check as we prepare for your sojourn upon the veranda. Just consider all the raised eyebrows upon the foreheads of the good citizens of Clarksburg!"

"To hell with the good citizens of Clarksburg!" exclaimed Edna. As Burris lifted her emaciated body in his arms, Edna touched his chin with her thumb. "Think on it this way. If the constable hauls me off to his jail for creating a public nuisance, I might actually receive my first decent meal in a decade!"

While Burris held Mrs. Ford, Ramona and Emma spread open the canvas litter on her bed. Then, Emma lined the stretcher with a folded blanket, placed Edna's pillow at the head and prepared to cover her with a tattered, handsewn quilt in a log cabin pattern which Edna's mother had made for her daughter some sixty-five years earlier.

Settled onto her new conveyance, Edna commented, "It feels a bit drafty down around Alabama."

"What dear?" asked Emma preparing to take up the wooden handles by Edna's head.

"I said it feels like my bare ass is hanging out!" Turning to where she believed Burris stood, Edna added, "My girls are so used to my salty ravings that they cannot understand me when I speak sweetly to them," laughed Edna.

There were several seconds of silence while Emma readjusted Mrs. Ford's hospital gown and her quilt. "Why does the bastard not answer me? Has he already escaped?" Edna asked, touching Emma's arm.

"Like gas after a bean supper," Emma chuckled.

"You have been hanging around Dame Edna so long, you are beginning to sound like her," Ramona cautioned Emma.

"Bring my ciggie papers and tobacco," Edna instructed the two women as they began to carry her down the ward on her stretcher.

"Absolutely not!" responded Ramona emphatically. "It is already risky for me to allow you to smoke on the ward but I have jurisdiction within these four walls. Outside, however, there is a town ordinance against women smoking in public."

"What a pity!" exclaimed Edna.

"Would you look at that!" called another elderly woman patient as Edna passed by on her stretcher. "They are taking old Edna out feet first! I wondered what all the commotion was at the other end of the ward."

"Sorry to disappoint you…you old squirrel," snarled Edna, raising her head, "but I am still among the living."

"Dame Edna looks more like Cleopatra being carried by her slaves to a barge on the Nile," quipped another.

"Was it the Egyptians or the Vikings who used to burn their dead kings and queens on barges out in the river?" asked Ramona.

"Shut up, Ramona!" ordered Mrs. Ford. "You are not being paid to give me a history lesson."

Emma and Ramona reached the top of the staircase and began their slow descent with Edna Ford constantly admonishing them, "Do not drop me! Be cautious there!"

Once at the foot of the stairs, the two women carefully positioned Edna on top of the waiting hospital gurney, readjusting her gown, pillow and quilt until she was comfortable.

"Thank you, Ramona," said Emma.

"Will you two be all right from here?"

"We shall be just fine," Emma responded.

"Well, I for one am not so sure of that," Edna said weakly.

Emma began pushing the cart with its frail cargo toward the front door, where she paused to lift the front and then the back wheels over the sill. "You are going too fast!" insisted Edna.

"I am creeping," replied Emma, pushing the cart to the far end of the veranda, well out of the way of the ebb and flow of the hospital. Next, Emma positioned Edna's gurney at right angles to an exterior hospital wall, securing the foot of the cart with a wooden chair. Then, Emma dragged over another heavy wooden chair for herself and sat down to wait for the elderly woman's reaction.

"What are you doing?" asked Edna curiously, turning her head toward the scraping noise.

"Sitting. What are you doing?"

Edna's nostrils began to flare, "What is that smell?"

"Which one?" asked Emma with her eyes closed.

Edna turned her head to the left and drew a deep breath, "That one."

"Which direction?" Emma asked.

"What in the hell is the matter with you?" Edna asked impatiently, turning her head in an exaggerated fashion to the left. "The smell coming from my left. Can you not see the direction in which I am facing with my head?"

"No."

"Why not?"

"Because I have my eyes closed."

"Well, open them."

"No."

"Why not?"

"Because this afternoon I intend to experience life as you do, without my eyes."

"Oh great! The blind leading the blind!"

"Mmm...something like that. Now, about that smell...my nose tells me there is honeysuckle blooming nearby," replied Emma breathing deeply.

"What is honeysuckle?" asked Edna.

"Flowers. Hundreds of them, all creamy white and pale yellow...flowing along a vine covered with green leaves and coiled about a fence somewhere. Pluck a wee flower from its vine, then nip off its bottom and pull down gently to reveal the tiniest drop of honey," Emma explained going through the gestures with her fingers.

"How do you know that?" asked Edna incredulously.

"I learned it as a child from my father. During the long summer evenings of my childhood, Papa would take my hand and the two of us would go in search of our favorite 'dessert' as he called the tiny flowers. After we had satisfied our taste buds, Papa and I would gather up an armful of the flowering vines and take them back to Mama to put in water on the dining room table. By the next morning, our whole house was fragrant with the smell of honeysuckle," Emma explained wistfully.

"Extraordinary!" exclaimed Edna, fascinated with Emma's explanation of honeysuckle.

The two women spent the next hour on the veranda identifying smells and sounds. A horse relieving itself upon the dirt road out in front of the hospital produced an especially foul smell that intrigued Edna. "Who cleans up the mess?" she wanted to know.

"You mean from the horse?" asked Emma.

"Yes."

"No one does," responded Emma, eyes still closed.

"Well…what if someone steps in all that…horse shit?" whispered Edna.

"People step in it all the time, children mostly, because they are not paying attention to where they are going," explained Emma.

"I have smelled that odor at my bedside before and now I realize what causes it. I swear that dumb bugger Palmer, the orderly who is habitually on duty in the women's ward, reeks of horse sh…excrement," added Edna, toning down her remarks. "Are any provisions made for cleaning off your shoes?"

"Oh, of course. Nearly every home and every business, which includes this hospital, has a boot-scraper outside the door. The polite thing to do is to avail oneself of the boot-scraper to rid one's shoes of mud, excrement, snow and the like before entering the premises," Emma instructed Edna.

"Well, judging from the way Palmer generally smells," laughed Edna, "he has taken a fancy to wallowing in the stuff!"

After she was once again safely ensconced in her bed on the women's ward, Edna thanked Emma profusely for the hour that they had spent together on the veranda of the hospital. "I can honestly say," began Edna, "that the past hour was the best one I have spent in more years than I care to remember."

"Does that mean that you are willing to put up with my company on the veranda for another hour later in the week?" laughed Emma, noting the smile on Edna's glowing face.

"You bet. Now, do two things for me. First, roll me a ciggie and second, fetch Palmer for me. I have learned this afternoon that I definitely do not like the smell of horse shit at my bedside," Edna chuckled.

Later in the evening of that same day, as Emma joined Mary, the boys and Heath at the supper table, the conversation turned to Mrs. Ford.

Intrigued by his mother's description of Mrs. Ford's blindness and with his mouth still full of ham and beans, Will waved a buttered biscuit in the air as he asked, "What's it like bein' blind, Ma? "I ain't…I mean, I haven't never knew anyone that was blind."

"You can just bet blind, old Mrs. Ford speaks better English than you do!" admonished George, wiping his mouth with his napkin.

"You don't need eyes to talk with, Georgie. All's you need is a tongue," and Will wagged his food-covered tongue at his brother.

"Being blind is sort of like being dumb," George countered. "Everybody makes fun of you."

"George!" scolded Mary.

"What your brother means, my darling Will," Emma responded, narrowing her eyes at her first-born and then addressing his twin brother, "is that even though Mrs. Ford cannot see her surroundings, she is very much aware of them because she has other senses, such as hearing, touch, taste and smell. All of Mrs. Ford's remaining senses are more highly developed...stronger than ours."

"You mean kinda like my readin'? The more I practice it, the better it gets?" asked Will of his mother.

"Exactly, dear," Emma concurred.

"Unless you do not have ANY SENSE to begin with!" George taunted his brother.

"There he goes again...callin' me dumb!" Will complained forlornly to Heath.

"Will, you are not dumb by a long shot," interrupted Heath. "Anyone who can saddle and bridle a horse as fast and accurately as you can, is very smart indeed. Why, I have watched grown men working for me over at the ranch who thought stockings on a horse referred to clothing and I have seen men who thought the pommel end of the saddle should face the south end of a horse going north!" exclaimed Heath, reaching out to tousle Will's dark hair.

Everyone at the table laughed, including Will. "Okay, Georgie! No more calling me 'dumb'. Understand?" Will admonished his brother, pointing at him across the dining room table with his fork. "Unless you'd like for me to beat the piss out of you...which you know I can because I'm stronger than you," Will shot back in his own defense.

"See!" George complained to his mother. "He always has to have the last word."

"As I was trying to explain, we use what we have the most of to help us through life," Emma commented.

After dinner, Will cleared the table for Mary and then disappeared.

As dusk approached, Emma finished drying the dishes for Mary and stepped out onto the front porch to watch as Heath, George, Johnny and Brute rolled around in the grass. "Have you seen Will?" she asked Heath.

"Nope," replied Heath. "I thought he was helping you and Mary with the dishes tonight," he said, sitting upright on the lawn, grass and twigs sticking out of his blonde hair.

"It will be dark soon," fretted Emma, "and I wanted to get the boys upstairs for their baths."

"Should I go look for him?" asked Heath as Johnny jumped up and down in his lap. "Easy there, pardner," Heath cautioned the toddler.

"No. You already have your hands full. I shall just go around to the back of the house and ring the bell. That always brings Will," Emma added, walking down the front steps.

Out back, Emma pulled hard on the frayed piece of rope that dangled from the clapper of an old, black iron ship's bell which was affixed to one of the columns supporting the roof over the porch, just off Mary's kitchen. As the sound of the bell echoed into the distance, Emma listened intently for a response. She was greeted with silence, save for a lone whippoorwill in the woods behind the barn who trilled endlessly about the nocturnal smorgasbord of insects that awaited him.

Again, she jerked the clapper furiously back and forth inside the summoning bell. Again, the only response came from the hungry whippoorwill. Fear sharpened her senses as Emma set off past the barn, down the sloping lawn toward the river. "Will Richardson!" Emma called through cupped hands as she made her way hurriedly in the fading light. And louder, "WILLIAM JAMES RICHARDSON!" The whippoorwill sang on into the dusk.

Glancing back up toward High Point Avenue, Emma could discern that Heath and the other two boys had taken the dog and disappeared into the house. She quickened her step down to the river, where the dark water frothed around outcroppings of rock and scrap lumber from the mill bumped against the shore. Even in her haste, Emma could not help thinking to herself, "Papa never wasted a single scrap from that mill. There is enough wood here to heat a family's home for all of next winter."

"WILLIAM RICHARDSON," Emma's voice was edgy with panic. She stood motionless, listening and then resumed her forward progress toward the fallen tree along the bank of the river where she had told her sons about the disappearance of their father. It was a favorite spot of theirs. Just then she heard a faint rustling in the distance.

The sun was dipping below the horizon to her left, across the Southport River. Was it a wild animal approaching or was it her son? Emma paused, cupped her hands again and shouted,

"WILL RICHARDSON!"

"WHAT?" responded the child's familiar voice.

"YOU KNOW WHAT!" Emma shouted back in the direction of Will' voice. "COME HERE AT ONCE!" she commanded on the verge of hysteria.

"Watchya gettin' so riled up 'bout, Ma?" asked Will innocently as he approached his mother, peeking out from behind an armful of something that he cradled with both arms against his chest.

"You...you..." she sputtered, "ran off without telling me where you were going and you know, because I have told you and George a thousand times, that you must TELL ME WHERE YOU ARE GOING!" Emma shouted at her son.

"I wasn't lost or nothin', Ma. I knew where I was the whole time," explained Will.

"You may have known your whereabouts but I most certainly did not!" admonished Emma, taking Will roughly by the ear to lead him back to the house. "Is that honeysuckle I smell?" she asked, suddenly taking note of the heady fragrance that emanated from her son.

"Yep."

"What ever for?" sputtered Emma.

"For Mrs. Ford. You know...the old lady that's been in your hospital for a hundred years," explained Will, adding, "and please let go of my ear, Ma. You're killin' it!"

Emma stopped abruptly in her tracks and released Will's ear.

"You mean to say that you have been out here all alone gathering honeysuckle for Mrs. Ford?" Emma asked, finally putting it all together.

"That's what I mean to say," Will beamed at his mother's face in the fading light before adding, "I heard what you said at dinner so I figured maybe what Mrs. Ford needed more'n anything else in the whole wide world was for me to pick her a big bunch of honeysuckle so's she could feel it and taste it. I mean, it ain't...isn't very much fun just to go smellin' honeysuckle. Know what I mean, Ma?"

Suddenly ashamed of her outburst, Emma crushed her son to her, kissing the top of his head, "Oh, my darling Will! I do know what you mean."

"Don't mash the flowers," Will cautioned his mother, "'cause it took a long time to pick all this and I don't wanna hafto do it all over again."

In silence Emma and Will began to retrace their steps back to the house on High Point Avenue. When she could just make out the lights in the parlor, Emma spoke again, "Will, whatever made you go so far away to pick honey-suckle? It grows all around the barn."

"Yeah, but that's the wrong kind," Will responded knowledgeably, peering sidelong at his mother in the gathering darkness. "Papa Miller always told me that the biggest and the bestest honeysuckle in the world grows down by our tree. Papa always said he grew it special for me and Georgie and never told the hum-mingbirds 'bout it. These flowers have more honey than the stuff that grows 'round the barn," and will shoved the bundle under his mother's nose.

Feeling herself on the verge of tears, Emma turned her face and hurried up the hill to the house. Will spoke again, "And you know what, Ma?"

"What, Will?"

"I just knowed Papa Miller would tell me to pick only the bestest honeysuckle for that blind old lady patient of yours. Know why?"

"Why is that, Will?"

"'Cause Papa Miller was always tellin' me that if you short-change folks, they won't never do business with you again. So, I just figured that both me and that old lady been short-changed our whole lives...me bein' called the 'dumb one' ever since I can 'member and her bein' called 'the blind one.'"

Tears slid down Emma's cheeks in the darkness as she and her son, Will, returned home. For the remainder of the summer of 1890, Will Richardson, age eight, made sure that his mother carried a fresh bouquet of honeysuckle across the Southport each week to grace the chipped enamel water pitcher upon Edna Ford's bedside table.

"Emma, dear, we must talk," began Mary one afternoon as the two women busied themselves out in the back yard hanging up the family's dripping wash. Emma was enjoying a rare day at home and Heath had taken the two older boys across the river to the horse farm while Johnny stayed behind in Grandview with his mother and grandmother. The white sheets flapping from the clothesline were an irresistible attraction for the toddler who was amusing himself by running against their cool, wet expanses, alternately draping himself in a corner of dangling sheet or peering out from under a hem to shout "Boo!" at the women.

"Would you look at Mr. Silly over there, Mama!" laughed Emma.

"Yes, dear, I see the child and the dirty marks that he is leaving on my nice, white sheets which I have just spent the last hour scrubbing upon that infernal board in the tub," Mary groused uncharacteristically. "Please pay attention to what I am about to say," she admonished Emma.

"What is it?" asked Emma stuffing her mouth full of clothespins and grabbing an armful of dripping laundry.

"It is the matter of the church cemetery, which I mentioned to you some time ago," responded Mary, picking up a dropped shirt from the grass. Hummel and Pastor Nesbitt have approached me again to impress upon me their urgent need to create another cemetery for the church. They have offered a tidy sum for three acres of the meadow, just up the wooded slope behind the barn. Your father used to love to sit at the meadow's edge and gaze out across both sides of the river," added Mary wistfully, trailing Emma as she continued to hang wash.

"Must we do this, Mama?" asked Emma, taking the last clothespin from her mouth. "I detest the notion of selling off Papa's land. He loved it so!" she cast a stricken look at her mother.

Gently stroking the long auburn curls that cascaded down Emma's back, Mary replied quietly, "Yes, we must sell the land and we must sell it now. I have dragged my feet long enough over this issue. It has become a question of financial survival," added Mary emphatically.

"I see," Emma responded sadly, gazing at the meadow beyond the barn with its fringe of pine trees. "When do you contemplate the sale?"

"The papers are all drawn up for our signatures. The sooner the better as far as I am concerned," Mary stated matter-of-factly, pulling out the last of the wash from the laundry basket to hand to Emma.

"Is it still your intention to have Papa disinterred and reburied up there?" Emma asked quietly, gazing off into the distance at the green meadow.

"It is. I have made the relocation of your father's remains a condition of the sale of our land to the Methodist Church. An additional condition of the sale of the land is that James is to be moved at no expense to either of us and relocated in a spot of our choosing. So, we must decide very soon where to place Papa," answered Mary, picking up the laundry basket.

Emma shivered.

"This weekend, Emma, we must endeavor to pick and mark the spot," added Mary entering the screen door.

"Yes, Mama."

Saturday dawned sunny and hot in Grandview. The sale of the Millers' three acres to the Methodist Church was due to become final the following Monday. Emma crawled out of bed, dreading the day. She felt as if her father had died all over again. The same ominous pall hung over the house on High Point Avenue. All that was missing were the black swags that had draped the front porch the day that James Morgan Miller had been laid to rest in the little cemetery behind the Methodist Church following a massive heart attack.

The house was eerily silent as Emma made her way down the long staircase and back to the kitchen where Mary had prepared a bit of breakfast and was washing up dishes in the big soapstone sink. "Good morning, Mama. What has become of the boys?" asked Emma, pouring herself a cup of coffee from the old blue enamel pot resting on the back of the stove.

"Oh, Heath took all three of the children over to Clarksburg upon the invitation of Roselle. Seems she had something special planned for them...a picnic, or some such, by the lake and then a swim." Mary handed a plate containing a piece of toasted bread with cheese and a fried egg on top to Emma. "I do hope your breakfast has not grown too cold, dear."

It was then Emma noticed the dark circles under Mary's eyes. "This is hard on you too, is it not, Mama?"

"But of course, my darling. It is terribly difficult for both of us," and Mary reached out to take Emma's hand. "I do not relish the idea of selling any part of this land where your father and I lived together for so long. We were so happy here together as a family! And that meadow where you played as a child..." Mary began and then stopped, seeing the tears well up in Emma's eyes.

Abruptly rising from the wooden kitchen table, Mary went to the stove and poured herself a second cup of coffee. Emma picked at her food. "We must look at this sale as a business proposition," Mary advised her daughter. "We must stop viewing the sale of our land as a loss. Instead, we must look at what we shall gain by selling those three acres and we must rejoice because we shall be able to have Papa just up the meadow from our home that he loved so dearly. We must try to carry a vision in our hearts of how happy it would make Papa to know that he can once again gaze out over his beloved home, the river and his mill...to catch a glimpse of his family...and most especially of his three grandsons cavorting about the lawn would..." and Mary began to weep uncontrollably.

Weeping profusely herself, Emma rose to embrace her mother and together the two women shared anew the intense pain of their loss. "All right now dear," Mary spoke first, dabbing at Emma's face with the kitchen towel, "we must get about the business of selecting a spot for Papa. Let us dry our tears and be brave. Did you know that your darling Heath fashioned some stakes earlier this morning for us to use when stepping off the boundaries of our plot?" asked Mary, picking up the bundle of precisely whittled stakes, neatly tied with rope that Heath had placed on the back porch alongside a hammer.

Emma took the bundle of stakes from her mother and clutched them to her bosom as if cradling a baby while the tears coursed silently down her cheeks. Mary hooked her arm through Emma's and together the two women traversed the back lawn with its gentle upward slope to the fringe of white pines.

"Let us stop here a moment, Mama," suggested Emma, slowing her pace under the pines.

"Listen!" she commanded her mother.

Mary and Emma both paused to look back down the hill. The outline of their faces left little doubt that they were mother and daughter. A breeze off the river threatened to undo Mary's hair, tugging playfully at the pins that fettered the long silky black coil at the base of her neck. The same breeze that had already wrecked havoc with Emma's long curls was now enjoying a romp through the pine boughs overhead.

"Do you hear it?" asked Emma, still in profile with her mother, gazing far down to the river.

"Yes, of course dear. It is the river wind come to sigh through our pine grove," Mary responded, following Emma's gaze.

"Listen again, only this time with your 'inner ear', as Papa always used to say," coached Emma.

"Come dear," said Mary, placing her hand on Emma's shoulder, "it is only the sighing of the wind through the pines."

"No! Listen!" Emma ordered so sternly that Mary flinched.

"I...I...must confess, Emma," responded Mary, "that I do not hear what you hear and..."

"Do you not hear the child crying?" asked Emma, swaying slightly with her eyes closed. "When Papa and I would come up here and listen to the wind in the pines, he would always tell me that there was another part of the old judge's story that he had never told anyone before, except me. Remember," began Emma turning to look at her mother, "how Papa told us and everyone else that he had found the wooden cross over the spot where the judge was supposed to have been buried by the Confederate soldiers?"

"Yes, of course," said Mary.

"Well, that was not the whole story. One evening when Papa and I were up here all by ourselves and the wind was blowing as it is now, Papa told me to close my eyes and listen for a second voice. So I did and what I heard," announced Emma, "was the unmistakable voice of a little girl crying. When I told Papa I could hear her, he asked me if I knew who it was. Since I did not, Papa told me that it was the judge's little daughter crying after her father."

"Oh, Emma my sweet, that was just a story that your darling father made up to amuse you," smiled Mary, reaching out to touch her daughter's cheek.

Ignoring her mother's abrupt dismissal of the tale, Emma reached into the pocket of her long muslin skirt and pulled out a handkerchief containing something that she handed to her mother.

As Mary opened the folds of the handkerchief to reveal its contents, she gasped. There against the creases of the handkerchief lay a beautiful, white, porcelain doll's head with painted on black hair, blue eyes and a delicate pink cupid's mouth. "Where did this come from?" asked Mary.

"Papa found it buried under the wooden cross that supposedly marked the site of the judge's final resting place. When Papa excavated the site to look for the judge's remains, the only thing he found there was this doll's head. Papa was intrigued about what the presence of the doll's head might possibly mean.

So, determined to get to the bottom of the mystery, Papa searched high and low through the cemetery behind the church and then through old records in the basement of the church to try to determine the reason for the doll's head.

What he learned was that Judge Andrew Thomas Vickers had a little daughter, Annabelle Leigh Vickers, who succumbed to scarlet fever at the age of five. Apparently, Annabelle was his only child. Consumed with grief following the child's abrupt death, the judge reportedly became obsessed with the notion that his daughter's soul remained lodged in the body of her doll. This notion of Judge Vickers prompted him to stipulate in his will that the doll was to be interred with him at the time of his own death.

And, whereas, Papa found a headstone for the wife of Judge Vickers in the cemetery behind the church, he never located a burial site there or anywhere else for either the judge or his daughter," concluded Emma.

"But why was I never told?" asked Mary peevishly.

"He did not tell me until I was around twelve or so," responded Emma, taking back the doll's head from her mother and carefully wrapping it once again in the handkerchief. "Papa said he waited that long to tell me because he did not want to frighten me with the tale of the judge's daughter. Papa decided the two of us would have a secret that only he and I would share."

"But James and I shared everything," sputtered Mary. "There were no secrets between us."

"Yes, Mama, I know, but just this one tiny thing...this doll's head was my secret and mine alone to share with Papa," said Emma defiantly, closing the handkerchief in her fist.

"I see," said Mary softly.

"Since we are going to lay Papa's remains to rest here, I believe it to be fitting that we should lay that which remains of the judge and his daughter, namely the cross and the doll's head, to rest here also. Would you agree, Mama?"

"Well, quite frankly, my mind is spinning with all the details, but I suppose that you are correct," responded Mary.

"Their souls are crying out for a final resting place, Mama. What better place than this," and Emma gestured up toward the meadow, "and what better time than now?"

"Well then, come. We must get about the business of selecting a plot for your father, the judge and his daughter. Let us choose carefully," advised Mary, "as I do not relish the thought of making this a habit."

A week later, Mary, Emma, Will, George, John, Heath, Pastor Nesbitt, Hummel and his wife, Louise Bennington, Luke Crawford, Angus O'Malley, Fanella Walker, Burris, Cordelia and Polly McKendrick, Robert and certain select members from the town council of Grandview and the elders of the Methodist Church gathered on the meadow's ridge above the house on High Point Avenue at one o'clock in the afternoon. The sky overhead was a brilliant blue and white tufts of clouds scudded across the heavens. A light breeze from the river tossed about the long grasses of the meadow and the rain crows sang their warning of an invisible storm that crept silently toward them from the southwest.

Draped with an American flag, the casket of James Morgan Miller rested on a simple wooden bier by the gaping earth that waited to embrace him. Two shovels stood at attention in a nearby mound of the soil from the land over which James had exercised careful stewardship during his lifetime. James would be laid to rest facing south, with an unparalleled view of his home, the mill and the river.

At the far edge of the family's plot, was a small excavation into the earth meant to accommodate a box containing the judge's wooden cross and the china doll's head that had belonged to the judge's daughter. A small American flag, neatly folded into a triangle, rested on top of the box.

Clearing his throat, Pastor Nesbitt stepped forward with his Bible open in his hands. "Friends," he began, "we are gathered here today in the eyes of God to consecrate this magnificent ground as the eternal resting place for James Morgan Miller, Judge Andrew Thomas Vickers and Miss Annabelle Leigh Vickers and those of us who will most surely follow them in the sweet by-and-by when the King of Kings sees fit to call us to our final home. As of today and for all eternity this place will be known as 'Miller's Grove Cemetery'."

Referring to his Bible, Pastor Nesbitt read, "The Lord is my shepherd, I shall not want. He maketh me to lie down in green pastures. He leadeth me beside the still waters. He restoreth my soul..." At the conclusion of the Twenty-Third Psalm, the pastor raised his head to say, "George, William and John Richardson, the grandsons of James Miller, along with their, friend, Robert, have prepared a special moment for those souls which we are sending to their eternal rest today," and Pastor Nesbitt stepped aside.

The boys approached their grandfather's casket, each carrying a cage that bore one of Robert's white doves. Shyly, George turned to face the gathering and said, "My friend, Robert, has these white doves and he taught me that when somebody's soul needs to go to heaven, the best way for it to get there is on the wings of a white dove." George paused to hand his cage back to Robert. Unlatching the door to the bird's cage, George reached inside carefully to withdraw the dove with both hands and then turned to face the river. "So, Papa Miller, I hope that you will please have a safe trip back up there to God," and George released the white dove which soared above their heads, circled the gathering once and then flew south over the river.

Emma and Mary wept uncontrollably as did many of their friends. Will released a dove for Judge Vickers. Johnny, with the help of Heath, released his dove for Annabelle Vickers. After the American flag from James' casket was carefully folded and presented to Mary and the flag which rested upon the wooden box was presented to Emma, a young man stepped forward to blow taps on an old, tarnished and dented bugle. Finally, the casket bearing the physical remains of James Morgan Miller was lowered into the ground and the mourners were invited to sprinkle a token shovel of dirt over top.

Will, observing the proceedings, became alarmed that not enough dirt was being shoveled into the grave to cover his grandfather's casket. When at last the officials from the town and those from the Methodist Church had made their speeches and Pastor Nesbitt had concluded the prayers, Will rolled up his sleeves and grabbed one of the shovels, handing the other one to George, "Come on, we've got work to do," and the children began to fill in their grandfather's grave.

"Boys, boys! This is all quite unnecessary!" admonished Hummel.

"Beggin' your pardon, sir," responded Will, "but it ain't a question of UN-necessary but more like NE-cessary," and Will pointed at the clouds forming in the southwest and rapidly approaching from across the river. "We can't be havin' Papa Miller gettin' all wet," added Will shoveling furiously along with George.

Hummel made a move to pull the child back, but Heath intervened, "Let the boys be. This is important to them."

Emma and Mary departed, taking John back down to the house as the two women were anxious to put the finishing touches on a spread they had prepared for all those attending the consecration of the new Miller's Grove Cemetery. Heath remained behind with the boys and when the twins became exhausted with shoveling, he took over and finished the job for them.

"Well done, lads! Your Papa Miller is pleased with what you did here today," Heath congratulated the exhausted boys.

"How can you tell?" asked George, leaning against one of the shovels.

"Well, just take a look at those clouds over there," Heath said pointing to a patch of sky over the river. "Looks like a face smiling in the clouds to me. What do you think?"

The twins strained to find the spot in the clouds that Heath was indicating. "I see it! I see it!" yelled George first. Grabbing Will by the head, George directed his brother's gaze southwest.

"Oh, yeah! I see it too! Looks just like Papa in the clouds and he sure is smilin' mighty big!" exclaimed Will.

"I told you so!" laughed Heath. "Now, I do not know about the two of you, but I have just worked up a fierce appetite with all this shoveling and I happen to know that down yonder on your grandmother's table rests some delicious eats and the last one down the hill, gets a plate full of spinach!"

CHAPTER 18

▼

In the summer of 1890, Grandview was still enjoying its enviable status as a small town hemmed up at its southern boundary by the pristine Southport River and fortified on its remaining three sides by a stockade of some of the tallest corn in the state. Occasionally, folks continued to squabble at the tavern over a draft of beer about whether it was the Confederates or the Yankees who had prevailed at the Battle of Turkey Hollow. Children were admonished about the dangers of wild boars, bobcats, walking on lake ice before January, stampeding teams of horses, tornadoes, poison ivy, swinging from well buckets, touching the family cookstove and entering a privy before hollering, "Who's there?"

Women did not have the right to vote. Forbidden too was the public use of alcohol or tobacco by women and only whores wore make-up and used hair dyes. The married female population of childbearing age in Grandview averaged one live birth every third year and of those children that survived, just half reached the age of five years. Women could expect, on average, to have two miscarriages during their fertile years. Only whores sought abortions and fully one third of those resulted in death to the women.

The residents of Grandview were all on a first name basis with one another and that included their children and their dogs. Everyone made it a point to know their neighbors' business, primarily out of genuine interest and concern but, as in most small towns, there were also a few who made it their raison d'être to fabricate what they did not know about their neighbors. One such person in Grandview was Evaline Bushrod. Evaline could not discern the line between fact and fiction.

Five husbands were Evaline's claim to fame but only the first coupling had resulted in an offspring. The traumatic birth of that only child and the untimely death of the little girl a year later left Evaline a barren, devastated and embittered woman. Discarding bits of her past which no longer suited her and wildly embellishing upon her meager origins, Evaline sought to infiltrate the ranks of the wealthy and socially distinguished in Grandview. Like a circus chameleon, she assumed the colors of those who occupied prominent positions within the social circles that she sought to access.

Possessed of an uncanny knack for ferreting out wealthy widowers, Evaline honed her social climbing skills. She favored considerably older, wealthy men, bereft at the recent loss of a spouse and exceedingly vulnerable to her wiles. Candlelight suppers and feigned sympathy became her hallmarks. Hugely flattered by the attentions of a much younger woman and briefly distracted from his burden of grief, the unsuspecting widower would naively succumb to Evaline's ministrations.

Inevitably, Evaline outlived each of her wealthy benefactors and with the death of each successive spouse, she inherited their fortunes. When Evaline's fourth husband died, the man's eldest daughter arrived at the home of her late father to claim her mother's fine set of china. Enraged, Evaline barred her entrance into the house, shouting, "The china has been in the house as long as I have and therefore, it must be mine!"

Unwittingly, Emma appeared in Evaline's cross hairs the summer of 1890. It happened when Emma went into town to Hummel's to pick up supplies for Mary. Fortunately, the boys did not accompany her that day. Emma was busy selecting peaches for Mary's cobbler when Evaline walked up behind her.

"Welllll," drawled Evaline, her voice dripping with sarcasm as she stood directly behind Emma, "would you look at what the cat has dragged in this time!"

"Oh, excuse me, Evaline," began Emma in an attempt to deflect the tirade which Emma knew was coming, "did you want to see the peaches also? They appear to be excellent this season." Emma gathered up the fruit that she had selected and moved to the far end of the counter, ignoring Evaline.

"Not so fast, missy," began Evaline as she ambushed Emma at the other end of the counter. "Or is it 'missus' now? I hear you can't seem to make up your mind about the man living with you…and…under your very own mother's roof," sneered Evaline at Emma's face. Her voice rose as she added, "And three young children allowed to watch your shameful fornication! Those children should be removed from such an unhealthy home at once!" announced Evaline looking around the store for approbation from the other customers.

Refusing to heed Evaline's tirade, Emma paid for the peaches and departed Hummel's for home, with Evaline in pursuit.

"How dare you ignore me when I am speaking to you...you haughty shrew!" Evaline assailed Emma out on the street.

Never turning to look at the woman who pursued her, Emma said quietly as she continued walking down Court Street, "You are not speaking to me, Evaline. You are shouting at me."

"Well, someone had better yell at you about your atrocious conduct!"

"Since when did you become the self-anointed advocate of female celibacy?" asked Emma, beginning to feel warm around the collar of her summer blouse. "You who are always tripping over your bloomers before the last old goat has grown cold in the ground!"

"How dare you address me using such vile language!" exclaimed Evaline Bushrod, indignantly.

The two women stopped to square off at each other on the corner of Longmeadow and Elm Streets.

"You are a guttersnipe, Evaline, and I shall address you as such," responded Emma, lowering her cloth shopping bag to the ground.

"And you are a filthy whore!" screamed Evaline lunging at Emma with her nails.

A small crowd of passers-by gathered about the two women just in time to witness Evaline launch her assault upon Emma. Evaline's nails ripped into the delicate skin of the smaller woman's cheeks, spattering Emma's white blouse with red droplets of blood.

Momentarily stunned, Emma instinctively stepped back, raising her hands to cover her cheeks. What happened next would become the stuff of legend around Grandview for decades.

As Evaline's nails hovered about Emma's face a second time, Emma surprised the larger woman by grabbing both her wrists and lunging against Evaline with all the force she could muster. The impact of Emma against Evaline's torso sent the larger woman tumbling backward into the street, with Emma still gripping the wrists of her assailant. When Evaline's head struck the ground she was momentarily stunned, enabling Emma to bind the woman's hands together with her own hair ribbon. Seizing the sash that Evaline wore around her waist, Emma bound both of the woman's feet together also.

Winded and bleeding, Emma stood over Evaline Bushrod, trussed up like a cow for branding, on the main thoroughfare of Grandview. A sizeable crowd had swelled and encircled the two women during the brawl that began with Evaline Bushrod's physical attack upon the much smaller Emma Richardson. As Emma began to defend herself, the crowd cheered. The entire skirmish lasted no more than a few minutes but just long enough to attract the attention of Constable Luke Crawford.

"Make way! Make way at once, I command you!" thundered the constable, a hand already on each revolver, as he waded into the crowd to where the two women remained.

A look of bewilderment spread across Luke Crawford's face, "Emma?" Recovering quickly, Luke asked, "What in blazes just occurred here?" Looking angrily around at the crowd of rapidly disappearing potential witnesses, Luke added, "Who did this to these women?"

Before Emma could reply, Luke unholstered one of his revolvers, raised the gun high above his head and shot into the air. "Halt, I say! No one moves unless I say so!"

"Now, Emma, who did this to you?" barked Luke, surveying Emma's swollen and bleeding face.

"She did," replied Emma pointing a finger at the still dazed Evaline, lying on the boardwalk.

"And who did that to Mrs. Bushrod?" he asked.

"I did," confessed Emma, pointing a finger to her own chest.

Trying to keep from using expletives in front of so many female onlookers and ever mindful that he was up for re-election that fall, Luke asked, "All right then. Who saw this happen?"

"Me and her did," came one reply.

"I did," and a hand shot up into the air.

"Very well then, you three accompany me and these women to the jail and the rest of you get back to your business. The show here has ended." Turning to look at Emma and then Evaline, Luke announced, "Emma Richardson and Evaline Bushrod, I must now escort you to the Grandview Jail for disturbing the peace," and Luke handcuffed Emma. Then he knelt down and untied Evaline's ankles, pulling her up by her hands, still bound with Emma's yellow satin hair ribbon. "Now march! Both of you!" thundered Luke at the backs of the women as he prodded them along Elm Street to his jail.

Once inside the jail, Luke removed Emma's handcuffs and the satin ribbon that still bound Evaline's wrists. "Emma," ordered Luke, "you sit over there and

Evaline, you sit over here," as he motioned to chairs on opposite sides of the jail. "And witnesses, you have a seat out front on the bench, and mind you, don't move a hair or I'll lock you up in one of those cells over yonder."

As the two women and one man went back outside to wait, Luke barked at Shorty, one of his deputies, "Go fetch Heath Hamilton at Miss Mary's and then see if you can rouse old man Bushrod from his afternoon nap and cart him over here. Begging your pardon, Mrs. Bushrod," explained Luke when Evaline shot him a disapproving look, "but everybody hereabouts knows Mr. Bushrod spends most every afternoon asleep in a chair on the back porch with his coon hound at his feet to keep him company."

Shorty hustled out the door and Luke addressed the two women, "Now, I would like to know just what in tarnation happened out there this afternoon," and as Luke poured himself a cup of coffee from the stove, both women began to talk at once.

"Sheattackedmewithhernailssheinsultedmebycallingmeaguttersnipeandshekno ckedmetothegroundandallIwasdoingwastryingtobuypeachesatHummel's..." Sitting in the wooden chair with his cup of coffee behind the scarred wooden desk at the center of the jail, Luke said, "Both of you, be quiet now," and the room fell silent, save for the "clink, clink, clink" of Luke's spoon against the metal sides of the cup as he stirred sugar into his coffee.

Taking a drink of the scalding coffee, Luke commented, "Damn! That's hot! All right now. Emma, you begin by telling me what happened first since you seem to be the injured party."

Evaline began to protest, but Luke pointed the spoon at her and ordered, "Shut up!"

For the better part of a half hour, Luke listened as each woman recounted her version of what had transpired on the streets of Grandview. Just as Emma was launching into a rebuttal of Evaline's version, the door to the jail burst open and there stood Heath Hamilton, blue eyes blazing, golden hair wildly framing his handsome, stubble-covered face. His shirt-sleeves were rolled up above the elbows, revealing the ropy muscles and prominent veins that ran the length of his arms. Sweat dripped from his thick neck onto his shirt accentuating the size of his shoulders. He was barefooted, trousers rolled up to his knees, revealing the tanned skin of his bare calves and tops of his feet. Whitewash splatters adorned his shirt and his trousers.

Surveying the damage to Emma's face, her matted hair and dirty, disheveled clothing, Heath exclaimed, "My God! What has happened here?" Dropping to his knees in front of Emma, he began to pick long strands of her hair from the blood-encrusted gouges that ran from just below her eyes to just above her chin on both sides of her face.

Turning his head to look over his shoulder, Heath barked, "Damn it, Luke, these wounds need tending or they are likely to become infected. Get me a clean rag, some soap and water."

"This isn't a hospital, Heath. Emma's not in any danger of dying and we have some issues that need to be resolved here before she gets her face washed," responded Luke.

Heath jumped to his feet, jaw set and fists clenched. Looking Luke in the eyes, Heath reached for Emma, picked her up and turned to walk to the door. "That's far enough, pardner," cautioned Luke.

"You can shoot me in the back if you like, but I am taking this woman home, NOW. She has been through enough for one day," said Heath never slowing his step. Carefully he lifted Emma up onto Grit's bare back, mounted the horse behind her and rode off toward the house on High Point Avenue.

George and Will were still slapping whitewash on one of Mary's fences around her prized flower bed along the east side of the house, when they glimpsed Heath returning with their mother. Happy to have an excuse to abandon their brushes, the twins flung them into the bucket of whitewash and ran eagerly toward the figures approaching on horseback. The boys' smiles faded rapidly as they caught sight of their mother's appearance.

"What happened to you, Ma?" asked George trotting alongside the big horse.

"Did you get runned down by a buggy?" asked Will as he jogged backward up the hill to the house.

"Your mother has been in a cat fight," Heath responded, stopping the horse at the front steps.

"Criminy!" exclaimed Will, turning to run full tilt up the steps. Banging open the screen door, Will tore through the house yelling, "Naanaa! Naanaa! Ma been attacked by a tiger!"

Startled by the sudden commotion and his brother's obvious agitation, Johnny began to wail in fear in a corner of the kitchen where he had been quietly playing with his wooden blocks.

"Will Richardson! Just look at what you have done now!" admonished Mary, reaching down to scoop up the toddler. "Shush, now, and tell me what has you so stirred up but please do lower your voice as you are absolutely terrifying your brother," Mary warned as she swayed the baby back and forth on her hip.

"I said," gasped Will, "that Ma been attacked by a tiger!"

"Oh, how ridiculous! There are no tigers around here. Have you been smoking grapevines again?" Mary asked, suspiciously squinting at her grandson.

"Just come see for yourself!" responded Will, pulling his grandmother down the front hall by her apron.

At that very moment, George nearly ripped the screen door from its hinges as he pulled it wide open to allow Heath to enter the house with Emma in his arms.

"Dear heaven!" exclaimed Mary, still holding Johnny who began to cry again. "What has happened?"

"Old biddy Bushrod tried to scratch out Ma's eyes!" announced George, running up the staircase behind Heath who was wordlessly carrying Emma up the long flight of stairs toward her bedroom.

"Yeah, and that's when the tiger jumped on her and…" gasped Will, still short of breath.

"What in hell are you talking about?" asked George, suddenly turning on Will and bringing the forward progress of Mary and Johnny up the stairs to a halt.

"I'm talkin' 'bout that huge tiger that made them big scratches on her face," Will responded defensively.

"Heath said and I said it was old biddy Bushrod that made the scratches on her face," retorted George in a loud voice.

"He didn't say no such thing…he said Ma been in a cat fight! Are you damned deaf?"

"All right…all right, boys! Stop this arguing and get a move on up these stairs so that I can tend to your mother," Mary said, running out of patience.

Gently, Heath placed Emma on the pink covers of her childhood bed while Will and George scrambled up beside her for a better look at her face.

"Oh, Ma!" exclaimed Will sadly, surveying the damage to the skin of his mother's face. "I'm afraid to tell you this…but I think you're ruined!"

"Holy horse poop, Will! What a terrible thing to say to Ma!" George chastised his twin brother.

"Nonsense!" said Mary, bending over to scrutinize Emma's face. "All I need is some soap and water and some of my fine, homemade ointment and your mother will be good as new in about two weeks," Mary added reassuringly and she bustled out of the room to fetch her supplies.

Heath propped up Emma's head with extra pillows and removed her shoes while Emma tried to reassure her three boys that she was not in any imminent danger of expiring.

Mary returned to order everyone away from the bed. "Mind, you do not have to leave the room," she said, spreading a clean towel on the covers next to Emma, "but stay out of my way." Cautiously, Mary began to wash Emma's face with soap and tepid water, wringing out the cloth at last and placing it for a few seconds upon each affected area of the skin in order to dissolve the clotted blood. Mary carefully pulled hair and debris from the distinctive wounds before unstopping the bottle of alcohol.

"Now, Emma dear, this will sting like a hive full of bees but I absolutely must sterilize those nasty gouges as they run quite deep. Makes me wonder if the bitc…the biddy had just recently sharpened her claws! Now, close your eyes and hold your breath for a moment," instructed Mary wrapping her finger in gauze and dipping it into the bottle of alcohol.

"Ouch!" complained Emma.

"Here, Ma, squeeze my hand when it hurts," sympathized George offering his right hand to his mother.

"Yeah, and squeeze my other hand," echoed Will offering his left hand.

When Mary finished, Emma's face was clean but bright red from all the trauma of the wounds and the cleansing Mary had given them. "Now, to work some magic," smiled Mary for the first time.

"Oh, boy," smiled Will, "this here's my favorite part. Nana's gonna have you lookin' and feelin' better just like that," and Will snapped his fingers. Emma smiled weakly at her son.

Mary took the lid off a crystal jar and with her fingers, scooped out a dollop of aromatic, pale green ointment which she began to rub lightly into the affected skin of her daughter's face.

"Exactly what is in that concoction of yours, Mary?" asked Heath, finally conquering his consternation at the damage inflicted upon Emma.

"Oh, a little of this and a little of that," replied Mary vaguely.

"Come on, Nana. Tell us what the magic ingredients are," begged George. "Everybody in town always comes to our house to get some of your icky ointment whenever they get burned or hurt like Ma."

"Yeah, and everybody's all the time beggin' me, 'What's in that stuff, Will?' and I always have to tell 'em, 'I dunno.'"

"Face it Will, you are always telling people, 'I dunno,'" replied George, mocking his brother.

"Boys!" admonished Mary wiping her fingers on a clean towel. "All right then, I shall tell you what is in my magic ointment," and the boys leaned forward. "But," cautioned their grandmother, "if you go to copying my ointment, selling it and making hundreds of dollars, I shall be forced to take you to court," Mary deadpanned.

"Is she kiddin' us, Georgie, or not?" asked Will.

"Do you really think Nana would take us to court for making her dumb old mustard plaster? Honestly, Willy, you believe everything!" George admonished his brother and then asked his grandmother again, "So what is in that stuff?"

"Well, here is the recipe. Now pay close attention. First I boil up all the fatty pieces that are leftover after the butcher has finished cutting chops, roasts and the like from a hog."

"Yecch! That's disgusting!"

"Then," continued Mary ignoring Will, "I let all that wonderful liquid, with the meat still in it, cool overnight. The next morning, I skim off all that nicely congealed, white fat and boil it again. Oh, and by the way, I use the broth and meat to make that vegetable soup with my homemade noodles which you like so much, Will. Waste not, want not! Now where was I? Yes...and next, I strain the second pot of liquid containing all the fat through cheesecloth after fifteen minutes at a hard boil. Again, I cool it overnight and repeat these steps two more times."

"Sounds like a lot of work to me, Mary, for such a small jar of ointment," Heath added, picking up the crystal jar and sniffing at it contents.

"After that process, I go out to my gardens and begin to pick an assortment of flowers and herbs which I then mash in my stone mortar until they are indistinguishable, one from the other, mix the pulverized flowers and herbs into the rendered fat, and," here Mary snapped her fingers and picked up the crystal jar, waving it around in the air, "voila! The magic potion!"

Emma laughed.

"Yeah, but what kinds of flowers and herbs?" persisted George.

"Oh, a quarter cup of moonbeam buds, three tablespoons of dried dragon's breath, forty-two drops of liquid sunshine and a pinch of toejam," Mary responded without cracking a smile.

"Nana, that can't be right! Can it, Georgie?"

"Your grandmother's ointment has been a closely-guarded secret since her mother, your great-grandmother, passed it on to her," interrupted Emma. "Nana has not even given me the recipe," she added.

"And I intend for it to stay that way. One of these days, I shall give the recipe to your mother, but for now, I like being the only one in Grandview who knows how to make my magic potion," stated Mary. Laughing, she added, "I fear that in the wrong hands, women would be using my magic concoction to appear more youthful and men would be using it to enhance their...virility, shall we say."

"Sounds a bit like snake oil to me, Mary," laughed Heath. "You know…sort of like the stuff that traveling huckster tries to unload on both sides of the river every fall."

"My ointment has proven medicinal properties. His does not!" sniffed Mary defensively.

Heath bent to kiss Emma on the forehead with George and Will imitating the gesture. "Weil," smiled Heath, "I expect we shall know soon enough if Miss Mary's patent medicine…er…I mean, Miss Mary's Magic Moonbeams will live up to all our expectations. Now come on, everybody, let us allow this good woman some peace and quiet after a most disturbing day."

Heath took the lead for the door, pausing to turn and say, "But, let us all take one final look at your ma now because when we return, she will probably look a good ten years younger."

Mary swung a towel at him saying, "Shush and get on down the stairs this instant, Heath Hamilton!"

Everyone was laughing as they made their way down the long flight of stairs to the foyer, until Heath caught sight of Luke Crawford approaching on horseback up the front lawn.

"Mary, you keep the boys inside while I deal with this," and Heath shut the heavy front door as he walked out onto the porch to wait for Luke.

"You son of a bitch!" Heath exploded at Luke the moment the constable was within earshot. "Get down off that horse before I knock you off!" he added, clenching his fists at his sides.

"I did not come out here to pick a fight with you, Heath," said Luke quietly as he dismounted.

The two powerfully-built men stood facing one another on Mary's front lawn under the protective sprawl of an ancient oak tree.

"I hope you have come to apologize to Emma for humiliating her before the entire town," said Heath through gritted teeth.

"No, I don't make it a habit to go around apologizing to those who disturb the peace in Grandview," replied Luke, tying up his horse.

"Are you blind to the fact that the Bushrod bitch attacked Emma…inflicting serious wounds to her face?" Heath asked heatedly.

"I'm well aware of the circumstances of the encounter between the two women. I made it a point to obtain statements from eyewitnesses," declared Luke.

"Then why in the hell would you shackle Emma and drag her to the damned jail like that? I mean, Emma is scarcely bigger than an eight year old child and weighs about as much as my right leg! Explain that to me!" thundered Heath.

"Heath, this can either become a shouting match between the two of us, or we can behave like the civilized men that we are and sit down to talk out this situation," Luke warned.

"Right now, I am so angry I would just as soon draw your blood as talk but since you came here wearing side arms," and Heath pointed to the revolvers hanging prominently from the holsters around Heath's waist, "and I am unarmed, it would hardly be a fair fight, now would it?"

"There is no need to fight...only to talk," persisted Luke.

"Will talk heal Emma's face? Will talk restore her dignity the next time she has to shop at Hummel's?" Heath asked angrily.

"The issue here really isn't about Emma, or even Evaline. It is about law and order in Grandview," Luke tried again, choosing his words carefully.

Pounding his fist into the air before him, Heath raged, "How about if I show you my idea of law and order?"

"Maybe I should come back tomorrow after you've had a chance to cool off," offered Luke, preparing to untie his horse.

Just then, Emma opened the front door and walked out onto the porch. "Dear God! I can hear the two of you shouting at each other from all the way up in my bedroom and I daresay so can the rest of the neighbors along High Point Avenue. Stop it at once! You are making my head ache so badly that I feel as though it will split in two!"

"I apologize, Emma," said Luke, removing his hat.

"Please, Heath, you and Luke go away and take care of whatever it is that you must say or do to one another. But, do not conduct your business around here in the presence of my children and my mother," whereupon Emma turned on her heel, re-entered the house and slammed the front door.

Both men stood silently looking at the front door, unsure how to proceed next.

At last, Heath turned, walked silently past Luke and continued walking down the lawn toward the Southport River.

When Luke caught up with him, Heath was sitting on the bank of the river, within a few feet of the swiftly moving water. Aimlessly, he tossed pebbles into the dark depths of the Southport. "I never thought it would come to this," said Heath to the river.

"Come to what?" asked Luke, sitting beside him.

"Come to blows between you and me."

"We haven't exchanged any blows, Heath, old man. Only some heated words," and Luke rested his hand on his friend's shoulder.

Turning sharply to look at Luke, Heath asked, "Exactly what went wrong on the street there in Grandview today?"

"Heath, I don't know how you all do things over there in Clarksburg, but over here, we have a town ordinance against disturbing the peace and it was reported to me by the eyewitnesses, that both women were actively engaged in disturbing the hell out of the peace in Grandview!" Luke chuckled lamely.

Heath cocked an eyebrow at Luke who continued, "Since I am the elected law enforcement officer here in Grandview, it is my sworn duty to uphold the laws and enforce the ordinances of our town."

"Yeah, especially before an election," Heath reminded Luke.

"Right you are, friend, because unlike yourself, I have no horse farm to inherit from a rich pappy. I'm making my own way in the world, and this star," Luke tapped the tin badge pinned to his chest, "puts food on my table and will soon put a roof over my head and that of Benni as well."

"Leave my father out of this," warned Heath.

"I intend to remain as town constable for many years to come. It's a job for which I am well suited. However, if I don't enforce the laws and ordinances of Grandview, its citizens will vote me out of office," Luke reminded Heath.

"So?"

"So, when men, or, as in this case, women, disrupt the peace, I'm under oath to take charge of the situation, at once. Had it been two men instead of two women, I would have acted in the same fashion," Luke assured Heath.

"Like shit you would have! You would have pistol-whipped the bastards on the spot...you and that ghoul, Shorty, and then handcuffed them," laughed Heath at last.

"Right you are, my friend," responded Luke, placing his hand back on Heath's shoulder again.

"I want the people of Grandview to know that I am tough on anyone who violates our laws," Luke added.

"Well, I think you surely made your case this afternoon! Men and women will definitely think twice before they thumb their noses at each other in Grandview!" opined Heath.

"There is another matter which the two of us must address," said Luke, rising and brushing off the seat of his pants.

"Oh? And what is that?" asked Heath, also rising.

"Emma and Mrs. Bushrod will be required to appear before the judge in court next week."

"What?"

"Undoubtedly, the judge will levy a fine against each woman, as is customary."

"I do not believe this!" shouted Heath across the turbulent waters.

"Both women must appear and both will be fined, provided they both admit guilt," advised Luke.

"And if one or the other does not admit guilt, then what?" asked Heath.

"Then the judge will order the witnesses into court to testify as to what happened this afternoon," answered Luke.

"Holy crap! It just gets worse by the minute!" yelled Heath angrily at Luke. "You know that old bitch Bushrod will never admit to any wrongdoing! Hell, that whore thinks the name 'Bushrod' automatically grants her immunity!"

"I realize that she's a huge pain in the collective ass of our community and that folks hereabouts snicker behind their backs at her antics and her pomposity but she, like Emma, is entitled to be heard. Neither you nor I can tell her what she can or can't say in front of the judge," concluded Luke.

"Why are you making such an issue out of such a trivial incident? Do you not have more urgent matters that require your attention than flaying Emma twice, once on the main thoroughfare and again in a courtroom?" asked Heath, his face crimson.

"I'm setting a precedent. As the Constable of Grandview, I uphold the town's laws and I don't play favorites," Luke announced.

"You are setting a precedent, all right," growled Heath through clenched teeth. "You will forever be known as the biggest asshole this town has ever seen!" and Heath turned his back on Luke, striding up the long, green expanse of sward back to the house.

Emma was distraught when Heath broke the news to her later that same evening of the possible fate that awaited her in court the following week. "And here I thought Luke was our friend! Why is he doing this to me? Why has he singled me out for such cruel treatment?" she wailed.

"Luke has decided to make an example out of you in order to assure his re-election, plain and simple," said Heath quietly.

"But I was only defending myself!" protested Emma. "What was I supposed to do, just stand there and let that ogre rip my face to shreds?" asked Emma, reaching up to touch the sore, discolored welts that still lined both sides of her face.

"You did the right thing, Emma, and because I am so incensed about this mess, I have plans to hire a lawyer to appear with you in court next week. If Luke wants a fight, then it is a fight he will get!" and Heath pounded his fist on the kitchen table where he and Emma were speaking in hushed voices so as not to awaken Mary or the children, already asleep upstairs.

Emma remained wakeful most of the night and Heath paced up and down the front porch until well after two in the morning. As usual, the three boys arose early the following morning and clamored after their mother and Heath to join them around the breakfast table. Mary immediately saw that something was terribly amiss between the two but held her tongue until after the dishes were washed and dried and the boys were running wildly about the front lawn.

"Out with it, now," said Mary as she put the last dish away and poured more coffee for all of them at the kitchen table.

Briefly, Heath explained the sum and substance of his words with Luke Crawford while Emma sat listening, on the verge of tears, sipping her coffee.

"Why, that scoundrel!" exclaimed Mary. "And to think that I made him welcome in this home!"

Just then, the front door banged open and in marched Angus O'Malley calling, "Where is she? Where is our darling girl? Come to Angus at once!" accompanied by a vigorous clapping of the hands.

"Good grief! It is only seven-thirty in the morning! The man has no mercy!" protested Heath.

"All the saints and angels preserve us!" Angus sucked in his breath hard upon seeing Emma's face for the first time. Flinging his notepad and pencil aside, he dropped quickly to one knee beside Emma and taking her hand placed it against his cheek. "Oh, my poor darling girl!" Angus repeated several times before drawing up a chair right next to Emma. Without taking his eyes from Emma's face, Angus added, "Miss Mary, at this moment in my life, I am in desperate need of a cup of coffee. And by the way, I told the babies to stay outside so that Uncle Angus could speak privately with their tragically wounded mother."

"How thoughtful and kind of you to come so quickly, Angus," began Emma, smiling wanly at the reporter.

"Oh, the tragedy of it all! But such utter rubbish, if I am to believe what has been reported to me," Angus said, his voice full of scorn.

As Angus filled his coffee with cream and sugar, Emma unburdened herself to him. Mary rose to make a second pot of coffee and the boys peeked in at the back door. "Can we come inside now?" asked George. "I have to piss."

"Go relieve yourself behind the barn as I taught you to do," answered Heath.

"So, whom have you chosen to represent Emma in this mess next week?" asked Angus, turning to stare at Heath.

"Josiah Tweedle. At least it is my intention to call on him today about this matter. Do you know of him?" asked Heath, rising to pour a fourth cup of coffee.

"Everyone knows Josiah Tweedle to be one of the finest lawyers in the state!" beamed Angus. "Years of experience...good grip on his emotions in the court-room...aggressive as hell...knows his law forward and backward and hates to lose," Angus ticked off the barrister's attributes. "Splendid choice, Heath!"

"Josiah enjoys a fine reputation on both sides of the Southport," added Heath, "and is actually a longtime friend of my father's."

"Very comforting to know that, Heath, but what about strategy? Do we know what strategy we are going to use in the courtroom?" questioned Angus.

"I thought of little else as I walked the night away out on Miss Mary's front porch. I mean the whole thing is so absurd and should have been relegated to the shit pile out back, but oh no! Luke Crawford has decided to use Emma as his pawn in his bid for re-election. And by God, I am going to fight him to the death over this!" roared Heath, slamming his hand down so hard upon the wooden table that Angus O'Malley fairly jumped out of his chair and the coffee cups leaped in their saucers.

"But, to answer your question, Angus. While I have some definite thoughts as to what strategy we should employ, I want to hear first what Attorney Tweedle has to say. After all, I just breed and raise horses," replied Heath.

"Yes," chuckled Angus, "but you both have quite a flair for slinging horseshit!"

The reporter's humor lightened the moment just before Will, George and John came racing into the house. "Aren't you through yet?" complained Will. "You been talkin' all mornin' and it's lunch time!"

"I am half starved to death!" groused George.

Surveying the boy from top to bottom and back again, Heath was prompted to ask, "Oh yeah? Which half would that be?"

When Emma reported for work at the hospital the following Monday, the patients, doctors, nurses and ancillary staff at Angel of Mercy Hospital in Clarks-burg were aghast at the angry, red slashes they saw upon her face. Repeatedly, Emma paused to offer a brief explanation of her altered appearance to her patients and fellow workers which explanation was invariably followed by expres-sions of concern and anger.

"Just because I cannot see that mangled face of yours does not mean that I am unaware of what the insolent bitch did to you over there in Grandview!" Edna Ford exclaimed loudly as soon as she heard Emma's voice from the far end of the women's ward. "Come here at once!" she commanded, raising her head and shoulders from the bed.

Obediently, Emma walked briskly to Mrs. Ford's bedside and immediately began preparations for Edna's daily bath. "Stop all that crap, this instant," ordered Edna, "and come over here where I can assess the damage for myself."

With gnarled, shrunken and bent fingers, Edna Ford began a silent tracing of the contours of Emma's face and hair. "Mmm," said Edna finally after a prolonged stillness, "I did not realize just how beautiful you really are, Emma. Having said that, however, I am appalled at the damage that northern hussy inflicted upon you." And then, "Roll a cigarette for me at once!"

Emma obliged her favorite patient with a deftly rolled slim tube of tobacco and once she was contentedly puffing away, Edna amplified her reaction. "You know," she began after taking a deep drag from her cigarette, "it seems to me as if old Bushwhacker intended to gouge out your eyes."

"Bushrod," corrected Emma.

"No...Bushwhacker, I say, and do you know why?" asked Edna puffing and talking at the same time.

"I guess not," replied Emma, preparing Edna's bath.

"Because, during the war between the North and the South, the bushwhackers were the Confederate boys who hid out around Yankee encampments...waiting until the blue boys were all lollygagging around their campfires real nice and cozy like with their coffee and roasted venison and then...BAM!"

Emma jumped.

"Did I scare you?" laughed Edna.

"You most certainly did!" replied Emma, smiling.

"And that just proves my point. The Johnny Reb bushwhackers surprised the blue boys too...scaring them shitless by storming into their camps, guns blazing away...all whooping and shouting at once. Gave the Confederates the advantage every time."

"Oh, so you believe that Evaline acted like one of your cherished Confederate bushwhackers, eh?"

"Of course, I do. She hid out in that store, stalked you as you departed Hummel's and just waited until your guard was down and then..."

"Yes, I know. BAM! She attacked, right?" asked Emma washing Edna's face.

"Mind you do not wash my cigarette," Edna cautioned, scrunching up her face, "and yes that is why the relentlessly whoring old turd should be called Evaline 'Bushwhacker'."

"Oh, my dear Mrs. Ford!" laughed Emma uncontrollably. "Sometimes I wonder who dispenses the medicine around here, you or me, for I always seem to come away from our encounters feeling ever so much better."

"So do I, dear," responded Edna reaching out a hand for Emma to take in hers. "Should it not be thus among friends?"

It lightened Emma's spirits that those she knew and held dear were so supportive of her, although she found it increasingly difficult to concentrate upon anything other than her court appearance as the time drew near. To ease Emma's growing apprehension and to prepare her for the courtroom proceedings, Heath arranged an informal conference with the lawyer he had chosen to represent her. In a two-story office building just off the town square, behind an imposing piece of storefront glass that proclaimed in large gold lettering, "JOSIAH C. TWEEDLE, ATTORNEY AT LAW AND NOTARY PUBLIC", Heath and Emma found the cramped office of the barrister.

Heath knocked politely upon Mr. Tweedle's outer door.

"Make your entrance!" boomed a deep voice from the other side.

Once inside, Emma beheld her lawyer for the first time. He was taller than Heath, clean shaven, with a lion's mane of white hair, a bit too long around the edges and kept at bay only with incessant finger-combing. Impeccably dressed, it was well known that Josiah Tweedle favored red ties, highly polished boots and detested his spectacles. The barrister constantly fiddled with the latter, one minute pushing them up his nose, the next minute removing them, swabbing them with the end of his necktie, biting the earpieces, perching them atop his flowing locks and searching absentmindedly for them on top of his desk. Some said Josiah's obsessive handling of his spectacles could be attributed to his determination to overcome an addiction to tobacco after the much younger woman whom he courted assiduously before marriage informed him that his puffing habit all but rendered him disgusting.

Josiah Tweedle shook hands like someone used to splitting firewood. His grip suggested that Josiah knew only too well the importance of holding onto the ax handle while riveting one's gaze upon the intended target, lest a foot be lost in the process. Emma winced in pain as he enveloped her tiny hand in his huge one. Seemingly unaware of his client's discomfort, Josiah continued to hang onto Emma as his eyes searched hers during his introductory remarks.

"It is my very great pleasure to meet you, Mrs. Richardson. Indeed, you have become something of a legend in our town and it is not every day that one can hope to meet a living legend, especially one of such diminutive stature. Heath was quite right to contact me about your forthcoming court appearance as it would never do to have the reputation of one of Grandview's most prominent citizens sullied with such deliberately trumped up...frivolous charges," and he released Emma's hand.

"Sit," he commanded them both.

While Josiah exchanged pleasantries with Heath, Emma had a chance to glance about Attorney Tweedle's office. Two walls of the cramped office were lined with bookcases that ran from floor to ceiling and each shelf sagged with well-worn volumes of law, appellate briefs, poetry, almanacs, the barrister's daily diaries for the past thirty years, a smattering of fiction and even a cookbook. A copy of "The Adventures of Huckleberry Finn" lay open on the neatly appointed desk of Attorney Tweedle. A third wall of the office was lined with wooden file cabinets, all the drawers of which were boldly labeled with handwritten letters of the alphabet. An oil lamp burned brightly on the far corner of Josiah's desk and a leather satchel occupied the third client chair, next to Emma. Since its buckle was undone, Emma could see that the interior of the satchel contained reams of papers, carefully organized into categories such as, 'To File', 'Research', 'Trials' and so forth. Covered with what she assumed to be the attorney's own flowing handwriting, she could just discern the first sentence under the heading of the first page, "Comes now the Defendant in person and by his attorney, Josiah C. Tweedle..."

"Mrs. Richardson?" Emma realized that Josiah Tweedle was addressing her.

"Oh, please forgive me, Attorney Tweedle," blushed Emma at being caught surveying the barrister's office and peeking into his briefcase, "but it is my first time in a lawyer's office."

"I understand, my dear. And while I hope it will be your last, do take my card in case the fates decide otherwise," joked Mr. Tweedle, giving Emma a handwritten business card with his name and address.

"Now, let us turn our attention to the matter at hand," and for the next hour, Emma, Heath and Josiah C. Tweedle planned their courtroom strategy.

At nine o'clock on the appointed morning, Emma and Heath appeared in the imposing Grandview Courthouse which dominated the northeast corner of Court Street and Longmeadow Avenue. Completed late in the fall of 1884, the three story limestone edifice was punctuated with five copper domes that were beginning to oxidize to a mossy shade of green. The four smaller domes delineated the north, south, east and west corners of the building while the fifth, and largest dome, occupied the center of the building and housed a clock whose voice could be heard across the river, boldly marking the passage of time. High atop the fifth dome with its clock, flew the American flag.

Emma trembled as she and Heath walked up the limestone steps of the courthouse. They were met just outside the courtroom on the first floor by Josiah Tweedle.

"I am afraid I have some bad news for you, friends," announced Josiah, waving a piece of paper at them. "The clerk has just handed me a message delivered by a roughrider from Judge Theodore Freudenberg. Seems as though the judge's horse took lame some distance north of town which means the judge will not be able to preside over your matter until later this afternoon."

Seeing the stricken look on Emma's face, Josiah added, "I am terribly sorry for this inconvenience, folks, but it happens all the time. Makes me darn sore too. Here we have this magnificent new courthouse," and Josiah waved the handwritten message at his polished wood and marble surroundings, "and no sitting judge."

"What does that mean?" asked Emma.

"It means that our judges ride the circuit to preside over matters throughout the southern one fourth of our state. Hardly efficient. I am lobbying hard for a sitting judge in our own county. Now then, I must ride out to the Dillman farm and take old Herbert's last will and testament before another stroke renders him non compos mentis. Meet you back here at two this afternoon...provided my old nag does not pick today to expire," and he strode down the hall.

"Sir!" called Heath after the rapidly disappearing attorney.

"Yes?" asked Josiah, reversing his gait.

"Would it help if you took my horse? I believe both Emma and I would breathe easier knowing that your return would be assured."

"Most kind of you, lad. Yes, I accept your offer. Any time I can avail myself of the fine horseflesh raised by your father, you and Payne, I consider myself a fortunate man indeed."

Josiah Tweedle clapped a hand on Heath's shoulder and the two of them headed for the door and the long flight of stairs down to the hitching post on the grassy lawn, out in front of the courthouse. "You know," chuckled the attorney, "if my clients would pay green money commensurate with the services I perform for them, I might actually be able to afford a decent horse. I had a woman come in my office the other day and set a chicken in a cage upon my desk as payment in full, so she claimed, for a deed that I had drawn up for her mother. Can you beat that? I mean it is 1890 and folks are still paying me with chickens and turnips! And I detest anything with fins or feathers!"

Emma listened to the fading banter between the two men as they turned their backs to her and walked downstairs and outside the courthouse. Within minutes, Heath was back at her side and he could see immediately that Emma was fuming.

"What an impossible situation!" she complained. "First the judge fails to appear, then you pack my attorney off with your horse for another appointment some distance from Grandview and just look at this." Tugging at Heath's sleeve, Emma led him over to the doors of first floor courtroom. Pushing the door to the right open slightly, she motioned for Heath to look inside. The courtroom was packed with people.

"Do you mean to tell me," asked Emma, closing the door, "that all those people in there are going to go ahead of me? At this rate, I shall be here until this time next week!"

"Well, you heard Attorney Tweedle. The judge rides the circuit and when it comes time for him to appear in Grandview, everyone for miles around comes forward with issues to be settled by the judge."

"Am I just supposed to sit and wait all day? What an enormous waste of my time, and yours. You know how I hate sitting idle!" groused Emma.

"Say, I have an idea," brightened Heath. "How about if you march in there to the front of the courtroom and announce that you, Student Nurse Richardson, will hold a free clinic for anyone needing nursing services until the judge appears?" Avoiding her gaze, he added, "Why you could offer to bathe and feed the multitude, wash and dress their wounds, administer enemas, clip hangnails, mix powders, apply mustard plas…"

"Heath Hamilton!" she hissed. "You are not funny!"

"Oh, yes I am!" Whereupon, Heath turned to a woman who was passing by in the hall, smiled and asked, "Madame, do you not find me highly amusing?"

Ignoring Heath, the woman hurried on her way down the hall.

"Oh, heaven save me!" whispered Emma, placing both hands briefly over her eyes. "I have aligned myself with a lunatic!" And then she began to laugh, inaudibly at first behind cupped hands but as Heath began to make wry faces at her, Emma lost control, laughing hysterically.

Taking her by the elbow, Heath cautioned, "Come, let us leave this place as we would not want that big bad constable to appear and lock you up again for disturbing the peace," and the two of them fled as their laughter reverberated off the marble walls of the courthouse.

Back in the courtroom by one-thirty that afternoon, Emma and Heath squeezed into the end of one of the wooden pews occupied by a tall, dust-covered man, his wife, wearing a brightly colored sun bonnet, and six children. The man immediately extended his hand to Heath,

"Howdy. Name's Delbert Ketchem. This here's the missus and them's the young 'uns," Delbert announced proudly indicating his brood.

"Heath Hamilton," he responded shaking the man's hand vigorously.

"And that would be?" asked Delbert leaning forward and pointing to Emma.

"That would be Emma Richardson," said Heath.

"Oh," responded Delbert. Quiet for a few minutes, he added, "Not Hamilton?"

"Not Hamilton," smiled Heath.

"Oh."

At that moment, Angus O'Malley appeared at Emma's side. "Just wanted to let you know that I am here, sweetest, but I am stuck way over there," and Angus pointed to a far corner of the courtroom.

"It makes me feel better knowing that you are here, Angus," smiled Emma, patting O'Malley's cheek.

Angus retreated back to his seat on the other side of the courtroom.

Delbert leaned forward again, addressing Heath, "That one be Mr. Richardson?"

"Nope," responded Heath, eyes forward.

"Oh," said Delbert falling silent for a few minutes before adding, "Kinda confusin'…don't you reckon?"

"Very," responded Heath, never looking at Delbert.

Delbert turned to his wife and with a perplexed look on his face, began to scratch his head until the wailing of one of his offspring occupied his attention. "Shesh, Wilhelmina! Afore I take you across my knee," Delbert warned the child.

"But Caleb's sittin' on my dolly," protested little Wilhelmina.

"Gimme that doll right this here second," ordered Delbert, arm outstretched in front of his wife's thin chest, palm upward in anticipation of receiving the toy. "And jest fer that, Caleb, you'll be a splittin' the wood for supper tonight," Delbert said sternly to his son.

"Aw, Pa!" protested the boy, delivering the mashed doll into his father's waiting hand.

"And I reckon you'll be a splittin' the wood for tomorry's vittles too, jest fer that."

From a side door, the judge's bailiff entered the courtroom to announce loudly, "Hear ye! Hear ye! Hear ye! All rise! The Honorable Theodore J. Freudenberg, Judge of the Southern District, is now presiding."

Judge Freudenberg, in a long black cloak, ascended the bench and immediately rapped his gavel twice. "Please be seated and allow me to express my apologies for the lateness of the hour but due to circumstances beyond my control, I found myself quite suddenly without reliable transportation for several hours. However, I am here now and ready to proceed. We shall endeavor to hear from everyone present, but in the event that time runs out on us today, we shall reconvene here tomorrow commencing at nine o'clock in the morning."

An audible and collective groan filled the courtroom accompanied by murmured complaints. Rapping his gavel upon a small square of black marble affixed to the lower right-hand corner of the judges' desk which dominated the podium centered along the west wall of the high-ceilinged room, Judge Freudenberg barked, "Silence in this courtroom." A hush immediately fell over the gathering, save for the wailing of an infant in the arms of his mother near the door.

"Madam," scolded the judge, pointing his gavel at the woman, "you and the child are welcome in my courtroom but only if you can keep the babe quiet. May I suggest that you remove yourselves to the corridor just beyond the doors until such time as you have pacified the young one," and Judge Freudenberg banged his gavel again while the hapless woman and her infant disappeared from view.

Positioning his glasses on the end of his nose and shuffling the papers before him, Judge Freudenberg began, "In re Delbert Ketchem versus Cletus Donohue, are the litigants present?"

At the mention of Cletus Donohue's name, Emma dug her nails into Heath's thigh, causing him to start. Placing a finger against his lips, Heath warned her to keep silent.

"Beggin' your pardon judge, yer Honor, sir," began Delbert rising from his seat next to Heath, "but the name's Delbert Ketchem, not Ray Delbert Ketchem, your Honor, sir," and the man stood nervously fingering his hat.

"I so note that you are the plaintiff, Delbert Ketchem," replied the judge with a slight smile. "And is Mr. Donohue present?" Since no one stood, the judge ordered his bailiff to call the man's name out loud three times in the courtroom. Still no one stood.

Turning to the courtroom scribe, the judge said, "Please note that the defendant, Cletus Donohue, having been called three times in open court, appears not in re...I mean, in regard to the matter of Ketchem versus Donohue." Addressing Delbert again, the judge asked, "Do you have counsel...an attorney, Mr. Ketchem?"

"No sir."

"Are you prepared to proceed with your complaint against Mr. Donohue?" asked the judge.

"Yessir."

"Would you prefer to testify from your seat there beside your family, or would you prefer to come up here and sit in the witness stand?"

Delbert looked down at his wife, who nudged him forward, "Believe I'll jest come set a spell up there where you can hear me real good, yer Honor, sir," and Delbert excused himself as he squeezed past the knees of Heath and Emma.

As Delbert was about to sit in the witness chair to the judge's left, the bailiff stepped forward and said, "Remain standing. Place your left hand upon the Bible, raise your right hand and repeat after me."

Delbert fiddled with his hat, looking suddenly stricken over at his wife, before deciding to hold the tattered, wide-brimmed hat in his upraised right hand, while his left hand rested on the Bible, as he repeated, "I promise to tell the whole truth and nothing but the truth, so help me God."

"Be seated," said the bailiff.

"I have read your complaint," began Judge Freudenberg. "Did you write it?"

"Uh, no sir, yer Honor, sir. My missus over there done wrote it, fer I can't read ner write," confessed Delbert, motioning to his wife with his tattered hat. Mrs. Ketchem smiled broadly back at the judge at this unexpected acknowledgement of her composition skills.

"What I have been able to glean from your complaint," and the judge nodded to Mrs. Ketchem, "is that you allege a certain Cletus Donohue allowed a large dog, owned by him, to roam about your hog pens where you allege that the said dog killed two of your hogs. Is that the gist of the complaint?"

"Yessir, yer Honor, sir," and all the Ketchems, large and small, nodded agreement with Delbert.

"Do you have witnesses who can support your allegations…that is to say, your claim?"

"Sure do, sir. Them would be me and my boy, Caleb, over yonder," pointing to the boy who, moments earlier, had been grinding his buttocks upon Wilhelmina's doll.

"Tell me, Mr. Ketchem, exactly what it was that you saw which led to the demise of your hogs, but be brief," the judge cautioned the plaintiff.

"Well, sir, it went like this. Some time back, as I was just a finishin' my supper vittles and settlin' in with a good cup of coffee, I done heard all this dang noise a comin' from the first hog pen. I have two, your Honor, sir. One fer the boar and one jest fer the sows and piglets."

"Briefly, now," cautioned the judge.

"And when I runned outside to see what all the hollerin' was about, there was this danged black dog what runs with Cletus all the time and he done jumped into the first pen and was a killin' one of my sows what jest had a litter of prize piglets and she was defendin' them piglets of hers with her very life. And sir, lemme tell you, when one of my sows gets kilt like that, it's like the man jest took food out of the mouths of all my young 'uns," and Delbert paused to nod to his family all of whom nodded back in confirmation of their patriarch's testimony.

"Did you speak to Mr. Donohue about the loss of your sow after the attack by his dog?" asked the judge peering over his glasses at Delbert.

"I surely did, sir."

"And did Mr. Donohue offer to recompense…pay you for the loss of your sow?" asked the judge.

"When I told the bugger what his dog had did over to my place and told him he done owed me money for my dead sow, you know what he done?" asked Delbert, leaning closer to Judge Freudenberg.

"Please tell me what he did," instructed the judge.

"He went back inside that shack what he calls a house and I figgered he was gittin' me the money for my sow, but when he comed back out…Jesus! He pointed a gun to my head," and Delbert thumped his own forehead.

The courtroom erupted with catcalls, whistles and suggestions to, "Hang the bastard!" Angrily the judge slammed his gavel upon the marble until order had been restored. "I shall tolerate no further outbursts. Any more from anyone, and I shall clear the courtroom!"

"What did you do then, Mr. Ketchem?"

"I maybe can't read ner write, yer Honor, sir, but I ain't no fool. I took my ass out of there fast as these here feet would move," and Delbert raised his right leg to display a well-worn boot with a hole in the sole.

Those in the audience stifled their laughter as the judge waved his gavel and glared a warning at them.

"Mr. Ketchem, I am loath to have a boy as young as…"

"Caleb, sir, and he's goin' on eight."

"Yes, as young as Caleb take the witness stand. You mentioned a second hog of yours had been killed by Mr. Donohue's dog. Did Caleb witness that killing or did you?"

"Me and him both seen it, yer Honor, sir."

"Suppose you tell me about the second killing, but be brief."

Delbert Ketchem next described for Judge Freudenberg the vicious attack by Cletus Donohue's dog upon a second sow, leaving out none of the gory details.

Abruptly, the judge banged his gavel announcing, "Here is my ruling. I find that Delbert Ketchem has proven that various sows and piglets belonging to the plaintiff were killed by a dog belonging to the defendant, Cletus Donohue, causing substantial financial hardship upon Mr. Ketchem and his family. Constable Crawford, you are directed to consider filing criminal charges against Cletus Donohue.

I further find that Cletus Donohue has damaged the Ketchem family and that the amount of the damages is the value of the hogs that were destroyed by the dog and that value is five dollars per hog, and one dollar per piglet. Judgment is granted in favor of Delbert Ketchem and against Cletus Donohue in the amount of," Judge Freudenberg paused to scribble upon a piece of paper in front of him. "Seventeen dollars."

As Luke Crawford stood before him, the judge whispered, "You know, Constable, every time I sit in this courthouse, I am adjudicating matters in which this Cletus Donohue is involved. Every single time! The man's name has become as familiar to me as my own father's name. Can you not keep this miscreant off the streets of Grandview?"

"I shall endeavor to do just that, your Honor."

"I better not see or hear of this villain again, I warn you," concluded the judge.

The judge then banged his gavel and shouted, "Next!"

Looking confused, Delbert Ketchem remained seated in the witness stand to ask, "Does all that mean I won or lost?"

"It means, Mr. Ketchem, that you have prevailed in your cause of action and that one Cletus Donohue is ordered to pay you seventeen dollars for your lost hogs and their piglets. Next!"

A beaming Delbert Ketchem relinquished the witness stand, shook hands violently with Heath Hamilton and then ushered his family from the halls of justice.

"In re the matter of the State versus Emma Richardson," and the judge rapped his gavel again.

Trembling, Emma stood with Heath. Josiah Tweedle stood on the far side of the courtroom. "The defendant is here in person and with counsel," announced Attorney Tweedle, motioning to Emma that she should come forward and meet him at the large rectangular table immediately in front of the judge.

Heath took Emma's elbow and led her forward but Josiah whispered to him to return to his seat, adding, "Rest assured, Heath, I can handle matters from here."

"To the charge of Disturbing the Peace, how does the defendant plead?" asked Judge Freudenberg, looking only at Emma's lawyer.

"Not guilty, your Honor," and Josiah pushed a chair over from the end of the table for Emma as she seemed in imminent danger of collapsing.

"Is there something wrong with your client?" asked the judge, noting Emma's violent trembling.

"What is wrong with this young woman," began Josiah Tweedle drawing himself up to his full height of six feet and five inches, while pushing back the mane of white hair that threatened to obstruct his vision, "is the false charge that has been brought against her by the State," and Josiah turned to stab an accusatory finger at Manfred Crockett, the prosecuting attorney for the State, who was standing near the witness chair.

"Would you, Attorney Tweedle, and you, Mr. Crockett, please approach the bench," instructed Judge Freudenberg. Leaning forward, the judge whispered to the two imposing figures who stood before him, "Gentlemen, I am not convinced that a trial is in order here," and he began shuffling through the papers on the desk in front of him while the two men stood at attention.

"Rather, I believe that a pre-charge hearing would be more relevant, especially since the matter immediately following involves one Evaline Bushrod who has been charged with the identical infraction. I propose to consolidate these two matters. Then, gentlemen, it is my intention to proceed to determine if there is sufficient evidence to warrant charging either of these women with a crime. Do we agree?"

"I agree with your Honor," said Josiah Tweedle.

"Suits me," added Manfred Crockett.

"Mr. Crockett, please call your first witness," instructed the judge so that his voice was audible throughout the courtroom.

"Your Honor, I would call Miss Marjolein Beauchamp to the stand," said Manfred looking around the courtroom for the witness, who rose from the middle of the third pew to face the prosecutor. Carefully, the young woman picked her way past the cramped quarters of the litigants in her pew and without hesitation, walked to the witness stand, right hand already in the air and left one poised to place upon the Bible, having paid close attention to Delbert Ketchem's proceedings.

After Miss Beauchamp was sworn in, Manfred Crockett instructed the pretty young woman to be seated, "Please tell the Court your name."

"I am Miss Marjolein Beauchamp," the young woman with chestnut-colored hair said pleasantly to the judge.

Manfred Crockett addressed the judge, "Your Honor may now inquire."

"How long have you been a resident of Grandview, Miss Beauchamp?" asked Judge Freudenberg.

"All my life, sir."

"And exactly how long is that?"

"Twenty-two years."

"What were you doing on the afternoon of July the twenty-ninth?" asked the judge.

"I had just finished my piano lesson and was standing on the front steps of my music teacher's home on Elm Street, waiting for my father to escort me home, when I heard a loud altercation between two women," explained Miss Beauchamp.

"What did you see next?" inquired Judge Freudenberg.

"To further clarify the witness' testimony, your Honor, Miss Beauchamp just testified that she 'heard a loud altercation'. She did not testify that she saw an altercation, only that she heard it," observed Josiah Tweedle.

"So noted," responded the judge, adding, "Very well then, what did you hear, Miss Beauchamp?"

"I heard…" began Marjolein.

"Excuse me, your Honor, but would that not be hearsay testimony?" asked Attorney Tweedle respectfully.

"Counsel, this is an informal inquiry by the Court and I shall pose the questions that I consider relevant to this action," Judge Freudenberg reminded Josiah.

Judge Freudenberg then reminded the witness, "Miss Beauchamp, please answer my question. What did you hear as you waited on Elm Street?"

"What I heard, your Honor, was the sound of two women yelling at each other," answered Marjolein, nervously twisting her handkerchief.

"What did you do next?" inquired Judge Freudenberg.

"I walked over to where the two women were arguing on the corner of Longmeadow and Elm just in time to see the larger woman, who is over there," and Marjolein pointed at Evaline Bushrod who sat prominently in the front pew, "attack the smaller woman with her nails, like this," whereupon the witness demonstrated a gouging motion at her own face with her fingers curled up like claws.

"Do either of you gentlemen have any questions of this witness?" asked the judge, looking from Josiah to Manfred.

"No, your Honor," responded the prosecutor.

"Well, I do," announced Josiah, pushing his hair back with his spectacles before addressing the witness. Rising to his feet, Josiah moved closer to Marjolein.

"Now Miss Beauchamp, please describe for the Court what you saw occur on July the twenty-ninth at the corner of Longmeadow and Elm," Josiah instructed the witness.

"I saw that big woman over there, like I said, attack that little lady over there with her nails. She made long bloody gashes down the poor little lady's face," testified Marjolein looking sympathetically over at Emma.

"What did you see next?" prodded Josiah.

"That little lady put her hands to her cheeks, like this," and Marjolein demonstrated a covering motion with her own hands upon her cheeks, "and moved back away from the big woman."

"Wait a moment. Let me make sure I heard you correctly. Did you say, Miss Beauchamp, that Emma Richardson, the 'little lady,' my client to whom you refer, 'moved back away from the big woman?'"

"Yes, that is exactly what I said because that is exactly what I saw."

"So…"

And before Josiah could ask another question, the witness added, "That little lady was trying to get away from the big woman."

"Thank you, my dear," said Josiah flashing a smile at the witness and patting around his face, found his spectacles on top of his head before saying, "No further questions, your Honor."

As Marjolein returned to her seat, the judge asked, "Mr. Prosecutor and Counselor Tweedle, do you have any additional witnesses?" Hearing none, the judge then called Evaline Bushrod to the stand.

"Eh? What?" asked Elmer Bushrod who had accompanied his wife to the courthouse. Throughout the afternoon, Evaline's octogenarian husband had sat silently next to his wife while leaning forward on an imposing, hand-carved walking stick in the first pew, hand cupped behind his right ear as he strained to hear the proceedings. Several times, the elderly man had appeared on the verge of dozing off, slumping forward precariously. Only the swift intervention of Evaline had prevented Elmer from toppling onto the floor.

"Shush, Elmer!" whispered Evaline to her spouse. "It is my turn to testify," and rising importantly from her seat, Evaline clasped her hands piously before her as she walked dramatically to the witness chair, crocheted purse dangling from her wrist.

After she had been sworn in by the Court's bailiff, the judge said pleasantly, "Good afternoon, Mrs. Bushrod."

"Good afternoon, Judge Freudenberg," Evaline replied unctuously.

"Please be seated," the judge instructed her, "and tell me how long you have been a resident of Grandview."

Evaline tittered, "Oh, if I reveal that fact, I shall be revealing my age."

"You may whisper it in my ear if you prefer," replied the judge.

Leaning far to the right in her chair and placing a protective hand to shield her words from the audience, Evaline whispered in a coy and barely audible voice, "Fifty-five years."

"Let it be put into the record that the witness is fifty-five years of age," announced Judge Freudenberg to the courtroom scribe.

Loud laughter filled the room, prompting the judge to bang his gavel before continuing.

"Where were you on the afternoon of July the twenty-ninth of this year?" pressed the judge, appraising Evaline over the top of his spectacles

"I was shopping at Hummel's on Court Street," Evaline replied.

"Did you have occasion to engage Mrs. Richardson in conversation?" asked Judge Freudenberg.

"I did. The woman was standing in front of a crate of peaches and when I asked her to step aside so that I might select some fruit, the woman launched a scathing verbal attack upon me in front of all of Hummel's customers, causing me terrible emotional distress," and here Evaline dabbed at her eyes with a pale yellow linen handkerchief.

Regaining her composure, Evaline stated, "Then, when I tried to escape her vitriolic diatribe, the woman chased after me onto the main thoroughfare and oh…the horror of it!"

"What horror is it to which you refer?" asked Judge Freudenberg.

"That…that…" and Evaline pointed to Emma where she sat at the table next to Josiah Tweedle, "person jumped upon me with such violence that she knocked me to the ground and then tied me up with her hair ribbon and my own sash from around my waist. I was so humiliated and wounded, I really did not know if I would ever recover. At which point the constable, not realizing who was at fault, imprisoned me until my dear, sweet, elderly husband could come to collect me," and Evaline began to sob into her handkerchief.

"Would you like a brief recess in order to regain your composure, madam?" asked Judge Freudenberg.

"No your Honor. I consider it my civic duty to continue on until justice has prevailed," sniffed Evaline, still dabbing around with her handkerchief.

"Now, madam, as I understand your testimony," the judge began again once Evaline had dried her tears, "you contend that Mrs. Richardson abused you verbally in Hummel's store, followed you out into the street where she bumped into you..."

"No, that is not what I said," Evaline scowled at the judge. "I said, that person jumped upon me, knocking me to the ground and then bound my wrists and ankles."

"Ah, yes...in much the same manner one would truss up a cloven-footed creature. Now tell me, Mrs. Bushrod, did she completely hamstring you? That is to say, did she draw your ankles up to your wrists, either front or back, and tie all four together?" asked Judge Freudenberg, leaning down to scrutinize the pinched features of Evaline Bushrod.

Evaline removed a silk fan from her purse and began to wave it in front of her face as if overcome by a sudden rush of heat. Finally she replied, "I do not appreciate being compared to a...a...piece of livestock and your characterization of me as a trussed-up cow in the middle of Grandview is...insulting to say the least."

The courtroom exploded in laughter, prompting the judge to bang his gavel three times. Ignoring the crowd of spectators, the judge leaned even closer to Evaline to admonish her, "This is my courtroom and you do not dictate to me how I choose to clarify testimony which has already been written into the record," and he banged his gavel once, causing Evaline to jump like a mouse caught in a trap.

Leaning back in his chair, Judge Freudenberg next addressed Josiah Tweedle and Manfred Crockett, "Gentlemen, it would appear that this witness has made some serious allegations. Do either of you wish to inquire further, seeking clarification?"

"Actually," said the prosecutor from his seat, "I believe you have already asked the pertinent questions and I have therefore concluded with this witness."

"I should think so, but kindly remember to rise when next you address this Court."

Since Josiah Tweedle was already on his feet, adjusting his red tie and his spectacles, the judge looked over at Emma's attorney. "Your Honor," began Josiah, "I should like to ask some questions of this witness, if you please."

"Be my guest, Mr. Tweedle," responded the judge.

"Good afternoon, madam," began Josiah politely, bending slightly in the direction of the witness.

Evaline continued to fan herself silently, as beads of perspiration began to trickle down her forehead, where they closed ranks just above her eyebrows.

"Since the judge has already elucidated your initial testimony as to the circumstances of your encounter with my client, Emma Richardson," and Josiah walked over to his client and placed a protective hand on her shoulder, "I shall endeavor to avoid treading upon that same ground."

"How tall are you?" Josiah asked bluntly, standing off to one side so as not to obstruct the witness from view.

"That is an impertinent question!" snapped Evaline, visibly sinking lower in the witness chair, feverishly fanning herself.

Bang! Down went the judge's gavel. "You will answer defense counsel!" boomed the judge.

Flinching, Evaline peered out from behind her fan. "I...I...am not sure," she stammered.

"Oh, come, come, madam! Each of us present here today knows how tall we are. Stand up and I shall measure you if you cannot remember," suggested Josiah.

"No need," responded Evaline with a dismissive gesture of her fan, "I am five feet and five inches tall."

"At the risk of being labeled 'impertinent' by the witness again, your Honor," and Josiah bowed slightly to the judge before turning to Evaline Bushrod, "I should like to know how much you weigh."

The audience gasped in unison. Her face contorted in a moment of panic, Evaline hid behind her silk fan.

"Answer the question," bellowed the judge.

"In all fairness to the woman, your Honor, she may not actually know her own heft. Therefore, I would suggest that we employ the scales of Justica from out in the hall to..."

"One-six-five," whispered Evaline from behind her fan.

"Only sixty-five pounds?" asked Josiah in mock surprise.

"Speak up, madam. How much do you weigh?" asked the judge, gavel poised in midair.

"One hundred and sixty-five pounds," Evaline answered rapidly.

"Are you a married woman?" continued Attorney Tweedle.

"Yes."

"Is your husband present in the courtroom?"

"Yes."

"Where is he, madam?" Not waiting for her answer, Josiah turned to the people in the courtroom and, scanning the throng, asked, "Would Mr. Bushrod kindly stand?"

"He cannot," replied Evaline, snapping her fan shut.

"Forgive me, madam, but I did not hear you. Would you repeat what you just said?"

"My husband cannot stand without assistance."

"And why is that Mrs. Bushrod?"

"Because of his age and his constitution."

"What is Mr. Bushrod's age, please?"

"Eighty-four."

"And what is his constitution?"

"He suffers from a stroke that he endured last winter."

"I am sorry to hear that, Mrs. Bushrod," Josiah said, solicitously touching the back of the witness chair briefly before asking, "Whom do you employ to care for your husband?"

"Judge Freudenberg!" protested Manfred Crockett jumping to his feet. "I fail to understand what these questions have to do with Emma Richardson."

"The relevance of my line of questioning will soon become apparent," Josiah addressed the judge.

"See that it does," responded Judge Freudenberg. "Continue on, Counselor."

Walking over to the scribe, Josiah asked for a reading of his last question.

"'Whom do you employ to care for your husband?'" read the courtroom scribe.

Evaline sat motionless, fan closed upon her lap, forehead dripping.

"Answer the question, Mrs. Bushrod," warned the judge.

"I do not employ the services of anyone to care for my husband."

"Who cares for him then?" asked Josiah.

"I do. I am quite capable of caring for my husband by myself."

"I see. Did you and your eighty-four year old husband who suffered a stroke less than a year ago have assistance today in climbing up the twenty-two limestone steps that lead to this floor of the courthouse?" Josiah looked out over the expectant faces in the courtroom.

"No."

"Please tell us then, how you and Mr. Bushrod climbed that formidable flight of stairs, unassisted," Josiah Tweedle made a snapping noise with his suspenders.

"I...I..." stammered Evaline.

"Yes?"

"I carried him…piggyback," whispered Evaline.

The courtroom erupted again and Judge Freudenberg flayed the marble square with his gavel.

"Forgive me, Mrs. Bushrod, but I did not hear you. Could you repeat your answer to my question?" Josiah asked, feigning deafness.

"I carried him."

"You carried your husband upon your back all the way up the twenty-two steps leading to this floor of the courthouse, Mrs. Bushrod?"

"Actually, I paused to rest several times as we made our way up the steps," explained Evaline.

The spectators tittered. Judge Freudenberg threatened them with his gavel.

"What a formidable feat, Mrs. Bushrod. Bravo!" and Josiah put his hands together in mock applause.

Evaline's self-satisfied smile quickly faded from her lips when she saw the dark expression on the prosecutor's face.

Whipping his spectacles from his face, Josiah Tweedle announced, "No further questions, your Honor," and returned to sit next to Emma at the long table in front of Judge Freudenberg.

"Do you, Mr. Crockett, wish to call any additional witnesses?" asked the judge.

"Not at this time, sir," responded Manfred still seated.

Bang! Down went the gavel. "Rise to your feet, man, when you address the Court!" boomed the judge.

Manfred sprang to his feet, "Begging your pardon, your Honor. I do not wish to call any other witnesses."

"Very well, Mr. Prosecutor. Then Attorney Tweedle, please call your witnesses," instructed the judge.

"I shall call only one witness, your Honor," announced Josiah after standing to button his coat. Stanching the flow of white hair with his glasses, Josiah smiled over at his client, "Emma Richardson, please take the stand."

Emma had remained motionless in the hard wooden chair for the duration of the proceedings, hands folded on the table in front of her, mindful of her attorney's instructions that she was not to react to anything that she heard or saw. "Do not under any circumstances draw the judge's attention to yourself," cautioned Josiah.

Emma rose stiffly from her seat. Offering his arm to her, Josiah escorted Emma to the witness stand and when she turned head-on for the first time to face the rank gathering of humanity which overflowed the courtroom, there was an audible gasp as the spectators caught their first glimpse of the ugly red welts still visible on her face. Even the judge had difficulty tearing his gaze from Emma's injured face.

"Please state your full name for the Court," Josiah began, smiling confidently at his witness.

"Emma Miller Richardson."

"And what is your profession?"

"I am a student nurse at Angel of Mercy Hospital in Clarksburg," Emma responded, carefully maintaining eye contact with her attorney.

"How old are you?"

"I am thirty years old."

"How tall are you?"

"I am four feet and ten inches, sir."

"How much do you weigh?"

Without hesitation, Emma responded, "I weigh ninety-five pounds."

Josiah broke eye contact with his client to face the spectators, hands on his hips, "Tell us, Emma Richardson, were you required to take an oath when you became a student nurse?"

"Yes sir."

"Did you swear upon the Book of God," and here Josiah grabbed the Bible from the corner of the judge's desk and held it aloft, "as you took that oath?"

"I did, sir."

"What was it that you swore before Almighty God on the day when you became a student nurse?" and Josiah strode over to his client and thrust the Bible at Emma.

Holding the Bible with both of her hands, Emma recited, "I, Emma Miller Richardson, do swear that for the remainder of my natural life I shall endeavor to preserve human life, offer comfort to those who are suffering, assist the afflicted and facilitate the healing of the sick or the injured. I shall comport myself with dignity and good will toward all. I believe that each life is sacred and I believe that where there is life, there is always hope," and Emma handed the Bible back to Josiah.

"Do you believe in that oath which you just recited for all of us here today?" Josiah asked the diminutive woman whose feet dangled above the floor from the witness chair.

"I most assuredly do, sir."

"What lead you to become a nurse, Emma?" Josiah continued.

"I have a widowed mother and three small boys to support, sir," answered Emma.

"Do you have a husband?"

"My husband abandoned me and the children just before the birth of my third child."

Shouts of, "Rat! Scoundrel! Dog! Womanizer!" reverberated throughout the courtroom, prompting the judge to rebuke the onlookers yet again.

"Are you a church-going woman?" asked Josiah.

"I am, sir."

"And which church is it that you attend?"

"I have attended the Grandview Methodist Church for the past twenty-seven years, the same church in which I was baptized and married," Emma replied quietly.

The courtroom began to buzz. Down went Judge Freudenberg's gavel.

"What were you doing at Hummel's store on July the twenty-ninth?" asked Josiah of his witness.

"I was purchasing peaches for my mother."

"Did you have occasion to exchange words with Evaline Bushrod?"

"I did," began Emma looking directly out at Evaline.

"What was the gist of the verbal exchange between the two of you during the time you were purchasing peaches inside Hummel's?"

"Evaline accused me of fornicating in front of my children," said Emma, mincing no words.

The courtroom erupted with angry sounds. Loud hissing and booing filled the stagnant air and a tossed apple core came within inches of striking Evaline Bushrod.

Judge Freudenberg beat the marble square unmercifully with his wooden gavel, shouting, "Order! Order in this courtroom, I say!"

"What did you do in the face of such an unfounded accusation?" asked Josiah, pausing briefly in front of Evaline Bushrod before resuming his pacing.

"I moved away from her to the far end of the counter, paid for the peaches that I had selected and left the store."

"Where were you going?"

"Home," answered Emma simply.

"Did you make it back home?"

"No."

"Tell me why you were unable to return to your home, please," pursued Josiah, removing his glasses.

"Because Evaline Bushrod followed me out of the store and attacked me at the corner of Elm and Longmeadow."

"Describe the attack for me, Emma."

"She lunged at me with her claws and dug them into my face, ripping the skin all the way down my cheeks," and Emma demonstrated with her own hands upon her face.

"So that is how you acquired the red welts here and here?" asked Josiah, indicating both sides of Emma's face with his folded spectacles.

"Yes."

"What did you do to defend yourself against this heinous attack upon your person?" Josiah questioned Emma, pausing to replace his glasses and look over at Evaline Bushrod.

"When Evaline attempted to gouge my face a second time, I grabbed both her wrists and threw all my weight against her, knocking Evaline to the ground. Then, I bound up her wrists and ankles to keep Evaline from injuring me again," Emma stated.

"What happened next?"

"Constable Luke Crawford handcuffed me and took me and Evaline to the Grandview Jail," Emma concluded.

"With what did the constable charge you, Emma?"

"Disturbing the peace," Emma answered.

"I have no further questions, your Honor," concluded Josiah Tweedle.

"Mr. Prosecutor, do you wish to examine this witness?" asked Judge Freudenberg, glaring over at Manfred.

"Don't vote for that there constable!" yelled someone in the audience. "He picks on helpless women!"

BANG! BANG! BANG! Down went the judge's gavel. "Bailiff! Remove that man at once!" stormed Judge Freudenberg, leveling his gavel at no one in particular.

While the bailiff struggled to ascertain who the offender in the audience was, Manfred Crockett rose to his feet and muttered, "I have no wish to examine this witness."

"Please conclude your remarks then, Mr. Prosecutor," instructed the judge.

"I have your Honor," said Manfred, with a wretched expression on his face.

"Mr. Tweedle, please conclude your remarks as they pertain to this case then," Judge Freudenberg instructed Josiah.

"Your Honor, the prosecuting attorney over there," and Josiah pointed his folded spectacles at Manfred who was trying to disappear, "has not established that Emma Richardson committed a crime. Constable Luke Crawford arrested my client and then shackled her, like a common criminal, on the main thoroughfare of Grandview, the town in which she was born thirty years ago.

For twenty-seven of those years, Emma Richardson has been an active member of the Grandview Methodist Church. That same church where Emma Richardson exchanged wedding vows with the man whom she promised to love, honor and obey. How did her husband repay Emma's love and trust? With abuse and abandonment," Josiah answered his own question, while striding angrily from one side of the courtroom to the other, addressing first the audience, then the judge and back again.

"Emma Richardson," continued Josiah Tweedle, "made a noble and commendable decision. She would study to become a nurse in order that she might be able to support her three children and her mother. She took an oath to care for the suffering, the ill, the afflicted, the injured and the dying for the rest of her natural life. Indeed, Emma Richardson has already demonstrated her inspired skills and compassion to such an extent that people seek her out that they may be healed and comforted by her. Word has gotten around Grandview that Emma Richardson is gifted," Josiah paused next to Emma and placed his hand lightly upon her shoulder.

Resuming his relentless pacing, Josiah then asked, "But how do we, the residents of Grandview, repay this gifted healer in our midst? We curse her. We vilify her. We attack her. We cause her harm," and each time Josiah punched his folded glasses through the air at Evaline Bushrod, where she sat cowering in the pew with her drooling octogenarian husband.

"As if that were not sufficient," Josiah walked directly in front of Luke Crawford, "we shackle Emma Richardson, who stands four feet and ten inches tall and who weighs ninety-five pounds, because she has the audacity to defend herself," Josiah pointed at Evaline, "against the crazed onslaught of a woman who stands five feet and five inches tall and who outweighs Emma Richardson by seventy pounds!"

"Further, we repay this Florence Nightingale in our midst by charging her with 'disturbing the peace' when the only peace that has been disturbed is her own. And the only disturbance," thundered Josiah, "has been wrought upon her beautiful face," whereupon Josiah grabbed Emma by the chin and thrust her face around and forward so the judge could have a clear view of the gouges left by Evaline Bushrod.

"Emma Richardson acted in self-defense on July the twenty-ninth. Emma Richardson did not take an oath to allow others to mutilate her," bellowed

Josiah, hair flowing wildly unfettered about his face. "Emma Richardson took an oath to preserve life, and that oath included the preservation of her own life as well." Josiah returned to the long rectangular table and sat down without further ado.

At once the courtroom erupted with applause, whistles, foot-stomping and shouts of, "Hear! Hear!" Prolonged banging with the gavel brought no cessation of the din and the bailiff scurried about the room attempting to collar the worst offenders and eject them into the hall. Evaline Bushrod was struck in the head by a half-eaten leg of fried chicken.

"Ladies and gentlemen," began Judge Theodore Freudenberg, readjusting his glasses on his nose, "we have been gathered here this afternoon in the courtroom to determine if there is sufficient evidence to bring criminal charges against Emma Miller Richardson and Evaline Bushrod. Both the State and Emma Richardson have presented compelling evidence which merits further consideration by the Court. However, due to the lateness of the hour, I shall now retire to my chambers to review the evidence submitted, examine relevant cases and statutes in order to prepare my judgment which I shall render here in this courtroom tomorrow at nine o'clock in the morning. Court adjourned!" and Judge Freudenberg banged the gavel once, before rising from the bench to disappear in a swirl of black cloak.

Once again the courtroom erupted with the raucous and angry outbursts of those who were faced with the passage of yet another day before they too would have their say in open court. Many of the litigants had traveled long distances to have their grievances heard and adjudicated. The courtroom had been unmercifully hot that afternoon and that circumstance, coupled with the pungent smell of unwashed bodies, had prompted several onlookers to vacate their seats for some fresh air on the front lawn of the courthouse, which by early evening had taken on the air of a military encampment.

Josiah Tweedle took Emma by the arm and led her back toward Heath who immediately asked, "How do you think we did?"

"I think we did just splendidly," answered Josiah as he patted Heath reassuringly upon the back. "Do you know the old saying, Heath, that 'a picture is worth a thousand words?'"

"Yes sir."

"Well," laughed Josiah as the trio made their way through the doors of the courtroom and out into the marble corridor with the rancid throng, "this is our ninety-five pound, four foot and ten inch tall picture here." Josiah hugged Emma to him before adding, "In my book, she was worth about two thousand words this afternoon!"

For the first time since the proceedings began, Emma allowed herself to smile. "So you really think I have a chance?"

"I would be very surprised indeed," replied Josiah, "if the judge does not dismiss the charges against you."

"Emma! Emma!" shouted Angus, threading his way toward Heath, Josiah and Emma as they walked together down the long corridor to the exit.

Emma paused and turned around to wait for her friend, the reporter, to catch up with them. "Bless your poor, sweet, little heart!" exclaimed Angus, planting a kiss upon Emma's hand. "You were absolutely magnificent upon the witness stand and just look at all these notes I took," and Angus waved page after page of his cramped scribbles in pencil.

"Thank you for being present, today, Angus. Only a true friend would sit for that long and under such deplorable circumstances to lend support," Emma smiled, a sickly pallor tinting her face.

Rattling on, Angus turned next to Josiah Tweedle, "And I believe tomorrow's headline will be, 'ATTORNEY INVOKES THE SCALES OF JUSTICA.'" All three men laughed, except Emma.

"I fail to see the humor in that," she commented.

"Come with me," instructed Josiah. Still laughing, Emma's attorney turned around and waded into the oncoming swarm of humanity which was still exiting the courtroom. Pulling Emma with him, Josiah made his way back to an alcove to the right of the room they had just departed.

Stopping before an imposing bronze statute of a Greek woman dressed in a toga with flowing hair and a blindfold covering her eyes, Josiah said, "Emma, permit me to introduce you to Justica, the symbol of unbiased justice that we, who are so sworn, endeavor to attain."

"She looks like a Greek goddess," commented Emma, lightly tracing the hard folds of Justica's gown, noting the scales that the statue held in one hand and the sword that she held in the other.

"She is a goddess…a goddess whom I woo assiduously each and every day of my life in this courthouse," and Josiah bent into the alcove to kiss the blindfolded woman upon her cold hand. "And every day she says to me, 'Josiah, it matters not that you are a cunning flatterer or that you pay such shameless attention to me. I shall continue to hold my scales high and weigh the merits of each case set before me, heedless of all corporal distractions. I shall do so unfettered and undisturbed by your cheap ministrations to my femininity.'"

The men were enjoying a huge laugh in the now vacant corridor. Emma stood motionless, gazing up at the bronze woman who rested atop a marble base. She placed her hand briefly upon each pan of Justica's scales, permanently suspended in a neutral pose. "So, it was all a ruse?" asked Emma, looking at Josiah.

"What was all a ruse, dear?" asked Josiah, still smiling.

"When you said in the courtroom that you would weigh Evaline upon the scales of Justica."

"But of course. The woman was too ignorant to know who Justica is or that my suggestion to weigh her upon Justica's scales was a mere figure of speech," Josiah responded, the twinkle beginning to fade from his eyes.

"So, you tricked Evaline into answering your question?" pursued Emma, still looking up at the statue.

"Oh, come, Emma," interjected Heath. "The man has in all likelihood gotten the charges against you dismissed and you want to quibble about semantics?"

"He was untruthful," said Emma, suddenly sullen. "He duped Evaline into believing that he could ascertain her weight upon the scales of Justica if she would not answer his question."

"I apologize for Emma, Mr. Tweedle," attempted Heath, putting an arm around her shoulders, "but this has all been a miserable ordeal for her. You know...first being attacked publicly, handcuffed on the main street, marched off to jail and finally this hearing which has dragged on far too long. Now, she is being asked to wait overnight to learn her fate. Obviously, Emma is in need of rest and I must take her home at once." Heath stuck out his hand to Josiah, thanked the attorney and bid him farewell, escorting Emma firmly from the premises.

"Well, I declare! If that is not just like a damned woman!" cursed Josiah to Angus who remained at his side, pencil poised in midair.

Together, Angus and Josiah stood watching Emma and Heath disappear down the long corridor.

"Frightening, is it not?" asked Josiah, looking down at Angus. "I mean the way the female mind works. Not at all like ours, eh? It never ceases to amaze me that these lovely creatures, to whose external qualities we are so drawn, can be so lacking in rational thought. The good Lord obviously knew what He was doing when He gave us men the upper hand. Would you agree, my friend?" Josiah asked of his still-silent companion.

Angus nodded his assent.

"Say, Mr. O'Malley, how about joining me for supper?"

"It would be my pleasure," answered Angus, finding his tongue once again.

As Heath and Emma were descending the limestone steps of the courthouse, Emma paused, "Heath, please wait a moment. I must sit down as I feel faint."

At once, Heath gathered Emma into his arms and placed her gently between the paws of a recumbent limestone lion guarding the courthouse staircase. Standing before her, Heath held onto Emma's arms to support her and instructed, "Breathe deeply of the fresh air. Come now! Breathe in and out! Deep breaths!"

Heath inhaled and exhaled with Emma until she said, "I am feeling better now but can we sit here for a bit?"

"Of course we can," and Heath sat next to Emma with a protective arm wrapped around her sagging shoulders.

"I apologize for what I said to Josiah back in there," began Emma. "My remarks were inappropriate, in light of the fact that he did a most magnificent job in the courtroom."

Heath squeezed her slightly. The two of them sat silently taking in the scene below them on the lawn surrounding the courthouse. Since many of those who had been present in the courthouse for the past two days had yet to have their grievances brought before the judge and since most had traveled some distance to be heard, the unrequited throng was preparing to make camp for the night.

Horses were tethered to trees, quilts were thrown casually about over the long grass and the sweet smell of hardwood smoke from numerous cook fires permeated the early evening air. Small children chased after a tall boy rolling a metal barrel hoop along the dusty street. From a family's camp by a cluster of dogwood trees, drifted the mournful sound of a harmonica. A furiously barking spotted dog chased an orange cat up a nearby oak and crickets began to add their voices to the evening concert.

"It all looks so normal, does it not?" asked Emma taking in the scene before her.

"Umm," agreed Heath.

"One could scarcely deduce from our vantage point that anything was amiss among those down there preparing to cook their supper," she continued.

"What is it that you feel is amiss among Justica's dinner guests?" Heath teasingly asked Emma.

"Think about it for a moment. So much hangs in the balance for each and every one of us here today," sighed Emma contemplating the rabble just below her feet. "Delbert Ketchem was fortunate. His proceedings are over and the judge ruled in his favor but what about that man over there? Will he be so lucky tomorrow?" Emma asked, indicating a disheveled, unshaven older man who stood on the perimeter of his family's encampment, sipping coffee from a tin cup.

"I overheard him say that he and his family live on a twenty acre tract of land some distance from Grandview. Apparently some unknown upstart suddenly appeared out of nowhere waving a deed to the man's property. Our man down there has exercised squatter's rights to the property for the last twelve years and…"

"Our man?" Heath interrupted Emma.

"Well, I mean that as a figure of speech because…"

"Emma, you must stop this," cautioned Heath. "You are already a bundle of nerves over your own problems and those of your patients and now you are going to take on that fellow's worries too."

"I cannot seem to help it. The more I look at those around me, the more I realize there are so many who are in trouble, who need assistance…"

"And that is exactly why there are lawyers and doctors and nurses and grand-mothers and school teachers and good neighbors," Heath rattled on, leaning down to give Emma a peck on her cheek.

"But that man has no lawyer and he is in very real danger of losing his family's home," protested Emma.

"Then, that man has a fool for a client and speaking of home, let us go there at once," Heath stood and prepared to remove Emma from her perch under the lion's jaws.

"What is that supposed to mean? The part about the man having a fool for a client?" persisted Emma.

"It means," explained Heath, "that any man who is not a lawyer and under-takes to represent himself in a court of law has a fool for a client."

Heath gave Emma a leg up onto Grit's saddle and turned to untie the horse's reins.

"Does that mean, then, that if I apply a bandage to my own wound that I like-wise have a fool for a patient?" Emma continued belligerently.

"It means," answered Heath once again as he handed the reins to Emma, "that you are going to ride home all alone unless you hold your tongue. You are exhausted and just itching for a fight. Well, I refuse to engage in your favorite pastime. Now, get along home and I shall walk. The exercise will be good for me," and Heath strode past Emma out into the street.

Emma dug her heels into Grit's sides and trotted down Longmeadow with her nose in the air. That evening, a pall hung over the house on High Point Avenue. Emma refused to speak to Heath. Heath refused to speak to Emma. The three boys all spoke at once until Mary, sensing the discord, whisked them upstairs for bedtime. Emma locked her bedroom door that night and Heath slept on the back porch with Brute.

The strain of the all legal wrangling of the previous two days was evident the next morning as Emma, Heath and the boys assembled at Mary's kitchen table to eat their breakfast. Emma was pale and somber as she appeared in the kitchen dressed all in black. Heath had not shaved for the past several days and dark circles underscored the brilliant blue of his eyes, which were heavy-lidded with fatigue.

Looking up from the cracked blue and white bowl of cooked mush, thick with butter, sorghum and cream, George was prompted to ask, "Did somebody die, Ma?"

"What makes you ask that, George?"

"Well, you look sad and you got on those black clothes of yours that you always wear when somebody dies," responded the boy, shoveling the steaming mush into his mouth.

"Talkin' to that judge is what made her sad, Georgie," Will began to explain helpfully, "and when you're goin' to talk to that judge you're 'posed to wear black. Right, Ma?"

"Yes, Will, that is about the size of it," and Emma bent to plant a kiss on the top of Will's head.

Seeking to change the subject, Mary interjected brightly, "Heath, have you noticed what an absolutely perfect morning it is?"

Heath rose from the table to pour himself a second cup of coffee, pausing at the open window above the kitchen sink to inhale deeply. "Ah, Mary, you are so right. It is going to be a wonderful day!" and he winked at Emma, who ignored him.

Breakfast was difficult. Even though it was August, a palpable chill hung in the air. Johnny added to the contentious atmosphere by throwing a tantrum and refusing to eat.

"Here, give me that spoon!" George ordered, wrestling with his baby brother for control of the spoon.

"Boys! Boys!" exclaimed Mary. "There is no need for this. Johnny is obviously not hungry this morning," she reasoned.

"Oh, he's hungry all right," responded Will. "He just don't like mush but when I explain that it's good for him and feed it to him real nice and gentle, he'll eat for me. Just watch this."

Talking sweetly with Johnny in their oft rehearsed banter of baby prattle, Will convinced Johnny that he was the mama bird come to feed the baby bird a worm.

Each time the spoon drew near Johnny's mouth, Will would exhort, "Okay, baby bird, show mama bird how you make the worm disappear."

Will sat patiently feeding his baby brother while the adults, happy for the distraction that the antics of the children afforded, sat silently eating their own breakfast.

Wiping his mouth upon the checkered napkin, Heath rose to clear the table. "That, my young friend, Will, was showmanship training at its finest. I believe that you have all the hallmarks of a gifted horse trainer inside that head of yours. What do you say, pardner, should we maybe start educating you to help me train the colts at the farm?"

"You mean it, Heath?" asked Will, delighted to have been singled out for recognition.

"You bet I do, but right this moment, your mother and I need to be on our way back to the courthouse to hear the judge's ruling," concluded Heath, offering his hand to Emma, who ignored the gesture.

As Heath and Emma walked down the front hall and exited the house on High Point Avenue, Heath, seeking to lighten her mood, asked, "Now, madam, what is your preferred mode of transportation? Foot? Horse? Pig? Dog? Uh...I know!" and Heath knelt in front of her, "Piggyback!"

Emma stood looking at the handsome man who knelt before her in the sunlight on the front lawn of the house on High Point Avenue. Instinctively, she reached out a small hand to touch the stubble of his cheek and smooth the blond curls behind his ears. Her gaze never wavered from his as she leaned forward to kiss his lips. For a fleeting moment, Emma wished she could disappear forever into the depths of those blue eyes. Instead, Emma turned and began heading toward town, offering her hand for Heath to take as the two of them walked silently through the streets of Grandview for her nine o'clock appearance before Judge Theodore Freudenberg.

The rabble that had overflowed the lawn surrounding the Grandview Courthouse the previous evening had once again filled Judge Freudenberg's courtroom to overflowing. Since there was not a vacant seat in the room, Emma and Heath stood waiting back by the door. As the clock in the cupola atop the courthouse struck the hour of nine o'clock, the judge's bailiff entered the courtroom, calling, "Hear ye! Hear ye! Hear ye! All rise! The Honorable Theodore J. Freudenberg, Judge of the Southern District, is now presiding."

"Be seated, ladies and gentlemen," began Judge Freudenberg, taking the bench. With his glasses perched on the end of his nose, the judge scanned the papers in front of him and then tapping the pages in order, he announced, "In Re the Matter of the State versus Emma Richardson and In Re the Matter of the State versus Evaline Bushrod, are the parties present?"

"Indeed we are, your Honor," responded Josiah Tweedle adjusting his tie one final time before motioning to Emma to come forward and meet him at the rectangular table in front of the judge. "Remain standing," Josiah whispered to Emma as she prepared to sit in the wooden chair.

"And what of Evaline Bushrod?" asked the judge scanning the crowd. "Bailiff, call Evaline Bushrod," instructed Judge Freudenberg.

When Evaline did not come forward, the judge leaned over to his courtroom scribe and said, "Let it be reflected in the record that the Defendant, Evaline Bushrod, having been called three times in open court, appears not."

Looking at Emma and with only an occasional glance at his paper, Judge Freudenberg intoned, "This Court having taken under advisement the case of the State versus Emma Richardson and the State versus Evaline Bushrod, now makes its ruling thereon as follows:

I find that Evaline Bushrod is guilty of assault and battery upon Emma Richardson causing her bodily injury. There is sufficient evidence to warrant Manfred Crockett filing criminal charges on behalf of the State against Evaline Bushrod.

I find that the State has insufficient evidence to charge Emma Richardson with disturbing the peace. It is the Court's observation that Emma Richardson may well have the right to sue Evaline Bushrod in civil court for the vicious injuries that were inflicted upon her person by the said Evaline Bushrod."

Whereupon, the judge banged his gavel, announcing, "Case concluded and now in re the matter of Reginald Suggs versus Clement Bix, are the litigants present in the courtroom?"

Josiah hugged Emma to him and holding her firmly with one hand and his worn satchel with the other, walked Emma back to where Heath waited for them. Smiling, Heath opened the door to freedom.

Out in the marble corridor, Heath embraced a now smiling Emma and shook Josiah Tweedle's hand. "Just one second, my friends," said Josiah setting his satchel on a nearby bench. Opening the brass closure on the satchel's leather strap and reaching inside, Josiah produced two red roses.

Offering one rose to his client, Attorney Josiah Tweedle said, "Madam, may I present you with this token of my esteem?" Josiah next walked over to the statue of Justica and placed the second red rose upon her scales. With a slight bow, he murmured to the bronze lady, "Once again, my lovely, you have prevailed," and Josiah placed his lips briefly upon the cold hand that held the scales aloft.

Returning to his client who remained in Heath's protective embrace, Josiah announced, "I should like to kiss your hand as well, madam, but fear of being struck tempers my inclination," laughed Josiah.

Emma promptly offered her hand, returning the laughter.

CHAPTER 19

▼

Time is a great healer. With the passage of summer and numerous applications of "Miss Mary's Magic Moonbeam" ointment, the angry red welts left by Evaline Bushrod upon Emma's face, disappeared. Soon after the trial, however, it became apparent that the break between Luke Crawford and Heath Hamilton would take much longer to mend. Louise Bennington left the nurses' training program abruptly at the end of August without a word to Emma. Fanella Walker would later confide in Emma that she knew Benni was pregnant.

Emma continued to journey across the Southport River twice a day to continue her practical year of nursing at the hospital. Twice each month, Emma was required to work the night shift but because of the security measures that she had fought so hard for at the hospital, there were no further breaches of the nurses' safety after hours.

Several times each week, Emma made sure that her favorite patient, Edna Ford, was treated to a sojourn upon the hospital's front veranda. The two women had formed an enduring friendship that would last the rest of Edna Ford's life.

Burris McKendrick continued to challenge Emma's skills as a nurse. Singling her out for advanced tutelage, Burris recommended increasingly that Emma should audit certain classes for the medical students that he was teaching. He always prefaced such suggestions with, "You absolutely must know these latest techniques if you are going to continue to assist me in the surgery."

Already bored with bedpans, bandages, thermometers and nursing notes, Emma was only too happy to escape into the classroom and sit at the back, away from Dr. McKendrick's male students. From her vantage point, Emma would watch riveted as the brilliant surgeon strode back and forth at the front of the classroom, lecturing his students and making chalk drawings of the latest surgical procedures upon the board.

There were, however, several caveats that Dr. McKendrick imposed upon Emma. She was cautioned to remain inconspicuous, which meant that she was not to raise her hand to ask questions or to be recognized in the classroom. She was specifically forbidden by the doctor from any scholastic interaction with the male students. Emma was not allowed the use of a textbook and since she did not hand in homework, she took no tests on the subjects that she was studying.

What Burris McKendrick did not know, however, was that long after the rest of her family was fast asleep, Emma sat propped up in bed in the soft glow of her oil lamp, outlining everything the doctor had covered in class earlier that day, complete with pencil renderings of his chalk drawings. She simply made her own textbook.

Both Fanella Walker and Burris McKendrick had begun to use the term "gifted" when evaluating Emma. By virtue of its modest size, the town of Grandview was well aware that in addition to Percival Abernathy, the town doctor, it had student nurse Emma Richardson in its midst. When Dr. Abernathy was away on a house call and unavailable for emergencies, the afflicted trudged to the house on High Point Avenue.

Mary's household was alerted to the arrival of a visitor to the home when, during the course of dinner one evening, Brute rushed down the front hall, viciously barking and smearing the glass at each side of the front door with his nose.

"Easy boy...easy there!" called Heath rising from the dining room table and removing the napkin from under his chin.

"Who is it, Heath?" called Emma after him.

"I do not recognize the woman," he answered. "Some fella just dropped her off at the front steps and then rode on so I am going out onto the porch to see what she wants."

Fanning the dog back with his napkin, Heath edged through a narrow opening of the front door to greet the heavyset woman who had turned to move back down the front steps in fear of the snarling dog on the other side of the glass.

"Yes, ma'am," began Heath cordially, "how may I help you?"

"This is the home of Emma Richardson, isn't it?" asked the thickly rouged woman struggling to draw a breath.

"It is but she is at supper right now," responded Heath. When Heath noticed the immediate look of dismay that clouded over the woman's porcine features he added, "Do you have some sort of an emergency?"

"Indeed I have...or rather one of my girls has," responded the woman grabbing her blonde wig just as it began to slide off her head.

"So, I should tell Mrs. Richardson that your child is ill?" asked Heath, blue eyes riveted to the pudgy fingers which worked rapidly to pin the saucy curls back into place.

"I didn't say 'child'. I said 'girl'...one of my girls is ill."

"I am afraid I do not understand Miss...what did you say your name is?"

"I didn't say but the name is Hattie Garrison."

"The famous Miss Hattie of Miss Hattie's House..."

Heath was interrupted by his visitor, "Yes, yes. That Miss Hattie. Now could we dispense with the foreplay and you run along inside and fetch that doctor out here for me?" and Miss Hattie made a shooing motion with her bejeweled fingers.

"Mrs. Richardson is not a doctor," corrected Heath. "She is a student nurse and..."

"Listen mister, I know everything about everybody in this town and I know that Emma Richardson can stitch up a stab wound and birth a baby with the best of them. Now are you gonna get her out here or am I gonna have to shoot that damn loud dog and fetch her myself?" asked Miss Hattie reaching into her purse to pull out a small pistol.

"No need to get so riled up, ma'am," answered Heath, retreating inside the house and rapidly disappearing down the front hall.

"Well you'd be plenty riled too if some asshole kept you parleying out on the damn front porch while one of your girls was bleeding to death," Hattie called after Heath.

Emma grabbed her black bag from the hall table and joined Miss Hattie on the porch. "Please fill me in while Heath brings around the carriage."

Moments later, Heath pulled up in front of the house and assisted both Emma and Hattie Garrison up into the carriage. "I trust you know where my establishment is?" asked Hattie.

"Yes, ma'am I know where it is," responded Heath, immediately adding, "even though I have never been there," and he shot Emma a quick glance.

"Well, hurry up then. The girl is in bad shape."

At once, Heath slapped the reins across Onion's broad back and they set off at a brisk pace, following the back road to Miss Hattie's House of Splendor on the far north side of town. Heath was not anxious to be associated with the madam of Grandview's whorehouse.

Miss Hattie's was a two-story, non-descript, white frame farmhouse with tall, red brick chimneys at either end of the steeply gabled roof. Closely clipped lilac bushes wound around the house and a discreet red wooden sign with crisp, white letters that spelled out the word, GARRISON, welcomed visitors to the front porch.

"Drive on around behind the house and pull into the barn," ordered Miss Hattie. "I do not allow customers to leave their horses or carriages on the front lawn or I'd be too busy cleaning up horse shit to keep an eye on business. Stop at the back steps so Emma and I can go on inside. You, stay in the barn," she wheezed, jabbing a highly buffed nail at Heath.

Heath did as he had been instructed, leaving Emma to follow the tightly corseted Miss Hattie up the back steps and into the house. "This way," Hattie said to Emma. "I keep a room at the back of the house for my sick or injured girls so as not to frighten my customers away."

The two women passed through a large, cluttered, dirty kitchen before entering what was obviously a laundry room. Galvanized tubs were stacked against one wall. A soapstone sink and pump sat opposite the arsenal of tubs and clotheslines that dangled freshly washed bloomers, stockings, blouses and the like. Miscellaneous items of female attire lay soaking in a tub of water in the middle of the floor.

As Miss Hattie approached a closed, warped, green door at the far side of the laundry room, she turned to speak in a whisper to Emma, "Do I have your oath that you will not disclose what you are about to see in there," and she jerked her head at the door, "to anyone once you leave my place?"

"I cannot make such an oath for if I find that conditions merit, I shall have to summon additional assistance which would necessitate discussion of the patient's symptoms," responded Emma, holding the handles of her black bag with both hands.

As Emma's words penetrated her thick skull, Hattie Garrison stood silently contemplating Emma before she slowly pushed open the warped door, calling softly, "Nellie girl? The nurse I told you about has come."

When Emma attempted to correct her, Hattie whispered, "Tonight you are Florence Nightingale. Get my meaning?"

In the wan light that filtered obliquely through at the edges of the heavily shaded windows, Emma could barely discern the silhouette of dark hair against the stark white of a pillow cover. Moving closer to the bed, Emma realized that she was looking at a young woman on her side, shivering under a pile of quilts.

Silently, Emma pulled a chair to the side of the bed, set her black case upon its upholstered red cushion, opened the leather straps and abruptly left the room.

"Just where do you think you're going?" asked Hattie, in pursuit.

"To wash my hands," replied Emma rolling up her sleeves.

"What for?" asked Hattie, handing her a clean towel.

"Germs."

"Germs?"

"Yes," explained Emma. "Tiny organisms that might be on my hands which could, if transmitted to…"

"Nellie."

"If transmitted to Nellie might compound…worsen her condition," Emma tried explaining to the vacant eyes that searched hers.

Moving back to the side of Nellie's bed, Emma pointed to the windows saying, "Please pull up the shades as I shall need every bit of light in here that is available and that will include a lamp."

"But the light is too harsh for her," protested Hattie, "and her condition much too grave."

"How do you expect me to examine my patient in the dark? To determine what is wrong, I must first be able to see her," scolded Emma.

Hattie busied herself raising the shades and then scurried out to fetch an oil lamp.

Emma spoke softly to the dark hair, "Nellie? Nellie, it is Emma Richardson your…nurse. Can you turn toward me, dear?"

The quilts shifted and a tiny, white oval face appeared from under the mass of dark curls as Nellie turned toward Emma. "Oh, please help me, nurse, for I am bleeding to death."

"I understand, dear. Now, I am just going to pull down these covers and begin my examination…"

"Please don't!" protested Nellie feebly. "I am so cold and I can't stand to be uncovered!"

"Tell you what, Nellie. I shall only uncover the part which I must examine. I shall cover it up again before moving on to the next part and I shall begin at the top and work my way down. Will you help me, Nellie?"

"Uh-huh," mumbled the sickly white face.

Emma began her examination of Nellie Potter. "How old are you, Nellie?" asked Emma.

"Twenty-five."

Emma examined the young woman's eyes, nose, mouth and took her temperature. The thermometer registered one hundred and four degrees. Nellie shivered uncontrollably.

Hattie returned with an oil lamp. Striking a match, she lit the wick, rolling it up to illuminate fully the bedside where Emma worked.

"Miss Hattie," Emma paused, "I must mix a powder for her at once to lower her temperature. Please fetch a glass of fresh water for her."

"What's the matter with this?" asked Hattie, thrusting a dirty glass at Emma.

"I want a clean glass filled with fresh water, at once," snapped Emma.

Hattie disappeared.

"Is it because of those...germs you mentioned?" asked Hattie returning with a clean glass of fresh water.

"It is and thank you." Emma mixed a teaspoon of the white powder into the water and raising Nellie's head, prompted the girl to drink.

Emma continued her examination, stifling the horror that rose within her when she uncovered Nellie's blood-soaked undergarments and bedcovers.

"How long as she been bleeding like this?" Emma asked angrily, wiping up blood clots that resembled raw chicken livers.

"Since...since..." stuttered Hattie.

"Since when?"

"Since this morning."

"And no one had the sense to summon me before supper?"

"I thought..."

"You thought what?"

"I'll have you know that I'm an expert abortionist! I'm known far and wide for my skills with a knitting needle!" snorted Hattie.

"Are you now!" retorted Emma. "And are you also known for letting your patients bleed to death? Listen to me, Hattie Garrison. You and I are going to strip everything off this girl and her bed. I am going to wash her on that cot over there and then I am going to pack her birth canal with sterile cotton and gauze that I have in my bag here. You are going to flip this mattress over and apply fresh bedding. I am going to dress her again. We are going to place her back in bed. You are going to bring some hot soup in here for Nellie and when we have finished with all of that, you and I both are going to fall to our knees and pray like hell for her recovery. Do you have any questions about what I have just said?" Emma stood with her hands on her hips, glaring at Hattie.

"I'll have you know that bed of hers has already been changed once today..."

"Once is hardly adequate given Nellie's dire loss of blood. We must both apply ourselves immediately in order to attempt to save this young woman," retorted Emma.

As she was exceedingly weak, Nellie offered neither resistance nor assistance as Emma washed and dried the girl's pale body. After Emma had applied the packing and dressed Nellie in a warm nightgown, she and Hattie carried the girl to the freshly made bed, piled on clean quilts and Emma began spoon-feeding the soup to her.

"How long has it been since she has eaten or drunk anything?" asked Emma.

"I wouldn't know," replied Hattie.

"Well then, fetch the person who has been caring for Nellie so that I might inquire of her about what this girl has ingested," instructed Emma, continuing to spoon the hot soup into Nellie's mouth.

Emma's instructions were met with silence.

"Why are you standing there, woman? Go at once and fetch the person here!" said Emma sternly.

"There is no one to fetch," replied Hattie gathering up the soiled linens.

"Whatever do you mean?" asked Emma.

"I mean no one has had the time to care for her," Hattie replied sullenly. "I am running a business here, not a charity."

"For the good Lord's sake, woman! You did this to her in the first place and then you abandoned her in this dark, foul room to bleed to death!" Emma rose to confront the wheezing madam. "And furthermore, remove that corset so that you can breathe unfettered. Attempting to cinch up your avoirdupois with that instrument of torture is causing you to sound like a steam engine, to say nothing of what the combination is doing to your heart and lungs."

Whereupon Emma handed the empty soup bowl and spoon to Hattie. "Every half hour I shall require a clean glass of fresh water for Nellie and another bowl of broth. It is essential to her survival. I shall remain here with Nellie until I feel that she is out of danger but I must insist on help. I suggest that you get some of those other girls of yours off their backs and into that laundry room to begin cleaning up the unsanitary mess generated by your botched abortion," Emma flung the words at the whorehouse madam.

"Since Nellie is sleeping," continued Emma, "I am going out to speak with Heath and then I shall return directly," and she marched out of the house, leaving a speechless Hattie Garrison in her wake, still holding the empty soup bowl and spoon.

Emma found Heath in the barn trimming the hoof of a black horse. "Just what do you think you are doing, Heath?"

"Oh Emma, there you are. Well, I thought I might as well make myself useful, especially since the condition of this horse is deplorable. So tell me, are we here for the night?" asked Heath, the smile fading from his lips as he gazed upon Emma's contorted features.

"Nothing can possibly equal the deplorable condition of that poor girl in there!" and Emma thrust an arm angrily back at the house.

"That bad?"

"Worse! My patient is a very young woman! She has been savaged by Hattie's botched abortion with a knitting needle and I am not sure that Nellie is going to pull through," answered Emma sadly.

"Is that the girl's name, Nellie?" asked Heath, leading the horse back to its stall.

"Yes. Listen, Heath, it is imperative that I remain with this girl until she either succumbs to the loss of blood or shows substantial signs of improvement. It is painfully obvious that I am all that stands between her and certain death."

"But Emma," protested Heath, "there is a whole houseful of women in there who can tend to her now."

"Yes and half of those women are busy fornicating for their next dollar while the other half combined do not possess the brain of a inch worm, which includes their illustrious madam!"

"I see. So, what do you want me to do?"

"I need you to return to Mama's and help her with the boys. Explain things as best you can to the boys but do not mention the circumstances, except to Mama. Please get word to Fanella Walker that I shall be absent from the hospital tomorrow while I tend to a critically ill girl. Can you do all of that for me?" Emma asked, placing her hand upon Heath's arm.

Heath took her hand and kissed it briefly, "You know you can count on me for anything! But when shall we see you again at home?"

"Not until Nellie is better or dead," Emma answered flatly and she rushed back into the house.

This time when Emma entered the house, both the kitchen and the laundry room were beehives of activity. Two of the residents were busy in the kitchen washing dishes. Two others were rinsing out Nellie's bloody sheets and undergarments.

"Girls!" called Emma to the four women. "Please gather around me for a moment."

All four stopped what they were doing to follow Emma onto the back porch. "Permit me to introduce myself, I am Emma Richardson and I am here to care for Nellie who is in grave danger because of the blood loss she has endured as a result of the abortion performed upon her by Hattie Garrison.

I am going to need the help of each and every one of you to prevent our little Nellie from dying tonight. We five are like soldiers and together we must fight the demonic death that threatens to take her from us. Are you with me?"

"We're Nellie's best friends," spoke up a buxom redhead, "and we'll fight like hell to save her. You can count on us. Right, ladies?"

"Right!" chorused the other three girls.

"Just tell us what to do," spoke up a tall blonde.

"Cleanliness is imperative right now. Nellie's bloody linens must be washed with soap and then boiled. I need to keep forcing fluids into her mouth every thirty minutes, which means clean water and a healthy broth. Can anyone here cook?"

A brunette with mottled skin raised her hand, "I can make soup out of a stone."

"Splendid. Make a large kettle because it is going to be a very long night..."

"Pardon me, Nurse Richardson, but I found something in Nellie's sheets which I think you should see," interrupted the fourth girl.

"All right then, while I take a look, you other three get busy. Let us save Nellie!" and she returned to the laundry room with the fourth girl.

The brunette with waist-length hair led Emma back to the pile of soiled linens in the laundry room. Taking a bundle from the top of the heap, the girl set it in the soapstone sink where she carefully unwrapped the top folds. There in front of her lay the tiny, completely formed and unmistakable bloody body of an aborted fetus, still attached to its mother's umbilical cord.

"Ah...so there you are my poor little darling!" cooed Emma as she began to examine the aborted fetus. "Look here...forgive me but I do not know your name," said Emma turning to the pale girl with the waist-length hair who stood attentively at her elbow.

"Clementine, ma'am, but everybody calls me 'Clemmie'."

"Very well then, Clemmie, take a look here and tell me what you see," said Emma turning the stiffened fetus over and prying its legs apart.

"Looks like a poker to me," responded Clemmie.

"Right you are. I knew I could count on you to recognize a male child. So, our little Nellie was carrying a boy. Would you just look at his ten fingers and ten toes! Notice how exquisitely small they are but perfectly distinguishable. And such lovely little ears! However, judging from the rigidity of his body, I would estimate that Nellie passed him much earlier today. Do you happen to know..." and Emma heard something fall onto the pile of linens behind her. Clemmie had fainted.

Quickly, Emma washed her hands and then entered Nellie's room to retrieve her vial of smelling salts from the black satchel. As she waved them under Clemmie's nose, the girl's eyes flew open and she appeared startled by everyone bending over her.

"You fainted, dear," explained Emma, "while you were looking at Nellie's aborted child."

The other three girls gasped at Emma's revelation as she continued, "Yes, ladies, his small body is there in the sink. As soon as I can talk with Nellie about this, I shall endeavor to have her give the child a name and then we must give him a decent burial but until then, one of you pack Nellie's fetus in ice to keep him from spoiling."

"Can we look at the…baby?" asked the redhead.

"You may indeed, provided those who look do not faint! I must get back to Nellie at once," and Emma resumed her vigil at Nellie's bedside, glass of fresh water and broth in hand.

Night had fallen and the only illumination in the small room came from the half full oil lamp. Emma pulled the shades down in an attempt to discourage the unwanted attention of the moths that were attracted to the light cast by the lamp. Since Emma had been changing Nellie's packing every half hour, she was pleasantly surprised to note around ten o'clock in the evening that the girl's bleeding had substantially reduced in volume. Emma had been forcing fluids down Nellie for several hours but it continued to concern Emma that the girl had yet to indicate a need to sit upon the scarred enamel basin under her bed.

Hattie Garrison had not revisited Nellie since her retreat from the back room with the empty soup bowl and spoon. From the sounds that drifted to the back of the large house, Emma knew that Hattie's House of Splendor was enjoying a very busy night. Indeed, Clemmie and her three friends had all taken their leave around eight-thirty in order to prepare for their usual customers. Together, the redhead, the blonde, the brunette with mottled skin and Clemmie had washed and cleaned every inch of the kitchen and Nellie's room, in addition to the soiled linens and clothing. They had prepared a large kettle of soup and made sure that Emma had something to eat as well.

As Emma stood by the washstand in her dim surroundings mixing yet another powder for Nellie, she could hear the unmistakable, rhythmic creaking of bed boards just over her head, accompanied by the melodious groaning of a male customer in full rut. A slight smile played across Emma's lips and she chuckled to herself. "Men are such fools," thought Emma, "but we women are even greater fools for allowing them to desecrate our bodies for their own pleasure."

Emma sat in the chair next to Nellie's bed where she lay under her mountain of brightly patched quilts. "Nellie, dear. Raise your head and drink this for me."

Nellie's eyes fluttered open in the small, pale, oval face. Drinking all of the murky liquid that Emma offered her, Nellie belched. "Please excuse me, ma'am."

"Think nothing of it," replied Emma wiping the girl's mouth.

"What time is it?"

"Around ten o'clock."

"Sounds busy upstairs," observed Nellie.

"Indeed it does."

Just then, the sound of piano music reached the small back room. "Oh, do you hear that, Nurse?"

"Who plays the piano in the house?" asked Emma.

"Clemmie does."

Emma stood listening for a few seconds, "She sounds quite talented."

"She really is. I've told Clemmie many times that she should get away from this place and go study music. Don't you think that's a good idea?" asked Nellie, looking feverish.

Moving to her side, Emma propped Nellie up with a folded quilt on top of her pillow.

"Excellent idea, dear. But right now, it is time for you and me to speak of more important matters. That is, if you think you can manage it?"

"I'll try."

"I know that your given name is 'Nellie' but I do not know your surname," began Emma quietly, sitting by Nellie and holding her hand.

"Potter, ma'am. Nellie Potter. What's your name?"

"Emma Richardson."

Nellie's eyes flickered with recognition.

Emma continued, "Well, Nellie Potter, I must inform you that some time earlier today you passed a male fetus…"

"A male what?" interrupted Nellie.

"A male child."

"Is he alive?" asked Nellie, her dark eyes riveted upon Emma's.

"No, dear. The fet…child was much too young to survive outside of your womb," responded Emma tenderly, smoothing the hair from Nellie's face.

Tears formed at the corners of the young woman's eyes and slid slowly down her cheeks. "The wages of sin!" cried Nellie. "To think that an innocent must pay for my mistake!"

"There, there, Nellie. Do try to remain calm because I need you to be clear-headed so that you can select a name for your child. I must arrange for his burial in the morning. Can you think of a suitable name for your child?"

Nellie looked down at the foot of the bed for such a prolonged period of time that Emma, thinking she had drifted off to sleep again, rose from the chair beside her bed.

"No, don't go!" Nellie exhaled with all the force she could muster.

Startled, Emma sat down again.

"I know what I want to name my child."

"Yes, dear, tell me."

"Edward."

Emma flinched visibly.

"Is uh…Edward a family name, dear?" probed Emma.

"No. It was the name of my favorite customer who mysteriously disappeared a long time ago," responded Nellie, looking into Emma's eyes.

"How about your father's name, or your brother's as an alternative to…" began Emma.

"No. It should be 'Edward'," insisted Nellie adamantly.

Feeling uncomfortably hot, Emma rose and murmured, "I believe I shall fetch us some fresh drinking water, Nellie," and she left the room abruptly.

Leaning against the soapstone sink, Emma fought to regain her composure. Finding no relief at the sink, Emma dashed from the house and ran to the barn where she grabbed an ax and began to flail away at a pile of cordwood.

A male customer, returning to his horse after having concluded his business at Miss Hattie's, happened upon Emma as she sought to alleviate her omnipresent rage at Edward which was normally quiescent underneath the rehearsed serenity of her beautiful exterior. Like a volcano erupting, Emma exploded upon the woodpile, sending the oak logs flying about in the moonlight.

"Miss? Can I help you out there, miss?" asked Hattie Garrison's customer.

Startled to have been accosted unexpectedly in the dark, Emma leaped backward, ax still in hand, panting violently from so much exertion.

"How about if I just roll up my sleeves and chop some firewood for you, miss, before you hurt yourself with that thing," laughed the young man cautiously removing the ax from Emma's grip.

As the burley young man began to split firewood he asked casually, "You new here?"

"Yes," answered Emma breathlessly.

"Thought so. Maybe next time you and I could…"

"Now just a minute!" scolded Emma. "I shall have you know that I am a nurse here on the premises for the purpose of caring for a sick woman. Do not for one second confuse me with those...those...'ladies' in there!" railed Emma.

"Begging your pardon, miss, but I just assumed..."

"Well, your assumption was entirely erroneous! You can stack the firewood by the back door when you finish," whereupon Emma turned on her heel and walked back to Miss Hattie's.

"How much do you need, miss?" called the burley young man after Emma.

"All of it!" and Emma slammed the back door.

After splashing cool water onto her overheated face from the pump beside the soapstone sink, Emma walked serenely back into Nellie's room to resume her vigil.

"Nurse Richardson?" said Nellie weakly.

"Yes?"

"I know who you are."

"Oh? And how is that?" asked Emma, still fighting to maintain her composure. Pinning the errant strands of auburn hair back up on top of her head, Emma asked, "Just who is is that you know me to be?"

"You are Edward's wife."

Emma froze. With every swing of the young man's ax outside in the moonlight as he split firewood for the whorehouse, she could hear, "You are Edward's wife...you are Edward's wife...you are Edward's wife..."

"Even as you are Edward's whore?" blurted out Emma in response.

"Yes, ma'am. His favorite," the pale lips in the oval face twisted obscenely with the words.

"Well, how lovely! And how fitting! I, his abandoned wife, am called upon to treat his abandoned whore! But please do not try to tell me that your aborted child is Edward's because my husband has been gone entirely too long to have achieved that feat!"

"No, Nurse Richardson. My dead son was not fathered by Edward. Just my daughter was."

"Was? Was what?" asked Emma, her voice choking with emotion.

"Edward Richardson fathered my daughter, Sophie Potter," replied Nellie, sinking deeper into her covers.

"How could that be? I mean, how could you possibly know who the father was with all the men that you have...had..."

"A whore always keeps track of her mistakes, Nurse Richardson," Nellie said, drawing the covers up under her chin, "and I made two fatal ones. I fell in love with Edward and then I got pregnant. All whores know better than to do either."

"I quite understand, Nellie...I made those identical mistakes myself." Emma paused before asking, "Tell me, Nellie, did Edward ever...did he ever beat you?" Emma felt suddenly as cold as Nellie looked shivering under her pile of quilts.

"He tried, but there were always others around," Nellie responded feebly.

"Ah, how I wish I had known such protection by others!" sighed Emma.

Emma took Nellie's temperature and then rose silently to clean the thermometer with alcohol, her mind reeling with the young woman's revelation.

As Emma held a glass of water to Nellie's lips, she asked, "Where is your little girl?"

"In St. Louis with my mother and father."

"Is that where you are from?" asked Emma, wiping the pale lips.

"Yes."

"How old is Sophie?"

"Nearly four."

"I see," replied Emma, looking at the pitiful girl with the pale oval face, shaking beneath her covers.

Reaching under the quilts and drawing out Nellie's hand, Emma held onto her patient and looked deep within the feverish eyes, "I think, Nellie," began Emma, "that you and I are bound together in a very odd sort of way."

Nellie nodded.

"I have three sons by Edward and you have his daughter. How extraordinary!"

Nellie nodded.

"It takes a bit of doing to untangle that knot? Would you agree?" asked Emma wringing out a cloth in cool water to apply to Nellie's forehead.

"Yes, Nurse Richardson," whispered Nellie. "But whether Edward was yours or mine or everyone's doesn't concern me any longer."

"What then?"

"My concern is for my little girl and what will become of her if I die here in this bed tonight."

"I understand your concern, Nellie. What do you propose?" asked Emma as she continued to apply cool compresses to her patient's head.

"I've saved a bit of money. I always give my parents money whenever I can get back to St. Louis to see my little Sophie. Do you think you might...could you take the money and my possessions to my parents for Sophie if I do not recover?

I think there's enough money to bury me with my son and still have some left over for my daughter," added Nellie pathetically.

Emma reached across the covers to enfold Nellie in her embrace, "Yes, Nellie, I shall take your money and your possessions to St. Louis for your child. I shall arrange for you to be buried with your son in the new Miller's Grove Cemetery here in Grandview. But you must tell me how to find little Sophie and your parents," said Emma, laying Nellie gently back against her pillow.

"Clemmie and I share a room upstairs. She knows what's mine and what's hers. Trust her and no one else," cautioned Nellie feebly. "My money's sealed in an envelope and tied up with a pink ribbon in a stack of letters from my parents. Their address is on the outside of the envelopes."

"Is there anything else that I can do for you?"

"Yes, Nurse Richardson. You can tell Sophie that I made many mistakes in my life but tell her…make sure she understands that she is not one of them. She is the best thing I ever did! Tell Sophie that I love her more than life itself and that I'm going to go on loving her for all eternity," Nellie paused and closed her eyes.

Thinking that Nellie had drifted off to sleep, Emma again rose from the chair as Nellie whispered, "I feel so terribly cold and tired. If you don't mind, I believe I'll just go to sleep for a while. Good-night, Nurse Richardson, and thank you…may God bless you always." Nellie Potter's eyes closed for the last time.

"Good night, Nellie. Sweet dreams," responded Emma instinctively.

As Emma prepared to change Nellie's packing and feed her some broth around eleven o'clock, she realized that her patient was unresponsive. After a brief examination of the young woman, Emma determined that Nellie had slipped into a coma.

"Damn that Dr. Abernathy! What could have kept him this long?" she muttered to herself, as Emma stood helplessly looking down at the young girl who lay dying in a cocoon of quilts. Emma, however, understood that there was little Dr. Abernathy or even her mentor, Dr. McKendrick, could do at that point. Nellie had begun slowly bleeding to death from the moment Hattie Garrison violated her womb with a wooden knitting needle.

Emma sank heavily onto her chair next to Nellie. Reaching under the covers, Emma grabbed the girl's hand and held onto it with both of hers as if to pull Nellie back from the abyss into which she was inexorably sinking.

"Oh Nellie! Nellie! Please do not go yet! You must not do this! I beg you not to do this!" and Emma began to weep. "Think of your child, Nellie!" During her many months of training at Angel of Mercy Hospital, Emma had shunned death's embrace, but now in the dark of night, it had finally found her in the back room of the sleazy, creaking whorehouse and it pressed its advances upon her while she alone kept a silent vigil over Nellie Potter.

Dutifully, Emma recorded Nellie's demise in her neat script upon the tablet of paper with the carefully sharpened pencil that always accompanied her in the black satchel. "A good nurse must take good notes. Document every detail. Leave nothing out so that the attending physician has at his fingertips a meticulous catalogue of symptoms, intake, output, temperature, pulse, respirations, heartbeat, date, time," Emma's mind ticked off the requirements that Fanella Walker had drilled into her head.

After the word "heartbeat", Emma wrote, "None." After the word "date", she wrote, "September 15, 1890." After the word "time", she wrote, "Ten minutes past the hour of two, ante meridian." Emma closed the tablet of paper and placed it in the pocket of her skirt before rising resolutely from her post. Grasping the covers firmly, Emma bent down to kiss the waiting forehead, even as she had done a hundred times before with her own children when she tucked them into their beds for the night. Then, ever so gently, Emma pulled the wedding ring pattern quilt up and over Nellie Potter's face. Death had been requited.

Emma walked over to the windows and raised the shades. Moonlight came spilling into the room, washing over the body of Nellie Potter. Emma placed her hands upon the windowsill and leaned far out into the night, inhaling and exhaling deeply, trying to rid herself of the stench of death. The oil lamp began to sputter and as Emma turned back to look, its light too was extinguished. Alone in the dark with Nellie's corpse, Emma had to fight the urge to run screaming from the cramped room.

Realizing that she must notify Miss Hattie, Emma picked her way out through the green door into the laundry room and through the kitchen toward the faint glow of a lamp coming from the parlor toward the front of the house. For the past two hours, the only sounds in the house had been muffled laughter and snoring. When Emma reached the front parlor, she realized that Hattie Garrison was still awake, sitting at a highly lacquered table, drinking brandy and counting the evening's take with her pudgy hands, now devoid of their rings.

"Miss Hattie?" began Emma wearily.

Startled, Hattie Garrison called, "Who is it?"

"Emma Richardson," she announced, moving closer to the light.

"Oh, I see now. Need some more soup?" slurred Hattie, already into her second glass of brandy.

"No. There is no further need of soup."

"Well, what then?" asked Hattie impatiently, clenching a wad of bills tightly in each fist.

"Nellie Potter died at ten minutes past two this morning," replied Emma solemnly.

"She what?" screeched Hattie rising abruptly from a red velvet chair, nearly overturning the table which held her box of money and her brandy.

"She died at…"

"Well the very nerve of her to do such a thing! And in my very own house to boot!" complained Hattie, wavering unsteadily on bare feet, deformed toes splayed as if to grip the oriental carpet. "Do you have any idea what this is going to cost me?" complained the inebriated proprietress.

Exhausted from her grueling nine-hour battle to save Nellie Potter, Emma lost her composure and rushed at Hattie. Grabbing the madam by the lapels of her dark velvet dressing gown, she shook the woman, yelling into her face, "You fat, old whore! Have you not an ounce of compassion for anyone or anything but your own purse?"

"But…but…" stammered Hattie.

"Two lives were snuffed out here tonight. Two lives ended because of you!" and Emma drilled her finger into the woman's enormous left breast.

"I was only doing what the girl asked me to do," Hattie tried to explain.

"Like the devil you were!" swore Emma. "You sought to terminate Nellie's pregnancy in order to ensure the retention of her steady customers. No one pays good money to poke a pregnant whore. Might just as well go home and poke your own pregnant wife…for free!" Emma was enraged and becoming louder with each passing minute.

Clemmie was the first one downstairs, "Nurse Emma, what has happened?"

"Nellie has died," answered Emma, still wild-eyed and holding onto Hattie to keep her from falling backward.

From Clemmie and the others who now filed down the staircase, there arose a deafening cacophony of female wailing. Emma backed Hattie into her chair and then, releasing her hold upon the madam, commenced to shake Clemmie by the shoulders, "Listen to me," she shouted above the din, "I am going to take a horse from the barn and fetch Dr. Abernathy to certify Nellie's death. Then, I shall awaken the undertaker and tell him to come at once to collect Nellie Potter and her son, Edward. Do you understand?"

"Yes," cried the dazed girl.

"Do not touch her or the child. Absolutely nothing must be disturbed until Dr. Abernathy has a chance to examine both mother and child. Clemmie! Do you understand what I am saying?"

"Yes, I understand," but Clemmie crumpled onto the settee.

"Come here at once!" ordered Emma, dragging the weeping girl up by her arm and back toward the kitchen.

Once in the relative privacy and darkness of the kitchen, Emma pressed her face close to Clemmie's to say, "You must be in charge here during my absence. Nellie told me herself that you are the only one I can trust in this house. Gather your wits about you, Clemmie, and act responsibly for once in your life. No one must enter that room!" and Emma thrust her arm back at the warped, green door.

"Where is the baby?" sobbed Clemmie.

"In his mother's arms, for safekeeping," replied Emma, holding Clemmie's face tightly in her hands. "Look at me, Clemmie!"

Clemmie wiped her eyes with the back of her hand and looked into Emma's eyes.

"Do you promise you will not allow anyone to enter that room?"

"Yes," replied Clemmie, regaining a bit of her composure.

"Good! I am counting on you, Clemmie, to be worthy of the trust that Nellie placed in you," and Emma fled out the back door to saddle up a horse in the moonlight. This time, Emma did not worry about taking the road less traveled into town. It mattered little to her who saw her galloping along the road to Grandview on horseflesh borrowed from its infamous whorehouse.

Grandview's town doctor, Percival Abernathy, had just pulled the bed covers up under his chin when Emma arrived to bang upon his front door. A farmer had sustained a serious gunshot wound earlier in the day when he fell onto his loaded rifle as his foot caught in the fence that he was climbing. Treating the farmer and stitching up the nasty wounds had occupied all of Dr. Abernathy's time until well past one o'clock in the morning.

In spite of the hour and the degree of fatigue which were clearly etched upon the young doctor's face, Percival Abernathy stood quietly reading Emma's hand-written notes by an oil lamp on his front hall table. "What a needless tragedy," concluded Dr. Abernathy shaking his head as he handed Emma's note tablet back to her. "I'm called out to that damnable place so many times each month that all I have to do is whisper, 'Miss Hattie's,' into the ear of my horse and automatically he heads north on the road out of town. It has reached the point that even my wife is beginning to doubt the veracity of my incessant emergency trips to Miss Hattie's," complained Dr. Abernathy.

"And what do you find once there?" asked Emma.

"Well...similar to your circumstances this evening, I find botched abortions, diseases exchanged between men and women who have been intimate, alcohol poisoning and physical injuries to the girls from rough customers in addition to the more mundane complaints such as sore throats, skin infections, earaches and the like."

"Have you noted the deplorable sanitary conditions upon the premises?" Emma persisted.

"Indeed I have. Fouled bed linens, stacks of unwashed crockery and a smell that permeates my clothing to the point that my wife makes me bathe after I have been around Hattie's girls," noted Dr. Abernathy.

"I should like to speak with you at a later date about what could be done to improve the miserable living conditions of those poor women at Hattie's but due to the lateness of the hour, I must be on my way to fetch the undertaker. Shall I meet you there presently?" asked Emma as Dr. Abernathy opened the front door.

"Yes. It won't take me long."

"Good. Thank you, doctor. I shall see you soon." Emma untied her borrowed steed's reins and with a leg up from Dr. Abernathy, galloped off for the under-taker's house.

Harold Whinrey, Grandview's undertaker, was an elderly man and Emma had difficulty rousing him from sleep at three-thirty in the morning.

"Whadya say your name is again?" asked Harold Whinrey, fumbling with his spectacles as he stood myopically surveying Emma from the darkened interior of his house.

"Emma Richardson."

"Oh, Emma. Yes, yes, of course. The nurse. Right?" asked Harold, wiping off the spectacles with a handful of his crumpled nightshirt.

"Yes the...um...nurse. I must ask you to dress and come with me, Mr. Whin-rey, as there have been two deaths out at Miss Hattie's, one yesterday and one today. I have already notified Dr. Abernathy and he will meet us there," explained Emma.

"Good gravy! Was there a shooting or something? You know those fellas get kinda testy over those hussies of theirs," Harold commented. "Wouldn't be the first time I've been called out there to haul off a couple of stiffs that shot each other over a whore."

"No…nothing like that. One of Miss Hattie's girls bled to death following a botched abortion," began Emma.

"And the second one?" asked Harold.

"The fetus," replied Emma.

"Now, ma'am, I don't mean to contradict you or nothing, but in my book, I just write it down as one stiff. I mean, given the fact that the lump was not to term means there was no live birth, which means there was no live child, which means there was no second death. Get my meaning?"

"No, I most certainly do not get your meaning. The 'lump', as you call him, was alive when he passed from Nellie Potter's womb. The child, by the way, has a name…Edward Potter. Only after little Edward Potter left his mother's body did he die, which means you will write it down in your book as two decedents," Emma's eyes flashed in the darkness.

"Well, begging your pardon, ma'am, I'll just confer with the doctor in charge out there and he and I can settle this matter. No need for you to worry yourself about it any longer. See you over to Hattie's," and Harold Whinrey shut the door in Emma's face.

Sucking in a deep breath, Emma clenched her fists and stood staring at the closed door. "What appalling ignorance!" she thought to herself.

Emma was still seething when she reined in the horse at the barn behind the whorehouse. The house was ablaze with lights and she could see Dr. Abernathy in Nellie's room behind the kitchen as she approached the back porch. Clemmie was maintaining her vigil at Nellie's door when Emma strode into the laundry room.

"Oh, Emma! I thought you'd never get here. Doc's in there now with Nellie and the baby."

"Good girl, Clemmie! Stay at your post a bit longer while I speak with the doctor again," and Emma let herself into the tiny room after rapping lightly upon the warped door.

"It is Emma, Dr. Abernathy," she announced, entering the room.

The doctor looked up from the basin of pink water above which he was scrubbing his hands.

"You were entirely correct in your determination of the cause of this young woman's death. I applaud you for your valiant efforts to sustain her life after she had already lost so much blood. Even if I had been present, there was nothing I could have done to reverse the tremendous blood loss that Nellie suffered immediately after the abortion," said Dr. Abernathy drying his hands on a clean towel.

"That is of little consolation to me, Doctor," responded Emma sadly as she looked down at Nellie's pale face. "You know, sometimes after I have assisted Dr. McKendrick with a surgery at Angel of Mercy, I am inclined to marvel at the great strides modern medicine has made since the days of the Civil War. That is, until I am confronted by a case like this one and only then do I realize just how much further medicine has to go."

"Is it not the contemplation of those miles yet to be traveled which has bred a generation of insomniacs within the medical profession? Do we not all look upon the Nellie Potters slipping through our fingers and realize that we have not accomplished enough?" Dr. Abernathy paused to look into Emma's eyes before adding, "It is both a blessing and a curse to be charged with the obligation to search for answers to the remaining unsolved medical questions."

"Why did Nellie Potter have to die?" asked Emma sadly, looking down at the outline of the young woman under the wedding ring quilt.

"Because she lost too much blood, as you well know."

"I guess what I am really asking is what treatment would have been appropriate to save her?"

"It would seem to me that you have already formulated the answer for yourself, so how about if you put it into words for me?" encouraged the doctor, as he packed up his bag.

Emma grew silent. The sound of women's voices drifted back to the small room from the front parlor. "The answer, I believe, begins with the question," began Emma. "Given the degree to which the patient had exsanguinated, what is the procedure for replacing the lost blood from another source...a donor source?"

Percival Abernathy looked startled, "For a woman, you certainly do entertain some astonishing thoughts. My own wife frets over little more than the weather affecting the outcome of her divinity fudge but you...you are contemplating the transfusion of blood from one person to another. How extraordinary!"

At that moment, both Emma and Dr. Abernathy heard the distinct creaking of Harold Whinrey's wooden hearse as his mules pulled it to a halt next to the open windows of Nellie's room.

"Howdy, Doc," Harold greeted Percival through the open window, ignoring Emma.

"Morning, Harold."

"Hear we got ourselves a stiff whore," chuckled the old undertaker.

Sticking her head out of the window by Nellie's bed, Emma addressed Harold Whinrey, "No! What you heard me say is that there is one dead woman, Nellie Potter, and one dead child, Edward Potter."

"Says who?" asked the cantankerous old man.

"So say I," and Percival Abernathy waved the death certificates out the other window at the surprised undertaker.

"Well, far be it from me to come a cropper with our very own town doc!" said Harold, glaring at Emma as he slid down from the hearse to tie up his mules.

While the doctor and the undertaker carried the bodies of Nellie and her child to the waiting hearse, Emma took Clemmie by the hand and whispered in her ear, "Take me to the room that you and Nellie shared."

Hattie Garrison was lying upon a red velvet settee in the front parlor, one bulbous leg and arm dangling limply to the floor, while several of the girls alternately fanned her blotchy face and infused her with hot coffee. "Oh, my poor darling Nellie!" moaned Hattie, placing a fat hand to her forehead. "How I'll miss that child! Why, she was like a daughter to me!"

Ignoring the madam's histrionics, Emma pulled Clemmie up the stairs to the bedroom that she had shared with Nellie. The room was small, divided in half by a red velvet curtain embellished with gold fringe. On each side of the curtain was a bed, just large enough for one person to sleep or two to fornicate. The two girls shared a large chifforobe that obscured the damask wallpaper on the wall opposite their beds. Two small tables with oil lamps and two diminutive chairs completed the women's furnishings. Fraying velvet drapes were tied back with gold cords from the window to let in the cool night air.

Unlike Clemmie's rumpled bed, Nellie's looked untouched. Indeed, nothing on her side of the curtain was out of order. What the room lacked in accoutrements, Clemmie had tried to make up for by hanging scarves, draping beads and decorating with dried flowers. The room was heavy with the smell of cheap perfume and a recent sexual encounter.

"Do you like it?" asked Clemmie.

Heedless of Clemmie's question, Emma walked over to Nellie's bed and sat upon the Chinese red silk cover, heavily adorned with tourmaline beads around the edges. She let her hand glide across the cool, smooth silkiness of the cover and as she did so, she wondered how many times Nellie Potter had engaged her husband, Edward Richardson, in hedonistic pleasures of the flesh upon its slick surface. Was there still a trace of the moment's excitement that had resulted in the creation of the child, Sophie Potter? Emma searched the red sheen of the silk for some telltale sign.

"Emma? Emma?" Clemmie was saying. "Here are the letters that Nellie wanted you to have."

"Oh, forgive me, Clemmie. I was just lost in thought. Yes, yes…the letters." Emma took the packet tied up with the pink satin ribbon before adding, "Uh, would you mind if I had a bit of time alone in here to read through some of her parents' correspondence?"

"Help yourself. I'm going back downstairs to see if I can help the other girls. I'll make sure that no one bothers you," and Clemmie closed the door.

How strange it was to be alone in the boudoir of a woman who had once been a rival for her husband's passion and abuse! That very woman who had writhed across the red silk cover with pleasure and pain, now lay wrapped in quilts, jouncing upon the unyielding boards of an ancient hearse drawn by a couple of flatulent mules. Only a dead fetus curled at Nellie's breast attested to the fading memory of a compelling presence in the lives of so many men. Now that the symbol of Edward's wayward eye had a face and a name, the threat seemed almost laughable. Indeed, Emma began to laugh.

Only a giggle at first, and then uncontrollably, Emma laughed until she sobbed. Reaching into the pocket of her skirt, Emma sought her handkerchief and inadvertently pulled out her note tablet which fell open to the line, "Heartbeat: none." Instantly, Emma remembered the purpose of her presence in the house and she began to untie the packet of letters.

Blowing and wiping her nose, Emma sat propped up against Nellie's pillow and read the cherished letters from Lavonne and Lemmuel Potter, the doting grandparents of Edward's daughter, Sophie.

"Today the baby took her first steps!" wrote Lavonne in flowing, black script across the yellowing paper, and then in a letter dated two months later, "Sophie holds onto her Pappy's finger for dear life as they walk the length of the front room and back."

"She has begun to refer to me as 'Mama', Nell dear, even though I have done my best to discourage the term. Time and time again, I have tried to encourage little Sophie to call me 'Nana' but she has a mind and a will of her own! Please do not find fault with me for this, as I have done nothing to encourage it. She continues to call your father, 'Pappy'."

Another entry told of the little girl's diet. This time, it was the cramped ink scribble of Lemmuel.

"Dearest Nell,

I am so proud of the baby! She sat at the table with Mama and me today and ate your mother's mashed potatoes! Lots of spills and slips, but she ate them! Her favorite treat continues to be Mama's cinnamon applesauce.

Love always, Daddy."

Emma found herself smiling with each successive epistle from little Sophie's grandparents as they tried valiantly to chronicle the child's development for her absent mother. Nothing escaped the vigilant grandparents. Sophie's first tooth, her first words, her sleeping habits, her favorite toy, her illnesses, family outings, anything that concerned the growth and development of Sophie Potter had been meticulously recorded for the edification of the mother who continued to reside in another state.

On each of the envelopes, the return address in the upper left-hand corner remained the same, "35 Market Street, Saint Louis, Missouri." Four years' worth of cherished memories lay scattered across Nellie's Chinese red silk bed cover when Emma finished reading. Since the final envelope was sealed and bore no inscription, Emma surmised that it must contain Nellie's hard-earned savings. Emma paused, not knowing if she should open the final envelope. Then carefully, Emma gathered up each of the envelopes, including the heaviest one, still unopened. As Emma tied up the bundle again with its pink satin ribbon, she glanced out the window and realized that another day had crept over the horizon.

The noises of the whorehouse had faded. It had been a traumatic night for all of the residents and Emma imagined that the girls, including their madam, had all fallen into an exhausted sleep. Quietly, Emma pulled Nellie's carpetbags out from under her bed where Clemmie had described they would be.

Opening the chifforobe, Emma began to sort through Nellie's meager possessions, neatly stored and hung to the right. Touching the intimate objects that belonged to the deceased woman brought a new wave of sadness crashing down upon her. A peacock blue silk scarf that smelled of roses, white high-button shoes, a leather belt with its shiny mother-of-pearl clasp, a mauve velvet gown, a jar of lip rouge, Emma carefully packed them all away in Nellie's carpetbags.

Emma placed the beribboned parcel of letters atop Nellie's well-thumbed Bible and buckled the last carpetbag before tiptoeing down the broad staircase to see if anyone was awake to lend her a hand with the baggage. Harold Whinrey and Percival Abernathy were long gone. With Miss Hattie snoring safely in her bed, the whores were quick to anesthetize themselves with double rations of rum, all except for Clemmie.

Searching through the house for someone to take her home, Emma found Clemmie propped up on a couple of cushions by the back porch steps, smoking a cigarette and drinking coffee. She was barefooted, her loose, dark hair spilling carelessly about her shoulders.

"Clemmie? I have finished reading Nellie's letters and I have packed up her possessions in the two carpetbags from under her bed. Is there anything else of hers that I should retrieve before returning home?" asked Emma.

Scooting aside her cup of black coffee upon the peeling gray boards of the porch, Clemmie reached into her skirt pocket. "Just this," she responded handing an object to Emma who sat down beside her.

Emma took the handkerchief offered to her by Clemmie and realized that it contained something in its folds. Looking over at Clemmie, she asked, "What is it?"

"Nellie gave me this after Edward left because she told me she never wanted to see it again, but I figured that little Sophie should have it. Go ahead, open the handkerchief," said Clemmie, taking a long pull from the cigarette before dousing it in the remaining coffee.

Emma laid the small parcel upon her lap and began to peel back the corners of the lace-trimmed handkerchief. What she saw made her gasp. There in the center of the linen square was a cameo brooch trimmed with twisted gold, identical to the one that Edward had given to her the night of her parents' Christmas party when he had asked for her hand in marriage. Emma knew she still had her brooch hidden away in a dresser drawer so this one was a cheap duplicate or perhaps, they were both cheap duplicates and neither had ever belonged to Edward's mother. More than likely, both brooches had been purchased from some itinerant peddler passing through town.

"A family heirloom, no doubt!" exclaimed Emma sarcastically, as she bound up the brooch again.

"He told Nellie it once belonged to his mother," explained Clemmie ingenuously.

"Not likely," said Emma rising to her feet, "but I shall see that Sophie gets it nonetheless. Clemmie, I need a ride home. Would you be so kind as to help me carry down Nellie's carpetbags and then hitch up the horse to Hattie's buckboard?"

"I'll be only too glad to take you home, Nurse Emma, after all you did…tried to do for Nellie," said Clemmie, straightening her camisole and skirt.

"Oh, and do call it to the attention of Hattie Garrison that I have left my bill for services rendered on her lacquered table in the parlor. I have charged her fifty cents for each hour that I spent in this infernal place and I demand that my fee of six dollars be paid in full before sunset tomorrow evening or I shall undertake measures to have this rathole closed." As an afterthought, Emma added, "By the way Clemmie, when you finally decide you have had enough of this life, come to see me and I shall endeavor to assist you in obtaining more genteel work."

As Clemmie pulled the buckboard to a halt at the front of the house on High Point Avenue, Heath came from behind the house on Grit. "Oh, there you are Emma. I was just preparing to return to Miss Hattie's and seek you out as the boys, Mary and I had grown quite worried about your welfare."

Heath dismounted and tied Grit to the far end of the porch before hurrying over to assist Emma down from the buckboard. "What is all this?" asked Heath, pointing to Nellie's carpetbags in the back of the buckboard.

"I shall explain later," she said reaching out for his hand.

Heath placed both of his hands at her waist and lifted Emma down from the buckboard. As he did so, he noticed the blood on her skirt and blouse, the dark smudges under her eyes, the pallor of her skin, the unkempt auburn hair and the odor of whorehouse. Instantly he felt guilty that he had abandoned her at Miss Hattie's for the night.

"I must have those carpetbags taken up to my room, Heath. No one must disturb them, please," she looked into his blue eyes. "Put them under my bed." Then, she dismissed Clemmie, "Thank you for bringing me back home. Please remember what I said about having enough," and Emma walked up the front steps into a tumultuous welcome from her sons.

Will, George and Johnny ran at their mother full tilt from Mary's kitchen where they were eating their breakfast. "Ma!" exclaimed Will. "We thought you was never comin' back again!"

"Yeah, I figured maybe you were going to disappear just like...you-know-who," added George, glancing at his grandmother.

"Nah, Georgie. I been explainin' to you that Ma wouldn't never do that to us," said Will, face sticky with sorghum and a napkin still wound around his neck. "I told you Ma probably got et...eaten by a sneaky old bobcat like the one what..."

"Willynilly, you are a turd!"

"Well, didya ever think of lookin' at all that blood on her? Now, just explain that to me if some bobcat wasn't tryin' to eat her," reasoned Will.

Brute galloped around the gathering in Mary's front hall, barking his welcome and Johnny began to wail at all the commotion. "Ah, such music to my ears!" exclaimed Emma, smiling. "This is without a doubt the most marvelous place to be on the face of the earth! None of you can ever guess how much I have missed everyone!" and she gathered the three boys to her in a prolonged embrace before allowing them to pull her back to the kitchen.

"Lookit, Ma! Heath made your favorite pancakes!" Will exclaimed as he waved a sample dripping butter and syrup and thrust it under his mother's nose.

"I am so hungry, Will, I could probably eat a…"

"BOBCAT!" yelled Will.

Everyone laughed. "AND A HORSE!" chimed in George.

Johnny clapped his hands. Mary shooed Brute out the back door and then poured Emma a cup of coffee while Heath prepared a stack of pancakes for her.

Scrupulously avoiding any mention of her ordeal at Miss Hattie's House of Splendor, Emma joined in the cheerful banter with her family while she devoured four of Heath's huge pancakes along with fried fatback and a glass of cold milk.

"And now, my darlings, I am in desperate need of a bath and some sleep. Please excuse me, Mama," Emma apologized to her mother, kissing the top of her head.

"I understand, dear. After we clean up this kitchen, the boys and I are headed out of doors to weed my flower beds," said Mary, squinting at Will and George. "And you too, Master John! I expect your Nana can find something to keep those little hands of yours busy also!"

"Awww, Nana!" George groused.

"Look at it this way, Georgie," countered Will, "them worms is always hangin' around Nana's flower beds 'cause they figger we're too dumb to know they're hidin' in there, meanin' you and I can get a whole bunch of fishin' worms so's we can stick a pole in the river with Heath!"

"Oh really? And I suppose those worms told you all that!" exclaimed George, his voice oozing sarcasm.

"Even a dummy like me knows that worms don't talk, Georgie," answered Will.

"Well, how then?"

"How what?"

"Gravy, Will! How do you know that the worms will be hanging around Nana's flower beds?" persisted George.

"It's a fact that worms dry out in the hot sun, right?"

"Yeah," admitted George.

"And, to keep from dryin' out, them worms hightail it under rocks and logs and Nana's flowers! You'll see," beamed Will.

"Want to bet?" asked George, sticking out his tongue.

"Nope. I ain't got nothin' to bet with and Heath always says when your pockets are empty, you don't go makin' no bets with nobody."

While the great debate over the presence of worms in Mary's flower beds continued in the kitchen accompanied by the clatter of plates and silverware, Emma trudged wearily up the long flight of stairs to her bedroom, followed by Heath. "How about if I draw your bath for you, Emma, while you slip out of those clothes?"

"Uh-huh," she murmured.

When Emma turned to look at herself in the mirror, she was appalled at her appearance. The bloodstains on her garments were so extensive that Emma wadded up her skirt and blouse for Heath to burn. Her face looked haggard and her hair unkempt. Emma removed the few remaining pins and shook out her hair. Then, gathering a towel around herself, she joined Heath in the tiny bathroom and slipped into the sudsy, steaming depths of the copper tub.

"Anything you want to tell me?" probed Heath gently, as he knelt by the tub and began to shampoo Emma's hair.

"Plenty," responded Emma, with her eyes closed. "The only problem is that it will quite possibly require an entire day for me to tell you all that has transpired since you departed from Miss Hattie's," she responded wearily.

"In that case, perhaps we should postpone any further discussion of the matter until after you have slept," said Heath rinsing Emma's hair.

"Thank you. I desperately need some rest," she said, slowly slipping under the cloudy water.

Alarmed, Heath grabbed Emma by the hair and brought her head above the surface of the water in the copper tub, "Wake up!" he shouted.

"I am awake!" she laughed. "Just trying to get the stink of whorehouse out of my pores!"

For the rest of the morning and on into the late afternoon, Emma slept, sprawled out upon the pink covers of her childhood bed. Heath maintained a silent vigil over her, creeping barefooted up the stairs to peek through Emma's bedroom door every hour. Together, Heath and the two big boys cleaned out the barn while Johnny trailed Mary about the house as she did her chores. Around noon, the five enjoyed a picnic lunch out on the back porch, after which Mary put Johnny down for his nap in the swing with her while she sat and sewed, and still Emma slept.

Heath checked on Emma and then rounded up Will and George for a dip in the pond. "Come on, Georgie!" commanded Will. "Heath says we can go shiny hiney in the pond! He says Nana's too be occupied to notice."

"The word is 'preoccupied', Willy," answered George, already stripping off his shirt and trousers. Mary Miller had more than once expressed her dismay at witnessing bare male buttocks charging across the hill at the back of the house, past the barn to the pond just out of sight through the pine trees. "Good heavens, Heath!" Mary would exclaim. "Can the three of you not keep on your undergarments at least until you are out of sight of the house, beyond the trees?"

"Why Mary," Heath would chide Emma's mother, "you act as if you had never before seen a bare male posterior!"

"Oh, I have seen plenty of them in my day, albeit mostly under the age of ten, but you, Heath dear, are considerably older and need to be mindful that you are in danger of inflaming the passions of the women passing by on High Point Avenue," scolded Mary, with a twinkle in her eye.

"Well now, I surely would not wish to inflame those old lady quilting friends of yours that come traipsing to the house armed with their scissors and needles! They might just get riled up enough to inflict some painful damage to my gluteus maximus!" and Heath playfully rubbed his backside.

The repartee ended with Mary grabbing her fly swatter and chasing the three of them off her back porch, all the while calling, "Do not let me catch sight of your bare behinds or so help me, I shall consider it an invitation to use this," accompanied by exaggerated swishing of the fly swatter through the air above her head.

That afternoon, however, Mary was engrossed at the front of the house with her sewing and watching Johnny as he napped, thumb in his mouth, on a folded up quilt in the swing. She was oblivious to the three naked figures streaking across her back yard on their way to the pond.

After a leisurely dip in the pond ringed with cattails, the boys and Heath stole around the back of the house to dress, having first ascertained that Mary was still absorbed with her sewing on the front porch. It was around four o'clock when Heath stuck his head in the bedroom door to check on Emma, who by then had been asleep for nearly eight hours. As the door creaked open, Emma raised her head from the goose down pillow and blurted out, "Did you burn the letters?"

"Emma, darling, it is Heath," he announced realizing that he had startled her from a sound sleep. "You have been dreaming, my Sleepyhead," and the bed boards underneath the mattress complained as Heath sat down beside her.

"Oh," sighed Emma as she sank back into the softness of the pillow. "What day is this?" she asked rolling her head over to look at Heath.

"Friday," he reminded her.

"Oh. Did anybody explain to Fanella my absence from the hospital today?"

"I took care of it, just as you asked me to do," Heath reassured her.

"Thank you for remembering. Was she angry?" worried Emma.

"Not in the least. In fact, Fanella offered to come over and help you at Miss Hattie's."

"It was dreadful, Heath!" said Emma, clutching his hand and frowning.

"Perhaps this would be a good time for you to tell me what happened. I mean, provided you want to share that…or care to divulge that…"

"How do I smell?" asked Emma, rising to sit on the edge of the bed with Heath.

"Smell? Are you still asleep?" and Heath tugged at her long auburn curls.

"I mean do I smell of that place any longer?"

"You smell just fine, Emma. Remember, you had a bath after breakfast," Heath reminded her.

"It is just that I cannot seem to rid myself of the smell of all those women packed into that sordid house, coupling over and over again amidst the stench of decaying fetus and drying blood. The odors still fill my nostrils," and she walked over to her dresser to grab a handkerchief, furiously blowing her nose.

Heath walked up behind her and, turning her around gently by the shoulders, said, "Emma, Emma! The smell is neither on your person nor in your nose. The smell originates from your imagination. I think the only way for you to rid yourself of it is to tell me what happened last night. Would you agree?"

"I suppose," sighed Emma, rubbing her forehead, "but not in front of Mama or the boys. Let us excuse ourselves for a walk before supper. Please go downstairs and make amends with Mama while I dress."

Attired in fresh clothing from the skin out and with her hair done up loosely in a pigtail that dangled down the middle of her back, Emma waved a straw hat at Heath as she joined him on the front lawn where it lead down to the Southport River. The couple walked along hand in hand in silence for several minutes with Emma inhaling and exhaling noisily through her nose.

"Still smell it?" asked Heath, breaking the silence.

"Yes."

"Come on over here and sit with me on this rock," and Heath lifted Emma up onto a massive limestone boulder overlooking the river before scrambling up next to her. Planting a kiss on her bare neck, he said, "All right now, out with it! Let us begin to purge you of that smell!"

"It is so terribly difficult to tell," began Emma, avoiding Heath's eyes. "It is all so excruciatingly sad and…sordid."

"I assume that you are referring to the young woman whom you called 'Nellie'?" asked Heath.

"Yes," replied Emma somberly as her eyes filled with tears.

"Did she die?"

"Uh-huh," mumbled Emma, removing a linen square from her pocket to wipe her cheeks.

Heath placed his arm around Emma's trembling shoulders and hugged her to him, "I know that you did everything humanly possible to save that girl. You must not blame yourself, my sweetest."

The human contact prompted Emma to sob. Heath sat quietly holding her to him, allowing her to express her grief before she was finally able to regain her equilibrium and sit up straight. Emma blew her nose loudly several times before continuing.

"I really did everything by the book, Heath, but the poor girl had been bleeding since that morning and there was nothing anyone could do to save her...ten hours after the fact. It is so distressing to realize that even though it is 1890, women are still submitting to knitting needle abortions. Do you realize that no one was caring for Nellie until I got there?" asked Emma searching Heath's eyes.

"Unbelievable," responded Heath, releasing his grip upon Emma.

"Clemmie, Nellie's roommate at Miss Hattie's, found the fetus all rolled up in one of her bloody sheets and that bastard undertaker, Harold Whinrey, had the gall to tell me he was only going to record it as one death. One death! Can you imagine?"

Heath shook his head sadly, "Did you get ahold of Percival Abernathy?"

"Yes, and he certified that there were two decedents," triumphed Emma.

"Good for him but then, Abernathy is a younger and better educated man than Whinrey," commented Heath. "So have all the arrangements been made?"

"Yes...however...there is something else."

"What is it?" Heath asked, looking alarmed.

"Nellie Potter told me that she had been Edward's whore before his disappearance."

"What?"

"Yes, his whore...'his favorite whore' to quote poor Nellie." At this juncture, Emma turned to face Heath, crossing her legs like a pretzel under her skirt. Clearing her throat, she added, "And not only that, but she and Edward had a child together, about four years ago. A little girl named Sophie," Emma never took her eyes from Heath's face.

"Good Lord, Emma, how could she possibly know that it was Edward's child? I mean, given all the...the contact that she has had with men?"

"I know, I know. I asked her the same question but Nellie maintained that she knew the child was Edward's and at that point, I had no reason to doubt the confession of a dying woman."

"Where is the child?"

"With Nellie's parents in St. Louis."

"Is that where Edward is too?"

"No. Nellie could shed no light on Edward's whereabouts."

"Did Edward even know of this child's existence?"

"I cannot be certain," answered Emma.

"What a sordid tale indeed!" Heath exclaimed.

"There is more," added Emma, clearing her throat.

"Good Lord, now what?"

"It was Nellie Potter's dying wish that I should take all of her possessions and the money that she had saved from her...her work at the whorehouse to little Sophie Potter in St. Louis."

"Oh, no! Please tell me that you did not agree to such an absurd endeavor!"

"You already know the answer to your question, my darling," said Emma reaching up to stroke the handsome face before her.

Heath slid down off the boulder beside Emma and stormed angrily over to the water's edge. Raising his fists to the sky, he exploded, "Is there no end in sight to the messes that you are expected to clean up for this bugger? He tormented and beat you...cheated on you with whores...abandoned you and his three children and now we discover that Edward...the callous swine...has also left behind a fourth child...only this one has no mother. Dandy! Just simply dandy!"

"Please do not get mad at me, Heath," Emma implored, joining him where he stood rigidly at the edge of the river.

"I am not mad at you, Emma," he looked down at her, "but I would love to get my hands around Edward's neck, I can assure you. The man is completely devoid of a conscience."

"Be that as it may, Heath, a promise is a promise and I must go to St. Louis and seek out little Sophie Potter and her grandparents. I shall never rest until I do," said Emma quietly, slipping her hand into his.

Heath lifted her hand to his lips and kissed it tenderly, "Oh, my poor darling Emma! So much has fallen upon your shoulders! It just seems to me as though every time I reach a point where I sense that I am beginning to relieve some of your horrendous burdens, another load comes crashing down upon you!"

Emma managed a laugh, "Well, I guess I have become a sort of magnet for trouble of one sort or another. I guess it is my fate…perhaps even my destiny. Do you think?"

"Such a cruel fate, my lovely! For surely a face as beautiful as yours was meant to inspire all who gaze upon it." Heath caressed Emma's cheek lightly with his fingertips as he continued, "Only with our baser instincts in check, may we some day hope to realize our childhood dream of touching the stars, and until that magic moment, all I ask is to be allowed to bask in the glow of your approbation, for it is the sight of your face which inspires my heart to beat."

"Why, Heath, I never realized…"

"Just how much I love you," added Heath, finishing her thought. "Give me your hand," and he held her small hand over the left side of his chest. "Do you feel that?"

"Yes, of course. It is your heart beating."

Then Heath took Emma's right hand and held it over the left side of her own chest, "And what do you feel now?"

"My own heart beating."

After several moments, Heath asked, "Have you noticed that both hearts beat as one?"

Emma flung her arms around him sobbing over and over again, "I love you! I love you!"

"Possibly," smiled Heath down at Emma's tear-stained face, "but only about half as much as I love you," and his lips found hers.

After supper, while Heath and Emma cleaned up the kitchen, Mary washed the boys, tucked them into bed and excused herself early so that Heath and Emma might enjoy the September night alone on the porch. There was a notice-able chill in the fall air and Emma pulled the fringed shawl tighter around her shoulders as Heath cuddled her small frame to him for warmth.

"Ever since you told me about Sophie, I have been turning over something in my head and I would like to share it with you," he said looking down at her in the glow from the oil lantern on the wicker table near the swing.

"What is that, Heath?"

"You and Mary and the boys have suffered one hell of a lot. You two women work harder than any other women I know and I think you both need a rest…a vacation of sorts. So, I was thinking that I would offer to take all of us on a train trip to St. Louis. The six of us could stay in hotel for a few days. See the sights. Do some shopping. I know the Vendome Hotel over there serves excellent food in the dining room and I can imagine that Mary might enjoy getting out of her hot kitchen for a while. We could enjoy ourselves in the big city and you could have an opportunity to deliver Nellie Potter's possessions to her daughter. What do you think about that?"

"It sounds entirely too expensive to me. Think of it, Heath. Six train fares, at least two hotel rooms and meals for six people, three times a day!"

"I have the money to pay for it," responded Heath simply. "I want to give you and Mary and the boys a gift and I have decided this trip would fit the bill perfectly. What do you say?"

"I am not sure I could get the time off from the hospital just now..."

"Fanella Walker would understand your need for a few days away with your family," insisted Heath.

"But then there is the issue of school. Will and George go back to school the first Monday in October."

"Well, since this is only the middle of September, the timing is perfect, would you not agree?" Heath grinned at Emma, refusing to let her back out of his invitation.

"Actually," sighed Emma looking out across the river at the lights of Clarksburg that twinkled along the distant shore, "such a trip might be just what the doctor himself would order!"

"The very answer I had hoped to hear!" and Heath squeezed Emma, kissing the top of her head.

Since Emma had never traveled further than Clarksburg, the thought of traveling by train to St. Louis was both thrilling and disconcerting, especially when she considered the moment during her stay in the bustling metropolis when she would have to come face to face with Edward Richardson's illegitimate daughter, Sophie Potter.

TO BE CONTINUED...

0-595-33476-8

Printed in the United States
26663LVS00001B/478-495